The CANDY BOX

The CANDY BOX

Lock Cee Mangum

Library of Congress Control Number:		2021917905
ISBN:	Hardcover	978-1-6641-9223-2
	Softcover	978-1-6641-9222-5
	eBook	978-1-6641-9221-8

Print information available on the last page.

Rev. date: 08/30/2021

To order additional copies of this book, contact:
Xlibris
844-714-8691
www.Xlibris.com
Orders@Xlibris.com
827612

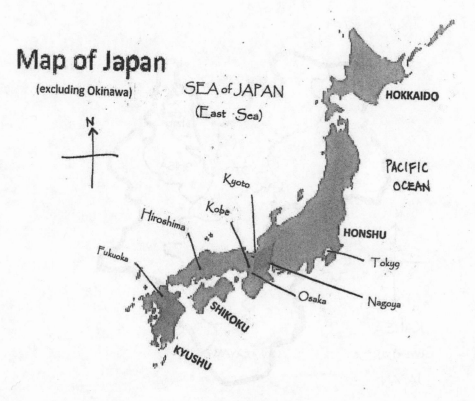

Map of Japan

(excluding Okinawa)

SEA of JAPAN
(East Sea)

N

HOKKAIDO

PACIFIC
OCEAN

Kyoto

Kobe

Hiroshima

HONSHU

Fukuoka

Tokyo

Osaka

Nagoya

SHIKOKU

KYUSHU

Map of Japan

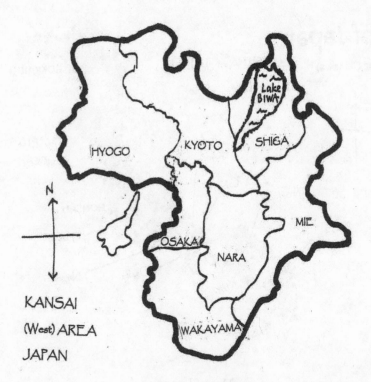

N

KANSAI
(West) AREA
JAPAN

Map of the Kansai Region

Map of the Prefecture

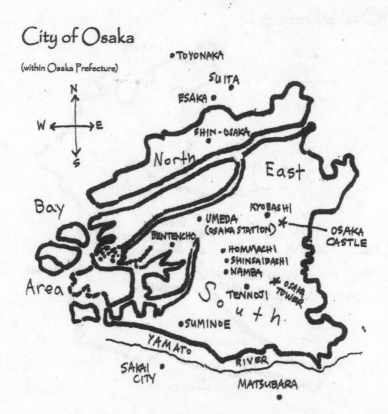

Map of Osaka

T HE MUSIC WAS uproariously loud in the club. It was dark, but rainbow streaks of light beamed through the crowd of frenzied dancers on the floor at random intervals. Hip-hop music was still much of a rare thing at that time in Japan, and places like the Candy Box were very special. This was because its owner—a *gaijin*, or "foreigner of Japan"—boasted it to be one of the few clubs in Osaka where people could go to party to this new craze, as well as the usual Western pop, drum 'n' bass, techno, or whatever scherzo enjoyed in the year that followed the Y2K, he realized it was a big deal. As a result, the establishment could also boast huge crowds on almost any night it opened its doors. Unfortunately, with big success came big troubles. There were lots of drunks, fights, drugs, even some minor gang activity, albeit not to the extent to which major league Japanese mafia, or *yakuza*, were involved, but serious enough to warrant concern for the club's management and ownership to eventually address. Their solution was to weed out the riffraff by upping the admission to a whopping four thousand yen (about forty dollars) for dudes, maybe two or three thousand for the women—of Japan—while all foreigners were allowed in for free. Again, this decision paid off, because not only did loyal patrons continue to enjoy the spot, but the clientele also seemed to improve. There were fewer brawls, a dress code was enacted, and although there were still drunken and doped-out visitors, it wasn't as brazen as it had previously been. Now it was a place where people could dress up exceedingly fancy, in fashionable attire, mingle in an "international" cluster under a resonant musical soundtrack, and basically pretend to be someone more special than they actually were.

People like Elizabeth Candace Amberbush liked this club only because she had become acquainted with the Middle Eastern owner, Tabriz Najaf, not to mention other members of the staff; and she could always enjoy a free VIP lounge seat, which meant she could sip champagne or any drink of her choice for free in a comfortable seat or booth regardless of how packed the place was, just like that particular night. In addition, in the almost three years she had been in Japan, this place was also in a rare category of spots that actually resembled what she knew to be a club. She had observed a great many decrepit holes from Tokyo to Kobe that were called clubs but were no more than a drab bar with a few feet of damp open floor accompanied by loud music and funky strobe lights. This place she was in tonight was pretty huge. It could accommodate the crowds it attracted and made it the maffick den that it was. As usual, she was treated like a queen, like some odd piece of royalty that had descended upon Japan and graced the country with her regal, pristine, and wholesome presence. The sight of her and others like her made the host country people feel privileged to be in their company, so much so that they didn't mind shelling out the loot for entrance fee. It meant a lot for them to be able to return to their Japanese lives and brag about having partied at a club with a lot of *gaijin*. It was like the English Conversation schools that she and other foreigners like her taught at, just without the textbooks.

As for Elizabeth, who had assumed a shortened version of her middle name, Candy, as of recent, the praise and worship she had received from Japanese people never ceased to amuse her, and tonight was no exception. She was going to drink for free regardless but allowed bewitched Japanese dudes to buy her drinks with a remote hope that they could lick her up and down from head to toe. Dudes who were hoping that they could get her drunk would soon get more than they bargained for. Despite her immaculate, chaste, virginal, and irreproachable appearance by the time she was all dressed up for after hours, she was far from the ordinary fairy-tale princess. Dudes would get the picture when they wake up after passing out; meanwhile, Elizabeth would be long gone.

She wasn't especially happy on this particular night, though. Here she was, approaching her late twenties, working and living in Japan and—get this—didn't really like Japan, its people, its culture; but strangely, she couldn't help but feel a tinge of sadness about leaving. She had finally made the decision to return to the United States of America, patch things up with her folks, and, more or less, quit while she was ahead. Tonight she was here to meet some old friends and acquaintances, who were unusually late.

She sipped champagne while a handsome Japanese dude in a black business suit tried desperately to communicate with her in broken English. What exactly he was talking about was a mystery. Liz was trying to figure out which taste she preferred: Dom Perignon or Moët? He bored her so much she likened his manner of talk to the children she used to teach English to and laughed at him to pass the time. He was determined, however, to woo her by showing that he was a big spender, so he kept buying and jibber-jabbering, and she let him have at it.

The only good thing about her experience is that her Japanese had greatly improved. This was a result of the efforts she finally made to study it and use it for her nighttime job. There, she entertained older and richer Japanese "sugar daddies" who had contributed much to the major stash of cash she intended to take back to America so she wouldn't leave Japan empty-handed by any means.

Saiko Yamabiko, her *mama-san*, or boss lady at the lounge where she worked, gave her the pseudonym "Candy"; but prior to that, she was always simply known as Liz, both in Japan and in America.

The auriferous, golden-blonde-haired California transplant girl looked like a typical "Brady Bunch" daughter, arguably beautiful by some but never the level to which it was elevated by the time she had settled in Japan. In the days preceding those, she was just an ordinary girl from an *arriviste* family background. Her already-somewhat-affluent father, Ike, had won a Multi-State Lottery in the late '80s, which allowed him to expand his trucking business to include boats and move his family, which consisted of Liz, her older brother Halbert, and his wife, their mother, from Iowa to California permanently, so they were like a real-life modern version of the Beverly Hillbillies.

Liz grew up pampered and sheltered. Her father's attention fell mostly upon her brother Hal, who was four years older than her. After his business took off, he tried to groom his son to become involved and help him run the company, which Hal eventually did. Liz's mother was a parttime substitute schoolteacher, a job she did not because she needed the work or the money, but because it was her pastime gig prior to becoming suddenly rich. Otherwise, she was a batty and fun-loving parent that Liz got spoiled by; and as Liz grew up, she learned that she could practically win her mother over on almost any issue by outbursts of hissy-fits and temper tantrums. She got almost everything she ever wanted, so it came as a shock to her mother when Liz decided to not pursue attending college at UCLA or USC and instead took a year off to goof around with her wild friends Becky and Mandy.

Liz, Becky, and Mandy would hang out, party all night, go on skiing trips, and frequent tanning salons. After a year of this, Liz would spend all her savings, which incurred the wrath of her father, who half-assed reprimanded Liz by reducing her allowance from five hundred dollars a month to three hundred. He then decided to put his foot down and make her get a job in a feeble attempt to teach her some responsibility. Liz's mother agreed with this discipline, for once being strict with her daughter, and further encouraged her to apply to a university, hopefully a prominent or distinguished one.

Liz would reluctantly get a part-time job working as a babysitter and then enrolled at Harbor College. It was there she met her Eddie, who became her longtime boyfriend. She and Eddie were similar but vastly different—similar in the fact that they were two typical Americans who had grown up off the fat of the land and the milk and the honey, without knowing hardly a day of despair in their entire lives. They were different because they were opposites in character. By the time Eddie had met Liz, she had already been corrupted by life whereas he was still a greenhorn to the real world.

Despite her mother's efforts to ensure that her daughter would be protected by sending her to the best schools and involving her with the best programs and activities, it still wasn't enough to shield her from the creeping societal decadence. Liz was able to successfully cloak her dark side from her mother for many years and have her believe that she was nothing other than the angel she had raised.

In high school, Liz wasn't the absolute treasure she now was in Japan. In fact, in those days, the only guys who were ever checking for her were dangerous-looking "ghetto people," often, Black dudes—scary ones too. The so-called seedy element was strangely drawn more to the round rear "balls" that appeared when she wore dresses or skirts than the ones on their basketball courts. Although these types of people were rare in her neck of the woods, the occasions she noticed the eyes on her by such individuals caused her to have a subtle disdain for not only them but men in general. This would grow over time and exacerbate tomboy tendencies her mother thought she had abandoned in her early childhood.

Back in Iowa, her father, who was originally an Okie, and her Hawkeye five-dollar-Indian mother—actually of Norwegian and Welsch descents, respectively—had fed both Liz and her brother Hal lots of dairies, corn, muffins, pancakes, and the best poultry from the pleasant farms of the area. Her active lifestyle had included lots of running around, climbing trees, jumping rope, hula-hooping, swimming, and playing softball with her brother and other children who were mostly boys. Her body would develop in ways not very ordinary for the average girl of her demographic. It was a deterrent for attracting boys in some situations, but she would occasionally get asked out on dates. These lackluster experiences, however, had dimmed her view of the opposite sex even further, not because she didn't enjoy making out with guys, but because in her own words, "they were such dicks!"

The Amberbush clan relocated between Santa Monica and the South Bay area, a proximity to Hermosa and Redondo Beach. Liz loved California right away and didn't miss Iowa one bit. She never had any problems fitting in and made friends with ease. Something a lot of people couldn't do, but remarkably she did. She was generally easygoing and tended to be a bit wiser than her peers. Such behavior was a result of her emulating her father, the aggressive, ambitious businessman, which made her appear authoritative; and some looked up to her.

She was voted class vice president one year. She attended high school near Marina del Rey, where she met Becky and Mandy, and they became best friends.

She joined the volleyball team, and life was permanently altered. On the day of the first practice, she decided then and there to be conscientious about her body and health. She learned quickly about the advantages of a healthy diet, balanced meals, and working out fanatically. When she wasn't spiking balls over volleyball nets at school, she was jogging, swimming, biking, and occasionally even playing with her brother's light dumb bells.

The lesbian assistant coach of the volleyball team secretly admired Liz's budding Grecian goddess-like torso as if she was Eurydice or a voluptuous Athena in the making, as voyeurism offered the twenty-something opportunity to spy on Liz and other girls showering after practice. This person was finally able to corner Liz in the locker room infirmary's training antechamber.

What was supposed to be a normal, after-practice rubdown of muscle cramps evolved into something more. Liz was introduced to the wonderful world of same-sex licking, in lascivious massage method around the female labia. A bisexual Liz existed from that moment, a trait that she passed on to close friend and teammate Becky, who embraced such lifestyle much like she had and with surprisingly little reservation. That assistant coach got either fired, married, or both; but Liz never ever saw her again and heard the chick moved back east and was still coaching.

The rest of the wild-side walk came when Liz was introduced to the booze, loud parties, the '80s music, Doritos, and all that accompanied it. Partying. Drinking. Dancing. More drinking. Happy dancing, singing, jumping up and down on expensive furniture. Lip- synching to hits from John Cougar Mellencamp, Bryan Adams, Bruce Springsteen—or was it, Rick Springfield? More singing and dancing. Hugging up with friends. Getting dizzy. Taking a toke of the grass. Smoking a cigarette or two. Sing. Dance. Scream. More booze. Take another hit of the pot. People suddenly putting their tongue in another person's mouth. Room spins. Wake up half naked from the waist down. Vomit. Puke. Gasp. Shit!

Somewhere between that first time and her senior year, she lost her virginity to some popular, upper-class varsity team member, a second-string bench warmer, but was hot enough to break Liz's ice. The romance was as short-lived as the ten minutes it took for him to blow his load all over her belly. When that chump graduated and moved on to attend prestigious Pierce College, a wilder side to her began to emerge outside of school: she adopted a stuck-up attitude and allowed her strange liking for girls to thrive.

Liz's mother noticed her daughter's tendencies and urged her to go on dates with boys, so to keep her mother off her back, Liz fake-dated a wimp named Carver Burk who had been handpicked by her mother from their church.

Carver's parents were happy to see their son go on a date with a girl—any girl, one that went to church even better—because like Liz's mother, they had concerns about their son Carver's sexual orientation as well, so the relationship looked good on the surface. Carver was Liz's part-time sucker that she used for alibis when she ran wild with Becky and her other friends. She would lie and say she was with Carver when she was in Hollywood Hills trying to hang out with hunks, studs, dikes, and weirdos too old for her and types her parents forbade her from interacting with.

Poor Carver knew he was being cheated on, but he was a good sport about it, and he played along with Liz's game. He seemed to know he was out of her league. Liz tried to hit him off with some gratuitous love sessions but was a bit too aggressive for Carver's taste due to his limited experience with women. He preferred the comfort and camaraderie of his choir boy peers.

One night she snubbed Carver to go on a sleep-away camp adventure. There was supposed to be some beer, booze, roasting marshmallows by a fire, ghost stories, and skinny-dipping and such. Problem was, there was one too many girls because Liz had ditched Carver, upsetting the four-girl-and-four-guy matchup. Instead, there were three dudes and four girls. Problem solved. One lucky dude got a chance to have a threesome with Becky and Liz in a tent.

After that, Liz was whispered about as being a somewhat loose chick, like a sort-of tomboy slut. Be that as it may, it did not ruin her socially. She was still known as one of the prettiest girls in school, a star volleyball player, and popular with the school body. The jollity of her character made it easy for her to befriend people, and she never had problems adapting to the West Coast environment. She fit right in.

She loved Los Angeles and the Marina del Rey nightlife. It was casual and yet festive, and she enjoyed it entirely. Life couldn't have been better. The daily pace was mellow but had its propensity for its own blend of melodrama.

Fast forward to 1997. It was a time in North American narration which would chronicle its youth for being proactive and vigilant to prove certain things. Some women felt the need to affirm that they could do anything that men could do. They could act as wild as men, they could play professional basketball like men, they could even dress like men. Simply put, they wanted to boldly go where no man had gone. Liz was in it full-throttle.

By now, with high school and volleyball long behind her, Liz would hit the beach in the summer of her twenty-third year. Her stunning starlet's sculpted hourglass figure in a candy hot-pink *Baywatch* bikini caused many heads to turn and mouths to drool. Not those young women such as her weren't ubiquitous, especially on California beaches; but roughly five years earlier, the Sir Mix-a-Lot anthem praising big butts still resonated greatly in the consciousness of many men, and Liz would be the rare anomaly—the type of chick one wouldn't expect to "have back".

After high school, she had taken a year off to go on numerous crazy, wild vacations and even went skiing in Colorado. Upon returning home, she fell back into her exercise regimen. She hit aerobics and yoga classes three to four times a week. She went swimming, jogging, and played beach volleyball. Her festive activities shaped and sculpted her mouth-watering, seductive figure even more.

Finally, when Liz could kick her tomboy—or keep it submerged—she managed to appear more feminine. She began wearing heels and walked with a womanly strut instead that of a gangling dude. Her Carolina-blue eyes had the ability at times to enchant others like the witch she was becoming and her hair, fifteen inches in length at the time, could have been the straw that Rumpelstiltskin spun into gold. Guys found her attractive, but a subtle tomboyish foible caused her to seem a bit rough around the edges—a little aggressive and extra—and not too many dudes wanted to pursue anything other than one-night stands. Basically, she had *the looks*—just not to the point where she'd be having Hollywood directors pump the brakes on their limos, hop out, and beg her to be their next Marilyn Monroe or star in one of their bonanzas.

Long before Liz's face would be likened to those of famous adult film stars—namely, Monika Starr—she tossed around in her head the idea of doing porn for a hot minute. While Hollywood directors like Michael Bay didn't seek her out to cast her in a flick as a love interest for a dude like Ben Affleck, a few smut film directors did approach her on the occasions she, Becky, and Mandy went to Venice Beach. She decided not to get into that business, though. She didn't need the money, but she wanted to have sex with some guys who were more interesting than those she had already been involved with.

To most of her friends, Liz was reluctant—downright scared—to admit the level to which she desired to be intimate with someone, if not boys, then girls. She was afraid of being slut-shamed. Becky, however, who was just as freaky as Liz, understood how Liz felt, and that's why she, and later Mandy, would be Liz's closest friend and confidant.

Detesting the type of work that would have her punching a clock, Liz continued to receive allowances from her family; enjoyed the use of a car which she wrecked; and she resigned herself to have babysitting jobs, which paid well because she would have affluent families from her neck of the woods as clients. So now she had her own money to jerk, and she would battle her carnal cravings with shopping sprees with her buds. She was living like a real-life *Clueless* Amy Silverstone in the '90s.

The ability to keep her diabolical hankering for the touch of human flesh a clandestine feature of her persona had its difficulties. This once came to a boil while she was babysitting an adolescent teen. She found herself becoming dangerously attracted to this fourteen-year-old because he was an unusual five foot ten in height, about an inch or two taller than her, who had to look up at him to order him to brush his teeth and get ready for bed.

This disturbing paroxysm to her otherwise sane condition struck when she saw the boy naked after one of his football practices. She was overcome by a Mary Kay Letourneau spirit. When the boy took off his clothes and got ready for his bath, he didn't feel any shame or embarrassment. He was still a coddled, upper-crust innocent kid who thought of his babysitter Liz as a regular adult, not unlike any other authoritative figure in his life—like a doctor, a nurse, or a sister from the church. Liz found herself watching the boy bathe in a way like how she was spied on by her high school volleyball coach, who ended up seducing her.

Luckily, she never acted on her impulses, and she was able to meet Edward Roman not long after. Their hooking up was more by accident than intentional. Her friends Becky and Mandy had found somewhat steady boyfriends and began spending more time with them, leaving Liz dateless often; and times when they did their girls'-night-out thing, once again, the only dudes checking for Liz would primarily be Black men and other "undesirables." Time after time, formidably framed, sweaty ebon hulks would stare at her with venomous cobra-like eyes -sticking out their tongues like serpents- if Liz and pals ever had the misfortune of passing a basketball court in the summer. Whenever they went to the shopping malls, or places in Carson or Inglewood where her father ran his businesses, the locals could be heard hissing and whistling at Liz. She thought she was in a perpetual snake den.

Becky liked Black guys, and even dated some secretly, but those were the "Oreo" types. Liz didn't have anything against Black men or Black people, but her parents didn't really like them, nor did Becky's parents either. Usually, LA people were thought to be open-minded, but Liz and her family weren't originally from California. They were some conservative Middle America hicks that suddenly came into big money and came out west, and along with them they brought their own form of white-supremacist mindset. Similarly, Becky's family shared that same code mentality, and Liz was so shocked to hear that they would disown her if she dated a Black or non-white that Liz decided to not even consider it as an option. So, for a while, it seemed that Liz was doomed to consort with lames like Carver Burk for the rest of her life. Eddie rescued her from that fate . . . sort of.

Edward "Eddie" Roman was a chump and regular loser from Sacramento, the son of some local Elk Grove suburban community pharmacists. Since LA was where all the action was and far more interesting than the capital city, it was the place he wanted to be after he graduated from high school. He was fortunate to have relatives who lived there. He chose an institute of higher learning close to where they lived, and it happened to be Harbor College. His relatives—a divorced aunt with two boys who was his mother's older sister—gave Eddie a rundown of the new city. He packed his bags and split to live with his aunt and two cousins, who were around the same age as him.

Although the campus ratio of women to men tripled the latter, Eddie couldn't score with the opposite gender if his life depended on it. He wasn't much of a lady killer—in fact, he wasn't much at all. He was a plain, simple gauche of a guy whose best compliments ever received pertaining to his looks had him being the ass baby result of a homosexual relationship between actors Steve McQueen and Jude Law. Otherwise, he wasn't much of an athlete: his build was like that of a life-sized cartoon character, possibly a Shaggy feature from the *Scooby Doo* series, or a Gilligan or bumbling Jack Tripper from the sitcoms *Three's Company* and *Three's a Crowd*. In a movie about real life, he would be the supporting actor for an extra. Old footage of him in his high school PE classes would make for good comedy blooper clip reels.

With a posture that resembled a boomerang, his dress code was strictly T-shirts and jeans. His sneaker collection was almost entirely Vans, except for a pair of black combat boots for dress and a single pair of black Chuck Taylors when he was trying to impress the ladies, to no avail.

At one point in time, Eddie tried to delve into the skateboarding scene. His cousins were into grinding and thrashing. After a few near-fatal accidents, he decided wisely to give up skateboarding and indulge in absolutely no hobbies at all for a while, thus severing ties with his cousins who were into that scene heavy. Instead of skateboarding or constructive activity, he elected to do illicit drugs whenever possible, go to comic book conventions, and watch weirdo pornographic anime videos with the new nerd pals he met who, like him, were reject skateboard posers or lousy wannabe musicians.

To support his budding interest in pot, comics, and cinema, he got a job at an "off the beaten path" video store. There he would be employed throughout most of his college days. By the time his junior year rolled around, he had worked his way up to assistant manager.

As for love life, girls would abuse Eddie and his boys at the video store. Sexy broads would come into the shop, bend over as if they were looking for some movie selection on a bottom shelf—directly before the counter where Eddie and his nerd pals would be working.

Eddie and his virgin coworkers would get tormented by all sorts of twats, panties, and even see-through pantyhose or, occasionally, no panties at all. On any given night, Eddie could see all sorts of gash, gaping cunts, camel-toe galore when the LA women wore short skirts.

There was a dive bar near the video shop and drunken dregs and sluts of all type would trudge in every now and then. Girls would sniff coke and drink lemon Coronas inside of the video store. They would shoot alluring looks at Eddie or one of his homeboys. They would wink, twitch their noses, and maybe even lick their lips.

As if almost in slow motion, the women would stride up to the counter and ask Eddie a question like, "Excuse me, do you have a porn section?"

With excitement likely to cause his hand to be removed from his crotch trying to hide his erection poking through his work pants, Eddie would respond, "Why, yes . . . we do!"

The chick would then say, "That's great. Then you guys can get to see naked women before you croak."

Then she would explode with a booming loud guffaw, which was so resounding with echo it seemed thunder or rain should have followed. For Eddie, or one of his partners, it certainly did feel like rain. Perspiration beads of embarrassment would polka-dot their foreheads when those things happened. Everyone in the shop would hear it; people would be laughing. Some hysterically. Eddie remembered the trauma of how he blacked out for a moment, and through a spinning, dark haze, he would hear voices laughing, but in slow motion, like people gagging on a dishrag. He saw the faces laughing, cackling, staring and pointing at him.

He would be awakened angrily from his daydream by a disgruntled customer at the checkout ready to have him tend to them. Eddie could recall several instances where he would have to take impromptu breaks and escape to the stockroom in back to dry his tears of humiliation. This mortifying experience would repeat itself all but too often during the first year or so, but gradually, he came to expect it and learned to condition himself to be indifferent to it. His coworker buddies weren't as lucky or strong.

Other times, chicks would come into the shop, talk all nice, clean-cut girl-next-door chit-chatty and seemingly square. They would shower Eddie and his boys with genuine-sounding compliments, praising them for their knowledge about cinema, film history, actors, and VHS cassette tapes. Finally, with starstruck eyes, she'd say something like, "Wow, you're so cool. You know a lot about movies! You must have a lot of girlfriends!"

Of course, Eddie and his crew would laugh, blush, or shake their heads like, *Gosh . . . wow, golly.* Or, *Gee . . .*

Then suddenly, almost as if on cue, a stunning Hollywood Apollo would appear at the girl's side as if he had magically appeared from the cover of a *Muscle & Fitness* magazine in invisible smoke. This dreamboat in a T-shirt with washboard, soap opera blond hair, and People magazine's Man of the Year looks pops up from out of nowhere talking. "Hey babe, here . . . I found the movie you wanted. Get this *boy* here to check us out. Take care of it while I get the Ferrari and bring it out front . . ." What would follow would be a sticky wet kiss that was over-the-top and sloppy.

When that was all over, she would walk to the counter with a pleased and satisfied look on her face accompanying a devilish smirk, the gamine would say, "You must have a lot of girlfriends because you just haven't found the right one, so you have to keep looking . . . but my boyfriend doesn't need so many girlfriends . . . all he needs is me!"

Cold pricks of rejection stabbed him relentlessly as he scanned the VHS video rentals for checkout while struggling to maintain a friendly smile and remain professional for business. Moments after flirting with Eddie and leading him on, the girl would greet a handsome boyfriend and suck face with that guy right in front him as if to say, *I know you wish you could have me like this guy is gonna have me and fuck my brains out tonight!*

Eddie's life would change upon meeting Liz. Almost immediately. Funny thing was it almost never happened. Being that he was assistant manager, he had to cover for one of his subordinates who called in sick one Monday morning. That was the day Liz visited that "off the beaten path" video store. She may as well have been a fairy godmother.

On that day, Liz had visited the video store and forgot her membership card. Without the card, in theory, a customer couldn't rent videos. Also, Liz was returning some videos, and these were overdue. Eddie was the assistant manager she greeted that day who was on duty. There was no automatic chemistry between them; neither was especially impressed with the other. Liz didn't think much of Eddie, and likewise, Eddie might have thought Liz was pretty, but he had to keep his feelings in check after so many times he would be led astray by wicked women who had visited the shop on previous occasions.

Eddie ended up waiving Liz's overdue-back fees. He fell sucker for the jive she fed him about not being able to read the return date on her original receipt she got when the videos were initially rented. Contrary to his pledge to not get "punked" by the female customers who would bait and tease, Eddie caved in and allowed himself to be finessed anyway. He sat with Liz at the service desk and helped her fill out necessary forms to get a replacement rental card. During this process, they ended up talking a lot about movies, about where they lived before coming to LA, and, throughout this conversation, discovered that they seemed to like a lot of the same things about California—the sunshine, the beaches, the life. And the rest was history. It was like a twist of fate that worked out in their favor.

This monumental moment was punctuated by Liz giving Eddie her telephone number. This time it was no trick, Eddie thought. This was real. Liz wasn't a dirty cock-teasing whore flashing beaver at him and then running away in the arms of a jock boyfriend. Liz of course gave it up on the first date and after she got reasonably intoxicated, she practically threw herself on lucky Eddie. This was an enormous achievement for him. He was a sudden hero to his nerd congregation.

Liz, at the time, was a party girl who peeped Eddie's lame existence and decided that she could use a boy-toy like Carver Burk again. Only, Eddie seemed a bit more rugged and masculine than Carver, even though he was somewhat nerdy and geeky. Despite that, he was reasonably handsome enough to compliment a chick like her, she thought, so she gave him a chance and knew he wouldn't turn her down. Besides, she needed a guy to spend time with like Becky and Mandy had boyfriends. Eddie was to be her windup plaything she could alter and manipulate at will, change like clothes on Ken dolls she found amusement with as a little girl. And of course, she was the Barbie doll that he would be devoted to. A relationship formed and blossomed afterward that neither of them would have imagined could last as long as it did.

Prior to moving to LA, Eddie was technically still a virgin—at least to actual intercourse—but he had been with a woman intimately, it could be said. He had been on the receiving end of numerous blowjobs back in Sacramento from a corpulent, unattractive redhead mutual female friend of one of his older pals. In fact, the woman was his chum's girlfriend at the time, and they eventually got married.

Fat Girl eventually came clean during a post–drunken-stupor-induced argument with the new hubby, and it was then that this guy learned the truth about how much of a double-crossing weasel Eddie really was.

Fat Girl admitted to her husband that Eddie had impregnated her via throat with his own blend of ball batter several times before and after they had gotten married, and it was the truth. It hadn't been Eddie's true intention to hurt his friend, but both he and his homeboy liked Fat Girl. But his dude was the first to smash her and subsequently became whipped in the process, so much so that he felt compelled to marry the bitch right away when he was a year out of high school. It was a big mistake—a stupid one of youth.

The friend, of course, felt betrayed and hated Eddie afterward. He didn't divorce his cheating partner, but he couldn't be friends with Eddie anymore either. He forbade his elephantine-breasted, cock-guzzling spouse from it as well. Surprisingly, or maybe not, Eddie didn't take it too hard. In fact, it would seem he didn't care because he knew he was leaving Sacramento all along anyway. He moved to Los Angeles and became more of a nobody. Liz would signal the first transformation in whatever category of male species he existed under.

Liz was the most gorgeous woman he had ever had the opportunity to speak with on a personal level. He could hardly believe it. Liz was all he could think about, and he bragged about it to his family every day and night. They began to see less and less of him because he was spending all of his time at school, the video store, and following Liz around. Spending all of his money was a given.

It was worth it. Liz was the first girl who ever let him enter vaginally. Fat Girl used to show Eddie her ham a lot but claimed she was saving her drippy, wide hole for marriage, thus Eddie settled for neck while his friend fell for the bait and slayed the pork.

Liz let Eddie hit it raw the first time, but when she saw how tender he was and the volume at which he would release on climax, she insisted he wear condoms, or settle for oral sex—something Liz had become quite astute at, at this point, having learned a lot about it since her first lesbian trysts in high school.

Eddie was cool with it. How could he not be? He was in a position his peers envied. It was beyond his wildest dreams in the beginning. His ego expanded a notch or two in the process. His macho was growing, and he insisted on lying to Liz about his past, claiming that he'd had plenty of experience with women prior to meeting her. With this in mind, she wondered why, then, did he always act so squirmy when she went down on him?

Quietly, Liz didn't really care too much one way or another, she knew Eddie was lousy in the sack. His lackluster performances and short-lived attempts to rock her were praiseworthy, but that wasn't the reason why she was with him. She just wanted to be close and intimate with someone; and with him, he was wholesome enough to not just be *anyone*. *So what if he wasn't stylish or trendy?* He was at least normal. *She* was the one who was *abnormal*, and Eddie helped her maintain that societally accepted image she wanted—and required. He helped her look normal. Nobody needed to know that she was a wicked witch.

Deep down inside, Liz had lewd and salacious lust in cold storage that threatened to overcome her on some rare occasions. It caused her to get a little freaky with her girlfriends or some strangers, and with all the talk of AIDS and the Magic Johnson bombshell revelation, around LA at that time, such lifestyle wasn't highly recommended by any means. Fortunately, Eddie came along at the right moment. Truth be told, admitting to herself and based on Eddie's show in the sack, she preferred women anyway. But there was room for improvement in him, and she knew it, so no reason for her to consider coming "out of the closet" even though in those days, it was a popular thing to do.

Romance flourished somewhat over a period of time. They both came from wealthy families, but the difference was that in LA, Eddie was a little poor. Unlike Liz's dad, Eddie's was really strict and authoritarian and wasn't as loose with funds. He didn't even buy Eddie a car after high school graduation. Eddie drove the same busted car he drove in his school days all the way to Los Angeles. Astoundingly, it survived the trip, to the disappointment of everyone, who had hoped he would perish along the way on such an attempt. Liz found it amusing and cute that he tried to appear roguish and attempted to conceal his affluent background.

Liz had previously conned her folks into sporting her a tiny pad apartment in a safe, clean neighborhood near Playa del Rey. Her excuse was that it was like a school dormitory, thus giving her the study space she needed without the distractions of home—whatever that meant—and of course, Mom fell for it. Once she did that, Liz and Eddie were practically inseparable. Eddie saw less and less of his family, and they were feeling a way about it. Eddie wasn't paying room and board to stay with his folks since he had come to live with them. He contributed very little to the household and spent all his video store money on his own personal goods, his car, and the rest partying with Liz. Eddie remained oblivious and devoted to Liz and didn't mind being her groomed boy-doll.

True to Liz's desires, she found she actually could dress Eddie up any way she wanted. She bought him clothes from expensive stores and made his look change from grunge to somewhat Waspy collegiate. She even decided which hairstylist he should go to and how to have his hair cut. At first Eddie didn't like it much, but when he noticed how people were starting to look at him differently, he grew to love it. It reflected in his attitude. He began to shun his old nerd crew at the video store and pretty much told them to fuck off. He was a total Liz slave and didn't care. No ideas of his own could be detected in his brain, or anything he considered better than being with her.

Eddie experienced his social metamorphosis during this time. Liz put him on to her friend circuit. He met Becky, Mandy, and an assortment of others. They would go clubbing and bar hopping and all the normal stuff. Eddie grew in popularity. He was beginning to be the star he never was back in Sacramento. It was amazing how a change of wardrobe and a haircut could expand his world from a prior scope of having only cousins at home and dork cronies at the video store, to now having a swell girlfriend, good friends, and also, other women were starting to really check him out. Now Eddie could exact some revenge and be the guy walking into a video store with a beautiful girl on his arm.

On several occasions, while partying with Liz's friends—who were now *his* friends *too* as far as he was concerned—Mandy tended to be a little bit too flirtatious with Eddie. He, pretending to be drunk, reciprocated, even though he had eyes for Becky in secret. Becky, who by now had grown her hair longer like Liz's, was like her twin, Eddie thought. And unlike the scandalous women who taunted and teased him back in the days at the video store, there was now touching and grabbing, and it was real. It gave him a game-changing high that no drug could ever induce.

When Liz realized Eddie's potential to be something more than what he was, her feelings for him changed immensely. Not that she had suddenly fallen in love with him—it was more a thing where she didn't want anyone else to necessarily have him. When she saw that other women—including her best friends, who already had boyfriends—seemed to want him or found him attractive or desirable, it caused her to feel a greater need to keep him to herself.

She loved her friends too and didn't want to lose them either. As for Mandy and Becky flirting with Eddie and possibly being attracted to him, she took it in stride. It was a compliment, really. She was determined to not become a nervous wreck with the jealousy, envy, and possessive feelings attached to a relationship. It was the high school stuff she didn't care to relive. She *accepted* it.

Life was about making mature decisions, wise decisions, she thought. Sometimes it seemed hard to make tough judgments, but she dared to do it. And when she did it, her reasoning was achieved by reminding herself that she too was attractive, beautiful, outrageously gorgeous, sexy, and so were her friends Mandy and Becky. Birds of a feather flock together, right?

As always, Liz was eager to prove herself. She liked proving things to other people too. Eddie was soon to graduate from Harbor College, and his birthday was on the same day. Liz came up with the idea to arrange a bizarre event to commemorate Eddie's graduation and birthday, and she wanted it to be something he would never forget. She wanted it to ensure that Eddie would devote himself to her for as long as she desired.

Liz damn near depleted her bank account, but she had to use cash because her mom had been giving her grief about all the credit card spending for frivolous activities or shopping. It had been reflected on the receipts.

She called Eddie at his job and told him to meet her in Downtown LA after he finished work that night. His shift at the video store ended at 10:00 p.m., but since he was assistant manager, he could make up an excuse to leave earlier and leave closing duties to a swing-man subordinate. Liz had supplied him with an address to a parking lot on a side street off Century Boulevard where he could stash his beater. With the purple-and-gray '74 Nova then stored, he walked a quick distance to a corner and hopped into a taxi,which took him to the Homewood Hotel.

Liz was already there and waiting for him inside the lobby. Jovial as always, she ran up to Eddie and bombed him with kisses following the big hug greeting. She also showered him with heartfelt congratulations for graduating the previous day and a premature birthday wish for his birthday, which would have technically been soon at the stroke of midnight that evening. Her mood was energetic, as if she had been jogging or finishing up a workout prior to his arrival. She made small talk like, "What the hell took you so long? Did you take the freeway?"

While Eddie made excuses about how bad traffic was, he looked around the fancy lobby, trying unsuccessfully to conceal his excitement. He could have sworn he had caught glimpses of a few famous subpar TV shows and low-budget sitcom stars along the way, and he was probably right. Although Eddie was from a privileged upbringing and his folks had money, they were prudes with the riches. Eddie was an only child, and his family vacations and outings were limited to trips to the Grand Canyon and Yellow Stone Park, which Eddie grew to abhor. They never stayed in any expensive hotels either. This was his first time at one, and he was impressed.

Liz shoved a hotel room key in his hand and told him to take the elevator to the tenth floor.

Eddie said, "Where are you going?" calling out to Liz's back as she had gleefully skipped away from him toward the lobby exit to the taxi port. She giggled like a Brady Bunch or Partridge Family happy, giddy young chick would, like she was up to no good. She blew Eddie a kiss innocently, but Eddie had butterflies in his belly and had a funny feeling that she was up to something—maybe a prank. He suddenly felt the need to take a dump. Was she breaking up with him?

"Just wait for me upstairs," Liz called back to him, and Eddie, believing that she would be back like she said, did as he was told. She dipped out the glass door and was gone.

Eddie waded through the elegant, posh, shiny marble floor's conglomerate of hotel staff, housekeepers, pages, bellhops, and kitchen staff. There was also a smattering of late-night arrivals such as himself, only now he was mingled with tourists set to be in studio audiences of random TV game shows, film crew gaffers, and hookers disguised as elite secretaries.

He finally found the elevator and got inside with a cluster of old tourist couples donning huge cowboy hats, toting fat clam-shell luggage, and reeking of Florida Water. He squeezed between them like an obstacle course to get off the lift and stumbled into his floor's corridor, wondering what the hell Liz had gotten him into now.

Eddie found the room on the tenth floor that the key was for. Thinking that Liz had put together a graduation-slash-birthday celebration gathering intending it to be an elaborate surprise, Eddie figured he would feign epiphany and wondrous shock and trudge up enough emotion to make a teary-eyed speech. Throughout their time together, Liz had never ceased to amaze, Eddie thought, and they had attended gatherings of this sort quite often with other friends—however, never to this level of ornamented extent. He was aware that Liz came from money, but he wasn't accustomed to her splurging for the fancy-shmancy five-star hotel overlooking the fantastic, breathtaking Manhattan Beach. He leaned his head ear-first to the door, attempting to try and detect activity inside. There was no stirring. After moments of hesitation, he finally decided to key in to the room . . .

2

AFTER THE GRADUATION and birthday celebration, Liz and Eddie were able to move on, and their relationship grew stronger than ever. Eddie's allegiance to Liz was solid, and he moved in with her.

It was a fine move for Eddie because his aunt was going to kick him out anyway, and his cousins were like, "Good riddance!"

After years of living with his aunt and not paying any rent, Eddie had saved up a little money, albeit not quite a lot. His parents would hit him off with some little gifts of money through wire transfer every now and then, but they were staunch in their decision to not create a dependent slacker of a son and didn't make such donations too frequently. It didn't do much good, though. Eddie spent his dough on marijuana, booze, comics, and novelties like *Pulp Fiction* movie posters as well as concert tickets where he and Liz would go see various artists like the Barenaked Ladies, Eagle-Eye Cherry, Cheryl Crow, the Wallflowers, and Third Eye Blind.

Liz had managed to recoup some of her expenditures by appealing to her ever-walkover-prone mother, who laced her daughter's pockets behind her husband's back, against his wishes. Eddie continued working at the video store for a while, but Liz knew that his income wouldn't be enough to support them by any means, nor would her babysitting gigs, so she shuddered at the thought of finding a real job, but had to anyway because she knew that her folks wouldn't foot the bill for her; and if she moved back home, she wouldn't be able to be with Eddie. Her parents didn't dislike Eddie, but they didn't really like him either; they were still

Team Carver and wanted their Liz to date high-class people from their section of town. Liz's father had the wrong impression of Eddie. He was a supercilious, *nouveau-riche* middle aged bigot who thought of Eddie as a lower caste who desired to marry up, seeking unsuspecting rich valley girls.

Still Liz was able to win her father over finally with the assist of her mother, her greatest ally, and agreed to support his daughter—and subsequently Eddie as well—until she graduated from college the following year. Her mother's supporting argument for Liz's case was based on her abatement. At least Liz was involved with a man, and even though he might not have been the finest of specimen in her view, she could have done worse; but he would have to prove himself.

Her college graduation wasn't the huge gala event Eddie's was, and he had no intention of trying to top what Liz had planned for his. Not in a million years. He was able to scrounge up some change to buy her a pawnshop bracelet—which ended up being an anklet as it was too wide for her wrists—made of white gold shined up to look elegant.

The job search after college was a dreary and futile hunt for a while. Following her passion for sports fitness and health, she tried to get jobs initially at fitness centers, swim schools, and tanning spas. She found a part-time job at the latter, but the pay sucked, so she had to keep her babysitting jobs, which were becoming scarce these days because all the kids were growing up and her clientele hadn't expanded very much. Some clients had reservations about referring Liz to other potential business because they had suspected her of using drugs after having found paraphernalia resembling bongs, small plastic bags, and peculiar odors in the air upon returning home. It was true, but Liz justified it by maintaining that she had only used while the kids were fast asleep. It was a poor attempt to clean up her tacky error in judgment, and failure to pass drug tests prevented her from getting jobs at the fitness clubs.

Becky and Mandy scored jobs right away. Because of nepotism and deep-rooted ties in the community, Becky was able to get a job working in the office of a gay lawyer who was a friend of her mother's. Mandy similarly got a job working in an office even though she couldn't type. More than likely, she was able to promise a little nookie to the guy who hired her on some eventual date. In the meantime, they could boast that they had somewhat professional careers working in offices downtown, preparing coffee, sharpening pencils, watering plants, answering telephones, and, most of all, dressing provocative and sexy in hopes that they could catch the eye of some sucker dude willing to wife them up, or, if not, that at least would take them out from time to time, or take them in and pay their way for an indeterminable period. Liz found herself in the same box as Eddie, to an extent. She too came from a rich family, but when they moved out to California, she was already in her teens, and her extended family was back in Iowa and Northern Oklahoma. She didn't have the influential friends in high places to hook her up so quickly like her pals. Ordinarily, she probably wouldn't have needed any special favors had she followed the instruction of her parents who had wanted her to go to UCLA or Southern Cal, but Liz insisted that Harbor was the only school who offered courses in her area of interest—fitness, or euthenics—but she ended up graduating with a liberal arts degree. She considered doing porn for a hotter minute.

Why she again thought of getting into adult entertainment arose was because it was the only offer for work that she didn't have to seek out. She would practically be propositioned by talent scouts every other week when she was in close proximity to a beach and sporting attire, which left her exposed from the waist down. Apparently, some directors wanted her for some interracial black-on-white "Queen of Spade" releases as she had ideal features bodywise that a lot of the so-called African Americans tended to adore. Nobody had ever explained to Liz exactly what her "ideal features" were, but she assumed very correctly it was the posterior anatomy. Yet another reason to consider porn soon came when Eddie lost his beloved job at the video store.

Just when Eddie thought his career at the video store was about to blow up, he was to instead learn that the place was going out of business. Instead of being promoted to manager, he would be getting his walking papers with a thank-you letter for his years of service and hard work. The painful irony was learned when Eddie got the news that the store was not really going out of business, but actually, Blockbuster Video was buying them out, as well as scores of other small-time local video stores like theirs.

Former owners of these local, unaffiliated video shops, just like Eddie's boss, the owner of "the off the beaten path" video store, couldn't compete with corporate monoliths and pretty much gave up without a struggle. Eddie was offered an optional position with the new company for less pay and ground zero demotion back to the level of the underling nerd former pals he had long ago shunned. Sparing himself the humiliation, Eddie left and found a job at a pizza shop, which had sucky pay, but as a deliverer, he could get good tips, plus free pizza and pasta at the end of his shift. He thought he was going to get a severance gift of appreciation from his former video store boss for never being late or missing a day of scheduled work—even if he was sick—but the older gentleman typed and copied a letter of thanks to all his former employees, signed his name, and the name of the person each letter was addressed to, and retired in Key West somewhere.

So how did Liz and Eddie end up in Japan? How did she end up here?

The idea to come to Japan was delivered upon her and then Eddie by proxy by a former acquaintance she happened to bump into while visiting the career services center at her former community college. She saw the scrawny but immaculately dressed man appearing to be in his his mid to late thirties due to his receding hairline and shiny baseball forehead emerging but was only two years older than Liz. She was a bit startled to meet him there. After their abject dalliances, Liz never thought she would ever see Carver Burk again. Miraculously, however, they remained cordial to one another and rather friendly. They even chatted for a while over coffee to catch up.

It turned out that Carver wasn't the type of guy to hold a grudge, and he had moved on with his life. He was a churchgoer and a forgiving type who expressed how he valued friendship more than holding on to how good or bad relationships might have been in the past. Relieved that he didn't, this made it easier for Liz to relax. Not that she feared him or anything—she simply wasn't in the mood for confrontations. Her job searching had dulled her feelings. Her babysitting jobs had dwindled to only one client, and tanning spa work was drying up too. She didn't spare an opportunity to spill her guts to anyone who would listen to her problems. Agreeable as ever, Carver was the perfect sponge he always was to suck up Liz's woes. She expressed to him the difficulties she was having to find work and wondered if he had experienced the same thing since he was there at the career services center.

Carver indicated that he had in fact gone through somewhat of a dead-end period where he was unable to land a job. But what he had to tell Liz about what happened after that had her ears extra tuned in.

He said, "Yes, a lot of companies don't like to hire us recent graduates. The reason they tell us is because we don't have any or enough experience."

Liz said, "Yeah, that's what I've been hearing."

Carver said, "Well, I've been working for almost six months. I just came back from overseas."

Liz said, "Where did you go?"

Carver said, "I went to Japan, Elizabeth. I was there for a year and a half. It would have been two, but I found a job here in the States. Had a phone interview."

Liz said, "What were you doing in Japan?" While thinking it was the last place in the world she could expect to see a guy like him and almost had to laugh at the idea of Carver wearing one of those fruity-colored kimonos.

Carver said "I did this work program—the CHET Program—it stands for Christians Helping Educate Together. They send people to Japan and have them work in public schools, community centers, and stuff. Easy work, really, and they pay about three thousand dollars a month. I was able to pay off my student loans the first six or seven months I was there."

Liz said, "Wow, lucky you. I haven't been to church in years. I was never as devout as you, huh? Too bad I wouldn't qualify for a job like that. But I don't know a lot about Japan, I never thought about really going there. What was it like?"

Carver said, "The people are really nice over there, and friendly. They seemed to love us American people. I was treated like a king. The food is nice if you care for sushi."

Liz said, "Oh, yeah . . . sushi does come from Japan, or China somewhere, right?"

Carver said, "And no, you don't have to be Christian necessarily. They really didn't stress the religious awareness aspect of it. I think they just wanted to base the program around the Christian principles and help people under a humanitarian umbrella . . . But the work itself was really easy. The easiest money I've ever made. I almost hated to leave, but I knew I couldn't stay there forever. It's a wonderful country, but not the place I'd like to grow old and, y'know . . ."

Liz agreed. "Yeah, I can understand what you mean, but for that kind of money, I'd be interested in trying."

Carver shrugged. "I would highly recommend it. Like I said, it's easy. Almost didn't even feel like work. I was always going to museums, castles, temples, shrines, y'know, historical sites, or excursions to botanical gardens—fascinating places you probably would have visited anyway as a tourist. It's practically a paid vacation. There's so much history and culture there to take in. At times it was downright overwhelming but at the same time, to top it all off, you're still getting paid for it.

"I know you'd enjoy it. You can party, have lots of fun, meet all kinds of people—especially in Tokyo. That's where I was. It's more international than most people would think. I met people from all over the world, not only just Japanese people. You don't even need to speak Japanese. Have you ever been to Mexico?"

Liz had been. She nodded recalling the year she stalled going to college, and Tijuana was one of the trips she made with Mandy and Becky. It wasn't the most fun vacation she had ever been on, but she was impressed with how far she could stretch a dollar there.

Carver continued, "Well, if you've been to Mexico, then you probably have a feeling what it's like, then. Imagine having all the money you need, party till you drop, enjoy the world to its fullest extent and still have money leftover saved. Like I said, I would have stayed the full two years, but when I was finally contacted by a company, I decided that it was a good time to come back to the States."

Liz was somewhat stunned to hear a guy like Carver talk like he was talking. *Party till you drop.* He never used to talk like that. In fact, he never even seemed like the party type at all. Carver had always impressed her as a church boy, one who sang in the choir, an exemplary, wholesome, and innocent type guy who didn't drink, smoke, or even curse, from the nearby gated community of Rolling Hills. It was amazing that he even struggled to get a job as he claimed, Liz thought; but then again, maybe his parents were strict too and were anti-slacker generation like Eddie's folks.

Carver then said, "Here's the kicker: when you come back to the States, you'll stand a better chance of getting noticed by a company hiring. You see, because by then you'll have that *experience* that those places always say we're lacking. The main thing is that on your resume now, you can put on it that you're fluent in Japanese. Because that will catch their eye!"

Liz squinted and said, "Are you fluent in Japanese now?"

Carver laughed. "No, not by a long shot. Sure, I can rattle off a few words, sentences, and phrases here and there, but fluent? No way. But who cares? It doesn't matter. Most of the time, neither is anyone at any of these companies you'd be applying to either—unless, of course, you're trying to get a job at a Japanese company, but I don't know anybody like that. Do you?" Liz shook her head no.

"The goal, you see, is to get your foot in the door. I don't think it matters whether you speak Japanese, Chinese, Russian, or anything at all. What matters is that your resume stands out in a pile among others, and that's the key. If they pick up your resume and see something different or more unique than anyone else in the pile, that's the goal, I think. That's what I believe got me the job I've got now. Anyway, a lot of people I know are doing it. It isn't bad at all overseas, and they even paid for half of my flight going there!"

Liz was flabbergasted. "That's crazy. I mean, it sounds awesome as fuck. I wish I could do something like that. Me and my boyfriend are in desperate need of real jobs. Right now I'm working at this tanning salon near Torrance, and the pay really sucks."

Carver said, "You should try the CHET Program, then. That's why I came here to the career services center today. I'm here to share my experience with this school's career service advisors."

Liz frowned and said, "Am I eligible for this program, though? You said I don't have to be a devout Christian, I got that part, but you graduated from college a year or two before I did, if I recall, so you must have applied and got accepted to that program immediately after graduation, right? Are they interested in recent grads?"

Carver's placid, tame Fred Rogers from *Mister Rogers' Neighborhood* facial features twisted up as if he had heard an unfunny, ridiculous joke. He stroked a beardless chin as if he was a wise old sage, and for a moment seemed perplexed before finally stating, "No, Elizabeth, I truly believe that the sole requirement—or requirements—are that you attended and completed the undergrad process, have a genuine interest in Japan, and attained a diploma. You have, haven't you?"

"Of course," Liz said. "My boyfriend has too."

Carver said, "Then you both should apply. I think the only restriction they have is that you not be over the age of thirty-five or something like that. All you need is two recommendation letters. That's a piece of cake. If you don't have friends or family in high places like most of the uppity folks where we're from, you can always go ask your former teachers, Since you're here at the career service center today, this'd be a good time. I'm sure you can track down a few of your former instructors.

"Like I told you before," Carver said, "I was treated like Mighty Thor when I was over there. With your looks, you'd be popular too. You are one of the only few natural blondes I know. Over there, you'd be more of an absolute goddess like the Hera that you are."

Hearing Carver speak of her that way warmed her heart. She could feel some warm fuzzies as she stared into his innocent blue eyes and almost felt bad about how she used to dog him out back in the day. She would get Carver to drive her to other dudes' cribs, perform some lewd act with them, then return to him still parked outside up to an hour later. She'd get in the car, wipe her mouth, slam the door, and be like "He had a *hard* time finding the book I needed to borrow. It was *hard for me to swallow* . . ."

The patient simp Carver would ask, "Well, did you get it?"

And with a look of absolute gratification, Liz would smirk. "Oh *yes*, I certainly did *get* it, all right . . . I soaked up every bit of it . . . every single drop!"

She abused him terribly, and she didn't know why she got such a thrill from it. Deep down inside, she knew that playing with people's feelings and emotions was wrong, but she had to do it. The hardest part was not laughing about it. Carver forgave her anyway. There probably wasn't a hostile bone in his entire body. The way he spoke to her and advised her proved it. She wondered if she would get back with him if he were trying to get her back. He was talking all nice, footing the tab for the coffee and cake, and forgetting that Liz was the chick who would excite him to rock-solid lengths and torment him with vituperation due to premature conflagration, leaving Liz's face looking like a wet Santa's.

Eddie seemed to have the same problem in the beginning, but he didn't seem to enjoy oral sex. *Seem* was the operative word. In truth, Fat Girl from Elk Grove was a hard act to have followed.

The problem with Carver was he would start firing away, prematurely, as soon as they removed enough clothes to do sinful acts. Then after a failed performance, he would calmly chalk it up to the fact that they needed not commit an unholy act as fornication and sex before marriage anyway.

Liz said to Carver, "Thanks so much for the coffee, Carver." They stood and leaned into one another and embraced in lurching stances so that only their shoulders met. Liz was quietly tempted to rub up against his fly. Today she was wearing a sporty thin-fabric A-line dress, and he would feel her warm lap. She was sure he would get in a certain mood but elected not to.

She took a step back and looked into his eyes and said, "Thank you for the advice and the information. I'll definitely look into it. The CHET Program, right?"

Carver took a white handkerchief out of his pocket and wiped his forehead,which appeared to be shiny, as if Liz's embrace—even a light hug with minimal contact—actually had excited him. He then said, "Yeah, and oh, and if you are going to apply, you'd better step on it. The application process is seasonal, and I believe that the deadline for this year is fast approaching."

Liz felt as if she was almost reeling from the earful Carver had hit her with. Like a bomb had been dropped on her head, her mind was exploding with ideas and possibilities. Maybe Japan was a viable option, like Carver had said. She had never thought in a million years that she would consider working in any other country, let alone one in the orient. She left the building and took a taxi to a nearby public library.

In the days before the Internet took over, the library was a prominent place where people like Liz had to go to acquire more detailed information about a particular area of interest, and it included job and career data. That day was no different. She did the research about the program Carver had told her about, the one that he had participated in. He was right—the requirement list stated that applicants need not be ardently religious and only needed a four-year college diploma to be eligible. No Japanese knowledge was required either. Reading all of this, it seemed too good to be true, especially when she saw that the salary paid would be equivalent to about three thousand dollars monthly. She wondered what the catch was.

The asterisk portion of the information piece stated that successful applicants would be required to commit to a minimum one-year contract. That would probably have been the catch, Liz figured; but then again, on the map, Japan didn't look too far from Hawaii, so how bad could it be? The only thing Carver didn't say or talk much about was *what did he actually do* while working in Japan? He mentioned teaching in public schools, but Liz had never been a teacher. Never thought about it either, unless it had something to do with health or fitness or euthenics. Still, if he could do it, she could do it.

Carver was also correct about the application deadline. It was only a month away from that date. Quickly she photocopied the career catalog page she had been reading about the program and raced downstairs to where the public telephones were. She called the toll-free number for the Christian Educators International's Christians Helping Educate Together Program. When somebody answered, Liz requested two applications, one for her and another for Eddie.

Needless to say, Liz reported to Eddie all about what Carver had told her that day, not sparing to mention that he was a guy she used to date, in order to "see if he was insecure." She gave Eddie the rundown about living and working in Japan. This came so suddenly that at first Eddie thought that she had been joking. But she wasn't. By the time she had arrived back to their apartment, she had a lot of time to think it over, and minute by minute, it had grown from a morbid curiosity to something of a probable necessity. In the least, Liz thought, just to apply and have an interview, to see what the gig was actually all about wouldn't hurt.

Liz began explaining it to Eddie, breaking it down to him in the same manner and fashion that Carver did, almost like she was selling the idea as a presentation for the program itself. Eddie shrugged off the idea initially, dismissing it as one of Liz's zany and over-the-top ideas that generally made for good laughs while getting drunk. He suddenly had a change of heart, however, when Liz emphasized that part Carver mentioned about companies hiring people with experience. Those that would stand out on a stack of resumes, or whatever the hell he had said. For whatever reason, Eddie took a bit of notice of that scenario, as he too must have heard something similar. He abruptly realized that Liz was indeed serious about this Japan thing, and if she went, then obviously, he would have to go too. He had nowhere to go; he had all but severed ties with his only family in the area, and he wouldn't be able to survive for long on a pizza deliverer's pay. The sound of three G's a month didn't sound bad at all if that was what they were paying in Japan.

For Liz, the more she talked about it, the more her mind was made up. Eddie was like a remote control, and she figured that she would be able to manipulate his decision before she even brought the idea his way. That's why she ordered two applications. There was no way she would ever consider doing such a thing, taking such a job, or attempting to even do so without her favorite boy-toy. Her living man-doll was Eddie. She had already decided his fate and hers. If they were going to be together and start a life, this was an opportune method for them to do it, she deduced. Moreover, it was a good way for Eddie to come up before the eyes of her family, especially her father.

Between the two of them, after a year of making all that scratch, they could amass a stash impressive enough to illicit acknowledgment from their parents, reassure them that they weren't slackers, idlers, goldbricks, or spoiled rich kids leeching. Of course, Liz knew that she was a spoiled little rich witch, but she would go through tremendous lengths to prove that she wasn't, especially bristling in defense of any criticism she'd receive.

Now with Eddie basically won over, the wheels were set in motion. Eddie too seemed to experience a gradual elevation of inquisitiveness and genuine interest in the program. It showed signs of surpassing Liz's. Eddie's aberrant curiosity about Japan was ignited in the days during his self-imposed exile from the skater community and found solace with similar others who had formed a nerd crew most of whom he worked at the video store with. After work and on days off, they would get together at one dude's crib, smoke pot, take shrooms, and sniff glue while watching this new genre of animation called Japanimation, or *anime*. The eerie and convoluted images portrayed of Japan and Asia mixed noxious with substance abuse at the time, but Eddie and his pals weren't the only ones. It was a popular, growing furor at the time, which would one day become a craze. For Eddie's experience, however, he and his pals became die-hard fans of the genre and could recount the good old days, the countless sleepovers—with his skater-reject nerd pals—watching hard-core, salacious adult-themed cartoons, sadistic episodes of slimy tentacles penetrating orifices of squealing naked dripping heroines—in 3D glasses—turned them on immensely. They would have circle-jerk contests before falling asleep with painfully throbbing hard-ons. Therefore, simply based on that alone, he surmised, Japan was as good a place as any in the world to see. Until then, surprisingly, his only visit outside of America was Germany, and he hadn't even ever been to Canada or Mexico.

With their minds made up by the time the applications arrived roughly a week later, both Liz and Eddie applied for the program. Liz took Carver's advice once more, and she hit up former sociology and English instructors—luckily both of them were females—and Eddie managed to contact his former supervisor at the video store, the actual manager he had been assistant to, for recommendation letters.

They each wrote somewhat plagiarized essays, as writing a three-paragraph composition on the subject of "Why You Would Like to Live and Work in Japan" was one of the application requirements. Also required were copies of valid passports, two passport-sized photo IDs, and the completed application form, which presented no big problems aside from the fact that Eddie had to request his passport from his family back in Sacramento. He was able to get it in three days, time enough for him and Liz to finish the process in the week's span.

As for the essay, they stole ideas from a newly established Internet system, and they subbed words here and there with use of a dictionary. Their basic reasoning for wanting to go to Japan echoed nearly everyone else who had ever applied in such a program or written about the subject of Japan: "Because of the ancient Japanese culture," "seeing the historical sites," "wanting to visit the enchanting cities of Tokyo and Kyoto," "seeing the cherry blossoms blanket the entire country's natural landscape," "the cleanliness," "the stunning architecture," "learning about Japanese language and culture," and so on. Some of the reasons rang somewhat true, but for the most part, both Liz and Eddie were ignorant about Japan and admitted that they didn't know much about the country besides the fact that it seemed like an advanced country in terms of technology but it had a lot of ancient historical roots that reflected every image they had seen of it as Americans living outside the country. So if someone were to have told them that in modern-day Japan people still walked the streets clad in kimonos, wore samurai swords and freaky haircuts with long ponytails and chopsticks to hold the buns in place, Eddie and Liz might have believed such to be factual.

In slightly less than two weeks, all the requirements needed to apply for the program had been fulfilled by both Liz and Eddie. Liz didn't have much trouble securing recommendations from two former instructors, with two factors in her favor: one of the teachers had a little time to spare; plus she slipped one of them ten bucks. Eddie, on the other hand, didn't get too many good grades, was absent a lot, and wasn't able to track down any former teachers. Instead, he got one from his former manager at the video store and another from his current manager at the pizza shop, who had, fortunately, taken a liking to him and was willing to lie that he had been acquainted with Eddie for years. With the hardest requisite out of the way, the passport photos, application form, and essay were the easy parts, so all they needed to do was mail the packages off to the CHET headquarters in Washington DC before the deadline and keep their fingers crossed.

In the meantime, Liz continued working at the tanning salon and babysitting and Eddie's gig at the pizza shop had picked up. Always a diligent worker, Eddie's job performance had impressed his current manager, who felt compelled to offer him more hours, which Eddie accepted, thinking he could work his way up to a higher position like he did at the video store. Instead of a promotion, however, Eddie got more hours and more delivery responsibility. In the beginning, this was good because his tips saw an increase, plus his standard paycheck too. The problems emerged when Eddie would have to push his Nova through some of the seedier, mussed neighborhoods of LA.

Eddie had lived in the city for years, but he still wasn't entirely familiar with the place, and his movement and knowledge was limited to the surrounding areas of where he worked, went to school, and stayed with his aunt and later Liz in Playa del Rey. At times, job duties would have Eddie delivering pizzas to spots that gave him apprehension, especially at nights when he worked most of his shifts. Mean-looking, menacing Mexicans muscular in wifebeaters would give him the shakes when he delivered to their area. They would seldom, if ever, give tips or offer him to keep the change, and he damn near had to pay kids money to watch his raggedy ride while he made house calls, or bribe them with free onion breadsticks. It was a wonder he never got robbed, but he shuddered thinking that it was only a matter of time before it actually happened.

Because money was rather tight, Liz and Eddie couldn't enjoy themselves like they usually did. She had seen less and less of her friends, particularly Mandy and Becky. They too were busy with their jobs and private lives. They would occasionally go to the movies, Angels or Kings games, some nice restaurants, and random concerts or shows here and there; but they didn't go buck-wild like they used to, tearing up the streets until the break of dawn. Instead of asking her mom for some more cash, she thought about what if she did decide to do porn? Could she just do one movie and get it over with and collect some big money? She didn't know who to ask about it. Of course, each and every time Liz would consider such an idea, she would also talk herself out of it. This time she took into consideration the likes of her brother Halbert, and maybe even her father too, and their habits.

She knew for a fact that her perv brother shopped for porn constantly. She caught wind of this from their mother, who complained about cleaning her son's room and always finding the shocking and lurid X-rated video cover boxes strewn about. For Liz's reasoning, it would have been her crummy luck that her brother Hal, or anybody who may have known her, would happen to pick up or discover a copy of a movie she had appeared in, and she'd bring disgrace upon herself and family.

In a span of time that seemed like eons but was only a month in reality, Liz and Eddie both received two separate postcards, addressed to each of them individually. The postcards were from the CHET headquarters. These cards, no doubt, supplied pleasing notification that they had been selected for interviews. The postcard supplied instructions, which were to call a telephone number listed on it and arrange for a time slot to be interviewed, provided that they were still interested in the program.

They were, and Liz wasted no time getting prepared for the assignation right away. She sped home to her family's estate and told her mother about her plan to pursue a job as a teacher overseas. At first, her mother, not surprisingly, rendered a lot of opposition and uneasiness about it. It was short-lived, as Liz had long ago mastered the art of persuading her mother to buy into her grand views through inveigling witchery. Liz was able to convince her much the same way Carver had been able to and used all of his talking points. When her mom heard that it was Carver who had recommended this program to Liz, and that he too had participated in it, she was won over. Carver was the epitome of credibility. He had represented purity and was known to be a good-natured church boy. With her mother on her side, it didn't take much to sway her father as well, who had also expressed his concerns in the beginning but decided to leave the decision up to Liz, as she was an adult.

Eddie's situation with his parents was similar, but he too secured their overall approval with the idea of him working overseas for a year. In fact, his absolutist father seemed to grant Eddie his blessing, citing that such an assignment might actually teach his son about responsibility and encumbrance.

Liz used the last money she had to get Eddie spruced up and copped him a conservative blue-and-gray business vine and a pair of shiny new stomps. They got in Eddie's whip and cruised all the way to Beverly Hills and halted somewhere on Camden Drive. There, she got Eddie all shampooed and styled up so that hours later, he sprang from Alma Salon looking like a fake younger Steve McQueen lookalike.

When the day of the interview finally rolled around, Eddie looked spiffy in his new suit, and Liz appeared tidy as well. Her mother, of course, had taken pity on her only daughter and saw to it that she too would be spruced up lovely for her big day. They had hit a boutique and got Liz laced up in a black, striped-fabric one-button business jacket and matching skirt with thin-heeled pumps. People actually thought she was a famous model or actress once or twice.

The interview was held on the campus of Pepperdine University in Western Los Angeles. Both Liz and Eddie would stun the two Japanese and one British interviewers for Christian Educators International. There were several other applicants among them, but Eddie and Liz were the most sharply attired. They looked like a hi-tech couple; other applicants there to be interviewed thought Liz and Eddie were the interviewers! It was an odd scene, as they resembled a set of high-powered young lawyers or urban professionals more than recent college grad slackers like the other applicants, some of whom had arrived for the interview in blue jeans and "boat shoes."

During the actual meeting with the Christian Educators staff for the CHET Program, Liz was energetic, spirited, and merry. She showed no signs of nervousness or jitters before, throughout or after the interview. In fact, her manner of addressing the two Asian inquisitors was somewhat minimally humble and offish, like she was talking to some people who might have been taking her order at a Chinese takeout restaurant. Apparently, little notice was taken regarding this, and it served as no deterrent or detraction from the overall impression she made on them. With glee, she answered every question with a bright and alluring smile and, along with witty remarks on the side, gave others a reason to smile, removing the tension otherwise associated with rigid and taut meetings like that. Her acceptance to the program was a cinch.

As for Eddie, he too attained successful marks during his interview. The years spent with Liz by now had swagged him out to his advantage, and he was aware of the charming effect he had on some women, especially when he was in nice clothes. With all three interviewers being women, Eddie was quick to notice that the British woman, who appeared to be in her late thirties, with a retro pageboy mop of hair, and a tad bit on the heavy side from what he could see, took somewhat of a liking to him. Eddie saw her suck her lips inward and breathing a lot through her nasal passage as her eyes darted up and down his body in the chair as he sat. At times, her gaze would rest upon his crotch as he was seated in slight 'manspread' position because his pants were tight and his balls made him look as if he was hiding golf-sized walnuts in his underwear. This English woman stated how Eddie resembled Jude Law, and one of the Japanese interrogators, who was familiar with the British actor, burst out in a fit of laughter but cited earnest agreement.

Today marked the first day Eddie had ever spoken to a real Japanese person from Japan, not a Japanese American or American of Asian descent. Although the English these women used was understandable, there was still a discernible accent when they spoke. It was obvious by then that they were very curious about Eddie. Apparently, they were expecting him to be a mild-mannered, epicene church boy type, but instead he came across as a slick, silver-tongued urbanite with charming Hollywood looks. Everything worked in his favor that would probably have eliminated any other candidate.

Eddie's interview was punctuated by the Japanese women asking about his relationship with Liz. They were aware that Liz and Eddie were together because they both listed each other's names while filling out the application section that inquired about whether or not they knew of any other applicants to the program, and what their relationship was to that person. Liz had listed two people, Carver Burk and Eddie Roman, as friend and boyfriend, respectively. Eddie had listed Liz only as a friend, thinking it wasn't in good form to categorize her as his steady.

The Japanese interviewers asked Eddie how long he and Liz had been a couple—a question they had neglected to present to the latter. They also asked if the two of them planned to get married, and other questions that seemed to border on what was deemed as too personal. Eddie would provide answers that indicated what he felt would suffice and merely offered the fact he didn't know about the future, but for the time being, eventually getting married was the tentative plan he had regarding the relationship with his significant other.

When the interview was finally over, they breathed sighs of relief and returned home. It did not take long for the good news to arrive. Not only did they both get the job with the program, the interviewers—who also doubled as advisor officials and placement officers—had seen to it that they both be situated in the same location, a city in the Osaka prefecture. They received the news via two thick A4-sized envelope packages.

Needless to say, Liz was overjoyed and exuberantly went into fits of screaming, yelling, and quavering with excitement. Although she had heard of Osaka, she didn't know where it was in Japan. The cities she was more familiar with due to her limited knowledge of the country were only Tokyo and "Key-Yo-Tow" (Kyoto). Other names she knew by affiliation with products she knew of like Sapporro (beer) and Kawasaki (motorcycles). She didn't remember where she had heard of Osaka, but she didn't give much care or concern to it because she and Eddie had gotten the jobs, and life was about to be good again. As far as she was concerned, if Japan was anything like what Carver had described, it would appear as though they would be going on a year's vacation with pay. She wasted no time sharing the good news with her family. Her father congratulated her and praised her efforts in finding such an engagement. Likewise, her mother dittoed her father's commendation although she was visibly saddened about the idea of her daughter not being close for such an extended period of time.

Liz's mother read the letter, which was inside the envelope pack bearing the good news:

Dear Miss Amberbush [Eddie's letter read the same only with name substitution *"Mister Roman"*],

This letter is to inform you that you have been selected to participate in this year's Christian Helping to Educate Together Program.

We are also delighted to inform you that we can grant your request to be placed in a host institution in close proximity to your significant other, contingent that you accept this location being Hannan City, Osaka. Every effort was made to satisfy your posting preference for Tokyo and Kyoto, however as these locations are currently saturated with participants just like yourself we ask that you understand the decision was made based on our present need.

You are adjured to confirm your acceptance to serve as an Assistant Language Teacher *by returning the enclosed reply form no later than two weeks following the receipt of this letter, or postmarked before that date. Please read all the documentation enclosed and should you accept this position, it would be to your advantage to already have a valid passport.*

Lastly, should you accept our offering position you will be required to appear in person at the Japanese Embassy in your city to apply for your Japanese visa. Upon arrival in Japan, you will attend a one or two week orientation in Tokyo prior to being dispatched to your assignment locale.

We here at Christian Educators International would like to thank you for your cooperation and patience with our procedures and selection process. We hope your journey to Japan is safe, wonderful, enlightening and pleasant.

Sincerely,

Oscar Gomimoto
Education Liaison Asian Division
Christian Educators International Institution
Washington DC / Tokyo, JAPAN

3

IT WAS RIGHT before spring, and Liz and Eddie's departure for Japan was less than a month away. Their friends and family treated the situation as if the two of them were planning some elaborate manner of eloping, or they joked as if it were true. Only Liz was confident that it was not far from the truth; after all, Eddie wasn't going anywhere—she made sure of that—and he knew it too. As far as she was concerned he was bonded to her forever, or for as long as she wanted him to be.

For their going-away farewell celebration, they partied like it was 1999, called up friends—mostly Liz's—and threw a barbarous bash at their crib. Of the several people who showed up, Becky and Mandy were decidedly present. There was a moment of uneasiness for Eddie initially when they appeared. He hadn't seen them since his graduation the previous year; it was the first time he had seen Becky again, now with longer hair, still looking like a shorter Liz, but on the thicker side. He was forced to look at her differently now. Liz kept a watchful, but playful eye on him during his brief interactions with her wild friends. Meanwhile, Liz carried on normally with them.

Accompanying Becky and Mandy were boyfriends both Liz and Eddie had heard about but never met until that time. Eddie now knowing the true characters of Liz's two cronies, determined the guys dating them to be more like benefactor sponsors than boyfriends.

A pinch of pain poked Eddie's gut when he saw the tall, six-foot-two mixed, mulatto dude Lamar. He was a black guy with a white European father from Bel Air, a pine warmer jock at some college, which had given him a free-ride scholarship, and he had, to his misfortune, hooked up with Becky and had his nose irreversibly opened for her. Little did he know that Becky was also seeing an East LA guy named Chavez, who was her fuck buddy until he had gotten locked up, then she went back to sporty Lamar with all the fresh fly gear, flat-top haircut, and fancy BMW but talked with rounded consonants and overcompensating proper English.

Apparently, Becky's secretly dating black guys was no longer a secret. But it also wasn't much of one that she had hopes of hooking up with a lawyer who wasn't gay like her boss, but nearly all his colleagues were also gay. No one took interest in her sexy ass except some of her boss's thug, hooligan clients of which Chavez happened to be. Lamar she met at a party and screwed after she was drunk. He fell in love with her, and the rest was current history.

Lamar wasn't looking too happy on this night, however. He appeared to be in a glum state, and Eddie could pretty much guess why. Liz recounted how Eddie had mentioned Lamar spending almost the entire night sitting in a corner of the room, long torso bent over his knees. His face was buried in his prolix yellow palms, gloomy, at one point seemed as if he was crying. Meanwhile, Becky was the party animal—social, jubilant, and paid little attention to Lamar, not moving to console or address his condition in any way, not even once.

Mandy's guy at the time was the dude Eddie accurately guessed was Steve. This guy was white but tried to claim that he was a quarter Mexican, quarter Puerto Rican and Irish. He spoke with a lot of bass and tone uniquely sharpened at certain intonations to sound black or like a radio hip-hop DJ. In fact, were he actually on the radio, without seeing his face, one probably would have assumed he was a so-called African American.

Steve was the guy who would have you believe that he was a gang member as he claimed. He had a series of tattoos on his hands, arms, and even some tiny ones under his eyes the size of rice grains, made to resemble teardrops but were actually minikin fish. Aside from that, however, he had a friendly and upright face that could stunt-double for Nick Carter of the Backstreet Boys. He too was dressed to impress in graffiti-decorated denim jacket bearing his name, and on his wrist was one of those illustrious timepieces from Emporio Armani, and Mandy had its matching companion because it had been his gift to her, like the twinkling, radiant new platinum bracelet on her other wrist.

Liz knew all about everyone's story, as did Eddie. He knew enough about Becky and Mandy to understand that as tempting as they may have been, it would do him no more good to consider anything flirtatious or otherwise with them anymore. Ever. Liz knew that he knew it. What she didn't know, or couldn't know, was the feeling Eddie felt seeing "top-notch" guys—Lamar a basketball guy who had the NBA future prospect looks and Steve the rich Vanilla Ice update—fawn over chicks like Becky and Mandy, two girls who appeared on the outside to be the prettiest flowers in the garden but in actuality were slimy, voracious man-eating weeds. It was shockingly amusing and perplexing his mind suddenly to then see his past days in the video store flash before his eyes again. Those fucked-up women—he thought—Becky and Mandy were just like them too. And, those unsuspecting hunks with them, with their Ferraris and BMWs and such, weren't so lucky after all—especially if their back stories looked like poor Lamar's and sucker Steve's.

Steve, however, turned the party out by whipping open his denim jacket, as if a flasher and actor from a movie scene, like "Hey, guys . . . wonder joints!" Then from the inner pocket of the garment, he produced a wooden case the size of a small A1 envelope containing several sticky-icky filled cones that had the entire place reeking the instant it was displayed. "It's from Jamaica, *mon!*" he said in a Caribbean-influenced pitch, another accent he could fake. It did the trick and upgraded the level of festivity. People cheered like they were at a school pep rally seeing star heroes.

The keg of beer ordered had arrived, and Eddie's manager at the pizza shop had blessed him with a little graciousness and donated several leftover pies to the jam. Steve's affluent Beverly Hills benevolence also provided a live DJ affiliated with Def Jef, or so he claimed—it didn't matter; nobody there knew who either of them were. He was just a black guy who looked the part and played good tunes to set the mood for the raucous occasion. It was nonstop weed, potato chips, dancing, drinking, root beer, vodka, shots, Absolut, ganja smell circulating the room like the stratus cloud of smoke from which they came. The party didn't stop until the break of dawn and somebody called the cops. Miraculously, no arrests were made. Life was good, and bribes could be paid.

4

JAPAN. FINALLY, THAT day had come. They made it there, and Eddie and Liz could have their short-lived version of a "Happily Ever After" saga. The flight was a little over twelve hours from LAX to Narita Airport in Chiba, Japan, outside of Tokyo city. Liz had never seen so many "yellow people" in one place at the same time in her entire life, and it was a bit unsettling at first. The flight had been a mix of all sorts of people, but by the time they had arrived in Japan, that seemed to dissipate into a sea of Asian faces. The writing and the language around her and Eddie changed, and suddenly, this strange new world had enveloped them.

Of course they were received at the disembarkation gates by a placard carrying representative from the Christian Educators group. Liz was relieved that this person was a non-Japanese, English-speaking individual who had greeted them with a friendly smile. Or he appeared to be so, at least. Regardless, his American accent and language was a comfort.

She had been to the ladies' room several times, and Eddie thought she was acting weird. He figured that it was her first time to have ever taken such a long and draining flight, the same as for him; but he didn't seem to be as worn out as Liz seemed to have been. When she was finally able to get herself together, the CHET Program rep, a *hapa* by the name of Oscar, who bore a resemblance to Keanu Reeves, but with a rounder head, crookeder front teeth, and glasses, took her and Eddie to the baggage claim to get their hulking luggage ensemble totaling five suitcases together with their carry-ons and shopping bags, increasing it to eight. Luckily, Oscar was all too nice and offered to help them carry the impediments all the way to a shuttle bus port, which he also rode along with them, to the actual city of Tokyo.

After another two-hour ride due to heavy traffic, they finally arrived in Tokyo, the big city. Oscar put the two of them up in a Ginza International Hotel and let them rest. He split and came back to retrieve them the following day. Jet lag didn't affect them too much because they had not slept on the plane, so by the time they had arrived, they pretty much were in sync with their normal sleeping hours and chose to not do too much exploring outside of the hotel's surrounding area. They found a Wendy's fast-food joint and went there, both pleased and surprised to see an American business in the country that was foreign to them. Eddie was glad that Liz was feeling better than she did when she left the airport.

The following morning, they got their first Japanese breakfast. They had been told they could get a complimentary meal in the hotel's restaurant on the ground floor. Liz was expecting toast, eggs, pancakes, and such, but not quite. Instead, there were strange square-shaped scrambled eggs sliced like a long row of cucumbers, thick slices of toast chopped into triangles, but no jam or jelly anywhere to be found. Instead, there was butter. No pancakes, sausage, or bacon. There was fish, pink salmon being the most prominent, and a series of small dishes that looked to them like various types of pickles and/or relishes that ranged in color from pink to green to yellow. Liz wasn't ready to be adventurous and try them; Eddie did and quickly regretted it. The only thing in abundance they could eat with little reservation was the rice, dispensed from a huge cylinder barrel that opened like a capsule with a lid at its top. Needless to say, they had a light breakfast, settling for toast, a boiled egg, lots of rice, and miso soup, something Liz had actually tried before and liked.

Oscar arrived later and picked them up in the lobby of the hotel. He had taken the liberty of ordering a minivan taxi that could accommodate passengers like Eddie and Liz with lots of baggage. The driver-operator was so friendly and rushed to the curb, opened the vehicle doors, and hastily loaded all their bags in the roomy rear compartment. Eddie and Liz had already exchanged some of their American money (via traveler's checks) to Japanese yen in the hotel and thought they should tip the driver, but the dude vehemently refused and rushed to the driver's seat on the right side—opposite of the US, which would have been the passenger's side—and started up the engine, ready to go. Oscar pulled the coats of the newbies that in Japan there was no need for tipping. Liz and Eddie were both happy and impressed.

Although they were only going from one part of the big city to another, the traffic was so thick, even at midday, that the trip took almost an hour. Nobody seemed to really mind. For Eddie and Liz, it was a comfortable, guided tour, which enabled them to see the city and the country up close for the first time ever. They got to see the crisscrossing crowded streets; strange new writing, or characters, of the language called Chinese Kanji, the likes of which they had seen in LA's Chinatown and Little Tokyo but was now etched in the landscape to the point of total inundation. Liz could finally also see that the Japanese people were very modern, dressed normally, and saw very few to no people at all wearing kimonos or samurai outfits. They were also happy to see that in a sea of Chinese writing signs, the familiar symbol of the popular golden arch of fast-food restaurants from the Western countries were abundant throughout the town tour.

They were checked into another hotel, but this one was less elegant than the first hotel they had stayed in the night before. They didn't stay, only long enough to drop off their luggage. They were then escorted to another part of town, where the first day of orientation was to take place. It was held on an academic campus area of a huge church in the Minato area of town to the southeast. There they met other foreigners like themselves, successful CHET Program applicants who had survived the selection process and made the cut. They were people from all parts of the United States, mostly rural areas or places neither Eddie nor Liz had ever heard of.

The orientation was a weeklong of intensive training, and it was basically a tutorial for first-time travelers and visitors to Japan and an introduction to the type of work that they would be doing. They got a brief, condensed history of Japan, then a summarized version of how their institute came into existence, and the usual speeches that welcome foreign people to the country.

They got schooled on how the US dollar converted to Japanese yen in the equivalent of approximately one hundred yen for every one dollar. Too bad they got hip to this on the third day in Japan when, after running late, Eddie and Liz decided to take cabs to the orientation spot thinking that they were still using the dollar and cents equations when in actuality, they were spending nearly hundreds of dollars on various trips instead of taking the bus or subway.

At night they would hang out at or near their hotel, which was ultimately like a temporary housing dormitory for the program participants for the week. The days were spent at the church campus orientation site like a normal workday, starting at 10:00 a.m. and ending around 4:30 p.m. Then after almost an hour's commute back to the hotel by train, most of them, Liz and Eddie included, were a little beat, so there wasn't much exploring. Some who dared would get hopelessly lost, not knowing the language and unaware of the way around and had horror stories to tell. Liz and Eddie were content to hang around the hotel and drink convenience-store beer and whiskey and eat snacks with the other program participants. It was like a nightly slumber party, but only Eddie and Liz were able to room together because they were given marriage status treatment. On their final night in Tokyo, there was a going-away party held in the Roppongi area of the city, where once again, they were able to see a plethora of people who weren't

Japanese and a lot of black people, and everyone was surprised to see them there, thinking that they were the American type but were actually Africans.

Eyes were on Liz the same as they had been back in California. Some tall, dark Black men dressed in fancy suits would stand in front of brightly lit signs on sidewalks introducing clubs of various sorts and encouraging the groups of foreigners like Liz, Eddie, and their fellow program entourage to check out their individual establishments. The orientation had warned them to stay clear of these joints, as some of them would charge ridiculously high entrance fees to unsuspecting new visitors. Or there were those places that had bartenders or shady lowlifes who would slip "Tuinal" or soporific drugs in the drinks of primarily female victims and rape, rob them, or worse.

While waiting for a light to change so that they could cross a huge, wide street, Liz was singled out and approached by a tall, well-dressed, but intimidating "negro," who touched her lightly on the arm, asking in a deep, Geoffrey Holder–reminiscent voice and thick non-American accent, "Where you from, baby?"

Startled and annoyed, Liz had replied, "I'm from Los Angeles, California." She looked to Eddie for some protection, and he reluctantly stepped forward and tried to position himself between the hulking mass of fear and his woman, but he did it in a comedic, non-aggressive way and smiled at the man like he had known him his entire life.

Eddie said, "We're all Americans," motioning his head toward the group of roughly seven people mixed with both men and women, most visibly shaken and nervous about seeing and talking to this black man, even though they were all foreigners.

The minatory man said, "I yam from America too, I yam from Bronx."

Eddie said, "You mean, like New York?"

"Yes," the man said. Nobody seemed to believe it. Someone from the group mumbled that the guy was lying and that he was probably from Africa somewhere. The light changed, and they scuttled off quickly as if they were escaping a stalker. The encounter with the man, coupled with the scary warning stories about the city, had Liz, Eddie, and their group hesitant about seeing the shiny, lit-up bars, and clubs, so they settled for a foreign-themed restaurant where they saw a lot of other Caucasian or white foreigners and appeared to be safe.

Now aware of the last train, where the subways ceased operation after midnight, they were mindful of the curfew and managed to make it back to the hotel in a timely manner. They had to wake up early the following morning to take a bullet train to the city of Osaka, and they couldn't miss it. So far, it had been a busy but interesting and an overall fun week. The people who they met during orientation were dispatched to various parts of Japan, and Liz and Eddie never saw them again.

5

THE PROGRAM HAD placed Liz and Eddie in Osaka, but not the big city part, the place they had arrived at when their train pulled into the Shin-Osaka Station around noon. Instead, they were to be stationed in the province, or countryside, another two-hour trip away. Like many foreigners who had never visited the country before and had only seen Japan on a map, TV, or movies, they thought Osaka was just the name of a city, but they discovered it was more. Atlas information had described Osaka as Japan's second largest city. Pictures they had seen of the place had Liz and Eddie thinking that Osaka, like Tokyo, was a bustling, phosphorescent city by night, not too much different than LA.

"Osaka is both a city, and then there's the state, or prefecture!" Liz exclaimed as she flipped through one of the manuals she had received during the orientation.

Eddie was trying to snooze as the bullet train, or *shinkansen*, raced past a breathtaking view of Mount Fuji, passing the Yamanashi region. Liz was enthralled reading more about Osaka, the place which would be their home for the next year. She discovered that Osaka tended to be especially rural in the southern region, where they were headed.

Oscar Gomimoto, the guy who had met and chaperoned them in Tokyo and the education liaison for the Christian Educators Institute, parted ways with them when they left the big city, but he hipped them with an easy way to get to their location by advising them to catch an Airport Shuttle Bus to Kansai International Airport from Osaka Station. That way, they didn't have to lug all their suitcases through crowded stations and streets to catch cabs to yet another station with similar conditions. The bus would furnish space for people like them with lots of baggage. From the airport, they could catch a train called the Nankai (main line), which would take them directly to the station they needed to arrive at.

It turned out to be good advice, albeit somewhat pricey. Hours later, they arrived at a station on the Nankai Line called Hakkotsukuri. Again, here they were, met by a program representative and members of the local municipal board and Board of Education (BOE), all of whom were Japanese, but only the CHET Program representative could speak understandable English. They welcomed Liz and Eddie enthusiastically and used two cars to escort the couple to their living quarters.

The location was officially known as Hannan City, situated at the farthest point south in Osaka near the border with the neighboring prefecture of Wakayama. This place was so far in the sticks Liz would later learn that people— even other Japanese people from Osaka—had never heard of it. It wasn't too far away from a famous place in the area called Kishiwada, but the Osaka they had heard and read about was an hour away by express train.

Aside from Tokyo—the big city and the capital—the Japan Liz and Eddie were first introduced to was the rustic, not-so-picturesque area. It could be said to have had beauty in some places (because it was new to them), but otherwise, it was a repetitive series of rice fields, empty lots, a mix of Japanese houses with triangular rooftops and flat-roofed neo-Western styles, a bunch of convenience stores of colorful varieties, and every once and a while taller apartment buildings, which could be seen for miles around, appearing closer in distance than they actually were. One of these buildings would be where Liz and Eddie would reside together.

To the average Californian from where they had hailed, the new home in Japan would have seemed relatively boring, but Eddie and Liz enjoyed the first few months. There was a slow, uneventful stillness of the locale that was kind of eerie, but that didn't stop them from having a good time.

When they were finally situated, unpacked, and ensconced in their living quarters, Liz had a big surprise for Eddie. She also was aware that she had dodged a major bullet, a feat that only someone like *her* could have pulled off; but due to her ignorance, she hadn't known how dangerously close she had placed herself in being in jeopardy of arrest by smuggling two dime bags of marijuana inside her shoes, underneath the removable inner soles.

In the days before the year Y2K, the security checks were not as intense and heightened. As such, customs agents and airport security had their suspicious, attentive, and cautious eyes on people like the black African Liz and Eddie encountered that night in Roppongi, Tokyo, and not blonde-haired, blue-eyed Disney princesses like Liz, who was able to skate through the customs inspection gate without so much as even getting her suitcase rummaged through. Eddie the same because he was with her. All they were asked to do was show their passports and answer easy questions about what country they were from and where they were heading to.

Prior to landing, Liz had removed the dime bags from her shoes and boofed them, a trick she had learned from Becky via Chavez. Upon arrival in Chiba, or Narita Airport, she had made several trips to the ladies' room to extract the contraband, which explained why she had appeared to not be feeling well according to Eddie.

During orientation, Liz had learned the extent to which she had gambled with her life as she and all the program participants were admonished about the use of illegal drugs in Japan and warned that possession of such could have them expelled from their position and arrested. The jail time for illegal possession seemed extensive, so much so that people like Liz thought that they were exaggerating. It was proven to her that it was no exaggeration when she heard more real stories of foreigners who had been caught with even small amounts of narcotics who got ten-year sentences. Such news had Liz shaking in fear and thanking all her lucky stars and uttering protective witch chants.

When all the apprehension and paranoia subsided about having the weed, Liz would finally show it to Eddie, who was overjoyed but at the same time very much relieved that Liz hadn't been caught and made her promise to not do it again. Liz was so used to doing it before on trips she took with Mandy and Becky she thought it would be the same when she did Japan; but she saw that she was wrong and did actually vow to not again try such a thing.

That out of the way, they thwarted the desolate boredom of their surroundings with impromptu parties. They would hit up the convenience store for beers and a strange new booze they took an immediate liking to called a *chu-hai*, a soda-like carbonated alcoholic beverage that came in fruity flavors and got them drunk quickly.

Eddie created a makeshift weed pipe out of aluminum foil. His skate-nerd pals back in Cali had taught him how to make it. Another stroke of luck they had was the fact that at the time, Japanese people weren't too familiar with the scent of marijuana to be wary or alarmed of its odor if it happened to seep from the cracks of Liz and Eddie's domicile. The Japanese neighbors chalked it up to the foreigners, or *gaijin*, preparing strange, smelly cuisine not of their country and were surprisingly open-minded.

The Japanese neighbors were so friendly, in fact, that the two residents who lived on either side of their apartment paid them a visit bearing gifts. Eddie and Liz would later learn that this was a normal custom practiced throughout Japan quite often. A new resident in a building would be greeted by people who already lived there and welcomed with a small gift, usually a household item they could use, like a set of sponges, dishwashing liquid, soap, or even a piece of fruit, a

Japanese snack, or maybe alcohol. Liz and Eddie both received a bottle of beer, and laundry detergent.

Their apartment was a two-bedroom place, already furnished with a small kitchen and dining area. It was very small, especially compared to the spacious spread Liz and Eddie had back in Playa del Rey, but they got used to it quickly. Since they slept together, the extra room they used as a huge place to store their things like a walk-in closet, freeing up space in the rest of the place so they didn't feel too boxed in. The furniture and household appliances were relatively new and still operational. These were apparently things that were left behind by previous program participants and occupants to be reused. They had a mini 68-inch-tall fridge, a 600 watt microwave, a toaster, an electric heater, a tea kettle, and a coffeemaker. In their small kitchen, they were also provided a series of pots and pans. They had no conventional oven, but they had a stovetop with four hot plate spirals.

True to Carver's words, their jobs didn't seem like work at all. They were treated like schoolteachers. During the orientation in Tokyo, they had received a crash course in the Japanese school system and stuffed years of training to be an educator into grueling cram sessions that filled close to eight-hour days, leaving Liz, Eddie, and everyone else fatigued and pooped. Now they were full-fledged teachers according to the Japanese BOE and thrust into their new positions expected to perform the miracle of turning Japanese schoolchildren into English speakers.

During Liz's interview back in Los Angeles, she had mentioned that she was good with children because she had spent years as a babysitter. As a result, she lucked out and got an assignment as a teacher at an elementary school. At that time, the Japanese Ministry of Education had not yet made it mandatory that elementary school students have English classes, so Liz barely had any work to do. She was more involved with accompanying a Japanese teacher in a classroom full of cute, animated children and served as a human tape recorder whenever a Japanese teacher needed her to articulate pronunciation of a certain English word for the entire class to repeat.

Eddie, on the other hand, was placed at a junior high school. His job was a little bit more active, busy, and somewhat challenging for, he actually had to try his hand at teaching and using the skill set he had been schooled on while in Tokyo. Luckily, he was handled with kid gloves, and the Japanese staff at the school wasn't too demanding of him.

Their schools, Liz's elementary and Eddie's junior high, were so close together in location the BOE thought it was a delightful idea to switch Eddie and Liz up every so often. At which occasion Eddie would visit Liz's elementary school and vice versa Liz visited Eddie's junior high. It couldn't be decided who made more of an impact, Liz or Eddie, but it was a given that they were overwhelmed with awe and praise. Although there had been previous ALTs to that region who were of foreign extraction, the program and others of its kind were still relatively new to Japan, and for many people—both Japanese students and teaching staff alike—it had been their first opportunity to ever interact and come into close contact with *gaijin*, especially ones like Liz and Eddie, who embodied that image of a foreign land to people accustomed to seeing black hair, dark (slanted) eyes, and the same pigmentation every day of their lives. Still, they went out of their way to make these visitors feel comfortable and at home.

At school or work, they would spend most of the day sipping green tea, coffee, or bottled water they brought from home. They would sit at their own desk, provided for them graciously by their schools, and at lunchtime, they ate a delicious meal that Liz agreed with, consisting almost always of some small slab of fish accompanied by an ever-present bowl of rice and the miso soup. While in the teaching staff room sitting at their desk, the room full of smiling and grinning Japanese staff teachers would constantly greet them with friendly "Hellos," which, for many of them, was the only English word they knew or could confidently use.

It didn't matter what kind of day it was—the hot, sweltering, sultry and humid climate of Osaka was new to both Liz and Eddie; it was like nothing Liz had ever before experienced, and it dulled her mood on most days, but not to the Japanese staff. While Liz and Eddie would have to change clothes at least once or twice, feeling stressed at some points, the overworked Japanese staff would never show any signs of agony or distress. They would smile at the visiting foreign teachers like everything was hunky-dory, make small talk with them (if such was possible with their English ability), and go out of their way to assist them with anything should they need it.

Neither Liz nor Eddie could speak Japanese as of yet, but the program had supplied them with numerous textbooks and provided one-hour intensive classes that took up the last hour daily at their Tokyo orientation. To Eddie's credit, he would spend his idle time in the staff room trying to learn the language whereas Liz would just sit, twittle her fingers, and basically do nothing until her mother sent her some magazines from home to read.

After a few months, Eddie had managed to learn and speak a few words, sentences, and phrases that were deemed understandable by Japanese people's standards. Although his speeches and talk would mean something close to nothing, like a baby's attempt to talk, the Japanese people praised him and offered heaps of encouragement for him to continue trying to learn. Liz eventually lost her stubbornness and decided to try and learn the Japanese language as well, amazingly surpassing Eddie's progress in a matter of weeks, and came to know all the basic greetings and responses. The best part about her studying was that it caused her to stop saying "Good morning" in the afternoon or evenings because up until then, it had been the easiest thing to utter a word that rendered the same sound as the American state of Ohio bearing its meaning. People thought of it as cute and funny she used the greeting at any time of the day. She became a favorite in no time. Carver was right: people grew to love her, and Eddie too.

To the locals, Liz and Eddie became celebrities. Little children at the elementary school Liz was stationed would draw pictures of her with yellow or golden hair and often depicted her with a crown or coronet on her head as though she was a royal princess. They were also showered with gifts. In addition, they were featured constantly in the small town's free press and community news rags. Anytime they were seen walking alongside the road, en route to the train station or from it to their crib—a fifteen-minute walk—they were offered rides, mainly from people they didn't know, or people they didn't remember they knew, or a combination of both—people they knew but whose names they couldn't remember. The hospitality they were shown was endless, it seemed, but this sudden VIP treatment they welcomed wholeheartedly.

During this time, they took a liking to Japanese snacks. Some were not too out of the ordinary, but different, like peanuts with spicy sesame crisps. Then there were odd ones like the dried squid, which was smelly and peculiar in the beginning but gradually earned a spot on their likable list of edibles. They would receive these and other types of gifts on a regular basis. So much so it reduced their need to buy them at the convenience stores.

They also received various household items, toys like the antiquated toy called a *kendama*, with a ball attached to a string and edged handle that they couldn't, for the life of them, have the former attached to the tip as was the purported object, unlike a traditional yo-yo westerners like them were familiar with, and bags of rice. The household item they liked the most was an appliance called a rice cooker. It was like the one they had seen in the Ginza Hotel back in Tokyo for breakfast, only much smaller and designed for home use.

Liz and Eddie spent so little on buying things because everything they needed they were supplied by gracious neighbors and co-staffers from their jobs. They marveled at how people would give them things like the rice cooker, a TV, a VCR, and other electrical items, including a boom box radio with CD and cassette players, which was fully operational. Most of the things they received looked almost brand-new or unused. Generosity furnished almost their entire living situation. Liz was to learn that it was a common practice for some Japanese people to buy all brand-new things after a short time, even cars, and giving them away if the option was available instead of throwing it away—something unheard of in her world where stores would lock up even their garbage dumpsters.

The teacher who had provided Liz and Eddie with the rice cooker had also showed them how to use it, how to measure the rice with a cup, and the amount of water they needed to fill up the contraption. It was so new and fascinating that Liz was dumbfounded as to how easily rice was prepared compared to how she knew it to be done back home. After this, both she and Eddie would begin eating rice more than they ever had before in their lives.

In addition to rice, their Osaka initiation demanded that they be introduced to a favorite cuisine popular in the Osaka, or Kansai (western) region of Japan called Okonomiyaki, or Japanese pizza as it was at that time called. For people like Liz, and notably Eddie, who had spent the last previous year in a pizzeria, this Okonomiyaki stuff was far from what their idea of pizza was! Still, it was a cherished dish that looked more like a vegetable pancake with fish flakes atop that people in the Osaka prefecture seemed to love.

At their welcome party to the city of Hannan, the BOE folks who met Eddie and Liz at the Hakotsukuri station had given them Okonomiyaki for the first time. They liked it *then*. Next they were treated to a complimentary dining session with Liz's school principal, whose family served Okonomiyaki. Liz made a friend at the local Laundromat—because the one appliance her and Eddie's crib didn't have was a washing machine—and that woman could speak a little bit of English and wanted to practice speaking it more, so she invited Liz to dinner at her place with her husband and small child. There she was served Okonomiyaki again. Finally, Eddie had participated in a cultural festival at a local community center where he learned how to make Okonomiyaki alongside some young kids, most of whom were students at Liz's elementary school. By the end of the first few months, both Eddie and Liz had had their fill of the Okonomiyaki stuff. Especially Liz, because at that point, she felt she was gaining weight. The food was very doughy, and she had been consuming a lot of rice, at practically every meal. She then resumed her jogging and sought a fitness club to trim the emerging poundage and urged Eddie to do the same. Eddie, however, declined as he stubbornly believed that he couldn't gain weight.

Occasionally Liz and Eddie would make visits to the city of Osaka. It was about an hour from their station, Hakotsukuri, in Hannan City, provided they change for an express train transfer at neighboring stations like Ozaki' otherwise the trip would be considerably longer using the local. By the time the train pulled in to the terminal station in Osaka called Namba, all the seats would generally be taken and the coach crowded.

They would most often take excursions to the city on weekends when they didn't have to work. The first time they went was a discovery tour, and they were in tourist mode. They saw all the famous sights like the Osaka Castle, the Osaka Tower (*1), and the Kabuki Theater, and tried to familiarize themselves with the various main drag areas of the town like Namba and Shinsaibashi, the two main areas for shopping, dining, entertainment, and commerce; Honmachi (or Hommachi), a business district with unique restaurants and coffee shops; and the main hub, Umeda (or Osaka Station), which was a combination of all the above, plus served as a connection point for several different trains, subways, and bus lines. Other places they would later discover would be Tennoji (a seond-tier version of Umeda but connecting the southern districts of Osaka and Nara); Tempozan, a harbor area with a famous aquarium; Nipponbashi (Den-Den Town), a place popular for electronics and later the Otaku element; and Kyobashi, home of the Candy Box Nightclub.

There was so much to do, much to see in Osaka City. So much so, it frequently became a cumbersome task to even go there. For the first time in their lives, Liz and Eddie became dependent upon public transportation. Back in LA, they never had to wait for a subway, a commuter train, or even a bus. They either had their own cars or used other people's cars. Eddie ended up giving his car to his younger cousin back in LA in an attempt to mend his relationship with those family members and the aunt who took him in. His token was appreciated, albeit with lukewarm reception, but he was somewhat regretful after enduring the task of having to walk everywhere and constantly needing a train to go anywhere. When he returned home for a visit, he would have to endure the same thing, and he dreaded the idea.

Once, while visiting Osaka City, they were so caught up in the exuberance of enjoying the sights and the scenes and bustling activity that they accidentally missed the last train back to Hannan City. They made a foolish error in judgment and took a taxicab all the way back to their place. The cabdriver was so happy that he took the job and retired for the rest of the night. It was a learning experience; they never did that again. It would have been cheaper for them to have stayed in a hotel for the night than spend almost three hundred dollars for a ride all the way back to where they lived. Luckily, they had a surplus of cash savings to bounce back quickly from such blunders.

Their salary was about $3,000 a month, or 300,000 yen. Since they lived together, they shared rent. Real estate was cheaper in the sticks, so that was another advantage. With rent split and utilities paid, they had over $2,000 to basically burn. They had very little to spend money on other than food, travel expenses, and entertainment like renting video tapes, buying music CDs, and seeing occasional movies.

What could possibly have been one of their better investments was their purchase of a telephone. They thought about getting one for their apartment initially, but Liz had a better idea.

The cellular phone craze had taken over the United States too at that time. Becky and the girls had theirs, but they were bulky and extreme compared to the ones Liz had seen the people use in Japan. Furthermore, she had heard that Becky had sky-high phone bills. Mandy had the same problem when she and Steve eventually broke up: he stopped paying her bills, so she changed plans to prepaid. She would pay in advance and be charged for only the time she used. It so happened that in Japan, the same could be done. The difference was that in

Japan customers wouldn't be charged for calls they received! All they needed was to show their passports as ID.

As time dragged on, peculiar things happened whereas Liz's duties and responsibilities had shriveled down to almost nothing involving teaching English. Instead, she would go on field trips to some old castle, a kids' park, outside playing soccer or dodge ball and watching the kids prepare for various festivals like Sports Day and Culture Day and the like. Sometimes her presence at school wasn't even needed at all, and she would be kindly dismissed for the day. It was a good and a bad thing for Liz. For one, it was good when Liz was hungover, disheveled, and feasibly reeking of alcohol and overall, not in the mood for being around all those smiley-happy slanted faces exacerbating her headaches. The bad thing was, even if she went home, there would still be nothing to do. Besides watch TV, the VCR, or stare at a blue sky and rice-field panorama, mountains, and trees. There wasn't much there to keep her entertained. The small-town "off the beaten path" video store couldn't keep up with Liz and Eddie's demand for foreign movies with English dubbing. They tried to watch Japanese movies, but these couldn't hold Liz's interest very much because she was hopelessly baffled by the language and simply gave up trying to understand it. She also became lazier about studying Japanese.

Eddie, on the other hand, had a different experience. As a junior high school ALT, he seemed to have more responsibilities. He would be inside of a classroom and teaching with the actual Japanese teacher. Often, it was fun, for both Eddie and the students. The students were very friendly, warmhearted, and attentive, both girls and boys. Eddie never had to come up with any of his own lesson plans—he just followed the instructions of the Japanese Teacher (JTE) of English, repeated words and phrases when directed, and occasionally he would teach and engage the students in Western games like hangman (*2) and bingo and likewise he would learn Jan-ken (rock, scissors, paper) and *achi-kochi* (here and there); and when he finally learned the *kendama*, he brought the house down with thunderous applause. He was a superstar instantly, and he loved going to work almost always.

Toward the end of the year, as the holidays for Westerners drew near, the appearances Liz and Eddie had to make at their schools decreased. Although it wasn't mandatory, Eddie would still attend the speech contests; go on the field trip(s) to the Osaka Castle and museums; go on little hiking jaunts to Inu-Naki Mountain, the famous Todaiji (Shrine) in Nara, even went to see a kabuki play in Ebisubashi. Sometimes Liz would go; sometimes she would stay in Hannan City and sleep, or go jogging, or try to keep herself busy on the fitness side.

Eddie was happy, living his best life and enjoying the Japan experience for the most part. He was still studying Japanese, and people told him that he was getting better. He enjoyed attending seminars and events where he and Liz could dress up in the ornate kimonos and ancient samurai armor and watch tea ceremonies and make origami cranes. It was a blast. So far, Carver hadn't been lying. They had saved a lot of money and had a lot of good news and stories to report to their families over the winter holiday.

6

THE HOMECOMING WAS a marvelous reception for Liz and Eddie as they returned to the United States with a lot of odd, fluky selected souvenirs for friends and family. They got an opportunity to let loose and enjoy things from their country that they missed while living abroad—real pizza, "real Chinese food," places to shop that had their sizes, and people who spoke English—yet compared to how they used to get wild, this time around was rather mellowed.

Liz was content to an extent, but she didn't know if she could remain in Japan another year, or if she would renew her contract with the program. Especially, she reasoned, if the conditions would be the same in the following term. She was growing bored and unimpressed, not with Japan, but just the "Japan" where they lived at. She had hoped that maybe an opening might have come about which might have allowed them to move to a more urban setting, like maybe Tokyo, or anywhere a bit more citified. If not, her home sickness was imminent.

Eddie was loving Japan more and more day by day. The way things were going for him, there was no reason to think that they wouldn't renew their one-year contracts. Up until then, Eddie thought that Liz was just as ardent as he was about the program and what they were doing. For him, the work and the money were easy—in fact, the easiest money he had ever made. He too started feeling himself and developing his own brand of ostentation, at times purporting himself as a real teacher.

Home for the holidays was now a tricky affair. Time was now split between two different hometowns. Eddie was allowed to visit Liz's family in LA; then he went back to Sacramento to be with his folks. Later Liz took a flight up to Sacramento and met Eddie's people for the first time. She also got a chance to see the snooty, upscale community Eddie came from for the first time and figured it out that it was his family in LA that were low-scale types. Funny thing was, Liz's father didn't like Eddie much, and Eddie's mother didn't think too highly of Liz; but there wasn't any turmoil. At that point, everyone was assuming that these two were planning to announce their engagement or wedding plans soon.

Liz's mom was especially happy to see her. She missed Liz, and Liz missed her too. She missed her friends, her father, her old neighborhood, and stomping grounds near the beach. Even her brother Hal looked as if he was glad to see her back also.

Eddie was indifferent about seeing his family. Hopes that his relationship with his family people in LA had ended on a positive note because he left his "junkasaurus" Nova to this cousin was unfortunately deflated. As fate would have it, the engine bit the dust, and so did any hopes of him ever mending his ties with his aunt and cousins; and although he was received with enough cordiality, allowing him to stay with them one day before heading back to Sacramento (upon initial arrival in LA), he was otherwise not too welcome there. Eddie didn't seem to care about that. In fact, prior to leaving the States, he had told Liz that it was harder for him to say good-bye to his ride than to his flesh and blood. And as for Sacramento and Elk Grove, it had been the same dull existence he wasn't interested in returning to. Whatever friends or pal-arounds or former versions of such had long since spread the word of how much of a reprehensible cretin he was. For cheating with his best friend's wife wasn't considered honorable, but old Fat Girl never bothered to mention that it was she who would sneak into Eddie's crib when her future hubby wasn't around.

In Eddie's family's basement, they would drink a case of Bartles & Jaymes Wine Coolers like it was ginger ale, smoke cigarettes, and listen to satanic punk rock music. Then Fat Girl would suddenly freak out, remove her whale panties, and then viciously unwrap Eddie's naked meat and cram it in her face like nuts and bolts. Eddie, obviously taking some reprobate liking to this, allowed her to do this on a regular basis. Of course, he knew his homeboy was seeing the cunt, but he never imagined that dude would marry her! But tie the knot with her he did, and one night, the alcoholic behemoth spilled the beans, and whatever else she had been guzzling that evening. The rest was history, and as such, Eddie never received much of a warm reception whenever he came back around his way. A permanent move back there was out of the question; he didn't care how rich his family was.

Now Liz, contrarily, had felt that she had almost achieved what she had set out to accomplish. She was halfway through the year—or the one-year contract. She wouldn't mind doing another year only if she could be in a "better" place; if not, she was fine with returning to America. She had learned enough Japanese and had amassed enough experience, in her own opinion, to use on a *curriculum vitae* that would catch someone's eye, as Carver had put it.

After a year in Japan with no recreational drugs, it would be a cinch to pass any silly drug test, Liz thought. Considering an opportunity to come home permanently weighed heavy on her mind. Now that she had returned to hear folks telling her how she appeared to be "gaining weight," it got Liz's mind back on fitness. With all the walking she had to do in Japan, plus the profuse perspiration inducing humidity at times creating sauna-like conditions, she would have thought that she had toned out a bit—and she did—but people who hadn't seen her for a long time couldn't tell. So she made up her mind that she would seek a career that revolved around health, fitness, or her field of study, euthenics. That was her dilemma, in fact, about Japan—improvement of conditions. If her conditions had improved, her attitude might do the same!

The only time during the visit home that Liz got to see old friends Becky and Mandy was once right before the big Y2K millennium New Year's celebrations. Nothing much had changed. Becky was still working at the gay lawyer's firm, still dragging Lamar around too; but if anyone had gained weight, in her opinion, it was Becky. Mandy had by then broken up with Steve, but he was still hung up on her and buying her nice things—perfume, jewelry, and gold-digging trinkets fitting for her ilk. While she did miss her friends, there was an underlying trend in behavior she felt she was outgrowing, and that was probably the kind of lifestyle she once shared with those main two companions. Her mistake was involving Eddie. Now the four of them would forever be connected in a weird way, thanks to her own misjudgment, believing that it would make her bond with Eddie stronger and fortified; but she could never see it as one of the many catalysts for its undoing.

7

LIZ AND EDDIE returned to Japan the second week of January amid a litany of unnerving rumors that the coming of the new century—Y2K, or the year 2000—would shut down all the world's computers and the resulting outcome would have delayed flights, chaos, and an overall life disruption. Fortunately, nothing like that happened, and they landed at Kansai International Airport (KIX) without incident. Neither Liz nor Eddie tried to smuggle any illegal contraband this time, although they were tempted.

They had had a lot of time to talk about their future plans before, during, and after their flight to and arrival in Japan. Liz was practically resolute that the two of them would be returning to the United States upon completion of their contracts with the CHET Program. Eddie, somewhat reluctantly, agreed; but he couldn't argue or disagree with Liz. She pretty much decided things for the both of them. The only thing that would have made Liz consider staying in Japan another year would be a change of location. This request she put in writing—typed up fancily and sent to the program institute headquarters in Tokyo.

In the meantime, Liz found out she could work out at a community center in the town of Izumi-sano near the airport. She didn't particularly like the thirty-minute ride (plus the additional fifteen-minute walk to her station) to get there; but fitness clubs like Bally's, Tipness, and other supercenters like XAX, were few far and between at the time. Liz felt she had endured one comment too many from people back home about how she had gained weight, even though it was far from the extent to which they were blowing her up. Still, she would make the

Liz wouldn't have been down for that. It was a disaster waiting to happen, and eventually Eddie's excitement would surely get him into trouble; and when it did, or even if it did, where would he take the lucky girl? Certainly not to his pad and have Liz walk in on them. This was before he had heard of the love hotels of Japan.

It wasn't that he didn't love or care about Liz any less, but she was perpetually refractory and stubborn. It was clear that she was the boss of the relationship, and while he didn't mind being led around like a puppy on a leash, he did seem to care about her perfunctory traits pertaining to fashion and upkeep. For a girl so obviously attractive, Eddie would later admit that he was shocked at how she hit the wall so fast, in his view.

Life in Japan had caused Liz's tomboy to reemerge, and Eddie had preferred a more feminine Liz. Becky. But she was another story.

Japan was, for most of the time they were there, either hot, humid, damp, or all of the above; and when it wasn't like that, it was rainy. Liz didn't like wearing conservative attire—business suits and heels—in that type of environment, and he didn't blame her because he didn't like wearing neckties and collared shirts and dress shoes himself. The walk to and from the train station had an uphill-downhill slope and precisely narrow sidewalks they had to share with speeding bicyclists. The terrain was somewhat rugged, and oftentimes, Liz's appearance reflected that.

Liz became the guy Eddie was in Sacramento: T-shirts and jeans, scant makeup, less perfume more perspiration and armpit stains to show for it. Her hair was growing longer, and she refused to go to a Japanese hairstylist, opting to take the matter into her own hands or wait it out until she took a break to go back to the USA. Her hair and hygiene laxity were deleterious to Eddie's attraction to her at times, and he couldn't help but entertain the idea of creeping around on her.

Liz almost never wore skirts, and day by day, she seemed to be dressing more and more boyish, and acting like a boy too. To her credit, she had a good reason—that being the lack of what she had deemed quality shopping centers and size selections available. Sometimes she seemed more masculine than Eddie and, because she was slightly taller than him, looked like his long-haired compadre with abnormally inflated breasts.

Were it not for her pretty face, essentially, long blonde hair when it wasn't in a tightly wrapped bun or ponytail, and rack, she would otherwise be void of female traits? Which, in turn, led to the unavoidable problematic issues with intimacy they eventually began to face.

Whenever she would put out, Liz was still the fulfilling love goddess of his life. But she was unyielding on her restrictions on him trying to perform without contraception, as she had no intention of taking birth control pills in Japan. The only products she had confidence using in the country were toothpaste and tampons.

Eddie would run through a box of condoms frequently. Not because he was having hot, butt-naked sexual romps in the sack every single night but because he claimed to rip through the smaller condoms available in Japan and, in one attempt, use about two or three in the process. Then there was an issue of the timing.

Sometimes their schedules clashed. While Eddie would be working practically every day, Liz would be required to show up at her elementary school maybe three or four times a week. The times she wasn't at her school job, she would be at the community center sports club in Izumi-sano or jogging-walking along scenic rural country back roads. When she came back from her outings all sweaty, she'd be the aggressor for Eddie's affections as she undressed for her shower. Eddie wasn't a particular fan of her in that condition and couldn't get as worked up as she had, and that ultimately didn't lead to either her or his satisfaction.

Their sexual incompatibility was imminent too, even though inconceivable in the beginning. Liz had for the longest time thought that Eddie was indifferent to or dissatisfied with her oral sex. She was wrong: her skill was up to par, but unfortunately, compared to Fat Girl back in Eddie's former world, Liz would be a runner up if there were a contest, whereas that other chick would win first, second, and third prize—gold, silver, and bronze. Eddie would still catch cold flashes waking up dreaming about how Fat Girl would quaff an entire bottle of wine cooler, then start singing Dead Kennedys or some other group and start dancing wild. Suddenly she would tear off her panties and jerk Eddie's arm, pulling him toward her. She take his hand and make him cram two or three of his fingers inside of her—he remembered how squishy she felt, like he was puncturing a slit of raw liver. She would pull his pants down as she sat on the carpet, then pull him on top of her, but covered her hole when Eddie tried to mount. She would yank his waist to her face, dig her fingers into his butt cheeks, and press him into her throat like she was squeezing and consuming fresh orange juice. This, repeated on a frequent basis, was hard for anyone to ever top as far as Eddie was concerned. So erroneously, Liz thought Eddie didn't appreciate her "top" artistry and expertise, and as such, she sought to increase her clout in the craft by continuing to try and please him in that department as opposed to the intercourse area. What she wasn't going to do, she was absolutely sure, was get pregnant! So it became unsurprising that a lot of their play time ended in 69 positions.

Eddie's oral finesse was lame, lacking, and overall pathetic as far as Liz was concerned as well, and that she wasn't faking or hiding from him. But similarly to Eddie, even if she had tutored him to pleasure her to her liking, no one had done it better than the chicks she had made out with, primarily the volleyball coach's assistant and Becky. Still, it was her proclivity to think that women knew how to satisfy other women in ways men couldn't know how to. If it weren't for her insatiable hankering for penetration, she probably wouldn't have felt any need for an Eddie, or a Carver, or any boyfriend. Maybe.

trip from Hakotsukuri (Hannan City) to Izumi-sano two to three times a week, sometimes even more, depending on her skimpy work schedule offering her more vacation days than ordinarily expected. It was fine otherwise because she had time and money to basically kill.

Their salaries were always directly deposited in this bank called Sanwa at the time, and they had a good surplus even after their enormous expenditures during the holidays. The money they saved, Liz figured it would be used by her and Eddie toward their building a future together. It was something they had a lot of time to discuss. The basic idea was that Eddie was to get a good job, they would return to the United States, buy a house—with the help of their parents if need be—and live happily ever after. This pipe dream had been conveyed to Liz's mother, and subsequently her father too, and it was supported, albeit tentatively. Regardless, she felt safe having the net of her family's support to fall back on in case cloud nine sent her crashing down.

Eddie was still experiencing a growing fondness for Japan, and he was low-key, hoping that Liz would change her mind about going back home and stick it out for another year. Participants in the program could renew their contract only once, so the maximum time they could be eligible for it was two years. Thus, Eddie figured, why not stay another year? It was easy money, easy work, and one hell of an experience.

Another reason Eddie was enjoying Japan was because just like back in LA, his life as a nerdy, gangling poser transformed into that of a hip and appealing socialite and productive member of society, so to speak. He exceedingly savored his new status as someone important in Japan. He, like Liz, was lionized—but more so him, for some reason, and people would stare at them everywhere they went and, in some cases, treated them like Hollywood stars.

Eddie wasn't around Liz at every stroke of the clock to vouch for her experiences in Japan, but for him it had been the ultimate rush to be popularized in ways that never before occurred. His sudden Academy Award–winning looks of a Jude Law made him a regional sensation. He was a local hunk, and some immediate-area high school girls in short school uniform skirts would purr delightfully at him whenever their paths crossed. It wouldn't be long before Eddie's dormant attraction to Asian women would creep its way to the surface of its hidden subconscious brain port.

His male acquaintances were his coworker junior high school teachers, generally a small group of overworked science, math, Japanese, and English instructors in their late thirties or mid-forties, who were warmhearted enough to spend time to welcome the *gaijin* to Japan. They would invite him to go to baseball games, karaoke, elaborate dining halls called *izakayas* (*3) and other fun outings. Liz would have a similar experience, only with matronly female teachers, and they would go to movies, coffee shops, and cornball shopping centers with antiquated style of fashion and whatever she could find that she liked would be too disappointingly small, and the dumb Japanese bitches would just laugh. She would grit her teeth, like, *What the hell is so funny about that, you cackling yellow jagged-teeth mice?!* But she kept it inside and shrugged the incidents away, rolling her eyes, like, "Ooooh-kay!" Basically, her moments with the mid-life wives of Japan was about as mouthwatering as chewing salty cardboard boxes.

For men, however, there was a different atmosphere, and this was probably what had been secretly eating away at Liz very slowly. In the beginning, it wasn't so blatant. She didn't notice it so much, but it became easier to recognize at the *bonenkai* (year-end party)(*4) at the close of their first year. She noticed that women were treated, in her opinion, as subservients. Moreover, men were allowed to be chauvinist and be familiar with women in ways that would grab them a sexual harassment claim or two. No one schooled Liz's flock about Japan any further than the country being an ancient place full of triangle box castles and temples, bald monks with a single lock of hair, and samurai swords that America went to war with.

At Tokyo's orientation, the Christian fundamentals were stressed, of course, so they didn't delve too much into the social issues of Japan. Of course, they were aware that sin abounded and was to be found everywhere, but they were admonished that the program participants' missions should not have been to change the world. Their premise was *Go to work, do your job, be the walking advertisement for your homeland, and then go home. You'll get paid.* When Liz learned how much different things were for men and women compared to the States, it was too late.

Too late.

Eddie had been introduced to these spots called the hostess bars. By the time Liz found out what these were and condemned them as being trashy lounges for high-priced hookers, Eddie had already been a couple of times and had kept it from her, which was a wise decision.

A somewhat youngish co-staffer at Eddie's junior high thought it would be a hilarious idea to get the *gaijin* teacher drunk and take him to a "snack pub," or hostess bar. These would always be in some seedy part of town, no matter how big or small. These places were, often, cheesy, cramped, and musty; but due to the fact that it was Eddie's first time to experience such a thing, it was curiously appealing, causing him to be drawn immediately to it.

The staff at the basically small bar were all women and presided over by a *duenna*, or mama-san, usually an aged woman or authoritative one, probably the owner but chief operator. The women were dressed meretriciously in evening dresses, silky gowns, and elegant garments, sometimes intentionally provocative. Their perfume was heavy, and it covered up the sweat, cigarette smoke, and spilled whiskey that the retro cushion furniture often reeked of; but this didn't detract from Eddie's enjoyment because these chicks would be into heavy flirting.

Now Liz wasn't around to watchdog him while an exotic broad sat in his lap. These hostesses were coquettish and flirty to the hilt; some even spoke a little English. He knew something was odd and peculiar because the co-staff teacher who took him to the first hostess bar ever was already married, or so he said. Yet he was there at the afterhours little pub just like him, with a girl in his lap, sipping on a scotch, and singing karaoke on a mic. The women were drinking too and rubbing Eddie's slightly hairy chest, and these weren't any teasing video store vixens either. The disheartening thing, however, was that at the end of the night, like the dreadful video store days, he'd have to go home with a blue-ball boner. Luckily, though, he would have Liz to soothe his tension—if she was willing—but he didn't think to pursue any type of arrangement with the hostess chicks for fear word would get out; and he assumed the same for his co-staff teacher. That is, until they went again, and the next time with one or two more male teachers accompanying them.

***

One night while Liz was at the gym in Izumi-sano, Eddie didn't get a chance to tell her that he would be going bowling with his male teacher pals. After bowling, they carpooled to the familiar snack bar that Eddie recognized, in the damnedest of locations, nestled between a tight bunch of residential cribs considered high-end with the decorative bonsai trees in the yards. The fancy-lit cube of a building had no windows, but a retro neon sign glowed absorbingly in a drab light green above its sole door. The only word of its intricate design Eddie could read was the English word "snack."

Inside there was the elaborate but exotic hole-in-the-wall lounge he had been to before. It had a high-counter bar, a few decorative highchairs, and several coffee tables and chairs. On this night, nearly all seats were occupied, and older Japanese gentlemen were drinking and singing old, haunting dulcet *enka* tunes on a karaoke setup.

Already tipsy from the beers consumed at the bowling alley, Eddie would fall into the gig and enjoy the atmosphere. There weren't as many girls there as there had been the first time, he was there. This time, the women seemed a bit older than the first time too, but they were still nice, and Eddie welcomed the change of another woman's attention and touch. To absolve his own feelings of guilt for feeling happy to get cuddly with other chicks, he would try to get piss drunk. At these hostess bars, he would be accommodated in that area as women would always seem to be around when it was time to refill the whiskey in his glass.

When it was Eddie's turn to sing karaoke, he blew a couple of Barry Manilow jams, and his performance tore the roof off the place. A lot of the old Japanese men a hop and a skip from being geezers thought they had witnessed an authentic foreign talent. The thunderous applause he received, along with the hard, fifteen-year-aged Hibiki whiskey went to his head.

He had excused himself to the restroom in the back of the high-counter bar. On his way back to join the festivity in the main room, he had a minor collision with one of the hostesses as they tried to pass one another in a small corridor leading from the side of the long-bar counter.

The woman was slightly older. Eddie's callowness about Japan would have put her in her thirties, but little did he know he was off by a decade younger; but still, she was stunning. She was a voluptuous, short beauty in a cleavage-revealing evening dress.

When Eddie and the woman tried to squeeze by each other in the narrowness of the passage, she pressed her fluff-jiggly, perfumed firmness hard into his chest. With heels, she and Eddie almost stared each other eyed to eye. Because they both had been drinking, she likely played the contact off as if she was drunk clumsy. Eddie was hip because he used to do the same thing back in LA, and most of the time, it was with Becky or Mandy, until Liz shut all that down. Then just like that night, however, Eddie's quick tumescence poked the woman in her soft crotch area.

The hostess hummed like a cat's purr when she felt him there. Eddie laughed like a sprightly, intoxicated imp and pulled her close to him in an embrace made to appear as if he had been trying to help her and keep her from falling down. Her warmth and touch tingled his senses so immensely he nearly nutted himself. That was around the time one of his coworker teachers casually interrupted, or basically cock-blocked the scene, dragged Eddie away, like, "Oh, there you are! I thought you got lost, Eddie-san! I've found my drunk foreigner friend, everybody! Come along, *gaijin*-friend!"

Thus, with Liz not around, a tempting urge to have a secret one-night stand with a hot Japanese babe tended to cross Eddie's mind. The hostess bar experience ushered in the compulsion heavily because it seemed to be acceptable in Japanese society. His foreign ignorance made him think that cheating was an unwritten norm, that it was ostensibly so, and he was warily intrigued. Now that he was in Japan, little did Liz ever suspect that there were times when women would actively approach him when they weren't together. He would be at a supermarket or walking through a park on his way back from the station and occasionally be approached by a cute young college-aged female soliciting him for private English lessons. He had liked the attention. He began to like it too much.

The idea to teach English privately was shot down immediately because the program forbade any endeavors to moonlight, or pursue employment or other sources of income outside of its entity due to bureaucratic minutiae too confusing to challenge. Off the books was a gray area, but not worth the risk. Besides,

Liz wouldn't have been down for that. It was a disaster waiting to happen, and eventually Eddie's excitement would surely get him into trouble; and when it did, or even if it did, where would he take the lucky girl? Certainly not to his pad and have Liz walk in on them. This was before he had heard of the love hotels of Japan.

It wasn't that he didn't love or care about Liz any less, but she was perpetually refractory and stubborn. It was clear that she was the boss of the relationship, and while he didn't mind being led around like a puppy on a leash, he did seem to care about her perfunctory traits pertaining to fashion and upkeep. For a girl so obviously attractive, Eddie would later admit that he was shocked at how she hit the wall so fast, in his view.

Life in Japan had caused Liz's tomboy to reemerge, and Eddie had preferred a more feminine Liz. Becky. But she was another story.

Japan was, for most of the time they were there, either hot, humid, damp, or all of the above; and when it wasn't like that, it was rainy. Liz didn't like wearing conservative attire—business suits and heels—in that type of environment, and he didn't blame her because he didn't like wearing neckties and collared shirts and dress shoes himself. The walk to and from the train station had an uphill-downhill slope and precisely narrow sidewalks they had to share with speeding bicyclists. The terrain was somewhat rugged, and oftentimes, Liz's appearance reflected that.

Liz became the guy Eddie was in Sacramento: T-shirts and jeans, scant makeup, less perfume more perspiration and armpit stains to show for it. Her hair was growing longer, and she refused to go to a Japanese hairstylist, opting to take the matter into her own hands or wait it out until she took a break to go back to the USA. Her hair and hygiene laxity were deleterious to Eddie's attraction to her at times, and he couldn't help but entertain the idea of creeping around on her.

Liz almost never wore skirts, and day by day, she seemed to be dressing more and more boyish, and acting like a boy too. To her credit, she had a good reason—that being the lack of what she had deemed quality shopping centers and size selections available. Sometimes she seemed more masculine than Eddie and, because she was slightly taller than him, looked like his long-haired compadre with abnormally inflated breasts.

Were it not for her pretty face, essentially, long blonde hair when it wasn't in a tightly wrapped bun or ponytail, and rack, she would otherwise be void of female traits? Which, in turn, led to the unavoidable problematic issues with intimacy they eventually began to face.

Whenever she would put out, Liz was still the fulfilling love goddess of his life. But she was unyielding on her restrictions on him trying to perform without contraception, as she had no intention of taking birth control pills in Japan. The only products she had confidence using in the country were toothpaste and tampons.

Eddie would run through a box of condoms frequently. Not because he was having hot, butt-naked sexual romps in the sack every single night but because he claimed to rip through the smaller condoms available in Japan and, in one attempt, use about two or three in the process. Then there was an issue of the timing.

Sometimes their schedules clashed. While Eddie would be working practically every day, Liz would be required to show up at her elementary school maybe three or four times a week. The times she wasn't at her school job, she would be at the community center sports club in Izumi-sano or jogging-walking along scenic rural country back roads. When she came back from her outings all sweaty, she'd be the aggressor for Eddie's affections as she undressed for her shower. Eddie wasn't a particular fan of her in that condition and couldn't get as worked up as she had, and that ultimately didn't lead to either her or his satisfaction.

Their sexual incompatibility was imminent too, even though inconceivable in the beginning. Liz had for the longest time thought that Eddie was indifferent to or dissatisfied with her oral sex. She was wrong: her skill was up to par, but unfortunately, compared to Fat Girl back in Eddie's former world, Liz would be a runner up if there were a contest, whereas that other chick would win first, second, and third prize—gold, silver, and bronze. Eddie would still catch cold flashes waking up dreaming about how Fat Girl would quaff an entire bottle of wine cooler, then start singing Dead Kennedys or some other group and start dancing wild. Suddenly she would tear off her panties and jerk Eddie's arm, pulling him toward her. She take his hand and make him cram two or three of his fingers inside of her—he remembered how squishy she felt, like he was puncturing a slit of raw liver. She would pull his pants down as she sat on the carpet, then pull him on top of her, but covered her hole when Eddie tried to mount. She would yank his waist to her face, dig her fingers into her butt cheeks, and press him into her throat like she was squeezing and consuming fresh orange juice. This, repeated on a frequent basis, was hard for anyone to ever top as far as Eddie was concerned. So erroneously, Liz thought Eddie didn't appreciate her "top" artistry and expertise, and as such, she sought to increase her clout in the craft by continuing to try and please him in that department as opposed to the intercourse area. What she wasn't going to do, she was absolutely sure, was get pregnant! So it became unsurprising that a lot of their play time ended in 69 positions.

Eddie's oral finesse was lame, lacking, and overall pathetic as far as Liz was concerned as well, and that she wasn't faking or hiding from him. But similarly to Eddie, even if she had tutored him to pleasure her to her liking, no one had done it better than the chicks she had made out with, primarily the volleyball coach's assistant and Becky. Still, it was her proclivity to think that women knew how to satisfy other women in ways men couldn't know how to. If it weren't for her insatiable hankering for penetration, she probably wouldn't have felt any need for an Eddie, or a Carver, or any boyfriend. Maybe.

January and February were a bit colder than usual, for the obvious reason being that it was technically winter by Western Hemisphere standards at least. However, to Eddie and Liz who were used to sunshine and the California heat, the winter in Japan was almost like a chilly breeze or extended fall—and furthermore, Liz's background in Iowa, the last place she ever lived that could get three or four inches of snow a year—the winter was refreshing. It was a welcome change from all the humidity. She didn't much like jogging in colder or rainy weather, though. She liked her gym, but it was a pain in the ass to walk to the station, take the train, transfer to an express (or remain on the local and extend the trip time), get off the train, and walk another ten to fifteen minutes (depending on street traffic) to the community center where the free gym was—and sometimes she would do all of this to arrive and discover that the place was closed that day!

Frustrated somewhat, Liz slacked off the gym activity the latter of February and into March. She started drinking more, staying around the apartment, and binge-watching episodes of *The X-Files*, *Star Trek*, and *Friends*. The "off the beaten path" video store of their village saved her life by introducing these episodes of TV shows in their inventory.

Eddie was oblivious to Liz's creeping melancholy. He was aware of her abbreviated work schedule compared to his, and he figured that she was enjoying herself as much as he was, if not more, considering she didn't have to work as hard as he seemingly had to. He would ceremoniously join her in the drinking and splurging festivity: okonomiyaki, more rice, hop and barley rich beer, and the fascinating *chu-hai* stuff; and as a result, both started to gain weight. More so Eddie, because he had never been as active as Liz in any sense, even though he trudged his way to work every day and walked the same bumpy, narrow sidewalks up and down the hilly Hannan City passageways. He snacked all day on the peanuts, crackers, dry squid, and other treats he would either buy from nearby convenience stores or he would receive as gifts from teachers or associates. The times when he and Liz could hit a McDonald's was almost a sacred occasion like Thanksgiving.

Liz was the first to notice Eddie's emerging little potbelly and pudginess around the cheeks, but it was a little cute. Her adorable Ken doll was slowly transforming into a tubby teddy bear, she would often joke—sometimes to herself, sometimes to Eddie.

Eddie didn't see it that way. To him, his bulking up was the result of him becoming more muscular and heftier. People around him at the junior high helped to blow his head up that way. So it wasn't only his guts that were being inflated. His ego was pumped up daily by gawking Japanese people in awe of the *gaijin*, who treated him like he was Harrison Ford with an Indiana Jones whip and hat—crafty, clever, and a bit strong. He now was starting to see himself as the Apollo who would swoop down the video store with a Ferrari or Porsche and scoop the ladies.

He would lift five-pound dumbbells at the junior high school, and all the kids would crowd around him and express their complete wonderment at his ability to accomplish the feat of ten reps. They would go so far as to declare Eddie to be the strongest man alive. He felt like an instantaneous superhero from one of his comic books.

When he played basketball with the kids at the school gym, he double-dribbled, walked, carried, air-balled, and bricked continuously; but the one time he threw up a "prayer" and the ball went through the hoop, everyone cheered like they had won an NBA Championship game. The kids would go back to their teachers, parents, friends, and anyone who would listen to them and brag about how their "*gaijin* teacher" Eddie-sensei (*5) was the best basketball player they had ever seen. A similar thing happened when he played soccer with the girls' team after school.

Of course, a fourteen-year-old girl goalie wasn't going to stop a charging bullish, intense twenty-seven-year-old foreigner with a determined scowl on his mug blazing a trail of dust toward her from scoring. Eddie kicked the ball through the net, and the World Cup erupted with applause from the heart of Hannan City, as enormous as Eddie's already-inflated selfdom.

News would always travel quickly in any situation, such as the one Liz and Eddie would be in regardless of the country, it seemed. They were in a small township of a small city in rural Japan, so it was to be expected that people knew them and who they were, like celebrities. It was awkward at times, almost as if they had little privacy. But Eddie didn't seem to mind being a star, and he basked in it. And since he was the most visible in the community—due to his appearances at work outnumbering hers—his popularity surpassed Liz's. News of this outstanding and fascinating Western male caught the attention of a budding, up-and-coming educator named Hiroko Okada.

8

S PRINGTIME IN OSAKA, Japan, dazzled the California foreigners with its breathtaking cherry blossoms, changing the landscape with sprinkles of pink. Liz was starting to become more social and participated in more activities with her elementary school and the kids there. She even went on joint functions where the BOE would team her up with Eddie and his junior high school. They would watch a school play or a chorus contest or something of that nature. They even went on a cherry blossom viewing picnic (*6). It was the first time they had ever been to one. Liz wasn't a big fan of Japan in a civil, communal, or collective sense; but the nature continued to impress her and caused her to have a feeling of serenity. It was times like that—when she could lie back in Eddie's lap, sip a beer, and look up into a sky of fuchsia and feel happy—that she had made the decision to come there.

The decision to remain in Japan, or events leading up to the decision, came sooner than either Liz or Eddie expected. The subject of staying in the country was treated as an eventual discussion they would have to have, but one they would always put off, assuming that they could wait up until the last week or day in the program to make their decision, whether or not to renew their one-year contracts. Liz's request to be relocated was denied solemnly by Oscar Gomimoto and the faculty at Tokyo headquarters, so Liz made up her mind to not renew. Question was, had Eddie felt the same way?

The easiest answer was no.

It was Eddie and Liz's first time to attend a cherry blossom viewing picnic, and it was also the first time they had met Hiroko Okada. She was a newly appointed Japanese teacher of English (JTE) and in her second year working in the district of Hannan City. Like with many other people who they had met, Liz and Eddie were greeted by an animated, excited Hiroko, who appeared so pleased to meet them. The only difference was she was closer to their ages and could speak English very well.

She introduced herself to them. "I am Hiroko. I'm so happy to meet you for the first time. I heard so much about the two of you. I was supposed to meet you last year at the station, when you had first arrived, but I was out of town because of my work, but I'm so excited to meet you now. I hope to be friends with you. I will be working with you next year at the junior high school, Mr. Roman!" Her last statement was predicated on the idea that Eddie had already made his decision to remain in his position with the program and his current post.

Already adored and loved by the Hannan City vale's local community as well as the schools where he made his appearance, Eddie's rep had preceded him by the time Hiroko had made her introduction. It was true she would be replacing the JTE Eddie was currently team-teaching with, and for whatever reasons unknown to either him or Liz, she was overjoyed to have the privilege of being able to work with them—Eddie in particular, of course.

Eddie figured Hiroko's eagerness to be acquainted with him and Liz and possibly be friends to be due to a possible desire to practice and use her English. Her overfriendliness could have been deemed inviting and flirty, but Eddie ruled out that possibility because she obviously could see that he and Liz were in a relationship. Everybody knew it. Liz, on the other hand, wasn't as dismissive of Hiroko's excessive congeniality.

Although Liz was highly impressed with Hiroko's English, she was still Japanese. And being such caused Liz to be borderline mistrustful of her, not because she was necessarily insecure or because she feared losing Eddie—it was because she had been in Japan for almost a year and had met few people who could speak English as well as she could and was almost shocked. But at the same time, the thought of having a female friend to kick it with appealed to her and entertained the idea somewhat.

Hiroko's English-speaking ability was leaps and bounds over almost everyone they had met in Osaka (not Tokyo), even Liz and Eddie's JTEs. So impressive was Hiroko's speech Liz almost took her for an Asian American, as she would put it. Her talk was unique and arresting, enough to make Eddie's jaws drop. He hadn't expected any Japanese to talk like that in English, and with such good pronunciation as well. To top it all off, she was *cute*—not exactly *pretty*, but cute.

Hiroko had somewhat paler skin, a little lighter—or "whiter" than the average Japanese person in their circumference of interaction. Or maybe it could have been the foundation she used? Whatever it was, she seemed like an off-color, lighter duplicate of a Japanese human being around where they were in Hannan City, and she kept her lips shaded in a pinkish color, as if she was a female vampire that fed only on the blood of peachy carnations. Her hair color was jet black, and had she not been wearing it in a professional-looking bun a majority of the time she was seen publicly, it would flow arabesque past the nape and tickle her back shoulder tops.

When she smiled for too long, it could be seen that her teeth weren't exactly straight by the standards of the average Californian, or American. Her bicuspids were, through nature of formation, carved in such a way that they appeared sharp, giving her the vampirish-type smile at times. Yet a faintly Lena Horne–*colored* girl—similitude of a smile in turn, would activate dimples on either side of her *takoyaki*-ball–shaped round cheeks as if she was being poked by an unseen ice pick.

Another remarkable trait setting Hiroko apart from other Japanese—as if what she already possessed wasn't enough—was her bigger and rounder eyes, but still with enough recognizable jagged curve to denote Asian features. This was complimentary of the wonders of plastic surgery. When her eyes lit up in excitement or similar, they would enlarge like those of a Disney character either, Chip or Dale.

Eddie was secretly trying to figure out what her score would be on a scale of 1 to 10, but had to put her in a separate category of "as far as Japanese women would go" and decided she was a 9. She did not get the perfect 10 because of her teeth, he mused silently. He imagined what the oral sex would be like, and then again, he couldn't imagine.

Meeting Hiroko came at a time when Eddie's fondness for Japanese women was growing rapidly. He had been, up until then and continually, doing a remarkable job hiding it from Liz. Likely, the only reason he had not stepped out on her already was because they lived together. Every minute of his time was almost always accounted for. They both now had the Tuka prepaid cellular phones, so even if they were apart, they were never out of reach.

The Tuka phones were among the coolest contrivances at the time. They were the size of a candy bar, or a fat cigar, but they could still transmit telecommunication and record voice messages. They had a small keypad with all the number digits and a screen that displayed the incoming calls, automatic redial, and everything a functioning cell phone required. They could fit in the pocket easily, were astoundingly durable, and had a resonant chime. Tuka was the name of the store, and a lot of foreigners liked this one because they weren't as restrictive as other Japanese companies at that time. Anyone with a passport could get one—even tourists—and the coolest thing was there was no contract obligation. So long as the user maintains a balance on the account, the phone was operable. Balance could be obtained through purchase at the Tuka store locations or at convenience stores. Liz's phone was pink, and Eddie's was green.

They were always within range of speed dial. Even if they weren't, in their neck of the woods the pickings were slim. Their area was sparsely populated even though Osaka boasted a head count of millions. Moreover, Eddie and Liz were both popular, and almost everyone around knew who they were. Trying to creep around there would have been big news and a big mistake. Eddie was just as disappointed as Liz when he discovered that the program denied their relocation request, but he was still game for renewing his contract.

On weekends they started to make more trips into Osaka City. Eddie thought that a change of scenery would do them some good and possibly warm Liz up about staying another year. For a while it seemed to work. Whenever they arrived in the town, she would seem to liven up; it was like the California Liz had reemerged. Then Eddie would see drop-dead gorgeous Japanese women. Would Liz be able to hold her own against them?

As always, because Liz appeared to be his significant other when they were together, women would flirt with him. In department stores, women's clothing shops, small cafes, diners, bars, or wherever they would go, places that had Japanese female attendants would be extra friendly and obsequious. They would be covering them with colorful compliments—in the best English they could produce—and eyeballing Eddie as if enthralled. Flirting with him the same way the evil broads did back in LA, back at the video store. He would sometimes lose himself and drift off into cold-sweat daydreams thinking about it. The encounters would make him flash back. He sometimes dreaded going to the city with Liz, if only he could get out by himself for once. All his one-nightstands were in abundance and waiting for him, but he couldn't make a move. His hands were tied, "cuffed."

Liz wasn't oblivious to the attention Eddie would get, but since she too shared the spotlight, her comfort zone wasn't too disturbed. It did, however, serve to stir up Liz's growing enmity for Japanese women. For someone with occasional desires to be intimate with women, she surmised that her lack of interest in Asian women was based on some deep-seated prejudice she may have had toward the people. She didn't hate Japanese people, but she couldn't bring herself to take them seriously enough for them to earn any kind of her respect. The women were a joke, she often thought. Maybe she was jealous. She had to work out in frequency she would describe as constantly in order to maintain her spectacular frame, but she had a feeling that a lot of her Japanese competition—if such a term could have been applied—didn't have to work at having that perfect body to fit in those perfect outfits, perfect dresses, perfect skirts, impeccable taste, slender waists. They were naturally predisposed to having smaller bodies and didn't have the same problems with calorie intake as most Westerners. Then to add insult to injury, plenty of the shops she dragged Eddie into, with ogling-eyed Japanese girls there both employees and customers, didn't even have her size in stock.

So, while Eddie was thinking that Liz was dressed bummy intentionally, it was really because her gear selection was limited. Or better, she just didn't know where to shop. Her time had been mostly spent in an armpit location of the prefecture.

Liz's problem was figuring out if she liked Japan or not. She felt happy and rejuvenated in Osaka City. The sights, the sounds, the busy feet on the concrete streets and colorful neon kanji signs, the odd characters both animated and human—it was just like Tokyo, she thought, but a lot more laid-back, maybe? *But I like it here!* she thought. She wanted to tell Eddie that she loved him suddenly, but for whatever reason, she couldn't bring herself to do it. Up until then, she thought everything had been fine, according to her plan, and she didn't want to ruin things. But it was true, wasn't it? She *did* love him.

Back when they were in Cali, or the States, she never worried about Eddie running around on her or sneaking off. She had to remember that she was going the route of a lesbo before her disastrous dating of Carver graduated her to Eddie. He was to her one of those dime-a-dozen, easily replaceable batteries in a dildo, only, attractive because it came in a fancy package. Eddie's package was courtesy of her.

The conflict arose because now their relationship had meant something to her. They had been together for a long time, and Liz felt that their union had mutual advantages. It was like a partnership in an odd way. She had a decent servile boy toy to accompany her, carry her bags, follow her orders, pleasure her, and prevent the world from harming her. In her fairy tales, the witch wasn't wicked and oftentimes came out on top.

The fairy tale she had composed surrounding her and Eddie went to the tune of her being the powerful sorceress trying to protect an earnest, beloved young lad, destined to be a king. Unfortunately, the lad stayed a lad and all the Japanese women started to represent a nation of Sleeping Beauties, or glass slipper–wearing chicks who were after the young man she wanted to protect because she wanted to keep him for her own. If he ever became a king, she would be queen; and since she was also a preponderant power wielder, she would, of course, dominate him too and rule the world.

The reality was Eddie was just human. He wasn't a thief, a serial killer, or a domestic abuser; therefore, compared to a lot of other dudes Liz could have hooked up with, he seemed decent, and it was for these reasons that her parents approved of him. As such, it did not seem illogical, in her view, to expect that Eddie would be the man who she would marry.

After all, she had done everything—she sacrificed her self-respect and superciliousness and sleazed him all the way down. It gave her cause to assure herself that Eddie's loyalty to her would eternally be solid. Fortified. The chink in the structure couldn't be detected. It was vicissitude.

Now in Japan, she saw a presage that everything was going to change, but for better or for worse, she couldn't predict. It would make her shudder at times.

Uneasiness thrust thorny gores in her sternum as they walked the crowded Osaka City streets on a Saturday afternoon. Japanese people stared and gawked at them sometimes, but Liz couldn't remove her mind from the fact that *here* Eddie *wasn't* a dime a dozen. He was like a rare coin, and a valuable one if she had to use the attention he got from the women there as a gauge. He had been successfully transformed. In Japan he had attained his superhero status and dare she even say it, was a *hunk*—for Japanese women anyway—and that was both the funny and tragic part. Were he to return to the USA, would he also return to being the lurching lank loser he was when she discovered him at a video store? She thought so, pretty much.

Osaka City was an unending discovery tour. The energy was intoxicating for Liz, alluring and addictive. The people were lively, animated, and seemingly indefatigable. While in Tokyo, she had heard that the city was dangerous with crime, and the locals were waspish, pugnacious types; but she immediately dismissed it as crap. She thought people in Osaka were very nice and funny. She had barely paid for a thing since she had come to Japan. Those Japanese Osaka people had given them a rice cooker, radios, electrical appliances; had taken them on numerous outings ranging from sports events to kabuki plays, field trips from Kyoto to Nara, and practically every historical sight in between with zillions more to go . . . and okonomiyaki . . . She laughed. She remembered suddenly grabbing Eddie by the shoulders and half-stated, half-asking (or requesting),

"Hey, let's not go back. Let's stay!" she said.

Eddie panted as if he was nervous due to being taken off guard. He said, "What, you mean stay here? In Osaka?"

Liz said, "Yeah! Just for a night. I don't wanna leave."

Eddie thought for a moment, as if it needed a lot of consideration. Liz was quizzical of expression. She hated to think of pouting all the way home on a dreary train ride back to the boondocks when they had been having so much fun.

Eddie said, "Well . . . fu-uck, why the hell nawt? It's Saturday, we don't got work tomorrow, yeah, let's fucken' dew it!"

Liz hugged him as if he had given her a diamond ring present. Then she wrapped her arm around his, and they walked the turnabout at Nankai Namba Station. "That's why I . . . love you!" she whispered, but there was too much noise from all the activity on the cramped and populous streets. Eddie hadn't heard it.

9

LIZ MIGHT HAVE at some point thought a few Asian guys were hot, particularly in the recent years or prior to her moving to Japan, but overall, she didn't go for them. Of course, she had seen and met plenty of them in America, likely the Americanized ones. She even went to school and attended classes with a plethora of them, but in everyday dealings, they were beneath her radar. Japanese men in Japan were no exception. Especially Japan's Japanese men, whom she saw as mostly weak, lame, and significantly feminine—and the ones who *weren't* like that were chauvinistic. She didn't dig the idea of men doing all the work and having the women stay at home doing the cooking, cleaning and household chores—like her mother—and taking care of kids.

In their living situation, both she and Eddie would take turns cooking—whenever they did cook—and that was limited to spaghetti, rice dishes, and okonomiyaki, which they had learned how to prepare when they came to Japan. Otherwise, they would get all their food from the already prepared food-stuff sections of the supermarkets and convenience stores. Liz, with her health regiment, didn't much like this selection, nor did she appreciate how expensive fruit and produce was in the country, but someone had pulled her coat it was like that because Japan was an island nation that had to import a lot of such goods, and the costs they incurred to get the stuff there reflected on the price for the consumers. Still, they endured and during it all so shared the cooking details. It was a cooperative partnership, not just the female doing all the work. All of Liz's conversations with Japanese women she could communicate effectively with seemed to indicate that the majority of them were obedient and subservient housewives or other, even her teacher co-workers, who should have been considered career women; but they too would convey the message to Liz that they would, without fail, go to work every day and then come home to make dinner, take care of their children, and maintain the upkeep of the house.

Liz was a product of the Hillary Clinton, Tipper Gore, and women's' rights advocates and other movements. Throughout the '90s, the empowerment of women in Western society was a recurring theme. It influenced not only her but also many people in Canada and Europe. Even her own mother put her foot down and went back to teaching when their family moved to California—albeit parttime—determined however to not just be a stay-at-home mother; and she, like Liz, was turning against the idea of being inferior to men in either home or workplace.

Thus far she had been able to hold Eddie in his place and never once got any man-biased dogmatic superior attitude talk. "Ken Dolls" after all weren't allowed to voice such mannerisms and in fact, they were at the mercy of their owners, who positioned them, dressed and groomed them to be well-behaved figurine so desired. Now it was changing.

Eddie liked being pampered.

When they dined with Japanese hosts—or forced to in some instances—Liz was equally impressed and alarmed at the hospitality they were shown. Just like at last year's *bonenkai* whenever Eddie's beer glass was empty, the fair Japanese maidens would quickly race to fill it up again, sometimes cartoonishly colliding with one another while doing so. When his dish or plate was empty, women would immediately inquire if he needed anything else to eat, even going so far in many instances as to prepare his plate altogether.

It got to a point once where Liz had to intercede. She felt it was her American duty to explain equality to the Japanese. She told them, "Eddie is a man, and he needs to get off his butt and get it himself. He needs to get his *own* food, pour his own drinks, and since he's a man, he oughtta be serving us, *because we're women!*"

Hiroko Okada would sometimes be around to translate, and for that, Liz saw her as a godsend. People would laugh when it was understood what Liz had said. Some had found it amusing because they didn't think Liz was actually serious. Hiroko could sympathize, as if she understood where Liz was coming from, the message she was attempting to convey; but unfortunately, as she knew, in Japan, such ideology didn't really wash. It was a battle she wasn't going to win, no matter how popular or influential she was, or *thought* she was. Still, she allowed Liz to dig her own grave and not get too enmeshed. Liz had hoped to gain her as an ally in this regard, and it would have enabled her to seek a better relationship with her, possibly leading to friendship.

Hiroko explained, "A lot of Japanese people are still a bit old-fashioned. I do not agree or disagree with it, but I understand the way that you feel."

These types of reassurances tended to suffice, and Liz would yield without getting too worked up about aspects of Japanese culture she failed to comprehend. Meanwhile, though, the same Japanese hospitality was continually rendered. Liz was uncomfortable about it, but Eddie couldn't get enough.

While women cleaned up everything after the party, the dinner, or the gathering of sorts, the men would lounge about, sip drinks, puff squares, engage in small, leisurely chat among each other sucking on toothpicks. They urged Eddie to do the same, like *get out of the women's way and let them do their work.* Eddie was completely fond of the idea.

Liz would finally go bonkers one occasion and started bitching and making a big deal about it. She was rattling off some "This is chauvinist! Oh, this is soo male chauvinist!"

She said, "In America, we'd never go for this anymore. Everybody helps, everyone lends a helping hand. People share duties, chores, and responsibilities. That's how the first Thanksgiving was in America. The Indians and the Pilgrims helped each other. Men and women helped each other."

No one was around to check Liz's bullshit, and most of the time, Eddie was too drunk with bliss he found Liz's rants as entertaining as the Japanese people did. The Japanese women would be washing dishes; wiping tables; putting away pots, pans, okonomiyaki hot plates; and laughing at Liz barking away, like, "What the fuck is this loudmouth foreign princess babbling about?"

Liz half growled, "It's not fair that you women in Japan slaved for hours preparing all this food, setting the tables, and pouring all those drinks for you to be here cleaning away like servants, while the men sit on their rumps, just relaxin' and smoking and playing cards!"

The men would be *chillin'* in a foyer somewhere playing cards, or *mah jong*, drinking heavy-duty liquor called *sho-chu*, from a famous place called Kagoshima. Eddie took a sip of this and got instantly wasted. Dude almost started hallucinating and turned into a walking zombie. But since he was Liz's bitch boy toy, she snatched him up and practically dragged him to the kitchen by his ear and demanded that he help the women clean up. She had been drinking too, and it caused a scene when she manhandled Eddie the way she did.

People were alarmed at how strong Liz actually was. It was a shock to see such a lovely-faced, beautiful girl suddenly behave as a hoyden yet perform an act of strength like lift a man, but Liz had always been athletic and active. Still, Hiroko Okada witnessed this as well and couldn't help but feel a little sorry for Eddie.

Surely he must be humiliated, Hiroko thought. But they played it off as a joke, so it served to assuage the initial tension it caused. People didn't know if

Liz had been serious or not, but since she was grinning—psychotically—people guessed it was a normalcy, or oddity of foreign habits.

The night would close in cataclysmic disaster of a dead-drunk Eddie trying to help wash dishes and collapse. Along with him, as he toppled downward to kiss the pantry floor, came an entire rack of fragile, object d'art China and ornate porcelain dishes, crashing like chimes of a hibernal storm.

***

All forgiven, as Eddie could do no wrong, he later decided to avoid those types of situations by drinking less at future outings. Further, he would try to keep Liz from getting worked up like that by trying to try and help people clean up or trying to pour his own drinks. In front of Liz, Eddie would agree with Liz's feminist ideologies and pretended to not enjoy all the surfeited pampering and attention he would get. This, as well as the weekend trips to Osaka City, seemed to placate Liz, and things were looking up. It kept Liz from being in dull and moody attitudes that the countryside had done much to influence.

More importantly, he also masked his growing desire to get some bedtime with a Japanese woman. His latent lust was a quiescent cloak denoting disinterest. To throw Liz off the scent even further, he would make caustic and derisive comments about Japanese women the same way Liz did about the men, pretending his disdain for the people matched hers.

He described, to Liz's contentment, Japanese women as "scrawny, sinewy, and unappealing." Liz was appeased a great deal. She even fell back on all her sententious tirades at the dinner parties and group outings. (*7) She wasn't prone to spewing all her feminist views, and they had a better time. Liz hadn't accepted defeat; she considered Hiroko and her colleagues to be lost causes, and so there was no need to pursue deeper or meaningful rapport.

The essential and relevant matter was Eddie was still on the reel, and she was still holding and controlling the line and the rod. She fixed her head to thinking that she was irreplaceable. She didn't know anything about Hiroko.

10

TRUTH BE TOLD, apparently, even for Japanese people, Hiroko was a stunner. When staffing shuffle was complete and she switched positions with the JTE at Eddie's junior high school, she was grouped with the same bunch of teachers she had taught with the year before, her first year as a teacher altogether. Unlike her peer novice teachers, Hiroko had not a single nervous bone in her body, and she confidently stomped through challenging territory and emerged victorious, gaining the instant respect of veteran instructors and faculty, which was a rarity by any stretch of the imagination in the Japanese public school system. That, of course, was another story.

As she gained much admiration, while the other new teachers would piss in their pants, cry their eyeballs out, or suffer an illness due to stress, even go the length and commit suicide, Hiroko remained humble. She finessed her situation well and baffled everyone, herself included. It was as if she had a burning secret inside of her enabling success. It had not always been that way, she of course knew, but she was grateful f0r what she was able to accomplish.

Along the way, other eligible or quasi-eligible young bachelor staffers like the soccer coach science teacher, and the badminton coach math teacher fell victim to Hiroko's allure. They would campaign hard for Hiroko's good grace. For a while, she could bounce back and forth charming the guys, allowing herself to be a ping-pong ball getting tapped back and forth between both dudes' attention. Eddie would come around, shut down the table, and interrupt the game.

Whenever Eddie was in the room, she would treat the Japanese suitors like invisible air or transparent oxygen. Hiroko and Eddie would begin speaking English to one another, and the Japanese guys may as well have been swallowed up by a trapdoor. The mad math teacher couldn't add it up and would slither away solemnly with his slide un-ruled. The soccer coach science teacher too stumbled sadly away with his deflated balls. When Eddie was around, she gave him attention that couldn't be divided with a samurai sword blade.

The cartoon chipmunk eyes trained directly into Eddie's prominent droopy eyes when he spoke. Every word that left his jib came into palpable existence, and she ate them up. She understood everything he would be saying, even if he threw in some taboo or cuss words or colloquial terms. Here was where she recognized where a considerable source of her power and influence was—not only just her ability to speak a language proficiently that her people couldn't match, but also her ability to communicate with a Japan outsider and be his bridge between his culture and hers. It was an unquenchable feeling.

Hiroko wasn't tall, nor did she have the dimensions of a Liz—a statuesque, fit girl with a gymnast's proportions, a lovely blend of an athletic, toned physique with tantalizing curves adored by plenty of males. If ever an actress was needed to play the role of an Olympian, or an Erika Prezerakou (in her prime), Liz would snag this hook, line, and sinker. Hiroko was the opposite of the spectrum, but still in the realm of attractive in her own right.

Hiroko was lean, wiry, yes, but a leggy type of limber, like she could have held her own were she to be the athlete that she wasn't. Her noticeable set of ripe apple hooters were proportionate to her slender skittle frame, which gave her a dumbbell-type look when in neophyte teacher's uniform—the standard black jacket, skirt, and white shirt ensemble. She had a plump little melon of a rump, though not as pronounced as Liz's, but it proved to be a head turner on many an occasion, both in Japan and abroad. As if it weren't already obvious, Hiroko had lived overseas in North America.

She wanted to be airy and often appeared graceful to Eddie in ways that Liz wasn't. He didn't mean to make unfair comparisons, but he found himself guilty of doing it anyway. There would be times when Liz was gawky and gangling. Hiroko walked like she was always on her tiptoes, but always in short strides to the extent where Eddie visualized her as floating or walking on air.

Where Liz was athletic, Hiroko was artistic.

Liz liked physical activities: she liked the outdoors, sports, the festive and active life, not excluding wild liveliness. Hiroko liked indoor, subdued enterprise such as music, playing piano and acoustic guitar and even *koto*. She wasn't opposed to the outdoors and did engage in hiking or such, but she was more of the homebody who preferred watching movies, either at home or in the theaters.

This was right up Eddie's alley, him being the film enthusiast he was and also considering his background.

Another thing about Hiroko that became obvious was that she wasn't originally from Hannan City. She was from the more populous and urban city of Sakai, the immediate border town south of Osaka City. She was no stranger to the metropolitan and didn't like the rural setting much either. Since she was in her home country, she could deal with it better than Liz or Eddie, though; but it was enough that she could relate to their discomfort living in places like Hannan City. What better candidate would have been better to show Eddie around? he wondered.

Hiroko was never detected on Liz's radar, to her misfortune. She managed to slip through the cracks because the handful of times Liz met her, after the fascination with her English speaking ability dissipated, Liz dismissed her into the category of another Japanese groupie, or sycophant, enamored with her and Eddie because they were *gaijin*. It was a mistake, but Liz had tunnel vision.

II

A S THE DAYS drew closer to the deadline for the program participants to declare decisions to renew their contracts, Liz was still tossing the idea around of whether or not to stay after changing her mind from definitely going back to still thinking about it. The reason for this was because they had done a bit more traveling around, exploring new places in the Kansai region, independently, without the accompanying people from their school- or work-related field trips. They went to Wakayama, Kobe, Nara, Kyoto, and other cities and absorbed more of the Japanese experience. Liz had learned to use chopsticks like a regular pro, while Eddie was still struggling; but they were enjoying themselves whenever they weren't in the depressing outland town they resided in.

On one game-changing occasion, they decided to stay an entire weekend in Osaka City, not just go on an overnight trip. They decided to leave Hannan City on Friday afternoon when Eddie finished at the junior high school and return home on Sunday night. They had a good time as always, and for the moment, it seemed that Liz would be conciliated like a vampire or drug addict until the time they next needed blood, a fix, or both.

As such, it would appear as if Liz's resistance to the therapy of Osaka City jaunts was growing, evidenced by the fact that she wanted to milk this one visit to the very end and take the last train back to Hakkotuskuri Station on Sunday night. Eddie somewhat reluctantly acquiesced, but then again, he was a remote-controlled entity anyway.

They spent their time in the immediate area of the Nankai Namba Station, the portal they would have to use to take the Nankai train, which delivered them home. They figured no reason to venture too far from the station when they might have to make a mad dash to catch a smoker homeward bound.

Not far away was the Sen-Nichi-Mae shopping, entertainment, *pachinko*, and dining district. There were several indoor arcades that were saturated with human traffic. Even on a Sunday afternoon, the city was flooded with city folks, rural folks like them in town for the day, and random visitors, even from other countries. Liz and Eddie would constantly see smatterings here and there of foreign people but never engage in conversation. The most they ever did for acknowledgment would be a glance, a widening of the lips to indicate a lazy smile, or a quick "Hi" if that foreigner was an English speaker.

Liz and Eddie had partied and hung out in Osaka on numerous occurrences, but never had anywhere in particular that they knew of or liked. It was as if their ventures there were continuous bar hops or pub crawls, where they would try a place, move on to the next, and never look back. They stumbled upon this place called the Hub in the Sen-Nichi-Mae building because they followed a group of foreign people there.

That particular *gaijin* bar was ample like a ballroom. It was on the second floor of a luxurious hotel. It had what appeared to be an even mix of foreign and Japanese (or Asian) patrons. The establishment was abundant with heads and mirth, but it didn't seem overcrowded because there was enough seating to accommodate everyone. Eddie and Liz found themselves a table and sat for moments, expecting to receive table service from the staff but went ignored by them. Finally, Liz stopped a portly, pallid Caucasian girl with dark hair and asked her what a person needed to do in order to get a drink around that place. The girl was friendly, and she told Liz that she had to stand in line at the long counter extending the length of the rectangular-shaped ballroom, and the servers would bring the drink to their table.

While standing in this long line, Liz struck up a conversation with this girl and discovered she was from the United States like her. Her name was Stephanie Pritchard, and she was from Arizona, a small town not far outside of Phoenix, and she had been in Japan for three years. She seemed happy to meet Liz, like she was relieved or something of the sort, as if she was being rescued.

Stephanie said, "It's a welcome sight to see and meet other Americans. Female Americans especially . . ." She laughed. It was obvious she had already been drinking a few.

Liz said, "Really? Are Americans that unusual?"

Stephanie said, "Oh . . . no, not really." She shook her head in quick jerks like she had been snapped out of a hypnotic spell. "No, not at all. In fact, the company I work for hires a lot of Americans—well, recently they have, but not too many American girls, y'know, like us, hahaha!"

Liz had long been aware of the foreign presence in Japan, Tokyo being her first pellucid example. It was the area of South Osaka where she lived that didn't have the melting pot. She had not been apprised of Americans being a rarity to the extent to which this girl Stephanie had alluded, for while in Tokyo during her orientation with the program, the place was crawling with them.

With curiosity and intrigue aroused, they began talking more. Their conversation continued until they had edged their way up in line and ordered their choice of drink. Liz ordered a pitcher of beer for her and Eddie and paid the attendant. That cashier handed them a miniature flagpole with a laminated number on it. They returned to where Liz had been seated with Eddie.

After Eddie was introduced to Stephanie, she invited Liz and him to a booth nearby that she was sharing with two other foreigners, a male and a female. As the booth was roomy enough to seat up to six people, Liz and Eddie accepted the invitation and joined the group, careful to remember bringing along the flagpole with the laminated number. The wait staff spotted the corresponding number they had attached to the heaping pitcher of beer at the booth and delivered it in front of Liz in exchange for that flagpole.

The male and the female greeted Eddie and Liz with moderate interest. They were Stephanie's coworkers, and that was how they were introduced, from Australia and England respectively. The Aussie was introduced as Keefer Lane and he already seemed a little drunk. The Brit chick had a pointy nose like a bird's beak, but she was still relatively elegant, queenly, and attractive. She had a long name, introduced herself initially as Jill but wanted to be called Victoria.

Keefer blurted out, "Aw, jeez fucken Chroyst, love . . . just call'er Vicky like the rest of us do!"

It was a friendly banter. Stephanie broke out in a berk fit of laughter as if she was watching an episode of *Saturday Night Live* after freebasing cocaine. Neither Liz nor Eddie knew exactly what to think until they were made aware that Keefer had been trying to keep Vicky company and cheer her up. As could be ascertained by the incessant laughter at his joking around, he did a fine job lifting her spirits so far. His jokes were difficult for the new Americans Liz and Eddie to understand because of his heavy Australian accent.

When the back-and-forth between her and Keefer settled down, Victoria welcomed the new faces, then said, "Oh, more Yanks, I see! What brings you two to the land of the slanty eye?" This was followed by a short fit of laughter.

Eddie mumbled an inaudible response because it was plowed over by Liz's sonorous voice. She said, "Adventure, something new, and a chance to get out of California." Eddie pretty much agreed as always, and both he and Liz shared a chuckle as they commenced to chug their beers.

In minutes, the foreigners were chatting away and had more drinks delivered without having to go all the way to stand in line waiting at the counter. This was due to the kindness of the Australian guy, Keefer, who volunteered for the job. They soon were carrying on in discussion as if they had been friends for years.

If it weren't obvious at the outset that Stephanie took an immediate liking to Liz, it became clear shortly thereafter, as she would incessantly announce her great love for California, Los Angeles, the beaches there, and, of course, Disneyland. Furthermore, Stephanie's joy at meeting another American girl appeared genuine. Likewise, Liz was very happy to meet other foreigners. Meeting other English speakers was like a relief for her too. Now she could possibly speak with another person who understood what it was like to be a foreigner in Japan. It was as if she had suddenly struck gold.

Stephanie insisted, practically demanded, that they exchange cell phone numbers, e-mail and contact information, even their home address. Liz supplied her with the first two, no problem. No need to supply her address, she thought; she probably wouldn't be living there for too much longer anyway. Even when she told the group where she lived, none of them had the slightest clue about the place—never heard of Hannan City at all. It was only when Liz explained that it was in the general vicinity of the Kansai Airport that they started to get a clue.

Livid scowls creased the faces of the audience, as if to say, *What the hell are you guys doing way out there? Here is where all the action is!*

Liz would then expound upon how she and Eddie had ended up in Japan in the first place. Then and there, both Stephanie and Victoria understood. They got the picture. Especially Stephanie.

Stephanie too had participated in a similar program as the CHET. Just like Liz, she had a similar story. "I was miserable because I was smack dab in the middle of nowhere . . . in the almost-void-of-human-life prefecture of Shiga. Salary was good, but the weather was unbearably hot, humid, and there were barely any trains or buses to whisk you away to livelier areas like the citified parts.

"Even on my days off, I still wanted to work, or be at school, or anywhere there was human life. It was that *boring*. And these were the days before we had laptops and cell phones! At that time, all we had were the computers at our schools or some computer lab school that you have to walk several miles on a no-sidewalk road to get to—"

"Aw, geez," Liz said. "Yeah, we can relate to that. We use the computers at our schools too. It's almost the only reason why I go to my school."

Eddie burped and added, "I heard that next year they are going to quit allowing teachers to use the e-mail and the internet thing."

Liz was alarmed. "What? Where did you hear that?"

Eddie said, "That new teacher told me—you know, the one that can speak English."

Victoria was resting her V-shape chin in her palm, stirring her fancy cocktail lazily, and spoke with a lazy voice. She sounded either very haughty or fatigued.

She was like, "Why don't you guys get a good laptop? You can get one in Den-Den Town, you know."

Liz said, "We don't even know where that is."

Stephanie spazzed out like she had heard an unbelievable story. "Oh, my gawd! You guys have been here for almost a year, and you don't know about Den-Den Town? No fucken' way! That's where you can get all your electronic goods and needs. It's awesome. You can get a real cheap digicam—"

Liz turned her attention to Stephanie. "So how did you end up here? Did you quit that program that you were with? Or did they transfer you? I asked our office for a change of location, but they couldn't do it. They said that all the big-city locations are all filled."

Stephanie said, "I found about this *eikaiwa* (*8) called Bozack, here in Osaka, and they hire from within Japan."

Liz said, "Wait . . . hold on, you're losing me."

Eddie chimed in, "Yeah, what'sa *eikaiwa*?"

Victoria said, "It's Japanese for English conversation school."

Keefer burped. "But . . . uh, technically, they're nottan English conversation school—they also teach French, Spanish, German, like the one your ex works for, hon," he said, directing his attention to Victoria, who frowned and turned her beak downward at the fancy drink she was toying with.

Liz said to Stephanie, "So, you got a job with this English school? They hired you, and then you moved here?"

Stephanie said, "Pretty much, that's how it went. Usually, all the other English language schools that pay the most money don't hire people who already live in Japan. I guess it's because of all the bullshit inconsequential visa stuff. They like to hire people directly from overseas. But apparently, our company, B0zack Language School, must have somehow sidestepped that ritual, and they hire from within the country. In the old days, people had to leave Japan, maybe go to Korea somewhere, while their visa documents got processed. Luckily, I didn't have to do that. They have preference for people like you, me, who did those programs like JET, Earlham, T-NET, or CHET . . . I came here with the PorkPie Program."

Liz said, "How did you find out about these English conversation schools?"

Stephanie, Victoria, and Keefer covered Liz and Eddie with startled expressions. Liz thought for a moment that she had said something to offend them all.

Keefer said, "How have you not ever heard of the *eikaiwa*s, hon?"

Stephanie said, "Well, I read about it in the *Kinki Rag*. You should get one of those, they're free. They're like these little news pamphlets that post all these job openings, used stuff you can buy—they even got personal ads."

Before Stephanie could even finish explaining about what the newsletter was to Liz in full detail, Keefer had already scrambled off and returned with a few of the pamphlets and magazines she was talking about. He threw several free press publications on the table. *Kansai Scene, Kansai Time Out, Kansai Flea Market*, the *Kinki Newsletter*, and the one that Stephanie spoke of, the *Kinki Rag*.

Stephanie grabbed the crude, A4 pages of paper folded into a miniature brochure-like tabloid absent of any type of illustration or design, just multiple rows of typed letters separated by horizontal lines to accumulate ads, or entries. She handed this to Liz.

Stephanie said, "Yeah, this is the best one. You can find these at all the *gaijin* bars like this one usually."

Liz took the rag and flipped through the pages, some of which spilled out on the table and soaked up some spilled beer. Eddie strained to get a glimpse at some of the papers. Liz was hogging it, so he looked at some of the other publications on the table.

Stephanie said, "Bozack doesn't pay as much as the other schools, but the salary is still competitive, and besides, I really didn't care. I would've screwed my stepbrother to get the hell out of that godforsaken place! Since I've been here, I've never been bored. Here is where all the action is."

Victoria said, "You'll also get a chance to meet other foreign people who speak English like you do—albeit mangy." A snobby, critical attitude interwoven in her tone could have been detected. She continued, "I can't speak Japanese at all, and I don't think I ever will."

Liz said, "I know what you mean." She didn't know if she liked this British girl yet, but this was one thing she could relate with her about. Japanese language was difficult for her, and she didn't foresee herself tackling and conquering it.

Otherwise, the idea of moving to Osaka and working at an *eikaiwa*, was beginning to appeal to her. After all, she had not been entirely opposed to remaining in Japan if it were possible for her and Eddie to move to a "better" place. One thing was for sure—she was not willing to spend another year in Hannan City, and that was pretty much a finality.

As for the salary Stephanie mentioned, it didn't sound like a big deal. She and Eddie had already saved up a lot. The sharing of the rent helped a lot too. Rent would be more expensive in Osaka City, she was already sure, but this was still no deterrent. A move to Osaka City suddenly crept with enticing fingers into Liz's head to tickle her brain.

Liz said to the group, "So what's the chance of me and Eddie getting a job at a company like yours?" She didn't see the sudden wrinkle in Eddie's forehead. Eddie wasn't necessarily interested in any *eikaiwa*, or language conversation school, or Bozack. He could bear to listen anyway, mere curiosity to hear the response.

Again, Stephanie, Keefer, and Victoria exchanged quizzical, aporetic looks at one another. Laughing, they turned back to face Liz. They all seemed to 'verbigerate' "You should apply right away, of course you can get a job!"

Stephanie said, "Bozack doesn't care at *all* . . . as long as yer a foreigner and yer'a native speaker of the language of your country, an' in our case, it's English!" Her drunken drawl was impeding her speech a little bit. "We're the Americans. They love Americans'pecially!"

She paused to laugh and drank all the beer in her glass. Meanwhile, Victoria and Keefer shot her playful "boos" and thumbs-down gestures in response to her final comment. Keefer finished with a middle finger.

Stephanie returned the obscene gesture with a pudgy birdshot of her own. She then said, "Fuck you, Keefer, time for you to go get us another beer., pointing to the glass she had just emptied.

Keefer mumbled something witty or grotesque in mock disgust at being bossed around but squeezed himself out of the booth. Apparently, he was all too eager to get his next drink as well. Before he left, Liz chimed in with another round for herself as well. When she was intrigued by something, she tended to drink like a fish.

Victoria added, "But seriously, our school—or company—is like the McDonald's of English conversation schools!" They all laughed. "No, wait . . . that's the other one . . . ours is like . . . I dunno, like a fast-food shop. They'll hire almost anybody!"

Stephanie said, "What I like most about working for Bozack is that although I'm a whole lot busier than I ever was in the program, my life now isn't like those long, drawn-out, monotonously trite and boring days in Shiga . . . oh.my gosh . . . I swear at times I wanted to either kill myself or just head back to the States and roast in Phoenix.

"Here, all we do is teach these goofy Japanese people who pay us top dollar, or yen, to come sit with us in a room about the size of a spacey broom closet. They sit with us for about forty minutes—not even an hour—sometimes fifty, and they stare, gawk, or ramble on and on about their favorite foreign actor, actress, or musician.

"Some might even be able to communicate in decent-enough English, or something understandable, about their trip abroad, but by the time they're able to accomplish all that, the lesson session time will have just about elapsed. So it might seem busy or overwhelming at times, but your time is so occupied that it seems to just . . . zoom!" She sliced the air with an empty glass in her right hand, narrowly missing golden honey–blonde strands of Liz's hair.

Stephanie said, "Time just speeds on by! The only bad part—if you wanna call it that—my daily routine got shifted out of whack." Just then, Keefer returned to the table with two huge pitchers of beer, and Stephanie's face brightened up as if she had been presented with gifts on December the twenty-fifth.

Keefer said, "Of course, you mates know you owe me some money, yeah?"

Stephanie said, "Aw shut up, Keefer." Her annoyed tone was beginning to sound serious as she grabbed for the pitcher and served her glass first.

Liz was a little perturbed by the spilled foam from Stephanie's careless "messy Marvin" bit pouring the libation but dismissed it in good tact and patience, being that it was her first time meeting this girl. Besides, she was getting her coat pulled, and the information was absorbing, just like her shirt sleeve was the beer suds.

Finally, it was Liz's turn to fill her glass, and she poured hers all the way up to the rim before passing the pitcher to Eddie. She turned her attention back to Stephanie, who was gradually becoming increasingly unbalanced and wobbly.

Liz said, "What did you mean by your daily routine being out of whack or whatever?"

Stephanie had paused to sip thirstily from her glass before finally answering with a wet burp that sounded dangerously close to a puke preface. She managed to state, "I guess, well . . . it'sa good and bad thing, I suppose. As opposed to waking up every day at six or seven in the morning in order to be at my school's desk by 8:00 a.m., I now don't have to be at work until about one o'clock. Sometimes even two!"

Victoria chimed in again. "Oh, absolutely. I never was involved with any program here in Japan. I applied for Bozack from overseas, but ever since I've been here, my average day begins at around noon."

Keefer finally added his two cents to the pot. He said, "That's a beautiful thing too when you have a hangover, mate!" He nudged Eddie seated next to him with a sharp, heavy, and bony elbow, causing the American to wince slightly.

Liz's eyes bulged momentarily. She said, "Wow, one o'clock . . . that's crazy!"

Eddie laughed as if he was entertaining the idea of actually having intentions of applying for the company they were speaking of, Bozack. He then said, "So what time would we finish work if we worked there?"

Stephanie said, "Generally about nine, get home around ten, depending on where you live, and assuming you'd be the type that went, like . . . directly home after work. We all live right here in the city, so any subway ride gets us home rather quick, but then again, we hardly ever go straight home."

Liz said, "Well, I can definitely understand that. With all the excitement you guys have here, why would you wanna go home?" Just as she said that, she reminded herself that she would soon have to make the lengthy, dragging trip back to Hannan City, and her spirit dulled a tad.

Stephanie said, "Everything I was accustomed to doing in the afternoons when I finished work while with the program, I now try to do it in the mornings, like go to the bank, pay bills, shopping, and all that stuff. Or I just do it on my days off, and . . . oh . . . shit . . . yeah, that's another thing . . ." She slapped a palm to her forehead as if she was slightly distressed with a tired smile.

Liz said, "Your days off are Saturdays and Sundays, right?"

The trio of new faces shook their heads furiously. Victoria was the first to comment on this topic. She said, "That's probably the biggest downside. More often than not, you'll be required to work on Saturdays and Sundays. They say the weekends are the busiest. Most people who aren't working or in school have more time on weekends, so they come pay us. They come and give us money to entertain them basically." She returned to playing with the same fancy cocktail she had been play-stirring the entire time.

"Furthermore," Stephanie added, "You'll probably—more than likely—have to work on national and public holidays. Maybe Christmas!

"Unlike the public schools we work at with the programs, the conversation schools like Bozack—and most *eikaiwa*s, for that matter—are privately owned and operated enterprises, so that means they don't have to recognize holidays like our Thanksgiving or Christmas—"

"Or early bank day," Victoria said.

Stephanie giggled. "So to answer your question, my days off now are Thursdays and Fridays, but that's subject to change. That's another grim, depressing reality of working at *eikaiwa*s too sometimes. Especially the big ones like ours. And you'll be required to work those holidays with no extra pay either. You two are a couple, right?"

Both Liz and Eddie exchanged glances as if they needed to affirm whether or not it was true for a nanosecond before finally nodding to convey a "Yes" answer. After hearing about having to work on Saturdays and Sundays, Eddie was leaning toward not applying and was betting on Liz feeling the same way, especially hearing that the pay too was slightly less than the program, roughly about three hundred US dollars less.

Stephanie said, "You two might not have the same two days off. We all work five days in a week and get two days off. They don't seem to accommodate couples like some of those programs do. Just like those programs, you're at the mercy of the company, and depending on their needs, you pretty much go where they say go and when to."

That instant, Stephanie shot a gander at Victoria, who appeared suddenly saddened as if hit with a hurtful memory. The beaklike nose twitched a little on the British girl, as if she was trying to fight back tears. She excused herself from the table. Eddie noticed her plump, round tush that could rival Liz's—only Victoria was a slight bit taller and more slender. As she squeezed by, Victoria said she was going to the ladies' room. When Eddie quit staring at her elegant shape, he noticed her wiping her eyes.

Stephanie leaned closer to Liz and whispered, "Victoria, she broke up with her boyfriend, or her fiancée, I forget which. But, they broke up because they didn't have the same days off, I think. Plus . . . well, it might be best not to go into that right now, but I think you get the picture."

She did.

For Liz, the thought of her and Eddie not being able to have the same day off seemed unfathomable. It would have seemed to defeat the purpose of changing jobs and remaining in Japan. Back in the States, she thought, it might not have been a problem, but in a strange new and foreign country's envir0nment, she could foresee bigger problems and issues. Namely, the situation Stephanie had alluded to regarding Victoria and what she had been through with her significant other. Whatever had happened between the Victoria girl and her boyfriend, Liz didn't hear the entire story, but she could just about imagine.

Victoria returned to the table several moments later in better spirits, as if nothing had ever bothered her. She had already gone to the counter and had acquired yet another fancy drink with a paper umbrella. She took short sips of her drink and squeezed back into the booth, over Keefer's lap, and sandwiched herself again between him and Stephanie, and, without missing a beat, fell back into the conversation.

The discussion continued until the time eased its way toward midnight. The once-crowded ballroom was slowly dissipating as people prepared to exit and file out to the streets to catch cabs or the last trains. The moment Liz was dreading had finally come.

The party of five decided to leave together. When Liz mentioned that they would have to head to Namba Station to catch the last train, Stephanie thought it was a good idea for them to all leave the Hub together. On the way to the station, they passed a series of bars and night spots full of vibrant activity, and despite the late hour on a day before a new business week, the streets and indoor arcades were still packed with heads.

Keefer and Stephanie were already pretty wasted; Liz was beginning to feel a heavy buzz as well. Keefer seemed to have taken an interest in Eddie, and likewise, Eddie was fascinated with Keefer. He had always had a captivated fascination for Australians, largely due to his fandom of actors like Mel Gibson in the *Mad Max* flicks and the "Crocodile Dumb D", B, and C movies; and Keefer was the first Aussie he had actually ever met and had an opportunity to speak with.

Throughout the entire time when Liz and the other two girls were engaged in an absorbing chat mainly about being a foreign female in Japan and how trying it could be, Keefer and Eddie too had struck up what had appeared to be an engrossing convo. Occasionally, Liz would glance over at the two of them as they all walked to the station. When she saw Eddie smiling and laughing a little too much, as if he was *happy*, she decided to monitor the dialogue.

Liz slowed her pace and fell behind stumbling Stephanie and vaunting Victoria to join Keefer and Eddie a few steps behind.

"Hey, Keith . . . is it?" Directing her attention and inquiry to the tall, lanky Aussie.

"It's Keefer, like key, and for, like the key for your heart . . . hahaha!" His face was pinkish red, facial features like a cochineal Rod Stewart in his '80s style, substituting the clean-shaven look with a stubbly beard, which looked as if he had dipped his sweaty chin in a bowl of dirt. Or, he had pasted his jaws with poppy seeds. He seemed to tower over Eddie; he was probably at or about six feet tall, but similar to the American, Keefer too had a crescent posture, with rounded shoulders lurching forward. His blond hair was puffy and matted, in some places around his sideburns a little curly as if he had shampooed and allowed his mop to dry naturally with no attempt to style it save for the occasional clammy hand run-through with fingers for comb teeth. A poor man's Rod Stewart or Phil Collins with considerably more hair. He was literally a hot mess, but according to him, he never suffered a lonely night, which would indicate that his appearance was no disincentive for finding romance.

Because of her officious nature, Liz had intentionally overheard parts of Keefer and Eddie's conversation. They had been talking about women, with Keefer randomly leading the topic to Eddie's jib, and that was when Liz thrust herself into the chat.

She asked, "Keefer, do you have a wife, or a girlfriend?"

Keefer's narrow eyes widened as if suddenly terrified by the thought of answering such a question with an affirmative response. He said, "Jesus Croyst, heavens no, *sheila*. Why th'hell would I wanna 'ave a girly for? With all the mut on tap here?"

Right away, Liz didn't comprehend what the hell Keefer was saying, but Victoria did. She in turn responded with a haughty grunt and snooty rolling of her eyes. "Typical of you men . . . ugh!" She turned away as to not face Keefer or anyone. As she did, her hand stroked her dark-brown hair, in length nearly the same as Liz's, only silkier in flow and much better kept, as if the British girl paid regular visits to hair salons. Eddie was checking her out, and a quick image of Becky flashed through his dome. Not because Victoria favored her at all, but because she, Becky, and Liz had the longest hair he had ever seen or been around. Liz had beautiful hair once, Eddie thought—if only she'd take better care or attention to it?

Keefer's rejoinder to Victoria was saturated with bellowing, drunken laughter. He said, "Oh, don't crack the shits on me, love. You'll be all right. Just join me an'ave 'nother cold one." He turned his attention to Eddie.

"Whadda'ya say, mate?" Keefer said as he started nudging Eddie again with the heavy elbow. "Hows about we shoot through to 'nother stubby hole before you guys head back to woop-woop land?"

Eddie looked puzzled but visibly diverted. Everybody was laughing; his ears were ringing. The alcohol he had consumed that night was beginning to take impacting effect.

Stephanie was already past her normal limit of intoxication but was still amazingly coherent. Having been around Keefer for some time, she could pick up his Australian manner of talk. She translated for him to Eddie and Liz to the tune of, "He says you guys should hit another bar before you head back to your town, but me personally, I don't think you have that much time."

Liz interrupted swiftly. "Nah, he can't—we can't. We've got work tomorrow, and besides, we're already here at Namba Station." She pointed up at the big Nankai Namba sign above the huge depot. She took the liberty of answering Keefer on behalf of Eddie as well. There was no way she was going to allow her pet boyfriend dog to wander off in that big city without her, and not with a potential womanizer as Keefer, who made no bones about claiming to be.

"Fair dinkum," Keefer snorted, not appearing the least bit bothered by their decision. He bade them all—Stephanie and Victoria included—a fond farewell and trotted off as if he already knew where he was next headed.

Victoria said, "I'm going to call it an evening as well. It was nice meeting you two. Maybe see you again in the near future?" Her cheeky and seemingly impertinent tone made it unclear if her sentiment was sincere, but Liz accepted it anyway, pleased overall that she had met other foreign women at least, and people who could speak English.

Liz said, "Fuck yeah, that'd be great. I mean, to meet up with you guys again."

Stephanie's eyes were now droopy, and she looked half insane, but she could manage to talk normally. She said, "We have to have to have to . . . keep in touch, OK? OK? Y-you have my number, I have your number, I'll tell ya'what . . . I-I'm gunna e-mail you some information. About Bozack Language School, OK? And the telephone number to the head office, it's right here in Osaka. In Tennoj. In Tennoji yeah, that's the main office headquarters. They . . . they used to hire outside the country only, but now the policy changed. They hire from within the country . . ."

Eddie said, "Uh, yeah, I think we heard that part already." He was looking at his watch; he was feeling antsy, thinking that he and Liz didn't have much time. They would have to dash up a huge flight of stairs to reach the platform, or risk missing the train by ascending via crowded escalators.

Stephanie clung on to Liz's sleeve, though, as if refusing to allow her to leave. She said, "Well, anywho . . . when I get the clearer details, I'll e-mail you."

"Awesome," Liz said with a smile of quickened relief as she liberated herself from Stephanie's grip, replacing her sleeve with a handshake and waving at Victoria, parting ways with Eddie in tow. They shuffled up the grand stairway, Liz with minimal strain due to her fit condition even after excessive drinking. Eddie, on the other hand, was breathing heavily and fought the urge to release his stomach contents on the station floor.

Liz saw Eddie was lagging behind and urged him to hurry the fuck up.

Through handheld megaphones or "bull horns", the stationers were bellowing admonishing announcements that final trains were boarding and preparing for departure within minutes. People were scrambling and ambling toward the ticket purchase contrivances and wickets. Train conductors were blowing whistles. It was pandemonium on the regular, the same way every night around the same time.

Liz made it to the ticket machine and bought two tickets—one for her, one for Eddie—at the cost of the minimum fare because she forgot how much it cost to get back to Hakotsukuri Station, and she didn't feel the overwhelming urge to glance up at the charts above to find out. When the contraption finally spat out the two tickets, Eddie had dragged himself over to where she was, panting and rubbing his belly. Liz wasn't in the mood to be a sympathetic motherly girlfriend at that moment. She grabbed him like a rag doll and led him along as if he was one of the adolescents she used to babysit.

Even on Sunday, the outbound Nankai Train from Namba station was packed, standing room only. Liz and Eddie jammed themselves on a rear coach, the closest one on the platform from the wicket entrances. Japanese people squinted and scowled as the two *gaijin* jostled and wedged through them to get to a comfortable space where they could hold on to a pole or stirrup overhead strap. The coach reeked of sour vinegar sweat, masked with combos of various cheap exotic perfumes, soy sauce, and rice wine. The train shakily left the station, and the ride was bumpy all the way to Kishiwada. Thirty minutes into the ride—that was when they could finally sit. Eddie was almost immediately knocked out, and Liz allowed him to rest his heavy head in her lap. Old Japanese people were staring at them, some shaking their heads and looking at Liz like she was a barmy screwball of unsound mind.

After almost passing their intended station, Liz, fortunately, had managed to hear an announcement that alerted her to change trains for the local; she too had dozed off. She handled the task of Eddie and made him walk on his own two feet for the connecting transfer. They miraculously made it back to their station. A loud alarm blazed as they made their way through the wickets, as 150 yen was insufficient fare for a train ride from Osaka City to Hannan City. The stationer on duty saw that the fare-ducking offenders were the town *gaijins*, so he grinned like an obsequious actor for a toothpaste commercial and bowed at them as he shut off the wicket alarm, allowing them to pass. This caused Liz to think that they might need not ever pay again if it was that easy.

They hit the convenience store nearby and cleaned the hot oven of *en papillote*, copped several bags of chips, dry squid, and drinks of all sorts, including more chu-hai—as if Liz intended to do some more drinking at that hour. Why not? She probably wouldn't go to work the following day anyway. Had it been up to her, she would have stayed an extra night in Osaka City and said, "Fuck that job, fuck that school, fuck this country village town, and fuck the program!" But she knew Eddie would whine and object to it, so she decided to spare herself the grief. Sparing them both an onerous, uphill fifteen-minute walk home, they took a cab.

***

True to her inclinations, Liz didn't report for work the following day, and it was OK. She wasn't exactly missed. Eddie, on the other hand, lugged himself to work, albeit reluctantly. He wanted to stay at home and sleep in with Liz—maybe even have his balls drained—but he also wanted to prove himself and impress Japanese people with his diligence. So he towed himself to work with an irritating hangover that had him feeling as if his stomach had swallowed knives and his legs were rubber. On top of that, Osaka decided to rain—heavily too.

Eddie did his thing, though. He went to school, assist-taught four classes, and helped tutor kids in the after-school English Club. He was completely pooped by the time he arrived home. The rain hadn't ceased until he was ensconced in his crib, soaking wet for the second time today.

Liz had been lounging around all day. She looked sexy in one of Eddie's long T-shirts, bare save for panties from the waist down. Her legs were glowing and unusually high colored. He noticed that she had also painted her toenails for a change, today a light-blue, turquoise color—her favorite. A towel was wrapped around her head; it appeared as if she had not long been out of the shower. She had done maintenance on herself, which was good, as far as Eddie was concerned. It sort of irked his nerves to see her maxing and relaxing, like she had probably done the entire day, while he was slaving at work, half sick and half-dead. Then upon his return home, drenched to the bones, she didn't even have hot soup for him. In fact, she didn't even greet him at all when he got back home. She was talking on her phone and watching a video on the box.

Subtle anger subsided, Eddie thought he could finish his rotten day by taking momentary rest and solace inside of the sweet Liz cave. Liz wasn't having it. She was more interested in chatting away with none other than plausible new pal Stephanie, who had also called in sick that day. She did hit Eddie off with a kiss or two, but when he tried to go deeper, she halted his progress abruptly, almost as if he disgusted her.

She said, "Go take a shower, you addlebrain. You smell like you crawled through a dumpster. You're all wet." With that, she gave him a forceful shove from the bed, which almost toppled him altogether.

He was like, "What the fuck!" A little agitated but accustomed to Liz's childish, prissy, obstinate demeanor. Like a disappointed dog unable to secure a treat, or bone, he staggered to the walk-in-closet designated room and disrobed, prepping for a shower as he was ordered.

An hour later, a vegetarian pizza had been delivered. They sat at their kitchen table for dinner. It was the first time they could have an intelligent discussion about the previous night.

Liz said, "So . . . what do you think about getting jobs in the city?"

Eddie said honestly, "I'm really not sure. It sounds fun, but we're makin' more money out here in the country."

Liz whined, "But, Eddie . . . it's so goddam boring out here! I swear to gawd if I spend another year in this . . . this cuckoo's nest, I'm gonna go cuckoo myself. I'm gonna die from the boredom. Dude, I didn't come to this country to be bored out of my mind. I could do better back in Torrance, Hermosa, or Playa del Rey! At least, back in LA we had the beach, or we had some friends."

Eddie sighed. This was a discussion he wasn't enthusiastic about having. But he did have to admit, "I guess you're right," strangely agreeing with her and not faking or pretending to. She did have a point, but at the same time, he said, "But maybe you're taking what that girl Stephanie said a little bit too serious."

Liz disregarded his statement like dodging a ball thrown at her in slow motion. She said, "Sweetie, I think we should apply to that Bozack Company. What would we have to lose? I mean, I don't want to stay in Japan forever, neither do you. If we were to stay here another year, I suggest we move to the city. We can be closer to where all the excitement is, and just like last night, we can make friends, people who can speak English, and people we can speak to instead of mumbling all these Japanese words nobody here understands, and likewise we don't understand them."

Eddie couldn't believe Liz was swaying him. He really was under her complete control, it seemed. He secretly acknowledged that the conversation with Keefer the previous night had been enthralling. The conversation Liz had not been entirely privy to.

Keefer had talked to Eddie about how he slept with different women almost every night. He bedded Japanese women mostly, and he met them at either his job or at the bars he frequented.

He had said that he barely even had to look for women. All he had to do was go to a bar—it almost didn't matter which one, just any one with women in it—and they would approach *him*, not the other way around usually.

Additionally, he would go to work and get propositioned by female students, sometimes even the staff female members would step up to him with a coochie offer. To top this all off, he would be stone cold paid. Life couldn't have been better, Keefer had indicated to Eddie.

He had said, "I get more pussy than I ever got back home in Melbourne, mate. Hell, I fuck so much it's sometimes hard fer me to even get a stiffy. My prick has got so much attention here it's flat out incredible, mate.

"What's even better? I can have the best choice of twat from all the lonely cunts about. Y'know chicks, like Victoria, the persnickety cunt here, lonely foreign girls. They break up with their blokes, because their boyfriends run off with these sweet l'il Jap arses, mate. Or these young, ambitious Sheilas will come here to Japan but can't speak Japanese. It gets bloody lonely for 'em, y'know? After a few months of that—imagine six or seven months, mate—their hormones are boilin' over. Their mats are hotter'n a barbi in the outback . . . feed 'em a couple of drinks, and they're yours, mate!

"Ha! Sometimes they even show up at your flat in the middle of the night, mate . . . lonely, depressed, sobbing, and horny! Maybe back in her country, she was the fuckin' Queen of Lollies . . . she could have her choice of the best mongrels or Bruces, whoever she wants, whenever she wants . . . but in this country, mate . . . hahaha! She'll be so broken in spirit she'll be crying and begging a guy like me she wouldn't have given the time of day to back in her home country . . . begging fer'a mercy fuck."

This sort of talk had locked Eddie's ears into its frequency and was not easily dismissed. He wouldn't understand all of the Aussie slang and other terms all the time, but he could get the gist. Around that time would have been when Liz had interrupted him. Having seen Eddie's sneaky grin and his happy, cheery expression, her antennas went up.

Eddie decided to sleep on the idea to move to the city and or apply to the Bozack Language School. All of Liz's points were valid. It didn't take too much convincing him, but he would still sleep on it. He liked the program; he liked his job, his school; and of course, he liked the money. Hell, he liked Japan altogether. He was certain that he wasn't leaving; he would do everything in his power to get Liz to stay on with him too. Even if he had to quit the program and apply to that company in the city just to please her.

Yet it wasn't entirely about Liz either. Eddie too had some curiosities that needed to be resolved within his own mind needing answers. He was wondering if what Keefer said also had validity. And with that in mind, he didn't object to having separate days off than Liz.

In fact, to be able to hang out with "cool" guys like Keefer would be a welcome change. He had needs just like Liz had hers to be with other females to pal around and have extended girl talks with. Eddie too had a desire to buddy up with those types of guys who had experience being in Japan, English-speaking foreign dudes. The only downside was that if he were to go through with the idea to move to Osaka City like Liz eagerly suggested, he would have to sever ties with that cute, new JTE, Hiroko Okada. They had only known each other for a few short weeks, but he could see himself growing attached to her quickly, as if she were a longtime friend.

12

A DAY OR TWO later, Liz received the e-mail Stephanie told her she would send. It detailed the application process for the Bozack Language School. It seemed pretty simple compared to what she had to do to get into the CHET Program. No photos needed, no recommendation letters, and no damn essay. All she needed was an ink pen to fill out the application she printed out and the postage to send it to an Osaka address.

Liz went to her elementary school, sang a few songs with the kids like "ABCs," "Row Your Boat," and "Itsy Bitsy Spider" and finished mid-morning, well before lunchtime (around noon). When done, she had the rest of the day to sit at her desk and do next to nothing or use the school's computer and internet. She chose the latter and did further research about Bozack and the *eikaiwa* industry.

Bozack was the new kid on the scene, but it gained popularity quite fast over many of the other longstanding heavy hitters and was still growing. Their home headquarters was based there in Osaka City's Tennoji Ward and not in the capital city, Tokyo. It had been nicknamed the Second Most Popular Language School because it was rumored to have been formed by disgruntled former employees of the Number One English School—which also boasted of the provision of other language instruction, such as French, Spanish, German, and Italian, but still primarily known as an English school—but never specific as to whether or not such rumor was substantiated. It did, however, make for a fascinating read during Liz's idle moments at work, if such term could have been applied to what she had been doing.

Liz had been talking a lot with Stephanie on the phone too. Stephanie told her that the reason she thought her company had gained such enormous ground in the English school business was because they were apparently more diverse with their hiring compared to other schools. She had based this opinion on her own empirical observations, however; but it was reinforced by student testimonials Liz would read.

While most other English schools hired primarily Australians, United Kingdom people, New Zealanders, and basically Caucasians, Bozack hired anyone from any English-speaking country, and that included places like Canada, Jamaica, India, the Philippines, and, of course, the United States of America, but including Guam as well. This indicated that it wasn't a white-only company, and at the time, it resonated well with the Japanese populous.

Americans, as Stephanie had alluded to the first night Liz met her, were hard to come by—not because they were completely unavailable, but because they had earned a bad reputation of quitting jobs mid-contract and dipping out on apartment leases. They became pains in the ass to businesses struggling to acquire reliable reputations.

It made sense, because Liz had once heard the same thing during her orientation seminar in Tokyo for the program. They had really stressed the stipulation of the one-year commitment and pressed every one of the participants to seriously make sure that the program was what they wanted to do before signing the contract. Still, she learned, many people would sign anyway, intent on the idea that they would see the entire year through but ended up being so homesick they would practically fold overnight and succumb to culture shock. She heard a story of an American girl from Boston who had barely unpacked her suitcase before deciding to quit the job and go back to the United States.

Like Liz, a lot of Americans had seen pictures and film about Japan and believed the hype. They thought they would go to Japan and view all the neon glitz and glam by night and the castles in Kyoto by day. Instead, what they got was like Liz and Eddie, stuck in the middle of a rural outpost surrounded by people who didn't speak English and limited access to the outside world. Even Americans from rural extraction were rattled by the same setting in Japan, as they lacked a comfort zone to maintain their sanity. As such, a lot of companies began hesitating to hire foreigners from America for a period of time. Bozack took the risk and lucked out in the strategy, one would guess, as did Liz and Stephanie.

So Liz hit the BOZACK website and got a printable application she filled out and mailed the same day. In fact, she left work early so that she could go to the Post Office and send it. She also made a copy of the printed application to issue to Eddie. He reluctantly filled out his but didn't get his out until that Friday. Liz got a call from an English-speaking, quasi-European—accented female named

Ruth—discovered later to be Australian—a representative of the Bozack School. It was fast.

Eddie got the same call from the same person the next day, which was Tuesday. Ruth invited both Eddie and Liz to attend a group interview to be held less than a week later. As luck would have it, that day was a Saturday, at 1:00 p.m., in Osaka City's Tennoji Ward, and of course, they both had that day off.

Eddie still had his doubts and reservations about leaving the program, but he couldn't shake off the reminder that Liz was the reason he was in Japan in the first place, and he was somewhat obligated to do her bidding. As for that, he went along with Liz for the interview in Osaka City.

Once again, they got dressed up in formal duds and sat in a group of five for an interview process that took about four hours. It began with a brief history of the Bozack Company and its philosophy, basically the same thing Liz had read on the website. They started in the early '90s by former employees of NOVA, ECC, AEON, GEOS, and Berlitz. Their ideology and doctrine was purportedly based around "opening the doors to the world via communication with language as the key" and other over-the-top drivel.

The candidates for employment were Liz and Eddie, of course, then three others whom Liz thought were Japanese at first but found out they were English-speaking Filipinos—one male and two females who looked to be in their early thirties maybe, but she didn't ask because they didn't have enough time to get acquainted before their individual interviews. They were all given separate interviews by several different Bozack representatives who were charismatic foreigners from Australia, Canada, and South Africa. Ruth, the Aussie female who had contacted Liz and Eddie, was present as well. She looked like a redheaded, older version of Stephanie, somewhat avoirdupois but many more facial freckles and more serious demeanor.

Ruth Worth was the rep who interviewed Liz. Liz was expecting it to be a rigid, grave interrogation requiring a poker face. Instead, it was a lot of cheery talk about how life was both bitter and sweet as a female foreigner in Japan. Through this topic, they immediately achieved common ground, and Liz found no difficulty at all purging her thoughts and experiences in the country. Without sharing much about her own background, Ruth indicated that she could relate to Liz's issues and basically did the unprecedented thing and pretty much hired Liz on the spot. In fact, Liz was the only person hired that day.

Liz was hired, but she didn't learn of this officially until a week later. She got a call late Friday afternoon and received the news and became immediately elated. Especially when she was informed that she would be working in the heart of Osaka City! The news couldn't have come at a better time too, because the following Monday was the deadline for the program participants to submit their renewal intentions.

Eddie, on the other hand, received a letter in the mail that Friday. It turned out that Bozack *had* in fact offered him a job; however, they had intentions of staffing him at newly forming offices in the Tokyo area should he accept the offer. This was out of the question, unthinkable, Eddie decided right away and shared the news of the decision with Liz who praised him for that, but wasn't much relieved.

They would still have to separate!

Since Eddie wasn't going to accept a position elsewhere, especially somewhere as far as Tokyo, he naturally assumed that would disqualify him for employment with Bozack. Liz called Ruth and tried to appeal to her, but Ruth was stern and a little brisk with her, not like how she was during their interview.

Ruth had said, "Unfortunately, we cannot accommodate placement requests at this time. To be quite frank with you, Ms. Amberbush, you were hired immediately because there was a sudden vacancy. One successful applicant hired from overseas had declined the job at the last minute."

Liz said, "So there's absolutely no possibility of Eddie being able to work in Osaka?"

Ruth cleared her throat and paused because she was a bit agitated. She said, "We're not in the business of granting favors, Ms. Amberbush. The point of the matter is that the company is expanding its operations to Tokyo as we are quickly growing. If the company decided that Eddie would be better suited for that area's endeavors, I have no authority to alter it in any way."

Liz said, "Well, how about me going to Tokyo too—I mean, since you, like . . . need people there?"

Ruth swallowed hard and exhaled, now clearly annoyed but patiently maintaining her composure. She gritted her teeth and calmly growled, "The decision was made, Ms. Amberbush. We reviewed your information, and I personally interviewed you and felt that you were the best candidate for the position. I based my decision also on our needs for the Kansai area. We feel that you would be an asset to our Osaka offices. But I have no say in placements. The best we can do is put Eddie on a waiting list, and when an opening comes up, he will be contacted."

After this conversation, Liz thought succinctly about going through with another year—in Hannan City and the CHET Program—and just as summarily decided, "Fuck no," against it. Eddie contacted Ruth and declined the job offer if he had to move to Tokyo but wanted to be on the waiting list she was talking about.

In the meantime, Monday rolled around, and he submitted his intention to renew his contract with the program another year. Oscar Gomimoto, the Christian Educators, and the Hannan City BOE were overjoyed at the news. Perhaps Hiroko Okada was pleased the most out of everyone.

Since Liz already had the job with Bozack, she had to begin right away, so she bypassed the formalities and procedures involved with her coming departure from the program by trying to remain as quiet as possible about it. It didn't do much good. It was a small village, and word got around quick. People talked, and nosy Japanese locals were always gossiping and asking questions. The same went for work too. The times when people actually would speak or try to talk to Liz, they would be asking her questions that would be borderline obnoxious or a little too invasive, like, "How much do you weigh?" or "What's your bra size?" even "What color panties do you like to wear?" Others included, "Do you take showers or baths?" So it wasn't far-fetched to find that word was out that Liz planned to not return to the elementary school.

It was a tear-jerking event that Liz almost capitulated to. People were crying, sobbing, and splattering her with heaps of praise, good-byes, and thank-you letters. The children drew pictures, so many that she had enough material to publish a library book on primitive art. The strange thing Liz couldn't kick was even though she really wanted to leave that place, that location, and that school, she felt a little wistful, curiously, a little guilty. She hadn't taken her position as seriously as she could have or should have. While some of the praise and admiration of some adults may have been some bullshit, a lot of the children she had interacted with had genuine feelings of enchantment and fondness. She would never see them again.

13

LIZ WAS NOT aware of it, but she had the Bozack job the moment she walked through the door. All she had to do was show up to the interview. In the Japanese *eikaiwa* industry, a blonde haired, blue-eyed foreign "white" was like the mythical leprechaun at the end of a rainbow with a pot of gold. Added the fact that she was an American made her all the more appealing. Ruth Worth, the Aussie foreign liaison staff, wasn't all too fond of American people—she had her own reasons— but following the letter of what the company deemed a sought commodity, she understood the Japanese customer base's enchantment with foreign pop culture, and America was the hotbed for such environment.

Unfortunately, due to the Kansai area being somewhat of an epicenter, in its own right rich in history and containing notable cities such as Kyoto, Nara, Kobe, Wakayama, and Okayama, this made it an exceedingly popular destination for foreign visitors. Much like the CHET Program in which Liz and Eddie had enlisted, lots of people requested to be placed in those saturated areas. This resulted in the waiting list becoming extensive, and apparently, the employees who had seniority were offered first dibs.

Liz had been able to slide in on a stroke of good luck or timing. The job opening at the Bozack Osaka City School location came about, as Ruth Worth had mentioned to Liz, as the result of a last-minute cancellation. Otherwise, Liz would have been offered a position in Nagoya, Japan's third largest city roughly three hours east of Osaka, or Tokyo.

Bozack had already hired two Canadians, a couple from the Calgary area, but one of them had decided not to come to Japan. A position was thus made available, and Liz happened along at the convenient time.

Additionally, Liz's "type" was eligible for special treatment. She would have gotten the job even if she had shown to the interview with mangled hair, dusty overalls, and flip-flops. There was no way Bozack was going to turn away a blonde, blue-eyed female from the United States of America; Ruth Worth's feelings were irrelevant. If they couldn't use her for the Osaka area, they would have dispatched her to Tokyo somewhere like they wanted to do for Eddie—it was a given.

Yet Liz was hired, and she received her intake instructions and itinerary information with lightning speed. As soon as she sent word that she would be accepting the job with Bozack, they had set the wheels in motion abruptly trying to get her started. They set her up to be working in their Hommachi office, the Business District of Osaka City. It was situated between the massively grand Umeda hub and Namba, Liz's favorite fun place of shopping, drinking, and dining, and at times could be as bustling and commercial as either place, especially during rush hours.

That was the "good" news.

The "bad" news was that Bozack had a stipulation that required its full-time employees to reside no more than thirty minutes away from the locations where they were to work. This wasn't much of a surprise, and Liz wasn't too shocked to discover that she would be assigned to live in a company dormitory, but she had never heard of the place, Bentencho.

She was, in fact, ordered to move into the furnished domicile promptly and with short notice. Since the move seemed to have to be so rapid, Liz thought about getting her own apartment. That way, she and Eddie could still remain together— maybe—but no dice there either. Conversation with Stephanie—who had her own apartment—pulled her coat quick about the real estate woes for foreigners.

Stephanie explained about the "key money" and extravagant costly rent deposits that had her broke for the first few months she moved to the city. While she had saved up a little bundle living in the boring country, the cost of moving and securing a decent apartment in the city that accommodated foreigners— outside the realm of "*gaijin* houses"—was a needle in a haystack. Moreover, she needed a "guarantor," human collateral, and although Bozack provided such a service, they didn't for new employees.

Long story short, Stephanie got someone from her old job to vouch for her as a guarantor. So if Stephanie was the type to split without paying rent or damage fees, this guarantor person would get stuck with the bill. Bearing in mind a lot of foreigners—not exclusively Americans—were notoriously infamous for such departures, it was easy to see why it was difficult to find a guarantor. Especially for someone who had not been in Japan for a very long time.

It wasn't likely Liz would be able to get anyone from Hannan City BOE to do the same for her, given her poor work record. Lastly, the talk got her so spooked that she removed the idea to get an apartment of her own from her noodle. For the time being, the dormitory would be fine.

The somber and dreary separation of abodes between Eddie and Liz was assuaged by the fact that they both were relieved in a way. For Liz, she could leave Hannan City and live-in exciting Osaka City. Furthermore, she had made some friends.

For Eddie, he was happy to remain with the program and in Japan, glad that Liz would no longer pressure him into going back to the States with her. The most glaring bonus was now that Liz would be somewhat out of the picture, he would be freer to be naughty if he wanted. Bottom line, however, it was decided and deduced that Liz's departure was a necessary adjustment, and one that wouldn't put any strain on their relationship. At all. Of course not. The "vow" they made, he remembered. Eddie could breathe a sigh of relief.

Eddie too had been a cinch to get hired with Bozack but ruinously unable to willingly relocate to Nagoya and ultimately Tokyo. He had not been interviewed by Ruth Worth, but he had spoken with her when he had to turn down the job. When he asked to be on the waiting list for placement with the Osaka-based schools, Ruth told him that she could comply with his wishes but that list he was referring to was ever-growing and exceedingly long. It could take up to a year, she had said. Eddie was completely fine with that. He had already renewed with the CHET Program, so he'd be there in Japan anyway for another year. And if he couldn't get a job with Bozack, who cared? They weren't the only show in town.

Since the CHET Program had a two-year eligibility limit anyway, he had set his eyes on other options. After listening to Stephanie and Keefer that night in Namba, he was considering the future; maybe Japan wasn't a difficult place to get used to, he started thinking. He and Liz had already been in Japan for a year, had saved up a lot of money, having a relatively good time—it wasn't the worst possible situation. So far so good. Living for the moment.

14

A DAY BEFORE THE company orientation Liz was moved into the company dormitory. Ruth Worth and a Japanese staff member of Bozack met her at Tennoji station and took her by cab to the location of the new residence in the Bentencho area. They also paid for Liz's moving expenses, which wasn't too much as Eddie was keeping all the appliances, and the dormitory was already furnished with pretty much everything she already had. Mostly, all she moved was her clothes.

The "new" place was a crampy but wide abode on the fifth floor of a building that looked cleaner on the outside than within. Technically, the room itself was one huge space of floor ingeniously able to be sectioned off with hospital-like shirring dividers, running along tracks on the floor and ceiling. There were twin beds on either side of the divide and, like a hospital, each with its own service table and a lamp. Basically, this one room could be made into "two" with the use of the sliding divider, which ran on a track the length of the room to where the kitchen started. Liz chose the side of the room that had the window.

She didn't like this place as much as she did the spacious, comfy two-bedroom spot she shared with Eddie while with the program, but she was prepared to endure this setback. She figured it would be like that, so she didn't bother to be too concerned. What she *did* appreciate was the location. She was now somewhere in the heart of the city, and she couldn't wait to get out and explore. She now could look out of her window and see tall buildings for miles around. She could now hear the cars, trains, horns, and sirens blowing as opposed to peering outside in the country and view only waves of grain, rice fields, and vanishing points leading to distant mountains.

The next downer would arrive in the form of a Black woman who Liz swore was about six feet tall. She was the tallest Black female Liz had ever seen or met in person, and she would be her new roommate! Bozack had neglected to mention this, but it was too late. Liz was already locked in a contract, and it was too late to try and go back to the program. She had to bite the bullet.

Ruth Worth introduced the woman, Denore Langston, when she arrived several moments later with another company representative. They exchanged lukewarm greetings. This was before Liz learned that this person, Denore, was one of the two Canadians that had been hired and the other had been her ex-fiance who decided to stay in Calgary and decline Bozack's job offer at the very last minute. As a result, Liz's placement in Osaka City was due largely in part to this woman.

Initially Liz was apprehensive about this setup. Her interactions with black people had been scant, and back home she barely knew any other than the ones she met who escorted Becky. When Ruth Worth and all the other Bozack staff finally left the two of them alone, Liz and Denore could sit and talk and get acquainted.

Eventually, Liz settled down and warmed up to Denore. Her apprehension faded quite a bit when she realized that despite Denore's initial foreboding outward appearance, she was, in fact, soft-spoken, gentle, and downright friendly. She seemed shy and reserved, but had a sense of humor. She could laugh at corny jokes and was chatty when engaged. Liz deemed her a "square" right away because in their conversation, Denore didn't come across as the type that placed a lot of importance in partying. She didn't smoke or drink. Liz had an idea to change that. Especially if they were going to be roommates and possibly be hanging out together.

Be that as it may, it didn't occur that evening. Liz and Denore became so enthralled in conversation the time sped by. The story about how Denore's fiance had basically dumped her at the airport had Liz shook. If Eddie had dared do anything like that to her, she would never have come to Japan. The more they talked, the more Denore opened up. Next thing they knew, the day turned into night, and there was no use to go exploring when the next day would be another orientation, and it was one they both had to wake up early for.

This time around, there was no fifteen-minute walk to a train station, there were no uphill and downhill treks to arrive at those stations, and there were more options in ways to travel to a destination here. In addition to trains, buses, and taxis, there were also subways. The train needed to deliver Liz and Denore to their journey's end in Osaka's Tennoji Ward was about a five-minute walk, maybe less with a bicycle, which Liz thought immediately to buy when she saw so many people in the city using them. They arrived at the Bozack headquarters (HQ) Tennoji-Honko for orientation.

Liz and Denore were joined by some other foreigners that morning who were to be dispatched to the budding Nagoya and Tokyo offices. Liz and Denore were the only new staff to be stationed in Osaka. As such, Liz didn't bother becoming too acquainted with them.

At the orientation training session, which lasted the entire exhausting day, Liz learned more about the job she was about to work, which seemed to be *work*, compared to what she had previously done with the CHET Program. The speech and talk and lecture picked up where the website and prior interview left off.

The Bozack School was typically an English conversation school where Japanese people came to learn, practice, and speak English. These students at the schools were referred to as student customers, and Liz and the others would be teacher employees.

As teacher employees (TE), they would administer lessons to Japanese folks—and sometimes children too, depending on the school or location—in English (or a foreign language of choice/availability) for a period of about forty-five minutes or fifty minutes. Students were divided into four levels: Beginners, Basics, Intermediate, and Advanced. Each level had its own textbook, which looked like a colorful *Forbes* magazine, but with a thicker cover and less pages.

Unlike the CHET Program, which made an actual effort to transform regular joes into academic teachers who would appear in public school classrooms, Bozack clearly didn't care. All they required was that the *gaijin* show up to appear in front of a paying customer, and the rest was whatever shit show they paid for. But, to make it easy for the foreign TE's, and to make it appear as if they were concerned with the student customer's progress, they came up with the four levels and a record system to chronicle stages of their learning. It was a numeric system and easy to follow, so all the TE had to do was follow the number associated with the student and find a section in the textbook that corresponded with it. Once the TE found that lesson, all s/he had to do was read the page—verbatim if need be—and upon completion, the session would be halfway over. Liz would find out all of this much later when she would eventually be able to finesse it—like a lot of other teachers did—so that it would be a process so elementary she could do it in her sleep.

Ability to speak the Japanese language was unnecessary, and it was not even encouraged for the foreign teachers. Every Bozack School had a Japanese liaison staff, and these were the Japanese people who, supposedly, could speak English and/or another foreign language, depending on the class and student. Bozack didn't want foreign teachers speaking Japanese because the goal was to keep the student customers out of the frame of mind that they were in Japan. Liz was cool with this because she didn't think at that time her learning to speak Japanese fluently was possible.

The rest of the day was a bunch of other stuff like schedules, how to call in sick, how to request days off, how many vacation days they get, how many sick leaves, and the penalties attached to breaches of conduct, failures to call in sick, and various ministrations. It was a load of information crammed into a feebly prepared folder book breakdown of the company and everything they covered in the orientation. Liz fought to not fall asleep. She wasn't as animated as the other geeky dudes about to head out to Nagoya and Tokyo. She also was beginning to see what Stephanie was talking about: there weren't a lot of American women around in the Bozack world.

15

TRANSITION WAS UNDER way. The orientation gig came and went. So now Liz was situated in one of her company's dormitories, or *shattaku*, which wasn't really a dormitory at all. It was a room rented by the Bozack company and leased in their name, which they subleased to their employees. The building was in an area considered by some to be a borderline ghetto for Japanese people, but for hundreds of thousands of foreign people who chose to call Bentencho, Osaka, their home, it was affordable housing—if not at least reasonable—and lesser propensity for the prejudiced, bigoted landlords that refused to rent to them. There were people from many different countries living in the area. The obvious foreigners like Liz and Denore stood out; but the other Asians like Chinese, Koreans, Filipinos, and other southeast Asian people looked like Japanese but were still considered *gaijin* nevertheless.

This melting pot was one of the first characteristics of the new *nabe* that Liz took note of. She wasn't a stranger to diversity—in Iowa not so much, but California had lots of it, and she was well adjusted. She just was a little surprised at how it looked in Japan. Comparing it to Hannan City would be like night and day. She would now meet people in her building from places like Indonesia, Thailand, or some other country that spoke English. Many companies similar to Liz's likewise had accommodations for their employees as well, and it wasn't uncommon to see them all heaped and stacked in one small building.

"This shit is crazy," Liz muttered to herself out loud as she looked out of the window of the Osaka Loop Line train. The awesome yet overwhelming sights and sounds were doing a number on her senses. How she was feeling then differed from how she felt in the past when she had visited the city on weekends with Eddie. Now she would be there full-time and all the time. The vista was permanently changed. Different.

Instead of rice fields and quiet roads, there were now bustling streets and the patter of many feet. Neon signs floated sideways across the train glass like screeching apparitions. Liz still couldn't read much Japanese, but her *hiragana* and *katakana* game was picking up, surprisingly because of idle time she spent studying while previously with the CHET Program. She was better than she gave herself credit for.

It was her first day of work. Again, Liz bellowed, "Fucken' crazy!" with the tone and inflection of a dude who might play hockey on ice. Or, to the unassuming ear, as was that of her new roommate, would think. Denore Langston's younger brother had played ice hockey. She knew about dirty laundry and all the bad habits of dudes; and for the last two days she had been in the company of Liz, all she could think of was that she was the prettiest tomboy she had ever had the experience of meeting.

Liz became gradually intrigued about having a black person as a roommate. Stephanie, who bypassed the need for company housing and a roommate, thought Liz should be worried about it; but after the initial alarm wore off and they began talking a lot, she warmed up to her.

Ordinarily, she would not have consorted much with black people—male or female for that matter—not for any particular reason other than non-interest. It was her parents who had the real issues with blacks, not her necessarily.

Thing was, Denore didn't fit the stereotype that Liz thought she was accustomed to. Although Denore looked like she was rough and could hold her own in a dirty, drag-out brawl, her personality was the complete contrary. She had a quiet voice, very soft-spoken, and sometimes it trembled like she was a bundle of nerves. She spoke with an accent that had the faint traces of a British twang and rounded her consonants when speaking. Liz laughed, amused, thinking that Denore reminded her of the people Becky called Oreos describing the Lamars and other types of blacks she would consort with.

Liz had hoped Denore was one of those sassy, bold, self-assured, take-charge wrecking balls, the kind she used to see on TV or the Ricki Lake–type talk shows. If not those, she would settle for an Oprah, or maybe even a Whitney Houston type to sing for her. Maybe, if she could sing and dance, Liz too could pick up a step or two. That would increase her sexiness and hip quality, she thought amusingly.

To her dismay, though, there was no "star power" in Denore, Liz realized. Denore was a Jamaican Canadian. Although Liz could eat spicy food occasionally, she wasn't into reggae music at all. She didn't mind the weed at all, but Denore didn't drink or smoke, so the chances of her pulling a Jamaican blunt out of her purse would be slimmer than Weight Watchers. Denore was a five-foot-eleven quasi-diva who would break down in tears at the drop of a hat. One minute she would be fine, chatting, talking normally, her voice like a canary's for most of the conversation, and then suddenly, she would appear as if she was coughing, then the next moment she would be practically bawling like a baby.

Liz could understand, though. When she heard the story about how Denore's fiance dumped her, she sympathized. The furnished dorm came equipped with a coffeemaker, and Liz calmed Denore down with the prep java. Liz understood better than Stephanie that color didn't necessarily matter. All girls, black or white, shared things in common. Denore, to her, was just another vulnerable human.

While she would appear to be consoling and supportive to Denore, in reality she was doing it for herself. They were really supporting each other. Liz didn't want to fall to pieces emotionally like Denore. Her relationship with Eddie hadn't yet hit the rocks, and she did not expect or want them to. When they had the discussion about them having to live apart for a while, he appeared visibly shaken, uneasy about it. Or so it appeared.

She didn't like it either, but she didn't have much of a choice. On short notice, where was she going to have found a guarantor person? To help her get her own apartment and not depend on this new "English conversation school company's housing, she needed someone to vouch for her, but she hadn't established any considerable friendships that would have provided one. Moreover, she wouldn't have known where to start looking for apartments, let alone the time to do the search.

After finally calming Denore down, she could calm herself too. It was so depressing if she had to dwell on it too much. She should have been happy, excited. After all, this was where she wanted to be, wasn't it? So, no need to allow some spoilsport sad sack to ruin it. Luckily, her seeming to care for Denore had salubrious effects for the Canadian Amazoness. Denore calmed down a bit in the three days she spent with Liz.

Now it was their first day on the job officially. They traded the Loop Line train "ell" aboveground for the subway belowground, not knowing that they could have taken the subway from their crib; it was a waste of a half hour. They stepped off the train onto the platform and got lost in a flood of Far East faces, mystified by mazes of winding paths to nowhere, elevators that took them to another level of subway but not the street level; but finally, they could find their way to the asphalt by following the only visibly comprehensible word of English called "Exit."

The station was Hommachi, and the subway line was the red strip Midosuji, which ran along an expansive boulevard avenue bearing the same name (as far as foreign people would estimate); the station was so large and confusing anyone could get lost. To safeguard against such hazard, the exits came numbered or with alphabets; and if the destination you needed was located near one of those numbers or letters, that would usually be the most ideal one to use. Of course, newbies to the city would not soon pick it up. Yet Liz and Denore were the luckier ones who had received good directions. Problem was, they had difficulty in finding the exit with the number they were supposed to use. They just chose any random exit and got spat out far away from where they needed to be, resulting in further tardiness.

The terminus was the Bozack School Hommachi Branch. It was situated inside of a slim four-story building in which it occupied all floors except the ground level, which housed only a stairway to the second floor (US), a janitorial closet, and a place that looked like it was a bicycle stash spot for people who used them to get to work. At stairway's end on the second floor were double doors, the entrance to the school; and upon entering, one would arrive directly in front of a desk, greeted by a Japanese staff member. To the right was a long corridor leading to a teachers' lounge, or break room, where a large group of people had been assembled. Liz and Denore were directed to join the others in that room space.

There were a lot of faces in the office that mid-morning, some familiar, others that weren't much so. Ruth Worth was there for a little while and stayed long enough to issue one of those stern warnings about what would happen if they were habitually late for work and all that sententious babble. Liz was beginning to like her less and less. Needless to say, the feeling was mutual with Ruth about Liz.

After Ruth split, there seemed to be a sigh of relief in the air, and everyone appeared to be less tense. Stephanie greeted Liz with a warm embrace like she was her fat aunt that hadn't seen a relative in ages and stopped short of smothering her with kisses. Liz still liked women, but for some reason didn't find anything particularly appealing or attractive about Stephanie. Still, Liz hugged her back and made a joke about her seeming like one of her loudmouth aunts from Oklahoma.

Liz and Denore were introduced first to the Japanese staff. The head manager and regional assistant head director of Bozack operations was a guy called Kenjiro, but he could speak a minimal bit of English, and he was like, "But please call me 'Kenji." And so it was for this skinny, frail-looking wide-nostril-nosed guy in a black suit. The reason why he had so many titles was because his "assistant head director" title had yet to be finalized, but it was common knowledge he had recently been promoted. The Tokyo offices had to take off before he could officially be the Osaka area top brass.

His hair was black, spike-needled with center parting held in place by mousse of some sort. He was clean-shaven, but the shadow was due any moment, denoting his age being older than he looked. His manner of talking, however, reminded Liz a tad of Carver: limp wrist gestures, feminine movements of his hips and shoulders, and excessive blinking of the eyes. Despite these characteristics, though, Liz would later hear word around the office decree that this man, in his late forties, had a drop-dead gorgeous girlfriend, or fiancée or whatever, to whom he was twice her senior.

A female staff member who notably registered in Liz's head was one chick named Kayo Terumi. She had been introduced to several other Japanese staff, but their names were quickly forgotten. These individuals were the staff that worked with the customers; took care of the bookings, schedules, and the general business side of the company; as well as provide feedback to the foreign teachers. Additionally, their jobs entailed assisting the foreign teachers if they needed help with anything, which they often did.

Kayo stood out because she was the one who showed signs of having the best English-speaking ability, and, while the other female staff members seemed shy and eager to retreat to their office desks and compartments in another section of the office, Kayo confidently stood her ground among the *gaijin*. There was nothing about her which suggested that she was intimidated by foreigners.

Liz's dislike for Kayo was almost immediate. Thanks to Stephanie, Kayo's reputation had preceded her. Liz had no idea that she and Kayo were about the same age, in the late twenties, because she assumed the woman was younger by appearance alone, like a kid trying to wear adult business clothes as if playing house. Seeing how some of the male foreign teachers were gawking at her cleavage and the split seam in the rear of her skirt, Liz understood the source of Kayo's confidence. Phone conversations with Stephanie had made mention of this person at a glance, but this was the first time she had put a face to her rundown.

Kayo was a little thicker than the average Japanese twenty-something female, but she wasn't fat—she was just one of the few that were blessed with fuller breasts than most, unless she was wearing padding in her bra; and she also had somewhat of a rump to catch the eyes as well. Her eyes were a little sleepy: she looked perpetually fatigued, and maybe she was, but she moved lively and appeared to enjoy laughing and talking to the foreign staff, especially the guys. Liz was checking her out and concluded that Kayo's desperation to sleep with any of the male *gaijin* teachers couldn't be more apparent if she had worn a sign across her spread legs reading, "Please feed white cock." No wonder guys like Keefer—who, to her looked like a potbellied parenthesis in a yellow sponge mop wig—had massive egos.

Liz also noticed right away how Kayo was so helpful, supportive, and accommodating to the male teachers. With the females, especially to Denore in particular, she was short, a bit indifferent at times, and other times altogether curt. Interactions with non-Japanese women for Kayo seemed glaringly superficial. Since Liz and Denore were new, it would have seemed that Kayo would have focused more of her attention on them and not the guys she was joking around with whom she was already familiar obviously. Liz could tell there was going to be no love lost between them. Women like her were the catalyst to the growing rancor she was developing for Japanese women. She began to despise how submissive they were, as she witnessed up close while a teacher with the program, and how they made themselves so easily available for the lustful desires of men.

Kayo would allow teachers like Keefer to flirt with her and make innuendos that would have been construed as sexual harassment were he anywhere in a civilized, "Western" society, Liz declared silently with a rolling of her eyes. In the five minutes she had been in their presence, Liz heard Keefer make at least three comments about her "boobs". All she did was laugh. Did she really know English?

Liz didn't like it, but she already formed an opinion about Keefer and figured she could guess how he would react if she said anything about his manner of talk. She just remained quiet about it, as guys like him were both lost causes and therefore non sequitur.

To Kayo's dismay and demise, however, none of the *gaijin* teachers seemed interested in her, so Liz and Stephanie and others like Vicky too found silent delight in this. For although she had a nice rack—as did Liz—her back package was a little too voluptuous bulky for the taste of the foreign males. Especially those who were into petite, waif, tinier targets, which were plentiful pickings around town. She wasn't ugly, just far from beautiful, and "lady lucky" to have a body that generated enough interest to grant her looks a pass (as opposed to a fail) by default. Her jet-black hair was short, styled in the shape of a common mushroom. A dark mole the size of a loose-leaf paper hole sat on her right cheek near her nose accompanying her shade of beige made her look like a chocolate chip cookie with sleepy Asian-face topping.

Speaking of cookies, the bitch would even bake for the guys. Liz laughed as she remembered the stories she was told by Stephanie about Kayo. She heard that the taste of her baking was so atrocious Stephanie and Vicky would laugh incessantly about it, so much so it once hindered their ability to teach lessons to student customers properly. They couldn't maintain their composure and repeatedly had fits of laughter outbursts while trying to teach their classes.

They laughed because Kayo had the blasphemous audacity to consider her disastrous kitchen creations worthy of human consumption. Her muffins were literally used as hacky sacks in the office rooms by the guys in between classes. Or, on other occasions, these so-called edibles were used as missiles to bomb cats or rats outside, hurled down to a slime-rotten alley below from the break room window. Cookies were used for frisbees.

It was evident Liz and Kayo weren't going to be as affable as how she was with Hiroko Okada back in Hannan City. Hiroko at least, seemed a little humbler, Liz thought, even though she had every reason to be overconfident. Hiroko could really speak English like a professional Connie Chung or television evening news co-anchor. Kayo was just an obsequious dog hoping to get a good bone and probably wouldn't think twice about being a home wrecker. The type of floozy that allegedly yanked away Vicky's fiancée .

Thankfully, Liz didn't have to exert much energy into being concerned about Kayo, her antics, or attitude. For word also had it that she was going to be transferred soon. The scuttlebutt around the stead was as juicy as an orchard full of citrus fruit, and Stephanie had all the behind-the-scenes info. The alleged claim was that she consistently gave neck to Kenji after hours. She wasn't the only one, though. According to whoever started the rumor, this was a common practice in Japan sometimes for such favors to be granted without a necessary need for intimacy or catching feelings; it was described as a business transaction, comparable then to a massage or shoeshine. Liz heard about this and wanted to retch. Her respect level for the Japanese female staff was reduced to a half, even though she had no evidence to substantiate what she heard was the absolute truth. She presumed it was.

Apparently, the thriving business depended on sales. It was like a pimp game where the goal was to have more whores enter a stable than leave. The Japanese staff like Kayo were responsible for trying to get the whores, a.k.a. student customers into the stable and keep the house paid. They had a goal for every month, and if they fell below the goal, sanctions would be issued. Low-level grunts like Kayo and some of the other female staff would suffer by receiving pay cuts into their commission. Already their salaries didn't match their long, stressful hours of work, which exceeded that of the foreign teacher staff by nearly double.

For those not desiring the slice into their pay, other options were quietly available behind the scene. Such staff as allegedly Kayo would do anything to appease certain managers or preponderant supervisors who could or would "postpone the reports to the regional office until the next deadline" or "embellish some reports here and there to alleviate the impending crisis." If ordinary means weren't enough, like working extra hours, hitting the streets to hand out flyers, or making random phone calls soliciting new customers, the Japanese staffer would arrive at a breaking point, at which time they would either quit, put in a request to be transferred to another location, or accept the pay cut. Others still would simply just fall to their knees; swallow their pride, along with seminal fluid; and report to work the next day with a smile on their face like it never happened.

As the introductions continued around the Bozack School, Liz had been made privy to the chain of command. The top dog around the office was Kenji. Next in command was a Mr. Yamada, who wasn't present that day. Following him was a jaded-looking attractive woman named Mayumi Kazegawa, assistant co-manager, whom Liz met briefly, but the chick was so busy she allowed Kayo to tend to the two new teachers, Liz and Denore. Ruth Worth, neither teacher nor sales staff but talent agent scout and foreign staff advisor, worked primarily at the Tennoji HQ when grounded, but was most often traveling back and forth between Osaka, Nagoya, and Tokyo and seldom, if ever, made appearances like the one she had that day.

Each Bozack School also had a head teacher among the foreign staff, and this was the captain among the non-Japanese, whose responsibility was to co-manage the *gaijin*, among other things. On this day, however, the Hommachi branch head teacher was on a vacation leave of absence, so in his stead, Stephanie was acting like she was head and took the liberty of familiarizing Liz with the office and the other coworkers. Denore sat quietly most of the time and was barely even engaged for conversation or acknowledged.

Stephanie practically took Liz by the arm and guided her through the room full of people, at this point, mostly foreigners. She said to Liz, "This is Radley, he's from Canada."

Liz shook hands with a tall, clean-shaven, blue-eyed, pale guy with a black, spiky taper fade. His smile gave him a Brad Lowe or Michael J. Fox look. He was wearing a dark-purple shirt, a thin black leather necktie, high-water pants of the same dark color, exposing bony pallid ankles, violet sole socks; and dark sneakers that cold pass for dress shoes if worn with dress clothes. He was relatively cute, Liz surmised, but his piercing stare and damp palms from the handshake made him seem a little creepy.

"Nice to meet you," Radley said in a ghostly tone of voice as if he was intentionally trying to sound like a slender Frankenstein singing oldie hit "Monster Mash".

Next was Eric Cravens. He was an American—though some Americans might not want to claim him. He was a short, bespectacled guy in his early twenties, a recent college graduate and newlywed. He was the classic nerd with the curly dirty-blonde hair in the skin fade, and his glasses had the round wire rim and thick lenses; in them his eyes were three times the normal size, so it was easy to understand why he always looked surprised more than the people who looked at him.

Eric was from some town in Wyoming that nobody, not even Liz, had ever heard of and didn't care to even remember. He wore a button-up plaid shirt, suspenders, on this day a bowtie, and on his feet were none other than the Buster Brown Hush Puppies. He was one of the few Bozack employees who adhered to the company's conservative business attire dress code. Liz didn't know what to think of him but narrowed his type down to either being a former Little Rascal that got abused or bullied at school because he was too smart, or he was a secret serial killer that slipped through the cracks and the grasp of the law's long hands. The more he spoke, the more Liz began leaning toward the latter, or maybe even both.

"Nice do meed anodder 'Merican, heh heh . . . an' I was beginnin to think we're a minoriddy 'round heah," Eric said with speech, drawl, and subsequent drool dribble that made him appear like a functioning down syndrome afflicted, granted a job by the March of Dimes. He would giggle after making statements that didn't normally merit such humor, like, "Wow, it's growded in this woom," or "Wow, two new fazes I zee!" His giggles reminded Liz of mad scientist movies Eddie used to bring home from the video shop. To her, Eric looked like the type who had just dismembered a gang of naked teenage virgins in a basement, featured on an episode of *Unsolved Mystery*. When Liz shook his hand, she quickly wished she hadn't. She caught sight of a small canteen in the adjoining portion of the room sectioned off to appear like another. There was a sink; Liz made a mental note to go wash her hands later.

Stephanie could sense Liz's repulsion toward Eric and whisked her away. Adroitly she whispered to Liz out of earshot. "Don't let this circus sideshow freak and its looks fool you. This nerd just got married to some beautiful rich, wealthy widow."

Liz boldly exclaimed, "Him?" She turned and gaped at the Eric guy, not caring if she'd given away the fact that they were whispering about him. Her disbelief was dolorously profound, shock widening her eyes to those of Eric in his specs.

Stephanie giggled and tried to shush Liz before quietly exhaling, "Yeah, the guy Mitch, our head teacher who isn't here now—he married a Japanese woman too who's rich. They're on a honeymoon now, I think. But this guy . . ." She snarled and pointed a hidden thumb over her shoulder at Eric.

"He married some Filipina who was married to a rich Japanese guy who died or something like that. A lot of those people do that to stay in Japan legally, like how they do back in the States. I guess she was lucky because she got a huge inheritance and citizenship."

Liz replied in a low voice, "And he must definitely be feeling lucky . . . I mean, what rich bitch would pick him for marriage back home in America?"

They laughed and embraced one another. The intros ended with people Liz already knew like Keefer, Victoria. There were a few random Japanese faces she met briefly but quickly soon forgot. Denore had mysteriously vanished but wasn't missed evidently. Peculiar it was how Stephanie had conveniently forgotten or neglected to recognize or introduce Liz to a set of two nicely dressed black dudes in a corner of the room, away from everyone else, and engrossed in their own conversation between themselves.

Liz squinted at them, thinking that she might have seen them before. That was because at Venice Beach, she would see flashy, slick-dressed individuals quite a bit. The two black guys looked to Liz like they should have been either gospel or R&B singers and wondered if they were there at the school that day to perform or something. The jewelry they wore caused them to seem dressed too immaculately to be in an office environment or teaching in a school classroom.

Liz said with a quick index point jab in their direction, "So who are *those* guys? Are they, like, rappers or what?" She looked around for Denore to seek her impression of the only other black people there besides her. Denore was absent.

Stephanie's face dulled at the motioning toward the two guys, who looked like they were dancers or performers from *Soul Train* or *American Bandstand*.

She said, "Oh, them . . ." with elocution of voice that seemed to suggest, "Geez, why would you want to know *them*?"

Instead of approaching them to introduce Liz up close and personal, Stephanie opted to remain a lengthy distance away and merely pointed them out.

One guy had a slight chubby, robust shape, but it was a muscular-type chubby, like he was a football player that liked to gobble a bit too much during the off season, but still rugged and didn't look sloppy with his clean white shirt tucked inside strait-laced slacks with a matching hickory-brown necktie. He wasn't too tall; he was stocky, and his overall stature appeared possessed by strength and endurance. His hair was cropped in a small, neatly and evenly combed "short-big" afro. Liz inadvertently stared at his waistline too intently. The guy's belt buckle was a gleaming silver beam with a bull skull. He had a ring on his right hand with a similar symbol of his Chicago hometown.

Stephanie pointed at him and said, "That black guy in the white shirt is Chucky. He's from the States, from Illinois, I believe, if I remember correctly. He's pretty nice, but the guy with him, he's a total asshole."

Liz said, "You said '*that* black guy' as if they both aren't black or something . . . and hey, I thought they had a restriction against men teachers having ponytails or long hair?"

She was referring to the tawny, almost-penny-colored cat with a lustrous long, slicked-back collection of hair braided into colorful interwoven beads, extended into a single formation that extended the length of his nape. Although he was wearing a sporty, fat silk necktie, his blue-collared shirt was worn really loosely, unbuttoned to expose his collarbone, where more colorful necklaces, or *collares elekes*, containing colors of orange, red, black, white, and green tones; this was all meshed with a single herringbone jewelry wrapped around the neck, spread like a line of a liquid, silver snake. This guy had a vicious, angry face and dark eyes that couldn't be hidden even with the friendly, tender smile he tried to force his face to render. His slender caramel fingers had three to four rings on each hand, and while he talked, they streaked the air like hypnotic blurs of flash, and he seemed as if he should have been in a rap video, Liz lamented.

Stephanie said, "Oh, Deon is black too? I didn't know . . ." Her face crumpled as if she was racking her empty brain for a *Jeopardy* game show question to answer.

She then said, "Well, I suppose so . . . if we were in America, he'd be . . . negro, I guess. I dunno what they call those people anyway. Negro? African American?

Black? I dunno . . . but anyway, I got told that Deon is some kind of Indian or something, so I guess that's why they allow him to have long hair like that.

"Funny thing is, the other black guy, the one I think you're replacing here, he had long hair too, but he had those *dreadlock* things . . . well, they told him to cut his hair, he refused, and he quit before they fired him. But this guy, yeah, I guess you're right. He talks and acts like a *nigger*, but Mitch the head teacher told us that he was an Indian."

Liz said with shock, "He's from India? Like *Indian* or Native American?" Her mouth almost dropped open.

Stephanie suddenly appeared nervous and cautioned Liz to simmer down a bit. She didn't want to be overheard. She stated, "I guess he'd be the Native American type, not those people who have the turbans and blow clarinets for snakes in buckets."

By this time, more people had filed out of the break room, and with less commotion there, it became easier to overhear Liz and Stephanie's careless outbursts. Chucky and the other guy, Deon, had heard the last of Stephanie's comment; after all, they were standing less than five feet away from each other.

Even so, Liz thought it appropriate to shout over at Deon, even though he would have heard her absolutely fine had she used a normal volume of address. When they made eye contact, Liz practically screamed, "You're Native American? Really? Bullshit! *What percent Native American are you?*"

The guy Deon didn't respond or say anything at all, but if the squinted facial expression spoke, it would likely have communicated, "Bitch, fuck you. None of your got'damn business." Instead, however, he trained his murderous Rufus Buck eyes on Liz like Crazy Horse about to bring the hatchet down over Custer himself. As if nothing would have made this guy happier than just slapping Liz dead across her pink face.

Liz was an original fire starter who liked playing in the blazes she created, was incoherent to the enmity she had aroused in Deon, and they had not even been in each other's company longer than a few minutes. Unable to read or comprehend the pure hate he was fighting to not launch, she kept pressing him cheerfully.

She said, "I'm Native American—well, I'm part Native American," laughing as she inched her way closer to him and the other guy Chucky who had remained quiet the entire time, but matched a baffled scowl on his grill seeing and hearing Liz for the first time.

Liz said, "My mom's a Native American, though I forget which tribe it was . . . but fuck yeah, anyway, my mom—see, she's originally from Council Bluffs in Iowa, and she grew up near a reservation . . ."

Fate interrupted what would have been a garrulous Liz rant with the school's chime. This would ring twice at hourly intervals with ten minutes in between to indicate commencement or closing of the school's lesson session for that period. This particular chime on that day, however, signaled a different occasion for its call to assemblage, a call to order for all of the foreign teachers. As such, Denore magically reappeared, as well as some others who had left now returned. Here again, Liz and Denore would receive the same intros Liz got from Stephanie earlier, only this time smeared with a fake, sugar-coated topping of politically appropriate grandeur— etiquette designed to conceal shit from shitty people posing as classy.

Liz received her teaching schedule finally. She would be slated to work five days a week. Like every other teacher, she was assigned to two different branches of Bozack, a method the schools decided to employ in order to offer students a rotation of varying teachers. Three days of the week, she would be at the place she was that day, the Hommachi branch, and her coworkers would be primarily the motley bunch of characters she had met. There were others she had yet to meet, because that day was their day off, or they were at another school location for their assignment.

The other two days, Saturday and Sunday, Liz would be working at the Umeda Bozack branch. For the first time while in Japan, Liz was informed that she would have to work on the weekends. Had that been in Hannan City, for her it would have been utterly tragic. Now it didn't seem too bad, since she was already in the city and didn't have to make an hour-plus trip to get to any action and excitement. Plus, even though her work hours were earlier than the usual 1:00 p.m. start time for the regular, normal workdays at Hommachi, it was still not as early as the time the CHET Program required for her to be at work, which was no later than eight thirty in the morning. Now her days off were Monday and Tuesday. Wednesdays through Friday, she started work at one in the afternoon. Saturdays and Sundays she started at 10:30 a.m. It was still a breeze! The best thing about that was even though she started work earlier, she finished earlier too, so she still had a bit of weekend to enjoy.

She and Denore received train passes, compliments of the management, as transportation to and from work was paid for by the company. Liz was one of the few teachers who received two of these train-pass cards, or *teiki*, and this was because, for whatever reason, Kenjiro, the top dog, decided that he had wanted for Liz to take the Loop Line (a commuter train and ell) when commuting to the Umeda office from her home and subway to the Hommachi School. This was probably to lessen the complexity new people to Osaka faced when arriving in the Umeda hub. The school's proximity to the loop line Japan railway was easier to navigate to from more so than the intricate, confusing patterns of the subway's tunnels and passages.

On the way home, Denore and Liz were hipped to the Green Line subway (the Chuo Line) they could use to directly get back to their dorm in Bentencho, as opposed to riding the train all the way to Umeda and circling back around to arrive there after transferring to the ell. Liz felt the urge to praise Eric Cravens with a heap of gratitude for showing her and Denore the way, but neglected to offer such because, as she put it, she was "starving" and was interested in getting some take-out curry from one of the many restaurants lined up on the block of the Hommachi and neighboring area back streets.

Denore was down for that idea as well, and they hit up a Coco's pop-in minimart. They both copped a curry chicken and rice meal in a Styrofoam box and went home. Liz decided to go ahead and get a six-pack of beer, assuming that Denore would join her in the festivity when they got home.

As they left the nearest Lawson Convenience Store to their residence, Denore said, "You're gonna drink all those?"

"Sure, why not," Liz replied. "You are too, right? I got these for us, I can share."

"Oh no, thanks," Denore said. "I told you earlier, I'm not a drinker."

Liz exhaled heavily and said, "Aw, come on," as if she was somewhat deflated at Denore's attitude. She said, "Loosen up a little, it's not gonna hurt. You need to relax a bit."

Denore said, "It's OK, I can relax with a good book and a cup of coffee."

Liz didn't feel like struggling with an uphill battle and decided to rest the issue. She wasn't going to be a bad influence on Denore on this day, so she shrugged, like, "OK, whatever," and thought, *More for me later*, remembering the huge refrigerator they had in their room, twice the size as the one she and Eddie had back in Hannan City. Speaking of Eddie, he had called her once or twice, but she had been unable to receive his call.

She looked at her Tuka phone and saw Eddie's number registered on the tiny screen as an unanswered call. She had been so busy the past three days she had neglected to check in with her subject. The good thing was that he had done so for her.

She called him up, and they shot the breeze for a while after she and Denore consumed all of their foam-box meal. Eddie and she chatted for almost an hour. Denore sat quietly on her side of the room, perched upon the bed so her massive back rested upon the wall, reading a novel in her lap. Her face was expressionless, but after a while of hearing Liz exchange lovey-dovey conversation with her man on the phone, she began sniffing like a crying spell was coming. She rose up from the bed and slipped on a light sweater as if she was about to leave the apartment. She got as far as the door, slipped on a pair of flats, opened the door, just to close it and stand there at the entrance as if she was debating something over and over in her head.

Liz noticed that she was leaving and called out to her, "Hey, where are you going?" She thought Denore was going out to explore the town, and if so, she wanted to tag along. She quickly ended the phone convo with Eddie, vowing to call him back later.

She stumbled to the door, where Denore had been standing, but the tall Canadian girl just turned back and returned to her bed.

"Nowhere," Denore said with a light trembling vibration in her voice. "I'm not going anywhere now," she said. Maybe she was feeling a little relieved now that Liz's telephone conversation had ended.

Liz seemed disappointed that Denore wasn't going out. In the past three days, the two of them had become very acquainted, almost to the point where Liz could call her a friend, but if Denore was to continue being in a sullen, mercurial mood, Liz was sure that the relationship would spoil rather quickly.

As Denore removed her sweater and placed it back upon a hanger, she remained quiet. Liz thought it was a good time to ask what she thought about the black guys they met at the office earlier that afternoon. Also, she wanted to know where Denore had run off to during that time she had been absent.

Denore quietly stated, "I wasn't in the mood to be around people." She rubbed her eyes; she wasn't in tears yet, but it appeared that she was on the brink. "I . . . I'm sorry, Elizabeth . . . I . . . sometimes get like that, and . . . I don't know why . . . I mean, I know why, it's just . . ." She was fighting back the tearful explosion. "It's just I . . . I was never like this before. I was always outgoing and happy being around a lot of people . . ."

Liz considered going over to Denore's side and patting her on the back to console her but decided against it. She determined that sooner or later, Denore would have to be strong, and babying her wasn't going to help much. Treating her like a special case was not going to do any good; after all, the young woman had made the decision to come all the way to Japan without her fiance or anyone, so that in itself she recognized as a strength even she couldn't muster were she to be honest with herself.

She said to Denore, "I really think you should have a drink. You'd be surprised at how it might relax you. If anything, it might make you sleep."

For whatever reason, Liz's last statement made Denore laugh, though she hadn't intended for the utterance to be humorous. She was serious. Just as surprised was Liz to hear Denore claim that she'd "think about it, maybe one of these days" as a response, to which they both broke out in a sudden laugh. Liz had successfully cheered up Denore again.

Liz cracked another beer or two and fell asleep while watching a movie on the VCR with Denore. She was so exhausted from the day's activities. Fatigue crept upon her silently. It wasn't the first time this would happen and definitely not the last.

16

THE FIRST FEW days on the job as an English teacher, Liz didn't do much or any actual teaching. Her day was spent observing the other teachers who had been on the job longer than her, so that she could get a feel for what her duties would be. She mostly watched Stephanie, who read the entire lesson script word for word, allowing for the Japanese student to respond wherever applicable to areas in the literature which called for a response to test their comprehension and speaking skills. Otherwise, it was a basic one-person show until about the last fifteen minutes of the session. At that time, the student would be left to their own devices and required to produce sentences in English that the teacher would spend the last five minutes of class critiquing or praising, depending on their individual performance. Liz noticed how pompous Stephanie could be when offering animadversion to various students, particularly young female students, making them feel as if they needed more effective study and influencing them to pay for more lessons. This pleased the school very much, and that was why they liked having teachers like Stephanie around. Liz watched Stephanie teach the one-on-one (or, man-to-man) lessons, and she watched Victoria do the group lessons.

The group lessons seemed a bit easier; this was more like free conversation, not based on the material of any textbook. However, if a textbook were to be used, the teacher could choose from plenty of topics, which ranged from A to Z. Victoria liked to talk about male and female issues. This was right up Liz's alley, and she couldn't wait until it was her turn to hold forum and speak her piece on the issue.

Teachers like Keefer were in charge of teaching newer students and beginners. Liz observed his class once, and it was one time too many. It was obvious Keefer enjoyed his job a bit too much.

Knowing he had an audience, Keefer failed not to entertain with wisecracks and tacky comments directed at his student customer-clients, which could clearly be construed as insults, but since the people were beginners with very little understanding of English, they obviously didn't understand what was meant when the Australian foreigner referred to them as "cunts" and "wankers." Liz would listen while taking notes but had to strain to maintain composure. Keefer was making her crack up, but she felt a little sorry for the Japanese people who paid their hard-earned money for this type of education. But, since the head teacher Mitch was out of town and not around, Keefer was having a ball acting a fool.

Overall, the atmosphere at this new job was like a party without the sizzle and spiked punch. It was festive, full of laughter, jokes, pranks, and strangely resembled an offbeat parliament collection of foreigners who gathered to decide the fate of the Japanese unorthodox education system. At any given time, there would be at least seven or eight foreign teachers at Bozack School branches like Hommachi, Namba, and Higobashi (near Hommachi), whereas Tennoji and Amagasaki Schools were huge branches. The smaller branches were in Nara, Kyoto, and Kobe.

The Umeda School was somewhere in the middle. It was relatively smaller compared to the Hommachi Branch, as it occupied only one floor of the building in which it rested. Its layout resembled a bottle with a long neck for an entrance and hallway, which led to the front-desk reception counter, the small office area occupied by the school's branch manager and Japanese staff. And a broom closet-sized antechamber served as a private office for the former. Several classrooms of similar dimension lined up the belly of the space and at the far opposite end was the luxurious waiting room, which was carpeted and stocked with elegant Western-style furniture; the place, in fact, was designed to resemble a living space commonly found in a foreign country to create the visual image for the student.

Liz liked it there. Umeda was quieter than Hommachi, she thought, but was informed that during the week, it was a bit more active. Since Liz worked there only on Saturdays and Sundays, she taught the few English lessons there for the students. Bozack was still the new institution on the scene, so they had to compete with the big dogs for customers, and Umeda was the intense battleground for popularity and supremacy. Bozack was holding its own, but it was a slow, uphill fight. but it had its own uniqueness as a bargaining chip because it was one of the few places that offered French lessons as well as English.

Unlike Hommachi, there was only one branch manager present—a warm, amiable older Japanese woman named Hitomi, and one other teacher of French, a female instructor named Taffie Jolie, who was, according to Liz, hands down the most beautiful light-skinned black she had seen anywhere outside of California. She would only be the second black girl that Liz had ever become acquainted with, and comparing her to Denore, Liz determined that Taffie was the more attractive of the two.

Taffie Jolie was tall, slender, and Junoesque like a runway model. Long curly locks of black hair dangled lightly down her back and shoulders like fluffy, coiling cotton serpents. Her unblemished smooth skin caused Liz to moisten her pink rope lips, craving suddenly a café au lait from STAR.BUCKS. Mesmerized by the sight of her, Liz couldn't easily remove her eyes from panning Taffie's shape over and over, top to bottom, and quickly went into the mode of repressing some lesbian feelings of attraction for her. She absolutely knew for a fact that she would have considered making out with her if she had some coke.

Hitomi could speak English very well, and she could speak a little French too. Liz was impressed with her as well. She looked to be in her mid to late 50's, short, stocky and could play the role of an adopted Japanese grandmother; full of spunk, cheery, laborious and strict when need be. She gave Liz the short, brief tour of the school and the immediate area of the building in which the school occupied. Still, Taffie was the one person there who had Liz enamored.

Liz was slammed by a *Flashdance* flashback thinking about Taffie as she viewed the Paris, France, native greatly resembled a rebooted version of Jennifer Beals in debut film prime. Graceful, ballerina, and jazzy dancer strut in her steps, Liz figured for sure that she had encountered a sexy *Soul Train* disco queen gangsta'90s chick to now befriend. It was not to be so exactly.

While they did become friends, Liz would find no Jennifer Beals, no Whitney Houston, or Jody Watley in Taffie disappointingly. She wasn't American, and she wasn't a sassy, power girl either; so in Liz's book, Taffie and Denore ended up in the same category—whatever it was, it wasn't the stereotypical image she had expected the Black women to portray—they were both soft-spoken, shy, gentle, and reserved.

Taffie could speak English, but it sounded unnatural, like it was something she had to practice. She had a shrill, almost-squeaky voice, which seemed more fitting for talking with tropical birds or canaries than singing an R&B song or a love ballad, despite her proclivity for looking the part.

Eddie dropped into the city for the first time since Liz made the move there. His days off remained Saturdays and Sundays, but Liz now worked on these days. Per their agreement, this was a glitch that wasn't going to hinder their relationship by any means. On her break time, Liz called Eddie and told him to meet her there in Umeda at the school. Eddie agreed but had to receive instructions on how to get to that location. Liz asked Hitomi to explain it or guide a taxi driver for him, and eventually, Eddie made it to the school. Hitomi was very friendly and cooperative; she even allowed Eddie to wait inside of the plush reception room with all the fancy furniture until Liz completed her work shift.

When finished, Liz and Eddie would leave and check into a hotel. He was aware that Liz had the roommate now. Additionally, Liz informed him that he wouldn't be allowed to stay or sleep over at her dormitory because Denore would always be around, a sulking recluse. Judging by the conversations they had, she guessed that Denore wouldn't be the partying type either; she was going to be the stay-at-home, TV-watching, and curling-up-with-a-good-book type, scared to go outside and deal with society.

By now Eddie would be quite horny and easily aroused, aggressively seeking sex or some sort of intimacy with Liz. This pleased Liz because it indicated that Eddie was still gravely devoted and attracted to her even though her busy schedule, life in Japan and poor diet had her appearing somewhat slattern on occasion. Still, however, because of her demented need to be the puissant, puppet-master, she decided it best to be fake-prudish as to not spoil her pet and remained stringent. She would then start to put on an act, pretending to be not in the mood, subsequently denying him access to her sizzling, sticky, hot love nest. She found new, barbaric amusement cock-teasing him. This would continue until Tuesday night, when she would finally give in and surrender to him, but by then, Eddie's performance in the sack was reduced to the status of a two-minute load-blowing washout.

Poor Eddie had his patience and poise pushed to its limit being the reason for his X-double minus in bed. After a week of an empty bed, random eye-candy every day to and from work, it made Eddie antsy. Back home he could solve his problems with a jerk or two, but in Japan, he hadn't found any good material—at least none that Liz would allow him to have. No *anime*, no freaky porn, even though there was an abundant source at the tip of his fingers, easily found at any convenience store or vending machine a stone's throw distance from his place in the sticks. Still, he had no time to go shopping for smut, so until then, he had staved off his intent to wank himself and became a little tense.

Liz had no pity for him, though. She could sense how needy and indigent he became the first time she took Eddie to the dorm. Fully aware Denore would come back to the room soon, Liz blue-balled Eddie further by undressing and taking a shower. Then she would order him to towel her off while she applied some type of glittery polish to her toenails. Eddie was a sex-famished fiend by now, so she allowed him to start in on her, kissing her shoulders. Then as his breathing increased in intensity, she would respond by kissing him back in short, wet, and loud pecks, but not with tongue. The closer he would get to some type of attempt at penetration, the more she would resist him and give aberrant warning that Denore would be coming back! She summoned a spell of the slimy slut tongue to slither in his ear to make him shiver, to her delight. She felt up his crotch and knew by the swollen condition that he was ready to have it wedged into her wet womb, and sure enough, the apartment door deadlock bolts would crack loudly. Heavy, giant steps bopped clamorously inside of the place, the sound of thick-soled shoes thumped the tile floor like bowling balls as Denore announced her return with something to the effect of "Hi, I'm back!"

Liz was tickled to almost death over this, seeing the look on Eddie's face, scrambling to zip up his pants before Denore walked to the portion of the room where he could be visible to her, beyond the shirring partition contrivance. She covered herself with a towel, giggled a wicked guffaw, and scrambled to the shower vestibule for clothing. Denore and Eddie's introduction was her returning to her dormitory to find some unknown, white male stranger standing beside her roommate's bed, fumbling with his zipper. When Denore freaked out, started crying and screaming, Eddie understood why he and Liz couldn't have screwed while this obstreperous bawling broad was about.

Of course, Liz would appear just before Denore did anything crazy like attack Eddie. She was taller than he was, so Liz had concerns. She assured Denore quickly that Eddie was harmless and that he was her fiance. Now she was rubbing in Denore's agony, brandishing her significant other, and referring to him as her partner to whom she was engaged. She neglected to feel any remorse for it, and additionally achieved higher pompous ascension, a higher level of fascination and pleasure to see Eddie's agony, sexual angst; but she didn't know why.

17

BOZACK WAS A fascinating place to work. So far, so good, Liz thought, and she explained as much to Eddie the entire time they were together. All she could talk about was her new roommate, her problems, and her new job, school situation, and basically her whole environment. Eddie was a keen listener; he did not lack any interest and subtly envied her. He was looking forward to finishing up with the program and answering the call of the waiting list—that is, if they would still have him. In the meantime, Liz was warming up to the new location, environment and fresh network of acquaintances she was developing.

Bozack had many branches in the Kansai area and employed hundreds of teachers from Australia, New Zealand, the UK, the United States of America, Canada, France, and sometimes even Jamaica and the Philippines. In addition to boasting a rotation shuffling system of foreign instructors, they were also proud of their omnifarious diversity. The shuffling system would dispatch an individual teacher, like Liz, to teach at different branches, and this would change every six months or so, or however the Japanese front desks saw fit.

The core group by which Liz would constantly be surrounded were Stephanie, Keefer, Radley, Eric, and sometimes Victoria, Chucky, and the other guy with the "weird hair and beads," Deon; but on some days, she met visiting teachers from other locations.

One such teacher was a guy named Kwame Chwaku. Kwame was a real "African" American, as he spared no opportunity to talk the hind legs off donkeys, to the extent he seemed boastful that his parents had immigrated to Orlando,

Florida, in the United States from Nigeria. That his ancestors "had never been slaves in America, and he went on to suggest that he was "different" from other black people. He seldom, if ever, interacted with the other black people in the school, and Chucky didn't seem very fond of him, because he never carried on with him the way he would when Deon was around.

Kwame registered himself on Liz's radar of repulsion rather rapidly as she found him nosy, officious, and meddlesome. He went out of his way to inject himself in every discussion around the office where he wasn't being addressed, welcomed, or asked to engage; his contribution to most of these discussions would not be acknowledged in most cases, and it became a running, secret joke among Stephanie, Radley, Victoria, and later Liz as well, to place a permanent Ignore sanction upon Kwame.

Another thing about Kwame Liz found unsettling was his looks. His skin tone was darker than all the other several blacks Liz had now met—Denore, Taffie Jolie, Chucky, and the other guy Deon. Kwame's eyes were also a little bigger, Liz thought, especially when something appeared to surprise him, like the sight of Liz's cleavage on the first day he laid them on her. His lips were thicker, and pink like uncooked hot dog pork franks, and they dropped as well, seeing Liz that first time at the Hommachi School. He was a bit plump, but not sloppy; he had slight paunch but because of his height—maybe the same as Denore—his rumen was a tolerable sight when his polo shirts were tucked in. He had neither afro nor a slick, ponytail, his head was clean shaven baldie, when reflected by light, shined in spots reminiscent of malted milk dud candy—this Liz found to be his only redeeming attribute.

Otherwise, she didn't like Kwame. She didn't really crave the attention she would get from black people, and this guy, undressing her with his golf-ball eyes, was no exception at all. In a short time, Kwame surpassed Eric Cravens in giving Liz the creeps. She felt uncomfortable at times being alone in the same room with him but was assured by Keefer—the only person around the office who seemed to get along with him—Kwame was harmless.

Funny thing was, for all of Kwame's vaunting his dissimilarities with American blacks, Liz found it ironic that the guys she met earlier—Chucky and Deon—didn't gawk and gaze at her busty bum. It wasn't the same with Kwame. His hot-dog lips parted as he muttered, "Dayum!" While his ogling orbs X-rayed her, he would brazenly care not to hide the gaudy, poked-out bulge expanding beneath his pants' zipper. Apparently, this would be his outlandish way of trying to communicate his lustful attraction to her.

"How gross!" Liz responded as she shuddered angrily at a garish display of sexual harassment. It was obvious that he had become complacent and comfy with such behavior, as had Keefer, because the Japanese women tolerated it so much. Liz, however, was determined not to take it.

She said, "You do know that if this were America, and you did something like that, I could have you fired for that, or worse . . ."

Kwame didn't seem fazed. He contorted his face into a cute, cuddly, and innocent smile. He said, "Well, we're lucky this isn't America, then. And by the way"—his face suddenly became serious—"do you have any black in you?"

Liz stopped short of saying, "Hell no." She was so offended. She couldn't fathom anything about her appearance or personality, nor any remote feature of her looks that would suggest that she was somehow mixed—and not with a black.

Kwame followed up with morbid humor, "Question is, would you like to have some black *in you*?" He slapped his bulge like he was dusting off his zipper, laughing wickedly and showing a clean row of teeth in between the pink pork franks for lips.

The question was posed with inflection and emphasis that Liz knew meant was related to sex. Again, had it happened in America, he would have been fired, lynched, or whatever, Liz mused bewildered. But in Japan, this was not uncommon. As the days passed, Liz could see why.

Guys like Keefer, Radley, and other foreign guys would often change clothes from afternoon, sweaty attire that the Osaka stifling heat would render drenched, to "work clothes" in full view of the Japanese female staff. The Japanese staff Kayo Terumi would typically stick around and actually take scope of all the raggedy underwear briefs, hairy legs, and polka-dot boxers. All the while, many lewd references would be made during conversation while the undressing and clothes changing was taking place.

Because of this environment, Kwame had probably felt comfortable using obscene means to convey his message of attraction toward Liz. She acknowledged this, but that didn't make Kwame's antics forgivable. Still, she had not wanted to believe that he was too much of a bad guy. The reason was because she thought that because of his height, he would make a good friend, possibly even a romantic interest, for Denore. She had to dismiss that idea, though, because if Kwame had that type of feeling about her, she would feel exceptionally more unnerved at him coming around their dormitory should he and Denore hit it off.

What a waste! she thought. After all, had he not been a pervert and a talkative annoyance, Liz would have taken him to be reasonably intelligent. He was clever, articulate, and from what she had seen on the lessons he taught, he was just as charismatic and engaging as any of the other teachers at Bozack whom Japanese student customers flocked to see with fistfuls of money. The times when Kwame actually was called upon to be a welcomed source of information, he always delivered a favorable contribution. She reluctantly struck him from her thoughts of trying to hook Denore up with.

Elsewhere on the Osaka, Japan, landscape, in rural Hannan City, Eddie wasn't enjoying being apart from Liz as much as he had anticipated. The first few weeks had him borderline miserable. Liz may have had her flaws, but she was thorough when it came down to thinking for the both of them. She was the one who decided what they ate and drank almost every day, and she was the one who conscientiously thought about doing the cleaning and tidying up around the place where they had lived. Now that she was gone, the place was slowly turning into a pigsty, and Eddie had no idea how to do laundry or where the place was that Liz took the clothes to be washed. He began wearing the same clothes over and over; and as a result of not having them properly spruced up, his garments would be smelly and somewhat rank. He had to resort to dousing himself with more cologne than actually needed. Luckily, no one seemed to take notice, or, at least, they claimed not to notice. Eddie was still the area "sweetheart" and could do no foul deed to be chastised or traduced. He was still a hero regardless of how he represented himself.

Problem was, when Liz moved into the company dormitory in Osaka City, he had thought it was going to provide him a wide window of opportunity to creep around on her, so he could finally get a taste of some Asian twat. He desperately desired to try some out. The amount of attention he received when Liz was around caused him to believe that the instant she turned her back, some exotic Japan broad was set to lure him into a room with a trapdoor equipped with a fold-out bed; she would dim the lights low, pull her panties off, and perform erotic, geisha girl sexual acts on him, he was sure. Conversations with Keefer had tainted his head. On some weekends, Liz had permitted Eddie to have a drink with Keefer and hang out with him until she finished work; Eddie couldn't remember the complex directions to the Umeda Bozack School location where Liz worked, and could only navigate his way to the Namba branch, as it was close to the depot from which Eddie had traveled to from the sticks, so he would wait out at the Namba School, where he would be entertained by Keefer and some of his pals. Liz had no idea of what kind of absurdity Keefer was filling Eddie's head up with.

Unfortunately, nothing of the sort was to happen along that storyline as far as the geisha girl fantasy was concerned. The closest Eddie would get to see normal-looking, nubile women would be at the Junior high school, his work site. There, he would meet Hiroko Okada every day and a small handful of other female teachers who could be said to have been attractive or pretty, but out of his league because they were either already married or too intimidated by their lack of English-speaking ability to pursue any type of conversation or liaison with him at the same capacity Hiroko would. In other words, Hiroko was the only person around that could understand and speak to Eddie at almost 100 percent, so everyone around relied upon her services when addressing him at school.

Outside of work, there weren't any places in his neck of the Hannan City woods to meet any loose chicks. There weren't any bars in abundance the likes of which Osaka City contained. Places like *Pig 'N' Whistle*, which had coined the "*gaijin* bar" description, were unheard of around Eddie's area. Those "snack bars" that his lecherous dirty old Japanese dude coworkers had previously taken him to were quite pricey and startlingly unwelcoming to him if he didn't have his former colleagues in tow when he visited. Without his Japanese emissaries, no one took interest in him the same way they did when he visited on previous occasions.

On one particular night, he fell into one of those spots—it was a Friday night, in fact—one evening where Liz had blown him off for a night on the town with her new friends and hopefully score some speed. She had taken the liberty of postponing his trip out to the city for the following afternoon when she finished work in Umeda. Feeling sore and lonely but not brave enough to venture into Osaka City alone for some incongruity and phobia about missing the last train—he had trouble reading the train timetables even after a year in Japan—and he didn't like the coffin-like capsule hotels. The only place he could feel comfortable was his own bed or one that Liz made for him. So he elected to stick around his own village, rent some of those freaky anime videotapes without the close scrutiny of a sententious Liz to razz him; he'd order a pizza and drink by himself. The small vale didn't have much in the form of entertainment, but it did have a video store and a Domino's delivery service, as well as an abundantly stocked series of convenience stores.

To his chagrin, his town video store didn't have the raunchy X-rated section that spanned a third of the shop like others closer to the big city. He was a bit shy, too embarrassed to bring a porn selection to the counter to be checked out for rental. Nearly everywhere he went, he either met someone who already knew him or someone who had heard of him. Every video he rented and everything he touched at supermarkets or stores, people jumped on it and had to know exactly what it was. At least, with the X-rated anime vids, he could feel excused for thinking it was a normal "cartoon," and he could play the ignorant foreigner card. Still, the videos didn't do the trick, because he was bored of these low-level, condensed version of entertainment around midnight. He had to face the facts: the selection was poor, he couldn't understand Japanese, and it straight up ruined his high.

He decided to take a stroll to the neighborhood Lawson (convenience store) for another six-pack of Ebisu Beer. He mistakenly assumed that the more expensive a beer was, the stronger it must have been, so he bought the highest priced drinks. On the way back home, he decided to take an alternate, scenic route to break the monotony of his mundane, usual scope of Hannan City. He stopped his hike when he found an abandoned little park, or playground, crude and dated compared to the massive jungle gyms and monkey bars found in his "native land," but he found a swing set to rest upon while he chugged his suds and chucked the empty cans. He would notice how the stars were so unusually brighter out there in the countryside. It unlocked a beauty and appreciative quality that could be easily overlooked. Before he knew it, he had consumed all his beers except for one. Feeling bloated, stumbling about, he decided to press on and make his way back toward home, but ended up making a few miscalculated shortcuts that caused him disorientation.

With a drunken condition gradually descending upon him, Eddie tried to summon what remaining cognizance he had and retrace his steps back to the convenience store, or the park he took a break at, before he became hopelessly lost. Instead, he stumbled upon a row of expensive-looking houses on a winding smaller street between a patch of trees. This small stretch had a seedy look, and one small building sandwiched between the houses posted a neon sign burning on its front side above a sole door that read, "Snack," which Eddie quickly recognized. As he approached, he could hear wailing, like an ailing ghost or apparition, coming from the inside.

Not to be deterred by any malevolent spirits, Eddie was still coherent enough to remember that he had been there before, and didn't hesitate to enter the tiny building.

Inside he saw the familiar rinky-dink retro-themed lounge, the old-school strobe light dangling menacingly from the center of the main space like a gleaming silver wrecking ball. The mirrored long counter bar decked with two or three stools. Vinyl, imitation leather ottoman chairs and two coffee tables that had seen better days took up most of the remaining space. Clearly, some remodeling had been applied since the last time Eddie had been there, but for the most part, it still remained the same in sight, smell, and subtlety.

As soon as Eddie opened the door and stuck his head inside the place, he saw an unfamiliar old geezer in a black suit with a bald head and glasses. Dude looked about eighty, maybe, but he was singing a song on the mic like a Japanese Frank Sinatra. Beside him, seated on one of those sunken ottoman seats, was an older woman clapping. She was in a fancy but naff long, flowing black maxi-dress with peachy pink flower patterns. Thickish shoulders seemingly bare but for a see-through shoulder jacket; otherwise her aged cleavage was revealed in a provocative display. Her hair was fluffed out and curly, jejune in style, and could have been a wig. Overall, she looked as if she might have been beautiful beyond recognition twenty years prior, but tonight she was one Eddie would have opted to pass in hopes a better selection would be available. Preferably the younger MILF that had rubbed up on him the last time he went there. Dismally, it didn't appear that she or any other women were around. Only the one mama-san seated on the couch with the old geezer. When Eddie popped in, they both looked up at him with utterly surprised design.

Mama-san Yoshiko wondered what the hell the *gaijin sensei* wanted. She didn't see any of his Japanese coworkers from the school with him, and he appeared to be alone and somewhat intoxicated. So her initial alarm seeing him was warranted. There were two ways she could have played it: She could have kicked him out flat, or, she could treat him like a paying customer and hope that in his condition, he didn't collapse, go wild, or possibly perish. Wisely, she decided upon the latter as it was obviously a slow night for a Friday, as was business in general those days. She was in an industry *mizu-shobai* (*9), which was declining around her way. Competitors with younger, cuter trim were cutting into her niche, profession, and establishment. It couldn't be helped. So instead of turning away the foreigner, she welcomed him, poured him a drink of the hard-core whiskey, and offered him a free pack of Lucky Strike cigarettes. Eddie had not previously been much of a smoker, nor had been Liz; but since he had come to Japan and couldn't get his hands on any good pot, his nicotine indulgence had greatly increased. He accepted the smokes from Mama-san Yoshiko that night, and so commenced his habit and preferred brand.

Mama-san Yoshiko could barely speak any English, but she could communicate the basics like "You drink!" Then shoved a thick urban phone book–sized karaoke selection catalogue in Eddie's lap. "You sing!" Then she clapped, laughed, and bounced merrily on the couch, threatening to shake the old geezer off and crumbling to the floor.

Eddie had already been drinking since the early evening, while watching videos at his quarters. Then after he started to consume the high-power scotch whiskey, Mama-san lit his Lucky Strike with a wooden match. Suddenly now he retracted his thoughts of skipping over her for a younger or better choice. A single nipple and breast carelessly dangled briefly when Mama-san Yoshiko jumped up from the couch to fix people's drinks. It was the closest Eddie had ever come to seeing a live, partially nude Asian woman, young or old. She was so divine to his fragile mind at the time that the sight of her breast for even one second caused his heart to palpitate thunderously for an instant. Long enough for him to disregard Mama-san Yoshiko's age, and if he had a chance, he would prove it to her,

Apart from that idea, however, Mama-san Yoshiko was a pro, and she could already see that Eddie was being a hormone-charged young stud. She hadn't intended to flash her old tit at Eddie; it was just that in her business, it didn't always make sense to wear clothing that wasn't loose and comfortable, or the type of clothes that could be easily removed. So partial nudity wasn't uncommon, and at times was expected, especially for the particularly lucky and high-spending elites—but those were few and far between these days. Eddie might have been the closest to being one, but there was no way she would risk her reputation by having word get around that she slept with the "town *gaijin sensei*," but she was content with "Let's don't and say we did" while he was there at her place. She let

Eddie play with her breasts in short, teasing intervals, as she skillfully divided her attention between her two clients.

Eddie was trying to keep the party going by singing nonstop Barry Manilow and Neil Diamond jams. He was trying to outlast the old geezer, hoping that the old dude would conk out and head home. Then he could be alone with Mama-san Yoshiko and she'd offer up some old-school nookie, Eddie thought. As if to foil and thwart Eddie's plot and scheme, the old man stayed longer and went song for song against Eddie like in a battle, even though at times while Eddie was singing, he looked passed out.

If it was a showdown, the old man had won because Eddie was the one stumbling around when he tried to get up to use the toilet. The old man was drinking and singing *enka* still. Eddie's legs became huge rubber noodles—he thought for sure he had become an octopus—so he was determined to squirm his way to the can if he had to. Mama-san Yoshiko laughed but at the same time sighed as she tried to help the sturdy young man to his feet, displaying improbable strength. Now she was handing him a slip of paper, and in the best English she had used the entire evening, she said, "Please pay this amount!" Eddie looked at the piece of paper with a bunch of numbers scribbled on it. It looked like a digital reading on a stopwatch at a grainy, quick glance. He took it with him to the bathroom, pissed on it, flushed it down the toilet and returned to the lounge, stumbling less but still looking like a rickety robot more than human, a corrupted grin on his chin. He limped toward Mama-san Yoshiko, almost expecting her to envelop him into her bosom. Instead, her warm smile was interrupted with a sharp wrinkle of her forehead as a frown slashed her face into a gnashing boar.

"Where ticket?" she asked in a loud and deep voice that contrasted greatly with a sweeter, softer tone she had assumed earlier.

The old geezer had already popped on his porkpie and beat it. He had a taxicab waiting for him outside; he hit it and bounced. Mama-san Yoshiko offered to call a cab for Eddie too, but he declined. He would have been unable to communicate or navigate his way to where he lived in his state anyway. He was determined to find his way home regardless of his piss-drunk state, without incident. But he was still waiting for Mama-san to take pity on him, show him some love, and show him more than a single breast perhaps.

Indifferent then about the slip of paper Eddie lost, Mama-san put on her overcoat and started turning off lights. The strobe went dim, and she grabbed a ring of keys—they jingled impatiently—with her eyes trained on him. She was speaking in Japanese words that Eddie couldn't understand in the slightest, but because of the tone in which the words invoked along with her facial expression and cadence of delivery, he figured correctly that Mama-san was uttering, "Hurry up, it's time to go! Party's over, closing time."

"You don't have to go home, but you can't remain here," was the understood conveyance of feeling at that particular time. Eddie had stuck around until the wee hours of twilight, drinking, and enjoying the merriment at the tiny lounge as if some younger, fresher-looking night hooker was going to show up, but none ever did. With all the liquor Eddie had consumed, and with his condition, she was within legal right—or quasi-legal rights—to charge him as a customer whatever price she wanted. Establishments such as hers had outlandish, and sometimes unorthodox, payments, and there were often no set prices for any services. Instead, she relieved him of all his wallet's cash, save for three bills so he could catch a cab home, which she magnanimously did call for him.

Eddie woke up on the floor of his place, not far from where he had collapsed at the door entrance trying to take off his shoes, as was the Japanese custom on entering homes. He didn't remember much else but did seem to recall he had at one time a bunch of cash in his wallet, but he now had nothing. He didn't know how much he got charged at Mama-san Yoshiko's place, but whatever it was ate out a weekend's worth of scratch he had set aside for buying a hotel in the city with Liz and other things. With access to his wallet, Mama-san was able to acquire his *gaijin* card ID with his home address so she could give it to Eddie's taxi driver. For that he was thankful, but the horrible hangover he endured, along with knowing he had spent a grip on just two hours of karaoke singing, a few glasses of whiskey, and a pack of cigarettes caused him to react in dolorous fits of whimpering and cursing. He hoped that Liz wouldn't find out, but sooner or later, she would question him about his spending when she checked his and her bank statements, as she did monthly. From that point on, nightlife in Hannan City was a no-go as far as he was concerned.

18

APPROXIMATELY FORTY MILES away, in the city of Osaka, Liz was set to party the night away with her newly close-knit clique and having a splendid time. Suddenly, life was once again a wonderful thing reminiscent of how it was back in Los Angeles and California in general. Japan was unraveling itself into a wonderland of amazement, gaiety and wealth. Even spoilsport sourpuss mood blowers like Denore finally loosened up. Liz was both a good and bad influence on her, because Liz's jovial, vivaciousness had meliorating effects on Denore's constant sullen state.

Denore had finally met Chucky Chilson at the Namba branch of the Bozack Network of Schools. Denore's main assignment duty was at Namba, and her secondary school was at Hommachi but not consecutive days, so she and Liz rarely worked together. Still, however, Liz took credit for introducing Denore to the "other black people" at Bozack, even though Chucky had pretty much become acquainted with the Jamaican Canadian precisely two days earlier.

When it became clear to her that she wasn't going to introduce Denore to that obnoxious creep Kwame, Liz shifted targets to the first of two black guys she met at Hommachi. Chucky Chilson seemed like a nice, wholesome guy.

Chucky and Denore hit it off well and became friends. Soon after this friendship was struck, everyone in Liz's immediate cabal and some random others thought the two—Chucky and Denore—were dating. Liz too was certain that this was accurate gossip even though Denore adamantly denied it, albeit through fits of seemingly uncontrollable laughter. Liz figured that Denore was being shy and secretive about it, but officiously pleased that her intervention had resulted in establishing a "love connection" for her roommate. After a month of seeing Denore sulk around the apartment, decline invitations to go out with her and Eddie, it was a relief for Liz to see her have a good time.

Everyone seemed to be enjoying themselves, even acquaintances like Victoria Hamlin, who had endured a similar situation with her boyfriend/fiancée leaving her as well. She too showed signs that she had successfully moved on and began to hang loose in improved conditions. Liz's relationship with her, Stephanie, and other coworkers became tighter, as they were generally together for a majority of the time they were at work.

Stephanie was one of those chicks that liked to party, and about the same as, if not more than, Liz. Her negative attribute, among many, was a lower tolerance for alcohol and susceptibility to getting trashed much quicker than seasoned party-girl Liz. Stephanie was a living, breathing tragedy that became what she swore she wouldn't, which was a clone of her alcoholic, abusive mother back in Cave Creek, Arizona. Japan was as much an escape for her as the beer and intoxicants she absorbed to assuage her sorrows. It only resulted in the diminishing of her once-charming and comely looks, weight gain, and drunken stupors that required the assistance of others to literally carry her to a cab to get her home upon end of a wild night on the town. Still yet she proved to be a valuable associate—dare she say friend—and confidante who had showed Liz the ropes around the workplace, introduced her to a coterie of English speakers and teachers from Bozack and other English conversation schools, popular places to hang out and basically became her willing sidekick.

Wild nights on the town would generally be every other night after the last lesson was administered at work. The playground was from one of the city's main vessel roadways, Chuo Odori Avenue, which ran from east to west to the Minami Namba main station, about two square miles with scores upon myriads of waterholes, shot bars, pubs, restaurants, *izakayas*, and karaoke clubs. Almost every evening was one of new discovery and memorable events people hoped would somehow enrich their lives. Their jobs concluded at the precise peak time of nightly excitement, regardless of whether it was a weekday or not.

Although places throughout the town and *gaijin* bar hangouts were copiously saturated with bewildered Japanese citizens eager to befriend them, the general consensus among Liz's faction always indicated disinterest in entertaining the company of the people. Especially if the Japanese people didn't speak English. Keefer would only be interested in talking to Japanese women, of course; but Radley, Stephanie, and others repudiated them outside of work. Some felt that these Japanese wanted to take advantage of talking to foreigners and in essence receive free English lessons, while others were exhausted after trying to extract English conversation at work all day and didn't have any desire to do the same when the job was done. The only teacher who deviated from this characteristic was Eric Cravens, who spared no opportunity to improve his Japanese-speaking skills. He wasn't a drinker, and he was known to be one of the most obsequious, brown-nosers on board at Bozack. He was more often than not shunned because of his sententious tendencies, but tolerated because of his propensity for generous spending—footing the bill, picking up the tab—and yeoman services, lending cash to a needy colleague or two here and there.

Mondays and Tuesdays now free, Sunday afternoon—early evening—became Liz's new weekend, and she would spend this time almost entirely with Eddie (after work) before he had to push off back to the sticks. On rare occasions, Eddie would stick around until Monday morning and catch an early-morning, crack-of-dawn smoker back to the Hannan area to be in time for work. When this became too much of a drag and energy killer, Eddie wimped out of this burden, and Liz didn't much blame him. They would both be wiped out from the previous night's antics. So much so that Liz too would begin to put off going out to her former hometown, Hannan City, on her days off, but opted to do occasional Tuesdays. Eventually, this would develop into her practically demanding that Eddie just visit her in the city as opposed to her going all the way out there to see him. Eddie protested feebly at first, but gave in like he always did. Liz's yammering convinced him that life for her there in the boonies was deleterious; he didn't wish to put their bond in jeopardy. It was true, he conceded, that Osaka was where all the fun was, and Hannan City was a boring place to let one's precious life dwindle away while watching darkness blanket rice fields with chirping bullfrogs, crickets, and solitude as a soundtrack.

19

RADLEY OWENS, THE shadowy Canadian from a place called Brampton, phoned in sick a lot. One Friday night, while Liz was working at the Hommachi School, he did it again. When this occurred—a teacher calling to request leave, either suddenly or in advance—the main office in Tennoji would dispatch a replacement teacher, several of whom would be on standby for such situations. On that particular Friday, a standby teacher from the bordering city of Amagasaki, was sent to replace Radley. That teacher's name was Timothy Valentine.

Tim didn't live in Amagasaki, he just worked at the Bozack branch there. Nobody knew where he lived but it was assumed he cribbed at as location which was within thirty minutes of his main work site, as per company guidelines. Tim too claimed to be from the Chicago area and was very amicable and congenial with Chucky, as they were from the same locale in America. Liz noticed that BOZACK hired a lot of Black people and from her observation, they all generally got along well with each other—even Denore—but with the exception of Kwame, who hardly interacted with other Blacks in the Hommachi office when he was there.

Tim was a different sort, however. He was, in fact, liked by everyone for some reason, and this included not only Black people, for even Stephanie and Keefer appeared happy to see him. When he showed up at the Hommachi School, the other teachers would crowd him and surround him as if he was an ebony Santa Claus or a Greek bearing gifts, often surfeiting him with eulogistic praise and attention. He was, as Liz would later discover, the only Black teacher that the white teachers would invite out whenever they would arrange their selective group outings, picnics, parties, or designated events of a gregarious nature. Liz had attempted to break this cycle by inviting Denore to hang out with her, Stephanie, and others; but Denore had always declined. Otherwise, Chucky, Kwame, and Deon were seldom seen outside of work with Stephanie, Keefer, Victoria, Eric, and other white teachers. To his credit, Kwame would try to wedge himself into some arrangements, but for the most part, he would be avoided by those other than Keefer.

Liz was baffled and needed to know why Tim was an exception and why he was a different story. After all, he didn't appear to be any different from the other guys she had met there. Again, he looked like an MTV or VH1 celebrity—a dapper, clean-cut, and muscular guy, with glossy russet-brown skin tone like a taller version of Chucky, absent the facial hair, with no mustache, sideburns, or beard. The beehive waves encircled his head in an effulgent black spiral with panther-like blue luster. Stud piercings gleamed in both of his ears; his smile was clear, shiny, and edifying; and he could remind one of a Tiki Barber or a young Bryant Gumbel type TV basketball announcer. He talked with a smooth, rhythmical timing and used occasional slang, which was as foreign to Liz as the Japanese drivel she heard every day, but twice as intriguing. However, she couldn't help but feel as if he was putting on an act—as if he was attempting to mask his background, possibly a humble, ghetto past, by trying to code switch while in the presence of white peers, seeking to blend in like a chameleon.

She came to this conclusion about Tim, silently observing him while he interacted one way with his pal Chucky and then how he would Oreo out when the white teachers mobbed him like paparazzi. His wording would suddenly become eloquent, articulate, and expressive. Still, Liz couldn't see how any of this made Tim special. After all, Denore spoke very clearly, didn't use slang, and could easily have been taken for an Oreo if they were in the States, Liz figured, yet Denore wasn't revered in any peculiar way as Tim was. It wasn't until after work that night when Liz finally realized why everybody gravitated toward him. In fact, she too would thereupon commence to love seeing Tim whenever he showed up.

That night, when the last lesson finished, Tim and Keefer called to order the group of remaining foreign teachers and lead them all to the roof of the building, Liz included. When the secretive conclave was secure that the coast was clear, Tim then produced a small leather pouch, like a fanny-pack, opened it, and began handing out tightly wrapped loose joint reefers. Liz accepted one as well. Now she knew the secret, and she tolerated his leering at her booty.

Keefer was in a celebratory mood. He said, "When the cat's away, the mice'll play, eh? Good thing Worm is still on his honeymoon! Otherwise, he'd be here spying and nagging."

Tim said, "When is Mitch coming back anyway?"

Keefer answered, "Fuck . . . don't know, mate. He's the company sweetheart. They'll let him get away with anything. He's their boy. Plus, he shift-swapped with Eric and had a shitload of vacation days accumulated."

Tim said, "Cool beans, dude. That's why I could hit you guys off with some of these complimentary goodies and guest passes for this new club down in the village tonight. Chucky can't go, he's got other plans, so I got an extra one."

Keefer said, "Oh, give it to the new girl, 'Lizabeth, from the States. She'd be happy to tag along." And with that, he formally introduced Liz and Tim. He was reasonably friendly, appeared to show interest in Liz's body briefly, but nowhere near the ostentatious and bizarre way Kwame had and shrugged it off as if to say, *Not really the type I go for*, yet was munificent enough to give her a free "loosy" and an admit to the club that night, for which Liz thanked him immensely.

Stephanie examined the club ticket: it had only Japanese printing upon it, nothing in English except the words "Admit One." She said, "Is this for that new place, the Candy Box?"

Tim said, "He-ell no!" With laced emphasis, he added, "The Box is way bigger than this one we're heading to tonight, plus, it's in Kyobashi."

Keefer said, "Oh, the Candy Box, eh? I haven't been there yet, but I've heard of the place. Lots of the swanky Japs frequent that place, yeah."

Tim said, "Maybe next time we'll check it out together. I go there sometimes. It's free for foreigners, but it's just a pain in the ass to get there."

Stephanie chuckled and rolled her eyes. She said "So says the big shot with a car!"

Tim shrugged and said, "Oh well, it's still a pain in the ass. Parking lot fees are high priced, bitch! Besides, I didn't drive tonight. I plan on takin' a drink or two or three." Everyone laughed.

Keefer then said, "Cool, man. Anyway, let's get going. A couple of mates of mine are headed to American Village right now. They're going to meet us at Triangle Park."

Tim agreed, and they all left, except for Chucky, who had other plans and split early, parting ways with them before the distribution of pot on the school's rooftop. Too bad for him, Liz thought, or, maybe Chucky simply wasn't a smoker, making him even more suitable as a companion for Denore.

Tim had been, for the last year or so, the party supplier of illegal drug. When the group had later hit a club in the notorious American Village in West Shinsaibashi, the drunk glazed, "zooted" Liz nudged Tim with a sharp elbow like she had seen Keefer do with Eddie and other people when he wanted to gain their attention. Tim had posted up by the club's bar counter like a boss, a fat cigar stuck in the side of his jib and cradling a cute, slender feline-featured Japanese broad who was clinging to his left arm.

After smoking the joint with others in a secluded alley off the beaten path of a Hanshin Expressway exit underpass, Liz was above and beyond cloud nine high. Until then, her only opportunities to achieve such a state of bliss were limited to mediocre alcohol and puffs on nasty cigarettes she abhorred. The weed she had "boofed" to Japan a year earlier was long gone, scarcely a memory. Attempts to obtain marijuana, coke, or anything stronger had been futile, embarrassing endeavors prior to then, and in one fell swoop, Tim appeared that night and became the answer to all her wishes. She needed to cut into him and was determined to not waste the opportunity while he was there.

Unlike Eddie, Tim didn't appear to be cool with people elbowing him, nudging him, or any type of unsolicited contact. He eyeballed Liz hard with one eyebrow raised after she did it, like, *Bitch, what the hell is your problem?* Because Liz stepped to him apparently thinking he was her "boy," or, as if they had been chums for years, and that certainly wasn't the case. Still, he allowed her to speak her piece. She was like, "Can I . . . like. . . have a word with you, without your chick? I mean . . . does she . . . like . . . understand English?"

The Japanese girl with Tim rolled her eyes and smirked in a way Liz couldn't tell if she was annoyed or pretending to not be. This Japanese Catwoman gave Tim a glance as she loosened herself from his arms, which when around her seemed more massive than they were. It also seemed that she could understand English. Like Tim, she patiently tolerated the drunken behavior and excused it at the same time. Tim shot a glance back at his chick, marveling at how sexy she looked in her tight, form-fitting black spandex body suit, looking almost like she was clad in a scuba gear, but her garment material was much silkier like pajamas. He hated to excuse her from his company for Liz, but he muttered something incomprehensible in the deafening surround sound of club music, in Japanese. Miraculously, she heard him and left Liz and Tim alone at the bar. Vanishing in the black of the room like a puff of smoke, the girl was gone, and now the smoke was coming from Liz's cigarette, and in her other hand was a glass of gin tonic. Tim glared at her.

"What's on your mind—Amberbush it is, right?"

"Yeah, Elizabeth actually. Just call me Liz, dude. Everybody does."

Tim didn't seem amused. He took his cigar from his mouth; it wasn't lit anyway, but still he did it to emphasize his hope that Liz would get on with whatever she wanted to rap about.

Liz beat around the bush with the small talk, thinking that she could warm her way into the subject without spooking the guy. She said, "Wow . . . that chick you're with is pretty hot, huh? I guess it must be awesome for guys like you . . . to . . . be . . . able . . . to . . . come to Japan and have . . . have chicks like that . . . that bow down to you guys, and . . . make you feel so . . . so cool and be . . . so submissive to you . . . hahaha!"

The conversation went left, and Liz was flowing into a rant. The effect of the joint on top of some quick tequila shots, and now gin tonic, was turning her brain into a whirlpool with electric sparks. Now she was running off at the mouth to her detriment.

A sneer crossed Tim's face. He said, "Is that what you wanted to talk to me about?" The club music was noisy, and Tim was wondering why he had to have heard what Liz had said.

"Here I am," Tim bellowed over the wacky music. "I'm the nice guy who gave you a joint of *my own* weed—I mean like my *personal stash*—no charge, on the love, and this is what I get hit wit' from somebody like you?"

As drunk and fucked up as Liz was, she was still accordant enough to realize that she had stepped up to Tim a little bit wrong. Unfortunately, that was how she was when she became intoxicated and in such a condition. Yet she wasn't used to getting checked on her conduct either. Rather than eat crow, she just apologized in a quick, haughty manner.

Liz said, "Hey, hey . . . don't get so uptight, man . . . I didn't mean for us . . . to get off on the wrong foot."

The sentiment likely fell upon deaf ears, either due to the lousy selection of noise orchestrating the capacious auditorium, or because Liz's time was up. Tim checked his timepiece, which must have been a Swatch, or one of those fancy new joints that illuminated in the darkness of the immediate area. Time revealed itself to be almost 1:00 a.m.

Tim sighed and shook his head as he peered across the club flooded with dancing heads. He was probably searching for his Catwoman girlfriend, wondering where she had ventured off to. His overall facial expression at that point indicated that he had grown bored and annoyed with Liz. His thoughts were along the lines of *Damn, this bitch is fine and all but unattractive as hell when she's drunk.*

Finally, as if she could read the signal, Liz got to the point. She expressed a weak but lucid gratitude for the weed stick. She liked the pot, but she was a freak for the coke, the speed, the shrooms, the dope; and she threw in "You know what I'm sayin?" to raise Tim's eyebrows even further. She had watched a few *Yo! MTV Raps* in her day and figured she could code switch as well. It seemed to work.

It didn't take her long to convince him that she was legit—she was just a fun-natured party girl. Tim relaxed a bit, figuring she meant no harm.

Liz said, "I just heard you're the guy to talk to about getting the goods, y'know?"

Tim said, "Yeah, OK."

He was known as the Duke and a street fixer, a risk taker, fence, and back alley power broker. This wasn't the career he had always aspired to having after graduating from Columbia Chicago College, but he fell into the gig so perfectly he saw no reason to stop enjoying the extra cash, the women, and the life as a decently paid English teacher by day and supplier by night.

People like Keefer, Radley, or any *gaijin* teacher who wanted to score drugs too verdant or petrified to find or cop on their own would place their orders through Tim.

Tim would take their money, a handling or service fee for himself, and score the drugs. Over time, he had learned enough "polite" Japanese to speak to people in the Kansai area, which was a sharp contrast to the reputed brash and aggressive way it was renowned there. This, in addition to the wardrobe, he always insisted in dressing conservative and dandy, suits, ties, pointy shined stomps and brims, extirpated any suspicion whatsoever that in his briefcase he could be carrying enough drugs to open a private store. In a short time, less than a year, he had enough scratch saved up to get his own car; even if it wasn't in his name, it was still his.

Now Liz, being the bold and brazen fledgling witch she was, anxiously entreated Tim to introduce her to his dealer. She didn't want to rely upon Tim's middleman services.

She said, "It would do us both a favor. I don't have to bother you or wait for you or anything, and neither one of us have to get in trouble."

Remarkably, Tim was down for that idea and approved, even though his Maurice DuBois TV announcer mug held its pokerface. His rationale came to the conclusion that people like Liz were toxic and irritating. Once they became addicts, they were dangerous. It was better, Tim reasoned, if Liz were to be someone else's liability, not his. After all, he wasn't a dealer.

Tim said, "A'ite when you wanna cop that white girl? It's gun' cost you, y'know?"

It took a moment before it sank in that he was referring to the drug she wanted, not him belittling or insulting her. He insisted they use "coden" terms when talking about narcotics. Just because they were in Japan didn't necessarily mean that people around them didn't understand it. Liz gingerly agreed, claiming to understand the need completely.

"How about tonight?" she asked.

Tim said, "How much cash you got?"

Liz inquired about the price, and similar to the United States, it was a concurrent six thousand yen, or sixty dollars, a gram. Liz shelled out two "itchy mans" (**10**) and told Tim he could keep the change. Tim simpered as he took her bills and simultaneously fished out a phone from an invisible pocket coming from the direction of his waist. His cigar was on the club floor under his boot now as he began punching keys on the cellular. A moment later, as he walked away desperately seeking a quieter place to conduct a call, Liz followed him. She could not speak or understand much Spanish, even though she was from Los Angeles; all she could do was pick up discernible words to identify the language, and she could have sworn Tim had been speaking it when his call went through. When the call terminated, the phone disappeared.

Tim glanced at Liz and said, "Let's move out. Hold up—on second thought, you go ahead, leave here and wait for me by the outside door." He pointed to the exit and doubled back into the mirth of club darkness and flashing strobe sparks.

Liz downed the rest of her drink and threw the glass to the floor. It shattered into thousands of pieces like glistening fake diamonds. The sound of the busted glass pierced the obstreperous techno selection roaring through the place. Japanese people near the perilous pile of pointed glass looked frightened and gaped at Liz as if she had lost her marbles. She didn't care; the drink was good. The gin burned through her loins and eventually warmed down through her entire body to make her feel nice enough to do what she did. She dauntlessly strutted out of the main ballroom and waited by the outside door as she had been instructed.

Tim was upstairs at the VIP section putting on his jacket. He bid good-bye to Catwoman, then Keefer and some other teachers that were still present. A drunken Stephanie found Liz by the exit and staggered over to her like a zombie from a George Romero classic.

"Where are you goin'?" Stephanie managed to utter.

Liz said, "I'll be back . . . I'm gonna grab a few white girls."

Stephanie had by now assumed that Liz had some abnormal sexual preferences and tendencies as such in her state had superimposed her idea to figure she was embarking upon some lesbian dalliance. Because Liz was from California, Stephanie figured it was conventional and modern: she was open-minded and had no intention of discriminating against Liz, or holding it against her, but she just wasn't into it. She was still interested in men and wasn't ready to freak off with girls.

A moment later, Liz and Tim were off. A shadow of cologne and silk brushed past Stephanie's nose like a curtain closing and whisked Liz away.

The destination wasn't even far away at all. It was almost as if what Liz had been seeking had all the time been under her nose. A short walk of not even two minutes from Triangle Park where the club they were in was situated, Liz saw Tim heading for a signpost that read "The Cellar" as she struggled to keep the pace with him.

She followed as Tim descended a flight of stairs leading below street level, like a jaw swallowing him into the earthen street. Underground, the sound of live music became louder as they neared a soundproof set of clear glass windows.

They entered the small bar-and-grill, which looked like a real dugout cave in a mountain, walls comprised of uneven rocks and stones but glued in place with cement. It was an eye-shocking masterpiece of architectural design, if Liz could have appreciated it more; but otherwise, it was a relatively small cavern compared to the club she had just left. The difference was this place had a live band, which was a quartet of Japanese dudes performing a sucky but distinguishable rendition of *Picking Up the Pieces* by Candy Dulfer. Liz recognized the old hit and felt better in mood than she was at the previous spot, although just as dark.

The audience was comprised of patrons both seated and standing, but almost everyone in the place had been focused on the members on the small, elevated stage before Liz had walked in. Before Liz walked in, they were nodding their heads and grooving to the music, probably too drunk or zooted to realize that the band sucked. Liz didn't care that the junkyard band was lousy; she just knew the tune and for once heard something she could dance to.

She started dancing around like a possessed, crazed lunatic slut, now drunk high and almost out of her mind. She was rubbing her breasts and shaking her head wild. Her hair flared out like golden flame in the darkened wide room. She stole the attention from the band, and people in the house started thinking that Liz was part of the act. Unlike the other club, this place was almost all Japanese except for one section where Tim had drifted off to. Rough-looking Japanese dudes who looked too old to be in nightclubs stared at Liz; some drooled and licked their lips.

Tim had distanced himself from her intentionally so that he could approach a table in the back of the crowd of live show onlookers, where five scary, intimidating men sat. Four of the men were white Caucasians who ran the gamut of "rough" looks from bald to bearded, patch over the eyes, scarfaced, tatted, and all muscular. In fact, they all looked like either UFC fighters in street clothes, or Hell's Angels. In the center was a thickset Black man that reminded Liz of that guy Deon she saw that one time at Hommachi School. They could have been relatives, Liz pondered, only the guy she then saw had longer hair, silkier, almost arabesque, and twice the amount of shiny necklace jewelry. He was wearing sunglasses even though the place was already nebulous with cigarette smoke and dim.

The black man stood up and greeted Tim the way Liz noted to be the way black people in America usually did—an elaborate handshake followed by a one-arm embrace and an intricate finger snap or two somewhere. Excusing himself from the table of white guys, the man stepped away and followed Tim toward Liz's direction.

Tim yanked Liz by the arm subtly but with enough tug to make her aware he wanted her to move with him. He led her to the restrooms and phone booths in a corridor rear the stage. One of the bulky, bearded white dudes from the table had escorted them then shielded the trio as they vanished from view of the public. Tim gave the shady Brazilian dude eighteen thousand yen from his own stash of bills. He introduced Liz to the man.

He said, "Liz, this is Mr. Luzio Silver. From now on, this is who you'll be dealing with. Now if you'll excuse me, I've other engagements." He was trying to sound proper and elegant again.

Luzio Silver took Liz's hand, pulled her close, and pecked her on both of her cheeks. His lips felt warm and bristly, but hard. He said "Nice to meet jyu, Leez" in strong South American form.

He handed Liz a business card, which was totally blank except for the black inking which read "SILVER LIGHT PARTY SUPPLIES" in English, along with a nine-digit cellular phone number.

"Call eeny-time, twenty-four hour a day," Luzio said.

And with that, he retrieved from somewhere on his person three tiny, capsule-shaped tin foils, shoved them in Liz's mitts like he was still shaking her hand.

"Have fun, *menina branca*," Luzio said, "but if jyu get busted, don'jyu ever say about me!"

Liz may have been the drunk fool that night, but she knew best to adamantly claim that she understood full well the importance of not snitching on anyone. That was while in the presence of whom one would claim to promise. In truth, were she to ever get caught with drugs, she would cry, kick, scream, cooperate, rat, snitch, stool-pigeon, double-cross, betray, tattle, narc, fink, weasel, squeal, turn coat, and even deep-throat if she had to, and give new meaning to "whistle blow" if absolutely necessary. Whatever she had to do to canary up out of trouble in any or every way possible; but for that moment, she had to pretend to be all hip and cool, wise to the ways of a non-square in the '90s chick, even though it was already a new millennium.

"Don't worry," she said while fumbling for a cigarette and enduring another rough lip, double-cheek kiss from Luzio.

Cigarette lit, Liz exhaled smoke and stared curiously at the three grams of coke tins in her palm.

"Put 'em 'way, *menina branca*!" Luzio uttered in an admonishing tone as he and the musclebound white-bearded dude disappeared back into the ballroom.

Liz stashed the gram foils in her bra cup and buttoned her shirt up and tucked it inside of her pants. She searched the audience and room for Tim, who was nowhere to be found and long gone. She crushed her square and split the Cellar. Climbing the stairs again, she arrived topside, street level, and back on the narrow artery in American Village. No Tim, no coworkers, Liz decided to head home because she wasn't about to try to find the other club she was at earlier. Luckily, in Japan, taxis could be found and hailed in the most ungodly of hours of the night and day, and even in unlikelier places, especially the city. Liz shrugged and waved one over, and it abruptly halted where she stood, whisked her back to the crib in Bentencho. She remembered that she had to go to work the following day (or better, later that day). The reassuring feeling of not having to wake up at 7:00 a.m. like she had to do while working with the program made the ride home all the better. What a score for the day!

20

A PECULIAR TRANSFORMATION WAS occurring in the life of Eddie Roman. It was his second term, or follow-up year, with the CHET Program and he could see his popularity not quite dwindle but settle down. people became accustomed to seeing him around. His appearances weren't anymore seen as a star-studded event, and he didn't draw the same amount attention as he had when he and Liz first hit the scene. It was a vagary of demotion from being a princely mystical, magical phenomena of foreign extraction to a funny but interesting small-town *gaijin* mascot. People would nowadays see him and merely wave, grinning horribly, scary teeth fitting for Hallowe'en season frights, shouting at the top of their voices "Harooo! Ahahahaaha!" These types of greetings daily, or every other day, and small conversations with old "crusties" using fucked-up English. Such interactions were beginning to have Eddie miffed, but despite annoyance he maintained a pleasant demeanor to everyone in his community. He was determined to be a good example of a foreigner and maintain his heroic status.

Some mornings though, when he was pressed for time and needed to be waiting upon the train station's platform for his commute to work, his path would be barred by some random, wretched individual, be they young or old, who had studied English in their past or current experience. They would talk a blue streak on Eddie's ears, or attempt to, and their subjects would go the entire spectrum of having lived overseas to studying abroad and licking human genitals for the first time.

Ill conversations with olden, putrid elderly dames with spider-webbed pudenda past their prime would offer random invitations of hot crippled sex, he righteously refused of course. Not that he had anything against screwing old broads if given the opportunity, the nights at Mama-san Yoshiko's Snack bar had brought him to that realization, but wrinkled, withered relics were beyond the scope of his ability for attraction. There was no way he would try to stuff an eighty-year-old senior citizen, no matter how impressive her English ability—or attempt—and in addition to missing the train because of wasting time talking to these jive goons, the thought alone of going to bed with some of them made him sick. He may have been horny and eager, but he did have his limits.

Then there were those "chicken twerps". These were the bevy of soccer moms, new moms, maternity leave moms, and pretty much all types of moms even single moms, all various ages, who would stand in front of the buildings in the morning holding conference. Their manner of verbigeration while talking sounded like a gathering of hens cackling, pecking and chirping away like yard birds. They too would sometimes talk to Eddie, plaster spurious smiles or roll their eyes imperiously. Most of the time, they would now inquire obtrusively about Liz; where was she? Why wasn't she there anymore? Did they get divorced, or did they separate? Many intrusive and nosy questions. Still, Eddie had to force a painted smile and assure everyone that Liz and he were still going strong, she had just decided to accept another job in the city. It was an explanation that sufficed for whoever could understand English enough to comprehend him. Otherwise, the twerps seemed to pity him.

His patience was tested finally when one twerp mother brought one of her small children not yet old enough to attend school with her to the daily Chicken cluck session in the lobby of the apartment complex where they lived. She was one of those suddenly affluent, supercilious housewife broads who married a stable job working businessman (or "salary man") and felt like she was more prosperous than she actually was; with her hubby's allowance she shelled extra loot for her young kid to attend one of those new, frilly and sumptuous English pre-schools for children. When she saw Eddie, she forced the child to say "Good morning" to Eddie in English, to impress her Chicken crew and brag about how she spent her money for good use.

When the four-year-old kid saw Eddie, pale as a ghost, blue eyes different from anything he had ever been accustomed to seeing in the short time he had been alive, he became terrified, frantic, and hysterical. Hiding his little face up underneath his mother's legs, he screamed, cried aloud like a howling hound hit by a bullet, with a shrill high pitch. From that day on, every time that child saw Eddie, the child would explode into frightened tears, thinking that he would have to always speak English, emotionally upset. Eddie didn't appreciate that the mother forced the kid to talk to him. Eddie really did like kids, he thought they were cute, and he didn't feel good about invoking fear. He could tell that the mother was a younger chick, and he fought the urge to objurgate. He almost slipped, but he maintained himself.

He hated to be a waffler, but he was changing his mind about his surroundings constantly. On the one hand, he was sympathetic to his woman "master" Liz, agreeing with her that the country was hell. Yet on the flip side, there were still times when he thought that the life there wasn't horrible. The perks of quiet nights he still enjoyed. On the more festive evenings, there was the night symphony of crickets and bull frogs in bogs and swampy rice pits. Nearby, a forlorn roadside would feature someone on a 50cc motor scooter, revving its engine with a twitchy, spine-curling cadence that buzzed like the worst type of flying insect one could imagine. Other than these sounds piercing the serene, country silence, it was bliss.

Eddie appreciated this world and this aspect of Japan but could not imagine living there for the rest of his days. His fear was falling between two stools and failing to achieve his goals because he couldn't choose between certain alternatives. Returning to the States and California was in the definite picture, he thought; but then again, making money in Japan was so easy he wasn't sure if returning to his home country would ever be as lucrative.

And what of his future with Liz?

If he and she were to ever get married, he would have to consider career advancement. How would he ever impress her posh family? All he ever was in America was a loser video store clerk and pizza deliverer. In Japan he was an instant God, and the money was practically being thrown at his feet.

Both he and Liz had saved a lot of money. He thought about investing, buying stock and other things he thought would be beneficial; but Liz would talk him out of it, citing that her father thought of such as a waste of time.

In somewhat of a dither about this train of thought, he decided to study Japanese harder and earnestly, figuring it would be worth his while to do so. It could do nothing but help him, improve him. His struggle was staying interested in the dull textbooks the Program supplied. He turned to the Japanese comics, or *manga*, and this would become a beneficial study technique. That is, before things took a circuitous turn when he accidentally bought a lewd one.

In those days, before the mandatory law inveigled change; magazines and publications with provocative, adult-themed content was not sealed with a protective tape or adhesive preventing it from being opened and viewed by the underaged or minors. These adult magazines and periodicals would be distributed in the racks and shelves randomly among the normal ones. The average foreigner who didn't understand Japanese couldn't tell them apart.

Eddie would grab up one of these nasty, pornographic comics one night thinking it was a regular pulp rag with hopes he could use it as an entertaining and interesting way to read and study Japanese. Instead, he had selected one of these ill, erotic jerk-inducing picture books that freaked his head out. His *anime* crush had already resurfaced on lonely nights to add fuel to the fire, he then became addicted to the cheap, porno comics. The images he absorbed were beyond the breadth of ordinary orderly imagination. They warped his view of real women, as if the women of Japan were transmogrified into what he saw on their pages and video reels.

He quickly became increasingly bothered with hankers to sample the nectar of human cherry blossoms in kimonos and *yukata* garb. The best part about going to work nowadays was being able to see Hiroko Okada daily. In the back of his mind, Eddie wanted to believe that Hiroko secretly had the hots for him and admired him like everyone in town did; but due to his past experiences with women, he wasn't hip to the vibes she sent his way. He couldn't endure any more humiliation caused by women who got their thrills cock-teasing him like women used to do to him back in LA. He refused to fall victim again in that way—never again. He didn't know what he would do if what he endured at the video store ever happened to him again. Would he snap? He thought so. Question was, what would he do? How would he react? He was sure that it would not be pleasant. His past, according to him, wasn't very pleasant. It had been traumatizing.

Vicious vixens came to the video store and tortured him to the extent where they would actually unzip his fly right in front of the counter. She would whisper softly in his ear, "Where is your restroom, baby?"

Eddie would beatifically respond, "I-In the back." He would point with a finger, which was as erect as his nether region, to the rear of the store, all the while thinking, *Oh my gawd! Omigawd! Sh-she's gonna go with me to the back . . . she's gonna jerk me off . . . Oh my gawd!*

Instead, he would utter in a trembling but excited mumble, "Yes, th-the restroom is in the back."

His hopes and desires would be fiercely frozen by the woman's gelid response. As opposed to leading him to the rear of the store, she would point to his crotch and said, "Well, you should head back there to that restroom and fix your problem!" Before walking away laughing savagely, in such a way that her D-cup breasts would wobble and careen like fresh fruit in the glare of a citrus California sun.

Alarmed at the sudden outburst, the entire store would turn and see Eddie with a white ghost peeking out from his unzipped pants slit. Quickly, he would escape to the back to dry his tears and runny nose while simultaneously performing excruciatingly painful maneuvers to fold the erection between his upper thighs to hide it until it limped down.

Eddie relived this nightmare over and over and would sometimes wake up in a cold sweat. This dream was so dreadful and disquieting because things like that had actually happened. Once or twice, bi-monthly it occurred in fact. As a result, this as well as another abstruse incident—his graduation/birthday celebration—changed his life forever. His radar was cold and ineffective to the signals women sent. Those who had coaxed him in the past wreaked irreparable damage to his psyche.

The dreams were occurring more frequently now that he no longer shared his bed every night. On extreme lonely nights, Eddie would drag his mind back to that fateful night—the night he and Liz never spoke about. He swore it would never come back to haunt him, but alas it did. But then again, how could he ever forget it? No way could he ever!

It was in May. His birthday. His graduation. The hotel. The night. The memory was to have been boxed away and treated like the dreams he was now being disturbed by. It was a factitious fairy tale within a fantasy story but happened to be the most exciting, defining moments of his life. Yet, he was ordered to discard what happened into the abyss of the forgotten . . . his graduation "party."

21

EDDIE'S GRADUATION-SLASH-BIRTHDAY PARTY . . .

It was more like a surprise party. Eddie had stepped off the elevator at the Homewood Hotel and arrived at the suite on the tenth floor as Liz had instructed him to do. He keyed into the room. It was a spacious suite with a high ceiling and dark flooring, with a plush dark Saxony–type carpet. A fresh linen smell mixed evenly with an exotic pineapple aroma bombed his nostrils immediately. A subtle assault of weed smoke would subsequently follow up with a smack when the door slammed shut behind him. As he made his way further inside, he saw a side pillar to his immediate right, where there was also a full kitchen with bottles of champagne in ice atop the island counter feature.

Glancing conjointly about the capacious suite, beyond a trio of rectangular windows that slid down the massive wall horizontally from the ceiling, as if to form a huge roman numeral *III*, Eddie could see a breathtaking view of the Los Angeles nightscape. Brilliant coruscating streetlights looked like a million lit candles across the dark plain until the Pacific Ocean vanishing point. However, it was not the marvelous view of Manhattan Beach that caused Eddie's mouth to drop and his heart to palpitate in instant machine-gun execution. No . . .

It was the sight of blonde bombshell Rebecca Dollymore and mouthwatering dark-haired Latina Amanda Montoya. Both were clad in sexy, enticing Victoria's Secret lingerie and lounging expectantly on the king-sized bed by the windows.

When Eddie walked in, the two girls looked at each other, then, burst out laughing in one of their uncontrollable fits. This lasted about two minutes. Eddie peeped at the service table beside the bed close to him and understood why they were so giddy and full of *joie de vivre*. An empty bottle of Moet was turned over on top of it, and there was the unmistakable sight of white powder. The girls had been drinking champagne and sniffing cocaine waiting for Eddie to arrive.

Eddie could feel his lips about to drip before he drew them inside of his mouth.

He remembered how he cogitated of his deep love for Liz, but Becky had always been Liz's closest rival for his affection. It was a running joke among them before that Becky could have passed for Liz's *Brady Bunch* sister, only just a little shorter, a couple of tramp stamps (one on her ankle, the other on her nape)—shorter hair than Liz, but still relatively long and flowing, and generally gorgeous. Oftentimes surpassing Liz in radiance, as far as Eddie was concerned, because she tended to be more feminine than Liz, who had a gamine, tomboy gait, or appeared to. Where Liz would shy away from cuddling and familiarity more often than not, Becky would be the opposite and seemed to gravitate toward affection and petting. Problem was, she wasn't Eddie's girl, Liz was. But . . . why was she there that night at the hotel? And why were she and Mandy practically naked and looking like they were about to *seduce him*?

Red Mapale Cage lace wireless bra and garter belt draped Becky's luscious frame. Mandy looked equally palatable in a black Chantilly Lace trim see-through baby doll. They both rose from the bed at the same time and approached Eddie with ethereal slow and deliberate steps, as if they were performers in some kind of sensual music video or mind-boggling TV commercial.

The tote bag Eddie had been carrying containing videos of movies he brought from the video store slid from his grip and hit the floor beside his palsied legs. His reverie was interrupted by Becky's blood-red-fingernailed hand, fondling and rubbing his work uniform crotch. Mandy joined the preliminary fun by nibbling Eddie's earlobe, capitulating his throbbing disposition outright like that of a popped switchblade.

Becky took a break and produced a bottle of Dom Perignon with her hand that wasn't fastened to Eddie's balls, raised it to her lips, and drained its contents into her gaping mouth. Without missing a beat, she then placed the bottle on Eddie's lips, and he drank from it like a thirsty baby in a desert. She laughed like an insane asylum banshee before pulling the bottle away from him. Champagne was then poured upon his face like a water spigot, drenching his hair and face as if he had rinsed it.

A then goofy-acting Eddie would say, "D-does L-liz know you guys are here?"

Becky and Mandy again looked at each other like two voluptuary felines accustomed to high-class, fine fish and crystal saucers of milk who had suddenly been subjected to low-class Kal Kan Street corner–bought cat food from an old rusty can when Eddie violated them with his stupid-ass question. Mandy nonchalantly brushed off his query and took to the task of unwrapping his black video store uniform jacket and loosening his necktie. She pulled on it playfully and used it to lead him toward the bed.

When the two girls sat Eddie down on the bed, it was Mandy who then handed him an envelope with a letter inside of it. It was from Liz!

Eddie figured that the letter was from Liz because it had her name written with her handwriting on the outside. It had been addressed to him. He opened the envelope. A crisp 'Ben Frank' note slid out and floated to the floor between his feet. He reached down to pick it up before finally unraveling and reading the letter:

To my DEAR EDDIE,

Happy Birthday and Congratulations for Graduating!

To show my love and appreciation for you I have arranged for you to have a night to remember with two of my best friends. You might be asking yourself: "Why is she doing this?"

Well, I'll explain it the best way I can. You see, I understand that you are a man.

Because you are a man, I know that you sometimes see or meet chicks you might have the hots for, or some you might be curious about. I'd rather it be with some people that I know. Some clean, good people like my friends. If you were to sleep with some random slut at a bar, or the beach, or anywhere, you could run the risk of contracting AIDS or some degenerative disease out there, and that would be a tragic thing.

This wasn't an easy decision for me to make, and I did a lot of soul searching.

This was the conclusion I came to.

I know that Mandy and Becky have probably flirted with you in the past, and that's okay. We girls never keep any secrets from one another. That's why we are friends. I'd rather you be with them and not have either you or them feel the need to do something secretive behind my back.

After tonight, I have only one request and that is come tomorrow, I don't want to hear about this, and I want it to be erased from the memory of our lives. I'm only agreeing to this because I love you and I want to make you happy no matter what. This is undisputed proof.

So, in closing, I want you to enjoy yourself tonight with Beck and Mandy and remember that this is a ONE-TIME-ONLY deal. If you love me the way I love you, you will honor my request. Let this be your forever reminder of my love and devotion to you and you'll never need anyone other than me. I want for us to move on with our lives after this.

Love always,

Elizabeth

And with that, Eddie crumpled the *billet-doux*. He saw writing on the back page and opened it up again to read the postscript: *"The hundred dollars is to pay for your parking!"*

By now Mandy had already commenced kissing Eddie's chest after removing his shirt. Becky was puffing out weed smoke from a miniature bong.

Mandy said, "So to answer your question, Ed, yes . . . Liz knows we're here. I'm your birthday present."

Becky chimed in, "And I'm your graduation present!" Then she laughed her batty cackling fit of an outburst before feeding Eddie tongue from her mouth to his.

The letter Liz wrote was again reduced to a crumpled ball. Eddie popped another bottle of bubbly, snorted a couple of white lines, and the party was on till the break of dawn.

***

The following day, sunshine crept its way into the room space and illuminated the dark crevices of the world. Eddie woke up glued astride Mandy's bare naked spreadeagled mass. Becky lay beside them, head nestled comfortably underneath Mandy's left arm as if they were all locked in a loving cuddle. All three of them were completely nude now. All the fancy lingerie and "fruit of the loom" garments had been abandoned, stripped, and strewn and was now decorating various parts of the room, across the bed, on the floor, stuck on lampshades, everywhere.

Mandy was the second to revive, astoundingly able to peel herself from underneath Eddie and remove herself from the bed altogether. Eddie tumbled over like a lurid human lumber log. He felt the faint warmth of Becky and snuggled up with her and embraced her tightly as his morning wood slowly became activated.

Mandy was already in the shower at this point, brushing her teeth and detached from slumberous waking moments. Eddie and Becky seemed to be the slow starters. It was just fine for Eddie. It took all night, but he was finally alone with Becky. Mandy was a favorable and satisfying piece of fun, Eddie thought, but Becky was his assured pleasurable delight.

He realized his pipe dream come true was approaching its conclusion stages. As Liz's letter had indicated, this tryst with Becky and Mandy was only to be a one-time thing, and it was approaching the end. He wanted to cherish the remaining moments. His swollen organ exemplified his desire to close the event with one last quickie before they all parted ways. He rubbed it on Becky's inner thighs, hoping such would wake her up to the sensation he was feeling.

Becky yawned, stretched, and revealed to Eddie she had considerably less armpit hair than Liz and, even in a hangover state, still smelled of rosy under-scent whereas Liz would be more sweat and citrus in odor. Both unique, in their own way, but that moment, Becky was more appealing for the obvious reasons. The slight tugs of sadness pulled at his heartstrings knowing that this would be their last time together if he were to abide by Liz's letter-perfect conditions.

Becky raised herself up after yawning twice. Her lovely 34Ds flopped down her chest. Eddie's hand raced to cup them as if he were trying to save her boobs from rolling down her belly. Smiling, Becky quickly slapped Eddie's hand away viciously as if he were touching forbidden items in a jewelry shop. She then produced a hair band from seeming thin air to wrap her dirty blonde storm into a makeshift pony-tail readying for a shower soon to come. All the while, she and Mandy had been tennis balling talk from the suite to the bathroom as Mandy toweled herself dry. Eddie felt like a spectator.

Before Becky could stretch her Twinkie gold sponge cake–toned legs to slide out of the bed, Eddie managed to position himself at the seam as the legs attempted to close. Becky laughed with sudden surprise as she felt Eddie enter her. He began humping desperately and oscillating slow and steady like he was rowing her boat.

He was trying to catch some romantic feelings, but Becky didn't seem to be 'wit-it'. While Eddie was feeling his determined hardness stroke her moist morning womb, she was tapping him on the back like, "OK, tiger . . . that's enough."

Eddie maundered like a kid about to cry after being grounded for the entire summer. He pleaded "Please, Beck!" as he kissed, suckled, and licked maniacally at Becky's cheeks, nose, and ropy lips.

Becky snickered at the ticklish agitation but was more interested in whether or not there was any drugs left to blow.

Mandy had stepped into the room, now partially dressed in a change of undergarments she had brought, looking like she was in a bikini ready for the beach. She snarled a bit because she was probably a little envious seeing that Eddie had shown more of an interest in Becky than her, and it was she who actually had the subtle hots for him. Becky had been, more or less, a willing participant at the behest of Liz. It wouldn't matter much, though. The previous night's idyll was at its final curtain. She was happy to service him anyway, without losing her friendship with Liz.

She had an expensive watch on; she tapped it and said, "Hey, Beck, hey Ed! You guys might wanna hurry along—check out time is in a half an hour."

Becky answered as Mandy retreated to the shower room and vanity, "You guys got any more of the coke?"

Mandy shouted out from under the noise of some type of hair dryer, "Look in the drawer on the table. Just hurry the fuck up. We gotta order a car for today."

Eddie was feeling a rush from his love sack. Becky slid her hips backward toward the exaggerated curlicued headboard of the bed, attempting to extract Eddie from her body.

She said to him, "Sorry, Ed, we gotta leave now, ya hunk!" more sarcastic in adulation.

Instead of releasing her, Eddie clenched her spongy bare bottom with an iron palm clamp and pulled her back to him. With a final urgent thrust to remain in her, he drilled Becky back to the mattress.

Frustrated somewhat, Becky reluctantly sighed and surrendered. She returned Eddie some sugar, her tongue reeked of stale champagne, sourness, and mannitol.

Eddie panted, gasped, and exhaled like a screaming demon had left his body. He tried to collapse in an arduous but affectionate embrace atop Becky after just spray-painting the back wall of her underbelly again. Skillfully, she shoved him aside like a stuffed animal or blow-up doll, slid off the bed, and jumped to her feet. She beat a hurried path to the shower. Eddie remained on the bed, amused by the sight of his sperm oozing down her inner thighs; it looked as if she had tried unsuccessfully to hide some sort of creamy clam chowder between her legs. She began wiping some of it in her palm and licking it sparingly. Donning new underwear in a mystifying speedy fashion, Becky continued the back-and-forth convo with Mandy, who had by now made her way into the kitchen of the suite.

Becky was like, "You'd better get a move on, Ed. We have to leave here soon."

She was picking up her clothes from various spots about the room. She found her large handbag and disappeared inside of the shower box. Anything else said was drowned out by the sound of a blender or other contrivance of machinery coming from the kitchen.

When the noise ended, Mandy was drinking some sort of concoction she had made with the blender. She said, "Yeah, Eddie, get movin'. Becky and I have to order a car. We have to do it before one o'clock, or else no more limos will be available for the rest of the day."

Eddie said, "Relax, you guys. I have a car, y'know. I can give you a lift."

Mandy knew Eddie had a car, but being a prissy, persnickety valley girl wannabe, she didn't want to be seen in any type of atrocious junk whip the likes of which Eddie was pushing. However, she demurred on this particular day as it seemed a viable alternative. The limousine service to which she was referring was an exclusive private company that privileged society individuals had access to, costly but relied upon by their wealthier clients. The problem was, they often snitched on the spoiled brats of their employers, and Mandy and Becky had lots of leftover sizzle to sample; she didn't relish the idea of paying in addition for the car and then offering hush money to the driver—if that could even be possible— thus, suffering the discomfiture and degradation of resorting to a one-day ride in Eddie's clutter on wheels was bearable.

It was a go.

There was no shower. Mandy had made some kind of prehistoric smoothie with leftover cookies, bananas, nuts, and rum. They packed up all of their shit and miraculously met the checkout deadline. They left no tip for any of the many Spanish-speaking maids who kept knocking on the door asking when they were going to bounce.

Eddie lamented how it sucked to have to split from such a swell and luxurious hotel spot like that and wished that he could have stayed longer. He started to feel sorry for Liz. She sacrificed her feelings so that he could enjoy the opulent getaway, and it was a massive heap of a thought that was planted in his head through his coked-up haze.

The trio flanked one another with Eddie in the center as they exited the crowded elevator and dipped into the hotel lobby. The place was crowded with tourist groups full of old people with dark sunglasses and assorted hibiscus "don ho" shirts, flip flops, and *panama jack* hats, because everybody seemed to be checking out at the same time.

Oriental people in a large tour group led by some doyen with a flag stopped in their tracks and stared at Eddie and the girls. Wearing his cheap sunglasses on, people thought Eddie was a star from a rock group like Journey with two gaudy groupie hookers. They started snapping flashing photos of them, and Eddie giggled, feeling like a big shot celebrity.

It was hot and sunny. Eddie remembered his head spinning like a top on a flat table. When it started slowing down, he felt droopy inside of his car. Becky waited until she got inside his whip, sat in the back seat, and puked out all the smoothie, bananas, and anything else in addition to Eddie's jizz that she had consumed the previous night.

Of course, she was immensely apologetic and offered to clean it, but to Eddie, that was not the point. The stench of its aftermath would eventually make him want to do the same thing she did. If it didn't come from his mouth, it would have gone in the opposite direction out of his ass.

Mandy had Eddie's car cleaned out at a car wash on Sunset and North Hayworth Avenue. They did a good job destroying the pungency, but Eddie's queasy feeling lingered on. When they were back on the road, Mandy tried to ease the tension by whipping out her miniature perculator bong hooked up with speed. She held it up to his lips when he stopped for a red light. She urged Eddie to suck in the liquid candy smoke while she lit it with her lighter. He obeyed and had to admit, he felt better when the hit jolted him back into alertness as if he had sneezed gunpowder.

The light turned green, and they were rolling along again, with no destination in mind. Mandy and Becky began treating Eddie like he was their private chauffeur. The convenience of having someone drive them around finally kicked into Mandy and Becky, and they forgot that his car was a public eyesore stunningly able to move.

Mandy's head was thinking that the money she would have to pay for the limo service, a taxi, or other private car she could offer half—or maybe none—to Eddie for just gas. She opted for paying him nothing at all. After all, he wasn't *her* man.

Eddie would get his crash test dummy lesson on women on this day. No one had ever taken the time to talk to him about women. He was an only child; his father was a busybody pharmacist with militaristic tendencies and married to a stiff woman who was much the same. They figured Eddie would learn about the birds and the bees through the natural order of development.

Thus, all Eddie ever knew about chicks he learned from watching '80s movies like *Fast Times at Ridgemont High, The Breakfast Club,* and Anthony Michael Hall and Molly Ringwald flicks. If not those sources, it would be those like his lard-head friends who would know as little as him and end up marrying the first corpulent community cocksucker that allowed him to melt his throbbing erection in her twat.

As if the torment from women in the video store wasn't enough, Eddie would now suffer a whammy of a revelation about Mandy and Becky, for starters. For months he had secretly fawned over Becky, only to find out that she was a nasty girl, *really* nasty—like, hygiene wasn't top on her list. After a night like last night, a woman should surely bathe or shower, right? But since Becky hadn't, he couldn't answer his own question in his mind. Additionally, he had to wonder, what type of pig slop had she spewed in his vehicle? It was an eye opener, and more was to come.

Eddie was ordered to drive back and forth, here and there all over town. Mandy and Becky chatted with one another as if Eddie wasn't even there. The only time they engaged him was to issue commands on where to drive to, which left or right to take, and where to stop for them to get out, buy something, use a restroom, or window-shop before returning to the car. They finally told him to pull up on La Tijera Boulevard, and he obliged obediently like the gentleman thirsty for appreciation.

Becky, without asking if it was OK, lit up a fat, stinky coolie spliff the size of a crayon in the back seat and started smoking it. While one of them talked, the other of either Becky or Mandy would puff steadily from the loco weed, and they would continue trading off, passing it back and forth before it dawned on them that maybe Eddie would be interested in hitting it. Prior to that, they had just been smoking, drinking, talking to one another, and blowing the smoke in Eddie's damn face as if his hairy nostrils were ventilators. The only plus in that was him getting a contact high that aided in beating back his sickly undercurrent. He coughed trying to smoke the roach Mandy mashed in his dilapidated ashtray.

A cop cruiser flashed by in the opposite lane as they drove slowly down the block. Eddie became nervous as hell and tried to find a place to park on the side of the street. It wasn't often that people engaged in nefarious activities in his car. A second cop car drove by, and this time the cops eyeballed Eddie. Mandy and Becky didn't seem aware, or they didn't care whatsoever. They were on cloud nine and above.

Slipping on pairs of designer *cat eye le spec* Hollywood sunglasses, Mandy and Becky jumped out of the catastrophically grotesque purplish-red-and-gray vessel and quickly strode their flip-flopped feet toward a Pann's Coffee Shop. All the dope they had was in a glassine bag adroitly tossed by Mandy into Eddie's lap as they egressed the vehicle.

Eddie nearly shit bricks as the cop car cruised past. A police officer in the car who resembled Tom Selleck eye-daggered him with a clear message that he hated punks of Eddie's sort. Eddie grinned and waved as sweat wet his neck like he had bathed in the car-wash's spray-down. Fortunately, the cops were too busy racially profiling spics and niggers and took no interest in Eddie otherwise. He exhaled like a hot air balloon that had nearly exploded as relief refilled his chest. He got out of the car and ran to the restaurant he had seen Mandy and Becky disappear into.

Becky and Mandy were already seated in a booth banquette and waved him over when they were certain that the cops hadn't followed and entered with him. Mandy was visibly glad to see Eddie because that probably meant that he still had the sizzle she dipped in his lap when the rollers came through. She was right; Eddie handed the glassine bag to her.

He said, "Hey, you forgot and left this."

Mandy didn't forget it, really. It just didn't dawn on him that Mandy's sink-or-swim survival mechanism kicked in, and he had been expendable. He skipped past the table and headed to the men's room. After taking a dump that made him feel ten pounds lighter upon completion, he rejoined the girls at their booth.

Mandy and Becky had already ordered pancakes. Their orders had arrived, and immediately they spread whipped cream on the pancakes instead of maple syrup. Then they got into a curious commentary about how nasty it was and how they hated pancakes, yet still they wolfed theirs down with even more nasty whipped cream and gulping aromatic coffee like a sweaty boxer would Gatorade.

Eddie stared at the two chicks he banged the previous night snorting and digging into their food like pigs, sharply contrasting the tantalizing and seductive babes he had seen them as before then. Becky was grossing him out more and more by the minute, and watching her dig up her nose, he wondered if there was an itch in her nasal cavity or she was digging for gold. She wiped her fingers on the crease of her jeans.

The tired, crusty waitress (before the days of "server") came and asked Eddie what he wanted. Eddie was still trying to seem cool in front of Becky and Mandy, so he pretended like he was a *Pulp Fiction* movie character and asked for a bran damn muffin and black coffee. He soon received his order. It smelled like shoe polish and probably tasted the same, but Eddie nibbled it anyway as he listened to even more putrid yawping from Mandy and Becky, oversharing their week in review to not only him but other diner patrons.

".Steve is the biggest spender, but Henry from San Fernando is my favorite glass dick. He works out a lot, so he can do a lotta interesting things, picking me up and like, flipping me over in so many different positions. Only problem is he likes to take these injections . . ."

"Yeah, Chavez used to like doing that too, but I think Lamar is probably my favorite junk food, but he isn't, y'know, hood enough. I like his friend Hakim. I heard he's really from Compton, but I only like those guys because they can always give me free pot as long as I can introduce him to more customers . . ."

Eddie sat there for minutes hearing Mandy and Becky name-drop scores of their simps, suckers, toy boys, sugar daddies, and friend zone captives. Some names he knew, like Steve, Lamar, Chavez. He knew, others like Henry, Charles, Hakim, Tom, Dick, Harry, and on and on, he didn't. But as he took it all in, the more he struggled to wonder if the tales they told were all true. Since he may as well have been a fly on the wall, he was becoming sick believing them.

"Dick has such a hairy ass, but he likes it when I ram my tongue in it when I'm sucking on his balls! He's suuch a freaky bastard!"

Becky didn't bat a single eye at Eddie as she purged her promiscuous bedroom antics. He heard her talk and shuddered at how insouciant and indifferent she was talking about such bitch dog tomfoolery within earshot of anyone around to hear. He himself was unctuous fighting back upchuck and tears remembering how passionately he kissed those lips of hers, but now as she talked, even with whipped cream traces, her breath reeked of ordure he could whiff from across the table.

"So what time is Carl picking you up tonight?"

".Around eight o'clock he said, but I haven't listened to his new message . . . shhh . . ." There was a moment of pause as Becky listened to a voice message on her gadget. A chagrined expression wrinkled her face abruptly, then she finished with a nonchalant rolling of the eyes.

Mandy lit a cigarette and casually ignored and completely dismissed any small talk Eddie had attempted to make, discussing the antiquated decorum of the diner. She was in her own trance, obviously still high. She blew smoke in Eddie's face as if it was a reflexive, normal action. She snapped out of her coma only when Becky had put away her gadget and resumed their conversation.

"Carl can't come tonight. His flight got rescheduled for whatever reason. Where are you and Steve going?"

". . . said that we were just going to take a drive. I love riding in his Porsche. We might go to his sister's place in Santa Monica. She's out of town again."

"Since I'm free, maybe I'll call up Lamar and have him drive me around. His father got him a BMW, it's a convertible too. When is Steve gonna ask you to marry him? How long has it been now?"

"About a year, off and on, but he still has a year left at Cal State . . .still buys me stuff . . . outfits . . . shoes . . . he lets me drive his car from time to time, but after the last time I almost wrecked it, he kinda doesn't like . . . let me drive it anymore . . . How about you and Carl? And what're you gonna do about Lamar? Chavez?"

"Chavez is going to jail. I'll probably never see him again. By the time he gets out, I'll probably have got proposed to by some decent guy from San Bernardino. Carl just wants me to be his beard, but who knows? Maybe I can condition him to women. I like anal. He likes to party, he'll do coke from time to time, but he tries to hide it . . . heehehehee . . .

"He might want to someday get married; I certainly hope so, but then again, would I only be a beard wife? As for Lamar . . ." Becky sat for a moment and then shot Eddie a quick, annoyed look, then grinned like an evil spirit as she whipped out her cellular gadget. She put an index finger to yolk yellow stained porcine lips. "Shh . . . hey, Lamar? *What do you mean, where have I been?* Where have *you* been?"

And that was when Eddie's heart dropped to the checkered floor of the diner. Up until then, he had patiently endured the horrific details of their private lives, but what he was next to hear would obliterate any type of desire or respect he ever held for Becky.

He knew Becky had her affairs, and it would have been absurd for him to think that other men, perhaps many men, weren't attracted to her. It was silly to think that she wasn't the modish, whistle-bait best friend of his steady girl who could turn heads at almost any beach. However, he would never in a million years have guessed that she was *this* immoral and duplicitous. Neither she nor Mandy would he have expected capable of such treachery had he merely scoped them out at face value. Their valley girl looks and upper-class goody good girls vibe betrayed what was shockingly hidden beneath. Hearing them speak so wantonly about all the men they had been seeing within the last few weeks, he wondered why they simply didn't do porn movies. He felt the shoe-polish rag muffin begin to crawl its way back up his esophagus.

"Lamar," Becky said, "I . . . I can't . . . we can't...anyway, look...We have a problem. I took one of those home pregnancy tests and guess what it indicated . . .guess what it told me....yeah, so I had to go to my doctor and guess what he told me? Yes...yes...what?! *How can you even accuse me of such a thing?* Lamar! [**Sob***] . . . I can't believe this . . . I-I've only been with one person, and that was with *you*! [Sniff*] I told you . . . I told you a couple of nights ago that I'd be staying over at Mandy's last night. You couldn't reach me maybe because I was out of range . . . but do we really need to be talking about this just now? I mean . . . we have a real problem . . . My . . . my folks would never accept this, you know that . . . not . . . with..you . . .

"L-Lamar, this is no time for us to argue . . . I need about eight hundred dollars for the abortion. I-I need . . . what? What do you mean? Do you know how much such an operation is? And on such short notice too? I . . . *we*...need to have this done right away. I mean, listen . . . I have to keep my job, and if I'm in this condition, it . . . might [sniff*] . . . it *will* affect my career situation.

"Y-you have to understand [sob*], Lamar . . . I don't have that kind of money. My parents are gonna ask me about it, and I can't tell them! My daddy hasn't been giving me my allowance lately, he's been away a lot . . . I couldn't just tell them about this! Ask your father, your basketball coach . . . your scholarship money . . . yeah . . . yeah . . . yes . . . OK . . . I feel better, yes, thank you. You make me feel better by saying that you will, baby. Yeah, Can . . . can you meet tonight? Really, yes? Will you bring the money? Oh, wonderful, baby!" [*Sniff**] O, yeah . . . I love you too. See you later, baby!"

Becky's face lit up. After a smidgen more of fake tear-stained talk, the call was terminated. She then finally involved Eddie in conversation.

She said, "Counting this morning, you came in me three times, you jerk!"

Becky's eyes narrowed to a squinting scowl, glaring across the table at Eddie.

Mandy laughed. "Oh, my gawd. . . three times? He must have more than two balls. I could have sworn he did it on my face and tits . . ."

The conversation became blurry as it faded from his ears.

Like someone suddenly stricken with a precipitous incursion of diarrhea and biliousness, Eddie removed himself from the booth and made a mad dash for the restroom again. He was holding one hand over his jib, and the other was patting the seat of his work uniform pants.

He banged through the door to the men's room and scared the living daylights out of a tourist, rendered petrified upon seeing Eddie, who appeared like a sudden Jekyll-turned-Hyde had emerged. Eddie managed to find a vacant stall to empty his dearth, bowels, and guts. Tears once again escaped his eyelids. His skull was rattling as if there was a grandfather clock's pendulum inside banging either side of his head.

To have just heard Becky say that she would accept some poor unsuspecting dude's scholarship money in fake desperation to pay for a future abortion. It may or may not have been Eddie's child, he didn't even know whether she was pregnant that very moment or not, but he did know that he had contributed to the kerfuffle regardless. It was true, he had blown his load within Becky's walls more than once during their brief encounter, and this was confirmed by the glare she lashed him with before she got on the phone.

"What a bitch!" he stammered aloud.

Then and there, in the face of stench and waste, he determined to man up. Forget about bitches like Becky and hold tighter to Liz for the time being. For all of Liz's faults, she had never sunken to the depths of which he witnessed from Becky—at least, not to his knowledge—and, if by chance Liz was of the same caliber, he was grateful that she had kept it hidden from him. Birds of a feather may flock together, Eddie thought, but he had been with her a lot and had never seen Liz not shower, bathe, and nor did she bite her nails, dig up her nose, or attempt to cover stench with expensive perfume. Maybe this was Becky's unusual day of deviation, but it certainly shocked Eddie, and moreover, how she was treating Lamar was, in Eddie's opinion, atrocious and cruel. He wouldn't meet Lamar in person until about a year later at Liz's graduation party, and by that time, he hardly had the *cojones* to look dude in the eye, even though neither Lamar nor Steve had any clue their beloved squeezes had been unfaithful freaks with him. Lamar had been sullen and glum the entire night. Of course, Eddie knew why, but for the fact that a year later he would still be with her, there was no telling what sort of agony Becky had put the dude's heart through.

Eddie didn't want any of that.

Snapping out of his flashback, Eddie fluffed his pillow and tried to go back to sleep. Although he had desire for other women sometimes, Liz held a guilty contract over him to ensure he would remain hers.

22

BEARING IN MIND Eddie's bizarre and recondite history with women, from the first encounter with whale-sized sperm guzzler back in "the Sac" until that moment in time, his inability to be moved by them twinkling their eyes at him was justified. How long he was immured by his self-branded invulnerability was a matter of time, however. At the core, he was still weak and at times could be downright indigent and needy. The attention Liz had heaped upon him caused Eddie to be dependent as an infant at times. Sure, he had a mind of his own, but Liz offered him a comfort zone of knowing that with her, he would always be needed, and he occupied a tactical spot in her grim, lurid, tart heart. To go to such a great length and offer him a rendezvous with her girlfriends was mondo unfathomable. The Gordian knot he faced was an inescapable dilemma that he and Liz were sexually incompatible, and their living situation was making this increasingly escalated.

They made a flimsy deal in the beginning that they would be together even if one of them were working. That quickly dissolved. Liz would be drunk, high, and in her usual animated state of jollification and then fall back into the country quietude with a clamorous crash on Sunday evenings. At a time when most people were settling down to prepare for Monday, the business and school week, Liz's was about to blast off into orbit, transforming into the weekend witch warrior, or the wicked witch. Period.

The once-deemed fairy-tale princess Liz would still get love out in Hannan, but she was steadily wearing out her welcome with her boisterous return visits.

160

Clamorous, muffled noise was a constant whenever she was around. Eddie had been a polite, quiet, and model resident. When their situation was learned and better understood, the ruckus was grudgingly tolerated for a time, but Eddie received his warnings to pipe down.

The chicken heads still got a kick out of meeting Liz. They would usually see each other on Tuesdays, or Mondays also, if Liz wasn't suffering from an intense hangover. The screeching, shrieking children didn't scream when they saw her. In fact, it was the opposite effect shown to Eddie: instead of running away, kids ran to Liz. They wanted to hug her, kiss her, smell her hair, fondle her face, and be curious about the beautiful stranger. So much so that sometimes the mothers had to pry their kids away from Liz, their unusual object of curiosity. Liz had always been somewhat fond of children, aside from the one time she was struck with that sudden lust for a teenage boy, this dated back to her babysitting days. This had not changed much since she had come to Japan, and the kids she taught at the elementary school had been adorable. She didn't dislike the children the way she detested some of the adults. With this being said, knowing some of those chicken twerp parents, she felt uneasiness when their filthy, snot-nosed kids slobbered all over her. She gradually made increasing efforts to limit contact with them and avoid meeting them altogether—kids and parents!

This was no easy accomplishment as Eddie would sometimes enlist her services in order for him to arrive on time to work. If Liz was able to wake up, she could help Eddie fend off the conversation fiends who stalked the apartment lobby in the mornings. Since they were either retired, not working, or whatever, they had time to saunter about, read newspapers, gawk at the sunrise, and make people like Eddie late for work when they engaged him in morning chats.

These determined individuals would attempt to pounce upon Eddie with their brainless conversation and IQ–lowering English-speaking ability. Liz would kiss Eddie goodbye and shoo him off to work while she ran interference and thwarted the siege of chatterbox zombies like a heroic movie character.

Crippled retiree Mama-sans with walking sticks dared not show their decrepit withered grills around Liz. Their days of offering "granny sex" to her property was put on permanent pause.

Inevitably, however, the gradual detest of the dull, rustic setting would reemerge. To the point where she decided to stop returning to Hannan altogether. Eddie didn't object much. While his work wasn't particularly difficult or strenuous, it had the propensity to reach such levels were he to continue trying to perform without proper rest, preparation, and overall focus. Hangovers and delirium tremens didn't help at all, and worse, Liz was trying out a new game that involved playing with his balls.

Eddie would be edgy, horny, and raring to rip into Liz like a hungry baby after mama's milk. But Liz would play sick, demented denial games with him in bed. She would make him use his hands a lot, while she would use her stroke mitt on him and pretty much do all the freaky sort of stuff without penetration. Or she would squeeze her muscular thighs tightly together and trap his efforts to the detail of massaging her outer vulva, his sensitive tip tingled by her bush tricked his brain into thinking he was really into her, but he wasn't. It was something she learned rubbing skin with other chicks. Eddie's condom would burst before he climaxed under her bare bottom. She would laugh wickedly and then feign anger and disappointment with his attempts to satisfy her. She would accuse him of being selfish and only considering his own fulfillment, not hers. Feeling guilty, Eddie would try to make amends by muff diving and using his index or middle finger operating under Liz's direction. The next day, he'd wake up with Liz finishing a wild ride on his morning rod like a human dildo. She'd collapse beside him sweaty, then slide out of bed for her a.m. coffee, and Eddie would spend the rest of the day with a blue stiff. He wasn't overly thrilled about starting his day in such a way, but at least Liz could no longer claim that she wasn't being "satisfied." In her own demented manner, she was getting her thrills out of it obviously.

One weekend when Eddie paid a visit to the Umeda Bozack School where Liz was working, he met a sensational, gorgeous "chocolate-chip" cookie he likened to LaToya Jackson. He couldn't stop staring at Taffie Jolie, the part-time French teacher. Liz wasn't very busy, nor was the school in general, so she asked the school manager, Hitomi, if Eddie could hang around until she finished. Hitomi was so nice, she was like "Of course," but then added "But, if we get some new customers, he must leave there." Her English was very good.

New customers didn't usually come in the afternoons; they would come from morning to around noon, and then it would taper off. If he was lucky, Eddie could catch a nap until she was done. When she finished, she was busybody ready to rip up the town. First, they would do a little shopping, then dinner, maybe a movie too if something good was playing—six to eight months after its original release in the States—and finally, a quick trip back to Bentencho to stash the haul, then off to the night frolics.

This was all fine and dandy, as far as Eddie was concerned, but he was in a bad way for her and desperately desired Liz's dank, moist muff, especially after a week of her calling him on the cellular before bed talking about how damp she was below the belt, just thinking of him and "missing him." When he made the trip to the city, all he wanted was for her to show and prove. They couldn't make it at Liz's dormitory, as already made evident; for if house hermit Denore wasn't already there, she was on her way there and always seemed to arrive just when he was about to mount his majesty and dig her out with male tooling.

Eventually they would hit a love hotel—if a vacant one could be found. Because of it being a weekend, Osaka would receive a gigantic increase of visitors far, wide, and beyond. Love Hotels being cheaper accommodation in most cases, the rooms would go pretty quickly. The one time they couldn't hit a love hotel, they sprang the extra chips for a regular, business hotel. It wasn't bad except for the stale cigarette smoke remnant odor from past business geezers and the like. Otherwise, it wasn't too bad other than the price being a little more than what they would have paid for a Love Hotel, which had other features like cable TV porn, room service that included dildos and sex toys, alcohol, soft drinks, cup noodles, and order menu for ice, food, or dessert. Some other ones had video games and karaoke. Eddie liked those, because after Liz would black out from all the drugs and wine she took, he would have something to do to pass the time.

Generally, that was how it transpired each and every time. On better nights, Liz would remain sober or astute enough to dome Eddie off quick and put him to sleep. Then, as always, the same thing . . . he would wake up and have Liz riding him like the Wild, Wild West and fall atop him damp with heat exhaustion. Sexual appetite appeased, she would get her coffee, snort some coke, or blaze speed, and she was up and about with a spring in her step. She would go to work and disappear from noon until about 7:00 p.m.

During this window of time, Eddie's choices were any of several. He could wait for her and explore his day away in a discovery tour of the city, he could hang out at Umeda School if Hitomi permitted him but found he couldn't do it in the morning, so he abandoned this choice soon after. He had struck a good accord with Keefer, and even Eric Cravens too, so he could sometimes go to the Namba School and hang out there, even though he wasn't a Bozack employee. The reason he could do that was because the head teacher, a guy named Mitch "the Worm" Swiggler was on vacation and the Japanese staff was too busy on their side of business dealings to care too much about the daily antics of the foreign teaching staff; in other words, they were preoccupied with other serious matters other than trying to babysit adults from foreign countries. On nights when Liz and Eddie bunked at a regular business hotel, they could just book one more night; the Love Hotels had a mandatory checkout policy with no extensions. These were the days before the "internet cafe" would boom its way into the fast-paced jet set of Japanese mainstream central to the aspects of socialism. Had Eddie been aware of their existence at that time, he would have been tremendously aided by their convenience and usage.

Prior to those elaborate internet cafes with private booths, reclining seats, cushions, and blankets, those in Eddie and Liz's time were basically limited to a series of tables and chairs decked out in sectional booths similar to a library. Sometimes there was a divider between one customer and the next, sometimes there wasn't, but these were the spaces where Eddie and Liz could use the internet or take care of some printing needs. Sometimes Eddie would hit these spots up to kill time while waiting for Liz, but he never had the patience to endure an entire day with the uncomfortable seating.

He tried sitting in some of the crowded coffee shops like *DouTour* and *Hironoya*, but quickly grew to detest these dens of desperate, despicable English conversation dick riders. Not only did those spots have cramped, barely clean seating, they were also smelly and smoky from square puffing patrons. In those days, only ornamental miniature railing and imitation shrubs were the dividing borders separating the smoking section from the non-smoker. In many cases, the smell of cigarette smoke overshadowed the aroma of the coffee beans and brew. Eddie would always get mistaken for some Japanese weirdo's English teacher or tutor who was supposed to meet them there, or some other dumb, miscellaneous trite bullshit. And he would sometimes get propositioned to be a private lesson teacher. This would be old, elderly geezer types the likes of which he had seen at the hostess bar, Mama-san Yoshiko's Snack Pub, those types, but it only spooked Eddie out, and he mistakenly thought that they wanted to be on some gay Boy Scout business, in which he wasn't the least bit interested. As such, he decided to stay clear of these places in the long run.

There were scores of video game arcades to waste away inside. The most amusing one for Eddie was the Sega Arcade near the Hommachi School's indoor arcade. He had seen bigger ones in Venice Beach, and even in the Sac, but the amusement was still abundant. The place had three or four levels (he couldn't remember, of course). He spent a shitload of money there, again thinking that his 100 yen coins—equivalent to an American dollar but looks slightly bigger than a US nickel—were actually the quarters of twenty-five cents he was accustomed to paying to play video games in his country.

When 7:00 p.m. rolled around, if Eddie didn't get completely lost during his day tripping about by himself, he would already be somewhat bushed from his frantic, fast-paced day in the Umeda section of the city. There literally had to be millions of people in that area, Eddie mused with veneration. For some strange reason, he couldn't bring himself to dislike it. He understood why Liz was loving it, but he couldn't hang with her energy, unfortunately.

While Eddie was in the mood to wind down, Liz would be ready to rock and roll and let her hair hang loose. From the moment she acquired her own C contact, she would explode into party mode at will. Her weekend working hours were ten to four on Saturdays and noon till seven on Sundays. Of those hours, she would work about three or four; otherwise, there were many cancellations, no-shows, and empty slots. It reminded her of the boring days working with the CHET Program, but now it was better because in between the dull hours of downtime, she had people to chat with—Taffie, some other teacher, or Hitomi the manager.

Nice as could be, Hitomi was the sole Japanese staffer who operated as both secretary and manager on the slow weekends. Occasionally, another staffer would show up, or every now and then, but Hitomi was almost always the only officious Bozack faculty around when Liz was there. She allowed Liz and Taffie to kick back and relax in the teachers' lounge or the customer waiting room. Sometimes Liz could even cop forty winks, or a double, depending on the flow of customer traffic. On these occasions, she would be refreshed by the time her shift was over. So Eddie would show up low on vitality gas, ready to check in to a hotel and chill for the rest of the night—to relax, veg, and maybe some extra personal time.

But no.

Liz would be in the mood for dinner, maybe sushi at the "sushi-go-round"(*11), or a *"gaijin"* bar" where her Bozack pack would congregate to watch some sporting event, throw darts, get smashed, or maybe even sing karaoke, and *then*—a hotel.

Eddie simply was no fun.

Due to his weakened state, having nowhere near the tolerance Liz seemingly had for alcohol, Eddie would tend to get smashed at lightning speed. Sometimes it appeared as if Stephanie and Eddie were having a contest to see who would pass out first. Some even took bets, but Stephanie frequently won. They both, however, shared the ability to spring back into life regaining consciousness for a span of indeterminable intervals to ingest more libation, then blackout, "url" all over the spot and, needless to say, spoil whatever pleasurable or romantic aspect of the night to be gained. If this was on a Sunday, what a quandary would it be for Eddie who had to work the following day, and a dreary, dreadfully drab train ride back to Hannan City awaited him; he could either brave it out that night or wait until the following morning and wake up at the dawn's ass crack to catch a train to a bus, a bus to whatever to get him back to the woods, to get to work on time. Liz would urge him to call in sick every time, but Eddie sternly refused for he wanted to remain the exceptional and honorable example of a hardworking foreigner to impress the Japanese people around him. Liz scolded him that it was a waste of time. Eddie refused to give in to her on this one thing, although he really wanted to sleep in. What killed him more than anything else and the irritating feeling of sour belly, was the ache of his tortured genitals that weren't allowed to release properly; it was as if Liz had filled them up like water inside of a balloon and then allowed them to just—hang. She wouldn't even offer him a joint to smooth him out on his way back to work and the sticks.

By the time Eddie got home that night, he would have then received a call from Liz explaining how she was postponing her visit to Hannan until the following day, or that she wasn't coming at all. She had spent that day sleeping until hotel checkout time, going home and maybe sleeping a bit more, and then kicking off the whispering campaign with her crew, all of this while Eddie was grinding away at work. Fine by him if she wasn't coming, it gradually came to be; Liz got to be too much of a tantalizing tease and hoyden dynamo when she came out, interfering with his rest and putting his patience to the test. Eddie was in such bad shape, he thought of returning once again to Mama-san Yoshiko's spot and offer her a little scratch to see if she would "act right," if worse came to worst, maybe he would even take one of those dusty, battered aged hags up on their invitation to the bed—no, in the nick of time, he discovered those *pink chirashi* (*12), the leaflets he would find overstuffed in his mailbox almost every day, with photos of sexy women, sometimes nude ones, advertising some delivery hooker or escort service known as "health."

23

IT WAS KEEFER who had pulled Eddie's coat to delivery health. This was something Liz never had privy of knowing about. On the occasion when Eddie was able to camp out at the Namba School while waiting for Liz to finish her Saturday shift, he and Keefer were able to kick it for a spell. When feasible, Kayo Terumi of the Japanese staff who often arranged the teaching schedules for the foreign teachers would fix Keefer up with a mollified schedule, giving him more free time to relax, take breaks, sleep on the floor in the teachers' lounge, or chew the fat with his "cobbers," or amicable coworkers.

Although Eddie wasn't Keefer's coworker—neither were his Aussie mates, a set of cousins who each had similar buck teeth like beavers, squirrels, gophers or rodents, guys named Ricky Exmouth and Simon Bunderburg—they all used to hang out at the Namba branch if it was Worm's day off and usually on Saturday it was for a period of time. Simon and Ricky worked for a rival English conversation school company, but that didn't stop the Australians from all becoming friends with one another.

The cousins Simon and Ricky were also of similar stature, height, and personality traits. They differed only in hairstyles. Ricky had the dirty blond mid-fade with angular fringe, while Simon had the sandy blond somewhat retro-looking hockey cut. Both were slender, ectomorph-bodied guys but swore by being tough guys, boasting claims to have mafia and "893" ties, which was rare but not improbable.

Neither Ricky nor Simon seemed to be overly fond of American people, and that would include Eddie as well as Eric Cravens, Stephanie, Chucky, and soon to be Liz also. Their company hired mostly Australians and people from the UK, Americans were rare and often traduced or damned with faint praise by both students and colleagues from other extractions. Bozack, they noticed, tended to hire lots of Americans. Peculiarly, however, they like Keefer, had taken a liking to Kwame. Keefer was the only levelheaded person impassive enough to determine Eddie to be one of the more tolerable Americans. Eddie looked up to Australians in a weird sort of way, and many of the insults heaved at him from the Aussie blokes Ricky and Simon went over his head anyway. Keefer decided to ameliorate tension between the beaver twins and Eddie, taking the American under his wing.

Keefer could spin a tale that would have Eddie instantly agog and tuned in like a child watching cartoons.

Back in his earlier and unenlightened days in Japan, he had indulged the delivery health service. In the beginning, it started as a prank. It was a joke, bluff phone calls the Aussie and his mates would pull. They would get a handful of the pink-chirashi leaflets, call the phone number on the pink-colored side of the paper, and basically request an unspecified count of whores as advertised. Most of the time, the receptionist who answered their calls would recognize that Keefer or fellow pranksters were exactly that—pranksters and obviously foreigners as well. As the high jinks continued and phone gags remained the drunken occupation to score laughs on bored nights, one receptionist answering the call would explain to them that their particular service wasn't available for *gaijin*.

As time went on, every now and then, phone pranks to the delivery health sources would still be the occasional post-party amusement. This would be roughly a year or two later, and Keefer's Japanese had improved at that point. His strong points were in the usage of vulgar, inappropriate phrases relating to sex, and he was once able to convince an unsuspecting receptionist into believing that he was a Japanese person, perhaps with a speech impediment, but a paying customer nonetheless. Still thinking that it was an innocuous prank to end a night of horseplay and drinking with a load of laughs, Keefer and his flat-mates would retire to their individual rooms.

About an hour later, the apartment intercom would chime. Keefer answered the door and after having supplied the receptionist with his address, a plain Jane thirty-ish *moot* shows up. Nothing would be too special, nothing extraordinary or glamorous about this woman. She would have passed for a bland schoolteacher quickly advancing in age, a banal housewife, or a simple, miscellaneous mug or wallflower that wouldn't get a second look within a crowd of people. Her fashion would be slightly retro, outdated, or plain vintage, along with bummy shoes or slippers suitable more for men than women. After having invited this into his abode, Keefer recounted to Eddie how he instantly had the "Fuck me dead!" jitters and couldn't believe what he had gotten himself into.

Too daring to bail at such point, or turn the woman away, Keefer would pay the chick an itchy-man and the show was under way. The woman would tuck the money away in a compartment of the bag she brought, then casually strip to her bare bones, once ensconced in Keefer's room.

He also admitted to Eddie how he was at a loss of words as "plain Jane" denuded every single garment of clothing, including all socks and leggings, in less than a minute. Garments were neatly folded on the floor placed in a pile near where she stood in birthday form. Keefer would describe how suddenly the *boiler* would transform from plain Jane to sexpot smut mag centerfold candidate—*just like that*—as soon as she had removed her clothes! Where did that awesome "nuddy" body come from? Obviously hidden by the fashionably challenged wardrobe!

After achieving a stiffy, Keefer would undress with the Jane's help, then she would suck him off. Keefer would get graphic and overshare his experience. He told Eddie, "Yeah, that first time ended with a sensational 69, mate!" He went into detail about how he made his tongue needle her, with alternating thrusts like that of an arrowhead into the woman's anus and vaginal aperture. Meanwhile on the opposite end, he described his "doodle donger" disintegrating into the murky maw of Jane's jib.

"The entire time she concealed my cock in her cheek and throat," he went on to rehash. "Bear in mind, my thing is practically massaging her epiglottis. She's moanin' and wincin' up a storm, mate." Keefer then claimed he brought the bitch to climax with just the usage of his long, scaly tongue as she banged her hairy bum against his nose. Her suction powered hot throat devoured his tempered, creamy man babies. By then, Keefer conveyed how he was howling, panting, and sweating as if he had bungee-jumped from Mount Everest.

As soon as this was all over, Jane would get up, grab a towelette or handkerchief from the huge *odekake* bag she brought. She would wipe off Keefer's junk, next her clacker, and then get dressed. As quickly and immaculately as she had made her appearance, so did she leave in the same manner. Quiet as *kunoichi*. Keefer's roommates had not even the slightest clue that anyone had actually showed up. Anybody seeing the woman coming or going wouldn't have suspected that the plain Jane was actually a hot-bodied hooker; she would have passed for a librarian or school tutor making house calls.

So to avoid beating the bishop, Keefer recapped how he would utilize this "delivery health" service a few more times in the days that followed. Each time, a different woman would show up, but her description would remain the plain Jane—a dull, insipid-looking mid-thirties chick with moth-eaten, outmoded wardrobe turned foxy freak once the latter was shed.

He eventually grew out of the necessity for delivery health, Keefer narrated as if he was telling his life story to a reporter or psychiatrist. This was triggered by his frustration with the service because these Janes wouldn't consent to actual-penetration intercourse. The Japanese crony he had at that time who had been teaching him all of the dirty language had explained the best way he could that if the woman was to have sex with him, that would make the encounter prostitution for real, and *that* was illegal. Whereas a nude person providing a massage for genitalia wasn't considered unlawful. That it was a slippery slope, more or less, hard to enforce and difficult to convict.

Still, Keefer had wanted for himself a proper "end way," thus he was able to graduate to actually picking up sluts and whores on his own. His specialty would become *gaijin* killers, the adulation harboring types who were also pet-named yellow cabs, who would open their doors to give practically anybody a ride. At least, as literature at that time from Japan would allege. With these types, he didn't have to pay at all and they would supply him with all the quim he could ever want. That was why he had been living so happily ever after all those years. Twelve years total, in fact with no intention of returning to Melbourne.

Curiosity appeased, Eddie was hipped by Keefer to the mystery of *pink chirashi* and delivery health. He didn't care about whether or not the whores allowed penetration sex; his utter contentment with fellatio was groomed early on; besides, it cut the risk of an unwanted pregnancy! No Becky "repeats" needed. Although he was awfully tempted to try the service, he chickened out and refrained from calling the number on the pink side of the leaflet. It was due to the embarrassment and fear of being discovered to have purchased its service. His popularity and reputation was at stake in town, and ruining it would be disastrous. He would instead look at the photos on the flyers and have extra material in addition to his favorite porn "manga and anime videos to jerk off to.

HIROKO OKADA

INTERLUDE (I)

IF ONE WERE to allow her attractive, beckoning and comely outer appearance to fool them, they would never have suspected that Hiroko Okada was a tragedy queen turned success story; she had auspiciously rebounded from a fairly hellish and calamitous past, and was then, at the time Eddie and Liz met her, among the brightest up-and-coming educators that the Japan School Board were overwhelmingly pleased to have among their ranks.

Behind the smiling face, however, was a sad tale.

Before her parents divorced due to alleged infidelities—both mother and father analogously—they had resided in an affluent Tezukayama area of Osaka. After the separation, Hiroko moved with her overbearing young mother back to maternal original hometown Sakai City, the town across the river from Osaka City to the south. Her teenage years were spent more with her grandparents than her mother. Her mom was either busy working to extract money from former hubby or out trying to recruit people for some pyramid scheme racket, like Amway, to make extra cash. She had married an older considerably rich, stable gentleman at a young age, then had given birth to Hiroko in hopes she would have been a happy, storybook mom but instead, upon cutting ties with her husband, single mom parenthood was cramping her style.

Since Hiroko was such an adorable moppet of a chit, her grandparents didn't really mind taking up the slack raising her. As a result, she was subject to better, traditional rearing. She came home directly after school and club activities, she didn't linger about in the streets. She also developed good study habits and thanks to frequent trips to Tokyo Disneyland, her desire to learn English was born. Some event happened where a staff dressed up like Goofy or some Donald Duck character made a big deal about her saying some English words and everybody freaked out. From then on, Hiroko saw herself as a special kind of genius.

She would then watch a lot of Hollywood foreign movies. In addition to the school's English textbooks, she studied actresses like Meg Ryan and Julia Roberts and practiced speaking like them. "Pretty Woman" was her favorite movie. She would dissect and emulate speech elocution, sometimes she would practice speaking for hours in the privacy of her room. Simultaneously, she began seeing her world and those of the fictitious to collide. Her head formed an innate expectancy for her own life to follow the outline of a fantasy, or romantic tale like the ones she studied. She may have seemed a little bit weird or out of touch, but she made stellar grades. How tremendously she excelled in English without ever studying abroad had baffled her teachers.

Toward the end of her high school days, she fell in love with a badminton champ. For most of her life, she was a gullible sort of girl, fun to be around, but not to be taken too seriously until it was time to get cheat answers for tests, or English homework help. Badminton Champ was pretty much the same. Only, he was thinking more along the lines of getting his English homework done (by her) on the reg and swiping her virginity in the process.

Unfortunately, dude was unable to close that deal as the task of compromising Hiroko's hymen was too painful an ordeal for her to complete. Additionally, she had been practically raised by an old-school grandmother who pretended like sex was something she had done in a past life, so she was lacking formal instructions to basic sex education. Thus ill-prepared emotionally for romantic encounters she was. Still, with what limited knowledge she had in the area of carnality, she successfully compensated for her shortcoming in the prior department. Applying her oral aptitude and slimy saliva-coated palms to his sensitive high school shuttlecock's tension, she triumphantly blasted him off.

This self-taught lollipop skill came suddenly, and on one or two more occasions, such a feat was again rendered to Badminton Champ, as a result of continued failed attempts to breach her sugar walls. He lost interest in Hiroko when he found another starstruck schoolgirl's nest to raid. He dropped Hiroko quick like a birdie smashed on the opposite side of an opponent's net. Her heart felt the impact, and she faded away from the social scene. The girl who flashed her gash to attract the Champ was supposed to be Hiroko's friend, but after this, she realized that she never really had any genuine friends. She only had people—male and female—who simply wanted to use her.

Rejection turned favorable in this occurrence she then could focus more on her studies. Truth be told, the local Japanese boys didn't turn her on anyway. If she were to have her own knight in shining armor, it would be one that looked like a Disney prince. Watching Disney movies made her believe that dreams could come true.

Proof of this would come when she destroyed an English speech contest. The judges from England, New Zealand, and Canada were left with mouths agape after hearing her recite some homiletic about John Lennon. They were so impressed they wanted to give all three—first, second, and third prize—awards to her and tell all the other babbling, nervous, trembling-mouthed sucker students to go the fuck home. This stunning achievement made her eligible for another prestigious Josei-Shinri-Shakai study-abroad program for girls. Out of the slim one hundred students throughout Japan who even qualified, it was, of course, she who was first selected among a small group of 10 to be granted an opportunity to visit and study at various Canadian cities.

Hiroko Okada was placed in the city of Vancouver. There she studied at the Vancouver International Language Embassy Institute. At that time, this independent academic enterprise was vying for annex portion of West Vancouver University, so some "swole" pocket execs cleaned up a patch of old abandoned edifices and scrubbed together a place that could pass for a school, or at least a learning retreat of some kind. Hiroko was oblivious. She was thrilled to be in a foreign country and fresh out of high school, awestruck and dazed thinking she was living out a Disney-like story.

Attending the VILE Institute, she made the most of the experience and soaked up every advantage living abroad could afford her. She met so many people she couldn't keep up with the names or faces. The only person she could remember succinctly was her Chinese roommate—a girl named Ming. She was getting banged on the regular by some sinister looking, puffy blonde haired guy with a scar on his chin, a guy from Quebec. She could never remember his name, but he spoke French, Ming spoke Chinese, and with Hiroko in the mix, their *lingua franca* became English.

Hiroko remembered Ming to be such a kind, sweet girl but a little bit too fast for her taste and she didn't roll too much with her and her paramour. She was admonished by Josei-Shinri-Shakai advisors back in Japan to avoid clicking up other Japanese people while studying abroad; being around other Japanese people could put her in a comfort zone of speaking her native language and defeating the purpose of her objective. She was somewhat a loner, but there was no oppressive feeling of neglect, because she was still enjoying the world outside of Japan and didn't feel lonely.

The residence she shared with Ming was the old dormitory, successfully renovated by VILE, furnished with bunk beds, antique escritoires and a tiny closet. The showers and bath were communal and the dorm itself was coed separated genders by floors. Aside from Ming's constant companion, there weren't any resident pervs about, so it was relatively safe. The location was abundant with nature. It had a cozy atmosphere, which made studying easier and pleasant.

A year later, Hiroko was practically fluent in English, but because of her tender young age of seventeen, her topics of discussion were limited, so there was still more work to be done. Advanced study was pertinent. She wasn't quite ready to return to Japan. Although she had received some promised credits to be considered towards college, the entire time abroad to her felt like an extra year of high school, dazzled with an international twist. What she really wanted to do was visit the United States of America. It was such a shame, to her, that she had been in Canada for all that time and was so close to one of the world's most famous countries and hadn't once yet been! Her schedule had been rigid and uniformed, so she had adhered to program requirements regarding attendance and participation.

As fate would have it, Hiroko returned to her dormitory residence after class late one afternoon, and an announcement on a bulletin board in the lobby caught her attention. In between various posts soliciting buyers for used bicycles, textbooks, items for sale, and "Babysitter wanted" ads, there were announcements for various home-stay opportunities in conjunction with organizations like Unicef, EF, Open Door, AFS, Youth for Understanding and others. Most of these home-stays were in Canada: Toronto, Winnipeg, Saskatchewan, and such. But there was one in Oregon, USA, that caught her eye.

Until that time, Hiroko had done a fairly good job distancing herself from other lazy Japanese countrymen, but she was still cordial and pleasant with her people. She would do the "Hi and bye" thing when she encountered them, and she tactfully declined invitations to their restrictive outings. Whatever interest she might have had in the other lame Japanese people at VILE was indefinitely discarded upon discovery that none of them had any interest in visiting the United States.

Apparently, those Japanese students had "drunk the Kool-Aid" about America being the most dangerous country in the world. "Bear in mind, an exchange student Yoshihiro Hattori had just got blasted in the American state of Louisiana, knocking on the wrong fool's door looking for a Hallowe'en party. They might have had good cause to be petrified of the States." America-hating Canadians didn't help much to not convince them that America was a death trap either.

Hiroko Okada wasn't to be intimidated, however. She had come this far—she figured she might as well continue. For truth be told, she had always been more interested in the United States than Canada. She couldn't help it. Of course, Canada to her was wonderful, but nearly everything she liked about the world outside of Japan had come from America. From the music, the movies, to the

Disney fairy-tale fantasies. The Oregon home-stay became her next mission. Problem was, her student visa was recognized only in Canada.

Hiroko contacted her mother, Eriko, back in Japan and told her of her plans. She wanted to remain overseas for another three months or so and do a home-stay with an American family in the States. Her mother didn't really object, as she was enjoying her life as a socialite, and not having a teenage daughter in her hair was a welcome luxury. Not that she didn't love her daughter; merely she was disturbingly inattentive to her and mistakenly came to some absurd deduction that Hiroko's ability to speak English so well made her a genius in all facets of life.

Hiroko applied to the organization that facilitated the home-stay in Oregon, USA. This company would later be investigated for fraud and mysteriously vanished from the public scene, likely purchased, renamed, and abnegated of all previous existence. At that time, though, the skulking entity was, by all accounts—at least to the public—a legitimate home-stay–slash–host program coordinating organization. Because these such operations were so abundant, it was easy for some of the bad ones to be submerged among the more honorable ones that really *did* seek to promote international fellowship and cultural exchange. Unsuspecting victims like a vulnerable Hiroko would be among the many who served as litmus tests to ascertain their levels of corruption and depravity.

Similar to the rigid interview process that yielded her the winning seat among a slim order of youth high school grads slated to study abroad in Canada, she met with representatives from the West American Council Kith for Intercultural Exchange (WACK). She was met in downtown Vancouver by her interviewers—two friendly middle-aged women, one was a short Japanese American called Nancy Tanaka-Ryan, who looked like every Japanese person Hiroko had seen her entire life in Japan, but this replica could speak almost zero Japanese because she had been born and raised in the streets of Portland, Oregon.

The next interviewer was a grotesquely large blonde woman with glasses who went by the name of Alice. Hiroko didn't know what to make of her besides considering the woman suitable for wrestling Sumo of her homeland. She tried to not stare too much at the inflatable tubing underneath the woman's shirt, the way the ruffles circled her torso was keek inducing.

Nancy was ill-prepared to meet a potential host student from Japan of her ancestors. Most applicants that came through WACK were from the Philippines—in fact, Filipinos dominated the program—and some other countries like Taiwan and Korea, with smatterings of Chinese. Because she couldn't speak Japanese at all, the heavyset Alice was enlisted because she was fluent in the language.

When Nancy heard Hiroko speak English, she was immediately impressed and decided right away that she would be perfect for the immersion project. A girl with her profound understanding and grasp of the language should have no problem residing in deciduous situation with an American family. Alice, of course, agreed wholeheartedly also that Hiroko was eligible, so they wasted no time getting the paper chase under way.

Basically, Hiroko was to pay a nominal fee to the tune of about six hundred dollars. Money was never a big worry for Hiroko or her mother. While her father was alive, he kept regular payments of quasi-alimony—because he wasn't mandated or required by law to do so—more regular than his visits or calls. Apparently, it was difficult for him to maintain two lives: one with his former family and the newer one he had begun with another young maiden. Still, however, he was generous with the funds, and Hiroko mostly wanted for nothing; she had no problem getting the fee and tuition covered.

Hiroko was also frugal. She didn't spend much, didn't eat or drink too much, nor had she ever partied much—at all. She had barely tasted alcohol her entire life, and in the normal order of things, it was proper that it be so according to many social orders of Western society. Because of these practices, she was able to maintain her size relatively well, did not gain much weight, and rarely got sick. This offered her further opportunity to save money—no need to buy too many new clothes, and no need for expensive medicine. The hardest part about living in Canada, for her, was the cold winter! Aside from that, it was a pleasant cake walk, and she was now ready for the next challenge.

Two weeks after the successful interview, Hiroko met with rotund regional Vancouver office supervisor Alice, again at a bakery disguised as a coffee shop. The enormous woman grinned emphatically as she practically inhaled a huge gulp of coffee through the hole in her face that wasn't one of her nostrils. She was extra cordial, kind, and rich with warm smiles; but there was a subtle oddity in the mood she was bringing to the moment. Almost like she was eager to see Hiroko speed up her filling out and signing the applications she had placed before her, finish up, and hurriedly arrive at any spot elsewhere that served maple syrup–covered fried potatoes and sausage—she'd had enough cake for one day. The process was ongoing, and the quicker they got the ball rolling with the paperwork, the sooner Hiroko would be on her way, and she could get her fat commission. Pyramid schemes were the same all over the world.

Lo and behold! Within the span of time for Hiroko's Canadian student visa to expire and the grace period needed to reactivate it, Nancy Tanaka-Ryan, Alice, and other WACK associates pulled some strings to conjure up a mendaciously legit "special educational visa." This would allow her entry to the United States. Her mother, Reiko, had received translated documents by fax, granted her permission slip with a Japanese "inkan" seal, illegally notarized, but who would know?

In Silverton, Oregon, Hiroko was placed with a Wilson family, a short distance away from the state's capital city of Salem. This host family consisted of host-father Fred, host-mother Margaret, host-brothers Brandon and Billy, who had turned eighteen recently and would soon turn twelve, respectively. Lastly, there was a sixteen-year-old host-sister, Cindy.

The home stay with the host family was scheduled for two short months, but it was cut short with ghastly exigency. In the first few weeks, Hiroko had enjoyed riding horses on the ranch with Cindy. She had a funny time gardening and cutting potatoes with host-mother Margaret. She helped Billy chase slow turtles and throw rocks in ponds. Then there was Brandon.

With Brandon, she would have an amusing time watching him and his bicycle-riding fancy friends at a park smoking cigarettes and eating caffeine-coated candy. This guy Brandon and his weirdo friends had a lot of stupid questions to ask Hiroko about Japan. Apparently, bootlegged copies of the Japanese animation flick *Urotsukidoji* and similar others had skewered the minds of Brandon and his like with irreparable obfuscation.

They asked her obtuse and tactless stuff like, "Does Japanese pussy squirt for real like it does in the animations?"

Which, at that time, was difficult for Hiroko to totally grasp. Vivid and vulgar terms had not been, up to that point, a focal area of her studies. She could hold her own in a high school–level conversation, but aside from Ming, her contemporaries in Canada were all as square as she was, if not more. As such, terms like "pussy" and "dick" initially meant nothing to her outside of being a cat's and a Richard's nicknames.

Life with the Wilsons should have been picture perfect to the letter. Things took a riveting turn around the third week when Hiroko appeared to be gaining weight. Never had she eaten so many potatoes in her life, or variations—she had heard of and seen hash browns but not tater tots. For breakfast it was sausage, eggs, and diced potatoes. Lunch was potato soup, or maybe potato chips with a sandwich; French fried potatoes were always available; and on Saturday nights, the steak and potatoes was in order. In between, there were scrumptious desserts with fresh apples, cherries, and often topped with fresh whipped cream. Of course she was bound to gain weight, Hiroko thought, as she quietly pitied host-sister, who, although cute Dakota Fanning–type looks might attract a suitor or two, showed potential to have linebacker thunder thighs develop in later years like her mother, Margaret.

If things couldn't get any worse, Brandon's gradient curiosity in her became a crush. The crush became something worse.

At first, Hiroko was receptive a little. After all, even though Brandon wasn't by any means near what her mind's image had drawn of a Western or American boy, he was still the first one she had a chance to talk to and coexist with within close range. She would become fascinated more than repulsed, but that was initially.

Brandon would hang out at a park with his maggot mooks. When Hiroko and Cindy walked by, he would run up on them, then start hugging Hiroko like she was more than just a host-sister. Finally, one time when he did this, he held her close, and Hiroko was like, "What the heck?," as if shrugging, and hugged her host-brother back. Immediately she felt his tumescence and understood what the nature of the embraces represented in his twisted young mind. For that brief moment in time, Hiroko thought about allowing him free range to explore her as he desired, but Cindy didn't seem too thrilled about that. It was as if she could sense what Hiroko knew to be the obvious. There was something oddly fortuitous about Brandon and Hiroko "coming together." Feeling sorry for her host-sister, Hiroko pulled away from the excited host-brother Brandon and tried to mend her damaged image to Cindy.

However, it wasn't any sibling jealousy that caused Cindy to be upset. In fact, her problem wasn't necessarily with Hiroko at all. Her issue was with Brandon.

"I hate it when he does that," Cindy told Hiroko. "He rubs his hard-on on me, and I got sick of it. I told him it was gross. I made him stop, I told him I'd tell Dad if he ever did it again. He stopped a year ago, but now he's trying to do the same thing to you. I can't believe you even like *him* . . ."

Of course, Hiroko was confused. Cindy spoke of her brother as if he was a bottom-of-the-rung common criminal or trash. In secret. When among other family members and on subsequent outings, they all acted in accordance to model family guidelines. Orderly behavior, conduct, and conversation befitting a standard upstanding household. When not in the presence of parents Fred and Margaret, though, it was a completely different scenario; Cindy talked of Brandon as if she loathed him. Behind the scenes, their entire family situation reeked of "disturbia."

It was now clear that Brandon liked Hiroko not as a sister in the name of cultural exchange and fellowship, but as a playmate provided by his parents. When it surfaced that Hiroko was not his first target and that his own sister Cindy was, a red flag should have appeared in Hiroko's defense system, assuming she had one in operative existence. Brandon should have also been reported to the proper authorities to deal with his problematic personality disorder and issues. This wasn't to occur because Hiroko was still brooding over whether or not she should go through with returning the same interest in Brandon that he was showing in her.

Fact of the matter was, her previous encounters of intimacy in Japan with Badminton Champ and witnessing the antics of sexually active roommate Ming in Canada caused Hiroko's snowballing curiosity for boys. Even if Brandon wasn't the proverbial Disney prince or Hollywood looker the level of a Richard Gere, he was still an American boy, and if she made out with him—even without going all the way—she would have accomplished a feat worthy of bragging rights, something her Japan peers would unlikely be able to boast.

Brandon had the build and size of a rugby player, but only surfeited with flab more so than the muscle of one. His facial mug was a Jim Belushi facsimile Blues Brother, but without the black hat and shades. He usually wore glasses, but not when he was at the park with his vermin heads where he was trying to act and look cool.

Hiroko was fixed up in the Wilsons' guestroom. They all lived in a big, cavernous wooden house. The host-father, Fred Wilson, was a highly skilled carpenter and ran his own small-time company. He was a friendly, kind man who was brawny and tall with a thick mustache and balding head in the center. He didn't look like anyone the average person would want to piss off or get on the bad side of, Hiroko thought; yet to her he was always attentive, polite, and tender. This being the case, she couldn't understand it, then, why she would wake up in the middle of the night—or better, the predawn hours and see bespectacled Brandon seated at her bedside glaring at her, his face reflected off the moon's half light beaming through the window.

In a sudden state of consternation, Hiroko was so startled she could not even scream. Her heart just smashed against her sternum like a wrecking ball.

Brandon's voice sounded like that of a robot possessed by a demon seed, in a hypnotic monotone with no rising or falling inflections. He kept saying, "I hate my father."

Hiroko understood what the statement meant, but she didn't understand why he was saying such a thing, and why to her? And why in the hell was he in *her* room?

The askew and sudden appearance of Brandon had Hiroko so spooked that she didn't notice her eyes were leaking tears. She tried to cover her breasts with her hands and wondered why she was half exposed from the waist up. Brandon had unbuttoned her pajama top while she had been sleeping soundly. How long he had been at her bedside Hiroko didn't know, but she almost cringed when Brandon's hand reached forward to wipe away her tears. He rose from his chair and sat next to Hiroko on her bed.

"Don't cry, my love," he said. "I'm here . . . I'm here. I'm here, and I love you, *He-row-cold*. It's my father I hate!"

Scared stiff, Hiroko had said, "Brandon, I do not understand why you are telling me this."

Brandon stopped repeating what he had been saying with regard to his father. He removed his glasses. His eyes looked like moistened gray slits in the darkened room. He leaned forward and kissed Hiroko's quivering lips. She didn't move away. It was a gentle kiss; it calmed her down ever so slightly, but enormous apprehension was still dominating her movement. She accepted and allowed his closeness in hopes that he would get it out of his system, leave her alone, and she could then find a way to lock and secure her door better. Brandon didn't let up, though. He pushed his weight upon her and held her down on the bed, seizing both of her wrists, pinning them to the mattress. Hiroko could feel terror begin to intensify but didn't want to panic. She wondered what would happen if she screamed.

Brandon was panting heavily, as if he was under siege of an asthma attack. In seconds, he had Hiroko stripped practically nude. His mitts had grabbed fistful clutches of Hiroko's pajama pants' fabric by the ankles. With a swift yank, he removed them completely from her legs. His skill at doing so was so adept it even surprised Hiroko more than draw her justified outrage.

He struggled a bit removing the already-unbuttoned pajama top but finally peeled it off, Hiroko's elbows and arms were twisting and contorting as if he was freeing her from a straitjacket. She was then left wearing only her pink Minnie Mouse panties. The entire time this was happening, she had not uttered any words at all; her English skill and proficiency had been rendered temporarily disabled. Ineffective. Inoperable. Practically useless.

She made no attempt to escape, flee, or unass the situation. Fear petrified her stiff like wood decubitus on the small bed as she watched Brandon liberate himself of his bathrobe, T-shirt, boxers, and bedroom slippers. His attentive, pink wiggly piggy in dense acclivity the closer he came to her.

As if in a state of ataxia, Hiroko watched as Brandon inched toward her on the bed as if he was crawling. He parted her legs, and she made little attempt to tighten up or resist his action. He was still breathing and panting hoarsely like a fatigued mule.

Still trembling with trepidation, Hiroko had silently prayed for strength to move muscles in her body other than the involuntary ones regulating the jowly clattering of her teeth. She went unexpectedly numb as her Minnie Mouse undergarment slid off. While removing her panties, Brandon took advantage of the opportunity to bury his Friz Freleng cartoon sheepdog face into Hiroko's mangy, morning moot, pleasuring her labia with his mouth moisture. In addition to the bawdy, erotic "animation," he also watched his father's X-rated porn, cleverly excavated from a hidden, secret stash, which had served to educate him in the service he was then applying to Hiroko's pudenda. His impressive talent in that department of "going downtown" was met with no resistance. She began to relax!

Hiroko's mouth suddenly dropped open to gasp for air. Brandon's taste test tour of her twat stimulated her with a titillation tingle. She was in a daze. Stars from the twilight sky emptied from the heavens into the room to circle Hiroko's head; her dizzy eyes struggled to follow them. Her legs collapsed weakly as if Brandon's mounting torso had split them in half like a slice of ham parting limply into two. The sharp pain of Brandon's attempt to pierce her intact hymen snapped her out of her state of enchantment.

Without missing a beat, she sprang into action, remembering the treatment she pacified Badminton Champ when in the same situation before. It worked then, and she was sure it would be equally effective that moment as well. A peculiar thing happened, though. When she took his tension into her hands and moved her face toward the target of his desire, he pushed her away at the final moment before her lips made contact.

Brandon had said, "No, wait . . . I can't let you do that. It . . . it's nasty . . . I . . . can't kiss you if you do that."

Hiroko didn't know what to think.

She said, "Please, Brandon . . . I'm sorry, but . . . I've never done this thing before. I'm scared. I don't think I can do it . . . it hurts me so much . . . there." She quick-jabbed a pointing finger to the area between her bare legs.

Hiroko expected Brandon to cease, settle, and be understanding. Instead, he seemed to become frustrated and increasingly riled. As if he had listened to nothing she had uttered, Brandon pounced upon Hiroko, and in a move that resembled a wrestler's, he turned her over on her stomach, he straddled her, and his weight was briefly hefted upon her. He eased himself lower and rammed his slimy tongue inside of her rump and rim. A jousting tongue invaded her orifice with the jolt of a javelin.

"OH!" Which was all Hiroko could exclaim when this occurred, in a truncated gasp. Her startled, Chip 'n' Dale' shocked eyes maximum-width wide, frozen in fright.

With all the attention he lavished upon her, she needed not have reason to bathe the next morn. But it was clear that Brandon wasn't done.

He said, "I sort of figgered you were a virgin, but that's 'cus you're pure. You're Jap'nese 'n' all. You girls're sweet 'n' good."

Brandon was fondling himself the entire time he spoke. Hiroko was still lying immobile on her stomach, her legs clamped in place by his bulky buttocks. From where he got the tiny jar of mayonnaise would forever be a mystery to her, but reality was it being there was a factual event her mind couldn't conjure up, for the simple fact it was beyond her imagination's capacity.

Brandon told her, "I'm not gunna . . . well, I could never take your virginity, Herocold." She couldn't clearly see him, but she heard him unscrewing the jar she vaguely could see read "HELLMAN'S." She knew the meaning of hell, and other words describing gender, she even knew mayonnaise and what its usage was for—or she thought she did—yet she couldn't fathom the significance of it at that moment in time.

Two of Brandon's pudgy fingers dipped inside the jar and reappeared seconds later with a generous gunk of it plastered to them. This index and middle finger set crept inside the crest with the contents, dabbed on the entire crevasse to crack. The rest was history.

It wasn't real sex, or was it? Hiroko was unsure but incompletely. Better stated, she lost a virginity other than vaginal.

The actual encounter was a relatively quick one considering the amount of drama that led up to the final moment where Brandon surrendered the stored lust from his sacks to soil Hiroko's buttocks and bedsheets. In a fit of heaving and wheezing, he had kissed her with bestial passion at intervals, but it hadn't been reciprocal. He vanished as suddenly as he had appeared, like a hideous night-stalking psychopath, eluding all clever detectives in the micro-nick of time for a clean getaway. Leaving Hiroko alone to piece together the chilling, traumatic ordeal she had just endured.

Instead, her mind changed the channel. She was suddenly hoisted into a mental vignette where her story was a parallel-universe sequel, or a modern reboot of some Shakespeare shit: Brandon was damn Romeo and she, Juliet. What happened to her wasn't rape, because they were a couple, right? Also, instead of families hating each other, this Brandon-Romeo hated his own family, or just his father? She didn't know because the story was fiction. Albeit so, she faced her rapist at the breakfast table the following day when the family facade made its daily appointment with the Wilsons.

Morning discussion consisted of a debate sparked by youngest host-brother Billy who popped the question to his parents, inquiring about the existence of ghosts. The facade family broke into a schism of believers and nonbelievers. Hiroko's vote that she believed in ghosts made the split factions a draw game. Of course, she believed in the supernatural. She would have ghosts and skeletons in her closet for the rest of her life, thanks to her experience with them.

Almost exactly twenty-four hours later, the assault was repeated. More mayonnaise, more pain and pleasure for Hiroko. The pain came from fear of the unknown, false education against reality. The pleasure came with the comforting thought that she and Brandon were in some kind of Shakespearean secret affair. But something loathsome about Brandon's expression of love confused her, throwing a monkey wrench into her thought consoles. It prevented her from loving him or what he was doing to her. She had imagined such intimacy to be more affectionate, but Brandon's heated thrusts and grinding into her felt like something void of love or passion. She was crying, so how could she be happy? she wondered. The fantasy was slowly dissipating, like pipe dream smoke in the sultry air.

Brandon climaxed. He released a flatulent groan that was made to sound like a vine swinger in the jungle. It was a wonder how his outburst hadn't awakened anyone else in the house, but Hiroko remembered how huge the home was: Fred and Margaret's master bedroom was in an entirely separate annex of the house. Furthermore, the tag team snored in slumber like battling chainsaws. As for Cindy or youngest brother Billy, Brandon may have been unconcerned.

Perhaps he should have been a tad bit more concerned.

The moaning and groaning noises emitted from the activity of bedsprings and creaky wooden floors had awakened young Billy from the jump. He had been situated in the next adjacent room over. On the first night he had heard sounds coming from the guestroom, Billy retreated to cower in his covers, fearing possible Poltergeist or ghostly activity in the house. Such was the reason his sudden interest in ghosts was sparked into a discussion earlier that morning. His mommy and big brother Brandon convinced him that ghosts didn't exist, so he fearlessly investigated the source of the noises as if he was Encyclopedia Brown or Conan the Detective like Doyle's characters, magnifying glass and the whole nine.

Just as Brandon had breached the locked door—Hiroko could have sworn she had locked with firm approbation—it had remained unlocked on this night, and Billy had dipped his head inside the door, slightly ajar, the instant big brother Brandon was wetting up the naked back package of Hiroko's body with his special white glue. Billy was instantly freaked out of his mind. He escaped and retreated to his room, locking the door and panting under the covers, hoping that Brandon wouldn't do the same to him.

Billy, unlike Brandon, had never seen a pornographic movie in his entire life. His mother, Margaret, babied him so much she would cover his eyes if there was a picture of a woman in a bathing suit. Which made little sense, but it was because she didn't want her youngest to be pervs like her older son and her husband. Still, the kid was lost in the dark about sexual education, so he would later run to his mother and ask Margaret, "Why do women need men to piss in their butts?"

Of course, she was like, "WHAT are *you talking about*, Billy?"

Billy said, "Well, this mornin' I saw Brandon pissing into the Chinese girl's butt."

Margaret choked. She tried to remain calm and not lose her poise. She ran her hands through her curly dark hair. She pulled herself together and said, "Do you mean Hiroko, Billy? And she's not Chinese, dear, she is Japanese, OK?" She sat him down in a chair and crouched before him in the kitchen, grasping both of his shoulders lightly, then releasing him.

She said, "Now, tell me again . . . you say you saw Brandon doing *what* with Hiroko?"

Billy said "He was pissing inside her butt. But his pee was a freaky white color . . . it looked like he was squirtin' musterd . . . only, it wasn' musterd, it was squirtin' white pee . . ."

Innocent yet graphic, Margaret found it difficult to believe even Billy's Calvin & Hobbes imagination could scrape up a tale like that. Ordinarily, she would have dismissed such talk to his elaborate imagery, but not today. For in fact, while doing laundry the previous day, she could have sworn she had seen semen stains on Hiroko's bedroom linen. Not that Margaret was a forensic investigator;

she had seen enough of it in her own bedroom, but that was another story. She had elected to ignore her findings, hoping that it could have been better if she didn't grasp thought of anyone who would dare engage in such activity under her roof, especially one who was a guest. Moreover, even if the unfathomable were in fact true, who in God's name would she have been committing sin with? Billy had, in fact solved the case like the miniature sleuth he was; he had confirmed what she had been trying to deny with his tale of discovery. Still, rushing to judgment never solved many dilemmas, she surmised. She decided a thorough, or at least a proper, investigation was in order. She had to see for herself.

Margaret had then said, "Billy, listen to me . . ." The hands she placed on his upper arms returned, this time shaking him lightly to let him know she was serious. "I hope you are telling me the truth."

"I am telling you the truth, Mother! I swear I am!" Billy cried momentously.

Margaret sighed uneasily. She said "OK, I believe you. Well, honey, your brother wasn't peeing on Hiroko. He was . . . doing something else . . ." *Dear God!* she thought. *How can I lie to him and teach him to not be a liar? Oh, Brandon! How could you? I hope he didn't get her pregnant! Is she under aged?"*

Billy composed himself quickly and said, "Well, Mom, it looked like pee to me. I mean . . . it was comin' outta his ding-a-ling. He was yellin' like ya do when ya gotta go real bad, but he sounded like Tarzan . . ."

Margaret didn't want to hear any more. She said, "Right now, I want you to forget about that. What you saw was simply your brother acting naughty. Your father and I will have a nice, long talk with him. In the meantime, if you ever catch your brother engaging with Hiroko like how you claim you saw this morning . . . if you *ever* see that type of thing again, you come and fetch me right away! Do you hear me?"

"Yes, ma'am," Billy said.

Before Margaret released him, she kissed the top of his stringy sandy blond head and made him promise to keep their conversation a secret until the next day or two. Billy promised, then he ran outside to resume playing. An agitated hand raked through the curly black topping of Margaret's head again. She was now beginning to see Hiroko in a negative light. When they had first met her, she and Fred thought that Hiroko was a bright, intelligent, and mannered young lady from Japan, incapable of what Billy had described. Were they wrong?

As for Brandon, how much longer could she ignore his problems? Cindy had told her some things that had disturbed her, but as a young woman who had grown up with male siblings in more rural times and settings, Margaret knew what life for a female could be like with them. As such, she could sweep his antics under the rug given the reassurance from Cindy that his aggressive familiarity with her had ceased. But now this . . .

INTERLUDE (2)

MARGARET WOKE UP earlier than usual the following morning. She made a point to do so after retiring early, following an awkward dinner table where she was unusually silent. Fred thought she was having a headache on a bad night, because he wasn't in the mood to retire to his man cave for sessions with his X-rated paraphernalia.

As she was up and about, Margaret guessed that everyone in the house was still sleeping. The crack of dawn had yet to arrive, and the sun was an hour away from slicing its golden rays into the twilight darkness of the Willamette Valley. Fred was snoring away like a Paul Bunyan tool was lodged in his neck. Her daughter Cindy was a shroud of silence in her bed. The last rooms to be checked belonged to the boys and the guestroom that Hiroko occupied.

The guestroom was the last room on the far end of the hall. Next to that room was the spacious room Billy and Brandon shared. Margaret cut through the chase and approached Hiroko's room directly, turned the handle, and saw the door was locked. She stood there for a moment, as if she contemplated knocking. If there was something going on inside of the room, knocking would disrupt the action taking place. The participants would be forced to cease the activity and open the door. She had to catch them in the act, otherwise the shadow of doubt would never allow them to be convicted; they would deny any wrongdoing.

On second thought, she decided to take no action at all. Feeling a pinch of guilt that threatened to consume her, she thought *What if I'm wrong about my host-daughter?* It was obvious there was no moaning, no groaning like "Tarzan of the jungle" or anything like that. Maybe Billy had gotten his hands on some of Brandon's head shop candies again, causing him to have hallucinations. She cursed under her breath and figured she ought to crawl back into bed and snuggle against Fred's Viagra-activated sculpt. She concluded her "rounds" by doing what she should have done in the first place, and that was check out Brandon and Billy's room. She chided herself for the guilty sentence she issued upon Hiroko's image as a clean, pure, and sweet girl from the Orient.

Just as Margaret was approaching Brandon and Billy's room, she heard the creaking footsteps behind the door. A second or two later, methodical turning of the knob could be heard in the complete morning silence. She decided to dip quickly into the bathroom beyond her sons' room. Silently, she remained there at the bathroom door threshold, shielded by the opaque of predawn. If the footsteps came in the direction of the bathroom, she would quickly switch on the light and pretend she was using the space to not appear like a creepy, nosy, paranoid parent. Her ability to see with accuracy was courtesy of felicitous night lights situated in various locations throughout the corridor.

Not to her surprise, Margaret saw Brandon emerge from his room, still dressed in his Star Wars pajamas, robe, and slippers and carried a small backpack or bag of some kind. She became stiff as a corpse. As opposed to confronting her son, she remained quiet and cloaked in the dark of the bathroom entrance way. She watched as Brandon crept silently to the guestroom to the immediate right of his own, basically incriminating himself! Yet Margaret couldn't be convinced of his culpable actions so instantly. She continued to inspect his actions.

Stopping in front of the locked door, just as Margaret had done moments earlier, Brandon reached for the door handle and turned the knob. Almost as if expecting it to not have opened, Brandon reached inside of his backpack to produce from it a small tool of some kind. Margaret could not, from her vantage point down the hall, make out what exactly the tool was until Brandon had applied said object to the doorknob. It was a type of jeweler's piece precision mini driver—Maragret couldn't see it, but she knew what it was and the function it was used for around their household. It was generally for the purpose of which Brandon was then using it for, likely something he had found among her husband's mountains of tools and accessories in the sheds.

The mini driver Brandon used had a shaft so tiny it could fit easily within a small hole in the ancient doorknob center. Once within the inner bulb of the knob, the fitted wedge of the mini driver could attach to a screw's slit in it that activated the lock on the other side of the door. With Dungeons & Dragons high-level thief's dexterity, Brandon unlocked the guestroom's door, thus solving the mystery of how he was able to gain entry despite Hiroko's earnestly declaring that she had locked it. Margaret saw Brandon then slip his tall, portly Belushi-like bulk inside the room and shut the door in a remarkably smooth motion, with extra silence too. The door was once again locked when the door was completely shut.

Margaret's heart dropped. She choked back tears and vomit and leaned over the bathroom's sink. What right had Brandon to enter the room that Hiroko occupied? She wondered. Or, was it that Hiroko had invited him to come? Had she done something to seduce her son? It seemed obvious to her then that if Hiroko and her son had been engaging in an illicit affair the last couple of nights, she was just as much to blame as Brandon. Had she done something to corrupt his "good Christian morals"? Her poor, innocent Brandon had just turned eighteen years old, but he still wasn't a very worldly young man. They had lived in the countryside and burbs his entire life; complexity of Margaret trying to envisage Brandon as a sexual predator caused her to believe Hiroko had been the real, true aggressor. Furthermore, with Brandon's upbringing, never in a *million* years would she have expected to see him take interest in or consorting with a colored girl of Oriental descent.

The object of her participation with the immersion project Margaret lamented as if she was reminding herself of something she seemed to have forgotten, 'the object of allowing immersion of these people into our society through home-stay, is so that we can groom them to function in our Western culture and society. We give them an insight to what our lives are like so they can use it for a model of their growth as they learn to assimilate into our society. The benefits are twofold: they can improve their model minority statuses and we can bolster our image in cities and towns throughout the West of America. We will be praised for our "open-mindedness," and none would ever suspect us, or accuse us of being racist. Not to mention a cut of the money the host child's parents paid didn't hurt much either. Such was the dogma of the Wilsons and other host families like them who fancied taking in guests when business was slow. Doing deals with entities such as WACK, they could receive about a thousand bucks for every head they took into their homes for two months. This also included a stipend for expenses related to food and hygiene supplies—especially if the host child was a female. Such compensation was barely needed for food as the Wilsons would supply their guests with potatoes and other vegetables from their own gardens. Anything else they supplied other than what little money was used was bread and water.

Now it was time for Margaret to put an end to the shit show. She composed herself and stood erect before the sink, then exited the bathroom. She approached the guestroom again and placed her ear against the door. Faintly she could hear what sounded like a struggle, followed by Hiroko's pleading voice. Margaret turned the knob handle, and of course, it was locked. Instead of knocking, she continued to listen at the door.

Hiroko's muffled, pleading voice went, "P-please, Brandon . . . I cannot do it again. My . . . my body hurts there, where you put in your penis. I . . . I think I have been bleeding there . . ."

Brandon's voice sounded equally muffled to Margaret from the other other side of the room's door, but she was more familiar with his voice than she was with Hiroko's. She could make out what he had said accurately.

He had said, "Stop wigglin', just . . . be..still," with intonation that reflected an authoritative cruelty, an agitated drill sergeant or yawping boss at the office was what he sounded like. "Just stay put, I'm not gunna hurt'cha." There was a rustle and squeaking of bedsprings, as if someone was jumping upon it. "You wanna stay a virgin, don'cha?"

Margaret felt like an eavesdropping pervert in her own home. She snapped out of her damn coma. What more proof had she needed? Inside the room, Brandon had pounced upon Hiroko like Romeo in a Shakespeare play would do, relieved her once more of her pajamas and panties waist down at the time Margaret started banging on the door. It was too late.

She heard Hiroko's chime tingly songbird–type tone of moan become a series of gagging contraltos cut short by a crisp staccato of shrill squeaking in between. The symphony of sin had a blend of Brandon's tempestuously heavy breathing for bass, practically hee-hawing like an ass donkey.

Margaret demanded that Brandon open the door, still banging loud enough to wake the entire house. She was possessed by so much determination she might have knocked the door down with her blows. Incredibly, Fred swallowed his buzzsaw and was awakened from slumber. He rushed downstairs to see what the hell was going on. Of course, Cindy and Billy woke up too. Margaret was crying by then and frantic. Neither Brandon nor Hiroko had opened the door.

As best she could, through tears she strained to conceal in front of her two kids with worried faces, she brought Fred up to speed. Incensed, Fred too began banging steady hammer fists upon the door while Margaret ushered Cindy and Billy back to their rooms. Easier said than done: Billy obeyed while Cindy stayed, peeking out of her cracked door.

"It's Brandon, isn't it?" Cindy stage-whispered to her mother.

"Get in your room as you were told, young lady, this very instant!" Margaret shouted as if she had snapped and gone batty batshit bonkers. Her insane look at the early dawn was chilling, and Cindy slammed her door shut with herself securely inside. Whatever demon she saw outside couldn't have been her mother.

Outside, when Brandon finally came to the door, he tried to put on a front like nothing had been going on. The lie he attempted to tell was a would-be plausible spin about him and Hiroko having a late-night chat playing Connect Four bullshit games, and he fell asleep in her room by accident. Margaret allowed him to spew his nonsense before slapping his face.

"Don't you dare lie to me, young man!" she said with a potentially lethal index fingernail inches from the slits Brandon had for eyes more or less.

"Mom, yer just overreactin' as always." He rubbed his cheek that got the sting of the zap. He was fully dressed, and even had his robe on again.

Fred was trying to seem as if he was confused and low-key, hoping that Brandon had been telling the truth. It wasn't going to be tolerated by his wife. Margaret had already seen and heard enough to make her decision about Brandon's action final. What was more shocking than anything else was Brandon's callous, indifferent attitude about what he had done, as if he was clinging to his story—sticking to it—and that was, nothing happened. And furthermore, if anything *had* happened, it was no big deal. So the fuck what?

At long last, Margaret decided it was appropriate to see to how Hiroko was faring. She sat upon the bed crying, clutching a pillow to her lap and face. Fred could be heard verbally chastising Brandon with some "You're in big trouble, mister, and got a lot of explainin' to do . . .." before she shut the door, leaving them outside so she could be alone with her host-daughter. Ordinarily, she wasn't with the idea of providing or offering illicit, psychotropic drugs or hallucinogens to minors in any way, shape, or form; but due to the grave circumstances that were present, she saw herself as having not much of a choice. From her own experience as a former hippie that had actually attended Woodstock in her youth, she knew it wouldn't kill her; but as a mother, well, she didn't have much choice and no time to feel guilty about what she was going to do. But she had to give Hiroko something for her nerves, to calm her down in the wake of the agony she had suffered. After that, Hiroko's Disney-Shakespeare romantic fantasy was fading into a rabbit-hole portal to a locale of bizarre characters smoking hashish out of pipes, grinning cats, and mushroom furniture. A very short time later, Margaret's ministrations had Hiroko practically feeling like, *What ordeal?*

INTERLUDE (3)

THE FANTASY WASN'T over, but the home-stay experience with the Wilsons came to an abrupt and abysmal end. Margaret Wilson did an illegal thing and laced Hiroko's Alka-Seltzer with an apocryphal Tricyclic substance. Later, after some rest, she gave Hiroko a weird-tasting lozenge coated with opioid analgesic with a combined effect of memory loss and anti-anxiety or depression being the desired outcome. A highly criminal offense to administer such to a minor still a child in the eyes of the law. Even if Hiroko wasn't a citizen of the United States, the visa she legitimately acquired provided her certain rights. Margaret had time to think about all of these things, but she still thought that the risk was what she had to do. After all, she was a criminal. She had to do what she had to do, according to her logic.

Hiroko, of course, was shipped out. First she went to nearby Salem for a couple of days. Nancy Tanaka-Ryan came down from the big city of Portland and took Hiroko under her care. They stayed at a transient motel just outside of town. She was unaware at the time that Hiroko was under the influence of some mind-altering antidepressants and slept almost the entire time under her care. Hiroko was considerably upbeat otherwise, yet reasonably dismal. It was peculiar, but Nancy didn't question it at the time. The sudden emergence of a need to cancel a home-stay setup was neither unusual or rare—no big deal—but to cover their tracks, reasonable investigations had to be made. Therefore, Nancy Tanaka-Ryan had to stick around Salem and get the details on what went down at the Wilson

Ranch. Meanwhile, Hiroko would be introduced to Nancy's two hapa teenage daughters Bianca and Dana. They kept her company at the motel.

After the investigation was done, Nancy Tanaka-Ryan was fit to be tied. They had a serious issue on their hands. It was a sobering situation, but she did well to keep her emotions under wraps. Phone calls had to be made, Vancouver, Tokyo, Seattle—Portland back to where they were headed. After the two days in Salem, Nancy arranged to have Hiroko put up at a one-foot-in-the-grave practically abandoned out-of-business youth hostel in a shabby, low-end side street around Pearl District.

This hostel was adjacent to Rusty B. Nail Mechanic School and served as a dwelling for some of its students and/or visiting faculty. The walls of the exterior halls had chipped paint of a gray color that might have once been light green. The stairs were rusty, and the tile floors looked like they needed a good mopping. A lingering odor permeated the air, suggesting every toilet in the building remained perpetually unflushed. The place seemed more suitable for the roaches that scurried about than actual humans, but some Puerto Rican–looking dude walked by wearing only a pair of white shorts easily mistakable for underwear and eating a bowl of cereal. He made his unique appearance just as Nancy moved Hiroko in. Of course, this residence hall was co-ed, but due to Tanaka-Ryan's pull, she was able to get Hiroko a safer, secluded quarter with no roommates, female or male.

Bianca and Dana were almost the same age as Hiroko. They took interest in her right away. They had always been interested in Japanese people, the pure-blooded ones that they apparently descended from. They, like their mother, Nancy, had absolutely no knowledge at all about the Japanese language because they were all from Portland. The reason Nancy brought them along was because Hiroko needed someone to be around her and keep her company until matters could be sorted out. The two daughters were unaware of what was actually going on, they thought they were merely spending time on weekends helping their mother with her job, which was babysitting the exchange students, a "job" they usually found enjoyable and fun. Mostly they would watch TV, play old-school games like Monopoly, UNO, and Scrabble and now, since they were coming of age, they added talking about boys to that list. It helped to cheer Hiroko up when she started coming down off the substances she had been slipped.

Meanwhile, unbeknownst to Hiroko at that time, the Wilsons had made the one-hour drive to Portland. They had agreed to have a meeting with WACK and Nancy Tanaka-Ryan at their headquarters there. Alice Gourd came down from Vancouver, Canada, as well. They had to have a discussion about the hush proceedings that needed to take place. The Wilsons were shitting bricks, and rightfully so. There were potentially cataclysmic ramifications involved, and steps were necessary to keep the cops, lawyers, and the press out of it. WACK was like, "Calm down, we've handled situations like this before," and they actually had.

Needless to say for the Wilsons, especially the father, Fred, they wanted to beat the crap out of Brandon, but they couldn't do anything like that because that would tarnish their "good Christian" wannabe disguise they scammed on the community. Margaret played it up to the point of fanaticism, convincing enough for Fred to follow along, so they never used corporal punishment. As a result, they raised a sociopath, but that was now the least of their worries. For despite their disappointment and state of being pissed off at Brandon, they didn't want to lose him to jail, a mental institution, or prison.

Their worry dilemma was on account of the fact that even if WACK—Nancy Tanaka-Ryan and Alice—could successfully sweet-talk Hiroko into forgiving Brandon for (the alleged) "violating" her, meaning to a point where she didn't press charges, not coming forward with any information about what took place at the Wilson's residence, there was *still* the issue of the statutory law.. Brandon was 18 and Hiroko—although not a citizen of the USA—was only seventeen! This they thought could present some serious problems. What's more, Margaret had concerns about whether or not Brandon had nutted up in Hiroko, and if he did and Hiroko were to get knocked up, the entire scenario would be over-the-top problematic.

Sensing this fortuitously, Margaret drugged Hiroko a little bit to cloud her skull a bit, damage her memory. That way, she would have questionable thoughts about what had actually happened. She knew it was wrong, it was a rotten thing to do, and were she to have been caught—which she never was—she would have gotten into more trouble—they all would have, in all likelihood. But she took the chance, and it turned out to be somewhat of a good mood on their end.

Reason was because when Alice Gourd spoke (in Japanese for clarity), Hiroko revealed that she did remember being intimate with Brandon, but also seemed to have indicated that the liaison was *consensual*.

This didn't compute with Nancy Tanaka-Ryan. For if it were so, then why the hell was Margaret freaking out and getting all unglued; cutting the home-stay short and such was odd, she reasoned.

Alice had spoken with Hiroko alone but had videotaped the session. She reviewed the tape footage with Nancy first, but since she didn't understand Japanese, she was still in the dark. Alice had to break it down to her.

"It appears that Hiroko is either delusional, or we've been hearing a totally different version of the way things transpired," Alice said, drooling and lightly snorting in between every three words or so, as if she had trouble breathing through her nostrils. "Either way, we have our work cut out for us."

Nancy said, "So basically, she and the son got a little fresh with one another, the mother thought it was a rape, but it wasn't? I'm sorry, but I don't get it, Alice."

"Neither do I," Alice said, "but based on the conversation you just saw on the tape, Hiroko was under some sort of impression that she and Brandon were in some type of boyfriend-and-girlfriend relationship. And what happened came as a result of them becoming overly fond, like you said. So it was basically consensual."

Nancy said "OK, if that sticks then the Wilsons are clear of one of their worries. I still don't get it. How can the mother think it may have been rape and then the would-be victim state consent? So resolute she was in her indictment, she decided to end the home-stay immediately. It just doesn't add up to me."

Alice liked Nancy, but at times the woman could be a dingbat that got on people's nerves. Her thinking was a little screwed. Alice said, "Nancy, you have two daughters, and around the same age. Would you allow them to stay under the roof of a teenage boy in heat? I think Mrs. Wilson did the right thing and brought the home-stay to an immediate end. Oh, and from what I gather, he sodomized her. They didn't have what we'd consider traditional sex . . ."

"How horrible . . ." Nancy paused to grieve somewhat for Hiroko, feeling sorry for her even more. "But at least that's yet another worry that the Wilson's need not stress. She won't get pregnant that way, if what you're saying is absolutely correct."

Alice said, "Yes. And the Wilsons are well aware that in the state of Oregon, an individual aged seventeen years or younger is not viewed to be able to consent to sexual intercourse. Of any kind. They are still seen as minors in the eyes of the law. So you see, this is the biggest hurdle we're now facing. Even if only one year separates Brandon and Hiroko, the law will still stand. Everything is riding on whether or not we can keep Hiroko quiet about what went on there."

Nancy shrugged. She didn't like the idea much, but she was a scumbag just like the others at WACK, and she had to remain loyal if she wanted to keep her "skate job." Her personal feelings were irrelevant. "OK, then," she said to Alice, "what do we do now?"

Alice said, "Well, I have to get this videotape, your report, the Wilsons' statements and documents, and shoot back up to the WACK HQ. They are going to decide how next we may, or may not, proceed legally or otherwise. You know the drill.

"In the meanwhile, Hiroko has to stay here in Portland. We still owe her what she paid for. She didn't really do anything wrong."

Nancy cut in. "Yeah, I agree. I feel like she's the victim here. It's unfortunate that the Wilsons' creepy son is the actual predator, the real criminal here, but we have to protect him. It doesn't seem fair."

Alice said, "Believe me, I get what you're saying. I mean, gee whiz, Nancy . . . how long have we been doing this? We've seen some terrible shit over the years, I understand, but the people like the Wilsons are our bread and butter. They get us paid, and they put food on our table. And there are a lot of 'em out there, and just as many of these desperate study-abroad seekers willing to shell out their last coins for us to place them with those host families. Without them, we couldn't be able to enjoy this dream job."

"Very well then," Nancy resigned, she knew Alice was right. "I'll bring the girls by here on weekends, but during the week, they have school."

Alice, who was of a higher rank within the company than Nancy, didn't like the idea of being strict with her subordinates. Being one of those, Nancy could sometimes be a bubblehead, and Alice tried not to bring it to Nancy's attention that this was the way she felt about her. Alice's beef with Nancy was that she was dizzy and remiss. Sure, it was altruistic for her to peel off time from the schedules of her daughters to "babysit" a seventeen-year-old visitor from Japan on weekends, but what was supposed to occupy the young guest during the week?

Alice asked, "By the way, Nancy, what's the schedule for our English school affiliate associated with this here hostel?"

Nancy gasped and clasped her mouth and grasped the sound of her voice spewing "Oh, shit! This school is for budding auto mechanics! I completely forgot to contact the English schools—there're several actually—but oh, I'm really sorry. It's just I've been having my hands full with mostly this case. I have to come back and forth all the way out here from Hazelwood to the Pearl, and I'm bringing the girls along and—"

Alice put a stop to Nancy's run-on ranting. She fucked up, Alice got it. She waved her massive mitt in a motion that seemed to read, *Down, pet, down . . . easy . . . easy! It's a-l-l right.*

"There's always the travel center on Thirty-Seventh Street," Nancy blurted out, but Alice swatted her talk away like toxic mist.

Alice said, "No, their accommodations are a bit better of standard than our budget can allow. We already looked that one up. I was thinking about the hostel on the southeast side. You remember the one on Hawthorne Boulevard? Hey— do they still have the all-you-can-eat one-dollar pancakes?!" Her face lit up in demonic excitement as she awaited the response.

Nancy gravely disappointed her. "Um . . . yeah, I remember that one. I'm not sure if they still have pancakes, but unfortunately, the real dilemma is WACK is no longer an affiliate of their network. We have no dealings with them, so we're regulated to these lodgment quarters of secondary community colleges . . . I . . ."

Alice gave Nancy the "Shh!" finger. She didn't have time to fuss or argue. She was hungry. She had work to do; they had that case to settle with Hiroko. Since realizing there would be no flapjacks or Aunt Jemima breakfast, her attitude changed. She wanted to eat something, so she was in a tad bit of a rush to leave. She had to catch a 9:30 flight that evening back to Vancouver, and she wanted to hit a buffet before she endured yet another flight and its cuisine. That being said, she had no reservations about leaving Nancy to her duties, albeit she was careless and negligent and reminders were needed to keep her on her toes.

The Puerto Rican–looking dude came by again, softly singing some Spanish tune to himself. Apparently, he too was residing at the hostel. He vanished inside the door to his room; his cereal bowl dropped a few corny flakes in his wake.

A fat roach like the size and dimension of a 'double A' battery glided across the chipped tile floor and began feasting away on the spilled flakes and milk. The two long, toothpick-length antennae on its head must have summoned comrades because three more of the insects showed up for breakfast seconds later.

Frustrated at the sight, Alice came up with an idea. She said, "Why don't you take Hiroko to your place out in Centennial Hills? That way, you can save yourself the trip and not have to come all the way out here to bring the girls to this . . . dump!"

Nancy had a look on her face like, *Wow, why didn't I think of that?*

Alice said, "Yes, because of this unorthodox matter, we can redo the paperwork and have you documented as the host-parent. You can take three hundred dollars bonus. I'll write it off when I get back to the Vancouver Abbot Street HQ. The sooner we all get out of this shithole, the better." She looked at the dark roaches positioned at various locations all over the cruddy wall, and instead of being disgusted, she thought of mint chocolate chip ice cream. She began to sweat. "Let's get the hell out of here! This place doesn't even look like a hostel—it's more like a fleabag flophouse." She looked as if she was going to have a panic attack.

They came out into the street. It was a bit noisy with cars, cabs, and buses, and the clatter of footsteps treading the concrete sidewalks. Shitty bums and homeless people were searching for treasures under garbage can lids on the block. There was a musty odor in the air, but a lot more lucid than the halls of that hostel they'd just left. Alice pulled out a long Virginia Slim 100 and lit it, and with her huge hand looked like she was smoking a piece of spaghetti.

Nancy said finally "OK, so I'll inform my husband. He will be away for most of the summer anyway, but I'll still need to speak with him. So we'll let Hiroko stay here for just tonight. I'll be back tomorrow and pick her up. We also have to prepare some guest accommodations too I guess . . . anyway, I'll take care of everything. Come on, let me get you back to your hotel."

They left.

After bidding farewell to her new friends, Hiroko was alone. Her fantasy was still playing out, only now she was feeling awfully strange. Like no feeling she had ever experienced before, and she didn't know why, or what was happening to her. She was oblivious to the fact that she had been drugged. The effects were still making her feel dizzy, but she could not have known the reason for it. She was aware that the home-stay with the Wilsons had finished. She and Brandon had "broken up"; she had "made love" for the first time, but it didn't feel very pleasant; and she was now in another hostel that resembled an insane asylum, one that made the refurbished brick dereliction in Canada she stayed in seem like an opulent getaway resort in comparison. All these things she was aware of, and she thought that she would be overwrought and sad about it, but strangely, she wasn't. It was a puzzling thing. But somehow, she was apparently still happy. And she was excited about staying with the Tanaka-Ryans, and she was just as happy to meet her new friends Bianca and Dana as they were to meet her. As for her "Romeo" Brandon, it was unfortunate that it had to end, she guessed, but that's the way tragedies go . . . sometimes no happy ending.

INTERLUDE (4)

NANCY WENT HOME and told her husband, Norman, about Hiroko coming to stay with them for the next month. He was cool with it. He was an easygoing baseball player, and his team would be away for a majority of the summer anyway because they had a series of away games. They didn't have as big a house as the Wilsons, nor the ranch or acres of land to run wild about, but the home was cozy, suburban, and had grassy lawns and clean parks around the way. Hiroko liked this atmosphere a little better than the country type outback setting she beheld when at the Wilson's in Silverton.

During the days following Hiroko's move to the Ryans', WACK representatives were busy like worker bees on Hiroko's case. In between hefty feasts, Alice Gourd was a workaholic juggernaut when she wanted to be. She busied herself contacting their wide network of affiliates and council members around the world. Their organization, and structure was not unlike a sorority. It began as a sort of social club of women who studied psychology and psychiatry; then it became incorporated, and chapters spread throughout the world. From each of the new chapters, a newer project was formed from the branch out and these trickled into organizations and foundations like WACK. In Japan, the society was known as the Josei Shinri Shakai, and in the Western United States, Heta Omicron Zeta, the Women's Society of Psychology. This was the program that was responsible for placing Hiroko in Canada, and VILE Institute. Because WACK had an existing conjunction with VILE, they were as such able to enlist their "special services" to deal with Hiroko's matter.

After Alice Gourd in Vancouver gave her the go-ahead, Nancy Tanaka-Ryan called in a team of specialists from accredited institutions of psychological, social, and criminal academia, one in each field; and all three spoke Japanese fluently. It cost a grip to acquire their services, but this time, customer Fred Ryan was footing the bill. He had to sell part of his property to arrive at the several figures it took to compensate the needed individuals, for duties, hotel accommodations, and travel expenses. It was a mighty sum of kopecks, but he was a desperate parent that didn't want his rectal cranial–inverted son to be sent to jail, prison, or worse. Hiroko, in the meantime, was persuaded into believing that she was required by a mandate of the WACK Home-Stay Program to meet with this trio of "teachers." The rundown hostel Hiroko stayed one night in had a conjunction language school located a few blocks away. The Heta Omicron Zeta Women's Society of Psychology authorities pulled up on Hiroko there.

Nancy Tanaka-Ryan was a short, small woman of five feet four inches, but for some reason, she liked to wheel around the streets of Portland in a glossy, light-plum limited edition 1978 Cadillac Sedan DeVille. She claimed to have grabbed it at an auction that featured seized vehicles of criminals and drug dealers. The antique, plush spaceship hog hummed like a negro spiritual dirge from a "mammy." The seats were so plush Hiroko felt she was being swallowed by a sponge. Nancy had a Chaka Khan CD in the stereo and cruised the ride along Northwest Lovejoy Street. Her vessel had enough room to haul everyone—notwithstanding the tight fit—and they hit the "slabtown" slums. Luckily, Alice didn't tag along for this meeting.

The Snow Job Dream Team consisted of a retired elder Japanese witch from Japan; a haggard, somewhat disheveled-haired middle-aged hapa who was from both Japan and the United States; and, finally, another American white woman, a heavyset, short-haired blonde but nowhere near as colossal as Alice. She had a thick New York back east accent because she was from Buffalo. These three "scholars"—Akiyo Sugimoto, Sindrala Wada, and April Roubous—respectively might each have had their own back stories, which alone would qualify for epic episodes of a *Ripley's Believe It Or Not*, but for that momentous affair, they were summoned together to join forces in order to carry out a diabolical mission. They first had to see where her head was. They had already done their homework and had seen the video-taped session she had with Alice Gourd. After they assessed Hiroko's mental state based on their interpretations and findings, they would advance to the more complicated objective, and that was to make Hiroko believe lies.

It wasn't as difficult as they had imagined. In fact, they would later reflect in retrospect how simple the mission had been.

Since they were all professionals in their own areas of expertise and had been through horse-and-pony shows of many shapes, sizes, and colors, their duties seemed to be cake-walk routine. Even though none of them had met previously, they still were bonded by an age-old sisterhood and had minimal difficulties working together. The hardest part of the desideratum was hoisted upon Nancy, who had to chauffeur the women around, who stayed at three different hotels.

Even the youngest of the three, glasses-wearing peg-top-figured April Roubous boasted a fabulous PhD in psychology. Out of the three, she was the one who seemed the most human. She actually joked, laughed, and smiled a lot. She was the most upbeat and, along with Nancy of similar jocose nature, served to lessen the tense atmosphere.

Sindrala Wada had come up from Salem and insisted on staying at the extravagant, iconic Heathman Hotel the entire time she was to be in Portland. She was some type of social worker who had her own collection of master's degrees to brag about. She was also a big-head bitch with some furtive pull in the capital city, as well as the neighboring Eugene area, so she was relatively arrogant. Wada was there more on behalf of the Wilsons than Hiroko. She was to be the damage-control agent for the "good whites of America." She was in her late thirties; she might have been a stunner decades earlier, and were she to update her fashion and hairstyle, she might have still been considered a looker to some. Mostly, however, when she appeared, she always seemed to be frowning due to her Asian-rooted facial composition, and her clothes were wrinkled, hair bedraggled as if she had finished receiving a hard quickie pummeling moments before seen.

Finally, Akiyo Sugimoto, a decorated academic scholar, former police liaison, and part-time professor from Kyoto, Japan, fresh off the boat who was decidedly the most convincing element of the crew. She was a hard-nosed, stern older lady, and her attitude reflected such. The closest offering of a smile from her came in the form of a tightening of her closed, wrinkled lips and rapidly blinking eyes that could have been interpreted as conveying the statement of *Hurry up, let's get this thing under way.*

Before that could happen, though, Hiroko had to be pacified, or "softened up." They didn't want to make her feel as if she was under any undue pressure. So they made it seem like they were all on a simple tour of Oregon, and as a part of the WACK Study Abroad Home-Stay Program, it was a feature that Hiroko was "invited" to tag along. She would have probably liked it much better accompanied by kids more around her age, like Nancy's Bianca and Dana; but she fell for the quasi-tour dupe anyway and was relatively stoked about it. It was her first time to really see an American city in depth.

With Nancy behind the wheel, they rode all over town and had a really nice time, or they made it seem as if they were having a joyful outing. In actuality, for the adults, it was work. They showed Hiroko a good time by taking her shopping for clothes, souvenirs, and gifts for family and friends back in Japan. They took pictures and checked out various statues and plaques and historical sites all over various districts and the famous Gateway Transit Center. Hiroko was pleased with the excursion overall, and she had no idea of the severity involving her. She thought everything was a part of the home-stay Experience. So far, she had had a much better time three days in Portland than she had three weeks at the Wilsons'.

Nancy's daughters, Bianca and Dana, who were twins, had been unwitting co-conspirators in their mother's game plan, which was to prime her and season her with kindness adding a dash of lavished attention, plus a glaze of genuine interest. In this way, any somber feelings Hiroko might have had would be trimmed off. People showing her a good time would have, hopefully, made her forget about the bad. It had worked all too well. Bianca and Dana were more intellectually stimulating for Hiroko than was Cindy back in Silverton. In fact, the more she thought about it, and the more she became less head-clouded. She began to see the entire Wilson family as peculiar. She couldn't put her finger on it, but by far, the new placement with the Ryans proved to be a more interesting place, as she was more or less a city girl herself back in Japan. The urban atmosphere suited her, she supposed. She was also growing fonder of the Ryans day by day.

Tanaka-Ryan's caddy wafted along West Burnside Street. How she, with a spotless driving record, could dip and swerve the humongous hog in and out of traffic patches without incident was mystifying. She defied every stereotype of an American of Asian descent, but Hiroko was oblivious to such labels. To Hiroko, she was just a friendly woman with a vibrant personality, and one who could drive really well. Because of her, Hiroko received a picturesque street tour of scenic, low dive, "slabtown." The CD in the stereo player had changed to Evelyn "Champagne" King crooning vibrantly about "needing action." Nancy sang the jam word for word like it was karaoke. Hiroko was tickled silly hearing and watching her mini performance from the backseat of the whip.

They finally found a tatterdemalion greasy spoon on the east side that had free parking, so Nancy pulled in. The place wasn't crowded, aside from neighborhood regulars, winos, drunks, vagrants, and derelict addicts; but the booths were roomy and spacious, so she decided this place was as good as any, despite the lackluster decor. A vintage, cello-formed hag waitress approached the table when the five were comfortably squeezed into the booth of imitation leather vinyl seats riddled with cigarette burn dots and a table that wasn't burnished with a cloth but wiped by hand, merely swatting crumbs and other matter to the sticky linoleum flooring beneath.

The scabrous waitress, maybe late forties, reeking of perfume-covered grill house farts, was smacking loudly on gum in her chapped lip jib. She repined at the table of assorted-sized people with a sneer of crooked, coffee-stained beige bites and glared at Hiroko impatiently, all the while tapping her pencil on the order pad as if to say, *Hurry up with yer order, fer crissakes!*

Hiroko had been peering indecisively at the diner's menu from the time they had been seated but couldn't decide what she wanted to have. After nearly a month of eating primarily potatoes, almost anything was a welcome change. She really wanted a milkshake, so she asked for one and passed the menu to the woman seated next to her.

Sindrala Wada, who may have been as impatient as both Akiyo Sugimoto and the waitress combined interrupted the silent moment of Hiroko's indecision took control and liberty to order for everyone. She said to the horrid server. "Just bring us the whole cake, yeah the one with the yellow frosting and gray layers . . . plus, four coffees, black. Any objections from you, ladies?"

There were none. Everyone seemed to be in favor of the selection, especially April who applauded Wada for choosing the frosted banana bread cake she had been eyeballing.

Wada was in her no-nonsense, cut-through-the-chase mood. Like everyone else, she was ready to get to work, complete the job as expeditiously as possible, and enjoy the remainder of her paid requested appearance like a mini vacation. She gave Nancy a nod, urging her to get the ball rolling.

Like her Triple A minor league baseball hubby, Nancy Tanaka-Ryan took the first pitch and started in on Hiroko. At the behest of the experts, they coached Nancy to use her trusted host-mother role to ease into the topics to be of discussion.

Nancy said, "So tell me again about what exactly happened at the Wilson home, Hiroko."

Hiroko said, "Brandon suddenly fell in love for me."

It was some sad shit, even Nancy had to agree. The girl was delusional, and were she an elderly person, she would be dismissed as senile. Nancy didn't have time to feel sorry for her; she had a job to do. She asked Hiroko, "Do you love Brandon?"

Hiroko shook her head. "I don't know," she said. "I think I could love him. Or, in a dream I could love him. But I don't know if I love him in this world."

Nancy's stomach was knotting up. She was in danger of allowing a dam flood to rise underneath her bottom eyelids. In all her years with that business, she never enjoyed this part of it, having seen it more times than she would have cared to remember. Only this time she was struggling to keep from retching from the trenches of her belly. From what she could tell from empirical knowledge only, Hiroko was mind-fucked. She asked her, "Do you want anything bad to happen to Brandon? Do you think he should be punished?"

Hiroko shook her head emphatically, declaring opposition. Then her innocent cartoon like eyes swelled up and became teary. Of course, Nancy consoled her, but she then switched seats with Sindrala, so she would be flanked by her and Akiyo. They began the tag-team interrogation on Hiroko; they switched off and on like random flashing lights with their questions, and Hiroko felt somewhat nettled.

April was the empathetic—effusive with humanitarianism—kinder voice in the group. Akiyo and Sindrala, who Hiroko was then sandwiched between now, were a bit different. They were the imperious, uncompromising sorts, tough minded and serious about carrying out their job duties no matter how easy or difficult. In so doing, they didn't feel the need to go out of their way to be extra nice.

Akiyo and Sindrala Wada employed such tactics as subtle intimidation, but in the form of staring with ominous glares. It was like good cop, bad cop, and Hiroko was getting double-tag-teamed as the cake arrived for the intermission. Nancy and April dug into the heap of conglomerated calories while they all drank coffee out of their ears, already trying to get refills. Hiroko took a bite of the cake and thought she was going to get instant diabetes. She slowed down, in addition to the table's conversation, the brick of baked sugar was leaving a bad taste in her mouth. When the break was over and all the casual talk was finished—"I used to come here when I was younger" bullshit, the interrogation continued. This time, Sindrala took the helm.

Sindrala said, "So back to what we were discussing," in a methodical, slow speech pattern so as not to be misunderstood. Again she tried to put a fast-forward on the proceedings. She added "You wouldn't want Brandon to go to jail, would you, Hiroko?" Her hand held a voice tape recorder. It was by Sindrala, clicked on Record, and placed casually on the table.

Hiroko was concerned and confused. She asked, "Why will Brandon go to jail?" as she felt a feeling of sadness suddenly grip a lump inside her chest.

Sindrala continued, "Well, there is a law here in America that makes it a bad thing for a boy and girl to be naked together in the way that you and Brandon were."

Time for Akiyo to cut in the dance with some old-school Japanese mystique and "wisdom of the ancients" liquefied into the flow of her language and speech. She said, "It is a serious thing, girl. Also a very critical situation we have here.

"We are Japanese," Akiyo stated with authority and pride, "and we, according to our culture, we do not want to be a burden upon our hosts. That is not our way. We are people who choose to avoid conflicts. Although your current predicament involves a paramour, or friendship, or whatever kind of relationship you had with the son of your host family, your ages are of particular issue now. While we realize that this may *or may not* have been your fault, and we are not here to accuse you, however, we must ascertain for certain that your participation in this affair was mutual."

Akiyo's presence was intended to influence Hiroko to apply her trust in another Japanese person, to ensure her propensity to be truthful. Problem was, Hiroko's drugging was something none of them had been aware of, and it had apparently affected her memories somewhat. The "truth" was based on her feelings, not precisely the facts.

The entire conversation was in Japanese, and throughout this time, April would quietly translate for Nancy, who would chime in intermittently, wherever applicable.

Nancy said, "Yeah, Hiroko, nobody's gonna be mad at you if you tell the truth."

April injected with a giggle, "Don't fret too much, honey. It's pa-a-rt of growin' up." Although she was a warm, lighthearted sort, her thick eastern accent made her sound gruff and tough like a dude, and her voice tended to boom across the table like she was speaking through a microphone, aggressive like throwing jabs and felt like punches when her words arrived to Hiroko's brain. Fortunately, the other diner patrons paid them no attention. They were mostly degenerate, incoherent transients busy swatting flies away from their plates or taking up space in the place to not sleep on the streets.

April said lastly, ".Growin' up can be a lifetime thing, honey . . . and, ow' hoa-mones, as women, sometimes we develop too swoon, or maybe at different paces, no two wav us a-h 'like, but as women too, we understand. Y'know, sometimes with ow'a development, we tend to get a little less inhibited . . ." She looked around the table as her colleagues nodded in support, but Hiroko wasn't exactly catching all the pedantic talk. It tended to slip April's mind at times that she was speaking to a non-native English speaker. She quickly switched from backstreet Buffalo boxing gym bearing back to a contained and cordial Japanese textbook speak, to translate what she had just said.

Sindrala expelled a listless sigh and said, "We-e un-n-derstand, Hiroko, if you had . . . feelings for Brandon . . . if you loved him . . . we understand. We get it. We're human, like Alice here just explained, we're women. It's OK if you wanted to show him affection. Trust me, we are not angry with you about that."

Nancy added, "Yeah, we're not angry with you at all," as soon as April could translate the words from Sindrala.

"Perhaps," Sindrala said "it would have been better if you had waited a bit until you were older . . . but again, we are not faulting you for what happened. We just want to make that clear. But, Hiroko, you said you loved Brandon, right?"

She didn't. Hiroko had never stated that she loved Brandon, and Sindrala knew it. The others did too; only Nancy was a little bit in the dark about what was going on.

Hiroko had given a vague statement about her feelings for Brandon, but she had not stated that she loved Brandon. The voice recorder would have reflected that, but at that time of the conversation, it had not yet been turned on!

Sindrala repeated the question: "Hiroko . . .you said you loved Brandon, right?" It was a coaxing, hypnotic inquisition as she leaned her face slightly, slowly in the direction toward Hiroko, with the trademark haunting, portentous stare.

Hiroko said, "Yes . . . I do," sealing her fate, not understanding that her answer was induced.

With a satisfied grin appearing ever so briefly and for the first time, Sindrala shot a glance to everyone at the table, like, *Yeah, we got it!*

She then said, "You also love the Wilson family, right? Were they nice to you? What did you all do together? Did they take you camping? Canoeing? Fishing? Horseback riding? Tell us . . . how do you feel about the Wilson family?"

Hiroko could remember having fun times with other members of the Wilson family, it was true. That part of her memory wasn't marred or murky. Such times as highlighted when brought up while speaking caused her to remember the event.

Of course, those pleasant times would more often than not be overshadowed by the horrid development of rape, or even "date rape," but those weren't the events Sindrala mentioned. Based on that information, Hiroko could render no response other than "Yes, I love my host family. They were very kind to me. I am indebted to them for allowing me the experience of living with them."

Akiyo swooped in like an old cawing magpie with ancient *katanas* for a beak, slashing Hiroko's brain with speech "Well, child, if you love the host family, the right thing to do, the honorable thing to do, the Japanese way of doing things, would be to let this go. Cease and desist with any ideas that might be formulating in your mind about taking further action regarding this matter. What happened at the residence of your host family was just as much your fault as it was theirs. They were very charitable and kind to take you in, urchin, you stayed in their home and used their facilities. Wouldn't you agree, child?"

In the verbal sparring match, were there to ever be one, Hiroko would have been stunned alone with the tone of Akiyo Sugimoto's voice pitch, like a male opera singer, low but booming, a quality of being loud even when trying to be quiet. Hiroko took a pounding and was becoming groggy, or maybe it was the after-effects of the powerful narcotics still lingering.

Whatever the case, Hiroko snapped out of it long enough to reply "Yes, I do agree." As if she were in a mesmerized state.

Akiyo's voice subdued Hiroko vocally, allowing her diction to dab the young dome up with darts of dynamic pinpoint definiteness. "Then you must do the right thing and implicate yourself as the aggressor in this matter. You must understand the arduous nature of *our* circumstances. You are not a citizen here. You are a student on a special permission study visa, a legal temporary ward of the WACK Institute as of now. A plethora of strings had to be yanked in order to put you where you are now, especially in so hurried a fashion. You have much to be grateful for and many to thank. For now you must begin with your hosts.

"Consider your love for Brandon. Surely, he must be in love with you as well. And also considering the fact you stated that you do, in fact, love Brandon and the Wilson family, it would be quite unfair for them to be penalized or even incarcerated, wouldn't it?"

Hiroko was done. She was over it. Now all she wanted to do was get out of the diner and get these people the hell out of her face. She wanted to lie down somewhere, take a nap, and hopefully dream of something more pleasant than her current surroundings. America had to be better than this!

Hiroko was like, "Yes, you are right."

Akiyo wasn't done. It was like she impressed herself with her own banter. She rallied on. "Of course, child. We have been doing this for unspecified years, but concurrently, long before you were born. We know what we're talking about, and you would be doing yourself a service by heeding our words"—the disquisition was punishing—"as this was a mutual affair. No need for punishments or sanctions to be imposed on the hosts.

"Thus we are counting on you to make the right decision and agree to our perspective of things. These benevolent American people would tell you nicely, but as a Japanese, I am bound by our time-honored culture and tradition to address you and this matter in a firm and rigid course."

There were no objections. Hiroko could read her loud and clear. Everyone seemed satisfied. Sindrala's eyes widened and her pasty, linear grin appeared as she clicked off the voice recorder and stuffed it back in her large purse. She was going to alter and edit it anyway if need be.

April translated whatever she could grasp. Poor Nancy didn't have the guts to look Hiroko in the eye initially, but she "agreed to agree" with Akiyo, loyal to the "sisterhood." Done deal. Hiroko ordered a milkshake, and the rest was history. With the exception of Nancy Tanaka-Ryan, Hiroko never saw any of those people ever again. The rest was history.

INTERLUDE (5)

JUST LIKE THAT, the bleak, dismal denouement involving Brandon and the Wilson family was buried from both Hiroko's reality, and from the rest of the world. The slate was wiped clean. Were it to ever drag its ugly face from the depths of buried cased closed paperwork, Sindrala Wada, a Salem nabob and respected consultant of Women's Psychology, accredited Psychologist; would have produced Hiroko's "official" statements on a tape recorder that she initiated an affair with Brandon, thus inviting him to her guestroom and subsequently to her sphincter. A written version of the same data was drafted by witness Akiyo Sugimoto in Japanese to make privy for Japan officials and later in English by April Roubous, finally, notarized with an official seal by notary public Nancy Tanaka-Ryan. Done Deal.

Mission completed, the three scholars branched out in separate directions, enjoying succulent steak dinners and fine cuisine for the rest of their paid "vacations" to Portland, Oregon, having grand-slammed the objective in one night's work. Everyone could breathe a sigh of relief.

Nancy gave Alice Gourd a call in Vancouver, British Columbia (not Oregon); and needless to say, the madame marshmallow was ecstatic. So much so that she would celebrate with a lavish company-catered feast.

The Wilsons, especially patriarch Fred, were beyond relieved. Even though he had to shuck a small fortune to get the strings pulled, he figured it would have paled in comparison to the ridiculous sum he may have been required to pay for the lawyers it could have involved.

Hiroko didn't walk away as an additional piteous footnote in the annals of horrific home-stay history, not in totality at least. In silent, unspoken gratitude for her playing ball and latterly keeping the controversy and the WACK Institute out of the news, public scrutiny and possibly even criminal investigation, Hiroko was granted a two hundred dollar "refund." She also was awarded a two-night three-day trip to Los Angeles that included a visit to Disneyland with a one-hundred-dollar spending voucher.

Nancy, who was also a community PTA chief, at a meeting one night arranged an under-the-table deal with a superintendent from the district her daughters went to school in. Under a table in the board room she massaged away his lap's excited agony and delivered on a promise to allow him a backstage dry-hump session when the other parents were oblivious to their absence. The fabric friction triggered climax achieved rubbing his erection tipped boxers against Nancy's tender up-skirt camel toe in panties was a welcome change from his older, alcoholic wife's rotted cave, but both he and Nancy were too chickenshit to go all the way or get a hotel and make their affair official. So with a bump 'n' grind' closed-set tryst and a hand job as payment, the superintendent on the extreme low managed to squeeze in three available seats on a school trip slated for a school in a neighboring district that her daughters Dana and Bianca didn't attend.

As for the home-stay with the Tanaka-Ryans, it was picture perfect. Even Nancy could feel a little better seeing how things had transpired. Hiroko was energetic, vibrant and zesty every day. Twice a week she would attend classes at a two-bit language school downtown, but the rest of the time she spent with Nancy and her daughters. They went to the movies, parks, and other outings like bowling and roller skating. Nancy was full of glee to see how well Hiroko and her daughters were getting along. Every night was like a slumber party; it looked like so much fun. Nancy was tempted to join in the festivity of popcorn, potato chips, soft drink, and videos instead of being a strict mother and tell them to pipe down and go to bed.

The three-day visit to California was a graduation trip for some high school seniors, some of whom Dana and Bianca were acquainted with, even though the Ryan twins didn't attend the same school as them. Hiroko had an especially eye-opening experience with the Ryan twins.

Dana and Bianca were a set of tall, slender girls who were already inches taller than their mother, because their baseball-playing father, Norman Ryan, was an elevated man of six feet two. Traces of their Asian facial features were so scant they looked like Caucasians; maybe they could have been the spitting image daughters of a Star Trek's Mr. Spock around their eyes. The distinguishing feature that allowed Dana and Bianca to be told apart was Bianca's auburn hair color and Dana's hair was dark brown and shorter. Personality wise, there wasn't much difference, to Hiroko, than Cindy Wilson was back in Silverton. Where they differed was Dana and Bianca were a couple of fast, hot pants chippies. They had interests in boys of epic proportions and had already been relieved of their maidenhood.

It was with the host-sisters, the Ryan twins, that Hiroko got her rundown about the ups and downs of life as viewed by a young adolescent female, transitioning to young adulthood. It was like an initiation into the cult or sisterhood of sleazy females. Their nightly pajama parties would extend past the midnight hours until almost dawn. They talked about the cute guys they saw at the bowling alley, or the handsome blond guy at the pizza shop. Discussions were had about what kind of guys they liked, types, heights, shapes, sizes, and even colors. No rock was left unturned. They also showed Hiroko how easy boys could be manipulated. With the promise of something sweet, they could always get what they wanted from them. As a result, Hiroko watched as Dana and Bianca collected soda, cassette tapes, gift certificates to ice cream shops, tickets to concerts and movies, even jewelry! Both Dana and Hiroko each had at least three suitors. The girls' room phone was almost constantly ringing. Dana and Bianca also had neighborhood friends, and they were a strange, awkward, but motley crew of girls when they walked through the mall, numbering six to seven; people would stare at them. Hiroko felt strong, like she was a member of a girls' gang. In a way, she was. For the first time ever, she felt very powerful, pretty and in control. Dismal memories of events at the Wilson ranch were eclipsed in a desolate chamber of Hiroko's brain.

With all the prior fuss about remaining a virgin, or the inability to endure the pain of the occasion, it seemed unfathomable in retrospect that Hiroko finally lost it to a nameless, random, blond-haired drunk high school senior, then his pal, in a hotel.

Bianca had supplied Hiroko with the element of alcohol, something she might have been missing all along. The twist, however, was that Hiroko thought she was drinking a ginger ale that had too much melted ice when in actuality she had been drinking Zima.

She had already been dancing to some loud, rap-infused rock 'n' roll music at that party—she and her host sisters—when the spirit overcame her. She was tongue wrestling with her dance partner, a team captain blond hunk. She practiced the techniques the Ryan sisters and the girl posse had instructed her to employ, including sucking and biting on the lips. She had dudes shook instantly. Team Captain's black team mate co-captain was hankering to give the Japanese Oriental chick a go, and she didn't disappoint. It was as if she had the kiss of Cupid.

The party was an otherworldly juncture. Hiroko's dreamy state was returning, but it was a lightheaded one, until she was feeling some unexplainable heat from the depths of her tummy. At first she thought she may have been ill, but those feelings ceased when she drank more of the "ginger ale" with a peculiar aftertaste, and the song blasted by the DJ changed tunes, causing everyone in the party to cheer and roar.

The day had begun with a trip to Disneyland. It was the place Hiroko had always dreamed of going to. Due to the crowded conditions, they were unable to experience every single attraction, but enough to create lasting memories. They also paired off with interested boys from the wrestling team. These cool guys invited the twins and Hiroko to their hotel room private party upstairs after a surreal pool gala. They went upstairs to see an entire hallway completely taken over by teenagers. The wrestling team guys had adjoined their executive suite rooms and rented some DJ equipment.

After all the wild dancing, drinking, and mouth boxing, Hiroko's crash course would continue to the mattress. Her bikini was removed by the fondling team captain nibbling intoxicated at her neck on the bed. She didn't feel too embarrassed; after all, there were other naked girls walking around, Bianca included. She and her sister, Dana, were reasonably wasted, along with every other underage drinker in the house. The music was blasting some Beastie Boys "You Gotta Fight" and other jams, hardly romantic but definitely fit the mood of the scene.

The hotel room became the orgy spot, like a busy train station, with lots of heated vessels pulling in and out of tunnels of teenage lust and discovery. Hiroko witnessed Bianca, a few feet separating them on the same king-sized bed, python her arms and long legs around some negro that Hiroko could swear was chiseled from charcoal. Bianca looked like she was drowning in molasses treacle. But she was pulling his naked collection of opaque muscle deep into her as they sank into the mattress. They were slithering and suck-facing like scalded dogs. Finally, the bed started bouncing up and down. Hiroko couldn't believe it; she was watching a few feet away. She viewed Bianca as she released a sudden shriek like a wounded horse, her face contorted in a sinister but somber series of curls, like she was laughing and crying at the same time. The black guy still imprisoned in solitary confinement of her vaginal valley let loose a muffled wail as he collapsed into the pillow like he had expired due to suffocation, Bianca nibbling his ear like it was fruit roll-up. They remained there glued and nude, and the dude allowed no other trains to run through Bianca's station for the rest of the night.

Concurrently in time, Team Captain was trying to claim his inebriated faculties long enough to keep making out with Asian Doll Hiroko. He had already removed her bikini top, his drunken drooling mouth dribbled all over her nipples, and she was reasonably heated in a good way for a dude, but she kept restricting his hands when he tried to get the bottom half panties of the bikini removed. Finally, she acquiesced to Team Captain's groping and hoping. He pulled his swim trunks down past his buttocks and began poking. Maybe alcohol made her numb, or she was actually aroused, it finally happened; and this boy that she never saw again, forgot his name as if she never knew it even at all—he was the one. It lasted a full one minute and fifty seconds. Team Captain got the quick pin and finished the match shaking his efforts from the balls on her belly with respect. Co-Captain, who didn't mind sloppy seconds, wiped his team mate's spilled essence away and drilled his will to fill in for the job of showing his comrade "how it's s'posed t'be done!" Before Hiroko blacked out, she saw Dana on a pullout bed next to theirs— she too was getting squeezed and humped rapidly. She was the type of girl who liked multiple losers. She and Hiroko made eye contact for an instant, and Dana gave a ghoulish grin with the whites of her eyes showing.

Stumbling away from the libidinal location after midnight curfew, they made it back to their hotel room undetected. It was a miracle, but then again, with the loose reign the adults had over the privileged rich teens, there probably would not have been a stiff punishment anyway. As long as palms could get greased, the fuckery never ceased.

Prior to the plane ride back to Portland, Dana playfully but solemnly made her twin sister and adopted sister Hiroko swear to an oath of secrecy. Hiroko pledged with earnest to not speak about what went down in Los Angeles. It was a no-brainer really, because she did not relish the idea of any further complicated matters, which would necessitate another visit from the three freaks WACK had called in.

Upon return, Dana and Bianca showed their folks only the pictures of them all posing in various poses and posts with *Mickey Mouse*, *Pluto*, and the *Goofy* cast. Pictures of them with wine cooler bottles in one hand and phallus in the other were never surfaced thankfully. Hiroko spent her last days in North America feeling deeply enriched and hopeful. She bid her teary-eyed farewells to the Tanaka-Ryans and did the ritual dance full of empty promises to "stay in touch," "You'll always be welcome with us," and "We're friends forever." This was a short-lived commitment, almost as brief as the oath bond that Dana made Bianca and Hiroko swear to uphold.

Future letters sent by Hiroko and attempts to correspond with the Tanaka-Ryans were unanswered and curtailed respectively. For, shortly after her departure from their home, it was later discovered that Bianca was pregnant with, as her father Norman put it, "a nigger's baby," and in lieu of Hiroko's track record, Nancy's dim-witted capacity caused her to believe that it had been she who influenced her angelic, pristine, and refined suburban daughters to committing sinful, immoral acts. She had no choice: Dana's account of how Hiroko urged her and *real* sister Bianca to drink "spiked punch to the point that they lost memory had convinced her. They woke up in the hotel room of some jocks after a pool party that Hiroko got invited to; and they had tagged along to find her after mistakenly thinking she had gotten lost. Upon attempt to retrieve her, Hiroko shoved laced libation in their faces to consume from cups. Hearing all of this in detail, Nancy regretted ever allowing the savage young Japanese girl into their home and excommunicated her. She severed ties, forbidding either of her daughters from contacting her as well. She would never know that it was actually the other way around. It was her falsely credited untarnished daughters who had been spoiled by their father, who in fact, corrupted Hiroko. Dana and Bianca said, "Damn the 'oath' blood is thicker than piss.

INTERLUDE (6)

Hiroko RETURNED TO Japan in time to receive the news that her father had died. It would not have been too solemn an occasion had composer Hideo Okada not left Hiroko a decent inheritance. The money had been set aside for Hiroko to pay for her college education. Her relationship with her father had been strained, and his lack of presence in her life caused her to believe that he didn't care about her, or that he rejected her. Whatever his reasons were, it also had to be factored in that he also had another daughter—her half-sister she had never met but knew resided somewhere in the neighboring prefecture of Hyogo—her feelings for her father had grown numb. But the inescapable sorrow was unavoidable when she attended his funeral, meeting her high school age younger sister. They never had a conversation, nor were they enthusiastic about seeing each other. It was a miserable time.

Hiroko's mother, Eriko, was dipped and dabbed in flamboyant, splashy duds at the wake and ceremony. She thought for sure she was going to get a chunk of Hiroko's money, but she was wrong. Hiroko decided to use the money for college like her father had wanted. Eriko did her best to maintain composure upon hearing the news, but it was also OK, because her deceased ex-husband had always been generous with voluntary alimony that he hadn't been required by any courts to pay.

This arrangement stemmed from the nebulous circumstances that caused them to separate in the first place. They were not the match-made-in-heaven couple due to their human shortcomings. He was a successful musician and composer, dedicated to his career for most of his life, and because of such neglected to secure himself a love or wife until he was approaching his mid-forties, Hiroko's mom Eriko. She was a recent junior college graduate, entrepreneur wannabe working temp jobs at a catering company in between being a roving Tupperware and mail order catalog–type sales venture.

Eriko had big ideas about having her own boutique of some sort, anything where she could be the boss. The hard work required to accomplish such a dream was lacking in her loins, so Eriko married the first rich guy that showed her attention, even if he was at least two decades her senior. It wasn't a bad arrangement, though. In the initial stages of their marriage, Hideo's drinking habits had not intensified to a level where his groupie-slaying days as a touring musician resurfaced. He was known to be a ladies' man; both in his youth and even in his mature stage, he was always crisp and clean whenever he was seen in public, and he took good care of his body whenever he wasn't defiling it with rare, splendid rice wines. Eriko had been a lovely, voluptuous honey with whistle-bait chassis as well, sexy enough to catch Hideo's eye when he could have easily had his choice of several, but some motherly type of grace she possessed had charmed him to offer her a wedding rock. They tied the knot, and after Eriko gave birth to Hiroko, his sexual interest in her deflated like her belly should have. Instead, she kept up with the binge cravings of Shu-Cream Puffs and Mister Donuts.

To her credit, however, Eriko never got really fat, but she had definitely sized up in contrast to her figure before marriage. Maybe Hideo had taken this into consideration before his alleged infidelities, none of which were ever actually proven. Sure, he would flirt, he asserted, because of his local fame, but it was easy for him to be a mark for being a "rakehell." So he would drink and party and occasionally host lavish carousals at their crib in Tezukayama.

One such affair, at a year-end party, Eriko would have the tables turned, and the finger of infidelity accusation pointed at her. Too bad it had come at a time when Hideo was drunk out of his mind. As a child Hiroko remembered the scene, and horrified expressions of the faces of their guests when her father spewed his drunken rant claiming that he had walked in on her mother and one of their younger neighbors. People looked at him as if he weren't playing with a full deck. Hiroko had felt so bad for him she had cried, because from what she recounted, they had all been having such a good time before it happened.

The then fifty-year-old codger claimed that when he went to take a leak in his two-story deluxe grand home, the place was so crowded upstairs with guests he resorted to using a commode tucked away from everyone downstairs. En route with wobbly steps to his "spare" toilet, the elegant Western-style home included a small foyer for a washing machine, dryer, and laundry space. This space could be ensconced by an ornate, *aquatex*-textured mosaic glass door. It was here, Shigeru alleged, he caught a blurry glimpse through the irregular patterns of the glass door of the laundry room.

Though imbibed at the time with some exquisite fifty-year-aged sake from Kyoto, Hideo denied claims he was either roue or debauched and asserted he hadn't been hallucinating when he spied the sight of his wife's rump in a rotation cycle on a young neighbor's rod, churning her butter as he reclined beside her leaning arched up against the washer. A rendition her mother to the present day denied all accounts with utmost insistence.

In Eriko's version—the one that stuck throughout the times and corroborated by friends, family, and other guests in attendance—Hideo was in a drunken state of phantasmagory and confabulated a tale of her being caught in a compromising situation and while committing unfaithful inappropriate acts, when in fact, she was attempting to revive a neighbor who had passed out after falling drunk down their flight of stairs.

The truth was never revealed to Hiroko. All she remembered was people looking at her berserk, frenzied father like he was off his rocker. Not only was Hideo known to have a thing for younger women, he was also noted as one who concocted wild embellishments to distract from and obscure his own infidelities. Neither Hideo nor Eriko was ever proven guilty of alleged cheating as far as Hiroko knew, but her father's quick, sudden marriage to a young violinist musician so soon after his divorce and that woman's consequent pregnancy, the arrows of doubt pointed at her father over the years, and his estranged position in her life didn't improve things.

Her father's passing didn't impact her in catastrophic fits of depression and sadness. She found solace in knowing that her brief but final conversations with her father were cordial and they ended on good terms. It was important that she kept the lines of communication with him flowing, her mother had reminded, for in this way, it ensured that the monthly emoluments would continue. So, she remained in sporadic contact with him. Even while she was abroad, she sent him occasional postcards. Who would have guessed that less than a month after her return to Japan, he would kick the bucket. Nectar of his new, younger inamorata's nookie proved to be too much of a fillip jounce that did more than just jumpstart his troubled heart. It put him in an urn.

Hiroko used her inheritance while studying at Asia University. While there, she continued to make outstanding marks, and due to her regiment of hard work and diligent application of herself, she completed her undergraduate program an unprecedented year earlier than the normal four years. The Josei-Shinri-Shakai Society had made good on their promise to apply credits she earned prior to enrollment studying abroad at authorized VILE Institute. She received her degree in education and minored in international studies.

Experiences both at home in Japan and abroad had Hiroko street poisoned and somewhat depraved. She was able to conceal it with an attractive and comely face and controlled exterior, but her level of corruption had risen to the extent where she held a subtle contempt and disdain for some men. To date, her experiences with men had all been one heartbreak after another. Those that weren't such were faceless, emotionless shags or traumatic ordeals that she desired to keep buried. The Ryans of her home-stay were long ago vanished from her life for reasons she would never know. The only "friend" she made while abroad had trickled down to a single one—Michelle Ching, "Ming," from back in the VILE Vancouver days.

Hiroko returned to Japan and was presented with letters from abroad that Ming had written her. They too remained in loose contact throughout the years. Occasionally Ming would send various postcards from around the world her wanderlust took her: Toronto, San Francisco, even Denver. Apparently, she was still with the same boyfriend, and all her postscripts would punctuate her vow to someday visit her in Osaka, Japan. That day never came while Hiroko was aware.

In essence, when Hiroko was sad, she should have been happy, and likewise happy when sad, but that made no sense. Life was puzzling her with its pricks of pleasure and punishments. She took time out of her schedule to write Ming back every now and then, and regretted not trying to get to know her better while they were roommates back in Canada. Maybe she could have taught her a thing or two about boys the way Dana and Bianca pulled her coat, only a year sooner. Who knows? It could have made her all the wiser. She thought about it a lot, but became so enthralled with her rapidly morphing life she neglected to remain in contact with her when she moved away from her Sakai home. She got a job as a teacher, as if nothing else of a career would suit her; and she lived alone for a while. Her assignment in the rural Hannan City was just as much a disappointment for her as it was for Elizabeth Amberbush, and maybe for Eddie Roman too, but she was Japanese and could handle it much better.

Relationships with people were few and far between when she was not playing the role at school as an English teacher, and Hiroko's intimate encounters were restricted to one-night stands or short-term arrangements with spellbound suitors. She avoided relationships for the obvious fact that she did not want to be hurt by a heartbreaker, and after living abroad, she had a burgeoning appetite for a wider assortment of male options, causing her to see foreign men in Japan as rare, tasty delicacies such as raw, bloody steak and she a vampire shark. When she and Eddie Roman crossed paths, he was instantly her target. Too bad he had a "wife."

24

S HE HAD TO test him.

Hiroko stood by Eddie's desk in the teachers' assembly room. As usual, they made small talk about the school, the students, the lessons, and upcoming events. These were boring and bland subjects, truth be told. Hiroko didn't really give much of a damn.

Behind Eddie was a window. Hiroko squinted her cartoon chipmunk eyes, pretending to be straining to see something outside beyond the glass. Eddie spotted the change of her expression and grew curious. He turned to see what she was looking at. Just then, she silently dropped several of her pens and pencils on the floor on purpose, but feigned to appear as if it was accidental.

Eddie squinted and said, "What were you looking at out there?" His face glowered in mock outrage as he swiveled back to face front and eyed Hiroko. After a respite in the chat, he resumed, not noticing the writing utensils Hiroko had dropped inches from his bum shoes.

Hiroko said, "I thought I saw a large crow. Outside the window on that tree there."

Then, using both of her hands, she tapped her fingernails lightly on Eddie's shoulders, urging him to back his chair up, scoot backward. Eddie complied and rolled his chair back like she was gesturing for him to do, until his back was to the window.

Eddie said, "Yeah, I've noticed that there're lot of crows around here . . ." but postponed the rest of his speech because he was captivated by the view of Hiroko bending over in front of him. She was picking up the pens and pencils, but she

218

was taking her time, picking them up slowly, one by one. The entire time she was bent, her posterior pent his pants zipper in place to the extent she was practically sitting in his lap. She felt the emergence of a tumescent poke. *She had him!*

Eddie had been in this situation before. This was the kind of thing women did. He couldn't help being aroused by their antics, but he didn't have to be a desperate, gullible sucker to fall for their fake flirting. He swallowed a hard lump in his throat; his forehead emitted microscopic spheres of sweat. If only she were serious, Eddie thought long and hard, even though the span of time didn't exceed two minutes.

Hiroko ended the ribald, pseudo-innocent act by wiggling her waist from east to west and back before picking up the last pencil. The friction of Hiroko's skirt polyester and Eddie's cotton khaki pants created more undeniable heat between the two of them.

Other teachers were too involved with their busy daily schedules to notice what was going on in the rear of the teachers' assembly room. After all, people bumped into each other, dropped things on the floor all the time. All day, every day.

Eddie couldn't hide his excitement in the wake of the gratuitous "rubbie" from Hiroko. Even though she made it seem accidental and innocent, he couldn't pretend as if he hadn't been turned on by it. His speech was interrupted by his growing attraction to Hiroko, noticeable by looking at his lap statue. But there was a voice in his head chattering to him: *Can't trust her. She's just like those video store bitches back in the States. She's tryna give you the dick tease treatment. Don't fall for it!* His facial expression was harried with the thought of being ridiculed, once again, spotted with a visible hard-on, for all to see, like before. He gritted his teeth and slid his chair underneath his desk, providing shelter to his embarrassment.

Recognizing what she had done and what damage she had inflicted—but pretending not to—Hiroko turned and said to Eddie finally, "Oh, oops . . . I'm very sorry," while trying unsuccessfully to not glance down at his pants' uprooted inguinal area. "Are you all right?" she asked wryly, as if she didn't know.

Eddie's face went florid. His heart was racing like a sprinter being called to return to his runners' mark after being called back for a false start. *Just fine, you bitch*, Eddie wanted to say, but kept it in his head.

Hiroko ruefully stared at Eddie briefly, then ran her hands through her jet-black needles of hair. She too had felt the heat between her and him. She said, "Well, I must be going now. I have a class to teach next period." She turned and walked away, but glanced back over her shoulders. "I'll speak with you again later."

A murmured, incoherent response was all Eddie could utter. Such a brash display of interest would occur from time to time, at least once or twice a week. Improper, but easily disguised as accidents or coincidental collisions. The frequency at which it would happen caused the incidents to be like running jokes. But it was no joke. Eddie's feverish desires, growing rapidly, threatened to pierce the protective wall he had erected to guard him against heartbreak and humiliation at the hands of wicked wenches who lived for the thrill of tormenting dudes of his type.

With all of this going on, by the end of the week, Eddie would be in the mood to have his tension relieved by his love, Liz. Creeping loneliness, amatory lurid anime, and Hiroko's nether region assaults to his crotch would have his balls icy blue indigo by Friday afternoon. At such a stage of utter anguish, he would be game to accept Liz just holding his thing and spitting on it, if she complained of not being in the mood, something she often did. He accepted Liz's "handiwork" with grateful repose anyway. It was better than doing it by himself—at least he could close his eyes and imagine.

Liz, however, wasn't always so accommodating. She decided once to tell Eddie to not come to Osaka City on Friday. She had said that she would be working later than usual, and afterward, she was going to party with her coworker crew. She decided—for them both—that Saturday would be a better day for him to come to town because she started work earlier and finished earlier, so they had a little more time to address each other's needs. Then there were Saturdays where special events were held and required Eddie to work. There was some type of PTA Open House festival where parents and/or family of students were allowed to enter the school and observe classes, meet the faculty, tour the school, and enjoy some fun, games, and divertissement.

Hiroko waded through a sea of black-suited uniformed junior high school students and their parents in the city school that resembled a minimum security reformatory. She found Eddie also roaming the halls of the school doing his usual gaijin pet celeb" bit, greeting students and their folks, making daffy faces for the kids, taking pictures with random people—even strangers—and accepting painful jabs to his rectum delivered from small brats with fingers formed in steeples.

By now at this moment in time, Hiroko and Eddie were in a play-pretend boyfriend-and-girlfriend–type relationship. They flirted "innocently" with each other. Any incidental bumping, collision, or contact and Eddie would overexaggerate himself having a fake orgasm or heart attack, almost always causing Hiroko to crack up laughing, but nothing beyond that. Hiroko would be like, "Oh no, no way! Elizabeth will kill me!"

Despite the obvious attraction between them, Hiroko showed signs that she respected the border where blandishments and bantering ended because Eddie was taken. Eddie would respond to the tune of "Yeah, she'll probably kill me too, hee hee!" But in the back of his mind, he would be pondering if Liz would go for a (another) threesome.

On that Saturday of the Open House, though, Hiroko was careful to not flirt openly with Eddie, but she did greet him with overflowing delight, more than usual. She grabbed his hand like he was her man and led him along, similar to how Liz would do, but more lightly and as quickly, she released him, and he followed as if by remote control. Hiroko was wary of not being detected of having a crush on Eddie by parents, students, or any of the other faculty members.

Hiroko got Eddie to follow her to a small room with bamboo-framed, rice-paper-paneled sliding doors. This small space of approximately one hundred square feet smelled like straw and wheat but was perspicaciously clean and neat—practically spotless save for the pile of flat, silky cushions, *zabuton*, in a corner and near those, some obsolescent ancient-looking kettle ware of sorts.

Eddie's heart rate did its fluttering drum roll. *She's gonna seduce me right here in the school!* his brain voice screamed.

Before he could rise to uncontrollable levels of excitement, Hiroko cooled his engines and commanded him with an immaculately manicured index finger, "Sit down there," pointing to one of the deliberately placed cushions on the floor. She followed up with, "Wait, we have to remove our shoes."

Before Eddie's fit of trembling and angry whimpering would commence due to him fighting to restrain his rage at being led on, he amenably complied to his surrogate master. He disengaged his "bo-bos" from feet that were wrapped in tattered white socks, a toe on each one peeked out like a finger puppet. He placed his chintzy footwear beside Hiroko's diminutive black kitten heels.

A moment later, as if on cue, a female student of about thirteen, decked out in a flowery brocade-ornamented kimono entered the room. Her steps were rigid and evenly paced as if she were performing a specific, rehearsed time-honored movement. She knelt before Hiroko and Eddie, bowed with genuflected benevolence, respect, and high regard. Eddie felt ashamed of himself for his prior thoughts, cooled down rapidly, and blushed as the young girl performed a Japanese tea ceremony.

Eddie scraped his brain to recollect where he had seen this type of thing performed before and arrived at the discovery that he had witnessed it in a movie, but this was his first time in person. He watched the little girl, a student he had seen many times in the classes he assisted teaching, but could never remember her name. Although she was a mere teen, Eddie was fascinated by how the traditional Japanese raiment seemingly doubled her age in appearance. He noted her as being so cultivated, graceful, and, quite frankly, stunning to watch, for she was in extreme contrast form to the boisterous, loudmouth hoyden she often was in class.

As the young kimono-clad performer carried out the stages of the presentation, there was an odd but quaint silence. During a series of tapered measurements and movement over the next few minutes, Eddie's knees were getting cramped due to the seating arrangement. While this ceremony was being performed, the viewer participants were required to squat with their knees forward, something Eddie as a Westerner from America was not accustomed to in any sort of way.

Seeing his discomfort, Hiroko leaned into Eddie's ear and whispered a sultry, near-wet advisory, "You can sit more comfortably. You can stretch out your leg to the left or to the right."

Eddie's body was tingling. So much so that if the student had not been present, he would have ceased with the masquerading as a counterfeit what-if boyfriend and jumped her bones then and there.

Hiroko seemed to be aware that her moist lips grazing the inner core of Eddie's ear as she breathed her words had turned him on. She could tell by his momentary seizure: he shivered and sucked in a gust of air through gritted teeth. A cheap Japanese cologne that Liz had bought for Eddie lingered around the stubbly area of his upper jaw below the earlobe. To Hiroko, even the old-geezer fragrance smelled good on him. She likely would not have dared make the first move and drop a wet kiss on Eddie, but had he followed through on his intent to do such, he would not have been met with any resistance. It was a peculiar situation, like they were both captives, imprisoned by invisible walls separating them, preventing them from making the contact they each desired. They were bound by societal rules and morals.

The mood was soiled when Eddie chose to stretch his legs outward, even though he positioned them in a direction away from Hiroko and the girl, the vinegar odor of his holey socks quickly invaded the chamber. In minutes, the small room was reeking, but judging by how the girl continued undeterred with her ceremony acts, she may not have been aware that the pungent smell originated from Eddie's socks. Hiroko may have noticed, but she carried on as if she didn't care as she passed him a small rice cake.

He watched Hiroko open the small cellophane-wrapped sweet and ate it, then Eddie himself mimicked her actions. He had tasted one of these *mochi* confections before and hadn't liked it much; it was during the time when he and Liz had first arrived in Japan, and they were being served okonomiyaki every other day. He remembered how he had been expecting to get ice cream or some sort of cake for dessert after the Japanese pizza, but instead, they received this sticky and viscous "treat" that was so chewy it tended to cling to his molars. But as always, trying to prove that he had a true appreciation for Japanese culture, he endured what he deemed a repugnant rice cake and grinned as if he was head over heels for its taste. Even overplaying it to the extent he would look like someone on a TV commercial praising its delectable goodness.

When the actual tea from the rite was placed before Hiroko and Eddie to consume, he watched Hiroko turn the bowl toward her, rotated it clockwise, and took a sip at a designated point. She then rotated it counterclockwise and slid it over to Eddie. Eddie's thoughts were banging around in his brain like pin balls against bumpers. What did this ritual symbolize? he wondered with seething awe and idolization. He could have sworn that he had watched one of those Mr. Miyagi–type '80s flicks and had seen this tea ceremony, but he was dangerously close to misconstruing its purpose to possibly mean it being a romantic preface to a love affair.

Instinctively, Eddie took the bowl to his lip and took his sip of the green tea. He wasn't thrilled with the flavor or lack of particular piquancy his eurocentric taste buds had him accustomed to regarding tea, but he had to admit that it was different in a unique way. As if to say it could grow on him in due time perhaps.

Just as he became lost in his moment of solitary thought, the kimono-clad young girl bowed to her two viewers again with reverence before she trotted out of the room with her familiar graceful and kinetic steps. Then for the first time ever, Eddie and Hiroko were alone. Alone!

The eerie silence returned. The split in time was broken by Hiroko. She asked, "What do you think about Japanese tea ceremony, Eddie-san?"

Eddie said, "It . . . was beautiful."

He had few words. There was a captivating silence, and he couldn't find anything to say that would enhance the moment. Now the young girl was gone, the moment he had waited for had arrived, Hiroko was there and his for the taking. He knew she wanted him, and he desired her too, but there was still a lingering shadow of doubt he had about Hiroko and her intentions. That eerie voice in his mind was still telling him that she might be like the women at the video store, or worse—a double cock clutcher like Becky and Mandy. Though he might be attracted to other women, and his desire to engage in hanky panky with them may emerge, but remaining faithful and true to Liz might be his best bet.

Before he could allow his voice to convince him to move away from her, their eyes locked. They were then trapped within each other's gaze, and neither stirred for that moment. And then the moment of truth seemed inevitable for as if drawn together by an uncanny magnet or tractor beam, their faces moved closer toward the other. When it appeared they would momentarily come into contact and be halted by the touching of lips, the kimono-clad student and several of her peers popped back into the tatami room like, "Surprise!" Interrupting the would-be amorous encounter with a finality.

The cute young teens numbered three in total. They snuggled affectionately up against Hiroko and squeezed in between her and Eddie to be embraced by them, a display of familiarity generally unusual for ordinarily shy students.

The youth who had performed the ceremony said with blithesome, starry eyes, "Teacher, teacher! Eddie-sensei, how was it? How you like tea ceremony I did?" Her English was better than Eddie had expected it to be. He praised her with genuine commendation and, like Hiroko, felt relieved that none of the girls had caught them about to lock lips. As soon as the students bust through the sliding panel, Eddie and Hiroko had resumed their original, poised seating arrangements, snapping back to position like rubber bands released after being stretched. No one had suspected anything, luckily. After the cacophony of teenage chatter consumed the air like the fume of Eddie's feet, he was odor numb as she squeezed back into his clodhoppers, just as an adolescent made mention—in Japanese—about the room smelling like sour pickles. Still, Eddie wasn't a suspect.

A minute later, Hiroko had slipped on her shoes and was being led away as if by chaise by the trio of kids. Voices were drowned out by the mirth and laughter of the school festival. Eddie stumbled along behind them, banging the cramps and kinks in his legs after the painful squatting. A sudden vibration tremored his shirt pocket. It was his Tuka phone ringing.

He answered his phone, and it was Liz. For the first time, he wasn't really happy or thrilled to hear from her. He had been having an amusing time, and the turn of events had progressed his situation with Hiroko from lukewarm to gradual steaming. He was walking a tightrope. He tried to not sound guilty or suspicious in manner as he found a secluded, less noisy place—one of the school's sparsely occupied hallways.

After exchanging the normal greetings, Liz's voice went, "Hey, where the hell are you? You're supposed to be on your way here."

A bit irritated suddenly, Eddie said, "Noooo . . . you said that I didn't need to come out there this weekend, remember?

Liz's voice impugned, "No, you dick, that was last week. What the hell's the matter with you lately? Are you fucked up? Did you take anything? Aw geez, fuck it, Ed . . . just hurry up and come on out. Steph is showing us this new club tonight. They're gonna have one-hundred-yen tequila shots from ten o'clock!"

Eddie was fuming as he terminated the call. He had been almost certain that Liz had told him to not come that night. He was quite sure because he had explained to her that he had to work that Saturday, because of the Open House festival he was then attending; as such, he could have sworn she had told him that it would have been better if he stuck around Hannan City until she came then.

Excessive alcohol and drug philandering had finally affected Liz's memory, Eddie was thinking. He didn't usually—if ever—hang up on Liz; he would never dare disrespect her blatantly. However, she had been still deriding and objurgating him when he switched off his phone. He thought about it and quickly called Liz back before she had any ideas he had hung up on her out of animosity.

When Liz answered the phone, he was like, "Uh, er . . . I'm sorry, hun, I . . . we got cut off . . . it's really noisy in here, an' I think there's a connection problem here." It wasn't really a lie. The Tuka phones had weak reception and antenna sometimes, and it actually was clamorous at that location. Liz seemed pacified with Eddie's apology, but she was more interested in his progress with regards to getting his ass to where she was in Osaka City.

Pouting, Eddie said, "OK, I'm on my way, but y'gotta undertand babe, it's gonna take a bit of time. I'm still at the school. I have to go home, take a shower, change clothes—"

Liz's voice went, "Fuck that. Don't. No need for you to take a shower. You can shower at my place."

Eddie was surprised to hear such a bit of information. "What do you mean?" He asked. "Isn't that roommate of yours gonna be around?"

Liz was noticeably vexed by the sound of her voice, an irritated tone that Eddie was used to hearing. She said, "Nooooooo! You're such a fuckin' *schmegge*! You don't remember a goddam thing I ever tell you!" She let out a long sigh exemplifying her annoyance. She continued, "I told you yes, I'd be hangin' out with Steph tonight, but I also included *you* in that plan. I didn't know Steph wanted to show us a new club at the time, but that's irrelevant.

"What's relevant is, after we all meet up at the Hommachi School, some of us are gonna pair off, that's Chucky and Denore. She's gonna hang out with him, she made a new friend."

Eddie was like, "Who's Chucky?"

Liz was trying to not scream. She really wanted to wallop Eddie's face with a hard pillow and hear him wince. She said, "We're gonna have the place to ourselves, asshole! Now hurry your ass along and get here!"

"Cool!" Eddie practically yelled, becoming suddenly animated. The idea of being able to go to Liz's place appealed to him. It was comfy, he could sleep as late as he wanted to without care of a hotel's checkout time, could go and come freely . . . and most of all, Eddie surmised, Liz was going to hit him off with the action he desperately needed. Especially considering how Hiroko was cranking up his hormones, revving him for bedroom excitement.

"I'm on my way, babe!" Eddie said.

That instant, Hiroko had returned, circling a corner of the building and finding him. She heard the tail end of Eddie's talking into his miniature cellular. Eddie spotted her deflated expression. Dimples caused her cheeks to look like punctured sugar plums.

Liz was still on the phone. Eddie tried to strain his voice so that Hiroko couldn't hear him, but before he could utter anything else, Liz had said, "Just hop on a train now. No need for you to go back to your place. Hey, don't even come to Umeda tonight, just head to Hommachi, it's closer. Go there directly, don't pass go, don't collect two hundred brain cells . . . You remember where Hommachi is and how to get there, right?"

After affirming that he did know, Liz said, "OK then, get your ass going. You should already be halfway to the station by now. I'll meet you there at Hommachi. If you get there later, I'll wait for you, so don't worry."

Duteously Eddie obeyed Liz's directives. He prepared to leave as Hiroko reappeared.

"You are leaving now?" she asked.

Eddie said, "Uh, yeah that was my, uh . . . fiancée, an' she wants me t'go to meet her in Osaka City."

Visibly displeased, Hiroko swiftly pulled herself together and said with a perky voice, "OK, well, see you next Tuesday. You do not have to come to work on Monday because you work today."

Eddie livened up as if he had been injected with an additional boost of jollity. He said, "Oh! Yeah! I remember. Cool."

Hiroko stared at Eddie as if to recapture the moment they had shared moments earlier. She puffed her cheeks in a childlike moue. Deep in her thoughts, she crammed to understand the reason Eddie hadn't tried to follow up on what they had attempted to start back in the tatami room.

On the flip, Eddie too was juggling thoughts heavy as shot puts. Weighing on his brain with a burden was the thought of moving forward now, in close proximity to Hiroko, and their working situation. Would it be a good or bad idea to try and push up on Hiroko again? Need he be reminded any more than his mind's hidden voice relentlessly commanding him to bethink his LA video store past. He was haunted by the reminder of how Becky and Mandy were such dishy dreamboats at face value, but opposite that coin, they were the most conniving and deceitful broads he had ever seen. Even his first encounter ever with a woman, the Fat Girl back in Sack Town—or Elk Grove—even she knew she was stringing along Eddie's pal at the same time she clobbered Eddie with her elephantine breasts and her esophagus engulfed Eddie's erections and discharges like a suppository. With the exception of Liz, *damn near all women* were potentially deceitful, trickery gamines! For all Eddie knew, Hiroko could have been leading him on. Maybe as soon as he tried to kiss her, she would report him to the principal, the board of Ed, the program coordinators and CHET officials. What she would gain from it, he knew not, but maybe it was the same thrill women get anytime they saw dudes like him suffer. Their agony was their amusement, Eddie inferred to himself, having a non compos mentis conversation with the voice in his head.

He rain-checked the scenario as an abrupt and unexpected sharp pain struck his belly like a nail-spiked baseball bat. Could it have been the rice cake? The tea? Maybe something else he had eaten earlier that afternoon or the beer he drank the previous night? He knew not, but what he did know, whatever it had been that had upset his stomach, it didn't agree with him, and he was in dire need of a lavatory. A cavalcade of jarring voices from students, teachers, and parents threatened to swamp him, but he detoured the hall they populated and skirted away in an opposite direction. He found a toilet in time before his shocking release from the anus spilled out into the streets. He remained on the porcelain for about 10 minutes before he was even remotely satisfied with the dump.

He missed the express train to Osaka City.

25

IN THE COUPLE of months that Liz had been in the big city, she gradually became familiar with the lay of the land. Like many of her peers and coworkers, she copped a bicycle. Nothing too fancy like she had seen in the United States, but something durable with two wheels and a bike chain with sprocket, which came also with a mesh metallic basket connected to the curvy handlebars. Many of them even came with their own locks so people didn't need to use the bike chains even though Liz felt the need to take no chances and bought one anyway. These bikes were recommended for short trips around the neighborhood—for example, to the supermarket or convenience stores and back—but eventually, Liz would find a way to use this means for traveling to and from work when applicable. She was still a fitness freak at heart.

Despite apparent addictions to limelight exuberance, substances, and strange relationships, Liz was conscientious about health and nutrition still. She got little help from her coworkers finding a decent place to work out, even though there were a plethora to choose from. She got hipped to one "Fitness Club" by one of her better English-speaking students. It was amazing, Liz thought, how helpful Japanese people could be at times. Especially when they knew a person was newly arrived in the country. When she and Eddie were in Hannan City, people poured on the welcoming gifts, okonomiyaki dinner invitations, and help with practically any situation whatsoever if called upon. So during one free conversation lesson with a high-level student, Liz mentioned how she was "worried about falling out of shape" or "getting fat" due to drastic changes in her work hours. The student pulled her coat to the Fitness Club, and Liz joined promptly.

Her lifestyle was experiencing a drastic change as well. She was hanging out late and sleeping in a bit later. This didn't seem to be a negative thing because since her work shift usually began in the afternoon, she needed not ride the nightmarishly overcrowded early-morning rush-hour subway or commuter trains. The weekend schedule was a bit earlier, but human traffic was lessened in the mornings, opposite what it would be during the business/school week.

In between, she got her "Sensei in the City" tutorial from her coworkers.

Stephanie and most of the female foreign coworkers put Liz up on the recommended spot to get their hair done. It was at this salon in Shinsaibashi behind the grandiose Nikko Hotel. The stylist was some short, five-foot-four-inch Japanese dude named Takaro with a medium windswept hairdo, caterpillar fuzzy "zappa" mustache with a goat patch. He could speak English decently, and it turned out he didn't do bad work either, although it was beneath the standards that many had been accustomed to in their own countries, it was more convenience than quality, so decided the general consensus. For Takaro was very flexible, didn't charge an arm and a leg—most of the time—and it was easy to communicate to him what they wanted. He smelled good, like peaches and oranges, and his clothes were silky and suave. He looked like a late-twenties or early-thirties Japanese version of Hugh Heffner, but Liz didn't like him because he acted gay, or fake gay. But she appreciated him for hooking her hair up without cutting it too much. Now she could rock her straight-layered hairstyle with balayage, and ombre color upped her elegance and gorgeous factor.

Poor Denore Takaro couldn't help. When Denore showed up at his shop, he damn near turned her away flat and hurt her feelings; but then again, Denore was somewhat sensitive anyway. Luckily, Chucky had taken the helm and became Denore's guide. He put her up on a network of African and others from the black diaspora with shops in American Village where they could go to tend to their grooming needs.

Next, Liz and Denore got the tour of Nipponbashi courtesy of Eric Cravens. It was a short walk from the Namba Bozack School branch. He took her to a spot where she could cop some electronic goods like a newer and better digital camera, laptop, portable music players, and discount phone card minutes for her Tuka phone.

Supermarkets and grocery stores were tough, but Stephanie and the others recommended the ones that had English names like Market World or LIFE even though they were more expensive. According to them, they had the same stuff you could find back home, only with different packaging, less volume, and a higher price. Liz had a LIFE supermarket near her, so it was one she and Denore used more often and tugged groceries to and from there either on her bicycle or Denore's brawn.

There were plenty of dry cleaners to choose from; these too tended to be pricey, but their service was quality and timely. As for normal laundry, their dormitory building had its own coin-operated Laundromat on the ground-floor lobby. This place got crowded somewhat on the weekends because there were only but a few washers and dryers, but since it was accessible at all hours of the day and night, it was still convenient. The cool part about the Laundry Room was the opportunity to make casual acquaintances with her building neighbors. They were people of Japanese and various other Asian nationalities. Most of these people could speak very little English, but enough to communicate. Denore benefitted the most from encounters with these friendly neighbors when they helped her and Liz shopping at the supermarkets—there they learned how to read labels and such.

Clothing and fashion was a continual challenge, but buzz around the workplace had it that Radley the Canadian was the go-to guy in that department. Liz barely ran into Radley as he wasn't exactly a "regular" in the crowd and he called in sick the times when she and he would have worked together. Wardrobe, however, wasn't an imperative concern. She dressed conservatively for work, but basic, not elaborate. The stuff she really liked was unattainable because of the size availability. Her curves were too shapely and oftentimes too size-burdened for the clothes she found cute in most of the shopping arcade boutiques. Casual days, she wore standard blue jeans. She had a small stack anyway, and workout clothes were the least problematic to get.

Denore, on the other hand, was quickly becoming a sister of a Star Wars Chewbaka character prior to meeting Chucky. But since then, he showed her a place in Yotsubashi where a Haitian woman ran a shop the size of a broom closet, yet still got Denore's hair to look bolstered and pleasantly styled. Back in the days when she watched *The Cosby Show*, she couldn't remember the daughter's name . . . the Tempest Bledsoe character, the least memorable one but cute in her own unique way—that was who Denore reminded her of, but only with glasses, and her hair hooked up generally looked like that. As for clothes, that was a nightmare in the making, because she didn't feel very comfortable wearing hip-hop clothes the African-run shops offered. There were some department stores that actually had clothes to fit her, but these were bell bottom, itchy polyester that ate skin on the humid, hellish hot days of Osaka, chalky colors, shirts that looked like clothes from a past era, and when it came to shoes, she was still heading for disaster.

Liz was fortunate in the shoe department: she didn't have a huge foot size and was able to find hers in Japan more often than the average. It was a constant battle.

Then there were things that were a little exotic and extra. Laundry Room chance meeting conferences with building neighbors hipped her to a Thai

Massage Parlor in the nearby Kujo area. This crazy little spot blew Liz's mind immediately. It looked like something from a Sho Kosugi or Chuck Norris extraneous Oriental martial arts '80s flick set piece. It was chinoiserie complete with the silky, ornamental curtain adorning strikingly foreign and fascinating dragon, tiger, or snake depiction embroidery. The smell of jasmine incense was so embedded in the air Liz felt she had consumed it to her lungs directly without the aid of nostrils.

From what Liz could tell, the place was run by two Thai women, probably relatives, and in their forties or fifties. They could speak pretty good English, to Liz's surprise, and took a liking to Liz right away. She was a rare sight around those parts, and the fact that Liz was considered by some to be beautiful, or had porn star–quality looks in the least, and as such was able to establish the start of what would be a regular pattern etched into her schedule.

The elder of the two, named Tok, would strip Liz like she was a schoolgirl play doll, bathe her down with some herbal, scenty soap, then rinse and dry her off with a steamy towel. Then the Thai woman's older, powerful arms would massage demulcent, efficacious oils deep into her muscles delivered by firm fingers. She got the head-to-toe treatment, and it felt so good she had a spasm.

Her feet were scrubbed and filed smooth, toenails clipped and cleansed with some abstract little brush. Then massage in between her toes with aromatic bramble balsam and yew, causing a burning tingle for a second before it became cool.

It was more than a massage—it was an experience, as she would put it. And all this would be done in about forty minutes! She could be in and out, and agreeable for her on days when she came from the gym or when she needed to be fresh in addition to the normal cleansing associated with women femininity. This place was so on-point that Liz decided to keep it a secret from Denore. It may have been a mean thing to do, but she could be impishly covetous and parsimonious with information as well as money.

Since Tim the Duke had introduced her to Luzio Silver, she could now get some occasional, recreational cocaine candy direct from the man himself and twenty-four hours a day, round the clock! This was contingent if the shopper was willing to travel to the location where the exchange would take place. Otherwise, the goods would be delivered by some scary, "white-trash-looking" dude with an Irish accent, or trailer-park Ozark inbred. This foreshadowed imminent issues regarding Liz's concerns for her safety, as these guys were a bit gruff and freely spewing foul mouths who accosted her with undressing eyeballs.

There were several occasions quickly becoming the norm in the lifestyle whereas they would remain out so late or all night long, they would go to work straight, directly in after a night of partying. Liz would learn from Stephanie that this had long been the regular thing, although it wasn't always the recommendable activity, but some *gaijin* never leave the comfort zone of their extended honeymoon stage of being in Japan. There were always new things to discover, new people or strange, quaint things to see; it kept curious foreign minds thirsty like sponges to absorb it all, and it kept them out late.

They would roll up into their respective Bozack English schools looking and smelling like the walking dead. Living corpses with the stench of alcohol and dried vomit spatter strutted—sometimes staggered—into their places of employment, often with the same clothes they wore on the previous day, with disheveled, wrecked hairstyles. This, along with melted eyeshadow encircling ominous orbs made them look like punk rock performers or rock concert backstage groupies more so than teachers of any sort. Were it not for their attempt at wearing business attire, conservative in dress code—that is, those who really adhered or complied to the dress code—it would have been questionable if Liz and the others were even teachers at all.

Having a bit more pride than some of her average party-animal coworkers, Liz—and later Stephanie—would cover their odor with an 84 spray (*13) and some really expensive perfume like Chanel, Samourai, Platinum Musk, and some other fragrances. And this was when they would finally discover what Radley Owen's *wonk* (talent) was. Shoplifitng.

His favorite things to boost, of course, would be smaller items like colognes, perfumes, and small bottles of anything sold in cases close to the doors or exits; but word had it he could lift just about anything and had secured a nifty side hustle for himself outside of working as an English teacher. True or not, he was never caught or apprehended. He once brought into the Hommachi School a boxed bundle of perfumes, lotions, bubble baths, colognes, and shampoos. Before Liz found out that he was a part-time maven of thievery, she had always thought him a cadaverous, ungainly laggard with a Josh Hartnet appeal who was having a garage sale of items left by former rich Japanese girlfriends.

Radley, like Tim the Duke, was a risk taker, yes, but he was also a fixer. He fenced stolen goods almost like a flash dealer. Not only could he get toiletries and perfumes, he could also get clothes and electronic items. Nobody knew how he did it. He, like the Duke, got so good at what they did they began to take "orders." Foreign teachers and coworkers would reach out to Radley when they had a special need or request to have a type of camera, or a type of music player, or anything that the shopper could get good information on for Radley to get it or one like it. His secret nickname for those who enlisted his services was the Labrador, because he retrieved items practically for hire, and had achromatic, black hair like the dog. This probably would explain the reasons for Radley's frequent absences. Liz wasn't as creeped out by Radley as she was by others like Kwame and Eric and had pleasant interaction with him on occasions they met. Since Liz was "new," he had given her some brand-name goods for free.

As for the drugs, most of the guys preferred speed mostly, but there always seemed to be weed smokers all over the place. Liz would indulge whenever invited by Keefer or one of the others in between classes, right under the noses of oblivious, unsuspecting Japanese staff who had no clue of what marijuana aroma smelled like. The only one who might have had a clue was Kayo, but since she was sweet on Keefer, if she did, that cat was never let out of the bag.

What Liz didn't like about the weed was the price. It was ten times the price it was in the States, and back in California, it was practically free—*for her*. It was more expensive than coke and less available too, but of course, Tim had the connects. Apparently, he got his sizzle from dealers in addition to Luzio Silver, and he was the best guy to go to around the Bozack circuit for any recreational needs.

Stephanie was a Bozack community human bulletin board quid-nunc with her ear to the ground about anything interesting and new for all to indulge in. She came across the news of a new spot called the Pink Carnation in Shinsaibashi that was giving away "buy one get one free" one-hundred-yen tequila shots after 10:00 pm. With the exception of Eric Radley, who did not drink or indulge in intoxicants of any type, almost everyone else there was stoked to pay the place a visit. The usuals—Stephanie, Keefer, his pals Ricky and Simon, Vicky, and a couple of other faceless foreigners whom Liz was faintly, if even, acquainted with—planned to check the place out after work on a Saturday night.

On that Saturday, Liz finished work at the Umeda School and fell up into the Hommachi School around 7:45 p.m. All the other teachers were still teaching classes; no one was around. The Japanese staff was busy as usual with their gig. She was hoping she would bump into anyone who knew how to contact Tim. Stephanie didn't have it. Keefer did, and neither Stephanie nor Liz had Keefer's number! Victoria (Vicky) might have had it, but she wasn't answering her phone. Liz cursed herself for not having Tim's number. They should have exchanged digits the night he took her to the Cellar to meet Luzio Silver. Not willing to cry over spilled milk, she decided, "Fuck it, catch him next time," and waited for Eddie to show, because she had told him in brow-beating fashion to hurry his ass up and meet her there. He should have already been there, but he had left a phone message for her with some pathetic excuse about him missing the faster express train due to some sudden case of the runs. He could not squat properly over the hole-in-the-ground–type toilet, accidentally soiled his trousers, another ten minutes was spent cleaning it, which still made him seem like he had pooped his pants with the wet stain.

Luck struck in the form and shape of a game-show microphone sculpted small afro donned by Chucky Chilson, suddenly appearing and bouncing around in the school coffee lounge space of the break room. He must have had a no-show lesson and had returned from outside. If anybody had Tim's number, surely Chucky would! Liz assumed.

With a silence-shattering shout, she startled Chucky with a shriek for a greeting, instead of the standard "Hello" or "Good evening." She yelled out his name loudly like she was a female cop. Chucky almost dropped the papers he was carrying to cock his fists. When he discovered who she was, he relaxed and frown-smirked as they exchanged friendlier, normal greetings.

Without beating around the bush, Liz asked Chucky for Tim's digits. Chucky glowered at her. "Why you askin' me? Why don't you ask your friends, they call him all the time for what you want."

While this was true, Liz felt the need to explain her position for she had already tried to contact her so-called friends for Tim's info.

She said, "Oh, spare me dude, I've been tryna get in touch with Vicky all day. She won't answer her phone while she's still working. Stephanie doesn't know Tim's number because I guess he never gave it to her?" Stephanie wasn't a big druggie, or at least not the "purchase" type. She liked to mooch off of other people's stash or collect their roaches or leftovers.

Chucky waved off Liz's garrulous tirade like a swarm of gnats, saying, "OK, OK, I get it. I'll write it down, hold up." He picked a pen from his shirt pocket and inked the number on a memo.

Satisfied, Liz looked around and surveyed the surroundings. The Japanese staff were busy with potential customers, clients, and office tasks. The other foreign teachers would still be teaching for several more minutes before the chime. She and Chucky were alone, so this would be a good time, she thought, to quiz him. She had a nosy desire to know details about him and Denore.

Liz leaned close to Chucky as he finished writing the number and was about to hand it to her. She sort of stage-whispered, "So where are you and Denore headed to tonight?"

Chucky squinted and turned his back to Liz, tending to the cream and sugar in his java joint. His mind was screaming, *Why is this bitch all up in my business?* Instead, he swiveled back around and faced her to state, "We're goin' to hang out at that rich white boy's house in Tanimachi Towns." The scowl through his wiry glasses smoothed out.

Liz pulsed like a dynamo. She said, "Who, Worm? You mean he's back? When did he get back?"

They surprised each other. Liz was taken aback to discover that Chucky was on such good terms with head teacher Mitch Swiggler that he would be extended an invitation to visit his home. Likewise, Chucky was dumbfounded that Liz even knew Worm at all, let alone his nickname. He hadn't been to work for months; he was one of those extended leave of absences because of a "marriage anniversary." He definitely hadn't been around when Liz first began working there.

Liz knew about Worm only through talk. Nothing special, just everybody called him Worm because he was skinny but wore oversized suits to compensate for his flimsy build. Also, he had married a rich woman like Eric Cravens did, but the difference was Worm married a Japanese woman who was already of money—plus, she had amassed a fortune of her own from career endeavors of her past. The first thing she decided to do was address the issue of ethnicity, which she felt Chucky had inaccurately described.

"He's not white," she said.

Chucky sipped his coffee, but then said matter-of-factly, "Oh yeah, I remember he's half Japanese." His voice was dripping with sarcasm; his annunciation fingers were raised.

Liz said, "You guys gonna stay there all night or somethin'?" She needed to verify Denore was not coming back to the dormitory.

Chucky was vague, but he said, "He has more than enough room to put us up for the night, if it came to that, that's for damn sure. That place is a mansion. I thought you woulda partied there before, but I just remember, you're still pretty new, only a few months workin' here. Anyway, that dude got dollars on his dollars. No side hustle needed for him."

Liz was a hater. She said, "*He's* not rich, *his wife is rich.* She's rich and Japanese. Worm's mother is from Japan, I think, but from what I was told, he was born in Canada, and no, I've never been to his Japanese wife's palace."

Chucky's face looked terrified by what he had heard, but he was simply appalled. He said, "What the *hell* does it matter? She's rich, they're married, he can freely spend her money. What the fuck difference does it make who is Japanese and whose mother is whatever?"

Liz rolled her eyes and brushed past Chucky at the coffee station, slid in beside him while doing so, gave him a playful bump with her hip. Chucky moved out of her way and allowed her room to fix her own cup of coffee.

She said fatuously, "You know what else? That rich Japanese lady is, like, ten years older than he is, isn't she?" Instead of coffee, she had elected to make tea. When she was done, she strutted away from the coffee station in a dancing trot, still rolling her eyes. She figured that Chucky would be checking out her ass like the black guys always did, and she was right. He wasn't disrespectful about it; his was just a glance that caused him to raise his eyebrows favorably as if he had given her some sort of unsaid approval. Liz had happened to turn and catch him staring while she pretended to innocently sip from her teacup. This time she didn't feel the need to be offended or outraged.

Chucky then said, "What are you doing here today anyway?"

Liz said, "Steph is meeting us here. We're supposed to meet up here and then go to that new place, the one that's gonna give the free tequila shots."

Chucky asked, "Who is 'us'?"

Liz said, "Oh yeah, Vicky, Keefer . . . oh, my boyfriend is coming. He's on his way here now. In fact, he should have already been here. Where the fuck is he? I'll call him again now . . . " She fumbled through her expensive little purse.

She said, "Where's that other guy? Your friend with the long hair, looks like a rapper . . . where is he? I haven't seen him around. Boy, is that guy weird."

Chucky snarled lightly as if he wished he could dash the last bit of coffee he had in his cup dead straight in Liz's face, then rinse it with spittle. Who was *she* to call any of *his* pals weird?

Liz's fatuity was a bit annoying to people at times, and then was no exception. She didn't feel, however, that she be made accountable for it, or face any consequences because of it either. She continued, "Yeah, you know who I'm talkin' about—he has a Spanish name, you guys say he's an Indian, but he's from New York and looks an' talks like you negros. I don't get it. That's weird."

An immoral grin flashed across Chucky's grill. He said, "You need to hook up with Tim, right?"

"No," Liz said quickly. "It's not Tim I'm talkin' about, silly. I'm talkin' about the other guy . . ."

Chucky shook his head like he was abruptly exhausted trying to get through to an alien. He held up his G-Shock watch and a round clock hung high on the break room wall to check if both times coincided. He then said, "You do know that *the Duke* pushes off at eight, don't you?"

At first Liz had no idea what Chucky was talking about. She then recalled certain code speak they had adopted so that English-comprehending Japanese people wouldn't catch on. She looked at her watch, which read 7:59 p.m., two minutes shy of the time shown on the break room clock. It was then, and only then, she faintly recounted mention that Tim ceased taking orders for sizzle at 8:00 p.m. That night she met Tim she had gotten so trashed the intricate data had slipped her mind.

After collecting orders from the people desiring drug and their cash, Tim the Duke would then go to some undisclosed location in town and cop the goods. The 8:00 p.m. cutoff time ensured that he could be back with all the filled orders by, or in between 9:00 p.m. and 9:30 p.m.

The Bozack chime sounded off, signaling the end of all the class sessions for that particular night. This showed that the clock in the breakroom was one or two minutes fast.

Panicky, Liz punched keys into her Tuka phone that Chucky had just supplied her with moments earlier. Just then, the school's narrow hallways became slowly crowded with footsteps of random, just-released refugees of human aquariums they called classrooms. Fatigued *gaijin* teachers rushed to the teachers' breakroom, and the noise of their chattering voices was growing as Liz strained to hear her phone ringing Tim.

Several city sectors away, an annoyed Tim the Duke regretted answering Liz's phone call. Liz was accustomed to dealing with Luzio Silver directly. He delivered, or made his product available, twenty-four hours, and that was for the C, not the other stuff. Tim, on the other hand, had established a cutoff time point for his unique services, but because Liz was new, he decided to give her a pass that one time. She missed the deadline, he figured rationally, because she wasn't aware of closing time. That didn't stop him from being pissed off, however. He didn't like delays. He had gone through tremendous lengths to ensure that he ran a smooth operation, and this coincided with the precise timing and arrival of public transportation, getting him to and from where he needed to go in a timely manner; staying on schedule was of importance to him, his connects, and the customers.

Frustrated, Tim told Liz to meet him at the Candy Box Lounge in Kyobashi town near Osaka Castle. She was to either meet him there in thirty minutes from that time, or no deal. She would have to wait until next Saturday.

Fortunately for Liz, she knew where Kyobashi was. She had been to the area before with coworkers and remembered it vaguely. The club itself would be a problem to remember. Just then, as if conjured by mere thoughts of her, Stephanie had arrived at the Hommachi School and had made her appearance in the break room where everyone was. She was dressed like the regular Saturday night foreign hooker: skirt, cheap high heels, unfastened snap-shut Western-style Oxford shirt revealing cleavage and a skimpy blue plunge bra, tons of makeup, hair full of sticky spray, heavily perfumed. Accompanying her was bummy, walking sponge mop–topped Keefer and stunning Vicky, who had recently paid a visit to Takaro's salon and had him lace her flipped layers of dark hair with a deep part, tons of volume and bounce, creating a dramatic, sultry look with her black polo-neck shirt of thin fabric and a pearly necklace. There were so many others around, and some people Liz didn't know well.

Stephanie spotted Liz immediately and rushed to greet her. That instant she had approached Liz, she was receiving instructions from Tim and struggling to hear his voice pitted against the clamorous backdrop that had erupted in the teachers' break room. Liz sumo-shoved Stephanie away from her with one strong palm striking the middle of the 32D breasts and readied herself to leave.

Terminating the call, Liz said to her, "Steph, listen, I'll catch up with you guys later. Make sure you answer my phone call when I ring you later. In fact, put your phone on vibration mode instead of the ringer. Just in case you guys get to somewhere it's too loud for you to hear it ringing, you can feel your phone vibrating and know someone is calling. More than likely, it'll be me."

Stephanie was clueless but acquiescent, as Liz sprang out of the breakroom, to the long corridor to the main office room and exit and out into the street. She sprinted to the Chuo-odori Road and Midosuji Avenue intersection and hailed a cab. Luckily, she had worn flats that day.

Twelve minutes later, the taxi dropped her off at Coms Garden at Kyobashi near the subway holes. She threw three 1,000-yen bills at the cabbie and his 2,100-yen fare and shouting at him to "keep the change" as she jetted from the car and headed uphill in the direction, she saw trains from the Keihan Line dock the terminal. Per directions from Tim, if she headed to the Keihan Train Station, she was going in the right direction.

She bolted up the hill beneath the Keihan Railway underpass, saw the Koban police box, and continued two more blocks uphill and saw the decrepit, grubby backstreets teeming with after-hour pubs, brothels, cabaret clubs, and snack shops. The streets were lined with suit-clad individuals seeking female clients to work or patronize their bars or clubs. As Liz strode past them, some of their eyes would flick open wide as if they had seen a Hollywood starlet. One of the hosts tried to speak to Liz, but she didn't wait for him to make any ailing attempt to kick it to her. She asked him where the Candy Box was.

She almost didn't even need any directions because she was less than a block away from the building the club was located in, but the man was willing to show her where it was anyway. Because the place was popular and it had a catchy name, people who didn't ordinarily speak English could remember rather easily. She loosely thanked the man and brushed him off as she entered the building. By the time she approached the entrance, she was panting.

There was an enormous figure of a clown's head that sat menacingly before an orange, satin curtain-laced door. A pink tongue extended out of the hideous clown's mouth like a slithering, sliding board on a children's playground. Glued to the tongue was the artist designer's rendition of peppermint candy, toys, and a syringe. Two immaculately dressed Japanese staff stood before a podium of sorts. They spotted Liz and ascertained immediately that she was a *gaijin* and offered her a stamp on her pale wrist. Liz looked at the candy cane ink on her right hand. As she wasn't Japanese, she didn't have to pay the entry fee. She received a free drink ticket as she moved past the door attendants and approached another set of double doors. She could hear the loud music seeping from the cracks of the glass portal. When she pushed open the doors, a barrage of sound blasted into her face and eardrums like a flood of fugue. She was almost dizzy on the spot trying to follow the music's pattern due to the momentary disorientation. Electronic beats and robotic hymns floated a small cotillion of early Saturday night lunatic drunkards on a commodious, bowl-shaped dance floor. Although the place was exceedingly darkened, she could still make out its general structure, and it was rather clean and posh in appearance, and so were most of the people. She saw no one dressed "casually"—everyone seemed to be dressed like they were headed to or coming from an office job. People were in suits, ties, and women were likewise dressed in respectable attire, nothing sleazy or provocative like in some other clubs. Although foreigners could get in for free, Liz didn't see too many of them. In fact, she appeared to be the only white girl there as far as she could tell. Everyone else seemed to be Japanese or Asian in general.

Liz's athletic ability helped her avoid intoxicated Japanese women and men in their early thirties, office worker–attired and expensive-clothed, as they sailed the air like sky divers in practice. This activity was what they considered to be dancing. Heads and arms flailed frantically and offbeat to the obstreperously blasting techno, the dance floor looked like a boiling pot full of people fighting.

Groping hands from curious Japanese debauchees in business suits rubbed hungrily at parts of Liz's body as she squeezed through a conglomerate of inebriated human statues. Stationary effigies of human females remained still and motionless so as to intentionally block Liz's or anyone's path, pretending to be either too drunk or too listless to move out of her way. Gently, Liz wedged her way through these individuals and inched her way to the brightly lit, hollowed oval-shaped bar counter. The scene looked like a fiasco from a zombie and kung-fu genre crossover flick.

Liz was growing a bit impatient. She saw no sign of Tim, and she was fearing that she might have missed him. That maybe he got tired of waiting and had decided to split without her. A stroke of luck offered her the chance to grab a high seat at the counter; a drunk couple had hopped off their chairs and left before Liz propped herself up on one. Then she could see the place from a better vantage point.

The palatial space looked as if it could have previously been a royal kitchen for some European bigwigs. The walls were covered with the similar satin tapestries she saw at the entrance. Although the place was relatively dark, she could still make out through the flashing lights brocades of interwoven fabrics, with maybe gold and silver trim. The fiery orange color of the curtains gave the place a hellish, devil's den look when the lights randomly flashed on.

Finally, through a wildly cavorting smidgen of drunk idiots, Liz spotted Tim. On the circular bar counter, he was located at two o'clock to Liz's seven o'clock. Carefully, she made her way over to where he was. As she approached, she had to duck and dodge feral, flying hands, cloddish collisions and abominable dancers before arriving by his side at the luxurious, illuminated bar counter.

Dapper as ever, a lustrous short-sleeved rayon taffeta shirt caressed his muscular chest and cigar in his jib as usual. He was hugged up with his renowned companion, the Asian female Catwoman, dressed in black, snug leather pants and animal print sweetheart-neckline blouse gave her small bust line prurient definition. Tim puffed his licorice-aroma blunt while he sipped a dark, blood-red-colored wine from an impitoyable. He spotted Liz as she crept to his side opposite his woman and he issued her a vicious, lupine sneer.

The Duke said, "Amberbush, you gonna make me late. If I'm late, then everybody's gonna get their shit late, then that's gonna fuck up my business and my rep, you dig?"

Liz was by now a little winded from all the running around she had been doing to arrive within the thirty-minute time frame that Tim had instituted. Her momentary pause to catch her breath made Tim think that she was taking his admonishing lightly.

He said to her, "Oh, so you think I'm a joke?"

Liz pleaded, "No, no, Tim, not at all. I'm sorry. I'll never do it again, I promise. Please believe me." She had managed a smile while expressing her grief and was too distracted to argue about anything. Basically, she knew she had screwed up by not remembering to adhere to the cutoff deadline time, but all the same, she was delighted that she had made it in time before he dipped out.

Tim graciously accepted her series of bills and shoved them in his pocket, informed by her that she wanted half an ounce of pot. It cramped his style a bit because he was accustomed to receiving his orders on coded slips of paper, but he skull-noted Liz's request anyway. Catwoman helped him with his lightweight jacket, and he covered his beehive-waved dome with a trilby lid.

Tim said to Liz, "The delivery spot is gonna be in Umeda at around nine thirty, but probably closer to ten now because of you."

Liz was like, "Yeah, yeah, OK, OK," happy with herself for having enough foresight to have visited the ATM in Umeda earlier. Now that she had cleaned her wallet out, she would have to pay another visit to a withdrawal vestibule before the end of the night.

She called out to Tim as she followed him toward the exit, "Where in Umeda, Tim?"

Tim said, "We always meet up at the Big Shrine near the American Consulate General. Everybody knows where that is. All your crew is probably gonna be there anyway. Better make sure you be there, though, 'cause I ain't gonna be lookin' for you."

Liz nodded frantically as she watched Tim leave. His Catwoman companion vanished mysteriously into the liquidy silhouettes of the eclipsed ballroom as if she were never there at all. Suddenly she was alone at the bar counter feeling a tad uneasy, which was rare for her. She quickly realized it was because she didn't often venture into places such as this without her cronies or Eddie to lean on like a crutch.

An unexpected *pop* exploded several feet away from where Liz stood, and her heart raced for an instant. She turned to see a small group of dandy-threaded Osaka girls and guys who had just popped a bottle of champagne. They were all laughing spasmodically watching the bubbles jet out of the nozzle. It was by now somewhat obvious to Liz that this particular place was full of weirdo Japanese, according to her. When Tim left, she was almost certain she was the only non-Japanese person in the entire place.

Finding the empty seat Tim left behind still vacant, she climbed into it. Upon doing so, she decided to use the free drink ticket she was given when she entered the club earlier. She figured she may as well kill some time. A slim bartender sporting a jaunty, jet-black assymetric short-cut spotted Liz. He flipped a limp wrist across the side of his shaved head and pranced maidenly toward her, a gait similar to how Liz had seen the hairstylist Takaro gallop around his shop. The guy ignored two thirsty suits waving empty glasses at him demanding refills as he approached Liz. She couldn't communicate well with him, though. The music was still loud as hell, plus his English was just as inept as her Japanese. He then extended both of his bare palms toward Liz's direction as if to say, "Wait!"

In English, the man said, "Just wait a minute." He trotted off with a prissy twist. Seconds later, he returned with a tall man with curly blond hair and what appeared to resemble a John Travolta–type depression on the flesh of his chin. When he and Liz made eye contact, they smiled at each other immediately. It would have been a love-at-first-sight" moment if Liz wasn't already hitched, perhaps. For the entire year and almost a half, this man was the first foreign guy that she could actually describe as a hunk, or with handsome features. He appeared to be well built, as if he worked out, and he wasn't a scraggly, unkempt Keefer; an awkward, lumbering Radley; or a geeky like Eric. He was the most masculine man she had seen of foreign extraction, aside from the black guys at work, admittedly; but he was pleasing to her eyes enough to cause her to grin.

Likewise, the man had probably seen many women because of his job there at the club, but apparently, he must have seen some sort of quality in Liz's features that enabled a happy look to crease his face. Besides, she was a foreigner like him.

Liz shouted to him over the tumult, "Hiyeee! You speak English, huh?"

The man squinted and tilted his head to the side irresolutely and said, "Very little, but maybe Yes." Liz didn't hear him thoroughly, so she leaned forward and exclaimed, "WHAT?!" And he leaned in and explained to her that he was French, or something like that. His story was blurred within the flood of sound that relentlessly pounded Liz's ears. She could make out about 2 percent of what he had said before she decided to cut him off and order a drink. She handed him her free ticket.

The man asked her, "What vould you like?" in a thick, Euro-tinged accent.

Liz wasn't much of a beer drinker, but she did because it was often the most accessible alcoholic beverage for her. Tonight she figured she needed not waste a free drink on a beer when she was into shooters, tooters, bombers, slammers, shots, and cocktails as well.

She said, giggling, "Can you get me an Alabama Slammer?"

The man shook his head no with a piteous look. Then he explained that he had never heard of such a thing. He was not familiar with the various names of cocktails in English. He gave the same response after Liz ran off the names of every drink from a Charlie Chaplin to a Melon Ball to Tequila Sunrise to Sex on the Beach before settling on the only thing he knew, which was a normal, standard Gin and Tonic. Liz was resolved to accept that and felt happy Japan bartenders and servers didn't receive tips. A moment or two later, her drink arrived. She guzzled it like the thirsty fish she became and quickly ordered another, offering to pay with what money she still had left, which wasn't much.

By then, the foreign hunk had vanished, and the slopey banged toothpick guy in black had reappeared in his place. He placed a loaded highball glass in front of her. Now that he knew what she wanted, he fixed it stronger and told her it was "no charge." Which was good, because she only had a one-thousand-yen bill left. She eased herself off the high chair and stood while she sipped the drink.

Eddie had been ringing her on her cell, but she couldn't hear the phone because the club music had drowned out the sound of the chime tone. Liz had failed to follow her own instructions she had issued to Stephanie earlier, to put her phone on vibration mode should she be in the same predicament she was currently in.

That time was a quarter to nine or thereabout, and Eddie had arrived to a closed and boarded up Bozack School in Hommachi, where he had been ordered to go to. He was ill and pissed off. Something he had digested earlier had given him diarrhea. Hiroko had noticed his discomfort and went through tremendous lengths to help by giving him some chamomile tea. A school nurse offered Eddie some water-soluable bismuth, which he happily accepted because it tasted like the Western Pepto product he knew from back home, but differing only with its foamy gray color. He felt a little better for a period of time, but had to rush to the train station toilet once more before finally catching a speedier train to the city. The unstable rumble of his bowels still threatened to stampede again from his rectum. He raced from the Hommachi School back to the subway station below the streets where he knew there would be a bathroom for him to use. To his chagrin, the only toilets available were more of the squatting types. Having obviously not mastered the method of taking a crap, he decided to avoid the humiliation of walking around anymore with shit or a wet spot from cleaning it on the seat of his khakis.

On Saturdays, business hours came to a close a smidgen earlier than on weekdays. Thus, a half an hour after the final lesson ended at 8:00 p.m., Kayo of the Japanese staff informed the collection of *gaijin* teachers remaining at the school that they were about to close and lock up the school. They didn't have to go home, but they couldn't stay there. Eddie hadn't arrived yet then, but unfortunately, they all couldn't stay there and wait for him.

Stephanie too had tried to call Liz. She wanted to inform Liz that the school was closing and receive further instructions about what to do regarding Eddie, who, according to Liz, was already supposed to have been there. Like Liz, a couple of people—namely Simon and Ricky—had also placed orders with the Duke and wished to get to Osaka Umeda by 9:00 p.m., giving them enough time to reach the Big Shrine(or Ohatsu-Tenjin / Tsuyuten Shrine) by the 9:30 p.m. delivery drop-off time. No reason to hold everyone up, so they had decided to leave.

Around 9:15 p.m., a tipsy, half-stumbling Liz hopped out of a cab near the East Osaka (Higashi Umeda) Station. She teetered over to the rendezvous spot and met up with Stephanie, Keefer, Vicky, and assorted others familiar and non-familiar faces. The group numbered about ten people in total, like a soccer or baseball team waiting to take the field.

Stephanie scooted quickly toward Liz as she made her way up the long, wide street heading toward the direction of the huge intersection of Midosuji Avenue and First and Second prefectural roadways. Both of them were steeped in wonderment upon seeing each other.

Liz said to Stephanie, "What are you doing here?"

Stephanie said in an antithetical sort of way. "What are *you* doing here? Didn't you get my message?"

She hadn't. As if she had awakened from a deep slumber and regained a lost memory, Liz took her phone out of her expensive purse and read its screen. Sure enough, she scrolled through a series of at least ten missed calls. The list of received calls were an equal number of both Stephanie's and Eddie's. Liz gasped as if she had just been punched in her stomach.

"Oh shit!" she exclaimed. "Eddie! Steph, did he come? Where is he?"

Stephanie said, "Sorry, Elizabeth . . . I . . . I tried to call you more than once. We had to leave because they were closing the school. A couple of the guys, Keefer's friends, wanted to meet Tim here too, and we all need to be at the Pink Carnation before or around ten. We have to get out entry stamps before the drinkin' festivity starts."

Just then, before Liz could speed-dial Eddie and check on his status, she spotted Tim's hulking, six-foot heavyweight boxing champ–toned physique emerge from a portal of back alley shade. Several non-Japanese individuals with their small, memo-sized sheets of paper approached him carefully but cheerily eager. Liz then brushed off Stephanie and followed Tim like the other zombies wishing to get dope down a narrow winding thoroughfare intended for only pedestrians. This passage was nestled between dark, tiny shops with bay windows and electric signboards in front blazing the establishment name. Tim found a darkened corner beside a set of vending machines. His black silk glove–laden paws produced a suede satchel bag with snap-button straps.

The first "zombie" in succession of many handed the Duke their slip of paper with a number. Tim glanced at it and dipped his hand inside the bag. A mini-instant later produced from it a corresponding digit attached package of sizzle bearing whatever the shopper/customer had ordered. Whatever ordered was cleverly concealed, disguised, and tucked away inside of an emptied-out vitamin bottle or something of that sort. When it was Liz's turn, she didn't have a "memo," but Tim remembered Liz, and he eyeballed her with blank, icy irreverence. He reached inside of the suede satchel to whip out a small bag of what looked to be what the wording read on its surface: "Calbee Potato Chips." When he tossed it to Liz, she squeezed it, and it felt like a Brillo pad or sponge was inside of this polyethylene bag, not chips.

Tim sharply admonished, "Don't open that shit here, girl. You fuckin' crazy?"

It took a moment before Liz could snap out of the awe trying to figure out how they were able to seal the bag again like it had been just bought from a store. Relieved to be the last customer, she turned to reunite with Stephanie and the others.

Tim the Duke said "Yo, Amberbush, just remember for future reference, if you gon' do business with the Duke, you gots to place your order from Friday night until Saturday at 8:00 p.m. sharp, no exceptions next time."

Liz said, "What about that little piece of paper that everybody gives you? You didn't give me one to give back to you . . . oh, wait, because I was late, right? Hey, do you think you can score somethin' like ecstasy or that sort of stuff? A friend of mine wants it." It was a lie—she had no such friends who had requested that designer drug; she just didn't want Tim to see her like the other drugged-out zombies who were his regulars, although he already had the feeling she was.

Tim waved his gloved hand in front of Liz's face like he was wiping the wind away from her lips. He said, "Any piece of paper is cool, as long as you use the code. Coke, as you already should know is white girl, the speed is turbo. Weed is green, shrooms is veggies, and that other stuff you just now asked about is laxatives." He chuckled at the last one. Then he said, "Those are five thousand yen a pop, so get your purse ready to spend if that's what you want. Plus, I'll need twenty-four hours' notice on that one, so don't think of trying to do what you pulled tonight, girl."

His voice faded as he drifted lightly away, dissipating in the alley mist leading him back toward the Shin-Midosuji Avenue, where Catwoman in a car awaited him underneath the 423 Highway underpass.

Liz tucked away her "chips," stashing her package in her jacket's inner pocket and caught up with Stephanie and the others. They had been waiting for her impatiently back at the Tsuyuten Shrine gate entrance, facing the side street parallel to Prefectural Road 1. No cars there.

Keefer's "cobbers," Ricky and Simon, had copped some coke, hashish, and other illegal substances. They were giddy and full of excitement. For a couple of guys that detested Americans, they were certainly happy to see Tim that evening. Liz didn't need to guess why.

Vicky and Stephanie were close by with two random Japanese girls—one named Rena and another named Chikako. The J-girls were sycophantic students Liz had seen before from the Hommachi School. She had taught them once or twice, and they were relatively intermediate levels at speaking English. But they were more interested in having lessons with the male teachers like Keefer or Radley or any other white male available than female teachers. They surely had their reasons, but for women like Liz, she figured them to be hang-arounds, not much different from groupies for rock stars. Now, they were trying to cling closely to their Bozack English teachers, seeking to further their study of the language without spending extra money for actual lessons, as well as pursue any option of hooking up romantically with Keefer or one of his pals.

When Liz rejoined the group, Stephanie looked relieved. She crushed the cig she had been smoking underneath her worn-out T-strapped heels and grabbed Liz by the elbow. She said, "C'mon, we gotta head back to Shinsaibashi."

"Wait!" Liz uttered in a whiny, drunken-bound protest. "I have to get in touch with Eddie," she said.

Stephanie said, "You can call him on the way. We've gotta catch a cab. Now let's move!"

Keefer heard her and then said, "Aye, aye, Cap'n!" in an acrimonious, mocking military-salute style, causing the small group to laugh and Stephanie to shoot him a stiff, pudgy middle finger of hers.

He replied, "Oh, hurt me, love! I likes it in me freckle while givin'a go!"

Such ribaldry was common from him; everyone was entertained by it, Liz included—but not tonight. That time, she was becoming agitated. Seeing Keefer with his fan club of ignoble Japanese groupies didn't do much to simmer her nerves either. She didn't want Eddie to be around guys like him. She kept trying to call Eddie's phone, but she kept getting the same recording.

The recording was in Japanese, and of course, Liz could not understand what it was saying, or why she was unable to leave a message like she ordinarily could. She decided to then put one of the bemused, giddy J-girls to good use and stepped up to the first one within the immediate reach of her pink-coated fingernails.

Grabbing Rena roughly by her balloon sleeve, Liz yanked the young J-girl, causing her to stumble over to where she had been standing. Roughly she ordered, "Hey, translate this for me, what's this saying?" She shoved her phone to Rena's ear.

Rena exchanged a nervous sentence with her partner, Chikako, then listened to the phone message. A moment after, in relatively good, intermediate-level English, she responded, "This, person, phone . . . is . . . not use . . . now. Maybe they . . . turn off . . . phone . . . so you cannot leave message now."

Utterly disappointed, Liz retracted her arm with the phone and stared at it.

She said to the girl Rena, "OK, thanks." But didn't apologize to her for the rough handling.

Liz then noticed that her own phone's battery had an indicator which denoted its power had shrunk to two bars of connectivity from a maximum of four. She had left her charger at home.

On a Nankai Honsen (Main Line) Train headed back to Hannan City's Hakkotsukuri Station, Eddie was aboard literally "feeling like shit." Additionally, he was highly pissed at Liz. If things couldn't get any worse, his Tuka phone too had a depleted battery. In such haste to arrive in Osaka City as Liz had ordered, Eddie hadn't returned to his pad to retrieve his phone charger. On top of that, he didn't remember where Liz lived in the city. He forgot all about the name of the Bentencho Station or the address of Liz's housing spot. So when he had arrived at the Hommachi School to find the place boarded up and closed, Liz nowhere to be found or contacted, he felt no other recourse but to return home. Mad.

26

AT 5:59 A.M., outside the all-night diner Roastal Horse, sunlight oozed onto the landscape like soapy lather attempting to cleanse, scour, and purify rancid Shinsaibashi Osaka streets. Sunday morning was crowded still with early-bird dwellers. The avenues looked like littered spaces after a parade or carnival. Ornamented party people from the previous night's festivities stumbled along concrete footpaths and indoor arcades like freakish ghouls searching for holes in the ground to inhabit. The humidity was already like a thick blanket of heated moisture. From Namba Station to the Dotombori Channel, sepia-colored taxis swarmed the streets like motorized cockroaches eating up lanes and spaces of the road, blowing hysterical horn screams as would an imp toddler when aggravated. Nobody gave a damn about the early hour; quiet was not enforced here. The sounds of traffic, construction, screeching of bicycle tires, and people retching in short alleys dominated the air. There was also a couple yelling and screaming at each other in front of the diner, or "family restaurant."

Inside, Liz woke up with her face halfway stuck inside of a big bowl, which had contained some type of noodles. It was Stephanie who was waking her up, shaking her shoulders. Alongside her was a distressed Japanese worker, recognized later as the manager of the place, and he was uttering something exclamatory in his language.

As best she could, Liz tried to quickly pull herself together and clear her head. Difficult. Somehow, a Marlboro Light square found its way to her parched lips. Stephanie had plucked it from her purse and had intended to smoke it herself until Liz snatched it from her. Stephanie lit the cig for Liz like she was her flunky lackey. Liz didn't really like cigarettes; she would rather have had a joint, but she didn't know how to roll them. She didn't even know where to buy the paper to roll joints. But that was another problem for another time.

A quick scan of the room would help her spot one of Keefer's cronies, Simon, knocked out on the floor underneath the table, using the crumpled mass of his jacket as a pillow. Snoring.

The table they sat at was trashed with rice, soy sauce, beer, and coffee in what little space left available. A heap of multiple napkins were lodged where someone had attempted to clean up many spills. There was a crudely stacked convention of almost every sort of dish imaginable: dinner dishes, salad and bread dishes, serving platters, soup crocks, saucers of various shapes and sizes, fruit bowls, bread-and-butter plates, pasta bowls, several glasses, some of which were overturned.

On the floor, Liz's foot almost kicked Simon in the face accidentally. When she retracted her leg from the area near his face, she felt a sticky, pudding-like sludge underneath her shoe. It looked as if someone had vomited clam chowder with raisins.

Liz squinted at the big mess and struggled to piece together a timeline that connected her here and the last coherent memory in her brain. It was still difficult. She puffed smoke in the air; the room became a little cloudy. The frustrated manager rambled off a lengthy series of sentences in Japanese, but to the American citizens, he may as well have sounded like one of Charlie Brown's Peanuts' teachers speaking through helium throats.

Stephanie looked tattered, torn, and worn like she had just got a train run on her. Her blouse was stained and ripped along the sleeve, so many runs in her stockings they looked like designer spiderwebbed lace leggings and through smeared pink lipstick, she said, "I . . . I can't speak Japanese, Liz . . . are you woken yet?"

Liz grumbled in a lower contralto. "I don't . . . speak Japanese either. Ooooh, my head!" There, she ached like her brain was receiving acupuncture with porcupine quills. She reached for the nearest glass of what looked like water and gulped it down to the last tiny cubes without verifying what exactly it was. She wretched at its taste, some sort of tea. She wasn't particularly fond of Oolong.

The Japanese staff was waiting impatiently. He was trying to be cordial, but one could tell that he was nearing the end of his rope. His Japanese affability could only extend but so far. Other restaurant patrons at this early time of the morning, mostly Japanese, looked at the crazy *gaijin* like the spectacles they were, shaking their heads. Some laughed while others merely stared curiously, feeling grateful that they didn't live in the countries those foreigners came from.

Liz still had no idea how she or any of the others had arrived here, or better, she had little recollection. She did remember having several tequila shots at a peculiar bar with an all-female staff, and they had all been dressed like sports cheerleaders. She remembered puking the first time when their cab convoy dropped off their posse of ten heads after picking them up in Umeda. The blackout occurred when they reached Shinsaibashi, but the pieces were slowly coming back into place.

Liz noticed a clear cylinder tube of fiberglass placed dead center on the table, amid the junkyard mountains of dishes. The tube was half the size of a 12-ounce can (355 ml). A slip of paper was rolled inside of the tube. This she knew to be the bill, recounted from outings had with welcoming committees back in Hannan. She reached for it to peek at what the damage was, at the same time exhaled smoke into the air again. When done, she extinguished her cig not in an ashtray but inside of the drinking glass from which she had sipped the Oolong tea. The ash fizzed out, and putrid fume pierced the immediate area.

The Japanese manager was visibly upset now. His face had flushed into a ruby-red grapefruit with rage. He ran into the kitchen. This would have been a good time to dine and dash, because Liz checked out the bill and saw the tab came up to a whopping 57,000 yen. She almost screamed. It must have been some party!

The manager then returned, after having emerged from the kitchen with a waitress-uniform-clad young girl in tow. She appeared to be so nervous she was at the brink of tears. When the manager appeared before Liz and Stephanie, the young woman had followed, and he pulled her forward, reluctantly. The waitress started speaking in English:

"Manager said, you, must, everyone, pay money and please, you, go!"

This Liz and Stephanie understood loud and clear. An agitated Stephanie plaintively cried, "But . . . we can't leave without the others!"

While Stephanie rambled utterances with expostulatory whining, Liz was like, "What others?" And that instant, as if struck by lightning, random recollection and concomitant abilities restored the memory of Keefer splitting with Chikako, the friend of Rena who had translated the phone message, Liz recounted. Vicky had parted ways with them and skipped off early with a weird but handsome Japanese boy, who was one of her students at another Bozack English branch. Simon was snoozing away underneath the table still, and the arguing couple on the sidewalk outside the diner were Ricky and Rena.

Although Liz didn't know this, Ricky and Rena were screaming and yelling at each other because the latter had put up a hefty sum of loot for the cocoa puffs, 3M, hashish and other dope delivered by the Duke. This was done obsequiously by Rena in hopes that Ricky would commit to her. Claim her he did as his girlfriend, but as soon as they had arrived at the all-female bar, the Pink Carnation, he got too happy with the tequila and flirted with the receptive women. Having assumed that her gracious offer to pay for the hard merch would solidify her as Ricky's woman, Rena would then go frenetically berserk when she caught wind that Ricky had got his willy wonk up a barmaid's turd space in the ladies' room.

Back inside the diner, Liz was thinking that everyone else who had dined with them had already dipped out. So everyone else, those remaining, she didn't have to give a crap about. Simon and Ricky weren't her friends—they were Keefer's. He was gone. They were not her responsibility.

She said to Stephanie, "Hey, we have to blow this joint."

Stephanie was looking all scared.

Using her Los Angeles, California, girl acumen, Liz assessed the scenario. Liz's tentative plan was to dip out, to assert the classical dine and ditch, chew and screw. Problem was, Stephanie had a tendency to be somewhat of a chicken shit. Liz found another cigarette from Stephanie's purse, thinking that another smoke would calm her nerves because of what she was planning to do. She was uneasy, but in her mind, there was no way she was going to pay that enormous tab.

When she lit up again, smack dab in the center of the non-smoking section—again—she immediately realized why everyone had been glaring at her with horrified, silly faces. Now the short, balding ruby-red faced manager was practically in tears, still rambling on wrath-laced sentences only other Japanese people could comprehend. Of course Liz didn't know what the hell he was babbling, but she could certainly get the gist. She exhaled smoke in the direction of an elderly couple seated nearby. A bespectacled gray-haired old man grimaced and tried to wave away the smoke. Liz was like, "Sorry," then placed another shank in the same cup she put out the previous one in.

Stephanie said "You mean . . . we should . . . leave?" Jerking her plumb thumb toward the storefront's dual exit-entrance like she was hitchhiking for that destination.

Liz got heated. *Don't gesture, you dumbass!* her mind screamed at Stephanie. *How can she be so dense?* Liz recalled her peeps back in the States: Mandy and Becky would have followed along with the plan without giving away their intentions. To levant was their specialty.

Liz slapped Stephanie's wrist down and forced a strained, grit-toothed grin "Put your friggin' hands down. Yeah, we should get the hell outta here."

Liz carefully and methodically began to gather all her things. She did not lose her phone. Good. She found her purse still next to her right buttock on the bench-like banquette upon which she was perched. She looked at her watch. Dammit! She had to be back at work in the forenoon in Umeda.

By now, pandemonium had all but erupted at the diner. With all the commotion outside the store glass window and inside with the antics of Liz and company, the other diner patrons had become agitated and unsettled. Some had looks of disgust, others were preparing to leave. Angrily they called for the service of the manager and other staff. The bungling manager had to bounce back and forth to tend to other customers and was extremely apologetic. He ambled back to Liz and Stephanie at their table.

Liz said in a slow and lethargic manner, as if she was speaking to a special-needs retarded, handicapped child, "HE . . ." She was pointing to Simon the sleeping Aussie on the floor. "HE . . . WILL . . . PICK . . . UP . . . THE . . . CHECK . . ." She kept pointing at Simon.

She said, "HE . . . WILL . . . PAY . . . FOR . . . EVERYTHING!" Her hand movement was karate-chopping the air in some arcane or nonexistent sign language.

Apparently, it worked. The waitress said "You will wake up him?" As she spoke, she approached Simon and crouched down as if she was going to rouse him herself. The manager would then mimic her action of crouching down. Both the manager and the waitress looked up at Liz and Steph as if they were expecting them to assist with the revival of their party's companion.

On the contrary, Liz stepped off, pretending to be having an important, pleonastic conversation in English. Stephanie followed nervously, as if she finally got the point. The manager wasn't as much a fool as they had taken him for. He knew what Liz and Steph were up to, having seen the large group file out all morning and had trickled down to just a few remaining.

The manager rose to his feet and looked like he wanted to give chase as Liz and Stephanie got closer and closer to the doors. He told the waitress to go call the police. She obeyed his command and as she went for the phone, a young male waiter emerged from the kitchen. The waitress told that waiter to block the doors so that neither Liz nor Stephanie could leave. The boy stood there frozen with his mouth wide open like he was watching a shocking show.

Stephanie groused, "We can't just . . . leave . . . can we?"

Liz was done. She was already out the door and glided by the useless waiter who was a mouth-agape statue. Her attitude matched her statement: "Do what you wanna do, I'm history. I'll see ya later!" Of course, her heart was pounding, but she was resolute in her actions.

Stephanie emboldened herself and slid her feet out of her heels and ran after Liz on the slimy, wet sidewalk, barefoot over brine seawater merchants used to cleanse concrete. When she caught up to Liz, she was told by her to not run but walk quickly.

Liz said, "If we run, we'll look suspicious. Let's just quicken the pace." She had seen the waitress grab the telephone back in the diner. Judging from hijinks experiences back in the States, it was a pretty fair assessment according to Liz that she was calling the fuzz. As she remembered the "potato chips" in her jacket's inner pocket, there was all the more reason for her to hastily depart.

Easily, they slid past Ricky and Rena who were still arguing, because their public display had drawn a small crowd of onlookers. Ricky now looked embarrassed as hell. Rena was trying to speak with him in English. He was still drunk sick, so he pretended as if he didn't understand what the fuck she was talking about, and he clowned her broken English attempts. This caused her to get angrier. Her teary-eyed chastisement squeaked imploringly, aggravating to the ear like nails in a blender.

Liz didn't feel the slightest bit guilty for leaving the Aussies behind as she patted the bulge in her jacket. As far as she was concerned, if those guys had enough cash to shell out for all the dope they bought, they should also have enough for the tab. And shame on all the others who had dined and decided to leave without leaving any contribution of payment as well, she repined.

They made it to the Sen-Nichi-Mae Road, Hanshin Highway underpass. There, Liz waved her hands frantically like she was front stage at a Prodigy concert for a taxi. At least three cabs spotted the two white foreigners and almost toppled the curb like wrecked matchbox hot wheel cars to pick them up. Selecting the closest one to where they stood, Liz and Stephanie got swallowed inside of it and sped off. Liz told the driver to take her to Bentencho where she lived, while fractiously listening to Stephanie beg her to be allowed to crash there for a few hours.

The cabbie turned north on Naniwa-Suji Lane. Liz told Stephanie to shut the fuck up because her headache had advanced from acupuncture pokes to shish kebab piercing. Plus, she had to go back to work in Umeda in a few hours, her shift beginning at 11:30 a.m. Stephanie dozed off after a moment of quiet in the cab as it sailed along past Osaka Dome. By the time they had arrived in Bentencho, Stephanie was snoring away. Liz woke her up roughly, deciding to allow Stephanie to crash for a while at her place for two reasons: one, she knew Denore wouldn't be there, and two, Stephanie could pay the cab fare, and she did.

They endured a weary walk back to Liz's dormitory building. Even if Denore was there, she was sure she wouldn't mind letting Stephanie sleep off her hangover. She didn't plan on Stephanie using Denore's bed, however.

After half carrying the still- barefoot Stephanie to the elevator, then lugging her inside of the apartment, she went back downstairs to the lobby. She used the remainder of her coins to buy bottled water and soft drinks from the vending machine there. She went back upstairs, and Stephanie had already made herself at home underneath the covers of Denore's vacant bed. Snoring.

Liz removed the bag of weed from her sweat-dampened jacket as she removed it, placed it on the table. She sat down and sipped heartily on the bottle of water she had just bought, trying to keep her upset stomach and queasy feeling at bay. She was lucky she was in shape, or at least tried to be. Lugging Stephanie around was a mammoth-sized job. Her eyelids were heavy and strained as she yawned continually. She had to get some rest, so she began shucking her clothes. She tucked the dirty garments away and found a pajama shirt and short-cut sweats to sleep in, deciding to skip a hose-down.

When her head hit the pillow, thoughts of calling in sick floated in her head. So what if Bozack docked her pay? As such was the penalty if a teacher were to do so on a scheduled day of work. Her feeling was awfully unstable. It would do no one any good to have her around if she were prone to regurgitate remnants of ramen, *larmen*, tequila, or anything she might have ingested the previous night. Call in sick she decided to do. She closed her eyes to take a quick nap. She'd make the call as soon as she woke up.

27

L IZ WOKE UP around noon. She was awakened by the return of Denore, her heavy feet stomped the floor like a WNBA pro ball player. She made a lot of noise cleaning up the kitchen table.

Stephanie's "girly bag" had not only her shoes, but a shopping plastic bag from a convenience store like Lawson's or Family Mart that contained a bunch of "healthy" junk food: yogurt, carrot sticks, peanuts, and oval-shaped breadsticks. Also included were small vials of energy potions and stamina regulating drinks. Stephanie had emptied the contents on Liz and Denore's kitchen table while Liz had gone downstairs to grab stuff out of the vending machine. When Liz returned to the room, Stephanie had decided to postpone indulging her "munchies" and took to sleeping in other people's beds like she was Goldilocks.

Amazingly, Denore didn't raise hell about it. She was in good spirits, as if she had had a wonderful night and in a positive mood. Although she was a bit surprised seeing the lump in her bed, she assumed at first it was Eddie.

Denore saw Liz emerging from slumber and said, "Oh my goodness. Liz you look like you've been through hell. Aren't you supposed to be working in Umeda today?"

Liz was still groggy. Denore's words weren't immediately registering. The good thing was that her headache had subsided. When Denore mentioned the "working" in her addressing Liz, she looked at the alarm clock on the flat surface of a mini drawer set beside her bed. She groaned and pasted the palm of her hand to her forehead, realizing that she had pulled an "NC no-show" ("no call,

254

no show") which, at companies like Bozack was a serious offense, punishable by dismissal, suspension, or termination of employment if too frequent.

Liz said, "Fuck it . . . I couldn't make it in today the way I felt. Big fucken' deal." She rose from the bed in her cutoff sweatpants and Britney Spears pajama top. She walked to the kitchen, ignoring all the drinks and snacks on the table Denore had straightened up to look presentable, went to the fridge, and opened it up.

Denore sat down at the table. She said, "Did you call in sick?"

"Nah," Liz said, closing the refrigerator after extracting a container of Blendy Ice Coffee. "I didn't call. My phone has been dead. It's still charging."

Denore stretched her long arms to the kitchen dish unit because the place was so compact it was within her reach. She managed to grab a cup to slide it over to Liz in expectancy of receiving some of the Ice Coffee Liz was pouring. After all, it was hers.

Denore said, "You did a no-call no-show? Thanks." She lifted the cup to her lips after Liz poured some.

Liz said, "Yeah, I know it's a shitty thing to do, but they're not gunna fire me. I mean, it'd be my first offense, right?"

"Nah, they're not gonna fire you," Denore said, shrugging and shaking her head indubitably. "They'll probably give you a warning, or something like that, but that can't be good on your record, though. I mean, golly, you just started, same time as me, just about three months?"

Liz said, "Something like that," while thinking, enough about her situation. It was time to interrogate Denore. Stimulants from the coffee drink gave Liz a warm, buzzy feeling. She reached for one of Stephanie's Marlboros peeking from her sack and lit it. Denore tried to look disappointed.

"I wish you wouldn't smoke in here," she said, waving the air like nonsmokers do.

Liz said, "Shut up, oh wait . . . !" Before Denore's expression of outrage for being ordered to clam up registered, Liz had already raced over to grab her potato chip bag full of weed. She opened it. All the while, she was saying, "Yeah the only thing they're gonna do is probably I'll get docked an additional five thousand in addition to the ten thousand you get penalized for a regular no-show when you call in sick. It's like a hundred and fifty bucks dock of pay. Radley does it a lot. He inadvertently gave us the rundown. No big deal. Make it up with some overtime." She sat back down.

When she had opened the potato chip bag, the odoriferous zephyr of ganja blasted their nasal passages as if a tiny radiation bomb had discharged. Denore didn't like this at all, but she remained quiet about it. Her ex-fiancé and friends back in Canada occasionally indulged, but it wasn't her thing. She disliked the smell and shuddered at the thought of it seeping into what little wardrobe she possessed. She stood up and towered over the table, finishing her drink.

Liz said, "Geez, do you know how to roll a joint, Den?"

"Absolutely not!" Denore replied with an appalled expression on her mug. She split the kitchen and made her way to her section of the quarter.

Liz pouted. "Jeez, fuckin' . . . I thought you were Jamaican!" she said grumpily as she disposed of the cigarette in the low remaining water bottle of Volvic she was drinking earlier.

Denore bridled hearing the culturally disrespectful comment Liz uttered and chalked it up to her being an ignorant American. That, or she must have been a grouchy person after she woke up.

Stephanie was still asleep in Denore's bed, but Denore still started disrobing as if she was going to take a shower. Naked for an instant before draping a plush cottony calf-length robe around her full figured, column frame, Liz got a chance to check out her body in raw form for the first time. Her walnut skin gleamed in the noon sunlight, beaming streaks through the closed Venetian-type "xyloid" mini-blinds. Liz stared at Denore's breasts and her chocolate-y dark nipples, which were slightly darker than but similar to the Ice Coffee they had been sipping. Then she thought to herself about how she had never made out with a black girl.

Changing the subject, Liz continued the small-talk inquiries. "So how did things go with you and Chucky last night?"

Denore smiled as if she had been reminded of something pleasant. "Good," she said. "We had a good time. We hung out at Worm's place."

Liz already knew that. She jumped up from the table and moved toward Denore like she was going to follow her into the shower.

She said, "You guys just hung out? He didn't try to put any moves on you?"

Denore U-turned from the bathroom and almost collided with Liz, who had been trailing her closely from behind, as if she forgot something. She said, "No, nothing like that. Eric Cravens and his wife also came. We played Trivial Pursuit and watched that *Blair Witch* whatever video."

"Piffle!" Liz said "Why am I finding this hard to believe?"

Denore found the toothbrush kit she was looking for and started back for the shower and said, "Hey! We're just friends. He's a nice guy, but he's the kind of guy I would never think about dating back home. Then again, back home, or at least where I'm from, there aren't any guys like him. Look at it this way"—she tried to close the door on Liz as if she were a bothersome reporter in pursuit of a story. "It's like this: we maybe have the same skin color, but he and I, *we're not the same*. I'm from a different culture."

Liz couldn't believe it. "No way," she said. "I was thinking you two would hit it off."

Denore said, "He actually has a girlfriend—a Japanese girlfriend—and like I told you, he's a nice guy. I think he and I should be friends. Platonic. You see, I don't date guys like him. Don't take this the wrong way, but you Americans . . . are too . . . rough around the edges for me . . . a little abrasive." She tried to laugh off her honest and frank perception. "It can at times be a little off-putting."

No offense taken. Liz was more interested in why Denore and Chucky weren't tying the knot. After all, they were only but two of a small number of black people in a predominantly white foreigner company—they had to fall in love with each other. When she had first heard about how Denore and her former fiance had severed ties, Liz's impertinent nature caused her to believe it was her duty, as a part-time mission, to cheer up Denore and fix her up with a guy. Part of the task, she was happy to see, panned out good. Denore seemed to cheer up and was in better spirit as of recent. The only other black men she knew about to introduce her to was Chucky, and if he didn't work out, the next option would have been that Kwame guy, and she didn't care for him at all. As for the other guy, Deon, whose name she "forgot to remember," his vote was "No way in hell."

Liz tried to speak to Denore through the closed door. "Well, maybe you guys need more time. You should go out on a few more dates."

Denore's muffled voice behind the door said, "We'll hang out from time to time, I guess. We work together at the Namba branch on Wednesdays. We have the same day off on Thursday, so he's trying to get me to go to Japanese classes with him."

Liz said, "Thursdays? They still have you on the split schedule? Thursdays and Sundays your days off? Damn. I hope they don't do that to me. It's hard enough trying to see Eddie . . ." Then she remembered. Eddie. She hadn't spoken to him since the previous night. She really let him have it too. Pins and needles of compunction poked away at her silently inside. She went for her Tuka phone, now fully charged, and slowly disregarded what Denore was saying in the bathroom. She had to eventually call Eddie.

"Chucky's sweet, but he's just one of those guys, y'know—he burps, he drinks a lot, he uses foul language and, quite frankly, a lot of jargon I'm not even familiar with. He's real *American*!"

Liz reclined on her bed, waiting for her Tuka phone to load. She said, "He's from Chicago, right? He's from a dump, whaddayou expect?"

There was a moment of silence. Liz thought Denore got tired of talking and finally got in the shower. She heard the water get turned on. The door opened back up, however. Denore stuck her head out and smiled with her arms folded. She stared at the floor, ruminating. She said, "I don't want to lie—we can relate about some things. I guess similarities in our backgrounds can exist, but that's where it ends. Our culture is different. I cannot see myself being with that kind of guy. And to be blunt, I've never dated black guys."

Liz felt a pinch of anger hearing her say that, but she didn't know why. She said, "Me either. But why not?"

Denore said, "Where we lived, there weren't a lot of black families. We were the only Jamaicans in our neighborhood. It was a mixed area, but—"

Liz cut her off and said, "So Chucky's girlfriend is Japanese?"

Denore squinted an aporetic frown and said, "As far as I know, yes, she is Japanese, but I never met her. She lives in another city. Nagoya. That's where he's been trying to get Bozack to transfer him to, but they keep denying his request."

"Fuck all that," Liz said. She wasn't interested in that department of her company's politics. She knew all too well about their waiting lists and placement issues. She said, "Just what did you do at Worm's house? I mean, like . . . where did you guys sleep? Did you sleep in the same bed or what?"

Denore gave her a look of mock consternation and said, "Can I like . . . take my shower?"

Liz was persistent. She said, "No, not until you tell me about last night. Come here, sit down. Hey, turn that off." She pointed to he bathroom. Denore snarled as if she couldn't believe she was actually complying with Liz's bizarre transformation into her commanding lieutenant.

"Come, sit," Liz said, pulling her knees to her chest in lissome, supple fashion, patting a space on her bed she made available for Denore to rest her robust bottom.

Stephanie had just then woken up. She said, "Good morning" to Liz and Denore, not knowing that it was almost one o'clock in the afternoon. As if in a trance, she rose from the bed, rubbing her eyes free of laucoma, and made tracks for the restroom, the same place Denore had wanted to take her shower.

Denore said, "Don't be too long, I've gotta take a shower."

"No worries," Stephanie said, "I'm just gonna potty . . ."

Denore rolled her eyes and tried to scowl away the rotten fruit odor as Stephanie passed. She said, "Gosh, you two look like you need a shower more than me!"

Liz laughed. She said, "We went to this place last night called Carnations, right, Steph?"

Denore said, "Yeah, Chucky was telling me about that place. It's an all-female bar, but most of the girls there are old women."

Liz stage-shouted, "They're not that old. Most of them are around thirty-five, I think? But the youngest one there I think was about twenty-eight, I think she said."

Denore said, "They have that many women there?"

Just then, the bathroom door opened, and Stephanie emerged from it looking like a somnambulist, as if to say, "All yours," motioning her unwashed hands. Denore hesitated as if she needed a few extra minutes to allow the room to ventilate, due to the humus-like odor in Stephanie's wake.

Stephanie said, "I comp*l-e-t-e*ly blacked out after about the fifth shot of tequila . . . oh, my gawd!" She gasped. "Liz, you didn't go to work today?"

Denore chuckled and used that statement as her cue to dip away into the bathroom, or else she would never take a bath. Liz and Stephanie commenced into their small talk before Liz's charged Tuka phone rang. It was an unfamiliar number. Liz answered it and heard the voice of Hitomi Hasegawa, the manager of the Umeda branch of Bozack School. They had their conversation about the penalty for not calling in.

Affable Hitomi seemed regretful to even have disturbed Liz after discovering Liz's reason for not calling and following company protocol. She sought not to aggrandize the situation. Still, she had to do her job, and she did. Not without letting Liz off easy on her own terms, mentioning to her that, as usual, business was still slow on Sundays and there had not been but one or two lessons for English that day, and Bozack was able to send a substitute to cover them. The rest were cancellations. That guy Kwame was the guy HQ sent.

Hitomi was like, "Sorry to have disturbed you. Please get some rest, and see you next Saturday."

After hanging up, Liz returned to the kitchen area with Stephanie, who was already there rummaging through her bag sack and looking at the many drinks lined up on the table that Liz bought and Denore stacked up neatly, like, "Can I have one of these?" Then she cracked open what looked like a carbonated soft drink.

Stephanie said, "Thanks for lettin' me crash." She took a sip of the drink, then a minute later, Liz heard the sound of a guttural, goose-like cackle. Stephanie had her face in the kitchen sink throwing upchuck.

28

DISHY AND GLAMOROUS young Frenchwoman Taffie Jolie called Liz's Tuka cellular phone that Sunday evening around 6:30 p.m. when her shift at the Umeda Bozack School ended. When the mousy French teacher heard of Liz's absence, and subsequent "NC-no show" she grew genuinely concerned. She didn't have many "Occidental" friends in Japan, especially those generally around her age, which Liz was, so she took a liking to her. She was relieved when she finally touched base with Liz and found that things were peaches and cream, as the American had put it, as well as other terms English speakers of the world used to express a good situation. There were times her English ability was lacking, but she had gotten a lot better since she came to live in Japan, ironically. But Americans like Liz were few in number in Japan. She was amusing and *sui generis*. Since the feeling was somewhat mutual on Liz's end, Taffie was enchanting and unique. She shot a beeline to Umeda to have a hobnob with her.

After Stephanie's calamitous sojourn, Liz took another long nap, but not before making a phone call—not to Eddie but to the Bozack HQ. Per her earlier conversation with the branch manager at Umeda, Hitomi, she was required to report and confirm receipt of her warning and penalty for no-call-no-show.

She was finally able to get rid of Stephanie, mendaciously hinting that she was leaving the city to go see Eddie. Stephanie took the hint and left while complaining about how they hadn't yet ever been invited by Worm to his infamous home slumber parties. Denore had filled her in about how she had spent her previous night after hearing about the Pink Carnation and that morning at Roastal Horse diner. Liz grew tired of explaining, guessing, and rationalizing. She damn nearly had to shove Stephanie out of the door. Denore spent the rest of her afternoon doing laundry—primarily her bedsheets upon which Stephanie had slept—and did Liz' previous night duds too as a favor while Liz crashed for winks.

Well rested by the time Taffie called, Liz was in the mood to get out. She had called Eddie several times and got no answer. She tried to dodge the attrition attack by showering, as if to cleanse herself of guilt. She got dressed in the sexiest clothes she thought she had: black pencil skirt with a high center slit, T-strap heels, and some white halter top, exposing her cleavage. Eddie can wait, she thought. Especially if he was going to be childish and puerile by not answering his phone. She knew she screwed up, at least give her a chance to apologize or explain her side of the story. Since it didn't look like that was to be, she didn't feel like waiting around for his response.

Denore had fallen asleep reading a book on her side of the room. She had stretched out the divider to separate the dwelling, but from the kitchen, her space was still visible. She had wanted to thank her for doing the laundry and folding her dried clothes but decided not to wake her and silently split.

For the umpteenth time, Liz got lost when she exited the Midosuji Subway Line. She had sheepishly taken a different route than the commuter Loop Line Train she usually took to Umeda. Reason being since she was not pressed for time as she would be on a workday, she could explore an alternate route and familiarize herself more with Osaka city. Bad move.

Even on Sunday, especially in the late afternoon, Umeda Osaka was an insanely crowded place, both in vehicular and human traffic. Liz tried to read faint English lettering and directional arrows pointing to points, places, or destinations she was familiar with high on the ceiling of the mezzanine underpass tunnels to avoid thick clusters of human statues going seemingly nowhere. To no avail, below the streets were the same slow-walking ancients, sloth-footed big-city bumpkins and human roadblocks of Chinese or Filipino tourists. She wanted to go to the Hankyu Train Terminal, a commuter that serviced the northern areas, Kobe and Kyoto. Instead, she ended up at the San Ban Gai Shopping Bazaar adjacent to the Hankyu Station below the platform. The walk back to the Hankyu Station was a five-minute walk, but for Liz it was a serendipitous one for she discovered a quaint tobacco, pipe, and smoke shop. It was on the far corner of the bazaar. This shop was a nonesuch compared to other kiosks and small shops she had seen elsewhere, because this one sold cigars, pipes, rolling paper, tobacco in pouches, chewing tobacco, and it even smelled of belvedere bouquet, snuff, and leaf. Basically, it looked like a legit head shop without the quasi-legal bongs, pipes, and substances.

Liz postponed her astonishment and copped several packs of *Rizzla* and *Zig Zags*. The shop proprietor was an aged gentleman who was entertained at the rare sight of a foreigner. He gave Liz a small pack of rolling tobacco as a lagniappe for her sizable purchase. She gave the man a dull thanks and left. She was happy to get freebies and thought it was kind of the man, but she wasn't a smoker—at least not a chain smoker—and she couldn't roll a joint worth a damn, let alone a rolled cigarette.

Swarms of predominantly Asian faces swamped every empty space in sight at the Hankyu and Japan Railway Stations connection point as Liz pressed on. Scores of other trains, buses, and subways that made Umeda their terminal continually consumed and dumped out new hordes of populace in increments of calculated minutes. Facing one of the most difficult things for newbies in Japan trying to meet up in that area of the city that was, getting lost in the process, Liz had no difficulties spotting Taffie. Being black she stood out and was easy to spot. Otherwise, she would have spent another ten minutes trying to find that Haagen-Dazs Ice Cream Shoppe Taffie had told Liz to meet her at.

For Liz, Taffie looked like the perfect blend of copper, bronze, and beige, and her trademark rose-pink lips made her think about caramel spread evenly over something wet, like a watermelon. Her long, sleek legs shone like cinnamon sticks with honey's glistening gleam. Liz had a weird appetite, both sexual and in dining. There were times she even considered becoming a vegetarian. Or something similar, but the combination of the Ice Cream Shoppe and Taffie Jolie was filling her with an uncanny craving to lick something sweet. Like ice cream off of Taffie's breast nipples. She was overwhelmingly attracted to her, and she didn't understand so suddenly why.

Taffie spotted Liz, and they greeted each other with a hug and a French-type kiss to either side of the face. Liz didn't really want to stop there. She wished to carry the act out a bit longer. She wanted to grab Taffie's round African-esque posterior like a dude on a basketball court would.

Taffie's recondite about the American girl Liz was the same attribute that attracted her. Liz she saw as a typical American beauty—the movie starlet, the Marilyn Monroe or whatever, who was a blue-eyed angel on the surface, but a devil underneath. It was exciting to know such a person, no problem for her. She ought to know—she wasn't much of an angel herself.

29

TAFFIE AND LIZ had some ice cream. Needless to say, Liz had chocolate, and Taffie tried some strawberry vanilla and shared a myriad of laughs and jokes as they poked fun at Japan and the people they saw walk by while sitting by the huge storefront window. After that, they went to have coffee; there were hundreds of shops to choose from. The challenge was finding one that wasn't jampacked. Accomplishing that mission, they found one next to a McDONALDs outside the bustling station underpass, and this time Liz took heed of the smoking section perimeters before she lit up. What she really wanted to smoke was some of the ganja she copped via the Duke, but since that wasn't a feasible option, she settled for a cig from a pack of Marlboro, a rapine from Stephanie prior to her dismissal earlier that day.

Liz and Taffie talked about working in Japan and discussed Bozack Umeda School topics. It seemed like they were going to get a new French teacher. His name was Serge.

Taffie said, "The French classes are becoming more, Hitomi said, so they hire more teachers of French now because they need new Tokyo offices. This man Serge, Hasegawa-san tells me that he will be training here, for first three months, something. Tokyo offices not yet are open. Maybe he can also speak English too. He was supposed to come today, but he don't come. I see a tall black man he teach instead of you today."

Liz said, "Kwame, right? He's a creep and an asshole. You like him?"

Taffie shrugged. She said, "I don't know, we did not talk. He say not to me anything much. He seem like nice, I guess. He is American, right?"

Liz was like, "I dunno, anyway . . ." She didn't feel like talking about Kwame much. She didn't owe him any particular token of appreciation for filling in for her absence that day. It was his job, he would have had to do it anyway. Instead she focused her curiosity on the new teacher.

Taffie was still talking about Kwame. "He seems like average, nice, gentleman. Not like other foreign guy . . . they are so . . . insolent?" She hesitated, as if she was unsure of the English terms she was using. "So . . . *orueilleaux* . . . ?!"

Liz was keen on Taffie sharing her opinion about foreign, non-Japanese guys. Not that she cared, because in her head, she still had Eddie already in her pocket, but guys like Keefer, she thought, fit Taffie's description well.

She said, "Yeah, from what I've seen here, a lot of guys get spoiled because they get to Japan, and women here treat them like kings, and they fuckin' aren't! By the way, is your boyfriend from France too?"

Taffie said, "I have non boyfreind, no." Her confection-smooth face became perplexed.

Liz twinged at the unbelievable. "No way, you serious? How kin'that be? You're drop-dead gorgeous. You're the most beautiful . . . *black* . . . girl I've ever seen. If you were in LA where I come from, you'd probably be datin' some rich professional basketball player, or some rich singer or rapper!"

Taffie could almost blush after hearing such commendation. Faint pink strawberries peeked lightly through her velvety caramel cheeks. Liz was mesmerized by Taffie's cute, delicate face, appealing and beauteous in a bewitching sort of way. Not only was she attracted, she was turned on by Taffie's presence, her close proximity. Her smell, her aura was, by all accounts, potentially magnetic. This had never happened to her before. Her interactions with Blacks or "African Americans" were extremely rare to nil in the States. Aside from the occasional person they speak to at a public place, a deliverer, a domestic at the residence of one of her other rich friends, and random faces met on the by and by, relationships of any kind with the black race was nonexistent. She was neither proud nor ashamed of it, it was simply the way it was. Now, in Japan, she had become acquainted with more black people in three months than she had her entire life in America. The irony was as stifling as the inflammation of a mutual, unspoken jealousy they had for one another.

While Taffie was embattled with a struggle to trust white people and wondering whether or not Liz's accolades were sincere regarding her beauty, Liz was once again questioning her sexuality. Was she really not a lesbian? Why was it she felt the sudden urge to kiss, make out, get freaky when she was near Taffie? Why not Steph? Why not Vicky? She was pretty—why not Denore, or any of ten or twenty little Jap girls? she wondered. Moreover, she admired Taffie's wardrobe.

She was always decked out in the finest raiment, quality material, high-end accessories—well, what did she expect, the chick was from France—but Liz and other English school teaching dames had difficulty shopping to get anything decent to fit, yet Taffie was already threaded down fabulously, as she was that day. With aplomb and finesse. Of course, Liz was a little envious. Why, Taffie was almost as tall as Denore, especially with heels. She was slender, proportionate to her height and size, but a curvier inverted triangle to Liz's top hourglass version of the same frame. So Taffie would have obviously faced similar, if not the same, dilemmas as the rest of them. So how did she do it? Where did she shop? Liz was determined, she had to leak her secret head stash.

She said to Taffie, "Amazing . . . a drop-dead gorgeous girl like you with no boyfriend . . ." Her feeling of incredulity was bona fide. "That's hard to swallow."

"Why drop dead?" Taffie asked unpretentiously.

Liz laughed at Taffie's cute, misunderstanding of American lingo. Taffie stared curiously at her, waiting for a response.

Liz stated, "Don't worry about it." She crushed her cigarette in the ash tray.

They left the tight coffee shop, which was more like an enclosed concession stand with a counter and chairs. Taffie suggested they have a real drink, and of course, Liz was game. Taffie was much more familiar with Umeda than Liz was, so she allowed her to lead the way.

Taffie took Liz to this spot called the Can of Pee, on Route 2 Road in the heart of Umeda's Kita-Shinchi area. Liz knew little of this part of the city; it was near where they had met Tim the Duke the night before. She remembered because of the huge, landmark neon sign depicting a colorful suited man with a cane reading the words Takazawa.

It was Liz's first time to ever visit this odd establishment. The restaurant bar's name had her questioning the sanitary conditions, but Taffie was persuasive in convincing her there was "nothing to worry about." Liz had to have a private laugh about the play on words associated with the name and the place's actual design. It was an open-air bar, but half of it was covered by an actual canopy. Half the seating was indoors, and another section had a sky for a ceiling. On sultry evenings as those, it was enticingly fetching. The customer patrons were both foreign and Asian—presumably Japanese—of equal ratio, somewhat a rarity in Liz's speculative assessments.

As soon as Liz and Taffie walked in, all eyes were on them as they stepped into the place. Not only the usual Japan male gawkers, but also other females. Liz got a head rush. She felt like a star. Rightfully so, one English-speaking patron dining with a Japanese woman got Liz's attention to say to her that her Japanese friend "thought you were a famous actress. And your friend a famous singer!"

Liz laughed immodestly. "Nah, I'm just a plain old country girl from California!"

Taffie said, "People say like this to me all of the time, and I tell them, 'No, I am not a singer,' or, 'No, I am not this American actress., Do you know her? Rae Dawn Chong?"

To Liz, the name rang a bell, but she could understand if people thought Taffie was famous, but not so much her. Even to Liz, Taffie reminded her of the kind of singer who was of a Janet Jackson affinity, or the type of alluring one who would sing with an artist like Prince. The funny thing was, when she walked alone, she hadn't noticed how all eyes were on her. Then, while with Taffie, it was strangely more recognizable. It had a magical yet sinister effect on her mind. She was headed for trouble.

When Taffie and Liz squeezed through a thicket of seating in the sky ceiling section of the bar and made their way to the counter with a sunken floor behind it, a fuzzy pepper-headed bald barkeeper with a fu-manchu greeted Taffie like he knew her, then immediately began fawning over Liz. His Japanese, characteristically slanted eyes bulged like the crotch of his pants, and his heart was beating in his chest through peachy flowers on a greasy don ho adorning his torso.

Taffie knew this cat. She called him Takuto and san for the Japanese title, but Liz wasn't much into all of that. Even though Liz wasn't attracted to Asian men—or so she would lead others to believe—she couldn't help but feel flattered by the attention this Takuto guy had bestowed upon her. Taffie formally introduced them.

Takuto was overjoyed to meet Liz. He reminded her of the bubbly, friendly elder gentleman at the pipe, cigar, and smoke shop earlier. But Takuto was reasonably younger, like he was in his early to late forties. He must have been considerably taller than the average Japanese male, for she could see his waistline above the counter and the floor on which she stood was lower than the chairs where she and Taffie sat. He became all the more appealing when he started giving both her and Taffie free drinks. They both had the casual gin and tonic squirt. Takuto made them loaded.

During the discussion that followed, Liz discovered that Takuto was the operating manager, the boss. He was so infatuated with Liz he offered her a job right away as a part-time bartender or a waitress.

Taffie made a mock face of distress and said, "Takuto-san, you never offer me no job!" And she pouted. It wasn't like she would have taken the job anyway. At that point in her life, such a gig was beneath her, she felt. As did Liz.

Although happily adulated, Liz had no desire whatsoever in being a waitress or server. Even in the States, she would try any job, but the thought of waiting tables was never prevalent. When she went to a bar or a party place like that, she went there to have a ball, not work. Fuck that. Anyhow, she was sapient enough to figure out that Takuto had a thing for her. Taffie could see it too. They shared this info through a tacit, coded laugh.

Takuto didn't give up. Liz noticed how Japanese men were whimsically persistent. Takuto told her that if she worked for him, she could get free food and free drinks all night in addition to an attractive wage boasting three thousand yen (about thirty dollars) an hour, because she was an English speaker and, "an attractive rarity". This sort of got Liz's attention. Not that she was strapped for cash and sought a side hustle like Tim the Duke or Radley the Retriever, but the idea of getting paid to party and "wig the fuck out" was undeniably fascinating.

Liz put on her "Humor me" ears, hearing Takuto in very uncannily good English, jaw on about the benefits of her working there. Good hours, only from six to nine, or seven to ten, flexible on any night she was available—seven days a week. Or she could work the midnight happy hour, and he'd throw in an extra thou to her wage in addition to the free drinks. He was really pouring it on.

Liz was like, "Wait . . . what if I get drunk while I'm at work?"

Takuto' catfish face and eyes swelled, his mustache twitched as he shrugged. He said "If you get drunk? No worry. You can just sit down." He exuded a contagious laugh that had Taffie copying him.

When his laughing fit died down, Takuto said, "I have been in this business for a long time. I have seen a lot of foreign people come and go. Over the years, I have received a great share of "free English lessons" with my customers of other countries." He explained about the revolving door of transients who frequented his place. "I have never spent a single day in an English school. I never paid for lessons. When Japanese customers come here, and they meet you, they can enjoy speaking English. It might seem strange to you, but it would be like an added feature having you here. Also, you can make this place more appealing to foreigner customers." Which seemed to explain why he could afford to allow her free drink and stuff from the diminutive kitchen adjacent left to the counter.

"I'll think about it," Liz lied.

Takuto reached inside the breast pocket of his don ho and whipped out his business card. Liz accepted it, and he left her and Taffie alone for the rest of the night, save to refill their drinks on the house. He and Taffie must have either had a venerable relationship, or Liz had knocked his nose wide open for her, like no other foreign chick he had ever seen. And if what he said was true about how long he had been around seeing people come and go, that boasted a lot of significance. It wasn't easy to ignore.

Because of Takuto's inadvertent flirting, the subject of Liz and Taffie's discussion suddenly shifted to that of dating older men. That's when Taffie started to drink a little heavier. Liz was taken aback somewhat to see her order and down a straight gin with a twist. Takuto remained generous with the pouring as he occasionally made his stop at their station in between assisting his small staff tending with the place's other customers.

Following events of the tumultuous evening and subsequent dawn that preceded this night's occasion, one would have thought that Liz would have taken it easy and followed the example of her roommate, Denore, and relax with a good book. Or relax and watch one of the three televisions their crib had. That would, however, be grossly incorrect. Instead of taking it easy, Liz took another glass of Tanqueray in heavy dosages within her tonic and indulged in further intriguing chitchat with her mysterious weekend coworker. This was the first time they ever really got to hob nob outside of work.

"En tout cas . . ." Anyway . . ." Taffie fumbled her speech in between her native language and English every so often as if her brain was struggling to remember she was speaking to an American. She said, "I . . . must apologize to you. For, I have not been completely honest...I..." She sounded a bit agitated, and her rate of deliverance would quicken with every sip of her drink.

Taffie said, "I . . . don't have a boyfriend, but I have a man, that he loves me. He lives in Tokyo. He is a doctor. A . . . *veuf* . . . a man who have no wife because she die . . . ?

Liz quickly filled the information gap as she would one of her Japanese students. "A 'widower'," she said. "Your boyfriend is a widower!" Bemused.

Taffie said, "No! He is not my boyfriend . . ."

The only thing Liz could think of then was that this man was her sugar daddy or something like that. But Taffie continued to deny any sort of affection toward this person.

She said, "He's not my boyfriend, but he is in love with me, I think. He buys me so many things, he take me shopping in Kobe City, at a very expensive place . . . They are all like this. It is not first time with me. My first almost husband was this way, but I cannot bear to endure another loss as . . . *grandiose et extreme* . . . as extreme as how I have lost before. He is an old, older man, he is in his eighties . . . I mean, how long could we enjoy our lives together?"

Now Liz was getting the picture, but it still wasn't enough. It was becoming clear to her how she was getting the expensive, flossy clothes she wore, some snazzy rich old doctor was taking her on shopping sprees. But where? And how did she become acquainted with such a person? Things weren't adding up, Liz thought. There was a lot of things Taffie was holding back.

They both paused and stared at each other like they were frozen and standing still in time. For a moment, they seemed paralyzed within trajectory of their glowing orbs trained on one another. To the untrained eye, they looked as if they were about to kiss.

30

LIZ SMIRKED TAUTLY. She said, "What's your story, Taffie?"

"Story?" Taffie tried to relax, but she still seemed sad at the same time. Her cute pink lips wrinkled into a luscious, miniature rose. "I do not understand the meaning for this story. What does it mean?"

Liz said, "I mean like, who are you, why did you come to Japan? A girl like you—you should be a major star, or a model . . . why would a girl like you go for older guys? Eighty years old? C'mon, *man*, you gotta be shittin' me fer sure . . ."

Taffie finally came clean and purged. Although she knew she should not have been, she was confounded hearing that Taffie was, in addition to a French teacher, also a hostess, yet another *gaijin* who moonlighted with a side hustle. She worked in a blasé, sophisticated gentleman's lounge in a high-class seedy part of town, literally a stone's throw from where they were sitting right around the corner. Liz hadn't a clue that she was into that industry, nor what exactly it entailed, but the only thing she could associate as its equivalent fell not much short of prostitution. In any case, it was then clear how Takuto had become familiar with Taffie. She frequented the Can of Pee quite often due to its location being in such close proximity to her nighttime gig.

Liz's relentless pumping of Taffie's queries did not cease or halt. She continued to press Taffie until her quest for more details was attenuated.

Takuto had stopped by, on schedule to refill the drinks and supply the two of them with some complimentary mixed nuts, which were as salty as the Dead Sea. Liz munched sparingly on these while Taffie surrendered to run her yarn.

As one such as Liz would had guessed, teaching French alone—four days a week, five hours a pop—couldn't pay the bills. Not in Japan, and not in a city like Osaka, where the real estate prices were not known to be very cheap. The hostess gig Taffie was hustling sideways came as an accidental result of the reason she was in Japan in the first place.

De mon temps…

When Taffie was twenty-three years old, she was a "domestique" in a high-class, sumptuous hotel in the city of Paris, France, where she was born and raised. This exclusive auberge was popularly frequented by rich Japanese businessmen. One businessman who looked like a slick Sonny Chiba in golden years fell into the digs and got shot with Cupid's arrow the same way done earlier on Liz's behalf to that barkeep, Takuto. It so happened that Sonny was a big fan of jazz, and he was closet nuts over singers like Gladys Knight, Aretha Franklin, and Diana Ross. He had a special sexual attraction for Patti LaBelle—popular in France in his time—and Chaka Khan, who Taffie reminded him of. No doubt he was smitten and didn't mind spending his extra scrap change on her in tips and dinner when his busy itinerary lessened.

At first, Taffie took it as a game. A joke. The man Sonny (Liz couldn't remember dude's name after Taffie recounted) could barely speak good French. She took him for yet another generous Asian customer guest who was very polite, and she didn't take his practically stalking her while she changed the linens on his floor as weird, nor did she consider him dateworthy. Besides, he was much too old for her, or so she thought at first. So when he departed for a return to his country, Japon, she didn't believe him when he vowed to return in three months. Before he left, in the persistent way Japanese men pester others—especially females—he made her promise to go out to dinner with him and spend some time. She promised him she would, thinking that she would never see the dude again ever.

She was wrong. True to his word, Sonny did come back to France three months later. His company business trips were no joke. Not only that, it seemed that Sonny had gone on a diet, done some jogging, got himself a shave, and copped some hipper duds distinguishable from geezer gear. Taffie was digging the Sonny with the makeover and found it easy to hold her end of agreement. She did spend some time with him. He took her to dinner and stayed for a while in his room, but they didn't have sex or anything. They just cuddled, kissed, and caressed. It would appear as if Taffie would be involved in a romance with an older gentleman, and it didn't feel wrong. That is, until she found out that he was already married, and had been for about thirty years.

This became a problem because Sonny's wife would sometimes accompany him as she—like a lot of vain women used to the glamorous life—absolutely relished France with a passion. She loved shopping in Paris and traveled with Sonny on some of his business trips taking him there. As a result, he couldn't spend time with her on future trips, at least not quality time or anything other than one-hour clandestine rendezvous at a side street cafe. The quality time Sonny had in mind included hot nuts in bed, and not the caramel sundaes and parfaits they shared at the cafe.

Taffie still wasn't taking "Sonny" too seriously. She was younger and didn't mind having a seasonal ditto of a "sugar daddy" and the money and gifts he was throwing her way. Her dealings with the older Japanese man made for good, entertaining conversations with what few friends she had at that time. But "Sonny" was dead serious about his burgeoning love and desire for the exotic "Soul Queen". Before he split to go back and be with his wife, he gave Taffie his business card. He told her to contact him anytime, he wanted to be pen-pals, but told her she could call him "collect" too.

Of course, she hesitated at first to call him, but she did write him an occasional letter or two. In the days that predated the electronic mail, Taffie relied on *lettres et timbres*. But writing letters was tedious and time-consuming, so on some nights, when her *superviseuse* wasn't keeping a watchful eye on her, she could sneak away for an hour and call him. They talked, Taffie used the phone of a hotel guest that had checked out. By the time they got their phone bill, Taffie would be long gone and beyond suspicion.

Sonny's French had improved tremendously. He had been taking classes! Reason being he stated, was because he wanted to better communicate with her!

Several months later, Taffie received a letter from him. Sonny invited Taffie to come to Japan. Taffie still believed he was joking until Sonny's offer to pay her fare wiped the smile off her face and then knocked the doubts from her dome. For her, this was an inscrutable offer. She was mystified.

Unfortunately, Taffie had been an orphan since her mid-teens. She didn't have many authoritative figures in her life outside of work. Nor did she have anyone around her of substantial kith to advise or pull her coat about life stratagems and *faucons de vivre*.

In the blindest of naivete, Taffie packed her bags and flew to Japan. It was her first time to ever leave her country. Sonny helped her pay for her passport and everything. Again, true to his word, Sonny, the fifty-six-year-old business elite man really did have Taffie picked up and taken care of at the airport. He had her put up in a fly Holiday Inn on the Midosuji Strip.

Taffie didn't question or complain about her being at the hotel, which paled in comparison to the elegant one where she was employed, Sonny had already done so much for her. He had paid for her to come to Japan, picked her up from the airport in his black, e-class Mercedes Benz and paid for the room the entire week she was to be there.

She also knew why she was there. She was to be Sonny's date. It was something she felt, by now, was dangerously close to an affair, something she didn't mind, but there was something about being a mistress that seemed unappealing to her. Still, if he had the bucks, or francs, to support his fantasies that included her, she figured she could go along with it for a while. Why not? Since he was married, she was to be his candy girl, he was Sugar Daddy.

Wrong.

Sonny had some big news for her. He had kept the news from her that he had divorced his wife because he had been going through some legal issues surrounding that case. He had also been having some complicated issues with his family as well—his two children who were about the same age as Taffie—and he figured that it would do him more damage than good to be seen around town with an unfamiliar woman publicly.

The news of Sonny's divorce did have stupefying impact on Taffie. Suddenly, or magically, her feelings for him changed quickly from benefactor to legit significant other—if not *petit ami*. He was technically too old to be a "boy"friend. With his wife out of the way, Sonny didn't have to sneak her around, she thought.

His French had improved leaps and bounds. Taffie, on the other hand, could barely speak any Japanese at all. She was a little dependent on him at that time.

The week she spent with Sonny was the most enjoyable trip she had ever experienced. Sonny took her all over the city, and they had all the popular tourist sights: Osaka castle, the Osaka City Tower, and many of the same places Liz had seen. In addition, Taffie went to the floral and rose gardens at Utsubo Park, where she enjoyed especially because here, Sonny poured on all the affection. People were staring at them as if they made a good couple. Taffie hadn't had many lovers or special romantic partners in her youth, she admitted, and being with someone like Sonny who took extreme fanciful interest in her meant so much. It was like a dream girls dream of: Sonny probably looked like a retired martial arts film star that had gained a few pounds with traces of gray and clothes that might have looked more suitable for a younger gent, but he was still clean, smooth, and suave for a cat his age. Nobody was fooled by his attempt to look young enough to be a man that was dating within a similar age range, but the fact that they were almost the same height—Taffie slightly taller, she liked to wear heels—they didn't look too odd.

Black people were rarer in those days as well. People honestly did think Taffie was a professional entertainer. Her perfectly sculpted melanin-infused version of a Barbie doll frame reminded some of the Japanese old heads of their Francie toy figure. Only differing features were Taffie's buttery beige skin, the same flip hairdo, long curly eyelashes, and seductive youthful foreign eyes to that of Japan. Many saw her as exotic, a rarity just as much lauded as blonde-haired trophy girls. Young people would stop Taffie on the streets around her hotel and ask to take pictures with her because some of them really thought she was R&B pop singer Aliiyah.

After a night of wining and dining in fancy bars, cafes, and patisserie spots all over penurious back streets of Osaka, Sonny and Taffie made it back to the Holiday Inn. Sonny's idea for postprandial activities involved getting some long-awaited sweetness from his honey dip.

When Taffie stepped out of the shower in the nude and dripping wet, it was the first time Sonny's eyes had ever beheld such erotic magnificence. He had purchased a great many whores in his day, but they were limited to low-quality broads or paltry Japanese or Korean hookers at soap lands. Seeing Taffie naked was like him having his own personal Donna Summer or Minnie Ripperton within reach. The feeling was so overwhelming he had no recourse other than to ejaculate prematurely. The sucky thing about that was his inability to continue or rise back to the occasion for the rest of the night.

At that time, miracle drugs like Viagra had yet to hit the market wholesale, and older dudes like Sonny had to rely on a lot of foreplay, whiskey, or coke. Since Sonny wasn't a dope fiend and only a moderate drinker, he took his instrument failure in stride and spent the remainder of the evening cuddling, fondling, and drinking expensive champagne.

The following morning, she woke up alone. Childishly, her first thought was that Sonny had abandoned her, but her doubts about his devotion to her were again dismayed. She received a phone call to her room. It was almost as if Sonny had a hidden camera in her hotel room and could see that she had just awakened. He told her to look inside of the service drawer. Inside it had an envelope in it that contained some money. Being the stolid, executive businessman he was, he had gone to work, but he told Taffie that he would be back later, in the evening. Said he would send a car for her around six thirty, but in the meantime, shop till you drop; he told her to get something nice for when he came calling for her later.

When she hung up the phone, she found the envelope full of cash that Sonny said would be there in the service desk top drawer. She didn't know how much money at the time but was to later find out the envelope was loaded with ten "itchy mans". She got details on where to go shopping around the way from the hotel staff front desk people, who pointed her in the direction of the Daimaru Department Store up the block, less than a five-minute walk.

Taffie went to the department store and felt better than a happy kid from a candy store. She waded through the non-French-speaking populous and found that there was no one who could speak her language, not even at the information booth. All they spoke was English. Luckily, Taffie had always been a good student in school about languages, and of course, she could understand it a little. She found the floor finally, which sold the type of clothes she was looking for.

She bought some inimitably racy and steamy lingerie. She was fortunate because at that time, she was less curvy and the Daimaru Department store had a deeper warehouse than the average shop or boutique, so she could find clothes sizes that could fit her. Even though she was still a tad bit more voluptuous than the average Japanese girl her age at that time, she was able to purchase everything she liked.

Taffie donned the suggestive getup when Sonny came by to scoop her up that night. She even modeled herself, spun around, and showed him what she knew he wanted to see. Sonny dropped the flowers he had brought, then his trousers, deciding to skip dinner and the foreplay.

They hit the bed. Sonny was so wound up that he ended up blowing his wad right at the time he removed Taffie's panties. She found it playfully comical and laughed. What happened next was Sonny looking at her with a stare she would never forget, because it had given her shivers. Like if murder was a dirty look, then she would have been smudged with crud.

Sonny's equanimity was a factor in his endurance of Taffie's lighthearted, blithe arrogance, but it ran its course, and he had to take a brief rest. Taffie playfully coddled him. They woke up later and took a drive. They went to Shin-Imamiya. The Osaka Tower was illuminating brightly, as were the streets of bustling Shin Sekai and grubby Festival Gate. There were a lot of shady characters around the place, derelicts, transvestites, and homeless bum winos, but with Sonny, Taffie felt safe.

After an exhilarating walk through filthy, pummeled streets and battered sidewalks, narrow thoroughfares crowded with mahjong dens and denizens, late-night kushi-katsu diners, alley cats and rats, Sonny was like, "I have something to show you" in damn-near-perfect French, which totally blew her mind.

They had cake and coffee at a devoid, scanty teahouse ACE on Abiko-Suji Drive. The old lady who ran the Lilliputan Cafe of only three tables apparently knew Sonny and issued him and Taffie a creepy, teeth lacking Hallowe'en hideous smile. "Sonny" gave the friendly beldam a 10,000 yen bill and told her to keep the change.

Moments later, the cadaverous old biddy came back with a decorative, oriental carved trencher with coffee and strawberry shortcake. The cake was as horrendous as the shop's decor, but Taffie could smile through the ordeal. Especially when Sonny broke it down about how he had grown up on those streets not far away from where they sat. She could relate to him and he to her as well, because they both had to grow up hard and grow up soon.

Before Taffie's heart could recover from the warm tale of his youth, it received another flaming arrow of alarming magnitude. Sonny asked for Taffie's hand in marriage. No sooner had he popped the question than he had produced a resplendent, shining piece of rock she knew had to be a diamond. Its radiant glimmer struck her eye with a nanosecond of stinging heat in a mesmeric flash.

Aroused like never in her years, she trembled from the reverberation of her quickened heartbeat.

Life was a funny yet saturnine sort of thing, Taffie had mused. She recalled her earliest, happiest years growing up. Her white French father would tell her that she was the world's most beautiful girl in the shower while he molested her. Innocently, she still loved her father, ignorant to the evil ways of the world. She remembered how she cried incessantly until her stomach emptied when her father left her and her mother, a black Caribbean immigrant. He never came back. That man she knew to be her father had split to live with his white real family. The man didn't even acknowledge her or dignify her with even a look when she tracked him down in Pantin, northeast of the big city where he had taken up residence with his erstwhile estranged wife. That racist, harridan cunt told Taffie's half brother and sister, "Ne regarde pas cet animal noir!"

"Don't look at that wild black animal!" she said as she called "le gendarmie."

The cops arrived and bagged the hysterical Taffie, longing for fatherly love and affection. She never saw that man again. Ever.

Upon hearing the news of Taffie's rejection, her mother drank herself into so much of a melancholy-charged stupor. She incoherently fell into a city sewer hole twenty feet deep, broke her neck, and died instantly. She was never claimed by anyone on her father's side of the family, and her mother had never taken her to native French Martinique, nor had she introduced Taffie to anyone from her side of the family either. She was literally an only child. She remained a ward of the country until emancipated at the age of eighteen and had been on her own since then, working menial jobs, but mostly as a domestic in hotels, where she thought she would spend the rest of her days career wise.

Until she met Sonny, no one had ever reveled in her presence the way he had. The evanescent feeling of the sublime, princess's world she enjoyed in Japan was surreal. Sonny made her feel that it would always be that way, even if he was a quarter century her senior.

Without hesitation, Taffie accepted Sonny's marriage proposal. She made him an extremely happy man. She too was overjoyed because she could return to France and tell the hotel to take the job and shove it. She packed all her bags and possessions and less than two months later, and she flew right back to Osaka, Japan.

Sonny never failed to impress her. The way he came through taking care of everything so Taffie didn't have to worry. He had an apartment waiting for her upon arrival. They still could not live together because his adult children were bitching about it. By this time, Sonny had come clean about his plans to marry a foreign woman, thus all of a sudden, his kids became some xenophobic, intolerant racists for the mere sake of convenience. Taffie was content, however. As long as she had a ring on her finger, accompanied by Sonny's love and good graces, she was quiescent.

The ominous moment was destined to arrive. No matter how much, or how long fantasy fairy tales attempt to delay calamity's date on the calendar, hard times on the horizon lurked in their timetable.

When Sonny, after a year of courting, and finally getting his Soul Queen to accept his proposal, he was finally able to be one with his sweet, luscious Taffie. Tragically, however, after his masterpiece performance in bed, it wasn't his penis that suffered failure but his heart. His ticker gave out, and he died in Osaka Chuo Hospital.

It was a dour and gloomy turn of events, which happened so rapidly that Taffie couldn't properly mourn. She was unwelcome at Sonny's funeral or any proceedings. Since they hadn't yet legally married, people viewed Sonny and Taffie's affair as simply that—an affair between a rich old dude and his side piece, or high-priced hooker live-in girlfriend. Taffie's obdurant insistence that she had been Sonny's fiancee had no bearing at all and his offspring's stalwart, steadfast opposition to her receiving anything from his estate was upheld by Japan's courts. She was subsequently evicted from the apartment Sonny copped for her.

As luck would have it, good fortune still lingering, one of Sonny's acquaintances, who also had not been allowed to pay her final respects to him, met Taffie by chance crying in the lobby of the ceremony hall where the wake was held.

Saiko Yamabiko was an old hooker Sonny had known while he was alive and had frequented her exclusive lounge in Kita-Shinchi quite often. Saiko recognized Taffie because Sonny bragged about her, and even carried a photo of Taffie around in his wallet when he came to her place of business. Saiko spotted Taffie and consoled her. Upon hearing Taffie's lachrymose rundown of her situation, Saiko benevolently took pity on her and figured as a final favor to one of her most beloved clients and friends, she would help his paramour. Maybe it was because she seemed to understand what Taffie was going through having been through similar circumstances her damn self. She could definitely relate. For she herself had fallen in love with a rich, powerful man a quarter century prior, when she was a young plummy fresh and naive out of Yamanashi, her original hometown back east. Her love interest didn't die, though—he just married a pristine and virginal chick more his speed and left Saiko where she was, and would be, for decades to follow—in the same place—a high-priced hooker simulated sex game den hostess, looking to bleed affluent and prosperous moneyed men, never married. She had not been the only one of her sort either, obviously. Many in her "industry" had similar stories.

Regardless, such an occupation as the one Saiko commanded did not offer equitable or beneficial retirement bonuses or pluses. Dealing with family members of deceased former clients was yet another complex can of worms, be they legit mistresses or not. The fact that Taffie was a foreigner didn't make her situation any rosier either.

Having absolutely nowhere else to go in the world except back to Paris, Taffie almost did return to France, preferring to be homeless in her own country as opposed to a foreign one. Saiko, however, showed up in the nick of time and offered her a job working at her lounge. Considering what she already knew about Taffie, based on what Sonny had told her, Saiko was aware that Taffie had been employed at a swanky hotel, so she was familiar with that industry and its penchant for customer comfort and satisfaction. This, Saiko thought, would be good qualifications for her to be employed. Besides, she was always in constant need of newer, fresher girls. The revolving door was moving rapidly; women were always coming and going. They would quit, get fired, or take jobs at rival dens and brothels. But with Taffie working for her, Saiko could boast of having the most variety in her stable. She already had women from not only Japan, but also Korea, China, the Philippines; and with Taffie, she would then have one from France as well! To think of all the new clients she would attract gave Saiko currency symbols for eyeballs in delight.

Taffie was in no real condition to refuse Saiko's offer. Saiko became known as her Mama-san, and she showed Taffie the ropes of her new job. In addition, Saiko set Taffie up to live in a tiny, but feasibly functional one-room flat where she still resided till that day. She made a deal with Saiko that she would work off her debt, then save money and return to France. Saiko then put her on, and like she had predicted, Taffie helped to add more flavor to her establishment. In no time, Taffie was meeting scores of Sonnys, and none of them were stingy about tipping her cash money gifts, certificates, and other pleasantries in the form of expensive jewelry, accessories, and trips to beautiful Okinawa vacation resorts.

In the process of working, she learned Japanese too. She eventually earned enough money to pay Saiko back for helping her but didn't quit working at her lounge. Truth be told, she was not in a big rush to go back to France. She had grown to love Japan, despite the bittersweet circumstances that had brought her there.

Fate would issue another favorable circumstance to Taffie's life when a Bozack Japanese employee higher up visited Saiko's lounge. This came during a time when the company had begun its expansion in services, offering additional languages other than English for students of foreign lexicon. That individual serendipitously offered Taffie an interview for a position teaching French, and she was hired practically on the spot, as the personnel department did not have to ferret out an instructor and have them flown in all the way from France, such painstaking a process was curtailed.

Two years later, she was still working three nights as a hostess and three or sometimes four days as a French instructor, making major boodle, considering the fact that her visa had changed from Visitor to Cultural. And one year ago, she met a rich doctor, who claimed to be stricken by Taffie—much like Sonny had been. He lived in Tokyo, but he was constantly back and forth all over the country, and especially Osaka for medical conferences. Garden-variety, vanilla chicks from foreign countries like Poland and Russia didn't turn the old doc on. He had his sights on the Chocolate. Taffie blew his old mind and was the only thing that had excited and moved him since the death of his wife. At least once a month, Doc would show up in town on a day Taffie was scheduled to work, and he would, as always, extend to her an invitation to come and live with him in the big, big city.

Just as Liz had lied to Takuto earlier, Taffie lied to Doc and told him that she "would think about it." But in actuality, she didn't want to fool herself into thinking that she could or would fall in love again with an older man. Especially one that could potentially die on her and she would again endure a circumstance where she faced eviction, or even worse, a savior like Mama-san Saiko Yamabiko wouldn't be around to help her either. So with that story being told, here they were today, on that night, sitting at a bar in Umeda, Osaka's Kita-Shinchi. Liz caught a hearty earful and felt drunk and intoxicated taking it all in. So then Liz could understand why Taffie became so livid when earlier she had used the expression "drop dead," She had an ordeal in her past in which someone close to her had done precisely that.

31

WHEN LIZ AND Taffie were ready to leave the Can of Pee restaurant bar, they almost tripped, stumbled, and fell over a collection of wooden floor chairs. The evening crowd had dwindled down to a few customers as night dwellers scurried off to catch their last trains departing most often around midnight. Of course, the crooning Takuto ran out to help try and carry the two women, but the combined strength between the two friendly sots was substantial for them to each scamper out into the streets, hailing cabs at the curb.

For Liz, this was her second night in a row getting piss drunk, but tonight wasn't as bad. She was still somewhat in control of herself, and she didn't black out. The only problem was she had a tendency to become obnoxiously loud. People were staring at them as usual, but on this occasion, they appeared to be exceedingly amusing.

Liz exploded in laughter. She said, "Woah! Hahaha! These Japanese people look like walkin' lizards in suits and glasses!"

Taffie could understand a little, and she joined in laughing. She had so much fun that night with Liz. It wasn't very often that she could enjoy herself with foreign women in her age group. The foreign women she worked with at the Lounge she did not associate with outside of work. Even in a drunken haze, she was of sound-enough mind to consider Liz a new friend. Or at least she hoped. She had trust issues that she was still dealing with.

Liz said, "I guess . . . I'd better go . . . home."

Taffie agreed. But Liz too had such a good time. The night was still young because she didn't have to work the following day. An idea struck her mind like a lightning bolt.

"Hey, Taff," Liz's voice simmered to a husky whisper. She said, "Do you like . . . pot?" She shrank her thumb and index finger to her lips like she was smoking an imaginary joint.

Taffie was perceptive enough to guess what Liz meant as if it were a game of charades with her delivering the answer in the form of a question: "What? Do you mean *marijuana*?" Her face lit up with excitement. "Do . . . do you have it?"

Liz was like, "Yeah . . . I got a whole shit ton! You wanna smoke?"

Taffie said, "Yes . . . *bien sur* . . . of course! Where is it? Do you now have it?"

Liz's face read bummer. Downcast somewhat. "It's at . . . my place. But I live so far . . . maybe next time we meet we can . . ."

Taffie became suddenly insistent. "Oh, but we must . . . we can go please to your home . . . oh, please, *mademoiiselle Americaine* . . . surely you can share . . ."

Liz disregarded her momentary spell of cold feet. She said, "Yeah, why the *fuck* not . . . Taxi!"

Such a loud yell was unnecessary because there were taxicabs pasted to the sidewalk curb. Taffie dragged Liz to one and pushed her inside. She also entered and squeezed beside her as Liz told the driver where to go.

Liz then remembered, "But . . . I don't know how to . . . roll a joint."

Taffie couldn't get it. "Roll? Joint?"

Liz started the charades game again. She twisted an imaginary, invisible spliff, applied fake saliva, held it in her left fingers, and with the finger on her right, pointed to the object and finally formed an *X* to exemplify the international gesture to mean "No."

She said, "I . . . can't . . . make . . . it."

Taffie laughed as if Liz had gone through all the trouble to make her comprehend for nothing. She said, "No problem, no problem, I can do it."

Liz was elated. "Oh, fuckin' cool!" she said. They started giggling in grating excitement.

The old cabdriver was looking at the two sexy foreign broads in his rearview mirror wishing that his salary could afford him a night with those two dazzling hookers. All he could do was confirm the destination to where he was transporting them. He was surprised as hell to hear the black woman answer his question in Japanese.

Taffie said, "Where in Bentencho do we go? The driver, just now asked us . . ."

Liz said, "Just tell him to pull up to Bentencho Station, it's big. We'll walk from there."

Taffie relayed the information to the cabbie, and he took Tosabori Street en route to the target.

Liz asked, "You don't have to work at the Night Bar this evening?"

Taffie said, "No, I don't work *dimanche* . . . Sunday, I do not work there."

Moments later, they arrived at Bentencho Station. The short walk to Liz's dormitory location was brisk in the humid, swampy air of creeping summer. It wasn't until they had arrived in clamorous fashion to her place that Liz had remembered Denore was home. She clicked on the kitchen lights. Upon seeing her roommate resting soundly on the bunk in her section of the place, Liz motioned for Taffie to stay quiet, pushing her "Shh!" finger to her lips. She closed the divider slide to shield the darkened slumber area from the glaring light emitted from the space they occupied. Liz disappeared behind the divider to grab her stuff.

Taffie said. "You have roommate?"

Liz nodded as she located her "potato chips" bag, acknowledging Taffie who was peeking through the crack in the slide. She returned to the kitchen, closing the divider slide entirely to isolate her and Taffie inside the kitchen. They sat down at the small round table.

Taffie was alarmed when Liz showed her batch. She said, "Oh my! It must be very expensive, no?"

Liz was sobering up somewhat with the scent of the sizzling ganja. She said, "Well, yeah, compared to America, hell yeah, it's expensive!" She broke off a few raisin-sized increments of the dried marijuana plant and placed it on the table in front of Taffie. From her purse, she extracted the plastic bag that contained all the rolling paper packs she purchased earlier that night.

Taffie chuckled lightly and went to work, opening a pack of Zig Zag and commenced rolling a fat stick with the contents Liz supplied. Despite having longer fingernails, she was able to put a well-constructed joint together in less than a minute, with excellent, near-expert artistry.

Liz was awed. She was like, "Teach me how to do that . . . where did you learn how to do that?" Of course, Liz might have had many opportunities to learn such a skill back home, but in the States, she, Mandy, and Becky always used pipes, bongs, or other ingenious contrivances to get high. Either that, or guys like Mandy's part-time boyfriends always came with pre-rolled apparatus. She never thought she was going to be in a situation such as this, where she had no one who could do it for her.

Taffie said, "I learn many things like this when I grow up in the *orphelinat* . . ." She paused, and for the first time, Liz saw Taffie's thick pink tongue apply a sinewy track of saliva to the adhesive section of the rolling paper to attach a second joint, thinner than the first, but with the same deft completion.

Taffie then said, "I wanted for long time to smoke it . . . but I know not where can I get this one." Liz fought the urge to not be turned on seeing Taffie lick her lips afterward.

Liz found one of many lighters she possessed and ignited the fat joint on her lips. She ingested the first of the smoke and started coughing. Then she laughed and passed that shit to Taffie, who copied the same action.

Liz said, "I can get this shit, anytime . . . just tell me, I can get it for you."

Taffie clenched her fists and raised them above her head in mock celebration. They sat there for a few minutes and roasted the smoke to a roach. With intention to smoke the second, Liz had to shake her head rapidly before deciding that she had consumed enough for the time being. Taffie seemed to be of the same constitution. THC components produced galvanic impinges on their brains, especially after a spell of heavy drinking. The room began to spin, and their heads became feather light. Taffie hadn't smoked in so long that she felt as if she was going to fall out of her chair and almost did. Liz couldn't help but burst out laughing. Taffie did the same. Liz's cloudy head recalled Denore.

"Oh, shit!" she whispered and tiptoed to the dividing slide and cracked it wide open enough to peer inside. She saw that Denore was still lightly snoring light motor scooter growls of sound. Relieved that their strident outbursts hadn't awakened her, Liz refastened the divider slide hitch. She returned to the table and considered Taffie. It was late, she didn't really want to part company, but they could not stay there, for they would disturb Denore. Moreover, Taffie couldn't really sleep over because the living situation at that point couldn't accommodate any guests. All that was available for Taffie would be a cold, hard floor with barely a pillow, unless she slept together with Liz!

Liz's mind and body was abruptly invaded with feverish emotion and excitement at the thought of sleeping beside Taffie. She sat down at the kitchen table again and contemplated asking Taffie to roll another joint and give her a tutorial.

As if empowered by a mind reader, Taffie plucked a small chunk of bud and started rolling up. Upon completion, she said, "Why don't we go out to the club?"

Liz said, baffled, "This time of night?"

Taffie giggled and said, "Bien sum, yes! Why not now? It is only after midnight—"

32

A TWENTY-MINUTE TAXI RIDE later, Taffie and Liz stood on the corner of Katamachi Street and Kyobashi Intersection. Taffie knew about the Candy Box and suggested they go there, for this was the only place which was really popping that particular night. It was a Sunday, so most people who normally attended on weekends were absent because in all likelihood, they would be preparing for work or school the following day. On this distinct evening, there would be a different crowd. Liz didn't really care, but she liked the Candy Box because the previous time she had gone there and met Tim the Duke, she got in for free. Tonight was no different. Taffie and Liz walked upon the horrendous, macabre tongue carpet leading to the gaping orifice of a clown's mouth but operating as a door behind the silky orange curtain.

Liz and Taffie met with the two door attendants, who were dealing with a small queue of Japanese people awaiting entry. One of the door attendants spotted the two foreign women and beckoned them forward.

Liz and Taffie pranced and strutted to the front of the line ahead of the people waiting and received the same candy cane stamp Liz got the last time she went. The ink of the stamp looked a little faint upon Taffie's honeyed shade, but detectable underneath an ultraviolet light scanner.

In addition to free admission, a jump to the front of a line to enter also, Liz and Taffie got a free drink ticket. As stoned and intoxicated as they were, it was just more fuel to a fire.

The place wasn't as packed as it had been on Liz's previous visit, but there was still a sizable crowd. The music was different tonight, and so were the inhabitants. There were no fancy dressed people, no business suits or ostentatiously elegant duds on the people dancing on the floor. Tonight, people were in jeans, rags, overalls, Converse sneakers, and blue dungarees with cuffs on the legs. Men and women were dressed generally alike, with mostly chicks wearing jeans more than those in skirts. Hairstyles ranged from normal to the absurdly abstract. Liz didn't think much of these folks but favored them more so than the gathering of hepped-up dotty people she saw there the last time.

Speaking of which, as they made their way to the sparkling, illuminated ovular bar counter, the same assymetrical hair styled spindly gent was present, shaking a shiny mixing glass. She recognized the familiar face of that hairstylist Takaro. His facial hair, "soul patch", and askew sloped hair was a distinguishing feature, making him easy for Liz to remember. She hesitated in consideration of approaching him to merely greet him, but decided against it, as Taffie was nudging her, stealing her attention.

Taffie must have been growing tired of the gin and tonic and ordered a martini cocktail. The sloped-headed thin star was occupied with his shaker at the opposite end of the oval island bar. Taffie was able to communicate her desired drink to the plain-looking J-dude who took her drink order. Liz took her eyes off that Takaro dude and used them to search for the same foreign bartender she met the other night there. As a matter of fact, he was French too if she remembered correctly. To her dismay, however, such person never emerged from the curtained entrance to the kitchen rear of the oval island bar.

Liz said, "Damn, that guy isn't here!"

Taffie was barely paying Liz attention, happy to be sipping another drink. She said, "What do you like to drink now?"

Liz was like, "Aw, fuck it, same as you." Then she turned to look around the club again. The music tonight was different. It was sort of old, but it was some tunes that Liz recognized. Sublime, Third Eye Blind, Chumbawamba, Smash Mouth, and other stuff. It wasn't the ordinary music she would associate with clubs, but the patrons there that evening didn't seem to mind. They were a bunch of happily, bouncing balls of energy and joy, elated to be hearing foreign music.

Liz spotted Takaro again, and this time he was now speaking with a tall man who made the hairstylist appear to be a midget. In fact, the man had to lean into him to hear what Takaro was saying.

The tall man looked like a foreigner, but Liz couldn't tell if he was a Latino or an Arab. His hair was a slick, curly version of an Eddie Monster do, equipped with a conspicuous widow's peak. He was wearing glasses that looked like shades with orange mirrored lenses. He too had a goatie but it was bushy, not stringy like Takaro's. Also he was dressed immaculate with a radiant, silky light-colored blazer, a green shirt unbuttoned to reveal a hairy, almost woolly chest, and a gleaming gold watch. Almost magically, his eyes underneath the mirror lenses laser beamed upon Liz. His head turned robotic and eerily towards Liz, but she didn't notice just as she had turned away to receive the martini Taffie had ordered for her.

A moment later, Liz received a light tap on her right shoulder. Startled somewhat, she turned to face Takaro, who was smiling in delight of the chance meeting. Liz was cordial at first, but in her muddled state, it was short-lived. She began rambling a harangue of the day's activity in review. She didn't notice the tall, staring man behind Takaro until he finally stepped forward to speak to her like a secret service man for a presidential figure, almost creeping Liz out.

Takaro introduced the man as his friend. But the man said to Liz and Taffie in grammatically perfect English, but with a foreign accent, suggesting that it wasn't his primary or native tongue.

He said, "G-l-eetings, ladies, please excuz my interruption of your subdued daint, but I could not help but notice the two most lovely women here tonight, and I had to come over and meet you."

Liz took the vampire-looking gent to be a toady with weak pickup lines, but he smelled good, she thought. Plus, he could speak English, so she entertained his conversation.

The man took Liz's hand and kissed it politely and did the same with Taffie in an extrinsic, genteel manner. As he did, he finally said, "My name is Tabriz. Tabriz Najaf."

Liz and Taffie spoke to the man and told them their names. Tabriz seemed like a nice guy, but Liz wasn't interested in him very much, unless of course, he was going to buy drinks. Her attitude, however, changed when Takaro told Liz who Tabriz actually was—the owner of the Candy Box himself. Then Liz turned to face him when she addressed him instead of shouting over her shoulder at him like he was a lowly peasant.

"Wow, cool!" she said. "This is a really cool club. And thanks for letting us get in for free!"

Tabriz said suddenly, "How about you ladies join me in the VIP lounge?"

Liz and Taffie looked at each other for a split second and then smiled, while nodding in agreement. They were like, "Sure, yeah, let's go!" All the while, Liz was thinking about how awesome it was, and what a stroke of luck to have been noticed by the club's owner. Now she and Taffie followed the splendidly attired foreign gentleman from the oval bar.

Takaro behaved and made moves as if Tabriz's invitation to the VIP Lounge had been also extended to him and attempted to follow the trio. Tabriz quickly turned to him and in Japanese uttered to the effect of, "Nice seeing you again, Takaro. As always, thank you for coming, and I will see you again. Please enjoy a drink on me. Taka or Nori here at the bar will take care of you. Good night."

Dispirited somewhat, Takaro shrugged and returned to the counter to get his drink.

Taffie had been to the Candy Box before, but not many times. She had been there with some clients of the Lounge. Occasionally, the customer clients paid for the hostesses as escorts, and they went out on dates outside of the Lounge itself. Taffie had gone with some younger dudes there who didn't mind spending money, but she never had any access to the VIP sections. She wasn't much of a club hopper, but enjoyed music and dancing on occasion and began liking this special club because the admission was complimentary for foreigners such as herself and Liz.

For Liz it was the beginning of yet another surreal experience. The club itself for her was a wonderment to the eyesight even without the enhancement of a doped-out injection. Bold heading tapestries of flowing lines, sinuous curves, and accordant forms indicative of Art Nouveau lined the walls and had captivating effects. Tabriz stepped through a narrow passage that led to a small flight of stairs ascending the dance floor to an elevated room behind a soundproof door.

After opening the room's gaudy door, Tabriz removed his expensive-looking shiny black shoes that Liz thought must have been a 'size 12' at least, and placed them in a box immediately to the left of the entrance. He urged Liz and Taffie to follow suit.

Reluctantly Liz abided by the custom of removing shoes, as did Taffie, who also took off her ankle-strap high heels and put them in like boxes as they saw Tabriz do. A tall lattice screen of an unknown light color with authentic plants stood beside the entry thoroughfare, creating a narrow portal to a pocket room. The shading of the décor was doing a number on the eyes of the newcomers. Multiple down lights of pink, blue, and green appeared jaggedly throughout the space with indirect, incandescent black light, which still created distorted effects occasionally, reflecting flourescent tones on white garments, making Liz appear to be glowing inside of her halter top.

The smooth, soothing feeling of silk embraced Liz's toes as she and Taffie walked barefoot on a plush woven Dhurrie carpet, which in the lighting appeared like a colorful mozaic of varying degrees of the pink spectrum and distinct patches of dark and black dots, making it seem like they were walking atop the surface of a watermelon with its seeds.

Tabriz sat in one of four encompassing fauteuil chairs with cushion so soft Liz felt she was sinking into it when she and Taffie took a seat. The pedestal table in the center was of an unusual dodecagon design with a pickled finish and was almost as high as their kneecaps when seated. A soundproof window separated the room from the ballroom at large, but the music was clear and broadcast through speakers in strategic locations. They had a full view of the club, but apart from it as if they were spectators in a sky box at a sports arena or balcony with glass enclosure in an opera auditorium.

One of Tabriz's Japanese workers appeared, and they exchanged a few words. Tabriz then addressed the curiously gawking foreign girls. "Would you ladies care for some champagne?"

"Sure, why not?" was the consensus between Liz and Taffie. Especially if it was on the house like everything else had been that night. Liz wasn't often a champagne drinker either, but she figured why the hell not since she hadn't indulged in the stuff very much in her days.

Tabriz snapped his fingers, and the Japanese fellow was off. A minute or two later, he returned with a bottle of Dom Perignon, followed by another attendant who dragged along an ice bucket on a pole and wheels in his right hand. Each of the staff had three crystal flutes between the two of them, and these were placed on the table before the host and guests. Tabriz dismissed the workers after the champagne was poured, and they raised their glasses to make a toast.

After the formalities were over and everyone got their head buzz from the bubbly, Liz tried to reel her brain back inside of her dome to engage in conversation with this mysterious proprietor.

Tabriz asked, "So where are you lovely ladies from?"

Liz was first to offer up her details, and Taffie had become quaintly silent, but did provide the man with the information he desired to know. He was like, "Oh yes . . . France, I have been there many times . . . C'est un plaisir de vous recontrer, mademoiselle!" Then raised his glass to salute.

Taffie could have been blushing, but in the color scheme of the bizarrely illuminated chamber, one couldn't tell. Her face had been distorted into a somewhat sinister legion of brown darkness with streaks of color looking like she had on war paint at times.

She responded, "C'est aussi un plasir pour moi."

Liz interrupted with a badinage of faux outrage and said, "Oh, come on you guys . . . this is *Japan*! We need to be speaking *English*!" They all laughed and Taffie and Liz playfully exchanged a light slap boxing series of attacks on one another.

Tabriz said, "Oh yes! You are a fiery spirited American woman. So beautiful you are, yes. What brings you to Japan? What makes a girl like you believe one of the world's greatest countries to come here?"

Liz said, "We're teachers. I teach English, and Taff here, she teaches French."

Tabriz said, "I should have assumed as much. I have many people who come here who are teachers. Mostly they are males, however. It's steadily changing, however. That's why I do not charge admission to the foreigners at any of my clubs. I have also a disco in Tokyo as well."

Liz was impressed. He didn't appear to be too old and seemed to be doing very well for himself, considering the fact that he too was a foreigner there in Japan.

She asked, "That's amazing. You . . . must . . . be awfully busy."

Tabriz said, "It is sometimes busy, but I enjoy this type of life. I like the night and the people of the night. I dislike the humdrum of a working day, and I don't like waking up early for rush-hour life. I don't want to work myself to an early death, or a stressful life leading to death as a merciful release, as do these Japanese."

Taffie joined the conversation. "How long you have been here? In Japan?"

"About ten years," Tabriz said as he poured more Dom into the receptive champagne flute-bearing hands of his female guests. "Ten long, hard years. I first started out in Tokyo, but because the capital city is very popular and overcrowded with foreigners, I decided I should come here to the second largest city to the west, and that was here. So far, I have enjoyed equitable results."

Liz said, "Yeah, well, it's a pretty rad place here. The music is kinda weird . . ."

Tabriz raised his bushy Groucho Marks–type eyebrows above his mirror glasses. "You don't like the music?"

Liz about-faced and was like, "No . . . I didn't mean it like that. Actually, tonight is pretty cool. It's kinda retro? I dunno . . . The other time I came here, it was kind of weird."

Tabriz said, "Well, I find your opinion and taste very interesting and useful. I like to have a different theme for each night we open. And opinions like yours are necessary for me to select the mood to cater to certain crowds. Like tonight, for example . . .

"On Sundays, we usually get the hairstylists and people in the cosmetology industries. People who mostly do not have to work on Mondays. A lot of shops are closed on those days. For some reason, the late '90s music seems to appeal to this gathering. On weekdays or other nights, the music can range from techno, the Eurobeat–type sound to nowadays hip-hop music. I would like to get more of this hip-hop music on Saturday nights because it is so popular now. It really attracts a huge number of people, both Japanese and foreign."

Liz said frankly, "Well, I really get a kick out of the free admission."

Tabriz shrugged again and flashed a dainty smile. He said, "Well, for some apparent reason, places that have a lot of foreign faces attract Japanese patrons as well. They see foreign people like you ladies, and they become curious. When they think that foreign people like something, they become drawn to it and become desirous to know about that thing and they follow, maybe they feel as if they discovered something new. It works out well. As for the foreigners, well, you can enjoy any of hundreds of clubs or bars or nightlife dens in this city, but the one that has free admission is the one you will always remember!" He laughed like Count Dracula at the sight of a virgin leaking blood from the jugular.

"Do you like hip-hop music?" Tabriz asked, wanting to direct the question more to Taffie because looking at her he assumed that she would be into that genre more than would the American girl of a different hue.

Liz said, "It's all right, I guess. I'm not into it much, though."

Waiting for Taffie's answer, it was like a guessing game over a moment of silence before she shook her head. "No." In fact, Taffie had no preference for any particular type of music at all. Like everyone else who had met her expecting her to be a singer or dancer or some type of entertainer, Tabriz was a little disappointed to hear that she wasn't.

He said, "In the beginning, this place was supposed to be a live house. I wanted to have a place where local performers could come and do shows. It was to compete with that club in Umeda, Ambush. Perhaps you have heard of it?"

Liz had not heard of the place, but Taffie had. That place was a notorious place considered the male version of the hostess gig Taffie worked. Male hosts would entertain affluent, pretty penny–distributing cougars of Japanese high society. The twist was this club featured foreign males as a majority of the staff, quite often black people who were, by most accounts, decent singers who often performed covers and renditions of old American Motown hits.

Taffie said, "Yes, I know about that place, but . . . I hear this place, very dangerous?"

Tabriz said, "I don't know much about that. This place too used to be somewhat like that description, but that was before I raised the admission price. Before, when the admission was cheap, anybody would come, and it often attracted the low-lives. As for Ambush, I don't know, but I do know that they get a very good steady flow of clients. But I felt I could do better.

"You see, I wanted to have real performers, authentic ones who were actually from that culture. You see, I did my research, and I found that most of the people working at that place are from Africa. They are from places like Nigeria and Ghana and Senegal. They aren't really Americans! They pretend to be Americans. Japanese people do not understand the difference, but I do. You see, I am from Mandali, in Iraq. I am from where you Americans call the Middle East. I know the African man when I see them, and those guys there are Africans pretending to be Americans when they sing their rap songs, their R&B covers, and the dance moves that they copy."

Liz was confused and losing interest in this topic of conversation really fast. She still felt the need to engage him a bit more to not seem like the ungrateful visitor.

"What difference does it make where they come from?" she asked.

"Maybe not much, my dear, but only to the untrained eye. Imagine if you had not much exposure to the outside world. You have no idea what gold really is, but you have seen and heard of this thing sparingly in your life. Then one day, I bring you a rock, and I tell you that it is gold. You are satisfied until you find out what it really is. Then you realize that you have been scammed."

Liz was confused with Tabriz's talk, which she was quickly dismissing as bafflegab. She said, "I don't get it."

"I arranged a production of performers from the United States of America two, no, three years ago, but that plan fell through. I had to scrap it because myself and the management of the ensemble were unable to come to agreeable terms. It was so disappointing because I had the hip-hoppers, the *capoeiristas*, the singers, the dancers—all from the urban cities of the US, Brazil, *authentic* people from the culture, the real gold. Japanese people would have been able to see the difference. It would really have set my place apart from all the other places. It was so disappointing that I was unable to put this together. What a waste of talent and resources, because we were all set and ready to go. I must say, dealing with Japanese and business and politics . . . argh! It can be so overwhelming, mind-boggling.

"But to answer your question, the issue is not so much the nationality of the performers as it is the authenticity. The Japanese are keen on authenticity like anyone else would be. Ask the Japanese if they prefer a natural spa or an artificial one . . . Or ask yourself, would you be happy with a real diamond, or a stone that resembles one yet is not?

"It can be imitated but not duplicated. Authenticity applies something more than a mere facsimile, and the performers, I felt, would have embodied an aspect of the culture that the imitators would fail to resonate, and fail to captivate audiences in the same way."

Liz had just about heard her fill. The champagne was almost finished, and the dude was beginning to sound like a comic book character descending into the role of a mad villain. Liz decided it was a good time to visit the ladies' room. She asked where it was, and Tabriz gave her easy instructions for one that was close by and private more so than the common one for public use at the dance floor level. She slipped her strap heels back on and was off. After finding the restroom, relieving herself with a tinkle, she washed her hands and returned to the noisy ballroom.

Instead of returning to the VIP lounge, Liz elected to venture back into the ballroom, and a quick visit to the ovular center bar. She was hoping that she could see the French guy again, but once more after waiting several moments for him to make an appearance, he never showed. Only the effeminate, rail-thin Nori was still working the bar. Giving up, Liz returned to Taffie and Tabriz.

When she got back, it was Taffie's turn to excuse herself. She and Liz exchanged incredulous but funny stares as they passed one another at the door. "He is very strange, but I like him," Taffie whispered. Liz winked as she returned to the cushiony French-style chair and received the last of the Dom.

Tabriz stopped talking about his business and ambition and began pouring on the sweet talk and suggestive propositioning. In minutes, he was sounding thirsty like Takuto was for Liz back at the Can of Pee spot. He went on and on about how beautiful Liz was, and how she was a Hollywood starlet, because he knew from Liz's supplied data that she was from California.

He said, "It would be a man's dream to be with a woman like you. Your hair is so extraordinary, as if it were that of an angel's . . . a Christian angel, of course. Where I am from, treasures like you are beyond rare." And he went on and on. By now, Liz was somewhat used to the compliments, for sure it had gassed her head up, but depending on who was spitting the rhetoric, she was gradually feeling such comments redundant. The bottom line was although he was attractive, classy, and sophisticated in his own way, Liz didn't feel particularly drawn to him or compelled to bed down with him for the night—or any night—but that didn't mean she couldn't be his friend or be on good terms with him. So it didn't matter how much he inundated the champagne-induced talk with sweet nothings, it would not gain him access to her womanly grotto.

Liz adroitly deflected the conversation by changing the topic. She asked, "Why do you have that big scary clown outside the door? It's so . . . *far out*, y'know?"

Tabriz laughed. He said, "I was not the designer of this but the artist rendition of a story I once heard a long time ago. I could appreciate it. It also coincides with the name—the Candy Box—it was about this performer, he was like a harlequin, or a court jester. But, he had his addictions. You see, we all have these addictions, be it champagne, fine wine, or anything that is pleasant, or gives us the illusion of something pleasant or sweet—even if it is bad for you, you still feel the urge to have it. Sometimes this is the driving force for some people. For some it is the only reason why they wake up in the morning. So we all have this thing. Whatever it is. So tell me, Elizabeth, what is inside of your Candy Box? What keeps you coming back to something for more, and more?"

It was almost like a trick question, for which Liz had no immediate answer. She could have stated many things, and she almost did, but she was interrupted by the return of Taffie, who had called her from the room's door. She beckoned for Liz to join her.

She said, "El-ee-za-beth, can you assist to me, please?"

Liz said to Tabriz, "Excuse me, Mr. Nay-Jeff? My friend is calling for me. We're just gonna go powder our noses."

Tabriz squinted oddly in an unfamiliar zone of what exactly it meant to "powder ones nose" as he hadn't heard this expression much in his travels. He cleverly figured it out that it was a time for women to consult with one another, not use the cocaine drug, so he stood up from the table to excuse them.

For Liz it was a great time to dip out anyway as that scene was getting a little dry and tired. Although she did enjoy the atmosphere of the secluded room above all the action, it became a bit too confining after a while, and she wanted to get out. Furthermore, the psychotic color schemes and trick lighting of the room was doing a number on her brain. It had mind-altering effects on her without the aid of LSD.

Tabriz's discussion was intriguing, but nothing he spoke of held her interest at that particular time, no matter how much champagne he blessed them with. Besides, she had just about had enough to drink. Taffie pretty much felt the same way as she lured Liz inside of the common restroom on the crowded level of the ballroom.

Liz said, "So what do you think of him?"

Taffie said, "Oh, he was so very . . . *aggresive*. He really talked so fast, telling me 'Oh, you are a beauti-fool African Queen, you should be one of my wives . . . ugh! So he is strange . . . I like him . . . but he is strange."

Liz was at once turned off. Once she heard that she explained to Taffie he was the same with me, he was, like, really pouring it on how he was into me, and how I was some kind of American Beauty and whatnot . . . he's a real creep. And he's from Iran, Iraq, or one of those Arab countries, so he probably has a harem of wives that have to wear blankets to come outside and they get treated like slaves! Ugh . . . I hate those."

The restroom was almost vacant, save for one or two chatty chicks trying to have a miniature hairstylist tutorial session before the vanity. They looked at the stumbling gargantuan females and packed up their stuff to vacate the spot. Taffie opened up a stall and was like, "Let's you go." And motioned for Liz to enter.

Liz said in an ornery sort of way like a bleater, "But I don't hafta go, I just went . . ."

Taffie yanked her inside of the stall with her and shut the door. She fastened the latch. In a whisper, she was like, "Where is that? The . . . " She used the pinched finger gesture to symbolize a smoke.

Liz remembered that she had stashed the last joint in her purse compartment. She took it out of a rolling paper pack enclosure, protected from damage or destruction.

Taffie said, "We should do it now here."

Now Liz had her lily-liver moment where she sounded timid and whiny, like Stephanie was notorious for being. "But won't they smell it? We'll get in a lot of trouble."

Taffie said, "Cigarette? You still have it?"

Liz closed the lid on the fetid commode and sat on it as she rummaged through her purse. She found the cigarette box and took its last remaining Marlboro Light. She passed it to Taffie, along with the lighter, which was stored in the now-empty box.

Taffie lit the square and puffed the smoke out into the direction of the ceiling before passing it to Liz. Liz started to smoke the cigarette, then Taffie took the joint she had placed atop the toilet paper dispenser's flat surface. She lit it up, and they started some awkward hot box session, passing the cigarette and the joint back and forth until nothing remained of the joint but a roach too small to attempt using. The smoke from the Marlboro was apparently intended to mask the strong odor of the reefer.

When that was over, Liz felt so high she sensed that she could float her way over the walled enclosure and swim in the air like mist. Japanese girls came into the restroom. Liz laughed at them because they were dressed like old-school Raggedy Anne dolls, complete with vertical chain gang striped leggings. She couldn't stop laughing until she almost had to keel over and upchuck her guts in the vanity's sink. The two Japanese girls looked at each other with widened, confused eyes as if they had done something wrong. Taffie also was now guffawing surpassingly at Liz. They decided to get the hell out of the restroom before more people came and started bitching about the smoky fumes.

They didn't go back to Tabriz or the VIP Lounge. Liz took Taffie by the hand like she was on a date with someone she had met online, ecstatic that they hit it off. The DJ was still infusing the site with the '90s tunes. Stephen Jenkins and Kevin Cadogan were blathering on about how they wanted "something else" to get them through a semicharmed kind of life, and Liz started singing along: "When you say, good-bye! Do-do-do-do-do-do-dewwwwww!" Then she led her date out on the dance floor. Taffie joined her in the festive movement of bodies, and they both showed off their moves. Together, they looked as cloddish as any other imbecilic oaf who had been dancing on the floor that night, but oddly, the other clubbers opened up a space on the floor for the two of them like they were putting on a presentation for the viewers' delight.

From the VIP Lounge perched above the dance floor, Tabriz could see the two women dancing on the floor. He didn't feel salty about them ditching him. He could have his pick of splendid selections of broads from Osaka to Tokyo. He did, however, have a special curiosity for Liz, though. She was, in his opinion, one of those Hollywood big-screen TV broads in their best form, before they hit the wall, of course, and the only women he had seen that looked better than the American ones were the Swedish, or maybe the Dutch . . . but it didn't matter. He knew that she would be back. They always did come back. But for now, he enjoyed having people like her there. As he watched her dance on the floor, she herself looked like a charming performer, a captivator, for indicative of his own spiel earlier regarding authenticity, in his opinion, Liz too was authentic white trash, but maybe a poor, broke Disney chick who became a princess by virtue of some miracle or divine intervention, but a treasure nevertheless. Oh, how he liked her, but he wouldn't obsess over her too much, and he chided himself for the desperation he had reduced himself to by appearing thirsty.

He made a quick call on his cellular. On the phone, he told someone below to shine the spotlight on Liz and Taffie dancing out on the floor.

People were clapping and cheering Taffie and Liz's ridiculous dance act and lip sync performance. Liz had never been known as a great dancer, but for tonight, she may as well have been Cher with the long blonde hair. She had an invisible microphone and a backup singer and dancer who was Taffie, who she would occasionally close in on, face-to-face with, as if they were seconds away from a kiss, then retract themselves and continue on. Song after song until finally, people clapped and rejoined the conglomerate of bodies in the center like a bowl of chili.

After another hour of this, fatigue finally crept its way into the energy of the party animals. A lot of the crowd had dissipated, and the music had slowed down, signaling the closing time. Liz and Taffie are practically slow dancing now to Shawn Mullins, Liz imitating his howling moan, telling Taffie "Everythingz' gon'be aw'riiiiight, rock, goodbye! Yeah!." With her arms around her shoulder, more for support than anything else. She saw the time on her Swatch read close to 3:00 a.m. Guess it was time to call it another day. And all this time, she had not spared a single thought for Eddie.

Taffie said "Would you like come to my home? It is closer than your home. What is better for you?"

Liz was like, "Oh, really? Thanks! Sure, I'd really like to come." With a plenitude of gratefulness faintly surpassing Taffie's own pleasure in her accepting the invitation. They left the Candy Box, but not before being seen off at the door by Tabriz Najaf himself, still the calm, collected, and smooth gentleman, kissing their hands and all that, like, "Thank you, ladies, and do come again!" Handing them his crisp, gold-painted-tip business cards, bearing his name, phone numbers, addresses to several of his clubs both in Tokyo and the only one in Osaka, the Candy Box, at the very top of the list. It was loaded with information, plus it was a little thicker like a baseball card from ToPPs or FLEER. No way she could lose that, unless it was on purpose.

While Liz was in an intoxicated state of blandishment over the biz card, Taffie had summoned a taxi for them. They were whisked away in the cockroach mobile. She told the cabbie where to go in damn-near perfect Japanese. The old man heard her, and his eyes flew open as if a hot poker had been run up his rectum. A black foreigner was the last person he would have ever expected to speak like that. He didn't know whether to be in awe or to be fascinated. He complied and drove speedily along East Kyobashi Higashi Drive.

"Can't wait to see your place," Liz said.

She was like an excited kid about to go watch a G-rated movie. Her stomach started growling. They then discussed getting something to cure the munchies.

The taxi driver took the Sakuramiya Bridge over the Tosabori River tributary. Taffie told him to stop along the brightly lit Ogimachi Avenue strip. They found a noodle shop that was still open and feasted on some greasy, oily, and salty larmen, fried rice, and some tea. Liz didn't feel an excessive need to moan about how unhealthy the meal was because for some unknown reason, its consumption had a sobering effect on her inebriated and stoned condition. After the late-night, early-dawn feed, they took a short walk through some winding mazes of backstreet footpaths, which, Liz could never retrace in footsteps should she be required to find again. A series of left and right turns and a thruway between two adjoining buildings would lead to a small street, and there Taffie led the way to a villa-style rowhouse that was sandwiched sideways so that the entrance faced the road and the long building stretched rectangular to the rear. It was a trick on the eyesight, and access to the building lobby was easy to miss.

Taffie lived on the second floor, but they took the elevator anyway. When they arrived at her room, Liz went inside and felt thankful to live in her Bozack dormitory as opposed to the midget, tiny room Taffie lived in. To her credit, however, it was very clean, tidy, and kept up. The floor had a stainless, sumptuous white carpet, a miniature divan bed, decorated with pink linen, stuffed animals, and a huge plush heart pillow in matching colors. The room was spaced off with a translucent rice paper shoji screen, dividing the kitchen area and the main section. A console and a hutch were lined along the walls to make use of every usable inch or centimeter of the perimeter to make the place ostensibly spacious. Still, there was enough room for Taffie to spread a futon out for her guest to recline upon.

Taffie produced a drop-leaf retractable leg table and two bottles of tea from her miniature fridge. They sat and talked for a few minutes. Taffie told Liz that this was her secret hideout that her rich sugar daddy, the Doc, had provided her, and in fact, this was her second apartment, for which she needed not pay rent for! This apartment had been formerly the separate residence of the out-of-town-doctor for when he needed to be in Osaka. The perks of being a hostess was appealing, Liz mused.

It was almost 4:00 a.m. Liz had one last trick up her sleeve, and she placed it on the table. Taffie's eyes lit up again when she saw the joint. She laughed as she went to place a wet towel underneath the crack of her door. The small talk continued as Taffie dimmed the halogen lamplight and her decorative comet and star glowing stickers created a luminous galaxy on her wall.

After this final joint session, Liz felt her head once again get light, yet her eyelids became heavy and slumberous. Taffie, who had by now grown extremely fond of Liz, made the mistake and allowed her head to playfully fall into Liz's lap while exploding into the smoke-induced fit of laughter now a regularity. Taffie's thick curly black hair smelled like a combination of sweat, coconut, and some floral scent traces from a hairspray. Liz inhaled her essence like an herbal bouquet of fascinating new discovery. A flame ignited from desires of an unaccountable origin suddenly sparked deep within Liz's foundation. It was spreading fast, coursing through her body at rapid speed. She didn't know what else to do but lick Taffie's candy-brown forehead. Then she kissed her saliva clean. In her warped mind, she was going, *Wow, damn! The bitch actually is sweet!*

A sinister, girlish chortle emitted from Liz's throat as if to distract Taffie from the kiss to her lips that was to follow. It was two kisses actually. The first was an exploratory peck to see if the second would be welcome or better received. The second was long, deliberate, and sticky and punctuated with a light smack taste.

Of course, this wasn't the first time Taffie had ever kissed a girl, and it would not be the first time she had done lesbian acts. But this would mark the first time she actually enjoyed it. And welcomed it as opposed to the older studs in the orphanage who more or less forced her to be involved in such intimacy. This time, however, it was different.

Liz said, "Hey, we should take a shower . . . it's been a long night."

After kissing and hugging and rubbing lathery soap all over one another under the hot steamy water jet for about thirty minutes, the party came back to the bedroom. Liz had not been naked with another woman in that way since the days she would go nuts with Becky back home. Her visits to the onsen spas and public bath in Hannan City didn't count. Naked Japanese women didn't turn her on—at least not as much as Taffie.

Taffie said to Liz as they were on her little bed, "I hope that you do not misunderstand. I like you. You are beautiful to me. But, this is not what I am . . . I am not . . . *une lesbienne*, do you understand it? It is not who I am, but I like you."

Liz had to admit to having the same feelings. She poured out her heart and came clean about her past and history being with women, stretching back to her first experience in high school with the assistant volleyball coach. Yet she still couldn't shake the fact that she had the hots for Taffie in a way that made her feel like a predatory stalking dragon lady.

Taffie said, "El-ee-zabeth, I really would like to be with a man. I want *un petit ami, un amant,* a boyfriend like you have, but not a man who is so much older. This man, this doctor, he won't marry with me, but he want me to come and live in the Tokyo, but I can't. If he die like my before fiance, I will be doomed. I have nowhere else to go.

"But if I had someone, we can be together, grow together, stay together. I can have hope. Do you understand me, how I'm feeling? You have a boyfriend. You have a chance, more so here than me. So that is why I wanted explain to you I am not *une lesbienne*, but I cannot help it. I like you very much for girl." She kissed Liz hard on the lips like she was a hot boy and she was a spice girl. Cinamon and

Vanilla did a battle of tongues as Taffie's and Liz's mouths connected in a fierce kissing combat. Passionately, Taffie hipped Liz on the real French kiss.

The Iowa girl from California then descended her head beneath the pink coverlet sheet with her still-wet blonde hair following her like Rapunzel. Taffie's woolly bush reminded Liz of pictures she had seen of the mystical Black Forest of Europe, but she fearlessly trudged through its murky, sweet edges. Her stroke paid special attention to all the stimulating parts she knew well. Taffie had to squeeze her confetti-cream kneecaps to crush the sides of Liz's head, in ecstasy, keeping her captive in the forest. So to free herself, the wicked witch of the west had to conjure a tingling tongue spell enabling her to penetrate the forest. When the desired solution was discovered, Liz used one or two fingers to thrust forward, to gain the desired effects. At once set free she could breathe normal air again, but captivity had made her into a savage. Now she was the aggressor. She mounted the dark witch of the east and assaulted her with rapid but deliberate diffusion, ingress to the entrance, Liz using her fingers there. Enabled by a limp but powerful wrist, techniques she had long ago mastered while batting volleyballs during her high school days, she applied the affectionate heat. The French girl couldn't take it anymore, so her forest exploded into a mucky avalanche, her sweet sap seeped from the lush environment. She kissed the nectar remnants from Liz's face. The two entities took a break, but as the freaky passion was yet to be quelled, the showdown rallied on.

They caressed each other's breasts, focal points on all paps were not ignored as their legs coiled around one another's like slithering serpents. They were moaning in contraltos and staccatos, like specters, exsanguinous banshees of the shadowy walls of secrecy. Two completely different directions of wind from the east and the west met at the eye of the storm and pressed against each other. Perfect timing the crash caused them both to be ejected into a suspended state of animation, neither alive nor dead, in an introspective parallel universe but immobile. Like swimming or floating in water, but outer space was the pool. It was a surreal, hypnagogic climax, the likes of which Liz had never experienced before in her life. All but too amazing, too good to be true, but too true to be just good—it was the closest thing ever to perfect. When the gasp was released, they returned to consciousness and collapsed uncoiled together.

33

SOMETIME AROUND NOON, Liz and Taffie parted company. The latter had errands to run pertaining to her circumference of life, so did Liz. They each took another shower—separately—and Liz had to be on her way, with a few parting gifts. Taffie had a surplus of used clothes she didn't mind parting with, and if Liz could fit them, she was more than happy to get rid of those. Now it was no longer a big secret about where Taffie could get her gear. From the high-priced department stores and ritzy boutiques. She had one of those rich doctors who was infatuated with her to sponsor her in the garment department—and, if what Taffie had said was true, she also didn't have to pay for her rent. How lucky could one be? But then again, after hearing Taffie's back story, Liz thought she deserved it.

Now Liz had connection to get all the opiates. If she needed some excess wardrobe, she could ask Taffie, for accessories she could go to Radley, for free night club entertainment she could go to the Candy Box (for starters), and if she ever needed a part-time job, she could work at Takuto's spot. What she was mostly grateful for was the clothes. Taffie hooked her up with a hefty-sized duffel bag full of regalia-type duds as opposed to mediocre, plain, ill-fitting apparel she'd be otherwise forced to acquire as an only choice.

The exchange was Taffie getting a network to get dope. She mentioned to Liz that she wasn't into X but was curious to try it. Liz offered to get her some of that the following week.

The elephant in the room was their relationship, or relationships. Because of what they did at Taffie's place, they seemed to be an unofficial couple, or part-time lesbians? Liz didn't know but decided she should play it by ear, because Taffie seemed sincere when she expressed her desire to be with men, and in so many words, somewhat laconically, that she preferred men to women, and what they decided to do with one another was one of those onetime-only flukes. Regardless, no matter what happened after that instance, Taffie had been elevated to "best friend" status undeniably.

As for Taffie's relationship with the Doc, there was no advice Liz could give her. As for her wanting a boyfriend, Liz knew not of anyone she could immediately help her out with. She had already exhausted herself trying to get someone for Denore—Chucky, and even that relationship wasn't a boy-girlfriend one—and Kwame was out of the question. They had already met when Kwame filled in for her at the Umeda School. Again, Taffie tacitly implied that she wasn't into him either. Besides, she had Kwame pegged as an asshole and a droll. Not the kind of guy she really liked hanging out with; he was sort of like Keefer, but where he surpassed the Aussie in obnoxiousness was his obsessive need to be the center of attention and playful aggressiveness. Keefer was just a drunk, vainglorious root rat who kept his hands and jokes to himself for the most part. Kwame had a tendency to be touchy feely, and she'd heard that he had been the same way with Vicky, and even Stephanie. So again, as with Denore, Kwame was not an option.

Tim the Duke? Nah, Liz decided. He was like Chucky. They already had Japanese girlfriends, and they were whipped. Straight "Oreos"-but then again—they would have to be a different category technically. But the same desperation and obsessed look Lamar had for Becky, she could sense these guys had for Japanese women. Besides Eddie, Liz knew of no other guys who would be faithful to a girlfriend who lived out of town, in a whole other city like Chucky. He either was lying, or he was an extraordinary, exceptional guy.

Speaking of exceptional guys, Eddie might not have been such, but he had been faithful to Liz even though his thoughts and intentions would remove even that merit. Liz called him, and they finally got a chance to speak to each other. Surprisingly—or maybe not—Eddie's justifiable anger had, by Monday evening, been attenuated with the soothing sound of Liz's raspy voice.

When Liz explained her side of the story, she acknowledged that she was somewhat at fault. They would argue back and forth about who carried the most weight in how things turned out, and Liz shrewdly would find ways to make herself seem the least culpable. Her reasoning was that had Eddie heeded her directive and planned his exodus from bumpkin-world earlier, he would have arrived on time, and the debacle would never have taken place at all.

The difference between this prolonged argument and some others was that the previous ones, Eddie would be the levelheaded, rational sort of pushover who would back down and allow Liz to be the dominant one. He was just a fickle follower, with a limited, narrow outlook or scope for his own life. Liz was quick to calumniate, especially during their shouting matches, phone or face-to-face. For the majority of their duration together, going on four years at this point, Liz had been the authoritative entity in the union. And it was always supposed to be like that. Eddie was a wind-up toy, her Ken doll, her Teddy Bear with a pouch was the role and received her attention whenever she was ready to give it to him. Eddie was growing tired of this role and began showing signs that he wanted to flip the script. To the Japanese, he was a hero, so why did he have to be reduced to a lackey, or secret identity loser alter-ego with his woman?

So Eddie asserted his powers and lashed back at the stubbornly tenacious, pertinacious drama queen for a girlfriend. He bristled in his own defense and applied added emphasis with plenty of "Shut the fuck ups" and "Now just you wait . . . Listen to me, DAMMIT!"

Deep down inside, Liz could see that Eddie's frustration was moderately warranted, plus she had technically cheated on him with a woman, so she felt it would be favorable if she apologized. Placate him with a vow that she would make it up to him because it was easier to do to make peace.

Eddie calmed down. Neither he nor Liz knew exactly how she was going to make good on her promise to make things right, to make it up to him; but given her past record, Eddie had no reason to believe she wouldn't come up with something, so he gradually cooled down.

When the conversation returned to normal, they were able to talk like they had never had a problem in the first place. Liz filled him in on what happened with precise detail all up until the point where she and Taffie did a birthday suit dance in bed. Likewise, Eddie told her about his tireless efforts to remain the "best ALT" his junior high ever had but omitted the magic moments and dry molestation flirting from Hiroko Okada.

Two weeks later, Liz had accomplished a series of tasks. She had copped some X for Taffie, but she didn't give it to her right away. In fact, she was interested in taking it herself, but she chicken-livered on that plan because she was afraid of doing it by herself. So she kept the two pellets to herself.

Tim the Duke praised her for remembering to follow the timetable when ordering. Apparently, the X was a little cumbersome to acquire more so than some other dope. She liked Tim. He was cool, he had the prettiest, gleaming white-toothed smile, he wore the most stylish clothes, and he always smelled good. He would be the perfect guy for Taffie, Liz assumed. What's more, since he was the Duke, he had connection links to all the underworld pharmaceuticals. Taffie could smoke all the weed she wanted to, or get anything she wanted, plus she would get what she dreamed of having, a steady partner, one within her age range, and someone with whom she could grow—like her relationship with Eddie—who cares if she couldn't speak English the best? Of course, she would eventually grow better. Damn. Why did Tim have to have a girlfriend? she wondered.

Being the quick study she was, Liz became popular at the Hommachi Branch with students in a relatively short time. Because of her animated personality, Japanese student customers were drawn to her. Many of the female instructors were either totalitarian, indifferent, or both. The authoritarian, oppressive teachers like Stephanie and her herd would establish themselves as the boss of the class, thus mistakes and errors even in the slightest form or fashion were required to be addressed. The indifferent ones like Vicky would simply show up for work, read from the script, and leave the students to their own devices, groping in the dark, clueless about how they had spent their hour with a *gaijin* and money. Liz was the type who remembered the names of some of the Japanese people she taught. The only reason this was stemmed from the fact that she liked poking fun and talking about them to the other teachers in between classes. This was one of several other attributes that sparked her rise in Hommachi notoriety.

She finally had her sit-down with the head teacher Mitch "Worm" Swiggler. Remembering the first time she had seen him, she had expected a Clark Kent type—bold, muscular, and facets characteristic of a heroic leader, especially the type who could be placed in charge of such a large, motley crew of personalities from multiple extractions. Instead, she met an osseous walking skeleton in a bulky suit, tailored with extra buff on shoulder pads to make him appear larger or ominous.

Worm, as he didn't mind being called, turned out to be more easygoing than she had expected. He was able to joke around and be casual with the staff as far as she could see. She did not have to work with him every day, or see him much, as his job duties did not require for him to teach or be at work on schedules like the subordinate teachers. She felt thankful for that, because nobody liked being micromanaged or spied upon and feeling the need to always look over their shoulders to check if they are being secretly evaluated. Liz was alleviated of this subjugation because Worm was pleased to inform her that she was "doing an outstanding job." She had been receiving good reviews in customer surveys, and, lastly, encouraged Liz to "keep up the good work." This was good, and because of this, Liz felt she could work off the blemish on her record that her unexcused absence and no-call had imbued.

The rest of the time, she had done regular chores, errands, and maintenance undertakings. She went to the supermarket—for her and Denore because she had a tendency to eat and drink up her roommate's stuff—did the laundry, some tidying around the apartment, and other busybody stuff. She started going to the gym at nights after work and did less hanging out with Stephanie and other coworkers. Even Taffie she shunned going swimming and doing some Olympic laps, because when she was locked into her fitness frenzy spell, it became her primary focus. Then, by the time the weekend rolled around, she paid another visit to Tok at the Thai Massage spot in Kujo. Tok's topically placed herbal ointments worked wonders on her joints: kneecaps, ankles, instep of toes; shoulders, elbows, wrists, and fingers. She would leave the massage den feeling like a walking sponge, revitalized and vigorous. Tok was like a miracle worker with her hands and technique. She aggrandized, it left her with lewd thoughts of debating who could make her "come" faster, Taffie or technique from Tok?

Reluctantly, two weeks after their major fallout and subsequent rapprochement, Liz took the trip out to Hannan City on a Monday morning. The condensed number of commuters and train riders headed away from the metropolis in that direction of Osaka Prefecture didn't cease to amaze her. It somewhat solidified her assertion that where Eddie lived—and where she used to live—was a pocket of dung where no one wanted to go to or visit. When she got off the train at Hakkotsukuri Station and not contrary to her expectations, the place was practically desolate.

Eddie had taken the day off. This was something he did not ordinarily do. Even if he actually was sick, he would try to tough it out and endure the day. He had received an award from Oscar Gomimoto and the CHET Administration for having a good attendance record. However, in an unconventional attempt to mend and enrich their relationship, Eddie went against his ethic and called in fake sick, because he knew that Liz would be coming.

Around 10:00 a.m., Liz showed at the residence quarters, which had been her former home, one she and Eddie shared. She skillfully avoided the chickens, twerp congregations, and the hideous, olden horny hens that stalked her man. Since the building was a Lions' Mansion, she found a rear entrance to the place that the maintenance people used. She still had a spare key to the apartment where she used to live, so she let herself in. Another reason Eddie dared not try to cheat and bring a broad back to his spot. He would hate like all hell for Liz to find him in a precarious involvement with a side piece.

Eddie, remarkably, was still asleep. She took a moment to marvel at how cute he was to her when he was sleeping before deciding to wake him up in style.

She found their old "boom box" which was one of the welcome gifts donated to them when they had first arrived in Japan a while back. She stretched it and its cord over from the shelf where it was to the bed where Eddie slept. Before switching it on, she made sure the volume was at peak level. Liz played whatever CD was still in the radio, so "Sugar Ray"'s Mark McGrath was wailing away about how he "wanted to fly" and pleading for some "baby" to put arms around him when the sound at full blast was broadcast.

Liz had also gone through painstaking efforts to roll an atrociously executed joint. She had been practicing throughout the weeks, she was getting better, but not quite yet at that particular time. Anyhow, she had already lit it up, but so poorly had it been constructed, the smoke extinguished after the draft of one pull she took from it. She held the smoke within as she fumbled with the radio inches from Eddie's ear.

When the surprise shock of the loud music jolted Eddie from slumber, his first waking moment was greeted by weed smoke blown dead in his face. Eddie coughed, cursed, and rubbed his suddenly stinging eyes.

Before he could announce his grievances, Liz had already gone down on him, dipped below to the subway. Her slippery, slimy mouth was what the doctor ordered—sick leave or not sick—especially for an ailing, horny, and lonely Eddie. The oral expertise she employed upon the specific area of his anatomy gaining her attention was still at an award-winning level as far as he was concerned—though she would likely never match that of the first Fat Girl, but that was a different story altogether, irrelevant at that time for all the undeniable reasons.

In minutes, his gratitude rocketed to the roof of Liz's mouth. She juggled their wasted children in her jib like some absurd creamy mouthwash before kissing him, releasing the entire load on *his* lips.

Without missing a beat, Liz sprang up from the bed and was like "How about some *real* breakfast?"

Eddie was acting disgusted as he wiped his mouth and then his hands on the bedsheets. His discharge was so heavy, he felt like he was moving in slow motion, like he had been drained of all bodily fluids.

"I haven't been shopping," Eddie said.

Liz was already in her old kitchen area and looked in the fridge. It was basically empty save for a couple of bottles of beer, sports drinks, and rice balls.

"No shit," Liz said as she took out one of the onigiri rice balls and took it out of its clear wrapper. She took a bite, spat that portion out into the garbage where the rest of it was discarded. She said, "That fucken thing was hard like plastic!"

She began doing the same with the others and ended up throwing all the rice balls in the trash. "These things are nasty as shit, Eddie. How long did you have these things in there?"

Eddie shrugged his shoulders and outstretched his arms as he made his way into the kitchen wearing only his yellow boxers with red polka dots. He said, "I just bought 'em a day or two ago, maybe last Friday."

Liz said vulgarly "Fuck that, dude. These things go bad real quick." She scooped up everything Eddie had in the fridge and proceeded to throw it all out. "What would you do without me? You would go to pieces, that's what. I can't believe you have no food in here. No wonder you got sick that time."

Eddie feebly protested, "I was gonna go shopping last Saturday, but you said that you wanted to go to the pool, don't you remember?"

Not desiring to argue or rehash the previous spat, Liz pacified him with a series of of assurances seasoned with her stating, "OK, OK, calm down," and "I got it." Then she would rub the smallish pot belly Eddie was forming.

She said, "For someone who doesn't have anything to eat around here, you sure do seem to be getting a little flabby." She snickered as she tried to pinch his gut.

Almost comically, Eddie didn't view his recent weight gain as being necessarily flabby. Instead, he preferred to be of the opinion that mirrored how the students at his school and folks like Hiroko had seen him. To them, he was a brawny, muscular athletic Adonis.

"Just you wait," Eddie said. "By this time next summer, you're gonna eat those words."

Liz let out an exasperating "Ha! You already did eat those words!" she said as she almost violently slapped his tummy, laughing.

Before Eddie could retort, Liz had switched gears and had begun to start tidying up around the apartment. She then imperiously started bossing Eddie around, ordering him to get dressed. As usual, or feasibly normally, he obeyed pliantly in underling fashion. He got into gear, squeezed into a T-shirt, and kicked his legs inside some faded jeans within minutes.

"Wait," he said, "I just remembered . . . since I called in sick today, it would look awfully shitty if I were t'be seen out and about walkin' around."

Of course, Liz scowled disapprovingly. "Who gives a shit?" she asked. "They don't control you. You have a right to have a day off every once and a while!"

Eddie said, "Yeah, but still, it looks kinda bad, y'know. I've been studyin' upa little about this Japanese culture, y'know. Hiroko-san, that teacher I work with, she's been givin' me a lotta interesting books to read. Well, I uh . . . I've sorta been getting' this feeling of admiration for how they do things."

Liz couldn't believe her ears. This wasn't the Eddie she had groomed. It wasn't his *job* to be reading up about *anything*. She continued to listen to his nonsense through inscrutable ears.

Eddie went on to the tune of, "Yeah, there's a lot of *honor* in Japanese society. Did you know? They go to work, even if they are sick? I only stayed home today because I knew that you were coming. But the things we Americans would call in sick about, I believe that the Japanese wouldn't complain about it." And he gabbled on. Liz was more interested in the growling coming from her belly than Eddie's brown-nose crusade.

"And if they do take an absence, they will return from their absence and give the whole entire staff room some cookies or a snack as a way of apologizing for not being at work and at the same time thanking their coworkers."

Liz had listened to everything he was jibber-jabbering patiently, then she said, "OK, so what do you suggest we do, then? Sooner or later, yer gonna get hungry, right?"

Right she was, Eddie concluded. He came up with a solution, though. He went to the kitchen and dug up some food delivery menus. Liz was unexpectedly fine with the idea of ordering something to be delivered. She commandeered this mission and decided that they both were going to get two Bento box lunches from the Hokka-Hokka Shop and two pizzas.

In America, neither Liz nor Eddie would have been caught dead with a Domino's Pizza box or anything that would come inside of one. But in Japan, it was like mother's milk for homesick pizza lovers. The grub orders arrived in entirety slightly in the forenoon. Eddie's place looked like a small party was in progress.

Like while in the United States, Eddie had amassed a collection—albeit considerably smaller than the one he had back home—of video tapes. Most of them he and Liz had already seen, but they were still enjoyable nonetheless as they smoked pot and watched. They both liked how their minds would distort the meanings and messages of the flicks and story lines within them as they watched under the influence.

They spent the afternoon smoking the weed Liz brought, drinking all of Eddie's beers from the fridge. When they got the munchies, they gorged on leftover pizza, fried rice, and chicken. They watched videos like *Die Hard*, *Natural Born Killers*, and Eddie's personal favorite, *Pulp Fiction*.

As they snuggled together for the first time in a while, Eddie's growing urges to be intimate festered perpetually while cuddling. The after-effect of encounters with Hiroko at school was eroding his composure and restraint. Now Liz and her warmth was upon him, and he desired to be even closer. When he started stroking and rubbing her in provocative zones, Liz would smack his hands away, as if she thought he was trying to be annoying. She would be like, "Chill out and let me watch this movie!"

But Eddie wasn't trying to be annoying. Nor was he trying to give up. Unfortunately, Liz was tired, and she had to drop the disheartening news that she was on the menstruation cycle at that particular time. In fact, she had silently suffered through menstrual cramps that entire day yet hadn't complained about it. The hectic, engrossing schedule of waking up earlier (than usual) for work and going to the gym at night and trekking all the way back to Hannan City had taken its toll and plum tuckered her out. Filling her stomach with several slices of vegetarian pizza, beers, and the toxic glaze from fat spliffs Eddie rolled up, the light feeling of slumber took control of her functioning capabilities. She rolled over and began snoring away.

Deciding not to awake her, Eddie considerately allowed her to rest. Beauty sleep wouldn't hurt her, he felt. In the meantime, he was delighted to smoke another joint of the grass Liz brought over. He was amazed at the quality. When he finished, he too became groggy and sleepy. So he too napped out, contented to have Liz back in his arms. The bliss of reconciliation enhanced his sweet dreams for the time being.

34

AROUND 5:30 P.M., both Eddie and Liz were awakened by a loud chime of the apartment doorbell. Eddie was startled because he didn't usually receive any guests aside from delivery people. Since he had received all his food orders for the day, he wasn't expecting any more pizza or anything to eat.

His scraggly Jude Law imitation face looked harried when the doorbell stopped ringing and the person outside the door switched to light knocking. It was too late to pretend to not be at home. They had fallen asleep with the TV still on. It could be heard from outside in all likelihood. As such, whoever was outside knocking didn't appear to be going away.

Nervous to the point of panic, Eddie was still haunted by the grim tales he had heard at the CHET Program orientations, about people caught with even the smallest amount of narcotics—of which marijuana was considered—who would be imprisoned in Japan. No bullshit, even a raisin drop worth, or dollop in a pipe, would catch someone at least a year of hard time!

Eddie shook Liz frantically. Normally Liz was somewhat a light sleeper, but today she had been totally relaxed and had been oblivious to the doorbell chiming away. Eddie's sudden anxiety as he roused her awake was disconcerting.

Eddie's voice whispered desperately "Wake up, y-you gotta hide your pot."

Still post-slumber incoherent, Liz was like, "What!?"

Stage-whispering, Eddie stated, "The weed! Your pot! Somebody's at the door. You gotta put it away. Somebody's at the door, I don't know who it is!"

Petulantly, Liz said, "No worries. Only thing I brought was that stash you rolled up."

She pointed to a golf-ball-sized sphere of foil on the kitchen area table. Eddie spotted it and was relieved somewhat to have it located, and although he had used most of it while Liz was sleeping, there was still some left. But he was still paranoid.

He said, "What if somebody smelled it and called the cops?"

Liz's aplomb wasn't reassuring to Eddie, but she said, "No way, man. You can smoke grass and walk down the street here and nobody'd recognize that smell." Confident and feeling accurate in her speculative argument, she chuckled because she had already, at this point, indulged with Keefer and the others to test out the theory she presented.

It wasn't enough to convince Eddie, who was still disconsolately nervous. He began trying to stall the persistent individual at the door, called out for them to "hold on, just a second!" In English, whether they understood what he was saying or not. He made Liz convince him that all the weed was stashed and gone securely before he ambled to the door and opened it.

Hiroko Okada stood at the door with a curious, worried look on her face. Eddie was both charmed and yet still surprised to see her. He didn't even know she knew where he lived. Too bad she never came while Liz wasn't there. Today, on her unexpected visit, she was carrying some type of Tupperware container ensconced in cutesy Hello Kitty bandanna.

Hiroko's warm, affable smile and zingy character was ever present, with curative effects on Eddie whether he was sick or not. She said, "Eddie-sensei, thank goodness you are OK. We heard you were sick today. Everyone at school was worried about you. Even the students. This is some fish, rice, and soup made special, for you. It may be cold, so you can heat it up in a microwave range." She handed him the Tupperware as well as a chalky-colored sports drink, Pocari Sweat.

Eddie sighed in a disgorge of relief as he took the bandanna wrapped container. Flattered and touched, he said, "Oh, that's . . . really thoughtful of you, Hiroko-san, but I'm actually fine now. I . . . I'm not sick anymore. I feel much better . . . heh,heh.."

Hiroko stood at the entrance alcove by the door. She looked past Eddie into the greater part of the room, almost as if she had wanted to come inside. Ordinarily, Eddie thought, he would have definitely allowed her, or invited her inside, but today he couldn't.

After hearing a female's voice, naturally Liz would then poke her head around the edge of a wall from one of the two rooms. Immediately, when she and Hiroko locked eyes, well concealed umbrage on both sides was present for a micro-instant before assuming overexaggerated pleasant greetings, leading to them hugging and embracing as if they were long-lost best friends. For the next minute, the talk in the air was full of "Long time no sees" and "How have you beens?" before Hiroko haphazardly slipped pink pedicured toes out of platform sling-back heels and stepped in the room. Liz embraced her again, leading the leggy and supple young Japanese teacher to the kitchen dining area.

Eddie was abated for the moment. A part of him wondered what would have happened had Liz not been there.

Hiroko did not stay for long. She too was thrown off—and subsequently chagrined—seeing Liz. Of course, the feeling was mutual for Liz too, and they both did Academy Award–level performances perfectly masking their true emotions. How it was not obvious that they were fake happy to see each other was stupefying, but they managed to spend the next twenty minutes in conversational "inconsequentialities" and pretending that they liked one another. Liz had learned to do this quickly while in Japan and put it to good practice while working at the Bozack Schools, teaching their students. For Hiroko, it just went with the territory, as *honme* and *tatemae* (*14) was something many Japanese people learned to master.

Liz wasn't too naïve, however. She was from LA, and she knew the tricks of the trade chicks used when they were sneaky hood rats, posing as dainty and lacy "respectable" types, but undercover, they would be the most distasteful, loathsome freaks the world had ever seen. Liz ought to have known, being the witch, she was. As such, she could feel suspicious energy coming from Hiroko. Oh yes, she knew something was up.

For Hiroko, it had taken a bit of doing for her to build up enough courage to visit Eddie's place that night. She was a confident girl, but for some reason, she had to psych herself into going. For the past few weeks, she had been giving him every subtle hint she could to let him know that if he were to make moves on her, she would be receptive. But that was the thing—she wanted him to make the first move on her, so basically, she and Eddie were suffering from the same problem.

When she was finally able to summon her guts to go check Eddie's crib out, she was almost certain something would indeed pop off. The coast would be clear, nobody would be around, no teachers, no students, no interruptions—but no, that was not to be. Liz deflated the pipe dream. Her worry for Eddie was genuine, but the food from the cafeteria was just a ploy; nobody was so greatly concerned for Eddie that they felt the need to make a special platter of leftover fish and rice. People were absent every day; this was just a concoction of Hiroko, a disguised excuse to get her to Eddie's place without scrutiny. She could duck suspicion from the community with that scheme, but perhaps not Liz, who she was not expecting to see.

The sentiment was not lost on Liz. Nor Eddie. For now, he was earnestly touched. He caught on to the fact that Hiroko veritably had concern for him.

Now he would be feeling guilty too because in reality, he had not been sick, as everyone else knew by then. Yet Hiroko had cared so much about him that she was compelled to bring him some food and see if he was better.

Hiroko checked out Eddie's causal demeanor and asked, "How do you feel now? Where are you sick?" She knew he wasn't sick by now but subtly tried to let him know by asking anyway.

Eddie tried to think of a lie quick. It was too late for him to pretend that he was bed-ridden, prone, or woozy. He was upbeat and reeking of pizza sauce the entire time Hiroko had been there.

"Like I said, heh heh, yeah, I feel . . . uh, better now." Eddie looked nervously at Liz, almost like pleading inaudibly for her help to concoct a believable fib. Liz wasn't receptive to his signal and instead decided it to be an opportune moment to clean up the two half-empty Domino's Pizza boxes, consolidating leftovers into one, then throwing one box away in the kitchen.

"My diarrhea became really bad." He laughed a silly cackle.

Hiroko's chipmunk character eyes expanded to a psychotic expression of disbelief. She said, "You can eat pizza when you have die-ya, die-ya-ree . . . *geri?*"

Eddie began to sweat a little. He tended to do so when uneasy. Why did Liz have to clean up now? he wondered to himself, frustrated. Those boxes had been tucked away out of sight, in another room of the apartment Hiroko hadn't had access to.

After cleaning up the boxes and tidying up the place a bit, Liz turned her attention to her Tuka phone which, at that instant, became chiming away. She grabbed it from atop Eddie's highboy shelf and uttered, "Steph? Oh, hey!" And she then excused herself to another portion of the domicile, loudly speaking the entire time.

Stumped, Eddie alone had to figure out what kind of untruth he could whip up to seem convincing. He said, "Well, I had a fever, yeah, I had, uh . . . a fever this morning! But yeah, it's gone now." Thinking that this was a foolproof excuse. It was plausible, he thought. Who needed proof of a high temperature, which had since dissipated from the morning? His only mistake was explaining how he put a thermometer that Japanese people ordinarily inserted in their ass or underneath their armpit, he had put in his mouth, to determine fever. It was a funny faux pas Eddie had not even realized.

It was OK, though. Hiroko understood that he had been lying, *as all men do*, she accepted, but she thought it was cute how he was trying to cover it up. It amused her how American people would pretend to be sick in order to miss work—like children.

Liz, on the other hand, thought it was a crock of shit about Eddie feeling the need to lie. As far as she was concerned, Hiroko's opinion or feelings didn't matter. Hiroko was not Eddie's boss, not even his supervisor, really. And even if she was, her evaluative input on Eddie's job performance would be of little consequence anyway, for this was Eddie's second and final term of eligibility with the CHET Program, which only offered employment contracts a maximum of two years. So, after that term was done, Eddie would be moving away from there anyway and, in all likelihood, joining Liz in the city to work for Bozack or some other English conversation school.

When she finished her jib-jabbing with Stephanie, Liz clicked the phone off and returned to the visitor alcove where Hiroko and Eddie stood close, face-to-face. She had already slipped back on her sling heels and was in preparation to leave, but the way she and Eddie were positioned made Liz think that she had almost interrupted them kissing.

Hiroko said, "Well, Eddie-sensei, we miss you at the school. I hope you will feel better and hope we will see you tomorrow at school. I must be going now."

Eddie wished her a heartfelt thanks and, assured her that he would be at school the following day. Liz and Hiroko once again engaged in their "Nice to see you again! Let's stay in touch!" hugged up, superficial emotion-laced ritual as the former saw the latter to the door.

Immediately after Hiroko was gone, Liz came with the heat. She hardly waited for the door to slam. She said, "I don't like that cunt."

Impetuously, Eddie came to Hiroko's defense, a little hurt and offended by Liz's remark. He said, "But . . . but she's so . . . kind!"

Liz said, "Yeah, but she's overstepping certain boundaries."

"What?" Eddie whined. "Wha'do you mean?"

Liz laughed all sly, rolled her eyes, and shook her head as she made her way back to the kitchen. She found the unsmoked portion of the spliff she hid in the refrigerator earlier before Hiroko showed up. She lit it up and started trying to get high again.

"Are you trying to tell me that you honestly cannot see that she's tryna come on to you?" Liz eyeballed Eddie questionably. For all she knew, with Eddie's puerile and quixotic thinking, she judged a slight possibility he could be playing dumb.

Eddie wanted to lie, but he couldn't. His hesitation was the confirmation Liz needed, which he supplied all but too easily. "I . . . uh . . .," he stammered. "Well, I . . . she, well, maybe but . . ."

Liz dropped the bomb query. "So did you fuck her?"

Eddie gasped as if an explosion had detonated his heart, and he looked as if he desperately needed cool air to extinguish the fire in his chest. He was actually gripping his breast like he was having a stroke. Even though he had not been intimate with Hiroko, the spontaneity of Liz asking him and the fact that he was actually thinking about it caught him slightly off guard.

"I absolutely did not!" he managed to say before further doubt was cast his way.

He stared furiously at Liz. She smirked somewhat wickedly and did her usual rolling of the eyes. The look that always seemed to suggest her disgust and disappointment. Eddie followed Liz back to the kitchen, expecting her to have passed that thing she was smoking, but Liz burned the spliff to a fat roach and coughed its fume dead center into Eddie's troubled facial expression. When mist hit his eyes, it caused them to water somewhat, and after it all cleared, Eddie looked as if Liz had made him cry.

Liz said accusingly, "Maybe you didn't sleep with her yet, but you were planning to, huh?"

Eddie was boiling on the inside. He wanted to scream out to her, *Yeah! Yeah! Maybe I am! Maybe I am planning to sleep with her! I'm a man, damn it! What do you expect? If you won't satisfy me, I have a right to look for satisfaction somewhere else, don't I? It doesn't mean I don't love you any less! I mean, it's just like how you lent me out to your best friends for just one night . . ."*

But he couldn't say anything like that. He was too much of a chicken at heart. Liz pulled all the strings, and she held invisible ones controlling him at times like he was a puppet. The security of being with Liz coupled with their history—time accrued—had grown on him, to the point of a practical symbiotic relationship.

Instead of speaking his mind, he said, "I have no such plans on sleeping with Hiroko. Hell, fuck . . . I didn't even know she was coming over here today!"

Liz was feeling a mite hazy and light in the head because the pot had given her the instant rush of a blindsiding euphoria. Her feet danced softly on the floor, and like a balloon, she drifted toward Eddie. Her eyes narrowed to a slit-like sneer and threw her arms around Eddie's sweaty neck.

She said, "So she doesn't mean anything to you?"

Eddie said, "Nothing."

He was starting to feel relieved, sensing that she had finally begun to believe him. If she did, then they could quit this bickering, and she would cease doubting him.

Liz tilted her head to the side, but kept her eyes aimed at Eddie's. "Even if she brings you dinner?"

Eddie thought he could console her, adjusting his pleading oratory to sound more convincing "C'mon . . . She can't do anything for me, even if she brings me scrambled eggs laid by a golden goose, dinner or whatever. She's Japanese . . . I mean, yer my girl. Me and you, remember?" He pulled her close.

They kissed. There wasn't much passion involved, but suddenly Liz was overcome by some unknown erotic spirit. The lusty craving increased. She kissed on Eddie's face wildly. It was like she was having an instantaneous flashback of the Taffie encounter. Eddie was turned on at this point, but he could barely keep up with Liz's offensive. She bit his bottom lip. Hard. She almost drew blood.

Before Eddie could wince, Liz paused for air and whispered in his ear, "Yeah, and don't you ever forget it. No Jap bitch can do it for you like I can." As if she was trying to cast him into a hypnotic trance.

She stroked the sudden hard bulge beneath his zipper, then pushed him forcefully against his room's door. Eddie was taken aback, alarmed at Liz's strength.

Liz said in a raspy, venomous tone that was unlike her. It was fearfully demonic "She can never give you this!" And she dropped to her knees before him.

Before Eddie could object and suggest they make it to the bed, she already had his fly unfastened. He was inside of her mouth again, melting like a suppository as her long, lizard-like tongue worked every angle of his heated extension. She took matters such as his rapture in the palm of her hands and squeezed lightly, tickling his pubic hair there. He quivered and trembled. All Eddie could do was remain stapled to his door, unable to move, only thinking how greatly his chick's head game had improved. He let out an agonized, shrill cry as he spewed splotches of alabaster all over Liz's cheeks, lips, and gaping face hole. She was rubbing it on her skin like she worshiped it. A pained, urgent look painted her grill. She bit her lips inward and pouted like she was about to cry.

Eddie recovered from his moment of blissful erotic sensation and dropped to his knees to embrace her. He cupped her face into his palms and kissed her on the lips, this time with more passionate emotion. His tongue entered her mouth, still stained with saliva and his scum.

He said, "I love you, babe."

They sat there for a moment on the floor, hugged up. When Liz felt she had expended enough emotional energy, and a nefarious entity exorcised itself from her consciousness, she rose to her feet. Confident she still had Eddie on his leash, she still felt the need to maintain her command sometimes by testing him too. Occasional fits of emotion and tantrums on her part would exemplify her own strong desire to keep him, which Eddie would have no choice but to take into account. When Eddie finally told her that he loved her, it was all the comfort and reassurance she needed.

Liz disrobed in preparation to take a shower. When she had shucked down to her black classic panties, Eddie couldn't control his nerves. It was the first time in weeks he had actually seen her plump breasts in the normal light of a room, not in the dark, or a brief flash before she dipped in the shower—like she was about to do. He marveled at her sensuous curves. He wondered how she did it, but he knew why. She was a health nut, of course, but she could definitely maintain her Grecian goddess physique, porn star face, Hollywood sexpot stand-in babe. He started taking off his clothes and followed her to the shower.

Liz reminded him that it was her time of the month. Eddie tried to plead his case that he was so horny and revved, he wouldn't mind lining his bed with towels, but Liz wasn't having it. She literally slammed the bathroom door in his face, left him looking like he was smelling it.

Thirty minutes later, they were relaxing on the bed wearing bathrobes they had ripped off from the Tokyo hotel they stayed in when they first came to Japan. They were watching Quentin Tarrantino's *Reservoir Dogs*, smoked reefer and drank beer until the goods tapped out. Liz's phone buzzed, and she picked it up, then pressed the Talk button.

Stephanie was on the other end of the line. Liz sprang up like a Jack in the box and slid off the bed. Eddie looked at her as if to say, *What the heck?* Squinting in an agitated expression as Liz left his side. He shook his head because with her abrupt rising and prancing around, she was about to miss a good scene in the flick featuring Harvey Keitel.

Liz flipped on the light switch. She kept rambling, "Oh shit . . . yeah, yeah, yeah, I forgot..." and then she started laughing and giggling. She looked at the clock on Eddie's upturned milk crate doubling as a bedside table. It was close to nine-thirty. The intermittent "Yeah yeahs" continued, an apparent response to Stephanie's incessant chattering. Approaching four minutes into the call, it was terminated. She untied her robe, and it dropped to the floor. She stood naked, save for her now burgundy classic briefs. Eddie stared in disbelief and stupefied watching Liz suddenly get dressed.

"Now what are you up to?" Eddie asked shakily, "Y-you're leaving?!"

Liz said assuredly, "Yeah, you are too. Come on." She found his jeans, picked them up off the floor and threw them to the edge of his bed. Eddie looked at her as if he was in the room with some kind of crazed lunatic.

He said, "What the hell do you mean *I am too?*" He numbly reached for his jeans, half assed though, as if he had never intended to slip them on.

Liz had gotten dressed almost like a minute man from the days of the American Revolutionary. She was wearing her pink chiffon harem pants, white cotton blouse. She had applied light lip glitter to her kisser. Then she splashed upon the bed where Eddie was still fumbling with his jeans like a stumble bum.

"Yeah, hun, I'm so soo-r-r-y-eeee!" Liz exclaimed with a look that was suddenly beseeching and repentant. "I'm so sorry, Steph called earlier tonight when Miss Hot-Pants came by. She told me about a movie party tonight at Worm Swiggler's place."

Eddie was like, "What? *Worm?* What the fuck?" His face was in total agony.

Liz continued, "Yeah, Worm—well, his real name is Mitch, or Mitchell, or somethin' like that, but everybody calls him Worm. Anyway, he's the head teacher at the Bozack-Hommachi, Namba, and Higobashi. I don't think you've ever met him, and I thought tonight would be the perfect night."

Eddie's disbelief was insurmountable. "Perfect night for what? Are you . . . serious?"

Liz rose up from the bed because she was dead serious. She said, "Of course I am. Now, let's go. Tonight would be a good night for you to get acquainted. It's about networking, remember? We're from LA, it's not about what you know, it's who you know. And if you get to know this guy, he'll probably hook you up. You said you wanted to work at Bozack, right?"

Eddie couldn't answer. It was true, he did want to work at that company, and also correct, networking and schmoozing was a part of the lifestyle they had adopted, but tonight he totally was not in the mood to go gallivanting.

"Liz, I uh . . ." Eddie hesitated.

"Aw, come on, Ed. It'll be great. I mean, for real, it's a movie party, fer'gawdsakes. You are the guru of celluloid yourself. Anywho, I've never been to his place either, and I'm really on the edge of my seat to check it out, because everybody says it's out of this world. I mean, I hear he has a Jacuzzi type thing in his house—heard it was awesome—like a castle. Steph hasn't been there either, so he's invited all of us. That was Steph again just now, calling to remind me. I forgot to tell you earlier, that's why I'm so sorry, hun!"

This had gone too far.

Eddie's patience and poise had been stretched to its maximum length. It was either now or never. He had to put his foot down. Otherwise, he would have to endure ill treatment and Liz's capricious affairs. In a resounding manner, he stated his reasoning for not wanting to go with her.

"Liz, babe, I . . . I can't just leave here and go with you to . . . some fifty miles away . . . to some guy's house!" Eddie almost screamed. "Are you out of yer mind? Is this another big joke?"

Liz had nearly completed her groundwork for departure, her lightweight cardigan draped around her shoulder, her wallet, keys, phone, and other items tucked in her purse strapped to her shoulders. She looked at Eddie as if he were a strange, poor pauper who was refusing an offering of riches and gold. Instead of trying to persuade him to see things her way, she decided to prompt him to come to her. She dropped her shoulders and opened her arms wide as if she was awaiting him to embrace her.

She said, "Ed . . . relax. He's *married!*"

Eddie shouted, "That's not what I meant. I'm not that insecure, thank you. What I meant was, babe, I hafta go to work tomorrow!"

Liz's entire face wrinkled in disgust as she flounced away from him about to hug her. She was beginning to raise her voice too. She said, "Aw, Ed, call in sick again, take tomorrow off. What difference does it make? That damn Hiroko chick isn't your boss!"

Eddie said, "It just doesn't look right, Liz." His face was now clearly bothered and disturbed, as if he was in excruciating pain. He continued, "I mean, she knew I wasn't sick. She had to. If I call in sick again tomorrow, they're all gonna know. Besides, you heard her, she said *they miss me*—the students—*they need me!*"

Coldly, Liz erupted, "Do you *really* think they need *you*?"

"Well," Eddie began, "if it weren't true, why would she have said it?"

Liz shook her head. She too had grown tired and felt her patience had been dragged to its outer limits, and well beyond normal capacity at that. She went into the bathroom and looked at her face in the mirror vanity. There, she would spend a few minutes picking away, plucking, touching up and various hygiene and makeup activity.

Eddie gabbled away in the adjoining room, but Liz wasn't listening. She was silently humming an "I will wait!" Tune with a mock Darius Rucker pitch. She was pissed at Eddie, but she did not feel like arguing at all.

They could continue to go at it for another half hour, or even an hour. Liz lacked confidence that she would change Eddie's mind. She realized he was resolute in his reasoning why he wasn't going back into the city with her. In a way, she could certainly understand how he felt, but at the same time, she had feelings too. It had been her day off that day as well, and Eddie knew without a doubt how much she detested being there in Hannan City and how she dreaded even making the trip there. To add insult to injury, she would make the dreadfully dismal train ride all the way out to the boondock village, and Eddie would choose to remain cooped up inside—like Denore—afraid to go outside, afraid to be seen, but the only difference being Eddie was dastardly afraid of going out for fear of being spotted by someone who would suspect him of playing hooky from work.

What had gotten into him? she wondered. Aside from the fact that he seemed to be getting softened up by some strange, weirdo Jap girl, but what in the hell had initiated such a different person in Eddie, which pushed him to defy her? She remembered that he used to be so adventurous and compliant with almost everything. Now he was abruptly *rebelling* against her authority. He was attempting to be a bad doggy, she mused. She had to punish the impious toy boy by not sticking around.

Before she split, she kissed him on the lips, where he sat motionless on the bed, his supplicating face still in progress. She pranced away from him full of pep and cheer, but it was a façade, an act she put on to obscure how incensed she was with him. She knew how to push his buttons. He may not have shown it at that moment, but eventually she would break him down. Her assurance was unfaltering.

Calmly and casually, she left. She told him good-bye without waiting for his response. Because of their deep and intricate past, she knew he would never leave her. He was just being stubborn, hell-bent on sticking his nose up the asses of the people involved with the program. Sooner or later, he would come to his senses.

He would see things her way. She needed to forgive his utter stupidity for the time being. But aside from that, she was determined to not allow him to ruin her joy. There was no way she desired to stay miserable remaining cooped up in that crap bucket of a vale Hannan City. She had to be out! The offering—the sacrifice—of the two bodies of Mandy and Becky she had presented and in exchange she expected Eddie's eternal loyalty.

Eddie, of course, did not walk Liz to the station. He too was in his feelings. He didn't feel as though Hiroko deserved to be disrespected or insulted because she cared about him. Simultaneously, his lonely feeling intensified when she left him. It was like a "Hi and bye" visit. He couldn't believe Liz actually wanted him to ditch work and go to some home party like they were still some college party bum socialites.

When was she ever going to get serious? Eddie wondered. He didn't even know this Worm person. One thing for certain, he really would be "ill" or uneasy if he missed another day of work the following day. He was disappointed that Liz couldn't understand that; and that he was only trying to do a good job. Hiroko's act of kindness had struck a chord with him; he felt strangely appreciated; validated.

The Namba Osaka City–bound train arrived at the platform of Hakkotsukuri Station. Liz took a final gander at the area outside of the wicket gate, half hoping to see if Eddie had chased her down and given in to her overbearing will, apologetic and acquiescent. The station was indicative of the entire village itself—deserted, a ghost town. She stepped into the coach and stood clear of its closing doors.

35

MITCH "WORM" SWIGGLER and his newlywed wife, Mikako after four years together, lived in an affluent area of Upper Hommachi. In an urban locale such as Osaka, in Japan, a city which has twenty-four sectors, or "wards," atmospheric localities as improbably named Tanimachi Towns and Upper Hommachi, or *Ueroku*, could easily be overlooked. A quick turn off the normal terrain recommended by tourist guides, the main avenue thoroughfares of the Sen Nichi Mae Road and the Uemachi Passage, Mikako (and Worm)'s mansion (for Japanese standards) lay nestled in the heart of a prosperous and upscale area, which was also home to some well-to-do gangsters, "893", quasi-mobsters, high salaried pranksters and normal looking business people to the unsuspecting eye. A short distance from 'Higashi (East) Kozu' Park, between Chikai Puku and Taenaka Temples, all a stone's throw—in essence—from major department store and train station terminal bearing the same name, Kintetsu, but by way of a roundabout walk led to the plush subdivision of residences like the Swigglers', which tended to differ in unique contrast to the lantern-lit, bustling city sidewalks, and otherwise crowded streets of Japan's second largest city. The place where Mikako was born and raised, and the place Mitch loved like a second home.

Now forty, former porn star and magdalen Mikako was finally happily married to her young, *hapa* Canadian, whom she met while vacationing in Hawaii. This had been in the earlier '90s when she still had remnants of her adult film body. She was a short, rare full-figured vase chassis, who turned a few heads or two in her day, albeit the sleazy types of men that had her licking their hairy anuses she would later enjoy doing in front of a camera on a film set. She almost tied the knot with a regular joe "salary man" but made the mistake of not telling him what she did for a living. Since she wasn't a regular actress, she only did "fluffer" acts like blowjobs, tugging, and her specialty, rim jobs and scatology. On the rare occasion she got work that required penetration, it would be with some elaborate dildo, vibrating simulation or other miscellaneous sex toy, but never a real penis. Frustrated, she would visit her repressed sexual rage from a day on a porn set servicing several male rods for hours, upon her paramour who couldn't satisfy her cravings and demands. He hit the road and wished her the best of luck, because he wanted no parts of the Japanese equivalent of the girl from the movie *The Exorcist*, who Mikako became in the bedroom.

When word got out that she had done dirty movies for a living and not a standard *gravure* model as she had always claimed, dudes fell back from her. Her suitors were repelled. She didn't give it much care or worry though, because she thought for sure that some unsuspecting lovesick rich boy would discover her and wife her up sooner or later. It didn't happen, though, and after a few years into her thirties, she was getting outdone in the industry by younger, leaner, and fresher faces and mouths; and as a result, she began to get less work.

Fortunately, Mikako was able to snag herself a foreigner who could speak Japanese because his mother was originally from Kyoto. They met in Hawaii while he was on his college graduation vacation celebrating. Mitchell Swiggler—nicknamed Worm even then—was so skinny he looked like the vermilliform creature or had a parasitic version living inside of him due to his practically emaciated, wiry build. He was roughly ten years Mikako's junior, but he didn't care. He even dismissed his own parents' reluctance to accede to his love interest. All he knew was when she threw her cat on his hot dog, he was miracle whipped. Mikako unleashed her porn set skills and rocked his world for good.

Mikako convinced Mitch that he should live and work in Japan because she would get antsy and anxious after his two- or three-week visits to her country, or vice versa, she visiting him in Queebec, Canada. The rest of the time, they communicated through e-mails, but Mikako wanted more. She wanted him there with her in Japan, so she filled his impressionable head up with ideas about how lucrative job opportunities such as teaching English was in Japan at that time. It wasn't hard to persuade him either. Worm eventually was granted his mother's blessing, because with her, he often made pilgrimages to Kyoto.

They moved to Upper Hommachi and into the grand, luxurious home of Mikako's deceased, eccentric uncle, who had been a wealthy loan shark. That uncle had also been a fan of foreign art and architecture, so the six-room mansion's interior was an apocryphal blend of gloomy Japanese Haniwa and nineteenth-century European. It was set up with regal decorative furnishings, complicated architectural elements, and tapestries with dark, rich colors, striking to the vision.

Splendid stone deities from various cultures ranging from Vulcan to Chango lined spacious halls. Such extraordinary, fancy décor blew Worm's mind, just like anyone else's who visited the place, he would be so fortuitous to call home and gave birth to his delusions of grandeur, feeling that he was to be a *puissant potentate*.

When Liz went to their house for the first time, her mind was straight nuked. She had expected to see the traditional Japanese house, like she had seen in the countryside, with a small yard. Bonsai trees", the small pond of carp and perhaps a huge *tourou*. She was partially correct, for that was what she saw outside the home. On the inside, she stepped into a portal that sent her to another world without the usual spaced-out way she achieved a good high.

Recessed alcoves were etched into the walls at the entrance, with one stair creating the barrier to where shoes are removed and placed in small cubbyholes. Retrieving a pair of cushioned pliable slippers, Liz faced a Parthenon-type archway with a series of mind-boggling crepidoma pillars. Centered above its architrave were angular triglyphs and ornamental cornice molding that launched upward to a tall ceiling. A light-blue-carpeted stairway led to dark halls containing other rooms on the second floor.

People were already gathered at the Swiggler home, and the kitchen, spacious compared to Liz's or Eddie's, was comparable to a small diner. They were making sandwiches and some freaky concoctions in a blender. Drinking was heavily in progress, with all sorts of alcohol, prominently Japanese sake, sparkling wine, and lots of beer. Occasionally, people could be seen doing whiskey or tequila shots.

Having no desire to do a repeat of the night of the Pink Carnation drubbing and subsequent Roastal Horse fiasco, Liz wisely stayed clear of the tequila shots. Furthermore, she had to also put a damper on the drugs and pot smoking too.

***

Before arriving, Liz had to return home because she wanted to change clothes. She needed directions on how to get to Worm's crib, so she needed to phone Stephanie. After charging her phone, she got Stephanie on the line. At that time, Stephanie warned Liz that Mikako was a well-heeled strict bitch who didn't allow any drug activity in her home. This dispirited Liz somewhat because she was ready to roll a few awfully accomplished joints and kick back, but resorted to respecting the wishes of the host and hostess, leaving her "bhang" at the crib. She did, however, fire one up before catching the cab.

During the cab ride, the harum-scarum Stephanie was on the phone with Liz almost the entire time. She told Liz to tell the driver to take her to Tanimachi Town District 6. When she got out of the cab, she was instructed to walk to the nearby Lawson Convenience Store. There, Stephanie came over and scooped her up, and they walked together to the Swigglers'.

As they talked, hearing Stephanie speak about how scrupulous Mikako allegedly was, Liz presumed right away that she wasn't going to like her. The disdain she had for Japanese women was growing, and meeting Hiroko earlier that night had exacerbated it. Yet when she arrived and had realized how kind Mikako was, her feelings changed. It made things all the easier for her to respect the woman of the house. She also determined that Worm wasn't too bad of a guy, despite some like Keefer and Radley claiming the need to "watch yourself" around him, insinuating that he might not be as trustworthy as he seemed. They were right, but Liz had no way of knowing the depth of accuracy their statements contained. All she knew was, he was the type that didn't beat around the bush, he explained things clearly and simply, he was to the point. Something Liz liked.

Also, Worm and his wife frequently threw home parties. From what Liz gathered, he did this to be popular among his fellow foreign squadron of English teachers, not only at Bozack, but sometimes other companies as well. There were so many "new" faces present that Liz had yet to meet, teachers, male and female, from other branches, but she didn't know any of them. In fact, the only people there she knew besides Worm were Stephanie, Vicky, and the two cousins Simon and Ricky., who later were joined by the smarmy J-girls Rena and Chikako. It was the first time Liz had seen those two since the Roastal Horse, and surprisingly, neither of them was salty about how they were abandoned. In fact, their recollections of the night were just as blurry as everyone else's, especially Simon's. The funniest thing Liz found was that Rena, Ricky's girl, had paid the entire bill!

Liz wasn't blown away by the ostentatious display of prosperity and cache of the Swiggler home. She was already accustomed to what life as "poor, bummy and rich" was like, as she was from such a background. What impressed her was how Worm and his wife were so altruistic and charitable. From what she could see, the abode had been transformed into a free kitchen and open bar with no cost to the guests. She would soon figure out why.

Worm would hold court among the few folks he governed at the Hommachi branch, and acquaintances like Simon and Ricky who worked at another English school. Half drunk on sake and the other half intoxicated with the thoughts of him being an influential baron, viscount, or magnate, he spoke of how he desired to be founder of his own English school and company.

Mikako was the one who put this bug in Worm's ear. Already successful in persuading Worm to lift his stakes and move to Japan, she figured the next step would be to convince him further to start his own business—his own English school. She made him believe that he could make bigger bank than what he could get at Bozack by having his own booming business.

Ricky asked Worm, "How do you expect to create an English school that will compete with all these bigger, huge companies, mate?"

Worm's answer was "It's quite simple. Many of you expats have jobs working at English schools like Bozack, Nova, ECC, Berlitz, and so on, right? But you guys also have your own side jobs. You have your own private students that you teach outside of your schools.

"A lot of you guys don't always remain in Japan. You'll probably stay two or three years max. Then when you go back, you have students with no teachers— like *ronin*—and that's where I'd come in. My school could take them in. Or if I hire guys like you, Rick, you, and your cousin Simon. You guys could bring students to me too. All of you could."

Simon laughed, swigging a beer and wrapping his arms around Chikako. "Why should we bring our students to you, mate? Chikako here's introduced me to a couple who has a building down by the docks. They allow me the use of the entire second floor to teach my students. They're thinkin' of expanding their business ... why ruin a good thing?"

Worm said, "Because, Simon, one hand washes the other. Of course, you are one of the lucky ones that found some nice Japanese people to sponsor you, but I can assure you, by contributing to the pot, you would benefit. Everyone would. Unlike all the big schools, we'd have only one school here in Osaka, one centralized location, no several branches right away. We'd just have one big place and cut out the need for the Japanese staff. My wife, Mikako, and maybe one or two of your girlfriends . . ." He was alluding to Rena and Chikako.

"With the elimination of the excessive Japanese staff, we'd have surplus earnings, which would go to bigger and better salaries for the teachers. Better than you make at your company, and more than you can hope to get from teaching private lessons at shabby, smoky coffee shops."

Hearing this, Liz didn't seem particularly interested in Worm's vision as the others were. Reason being that she didn't plan to remain in Japan for too long a time as Worm described the intended dateline around when this school was slated to come into fruition. She found it amusing to see people gathered at Worm's spot, surrounding him as if they admired him like a revered leader of sorts. Like suckling pups to multiple tits of a bitch mammal, hoping to get a drop of prosperous nourishment. There were those who mobbed Mitch the Worm. Liz laughed because at that point, she saw Worm's type as all too common, and it never ceased to gall her: a skeletal gaunt, standing hanger hat within an ostensibly oversized Toronto Maple Leafs hockey jersey, an otherwise lame person who rose quickly in fame when he came to Japan. In America—or Canada, for that matter—so invisible, inconsequential, and unnoticed that he may not as well even exist at all. But, in Japan, he aggrandized into the status as a mayor for expats and the *gaijin* community with whom he closely dealt. This was a heaven he could never enjoy back home.

There had to have been at least twenty people at the party, Liz accounted when she had arrived. Most of them congregated in the cavernous, acorn-shaped stone-floored sunken living room. A huge TV that looked like a monitor imported from a NASA workshop was positioned in the center and broadcast a Julia Roberts and Hugh Grant flick called *Notting Hill*, which only Japanese people like Rena and Chikako appeared interested in watching. Else ways other people were drinking, eating, talking, and lounging on the genteel sectional sofas that complimented the contoured shape of the concrete arc.

Liz mingled with the usual people, the familiar faces. The only person she didn't meet was Vicky, who had sometime before introduced her to the Japanese guy she went on dates with. He was a handsome guy, Liz thought, for a Japanese, and he could speak English pretty well. Word around the scuttlebutt circuit had it that Vicky was just using him to stave her doldrums and lonely feelings after her man left her for a Japanese woman; and to get even with him, she tried to make him feel a certain way by prancing the poor Japanese kid around to the bars and places she knew her ex would frequent.

Stephanie too had a friend of her own to introduce, and a story to go along with it. Deciding to follow Vicky's example, she too began to seek out—aggressively—Japanese guys who hung out at *gaijin* bars. She had not been in a serious relationship for years, and it was beginning to make her as screwy as Vicky. The week before, they had gone back to the Pink Carnation, and once more, Stephanie got drunk out of her mind from the cheap tequila shots. She became so cumbersome to handle that Vicky had to leave her "alkie" bibulous coworker behind. That was when Stephanie met this Japanese guy named Michio.

Stephanie had managed to stumble her way out of the Pink Carnation and made it outside. She reached the stairway entrance of the building where the bar was where she proceeded to throw up wretched prodigality. Michio who had seen her earlier drinking at the bar, followed her out when she left, concerned apparently that the intoxicated woman would destroy herself trying to descend the building's stairs. Relieved that she did not, he approached her when she was done "spilling her insides" in the gutter next to garbage pails and offered his help.

Immediately pegging him a gentleman, Stephanie was delighted to give Michio her Bozack business card, which had her telephone number and e-mail address on it. Taking it out of her wallet haphazardly her *gaijin* card (*15) and other valuable items slipped out. Mitch picked them all up and returned them to Stephanie, and even went the extra length to place them neatly back inside the wallet. Dude then walked her to the nearest busy corner and hailed her a cab.

When the taxi screeched to the curb, the rear auto door flung open, and Michio hoisted Stephanie inside and told the driver where to go, because he had seen her address on her "gaijin card". With pellucid understanding the driver had Stephanie off and delivered home in a jiffy. A day or two later, Michio called her up, speaking understandable English, reintroducing himself to a Stephanie who only vaguely remembered him, but overjoyed to receive his call nevertheless. They established a friendship, and this night was their official first date.

Stephanie had been excited the entire evening, from the time she had disturbed Liz when was in Hannan City with Eddie, until she picked her up at the Convenience Store. All she kept talking about was the Michio guy, and that's how Liz heard about how she met him at the Pink Carnation. Prior to Stephanie yanking this Michio guy by his arm to meet Liz, he had been sticking to Ricky and Simon, following them around and showing them keen interest—especially charismatic Ricky Exmouth. When Stephanie came and grabbed him away from Ricky, Michio looked a little annoyed for a brief moment.

It was Liz's first time to meet Michio. She shook his hand even though to her, he was far from impressive in any way shape or form. Stephanie and desperate, love-sick chicks might have found him adorable in his thick black polo neck perhaps, but Liz could not admit to seeing anything special other than a peculiar oddity which she didn't immediately detect, when describing his demeanor. His English was better than understandable, as Stephanie had put it. It was quite impeccable—not perfect, but one could ascertain meticulously that he had probably studied or lived abroad.

"I used to live in New Zealand," Michio confirmed her.

He and Stephanie were stood about the same height, five feet eight, or about 171 centimeters. He had a youngish, clean-shaven, and emotionless face, yet wholesome enough that he could very well be a stage performer or school play actor who snagged the leading role. His build was slender but rugged in structure, solid as if he was athletic—maybe he lifted weights along with playing futsal. The shape of his head was round, like the balls from the sport he played, and his hair was eccentrically styled in a horrendous medium flip out, making him look like a Japanese version of Fredrick Douglas. Aside from the disastrous choice of style, if Liz were to be honest, she could grant him a tad more winsome than the average Japanese guy, so she had to give Stephanie some credit. Vicky too, if dating Japanese dudes was the way that they were going to give themselves therapy to assuage heartbreak or loneliness. Both of their dates were fair, she supposed, but she didn't like the way Michio stared. His eyes squinted when people spoke to him. Others might have declared this to be like a voluntary-involuntary habit done when a non-native speaker of a language focuses on the speaker, watching their lips move and hearing the sound combined, to gain clearer understanding. Liz, on the other hand, was given the impression that it was a look that implied his disbelief of the speaker.

As the night went on, Michio would expatiate about his times abroad with the others. Liz's final assessment of him resulted in her taking him for an upstart who had traveled overseas, got jazzed up and hip, then came back to Japan "cool," more so than he had ever been before he left Japan as a pure first-class nerd. Now back in Japan, he was still corny, but more of a big shot now, though, because he had the unique experience of having traveled outside of his country, something a great many couldn't boast.

Liz was ready to dismiss Michio to the obviate category of familiars but did an about-face and started liking him when he spoke of how he enjoyed getting stoned while living abroad and had also once visited Liz's home state of California in San Francisco. She regretted not bringing an extra ganja stick.

Liz hit on Keefer's dopey Australian chums Ricky and Simon in hopes that they had brought some of the sizzle from their big bundle, but disappointingly, they had not. They had already been through the drill with Worm's wife, Mikako and her ardent restriction of dope and usage in her home. Occasionally, she allowed Worm and his pals to get away with a joint smoke here and there, but only in a secluded, tucked away area of the house and never on nights like tonight when they hosted plentiful guests.

Michi had taken a special liking to Ricky; it was obvious. They were laughing and talking as if they had been friends for years; but like Liz, it was her first time meeting him. Stephanie joined in the fun and laughter, and they engaged in a silly game of trying to see who could slam chu hais the fastest.

While the activity was going on, Liz managed to pull Simon to the side. She asked him about the possibility of making a call to the Duke. She used the code language and everything.

Simon vehemently shot the idea to bits. It was already past Tim's delivering time and he didn't dare risk the Duke's wrath breaking protocol. He said, "Tim's a nice guy, yeh, but I defo'ouldn't wunna have him get mad and crack the shits on me. I don't wunna get on the man's bad side, yeh? And one'a the ways to get on the Duke's bad side is to bombard him with phone calls on his private time."

Understanding this, Liz had to accept it and pout. She did enjoy the party and the gathering though. She wished Eddie could have come; she knew he would have liked Worm. Also, with the talk of bigger salaries and better career opportunities, she figured it would have been beneficial for Eddie to have been privy to that discussion as well. She thought of calling him, and almost did, but saw the time being past midnight and decided not to and allowed for him to rest, which was what he was more than likely doing at that time since he would have to work the next day. But not her. Tonight. she was free. Feeling good, tipsy, and with low guilt about Eddie, dangerously resembling how Becky and Lamar looked. Tossing such a thought from her mind, she sought to cleanse it by directing her steps to the kitchen, where she heard the grinding sounds of blenders in motion and grabbed a stronger drink.

Acquainting herself with the blender operating coworker, Liz was handed a strong mephitic daiquiri. In fact, she had a few of these.

36

LIZ GOT A chance to speak with her mother, Ida Amberbush, every so often. Thanks again to the crafty, naif individual known as Eric Cravens, Liz received a tutorial on how to purchase phone card minutes for her cellular, which included features that enabled her to call overseas. Once she was able to teach her mother how to dial her number using the country code, she was good to go. Her mother could call her direct to her Tuka phone with no charge for minutes. It was a good setup. The only problem at times was the time zone differential.

As usual, the mother, Ida, would go on and on about how much they (her family) missed her after the obligatory initial inquiries of "How is Eddie doing? How are *you guys* doing? How's things in Japan? Do you need anything?"

Then she would get filled in about the current events around the way back home. Her brother Halbert was finally getting engaged, and how nice it would be if Liz could make it home for the holidays. But Liz had been thinking about staying in Japan this year, or taking some time off and doing some traveling through Asia. A lot of her coworkers had spoken a lot about package tours and such. When she heard about how things were back home, she didn't feel too enthusiastic as she thought she would be.

She heard that Mandy and Steve had broken up but got back together after another dude she tried to fleece punched her in the eye. As for Becky, it was vague but something she heard from her mother about one of her "friends" getting kicked out of college. It sounded like a big mess.

Regardless, it was clear that she and her old pals were growing apart. Each of them was settling into their own lives, and Liz was too. She had a lot of time to think about it, even though most of the time she was under the spell of cannabis, but she pondered her life events heavily. She was beginning to like the Japanese lifestyle. She didn't like Japan itself, maybe, but she liked the kind of life she was living. Wake up late, hang out late, work with some funny and interesting people, enjoy good food and drink exotic or otherwise, and have plenty of money on the side. A little dope availability was an added amenity she greatly appreciated. Everything was just as Carver Burk had said it would be. She knew it wouldn't last forever, and she would not be living in Japan forever, but for the time being, she felt she could finally hack it.

The night after Worm's party, Liz was relaxing at the crib, kicking it with Denore. Eddie called, and he was moderately apologetic as he almost always was when he tried to smooth things out between him and Liz about an argument she instigated in most cases. Liz being the pompous queen witch she leveled up to, offered a wonted acceptance as if she was truly a royal subject.

Eddie was also insistent that he wasn't feeling Hiroko. Liz took him at his word, but deep down inside, Eddie knew he was lying. He credited himself for having the will to resist her and remain loyal to the bond he and Liz shared. He was trying to put his backbone into use.

To show his sincerity, Eddie told Liz that she didn't have to come out to Hannan, and that he would just visit her instead. Also, if she was busy, that was fine. He wouldn't gripe or complain. In fact, he even decided to purchase a hotel for the weekend, because he had some excess yen stashed up. In fact, looking at his bank account, there was more money than he had for his own in his entire life. There was close to nothing for him to spend his money on. After Liz and Denore got the Nipponbashi tour from Eric Cravens, Liz shared the info with Eddie. He got himself a computer (laptop) and stuff like retro video games. These would keep him busy during the dismally uneventful atmosphere of the locale that drove Liz to the brink of insanity.

Liz was more than happy to not go back to Hannan City and lauded Eddie for intuitively thinking of that. She would be so happy when the CHET Program stint for him was over. So then, he could move to the city, and maybe they could get an apartment. Which reminded her . . .

A guarantor.

Stephanie and most of the other teachers she knew had their own apartments and didn't live in the Bozack housing. Stephanie had ties from the Pork Pie Program who helped her. Vicky had come to Japan with her boyfriend Jack, who worked at another big-name English school. Bozack in turn provided housing for both of the Brits, which the boyfriend deserted and left her to have when he moved out to go live with his new Japanese lover.

Eric Craven's wife helped him out, and as for Keefer, Radley, and the others, who knew? Everyone had their connections—even Taffie—but Liz didn't have anyone like that she could ask for help like her colleagues could. She started thinking about making fake friends. Maybe, she thought, she should cut into Vicky as that seemed like her department. She made a skull note to invite her out for, coffee, tea, or maybe a jog in the park. Unlike Stephanie, Vicky seemed more like Liz, who cared about physique and gaining weight.

As for the people she and Eddie had met out in Hannan City, she would have been remiss to not acknowledge how nice they had been. They had given her and Eddie all sorts of gifts. Microwave, toaster oven, television set, radio, dishes, pots, pans, and miscellaneous items that they were going to throw away anyway, but still relatively in mint condition, no hackneyed goods. Additionally, they would either take them out to eat (okonomiyaki) or invite them to their homes (for okonomiyaki). The bottom line, the hospitality they had been shown was praiseworthy and thorough. That being said, surely there would be more kind, eleemosynary types who would eventually befriend her and do the same, Liz thought.

At Worm's party, with all the talk of opening an English school, Liz thought about Mikako. She would be a good target for a friend. She was harmless to her, nonthreatening; she was older, a little on the chunkier, stocky size, and already married. The best part was she could speak English. She would make the perfect fake friend. She thought she might have needed one, being that she was in Japan. Everybody seemed to have their own "Japanese pet." Guys like Worm and Eric Cravens married theirs, but Chucky had a Japanese girl; she believed Radley had the same, so did Tim. Keefer, of course, had any one of several, and speaking of which, at the party, Liz knew she had seen his buddy Simon get really snuggly with Chikako. It was peculiar because Liz could have sworn that Chikako had been Keefer's latest love conquest, because they were making out heavy that night at the Pink Carnation. In fact, she heard they left together. Yet at Worm's party, by the end of the night, Simon was swapping saliva with Chikako and giving her the stink finger under a blanket on a secluded section of that bog couch. Maybe they swapped chicks too, Liz thought.

Vicky obviously had decided to move on and get herself a Japanese boy, and Stephanie had now done the same. Even Denore had blossomed and bubbled into a personable individual, and while she didn't have any Japanese friends, per se, she did, however, come in contact with various Japanese volunteers at the city municipal center where she would attend the free Japanese language classes with Chucky.

Liz eyeballed Mikako. Maybe she would agree to be her and Eddie's guarantor if she played up to her and acted all nice. Just like everyone was sucking up to Worm at his place. If she didn't play ball, well, there was always Takuto. She had a small collection of biz cards now. Luzio Silver, Ruth Worth, Hitomi Hasegawa, Takaro the stylist, the glittery Tabriz Najaf—Takuto. Perhaps the part-time gig working at that Can of Pee bar he offered her was a feasible idea after all. She could meet some interesting people there. The possibilities baffled her senses.

What would really be nice, Liz thought, was if she could become acquainted with some rich, big-spending benefactor like Taffie had secured.

The more she was around Taffie, the more curious Liz became about her after-hours lifestyle. She wasn't interested in prostitution—which to her was what Taffie's occupation sounded like—but she was interested in what exactly the job entailed that would cause grown men to throw money and gifts at them for just a few hours of drinks and conversation. Of course, back home, she knew such establishments to either be brothels or strip clubs, but Taffie would insist that her job entailed none of that.

Taffie and Liz would hang out on alternate Mondays. Not because they had planned it that way, but it was just the way it happened to occur. Taffie would have her own errands to run; Liz too would have hers as well. With Liz, it was more about exploring the city and becoming familiar with particular routes to go back and forth here and there on her bicycle. She even mapped out her way from home to the Hommachi School. She was a health nut as always, so in addition to going to the gym and swimming occasionally, riding her bike to and fro also became a part of her workout routine.

Taffie and Liz never got intimate anymore, not the likes of which escalated into the heated tryst that went down at the French girl's pad. But they were still hugged up and familiar. When they walked the streets together, they would be arm in arm like girls on a date. Sometimes Liz felt some urges to be closer and remembered that she had some X waiting for Taffie at her crib, but she instead quelled her rising lust. Deciding instead to be on the lookout for some eligible bachelor for her to date, and that was when the epiphany's scheduled arrival crashed into her head.

She remembered that "weird" guy's name—Deon! Yes, that was his name, Deon, Liz finally remembered. She had only talked with him that one time, her first day at the Hommachi School. She had never seen him again after that, so he sort of fell out of her mind, out of sight. She had to inquire as to why he had not ever shown up at work at Hommachi. She asked Worm if he was still even working at Bozack.

Worm confirmed that the guy, Deon Clemente was still working there. The reason why he wasn't seen much was because he was a Roving Circuit teacher. Because of his unique deportment and presence, the company had elected to have him make rounds and visit several branches of the schools. One week he would be at the Higobashi School, the next he could be at the Namba School, and so on. Worm knew about Deon's scheduling and informed Liz that he would be making his rounds back around to Hommachi soon. Good, Liz thought, for then she could get a chance to talk to him and pick his brain. She wanted to see if he had a girlfriend too, but from what she could prematurely judge of him, she highly doubted he was single, or the type who would settle down with just one chick. But still, she wanted to try. Furthermore, she was quite sure that a hottie like Taffie would definitely grab his attention, even if he did have a shit ton of girlfriends.

In the interim, Liz would also volunteer to work overtime and swap shifts on occasion. This allowed her opportunity to visit other schools, meet other staff members and coworkers and other interesting Japanese student customers.

She would meet other teachers and forget their names and faces almost as quickly as she learned them. For the most part, she didn't find them as interesting and charismatic as the ones she considered the core group of her associates, mostly centering around Stephanie, Keefer, and Vicky and the teachers at the Hommachi branch. What surprised her the most was how busy the Umeda School was during the week. The place was like a busy train station like Grand Central in New York. So busy, in fact, that Hitomi had an extra staff member or two to assist her. It was fascinating because by the time the weekend rolled around, Saturdays and Sundays for Liz at the Umeda School was like a ghost building. So quiet one could hear the clock's ticking on the walls. The teachers there, some of whom she might have seen and partied with at Worm's place, or maybe the group dope pickup with Tim.

Even Taffie had more French students than usual. She worked only three or four days a week depending on the schedule Hitomi prepared. Everybody was wondering when the new French teacher was due to show, and that included Liz. If that guy was eligible, maybe Taffie and he could get to know each other and Liz wouldn't have to deal with that guy Deon after all.

Hitomi told them that the new French teacher had some paperwork issues, and he had to leave the country. Not to worry, she assured however, for he would return. He had probably flown to nearby Korea while his visa filing was processed in Japan. It was generally a normal procedure.

The day came when Eddie finally could meet Worm. The latter had put together a pool party and barbecue to celebrate the end of summer. The humid, paludal atmosphere of the Osaka summer was coming to a close, and it was a great relief to take a dip in a pool. Worm's wife still had some influential and prominent acquaintances that she turned Worm on to. One of these such individuals allowed him the exclusive private usage of their outdoor pool and patio. The entire event was sublime. Liz wasn't too big on meat or beef, but this was one of the rare occasions she indulged heartily. Maybe it was because the munchies had hit her hard after some festive pool antics and puffing cheeba. There was also a lot of good alcohol; she declared the Asahi Super Dry Beer to be her favorite. She had plenty on that day.

It was a private affair for Bozacks, but they were allowed to bring their friends or guests. Liz noticed that most of the foreign male teachers had Japanese or Asian girlfriends. What few foreign females came, they were alone or cliqued up with other female teachers, or maybe they had a Japanese female friend of their own. Liz was happy that Eddie could make it that day and clear his schedule. It was merely a lucky turn of events. Sometimes the CHET Program had random teachers' work days in which he was not required to report to the work site. Still, he came, and that way, she would have a barrier to keep creeps like Kwame—also in attendance—at bay.

Vicky, Denore, and Chucky hadn't made it. Vicky said it was due to scheduling or time constraints. Denore wasn't feeling the idea of being seen in a swimsuit, deathly afraid she would be ridiculed for her size, and she could have been right. As for Chucky, no telling what his excuse was.

Even Radley showed up, and yes, he did have a Japanese girlfriend. She was a plain sort of girl, but nice. Her skin looked almost a golden tint when she was hugged up by Radley's milk-white arms.

Eric Cravens was there with his thick wife, noticeably older than he, and appearing to be the more dominant one in the relationship. She would have him running roundabouts getting her napkins, a plate of meat, a drink, and throwing away her napkins, empty plates, and beer cans to get a burpy "Thank you, honey!" And he would respire his demented, hoarse donkey's hee-haw laugh.

Stephanie was there, but her Michio guy didn't come through. She said to Liz that he had to work, or some excuse. Prior to coming, Liz had to white-lie to Stephanie that she wasn't gaining weight and that she looked glam in her aquatic blue-green, spaghetti strap onepiece. She had a full-figured bust as did Liz, and at one time could have boasted a zatfig, but those days, she was becoming a cream cheesed in the legs, particularly around the thighs. It was not as appealing as she might have thought, but considering Denore's apprehension about displaying herself, she would have thought Stephanie would be the same, but she showed no shame. Liz had to give her props for self-assurance. Stephanie's rationale was based on some observation Liz had once offered pertaining to the Asian and Japanese girl having a natural advantage in size over Western women. As such, no need to feel self-conscientious around them because, according to them, the Japanese were of a "midget race" anyway.

Despite all this, however, there was one person who Stephanie was sure to turn on, and that was Kwame. Kwame was hulking and stood over six feet tall like Tim, Chucky, and Keefer, but he was quite a bit more stocky and solid. He wasn't exactly a bodybuilder in form; he wasn't intricately chiseled, but he looked like he would make a decent rugby player. He wore goofy goggles that made his eyes appear beady, and his pink lips made Liz think of funny rag dolls of negros she saw back in Iowa, or exploitative cartoons. He hadn't come with any Japanese girls like the other teachers, but he was tagging along with Ricky, Simon, and Keefer and the hang-on girls that followed them around.

It was substantiated then that Keefer and Simon actually had swapped chicks, because Chikako was holding hands with Simon. Ricky, of course, had Rena, and Keefer had a new girl altogether! Nobody seemed amiss. Apparently, everybody was cool with the arrangement.

Kwame and some of the guys would do some horseplay in the pool. Kwame tried to move in on Stephanie, but she made violent protest and shit got a bit turbulent for a moment. Kwame had a problem concealing his protuberant reaction being so close to Stephanie and other chicks in and around the pool. He wasn't the only one.

Liz was undoubtedly the star of the event. She unveiled her hourglass favorite black strapless twopiece. The few Japanese men who showed up were Worm or Mikako's friends. When Liz strutted her stuff poolside, they too had to take quick dips in the water to cool down their hardened reactions at the sight of Liz's melons. Eddie was too busy drinking and screwing around with Worm, Keefer, and other guys to notice all the eyes glued to his girl's ass. Liz did, she knew she was hot, but she wanted Eddie to know it too.

When things between Stephanie and Kwame had simmered, Liz decided to deliberately walk past Kwame and yell out Eddie's name at him while he was in the pool. The instant Eddie turned his head to acknowledge Liz, he would also see Kwame gawking and rubbernecking her backside. Kwame would have to continually readjust his tooling the entire time. Meanwhile, Eddie would be like "Yeah, Liz? What is it, babe? Whadda ya want?"

Then Liz would be like, "Oh, nothing, I was just wondering if you wanted another beer or something." Basically, Eddie noticed all right. Everybody did. Well, at least she knew she still had it and that she was a certified babe.

The party was yet another splendid detail describing how well Liz was enjoying this new Japan life. It lasted until the evening, and the sultry air became less dense and cooler. The only bummer was it was so far away up in Senri-Chuo, Suita City. They took the train back to Namba Station, Liz kissed Eddie good-bye until next time. Dare she say it, but things were good for a while.

37

LIZ WAS FEELING refreshed one Wednesday and decided to ride her bike to work. It was an exhilarating thirty-five-minute trek using the route she took to arrive at Hommachi. Arriving at school an hour before the start of her shift, she was greeted by a sour-faced Kayo Terumi. She told Liz, "Your first lesson today is canceled." Then she walked away. They never exchanged too many words.

With two hours to spare, Liz contemplated grabbing a quick bite, but then remembered that she needed (or wanted) to meet that guy Deon. According to Worm, he was scheduled to be at the Namba School that week. Since she had time, she biked to Namba two subway stations away.

She arrived at the Namba School, about the same size as the Hommachi school but slightly grimier and with more clutter. Other teachers started arriving for the start of their shifts around the same time Liz got there. She didn't see Chucky or Denore; they were off on this day. She saw Eric Cravens talking to a midget teacher, Jeremiah Ng, who was barely over five feet tall, but word had it he could bench press about 300 pounds. Eric spotted Liz and was surprised.

"Whaddaryu doin' here, Elizabeth?" he asked, his magnified orbs gazed oddly at Liz like a goldfish in a bowl. "You workin' here t'day?"

Liz said, "Nah, I gotta get back to Hommachi. I'm just here because I heard that guy from New York is gonna be here. I need to talk to him."

"Noo Yoke?" Eric wondered aloud. "Oh, you mean Deon?"

Just then, Worm walked in. Having overheard the discussion, he saw Liz and said, "Oh crap. Deon isn't coming here today. There was a last-minute shift swap, and he's out in Kobe this week."

Liz was disappointed. "Shit. I came all the way down here for nothing. Hey, do any of you guys know how I can get in touch with him?"

Worm said, "Yeah, I thought I had his number on me . . ." He took out his cellular phone and began touching keys on its pad. A frown covered his face as he tried looking through the list of names and numbers on his phone's database. Finally, he said, "Damn, doesn't look like I have his number, but I think one of the Japanese staff has his number on file up front. If you wait a sec, I can go and look it up."

Liz looked at her watch. "How long is it gonna take? I gotta get back to Hommachi. I had a cancellation, but I need to get back and do preparation and stuff."

Eric interjected, "Yer fine. Hommachi is only a ten-minute subway ride, you got plenty of time."

Liz said, "I, uh . . . rode my bike."

Worm stiffened. His authoritarian alter-ego was activated. He said, "Bike? You rode your bike to work? You are aware that riding your bike to work is against the rules, aren't you?"

Liz knew as soon as she uttered it that she had screwed up. She got so comfortable being around the fun-loving, jovial Worm—jokey and lively with the staff and his subordinates—that she forgot he was also her supervisor. She remembered too late that Bozack prohibited the use of personal transportation commuting to work.

Worm said, "You're required to use the public transportation transcribed on your train passes. This way, the company can account for your passage and whereabouts."

Liz snarled.

Eric said, "Yeah, if the train breaks down, or if yo're late b'caus of th' train, you can get a note slip fwom the station. But if you get in a bike accident, well, you put yoreself at risk."

Jeremiah quickly contributed his adolescent-sounding voice to the discussion: "I personally know of plenty of teachers who ride their bikes to work, especially at Tennoji Honko." Liz couldn't get over the fact that this Americanized citizen of Vietnamese descent could speak English so articulately. After so many months of seeing only Japanese or Asian faces, which Jeremiah resembled so closely, she had a momentary lapse in ability to distinguish.

Eric concurred with Jeremiah. He said, "Yeah, I guess so . . ." He looked at Worm beseechingly on Liz's behalf, stating, "Aw, lett'er slide, she'ztill new. Some of those vague rules are hard to r'member, huh?"

Worm smirked and rolled his eyes, wrinkling his thick Asiatic eyebrows.

"Oh, OK, I guess I didn't actually see you ride your bike, Liz, and for the fact that you're not on schedule to work here at Namba today, I suppose I can't really write you up this time. But let's not have that happen again. I hate to be a dick, y'know, but I have to make us all look good. If our area gets a 90 percent service rating, we'll all get some fucken awesome year-end salary bonuses!"

Liz breathed somewhat easier, but at the same time, she wasn't sweating bullets or agonizing over the thought of being written up for breaking another company policy. She had every intention of riding her bike to work again if the opportunity presented itself.

Remembering her purpose for coming to Namba that day, she reminded Worm about it too. She asked him if he would provide her with Deon's contact information.

Worm looked as if he had snapped out of a coma upon Liz's mention of Deon. Then he pouted promptly and said, "They're really busy now. They have a lot of new customers and demo lessons. Hey why don't you use the intra-office mail. It'll cost ya'bout one hundred yen, but it's pretty cool."

"Well, how does it work?" Liz asked.

Worm went to a nearby file cabinet and thumbed through folders. He pulled out the intra-office envelope and handed it to Liz. He said, "Just fill it out where it says 'Teacher's name.' Don't worry about the branch, the front desk will take care of all that. After you finish filling out the envelope, why don't you just give Deon your number. Have him call you or e-mail you back. Slip it inside the envelope, give it to Mayumi or one of the Japanese staff, and the one hundred yen. Deon'll get it. We sometimes use this when we need to send stuff to other teachers, usually for teaching materials, though, not often for personal messaging, but I figure you're contacting him about something to do with work, right?"

Liz said, "Yeah, well, sort of." She scribbled her name and number on a scrap memo she found lying around on one of several rectangles, library-style tables in the room. She had yet to receive her personalized Bozack business cards because she had not yet worked for a year there, so the note had to suffice as she crammed it folded inside of the envelope.

"It sort of has to do with work," she said, reaching into her pocket for loose change "I'm trying to hook him up with a close friend of mine. It's really important." She handed Worm a one-hundred-yen coin.

Worm took the coin, ignoring the fact that Liz was using the company courier system on personal affairs, was more interested in who Liz was attempting to matchmake with enigmatic Deon. Automatically, his mind went to thinking.

He said with a hungry grin, "Lemme guess, your roommate, right? The tall girl from my country Canada . . . jeez, I keep forgettin' her name!"

Liz shook her head furiously. She said, "Nope! Not Denore."

Eric said, "An' she'z been keepin' a lotta time wit' Chucky."

Liz made a mock piteous expression. "Yeah, and they make such a good couple I think, but they are just friends. Chucky loves Japanese girls an'shit. But I want to introduce him to the French teacher, Taffie. She works at the Umeda School."

Worm was electrified with wonder. He said, "Oh, Taffie Jolie, aw absolutely. Man, she's hot, huh? My wife, Mikako, loves her!"

A sudden heated streak of jealousy sliced a rill across Liz's heart for a split second. With emphasis on Worm stating that his wife *loved Taffie*, what did that mean? she wondered. Though unaware of Mikako's carnal past in porn, she had sensed there was more to her than met the eye. She stared a bit too long at times—it was either a ploy or creepy, Liz surmised.

"Yeah, well," Liz interrupted Worm's babbling about Taffie and his wife having tea together and them practicing French and other things. She said, "We work together on weekends at the Umeda School. Sometimes we hang out. I can tell ya, she has it all—but she's so lonely. She needs a guy her age, so I was thinking, there's no other black guys around except the ones we got here, and they all got chicks, right?"

Eric said, "Kwame dozen't have a girlfriend."

Jeremiah and others who had entered the room erupted with laughter seeing Liz's disgusted reaction to what Eric said. She spat out, "They already met, and she told me that he isn't her type. Thank gawd!"

Worm's face melted from silly to serious. "I always thought Taffie to be a little timid, shy when she was around me. She's been at the house a few times, not recently though. But Deon . . . I don't know, man . . ."

Liz was jolted into a wary curiosity mode. "What?!" she exclaimed, almost shouting. "What's wrong with him? Is he, like, an asshole like that Kwame guy? Or is he like . . . a womanizer like Keefer?"

Worm smiled and frowned at the same time, for even he didn't even have all the answers to the questions she was asking. He said, "In all honesty, I don't have a clue. Deon doesn't hang out with any of us. But I guess he's OK. He's really a good dresser, though."

Liz said, "Well, is he like a playboy or one of those guys that dates a lotta dif'rent Japanese chicks? I'll bet he does, huh?"

Worm said, guessing, "Yeah, maybe . . . but I dunno. Whatever, just give him a shot. He might go for her, or she might go for him, you never know. But anyway, I'll give these to one of the staff. But for future reference, try to use this for something that has to do with school lessons, materials or somethin' like that. Kenji, the big boss and his henchman, dick-face Yamada—those guys are real strict and always looking for a reason to be furors. Every other week, I have to sit in meetings with them complaining about us *gaijin* teachers. It's bananas!"

Mission accomplished, Liz said her good-byes to the people she knew and dry greetings to the ones she didn't. She returned to where she had parked and locked her bike and scared away a scabrous, urine stench adolescent youth trying to chisel away at the flimsy dime-store lock. She tossed some discarded trash from her bike's basket to the streets to blend with the other debris and pedaled into the thick cluster of Midosuji Avenue traffic. With professional athlete skill, she avoided pedestrians, pets on leashes, other bicyclers, and, of course, erratic drivers on the strips. In minutes, she was back at Hommachi.

As she stopped for a red light on the corner of Midosuji and Hommachi Avenues, she swallowed hard as she saw the familiar gait of Kayo Terumi on the opposite side of the street. She was walking to the corner and set to take a left to apparently return to the office as Liz was. However, in lieu of the previous reprimanding from Worm about riding her bike to work, she obviously didn't want to be spotted by Kayo. Worm may have been lenient, but Kayo most certainly would rat, Liz guessed. She remained back for a moment, when Kayo hit the corner, she was directly across the street from Liz. She chose to remain still and just cover her face and not risk walking her bike in another direction and bring attention to herself. Although it was a crowded intersection, foreigners liker her still stood out immensely, especially blondes with long hair gathered into a carnation-like chignon.

Kayo turned the corner, and her back was to Liz. The light had yet to change, but as long as Kayo kept walking, the likelihood of her turning around and seeing Liz race her bike over to the building garage, a safe place to park her bike with no seedy characters around trying to steal it. Suddenly Kayo stopped! She had received a phone call, took out her phone, and stopped walking.

The light changed, and Liz was already in the crosswalk, leading her bike on foot. As she arrived at the curb, several feet behind stationary Kayo talking on her cellular, Liz's plan was to pedal left and turn the next corner to the right, the rear of the huge building complex. Just then however, she would be startled by someone calling out to her.

"Oh my, Elizabeth? Hi!"

Liz's heart dropped, and she turned, flabbergasted to look into the face of some random bitch of Asian background, whom Liz didn't immediately recognize. "I'm Ingrid Avecedo. You remember me? We did our training together in Tennoji. Are you working in Hommachi? I was supposed to work here today, but they got a call from the Higobashi office, so that's where I'm on my way to."

By that time, this loud, bespectacled girl who looked like a Filipina version of the Velma cartoon character from Hanna-Barbera had already attracted the attention of Kayo, who turned around and waved at them while still engaged in the phone conversation. Liz didn't remember this Ingrid chick right away, but her reminiscing over training days was not what she wanted to hear, and she really wanted to punch the bitch in the gut for her bad timing.

Liz brushed her off gently and said, "Yeah, let's catch up sometime. Drop me a note in the intra-office mail thingy. Sorry, I'd really love to chat, but I've gotta beat it now. I'm gonna be late," she lied. She had time to spare still, but she had to split since Kayo had spotted her. She sped away, leaving the Ingrid girl wide-eyed on the corner block growing smaller as the distance grew between them. She stashed her bike in the building garage and took the service elevator to the main lobby. As fate would have it, Kayo arrived at the lobby at the same time. She had already seen Liz when she came through the building's door, so it was too late to push the button to close the elevator door. She politely held it open for Kayo to enter, and they rode up to the Hommachi School level.

On the way, Liz made conversation. Her brain quickly went into action and used the chance meeting with Ingrid as the excuse she needed. She said to Kayo preemptively, "Oh, a friend of mine, the girl you saw back there—I got that bike from her. Cool, huh?"

Kayo raised her eyebrows, fascinated. She said, "Ingrid teacher? Oh, she gave you bike? Wow. She is nice. I guess you are lucky?"

Just like that, Liz was in the clear. It was a good-enough excuse to throw off suspicion. What are the odds she would check if she had lied? Liz thought chances were slim because the Ingrid girl wasn't a regular teacher at Hommachi, or the Higobashi School she was headed to. She had successfully dodged another bullet.

Three days later, on Friday night when Liz was completing her shift at Hommachi and on her way home, she received a phone call. She thought it was Eddie, but instead of her boyfriend's Kermit the Frog–sounding voice, she heard a velvety, rhythm-paced voice, like someone was talk-singing to her.

Deon on the line said, "Yeah, hello, this is Deon. I got your note. What'sup?"

Liz didn't know why, but hearing him talk, she had a peculiar, numbing feeling of being starstruck. She almost stumbled over her words. "I . . . um . . . yeah, I'm Liz, you remember me, right, dude? I . . . um . . . well, I wanna ask you a favor."

"A favor?!" He sounded almost outraged. In his mind, he was likely figuring, *I barely even know you, and you're asking me for a favor?*

"Well, it's not for me, you see, it's for a friend of mine," Liz said. "She's a really good friend of mine, Deon. She's a sweet girl, dude, and I really would like for you to meet her. I mean, would you? Could you? Pretty please? I mean, what harm could it do?"

On the line, Deon could be heard laughing.

38

THE FOLLOWING DAY, Liz reported for work at the Umeda Bozack School. Upon arrival, she was greeted by a poorly restrained frantic Taffie. "He is here!" she ranted in a breathless whisper.

Liz did not know what to think. At first, she thought Taffie was either scared, drunk, or on some form of PCP. She was laughing and carrying on like a teeny-bopper at a concert of a cherished performer.

Taffie said, "Why not you answer mine phone call to you?"

Liz had to apologize to her for being too busy to check all of her messages on her Tuka phone. Besides, they were automatically deleted after twenty-four hours. She stopped listening to the messages after hearing the one from Eddie explaining how he was busy with something, could not make it to the city that weekend. No prob. In the meantime, however, Liz was interested in who it was that had Taffie's tailfeathers ruffled. She herself was excited about telling Taffie of Deon and the conversation she had with him the previous night.

As they walked down the narrow corridor that led like a long bottle or swan's neck into the main lobby foyer of the school, their arms were entwined like they were a couple on a stroll. Liz could hear the manager, Hitomi Hasegawa, having a conversation with someone. She wasn't sure if it was a man or a woman, but seeing how Taffie had been carrying on, shakily uttering—"He is here!"—she assumed that the mystery guest was a man.

Turning the corner of the hallway, entering the inner ward, Liz saw that Taffie was right. It was *him*. The familiar, perplexingly handsome face was hard to place but difficult to forget. The curly, short-cropped blond hair, the dimple under the chin, no mistake. This was the last place she expected to see a guy like him. In a "respectable" place designed to be a foster for education. She expected to see studs like him at places like that club, the Candy Box in the Kyobashi District, where she had first come into contact with him.

Promptly, Hitomi caught sight of Liz, and her bubbly smile widened further. Liz imitated Hitomi's expression as if she was a reflection in the mirror. The man and Liz locked eyes like magnetic waves.

Hitomi said, "Oh, good morning, Elizabeth. And Elizabeth-san, I would like you to meet Serge. He is the new French teacher, and he will be training here before transfer to Tokyo."

Serge and Liz shook hands. Now she had a name to put to the face, which was a lot more attractive in the exposure of a well-lit room as opposed to a dark and smoky club.

"We've met!" Liz said as she and Serge held fast to each other's hand.

Serge said, "Yes, I think I also have seen you on the train. You live in Nishikujo area, yes?"

"Bentencho, actually," Liz stated. "But they're really close, I guess. I mean, it's the next stop on the city Loop Line."

They finally released their grips. The two pairs of glowing blue eyes were like a collection of rare, brilliant gems for a Japanese person like Hitomi. Liz and the man's staring contest ended in a draw, but it was Hitomi who was awestruck and dazed. Taffie on the side had already fallen as the first victim to the mysterious man's charm.

Hitomi snapped out of her trance. "Well, I'll leave you all to get acquainted while I attend to some office work. Elizabeth-san, when you are done with everything, you can come to my office, because I have some forms that you have to fill out." She left.

Liz said, "Wow, I thought you just worked at the club. Taffie and I visited your club a couple of times, but you weren't there, though."

Serge said, "Oui . . . I work there also. However, I have just 'eturn to Japan 'ecently."

Taffie interjected with some dialogue in French. This gave Liz a brief moment to get a start on her own particular tasks. She began taking pencils and books out of her book bag and into the drawer of a desk she used. When she was done, she looked up to see Taffie's ear-to-ear glistening smile.

Taffie said, "He work at the club until 5:00 a.m. he said, and Hitomi will allow him to come to here early."

Liz was a little confused about what she meant until Taffie was able to explain that after Serge's shift ended at the club, he could, basically, pull up to the school before they opened for business and in all likelihood, catch a nap for a spell before he started work.

"Wow. Hitomi's gonna allow him to do that?" Liz wondered, bewildered. "I mean, like does she even have the authority?"

Taffie shrugged, head leaning to the side. She said, "I really do not know this, but . . . no problem. Why not?"

"Oh, don't get me wrong, I'm not upset or anything. I mean, she lets us crash from time to time," Liz said. She laughed thinking about it.

Serge said, "It really doing a big favor to me. I need a job like this, and I have now the visa. Salary is much better here than the club, but I still need also that job. But here I do not begin my work until nine o'clock. If I go all the way to my home, it is not convenient. If I can come here directly, would be much better. *La vieille dame* Hasegawa-san—Hitomi—allow me to use a key and security code."

Liz was amazed at Hitomi's benevolence and the amount of trust she put in this Serge guy. She only just met the man—in all probability, the same as the rest of them—but she was already giving him his own key to the entire school, the security code, and the rights to cop z's on the waiting room couch. She knew that Hitomi was a kindhearted soul, tender, and generous for the most part, but giving a new teacher the key to the school, for her, it touched on the bizarre.

Rather than question it further, Liz dismissed it with a shrug, then continued to arrange things inside the drawer of her desk. She was looking to see if she had stashed an extra lighter inside of it. She found it and put it in her pocket. Remembering that Hitomi had some forms or paperwork, she had said, which Liz needed to fill out, she dismissed herself to the manager's office, leaving Taffie to her training of Serge.

Hitomi was busy with a phone call and told Liz to hold up a minute. While waiting, Liz took a gander back in the room at Taffie and Serge, chatting incessantly in French. In Liz's warped sense of perception, she could notice that the interest Taffie was showing in Serge did not appear to be reciprocal. While Taffie was buoyant and enthusiastic about her duty of assisting Serge, he, on the other hand, smirked and rolled his eyes when her head was turned.

He assumed the demeanor of an arrogant rock star who was accustomed to having women fawn over him. He was just another Keefer, only just a stretch more appealing and better-looking. A rugged, well-built man, who might just deserve to have a fan club of women, sure, Liz admitted. Every night at a club like the Candy Box, where he also worked, such behavior from women was a quotidian occurrence.

Hitomi appeared again with her upper torso peering out of her office door. She called out, "Sorry, Elizabeth-san, but your first-class today is cancel. So please give me a few more minutes, I would like to speak with Taffie-san." Her stately face beamed to everyone briefly and motioned for Taffie to report to her office. Just like that, Taffie split, and Liz was alone with Serge.

Liz, as always, felt the need to probe and pick the brain of every new intriguing person she came across as if it was her duty. Serge was no exception. She felt the need to know him in more depth.

Her forehead wrinkled slightly as her brain concocted a kickoff to the discussion. She said, "When I met you that time at the club, you said you couldn't speak English."

Serge laughed. "It is not I cannot speak the English, but I just do not want to speak it. I hate English language, I am sorry. As you see, my English is not good."

They both laughed when he said that. Liz didn't want to agree with him aloud. She was laughing because as bad as Serge's English was, she was sure she had heard worse since she had moved to Osaka City. During her laundry room visits in her dormitory building, she met some Chinese, Russian, and Romanian types who could speak thick foreign-accented, shitty English, yet they claimed to be working in Japan teaching English, at rates of up to eighty dollars per lesson or more (if equated in US currency). Aware of this, Liz found it eerily amusing that poor, unsuspecting Japanese people shelled out good money to be duped. Misled by people like Serge and companies like Bozack who promised to supply their student/customers with native speakers of the language they were paying in attendance to study. Suddenly the conversation she had with the Candy Box owner started ringing chimes of familiar notes in her head, what he had said with regards to authenticity and the Japanese appreciation for it. Then again, Liz guessed that perhaps his qualification to be a legit teacher was irrelevant, nor was any other foreigner's that could not speak English well. They could still teach, she guessed. As long as the Japanese person was unable to discern, it could be achieved. They could get away with it. What a shame!

Liz shifted gears and asked him, "Where are you from?"

At that moment, he began appearing aloof and standoffish, almost as if offended. He was like, "Why?"

Liz could not understand the need for apparent secrecy. "Relax," she said with a comforting look. "It's not like I work for immigration or anything. I don't wanna deport you or anything." She paused to see him loosen up a bit, yet he avoided looking her in the eye. She then said, "I just wanna get to know ya, dude. Everybody around here must know I'm from the States."

Serge ran his fingers through his short-cropped curly blond strands then fumbled at his side pants pocket. He reached inside and wrapped his hand around his box of smokes. Liz had wanted to smoke too, but not tobacco. That's why she had been looking for a lighter in her desk earlier. Either way, they obviously could not smoke inside of the school no matter what their choice of puffing substance was.

Liz said, "Wanna have a smoke? Let's go outside in the hall. The smoking area is behind the elevator." They did.

Serge followed Liz outside of the school and into the outer corridor by the building's elevators. There was an enclosed area that looked like a huge telephone booth suited for multiple users. It also had a phone booth's retractable door. It opened to the right and shriveled up like an accordion's wedges as they stepped inside of the chamber. A fan began oscillating inside of a built-in ventilation system triggered by their motion as they walked in.

"Crazy technology of Japan, huh?" Liz said lightly.

Serge finally purged as they lit up. Liz had borrowed one of his nasty, Seven Star cigarettes. She settled for it anyway because she was not yet ready to reveal to him that she liked the pot. He said, "I am born in France, but I lived for most of my life in Canada. In Quebec . . ."

Liz said, "That explains everything." Even though it really did not. She blew out a puff of smoke as Serge rattled on about him living in a one-bedroom flat in the Nishikujo District and the things he deemed pros and cons about Japan.

She decided to not press him for too much information right then, as she most often, nosily did. Serge honestly, in her assessment, seemed to be the type of person who preferred to keep to himself. Introvert perhaps? Still, there was a desire within her, a curiosity that had to be settled within her. It lingered to discover what kind of guy could charm someone like Hitomi, the manager, into trusting him as a newcomer to open the school on certain nights a week.

Moments earlier, Taffie had completed some random task that Hitomi had asked her to undertake. Afterward, she returned to the teachers' area to the rear of the school lobby for the purpose primarily to retrieve Liz for Hitomi, ready to see her now. Finding both Liz and Serge gone, she figured correctly that the two of them were outside in the hallway having a smoke. She headed out to join them.

Outside, Liz and Serge's conversation had lapsed into dating, going-out, having fun topics. Liz felt it her indentured duty to drop it on his ears that Taffie had the hots for him.

Serge was like, "No, thank you. She is not mine type. I do not go for this type of girl, such as this, is beautiful maybe, yes, it is true, but we call her type *macaque*. Not good for me." He laughed a bit cold and invidiously.

Liz was like, "What? Ma-ka..."

Serge said, "Like how it in America, yes? You people say to African American 'nigger,' like that, we call to her." He laughed again as he took one last pull on his cig before shanking it.

Liz did not feel like laughing. She happened to care about Taffie, and although her friend was not an African American, she did not feel that she ought to be described in a disrespectful way. But at the same time, she was unsure if Serge was even aware of how offensive he might have been.

She then said, "Well, I don't call them that. Maybe my mom, or Dad, or my parents' parents did, but I don't use that word much."

Serge said, "Not much?" After tossing his shank in a dispensary tray, he whipped out a crayon-sized spray canister of breath spray.

Liz copycatted him with the disposal of her smoked square but quelled her smoke breath with a piece of chewing gum tablets. She said, "Only when they piss me off, I might call one of them that, maybe, but I mostly used to hear them calling each other that stuff. But Taffie, I would never call her that. She's my dear friend, I love her so much." She heard herself say that she loved Taffie. The same as how Worm said his wife Mikako said the same. Ordinarily, it would have been just a usual expression, exaggerated; this time, it could have been real. Regardless, she got her point across. Serge knew that the level of contempt in which he regarded people like Taffie slightly differed from Liz, unexpectedly.

They left the smoking room. Serge slid back the corrugating door and the automatic fan turned off as soon as they exited.

Liz said, "So are you seeing anyone? I don't even know why I asked. A guy like you, probably you sleep around with a different Japanese girl every night." She oftentimes surprised herself with how candid and random she could be.

Serge said, "Please explain what is meant seeing anyone . . . ? Why . . . what does this mean when American people say this?" His sudden quizzical look Liz found inexplicably cute. A wicked side of her subconscious hinted that she would definitely cheat on Eddie with a guy like him, contingent on the fling being a one-night stand or temporary thing. She wouldn't even need to feel guilty about it. After all, Eddie owed her one technically . . .

Liz modified her question rather than explain the expression. "Do you have a girlfriend?" she asked.

Serge said, "I do not, actually, have no girlfriend now." He sounded as if he himself did not even believe it, and he continued, "I see many women, yes, but I have not one just serious woman." That instant, he peered deeply into Liz's eyes of azure that matched his own. For the first time, attempting to cast a spell on a witch in reverse was spellbinding. He spoke in voice that was mesmerizing in low, melancholy tone: "But, I know it that you have a boyfriend. I think I see you together once, maybe . . ."

Liz broke the spell by blushing her way out of the trance. It was creepy how people recognized her, like that disaster girl Ingrid, and now this guy Serge, who indicated that he had probably seen her while riding the same train, yet she had not noticed them.

Staring at the floor tile as they approached the office, Liz said, "Yeah, we've been together for a few years now. We were college sweethearts . . . I don't know where we're headed, though." She did not know why she chose to throw that in.

Regardless, it served as a hint to Serge that there was a remote chance that *la beaute Americaine* was available. If not then, possibly in the near future.

Serge showed no signs of whether or not he would take the bait, for as they returned to the main lobby again, he was suddenly whisked away by Hitomi, who, on that particular day, was somewhat of a busybody. Liz approached Taffie. Around her eyes, her makeup was slightly blemished and needed a touch-up, Liz noticed. In fact, Liz's intuition told her that Taffie might have been crying. Her telltale sniffing was a dead giveaway. Liz had grown astute in recognizing the signs as she had been for so long a witness to similar tendencies from her now wayward roommate Denore.

"Taffie . . . what's wrong?" Liz's voice was abnormally caring and delicate, indicating genuine concern for the friend that she loved.

Taffie played it off like nothing had been bothering her. Liz did not have much time, she thought, to discern such matters. She figured that there was probably a little bit of jealousy because she had been keeping a little more friendly time with this new Serge guy. This, she could see how Taffie could get in her feelings as she had decided prematurely to be head over heels crazy about him. Considering his choice of terms describing Taffie's kind of people, she figured herself to be doing her friend a favor by averting his attention from Taffie to her. Besides, there was still the news of Deon that she had yet to drop on Taffie.

Deciding to put Taffie's mind at ease, Liz told her, "Hey, listen, me and that new French guy, we were just outside talkin' about this and that. The good news, he says he doesn't have a girlfriend."

In a baffling display of altered attitude, Taffie abruptly stated, "That guy? He!? No. Now that I have a time to think it, he is not my type any longer."

Which was the weirdest thing Liz had yet to encounter with Taffie. Capriciousness? Or could it have been a sour-grapes feeling? Still, it was a good look, a mature way of seeing things, Liz lauded Taffie if such was the actual case. Brilliant ideas banged the insides of Liz's clever and deleterious dome.

"Yeah, fuck that guy," Liz said. "I know the perfect guy for you!"

Taffie stared emptily at Liz. On the inside, her mind wondered if she, this American *la poule Americaine*, was worthy of her trust. After overhearing the talk with the arrogant racist Serge, she was able to deduce that Liz had not shared the same attitude about her as he did, but she seemed to condone it nonetheless. But she remembered their special night together and recalled how Liz had made her feel so special. She was the only genuine friend she thought she had ever made in either Japan or France. Liz never bullied her into a dalliance like others in the past had done. She was just as fond of Liz as the other was of her. So as such, she did not want to lose her; she deserved another chance, but never that Serge scum. And she vowed to get even with his type in one way or another.

Finally, Taffie cheered herself up. She interrupted Liz about the Deon hookup and said, "*Mardi* night, I will meet Takuto—do you remember him? It will be his birthday. I will celebrate together with him. Would you care to join with us? It will be some fun, and"—she leaned her strawberry pink–coated lips to Liz's perfumed ear—"maybe we can sleep together after . . ." Then she giggled like an imp minx.

Liz was ignited with coquettish emotion, and she excitedly accepted the invitation. Finally, Hitomi was ready for Liz to fill out the paperwork she had been softly badgering about the entire morning. When it was completed, she went back to tidying her desk. Her Tuka phone rang. She activated her cellular and began speaking with Deon. The conversation lasted about two minutes. As if electrified by shock, Liz jolted in frenetic motion to grab Taffie and tell her, "I have this cool guy I want for you to meet. Please, and you can't say no." She had already terminated the call. Now Liz was the one acting all frisky and frolicking like Taffie was when she came to work that day.

She said, "There's this American guy from my country, the States. He's a little . . . odd . . . but, I think he's pretty nice. I think you'll like him."

Taffie acted as if the matter required a moment of thought. But given the fact that Liz seemed to have a bit of good taste, she presumed that she could at least give it a shot. She said, "Sure, why not, OK." And she sighed. Liz gave her a loving hug. She stopped short of kissing her on the cheek before Hitomi and Serge returned to the teachers' area.

Liz barely acknowledged Serge, and Taffie resumed her training duties to him in a professional, detatched manner. Before Liz left Taffie to her work, she said, "Oh, he's coming tonight at seven o'clock. Says he can meet us at some place called Toca-Tte'."

Taffie nodded. "I know it, yes," she said.

Liz left and entered her broom closet–sized classroom, equipped with a whiteboard on the wall panel, a small round table with four chairs, and watercolor markers that always seemed to be out of ink. On weekends at this school, the first two hours were almost always without event, and she was without fail, the only English teacher. Now that Serge had joined the team, the usual cotillion of three had grown to four.

At six-thirty, Taffie was ready to leave exactly that time. She and Liz left together and bade farewell to Hitomi. Serge had to remain behind to tend to some matters with Hitomi. Taffie ignored him while Liz gave him an abbreviated smile. They headed to the Kita-Shinchi area. High-priced hookers were jumping out of cabs adorned in fur coats—despite the remnant heat of a relentlessly hot summer refusing to make a hasty farewell—high stiletto heels, heading for their lounges to greet more big-spending doctors, lawyers, chemists, and politic johns.

They crossed the street using the Shin-Midosuji pedestrian overpass. She stopped at the stair landing on the north side and walked a few paces to stand before the entrance of the Dining Hall and Bar called Toca-Tte.

Taffie asked Liz "So who this man again? His name is?"

Liz let loose with one of her trademark devilish outbursts of laughter. She said, "He's Deon. He teaches at other Bozack schools. Anyway, he's meeting us here at seven, he said. Don't worry, you'll like him!"

39

EXHAUSTED. DRAINED. TIRED. All energy expunged. A plum-tuckered-out Liz laid fatigued on the Hommachi School floor. Supine. On her back. Her hands were placed over her chest like a stiff in a funeral coffin. Taffie and Takuto were the reason behind her condition. Taffie and her damned penchant for mixing French words when she was talking to Liz. Mistakenly, she cleared her calendar for Monday night, the night she thought was Takuto's birthday, but no—Taffie had said *Tuesday* in French! It was just a habit of hers (and Serge as well). Needless to say, Liz was puzzled as she sat around on her day off waiting for Taffie's call, which never came until the afternoon that followed. Liz, having work the next day on Wednesday, thought, *What the hell!* And decided to join the festivities thinking she would be back at a reasonable hour—her shift didn't begin until the afternoon anyway. Another reason she could not back out was because Takuto had made reservations at the splendorous Des Os five-star French bistro atop the MARU Building. For Liz it was the first time she was able to see how beautiful Osaka was from the skyline. The city lights polka-dotted the scene like a galaxy on earth.

Takuto really knew how to celebrate. Or maybe he was trying to impress Liz.

Bottle after bottle of Moet champagne was served. Liz lost count after the fourth. Multiple-course meal, which consisted of filet mignon and a side relish tray of coke. As if that wasn't enough, the afterparty was held at Saiko Yamabiko's Dream Lounge where Taffie worked. Liz was so wasted she hardly even remembered meeting Saiko. Her ordinary strong tolerance for alcohol was defeated by upset. Luckily, Taffie could look out for her when Takuto tried to take

347

advantage of Liz's vulnerability. The party didn't stop until the break of dawn. The broad daylight was when they made it back to Taffie's place. Liz would wake up and gulp a bottle of water and induce vomiting to feel not even halfway revived.

Naturally, she thought about calling in sick but opted to soldier through her aching hangover blues. But by the time the cab dropped her off at Hommachi, heavy eyelids set in, having had only two hours of sleep.

Noises of other teachers congregating in the teachers' break room did not bother her. Likewise, the garrulous small group of Bozack teachers weren't disturbed or deterred by the sight of zany Liz lying on the dirty carpeted floor. Such antics were nothing awry or out of the ordinary there; they were all a general collection of goofballs.

Additionally, with the head manager Kenjiro away on vacation, Worm not there either, they pretty much had *carte blanche* to cut up as they pleased.

Mayumi Kazegawa and Kayo Terumi were in charge. These two, submanagers were notorious for allowing the foreign teachers to get away with murder. Especially if Keefer was working; allegedly, he and Kayo were having a secret affair, but no one positively substantiated this rumor. Whether or not it was a valid claim, they still evaded disciplinary actions for rule infringements. The Japanese staff maintained their position that they had job duties in tremendous abundance and no time to babysit so-called adults; they disliked being keepers of a human *gaijin* zoo.

As luck would have it, Liz was yet again afforded an opportunity to rest a couple of sneaky hours due to a cancellation and a student no-show. Had Worm or Kenji been around, they would have assigned such person a clerical duty like stapling papers, writing English postcards for students, grading papers, or English proofreading, so as to maximize the efficiency of the hired worker. Sitting around idly was frowned upon, but rarely enforced if the proper authorities were not around. As such, Liz could spread out and take a nap.

Too bad Hommachi wasn't set up like the Umeda School, Liz complained to herself. This breakroom at Hommachi was decently comfortable, but there was no sofa! It had a canteen in the spacious chamber, a sink with coffee cups and dishes, some bookshelves, and thin rectangular tabletops that circled the room, leaving the center of the floor an open space. Liz closed her eyes and helped herself to that spot there, dead in the center.

Other teachers stepped around Liz as if she was not even there, carefully avoiding her with their grimy bottom shoes and heels.

Liz opened her eyes when she felt Eric kicking her leg. She saw his psychopathic, mad scientist eyes ogling down at her in a sinister way. She squinted while hoping that he didn't drool slob and have it land on her cheek.

Eric had said, "What z'matter, 'Lizbeth? 'Nother busy night?"

Liz's hoarse voice rasped, "Oh . . . I went to my friend's birthday bash . . .Ugh! Almost forgot I hadta work today."

Eric said, "Radley called in zick 'gain too. Was he with you guys last night?"

Just then, adorable Brit Vicky took notice of Liz for the first time and chimed in. "What time do you start, love?"

Liz groaned and lifted a forearm above her face as if to shield her eyes from the light. "After next period," she said. "And no, I haven't seen Radley for weeks." Finally answering Eric, growing frustrated that her colleagues wouldn't allow her to sleep.

Vicky rather unsympathetically said, "Oh, you have at least an hour. Enjoy your rest, dearie. The rest of us working people have jobs. Ta ta!"

Smugness from Vicky was not going to get under Liz's skin. She said to anyone who would listen, "Would you mind switching off the lights when you guys leave?"

The school bell chimed. The four teachers—Eric and Vicky comprised— filed out of the breakroom, and someone among the group obliged Liz's request and turned the lights off. Liz mustered enough energy to get up herself and close the blinds to the windows, and the room was reasonably dimmed. It became quiet again. Drowsiness soaked Liz's eyelids heavily; her senses shut down along with all awareness. Slumber commenced.

That instant, footsteps entered the school's entrance. Timberland hiking-style boots lumbered their way along and led their bearer, Kwame, through the door of the Hommachi Bozack, greeting the Japanese staff as he passed the front desk. He was received with a dry "Welcome!" by the Japanese staff, in their language, before they busily returned to their office work.

Because of Radley's absence, Kwame had been summoned to fill in for him. Like Liz, the first class he was scheduled that day was a no-show—or better, a reschedule, as Radley had called in sick on short notice.

Kwame, like a lot of other teachers deemed dependable, arrived one hour earlier than their shift, unlike some teachers like Keefer or Stephanie who had tendencies to show up five minutes before their shift started. Kwame used the hour to prepare for the upcoming shift by checking the levels of his students, assigning them appropriate lessons, and gathering materials. The last thing he expected to see that day, however, was the sight of a seductive, sultry Liz Amberbush, spread across the floor as if she was a sacrificial offering for a freak sex cult. He nearly dropped his bag in shock.

He said, "Oh, my god . . . Elizabeth?"

Abruptly annoyed, Liz didn't open her eyes. She knew who the voice belonged to. She growled icily, "I'm OK. *OK*!? I'm just so fucking exhausted."

Kwame entered the room slowly, placed his backpack bag on one of the tables. "Didn't you get enough sleep last night?" Although his face was flooded with concern, the wide and curious eyes combined with his hulking stature created a mood which caused the room to seem darker than it actually was.

Liz tried to brush him off. She was not impressed by Kwame's attempt to be amiable with her, nor was she appreciative of his care or concern regardless of how considerate he tried to be.

She said, "Look, I have just an hour before my shift starts, do you mind if I just take a nap? You can be a pain in my ass later. Just . . ." She waved her princess-manicured nails in the air, directing the wind—"Shoo! Go away"—in Kwame's direction. He felt the gust, and it incensed him.

He mumbled, "If you want to sleep, you ought to do it in your own bed, not the dirty floor, but OK." And he paced the room, as if undecided about something.

Kwame wasn't usually interested in white women. Sometimes he wasn't even into women at all. Other times, he was confused a lot. As a child in Nigeria, Africa, he grew up surrounded by Africans and his close relatives. When he and his family moved to the United States of America, he was introduced to a diverse setting. Diverse people. Diverse ideas.

After sucky performances on the basketball court had him looking like a lead foot, chocolate Frankenstein, he would flee the sport amid seething teases and taunts from Native American Blacks referencing him as a Fake Manute Bowl or Dumbo Mutombo. He found solace in soccer, where he became light-footed and friendlier with white boys.

On the soccer team, there were no teases or taunts—outright. In fact, being the only ink dot on the team, he was a special person and was treated as such. The whites complimented him on how he was "different" and he basked in the honor. He was repeatedly commended for enduring "nigger" insults, as it never dawned on the taunting detractors that Kwame's personal history as "Black" in America differed from their intended object of hate. Thus, he and the white guys grew close, especially during showers after practice and occasional sleepovers. His "interest" in Asian women came as a fluke. He only did it because his buddies were into the "Oriental chicks".

After attending an HBCU via United Negro College Fund Scholarship for an "African" American, he was surrounded by mostly white and Asian friends. Just like in high school, he was one of the few Blacks in his social circles, and as such, an oddity at times; but it worked in his favor. People thought him to be a rapper or someone from the gritty streets of the American hip-hop culture. Although Kwame had grown up in the country a considerable time, there was nothing about the hip-hop culture that related to him directly, and he had spent most of his years with the white guys on the soccer team, he was more into alternative rock than he was into rap music. So a few girls—mostly white—would try to give him play, distracting him from his hungry eyes for torsos of his soccer team buddies. But it was no use.

Ironically, the white guys would grow tired of drunken, pervert college dorm antics and eventually found Asian foreign female students to give them fucks. Kwame would get some of these leftover chicks that his white buddies threw away.

Over time, with all their involvement with Asian women, they gradually became interested in the culture as well. Japan somehow became the predominant one that plucked at their strings. Kwame and his pals would eventually apply for the CHET Program, and similar folks like Liz, Eddie, Carver Burk and many others. All his white friends got jobs except him. Only one Program offered him a job on "Stand BY" in case there was a cancellation. Luckily, there was. He did a year with the program and did not receive an evaluation score high enough to qualify him for a contract renewal, so he was dismissed.

Eventually, he heard about the Bozack hiring frenzy and managed to climb aboard at the right time and was still going strong for two years of the three he had been in Japan.

Now here, white women still failed to impress him until recently. His luck with the Japanese women had not been as easy as it had been in America. In the countryside, he had an ugly frog bog chick, but he cruelly ditched her when he moved to Osaka City to work for Bozack, thinking that the city chicks would flock to him in abundance. Unfortunately, he had to compete with thousands of other *gaijin* vying for the same spot as Player of the Year and didn't receive the rave reviews he was expecting. By any stretch of the imagination. He had not noticed the effect of his dry spell until the night of the last pool party thrown by Worm. Kwame had not realized how easily he was affected by the sight of pale skin in abundance, seeping through skimpy swimwear. First, Stephanie Pritchard, then Laura Violi, then Elizabeth—Liz Amberbush.

Liz was different. Kwame could not wrap his head around why it was so, or what it was she was doing to him. Normally, women of her type would be so far off his radar they were nearly invisible, especially in Japan. Yet Liz was something else. She was a different kind of beast. In his mind, the silhouette of her frame illuminated in the half darkness of the room made her appear like an angelic African chick smeared in white face.

For also on this day, Liz was wearing odd, cyan Tiffany blue pegged pants, courtesy of Taffie's garage inventory. As she lay on her side, because of its tapered legs, this made her rear appear plumper and more pronounced. She shifted her position again to flat on her back. Kwame could see all the camel toe and back-door crack quicksand cleavage. His hand found the crotch of his pants, and he could tell that a change was on the rise.

Not much of a smoker or drinker, Kwame missed a lot of parties because of it these days, but seeing Liz spread-eagle, curvaceous body ostensibly yearning, he was considering a smoke because a stiff drink before work was an unwise option. Discernment becoming somewhat convoluted, he half staggered to the fore office to bum a cigarette from a male Japanese staff member he was cool with. He got his loosy and hit the side-door stairway and fire escape perch outside. He lit up and tried to calm down because he was actually beginning to sweat.

The sight of Liz failed to escape his mind though. He trembled slightly as he had remained in the same spot smoking for about five minutes and his crotch muscle was still pressing out from the zipper of his pants, as if begging for release, from confinement. Sweat reappeared at his dark, umber complexioned brow. That was when he knew: the witchcraft was attacking him. She was casting a spell on him. He had been unprepared for it, because he had no idea that the existence of such sorcery was real.

With what was left of his own will, he rearranged the position of his tension in order for him to return to the workplace without causing attention to himself. But what if she was still on the floor? He did not want to be the asshole who tattled to the Japanese staff and tell them to get her off the floor, into a desk, turn on the lights, so other teachers such as himself could get to work. He did not want to be that guy, but he was running out of options. His erect condition caused for discomfort.

Shrewdly Kwame removed his shirt's neat tuck inside of his khakis and allowed it to cover his front. It looked sloppy, yes, but better that than obscene, he reasoned. He made it back to the teachers' room, and nothing had changed. Liz was still in the same condition, same position. She was snoring lightly, sounding like a bumblebee. A satisfied smile seemed to crease her lips, her eyes tenderly closed.

Witchery emitted from her corrupted pores ejected sinuously through the air in supernatural fumes. Kwame consumed the draft and was paralyzed instantly. He could not walk away, nor could he leave the room. Enchanted. Hexed. He was spellbound. He was without choice or decision but to surrender to the sinister coaxing of the sorceress.

His heart now beating like a Japanese taiko drum, Kwame knelt between Liz's legs, her supple trait made it easy for him to slide his bulk underneath easily. Her trousers were cut full in the waist. Kwame cupped Liz's backside with his fiery grip. For a split second, he could feel some relief from his bizarre condition. His yearning had come to fruition, his painful pounding heart subsiding, and his dry throat regaining moisture. Even fully clothed, dry-humping Liz on the floor like simulated, reenactment sex, Kwame was in split-second heaven, it was true.

Alarmed, Liz woke immediately and shrieked. With apparent adrenaline, Liz was able to arch her back, formed a bridge, and rolled Kwame's massive six-feet of bulk off of her. Kwame fell over and lay to her right side. With lithe quickness, Liz sprang to her feet, athletic grace still remnant despite the hindrance of a hangover and weariness. She let out a scream of disgust, as if someone had played a cruel joke on her and had covered her with a feces-soaked, "sambo" mannequin.

Kwame sat on the floor, dazed as if he was coming down from an exceedingly oppressive high, trying to kick it cold turkey, sweat making him look like a moist eggplant. A spark of rage jammed Liz's head, and she kicked Kwame in his face. The bottom of her flat tagged his forehead between his golf ball eyes. He groaned loudly with the sound like a seal.

Liz yelled, "You fucking asshole!" Her tone was drenched in resentment. She came short of kicking him again, but by then, Kwame had gotten back on his feet. In anger, his eyes were bulged out like a grotesque golliwog. Blood trickled down the bridge of his nose, offering him a faint semblance of a colorful witch doctor from a dark jungle.

"Fucking gross!" Liz shouted as she viewed the inguinal bulging protrusion from Kwame's crotch, pointing directly at her. His breathing seemed strained due to a bronchial ailment.

Alerted by shouting and commotion, several members of the Japanese staff appeared suddenly. Kwame's cigarette pal and Mayumi Kazegawa came to him and ordered for someone among the staff to crack open the first aid case. Other Japanese staff present were very startled to see Kwame bleeding and holding his face. Liz was yelling and almost screaming. She could not remember when she had felt so violated and appalled.

Pointing and hurling accusations of sexual assault, Liz caused somewhat a stir. Kwame did not respond to any of the allegations; he merely allowed himself to be walked away by Mayumi and the other dude like a loser in a K-1 fight would exit the ring, tending to the wound on his face.

Liz would be given the rest of the day off with pay. Ruth Worth from the main office in Tennoji was contacted, oddly, not Worm. Ruth was immediately dispatched to the Hommachi School, where she had a conference with Liz and Mayumi, and Liz told her side of the story. Kenjiro was maniacally displeased with having his vacation interrupted by this incident, but he dutifully returned to Osaka from Shirahama Resort to preside over the matter and investigation. Better he did it now than the alternative of his superior, Kenjiro admitted begrudgingly.

Kwame told his side of the story too. Within the depths of his clouded mind, recalling the incident, Kwame realized what he had done. Regardless of his subconscious giving his thoughts validity of him being victim of some type of spell or wicked witchery, he was aware that his actions had been unscrupulous. Despite that, however, he could not admit to it. In a bid to save his own skin, Kwame constructed a canard and caused advocates for his version of events to believe that he had stumbled on Liz's feet—believable because he wasn't wearing his glasses and the room was actually dark—and he fell on top of her, as she was lying on the floor! He also added and embellished how thoughtful and considerate he was to have devised a way to break his fall, after tripping over Liz's feet, so that he did not crush her when his weight impacted down.

Kwame's equivocation was the version that seemed the most conceivable, although both reports reeked of the ludicrous. To Mayumi and those most privy to the investigation and basing information from variants of staff who were present at the time, Liz had been the one displaying odd behavior. For why had she been lying on the floor? it was asked. Management took note of this cohesive but came to the eventual conclusion that some type of lewd affair occurred in which Liz had taken offense, to the point she had to become aggressive. As a result, Kwame was attacked and harmed. All these offenses were grounds for termination, if not a severe warning. For both individuals involved.

The cold, untoward reality was lamentably disastrous for Kwame, who was nearing the end of his contract. Instead of firing him, Bozack management transferred him to the Hyogo Prefecture Offices, so that he and Liz would not again foreseeably meet. Defying their own company policy, which required their teacher employees to reside within a thirty-minute commuting area. With Liz pacified, they didn't stress about involving the police and inviting bad publicity to the company and the declining image of the English conversation school industry.

Accepting the transfer, and in an attempt to make amends, Kwame offered Liz a written apology. Two days following the incident, Liz reported to the Tennoji main office, accepted the apology letter, and signed a sheet of acknowledgment in the presence of Ruth Worth. Liz didn't see the part where Bozack School was exempt from any litigation possibilities before she applied her John Hancock. It didn't matter, as far as Liz was concerned, it was an isolated event, but due to how ill and irritable she was that day, coupled with the repulsion she felt for him, it caused her to react by kicking, screaming, and yelling. True, she may have detested him, but she couldn't think of herself calling the cops or anything. It had not become that intense or serious. She even joked casually about it to Denore when she went home the evening of. Denore thought she was telling a tall tale.

The following month, when Kwame thought he could negotiate his way into a contract renewal, the Bozack management was like, "Thank you for your service," and in essence, "No thanks for any future with this company. Fare well in future endeavors, good luck, and good-bye."

Kwame's pleading his case "What about my perfect attendance record? I came whenever I was called for substituting—whenever you needed me—I came! What about my observation evaluations which were nearly flawless . . . perfect. You all said so!

"I have never broken company rules. I have adhered to the dress code. I . . . I even helped the Japanese staff on my down time. I have proofread countless documents for you all, corrected all sorts of English papers for your overworked

Japanese staff . . . I even helped clean up the staff room and watered the plants in the lobby when I had class cancellations and . . . how? Can you overlook that?"

Although the truth was a glaring bitter, bleak picture, Kwame was offered this as opposed to a suitable answer to his question. That is, all his efforts had been appreciated, yes, but he was still yet a single brick in a monument. His loss would barely be missed, no matter what his position was in the concrete edifice of the corporation. In Japan, a blond-haired, blue-eyed female was worth more stock in a business like that of Bozack. Solemnly but promptly, Kwame was shown the door. Liz never saw him at the school anymore.

40

THE DISMISSAL OF Kwame did not make many waves around the Hommachi Bozack scene. Worm was instructed by Ruth Worth to keep news of the incident contained. Liz was given the same request, but she did end up spilling confidentiality to Denore. Denore told Chucky and also, Kwame was pretty tight with Keefer.

Keefer tried to be indifferent, taking the side of neither Kwame nor Liz, but Ricky and Simon were giving Liz the suspicious side eye. Otherwise, everything was normal.

In the weeks that followed, Liz saw less of Taffie outside of work. After introducing her to Deon, Taffie and he had become, as Liz astutely anticipated, somewhat of an item.

The night they met at Tocca-Tte, the attraction between Taffie and Deon was immediate. He had arrived late. Liz and Taffie were posted up by the bar counter. The Dining Hall had the look and atmosphere of a saloon in the old American West. Deon walked through the part-paneled, part-louvered bat-wing doors wearing all black and looking like a stylish Wanted poster. Taffie spotted him entering, then asked Liz, "Is that him?"

Liz turned to see Deon making his way through the smoke-clouded clamorous air and patches of Saturday Night bar hoppers. Japanese faces followed him through the crowd as if he was a famous celebrity. Colorful beads and a glistening silver necklace were tucked underneath a white T-shirt, concealed by a black button shirt with the sleeves rolled up to his elbows. Another silver chain dazzled his right wrist bracelet style and on the other, a James Bond G-Shock, pinky rings on each hand. Donning black attire shrouded his physique, but he wasn't very tall, neither thin nor too chubby, but generally seemed to be physically fit or in good shape. His complexion was about the same as Taffie's, but he was a little darker shade between tawny and ochre of the brown shade. He was like a living coffee creature.

"Yeah, that's him," Liz said, and she frenetically waved to get his attention, but he had already seen the two of them. He flashed a smile, and the whites of his teeth sparkled like the stud earrings in his ear. Liz tried to give him the business as she was accustomed to doing with Eddie, attempting to deride him with the "What took you so long?"

Deon was like, "Chill, I'm on CPT." All the while, his eyes transfixed on Taffie, checking her out from head to toe. Liz didn't understand what he meant when he responded to her playful half-serious chiding, but she could tell that he was digging Taffie. She and Taffie had just come from work, so they were dressed a little more elegant than casual, but Taffie was never a slouch for fashion. Her glorious shapely danseuse gams were caramel columns to her purple Mary Jane heels. Liz caught a cold shoulder and twinged with a short spell of jealousy peeping Deon's eyes molesting Taffie's round, reverse heart rearing, which in the shoe matching muave peplum skirt looked as if she wasn't wearing panties.

When Liz introduced the two of them, Liz could see that Taffie was sending out an equal message of interest in Deon. She tried to mask it by laughing. In truth, she was not expecting to meet an American who was of Deon's shade. Just like Liz and others like Sonny in her past thought of Taffie as a stereotypical R&B or soul singer, she too immediately took Deon for a rapper, or worst case scenario, a hoodlum. But this, to her, was not necessarily a turnoff. In fact, it excited her straightaways. His swag, at least on that night, was unbeatable. Even Japanese women there that night were checking him out. People walked by and asked both Deon and Taffie if they could touch their hair.

Liz found this amusing, but Deon got a little fizzled when a Japanese man or woman tried to touch his ponytail. Taffie did not seem to care as she was used to men and other types touching on her while working at the Dream Lounge nights. Deon's only detraction, Liz mused, was a seemingly thunderous mood swing tendency. One minute he smiled cheerfully, as if he was actually happy, and another he would appear to fly into a hateful, murderous wrath, indicative of his facial reading. It gave Liz chills—so much so she didn't know who she would be more afraid of in a dark alley—a guy like him? or a hockey-masked psycho killer?

For about a half an hour, Liz hung out with Taffie and the indecipherable American Deon, drinking and talking about Japan. Deon shocked Liz with his ability to speak Japanese. Furthermore, despite his slang, he was also articulate with an extensive vocabulary, something she would have never expected from a guy like him. To her core, Liz was somewhat appalled and outraged that someone such as he would even dare to partake of such learning. For what purpose would it have served him outside of Japan? she wondered with burning curiosity. Of course, she wanted to talk to him more, but he kept brushing her off and trying to hold a conversation with Taffie, with Japanese as lingua franca, which meant Liz was a bit shut out. It didn't matter, though, because Liz recalled her purpose was to get Taffie hooked up, and gleefully she recognized she had. Success.

Deon was one of those types who liked to drink red wine and take the entire bottle. No exception for that evening, and both Liz and Taffie drank Mouton Cadet Baron Philippe De Rothschild wine. A few glasses of this *Bordeaux Appellation Controlee*, and their brains were Ferris wheeling. Excusing themselves to the powder room Liz disappointingly had no weed for Taffie, but she was a good sport. She and Deon were hitting it off so well, she more or less explained to her that she could take it from there. Liz took the hint and ditched the scene, thinking that she was going to see Taffie the following day anyway.

She found out later that Taffie and Deon had indeed hooked up, but they didn't sleep together. Taffie shared with Liz that she and Deon had done the equivalent of making out, but there was no penetration or sexual activity. Later, they did. Liz was sure of it. Although Taffie was not forthcoming with the information, she was certain that Taffie and Deon had slept together. Taffie always appeared to be happy. Her interactions with Serge at work were cold and distant. After work, she would either split to her night Dream Lounge gig, or off to meet her new beau, Deon.

***

Finally, Taffie slowed down and took a break from all the action, making time to have a sit-down with Liz on a Wednesday. She seldom, if ever, in those days ventured into south town, but Liz had been in the Shinsaibashi District that morning, shopping for cosmetics, so Taffie met her there. They linked up at their favorite waffle and coffee spot, Eikokuya inside of the Namba Kintetsu Station.

Taffie had received some serious high-value gift certificates from her Doc boyfriend in Tokyo and wanted to take Liz shopping. The idea to ditch work and go to Kobe City with Taffie played jaunty temptation in Liz's head, but she decided it best to go to the job and try to smooth out her burgeoning firebrand reputation due to the recent events with Kwame. She only had time for coffee that day and met Taffie before work.

Taffie asked if Liz had some more weed. Then Liz remembered that she was running low and forgot to prepare an order for Tim the Duke.

She slid Liz an itchy-man from her Louis Vuitton leather purse and said, "Please get me. When can you get?"

Liz took the money and said, "OK. I'll intra-office the Duke today, I think Friday. I can get it to you on Saturday."

Taffie said "Vindredi, ees no possible? Can you on Friday night?"

Liz didn't see why not. She said, "I figured I'd see you the next day at work anyway. I'd give it to you then."

Then Taffie told her that she and Deon were planning a weekend getaway, and she was going to ditch work on those two days, Saturday and Sunday. That Serge fool would be like a chicken with no head sweating bullets only half trained without Taffie there to guide him, or maybe the head office would send a reserve fossil to come and fill in. Regardless, Taffie wanted to bum some rolling paper from Liz and her to cop some bhang. Liz agreed and they changed the subject.

Taffie started talking about the sexy lingere she was planning to buy in Kobe that afternoon. Something was bothering Liz about Taffie's decision to continue her relationship with the Doc geezer. But then again, if he was allowing her the use of a rent-free apartment, Liz figured it was not her place to try to impose her views on the issue. However, in light of her emphatic desire to have a serious boyfriend, and after finding one—assumed—why wouldn't she sever ties? Perhaps it was too soon to tell and she did not want to put all her hopes behind Deon, and whether or not he would be faithful. After all, Liz thought, he looked like a womanizer, a playboy, and why wouldn't he be?

Liz said to Taffie matter-of-factly, "I have that X that we never tried."

Taffie ignited in motion like a struck match. She said, "Oui! I forget you told me this! Oui, yes, we must do it. Have you ever tried?"

Liz wasn't sure if she ever had or not, she had experimented with a lot of different things from the times she was in LA and until now in Japan. But for certain, she wanted her first experience to be with someone like Taffie. She really didn't want to give it to her if she was going to use it with Deon. She still had some covetous feeling stirring inside of her and felt that Taffie was a shared possession of hers and Deon. And in a way, she was right. With that in mind, she realized she could not really get angry, critical, or upset with Taffie for maintaining her dealings with Tokyo Doc. She wondered if Taffie came clean to Deon about Liz's sexuality? And even if she did, would it matter? Would he spread it around the job? It probably didn't matter because Stephanie already knew she was part dyke. Everyone else knew she had a steady boyfriend, Eddie.

Liz asked. "Taffie, you really like Deon?"

Taffie's salient strawberry blush pressed through her creamy cheeks, a cute shy smile warmed Liz's heart, "Yes, I like, of course. You know, but maybe we should try together . . . like you did for your boyfriend, no?" Then she started laughing.

Liz was unnerved to hear Taffie mention that. She didn't remember telling her, but in case she didn't, Taffie assured her that on the night she blacked out of

Takuto's birthday revelry, she divulged the sorrowful backstory of her epic with Eddie.

Taffie said with bubbly animation, "Oh, relax you, I am *plaisanterie* joking you. But I want to do it, the X"

Liz brushed over the thought of a threesome with Taffie and some strange black guy, for that would be like blatant cheating on Eddie. Because he was soon going to be working at Bozack, how tacky would it have been to have a guy like that Deon to know that he had her, and heaven forbid he opt to blab the news all over the school. Liz thought about it, but with Eddie, she might have considered it.

Just then, Liz spotted her roommate Denore. She waved the somewhat bovine Jamaican Canadian over to the cafe. Denore was distraught because her appointment with Chucky that day had been canceled. Furthermore, the Japanese lessons that day had been discontinued until further notice. That instant, she was heading home, back to the dormitory, and she was en route to the Dark Blue Yotsubashi Subway line.

Denore and Taffie met for the first time. Denore was surprised meeting another person who was of the same hue. Of course, Chucky had taken Denore to meet black people who had been from African and Caribbean extractions, so she was not completely taken aback, but the entire time she had heard of Umeda's French teacher, she had always assumed that Taffie had been white. Liz introduced them to one another, and it was for the first time, like Deon, Liz received a shock that Denore could speak a little bit of Canadian French and Taffie found her amusing.

Time ticked away as the three women chatted. Liz was whisked away by duty for work, while Taffie dangled her invitation to her like a carrot to a hungry snow bunny. The brilliant lightbulb popped up in Liz's brain, after peering at the piteous-threaded Denore, clad in highwater tapered jeans, white mock-neck shirt, and sloppy green cardigan with only one missing button left. Her shoes looked like tissue boxes.

Liz said, "Hey, why don't you take Denore?"

Although Taffie was normally a shy person, so was Denore. She appeared to have an affinity for people of her similar kind, and likewise, Denore made it abundantly clear that although she liked Liz, it was also nice to meet another black person because there were some things that Liz could not help her with, and usually it pertained to hair and hair care. At once, Taffie, in an uncharacteristically welcoming fashion, agreed to invite Denore along if she was willing—of course, she thought this included Liz as well.

Liz said, "Taff, you know stores that have shit for tall, for her size, right?"

Taffie said, "Oui . . . why not? She look like almost same as me in height."

Denore said, "Oh, I appreciate the offer, but I couldn't . . ."

"Spare me!" Liz said and curtailed Denore's self-deprecating description of herself and humility-laced refusal to accept gracious charity. Both Liz and Taffie assured Denore that a warm, philanthropic sugar daddy from an esteemed medical conglomerate munificently donated some JCB (Japan Credit Bureau) Gift Certificates to the sum of "shop till you drop" onto the French.

A moment later, Denore was practically coursing with such vigor it was comparable to a child believing in Christmas, preparing to see the gifts under the tree or in the stocking. The thought of her getting new shoes alone thrilled her to the extent it shattered her attempt to conceal excitement.

Liz was able to throw up her hands like a star athlete who had scored a goal, or spiked a ball over an opponent's net, or a home run. Imaginary audiences cheered as Liz congratulated herself for being the champion of bringing people together. First, Denore and Chucky, then Taffie and Deon, and that day, Denore and Taffie. Wow! She was good, she had to admit. Something new she had to brag about to Eddie. But when Denore came home happy that night with her new duds, Liz thought, *All dressed up nowhere to go!*

41

IN LATE SEPTEMBER when the fall season whisked ghostly hymns of chill winds and colorful leaves spray-painted the landscape, fifty-nine-year-old Shigeru Watanabe, CEO of Bozack, was vexatiously awakened from a serene slumber with a seventeen-year-old *Chigo* by a scathing predawn chime of his hotline telephone. In fact, he received several such calls in succession—first from one of his direct subordinates, Kenjiro Tanimoto, then others followed: Suguru Yamada, Mayumi Kazegawa, Ruth Worth, and so on down the command chain. He immensely disliked these emergency calls but knew all too well that in such dire circumstances he was summoned, the crisis must indeed be severe and required his mandatory attention.

The catamite groaned in half-slumberous vapors, rubbing sleepy eyes seeing Watanabe get dressed. He said, "Where are you going, Daddy?"

Shigeru rubbed his "Ganymede" on the cheek and told him that he'd have to leave the velvety Ashiya *Besso* Mansion for Osaka. Due to the magnitude of the dilemma, he was unsure of when he would be able to return. For them, it was a sad moment because it was a tricky situation for them to meet, and the rare times in which they could be undisturbed were scant, due to the nosy, prying eyes of the witch-trial-poised public, with odious views of pederast unions. With this fueling his disturbance, he was not in the best mood when his chauffeured Crown Royal breezed into the Tennoji District in Osaka.

The polished ride dropped him off at the headquarters on Abeno Avenue, where he was greeted by his retinue of which Kenjiro Tanimoto was present.

Almost immediately Kenjiro was brown-nosing and apologizing for the pressing need to summon his presence. Like a royal king, Watanabe extended his wrinkled paws to receive information papers he could brief as they headed for the service elevators. Kenjiro was desperately trying to explain how he had the situation under control, all the while shitting bricks on himself, trying not to cry, having had to keep under wraps a lot of other growing issues: foreign teachers lacking professionalism, hygiene issues, horseplaying—the case with Liz and Kwame—and rumors of drug use and drug dealing; but this present situation was one which could not be swept under the rug.

Chucky Chilson sat, that instant, inside the Bozack Headquarters thinking of better places he would rather be early Saturday morning. Instead, he was there, fatigued and trying to hold back tears. He had not slept at all. After being questioned by the Japanese police, he was released to the watchful guidance of Bozack representatives. Ruth Worth was on the scene, she was overwhelmingly consoling, in contrast to her usual termagant tendencies and tried to get grieving Chucky to rest his now-frizzy afro on her inflated freckle specked bosom.

Chucky had not been a suspect, but the police claimed that they needed all the facts about events that had transpired earlier or the previous evening as it were. Growing frustrated, Chucky was jaded having repeated his story over and over. With his patience lost, he called the twenty-four-hour support line for Bozack foreign teachers, the 911 card for employees who could not speak Japanese. This connected the teacher with an English-speaking member of the Japanese staff. This company card was invaluable to all teachers who had run-ins with the law.

Even though Chucky could speak a smidgen of Japanese, at this conjecture, trauma might have caused him to have a brain freeze. Additionally, the Japanese he spoke might not have explained every intricate detail: The accident, as he thought it to have been, could be misconstrued. Just like being questioned by the cops in America, Chucky reasoned. He did not want to incriminate himself inadvertently. It was better to have the astute translators from Bozack assist.

Ruth Worth was the first to arrive at the police headquarters where Chucky had been questioned. She reported to Suguru Yamada, who in turn reported to Kenjiro. With Yamada and Ruth Worth as his translators, Chucky was finally able to explain everything thoroughly, in a way satisfactory at long last, and he was released into the custody of his visa sponsors. They gave a ton of paperwork to be signed, and when done he was whisked away by cab to Tennoji, accompanied by Worth and Yamada.

***

What was now a cataclysmic tragedy had begun earlier that week, Wednesday evening after work. Denore had broken down once again feeling lonely and hopeless. Her usual activity of spending time at the Japanese Lesson Center had been discontinued indefinitely, and Chucky had not been around because he was focusing his energy on the long-distance relationship by visiting his Japanese girlfriend in Nagoya City.

Liz noticed and thought it was yet another episode of Denore being weak and desperate for companionship. The shopping excursion with Taffie falsely foreshadowed improvement of Denore's condition. She was happy to get new shoes and clothes, but Liz could not read the signs that Denore was suffering from an acute form of depression. Then again, she was only her roommate, dare she even say a friend, but definitely not her shrink. More than anything else, Liz felt like Denore's overseer. That was why she encouraged Denore to hook up with Chucky in the first place.

When she got back to the dormitory that night after work, Denore was sitting in the kitchen area, elbows on the table, resting her head in her palms. She and Liz exchanged solemn greetings. Liz made some coffee and smoked a cigarette, a growing habit. She poured a cup of coffee for Denore too.

Denore thanked her and laughed away her tears. She tried to front like she was strong and coping with her fragile condition. She told Liz how she had spent her day off while Liz was at work, punctuating it by name-dropping Chucky. Liz used it as an opportunity to persuade her to continue pestering him.

Denore said, "Chucky? Ha! You just won't quit, will you? When are you going to get it? He's just my friend."

Liz said, "So what. She's a *Jap*, right?"

Denore hesitated. Frowning, she said slowly, "I . . . think so. Yes, he told me his girlfriend is Japanese. But I've never seen her. She lives in another city altogether. That's why he wants to get a transfer there."

Liz went on a rant. "I think it's a shame and completely disrespectful. I mean, like, who does he think he is, Den'?"

Denore's forehead crumpled as she raised her head from her palms and looking at Liz as if she had mentioned something utterly confounding. She asked, "Who? Chucky? How, Liz? How is he being disrespectful?"

Liz said, "Well, it's clear that you two have a thing for each other. I think it's disrespectful for guys like that to date outside of their race when there're beautiful Black women like you who are single and eligible.

"I mean, don't get me wrong, I come from LA, and we get all kinds of people. I know, I understand. I see a lot of mixed couples, I used to all the time. One of my friends was mixed, and he was dating my best friend. What I mean to say is, Den, the world is mixed up, and one thing I do know is, I'm pretty sure I saw black women like you all the time, like, on TV, y'know—the talk shows, that big Black lady, I forgot what her name is—but those kinda talk shows that we get in the States, and they always used to talk about how they never have any men to date because—"

"Too many Black men are incarcerated or living dangerous lifestyles," Denore finished Liz's speech because she too had heard of such before. But like her family, she had considered it to be of little concern because *they* were different sorts of Black people—by their standards—and as a result, did not consort with those of such *caste*.

Liz's face turned wicked, and she grinned like a daughter of Satan. She said, "Don't you get a little mad when you see black men with other women who aren't Black?"

Denore had replied something to the effect of being "used to it" as it was a "common" thing where she was from, even though there were few black families who lived in her area of Calgary, Canada.

"It doesn't bother me," Denore said. "You know, I told you my ex-fiancé was a white man . . ."

Liz interrupted her and said, "Yeah, I remember you tellin' me all about him. He was a rich white guy from some old wealthy family in Calgary, yeah, yeah . . . All I'm saying is, Den', you're a beautiful girl." *For a Black*, she injected under her breath. "I don't understand why a guy like Chuck would pass you up to be with a . . . Japanese girl. It just doesn't make sense."

Denore listened to Liz as if she was a hypnotized pet listening intently to its master teaching tricks. The fact that Liz had taken such officious interest in her caused Denore to believe she earnestly cared for her. Denore actually allowed her head to tune in and focus on Liz's discourse, as if to say, *Do you really think so?*

Liz said, "I love Eddie. We've been together for almost five years. I see how these Japanese women look at him. They are nothing but a bunch of sluts!" That exact moment, she had women like Kayo Terumi and that Hiroko Okada in mind. Her own harlot tendencies she neglected to take into account.

"Believe me, I know," she continued. "They are always trying to steal my Ed, like whenever we go out, but I don't let any of them get near him."

Denore managed to laugh and then say, "Well, good luck. You are outnumbered."

They both broke out laughing. Denore felt better and relieved, as did Liz, for she could once more use her charming, magical powers to heal the dismal and glum. Once again, she could hear the imaginary studio audience clapping for her as if she was a psychologist or psychiatrist on the panel of an aforementioned TV talk show, successfully psychoanalyzing a hopeless patient.

Liz then remembered that Friday of that week, the American teachers were on abbreviated schedules so that they could vote in their country's election if they wished. Afterward, there was going to be a gathering at Sapporo Beer Hall Yaki-niku spot. She recalled hearing Chucky at work stating that he planned to attend.

This caught Liz's ear because it was one of the few times he was even invited to hang out with the *other* teachers.

Liz suggested to Denore that she too attend the throng gala and hook up with Chucky again. Only this time, if he did not make a pass or show interest in her, Liz recommended to her that she make the first move and throw herself upon him. How could he resist? Unless he was gay, and everybody pretty much knew that Chucky wasn't.

Denore fell silent in her chair. She grinned imbecillicaly and stared down at her cup of coffee, curiously thinking that Liz was on to something. *Maybe she was right*, Denore thought. Perhaps her loneliness could be cured by being involved in a relationship. Maybe, she continued, Chucky *could* grow feelings for her, like Liz had alluded.

Liz's goading undertone was persistent. She lit another cig and said, "When was the last time you made out with a guy? It's been a while, right?" She rudely blew smoke in Denore's face.

Squinting, Denore waved away the cigarette smoke from her face and turned away. She sat silent for a long moment. The hushed stillness of the moment was shattered by Liz's wicked guffaw.

"I can see it in your eyes," she said to Denore, as if she had *magical* powers. "Even if nothing ever comes up between you and Chuck *romantically*, I'm sure he wouldn't turn a hot chick like you down, especially if you were to throw *it* in his face! You know what I mean?"

Denore told Liz in her jutting, whimsical way that she was, basically, "full of shit," but at the same time, duly noted all that was said and took it to heart. She attributed her constant, or intervallic, melancholy to the lack of intimacy with the opposite sex. Back in Canada, she and her ex-fiancé were sexually active, but Denore had been celibate since their breakup. As a result, she was stressed, she guessed. Not to mention, her e-mails and letters reaching out to the ex had gone unanswered.

After agreeing to attend the party that weekend, Denore and Liz were paid a visit by Radley Owens the following Thursday evening. Once again, Radley had worked his skill and with his shoplifting prowess obtained and procured several items, one of which was a dazzling, extraordinary Ferrari Red bandage dress that Denore was interested in.

Ordinarily, Denore was opposed to partaking in or encouraging Radley's occupation of stealing. However, over a period of time, she found that in the half year she had been in Japan, shopping for clothes and being a young woman of her size and stature was frustrating and oftentimes embarrassing. Having gone shopping prior with the French teacher Taffie Jolie, she copped herself some women's slacks and some shoes that looked better than other chintzy schlock footwear otherwise available; but she had not the time, patience, or funds to make frequent trips to the Sannomiya District in Kobe City, or Tokyo, like Taffie could. With this in mind, she was gradually won over by the idea of Radley "finding" items of interest for her should he have come across anything that might have fit her size while he was on his out-and-about rounds.

Denore hit Radley off with some cash for the dress, shoes, and a bag at a fraction of the actual cost. Liz grabbed up a sleazy but rousing black tube dress and some perfume.

There was one more item Liz needed that Radley could not help her with, so she tried to dismiss him without paying him, citing that she would pay him on the night of the Sapporo Beer Hall gathering the following night.

Radley insisted he receive his funds right then because he had no plans to attend the party. Irritated, Liz had to leave the apartment at the somewhat late hour to make a vexing trip to an ATM. Radley accompanied her to Shinsaibashi by the Green Line Chuo Subway, transferring in Hommachi. Liz was a bit unsettled trying to make conversation with him; they rarely interacted outside of work, and even at work, he wasn't in her primary core of socializing. He was the guy who sat back and silently laughed at everybody else's jokes, then occasionally chimed in when the subject was about how unfair something was, or something that compared Canada favorably when contrasted against the United States.

Liz tried to get him to drop some secrets on how he was able to lift so well. Radley would laugh, his eyes hidden by the black-curtain bangs of his hair. It was as if he was so proud of himself for being able to do what he did. However, he never told anyone anything. He would always change the subject. The last part of the thirty-minute subway trek grew silent save for the rattling of the coach on the rails.

In the days that preceded ATM machines being found in almost every convenience store throughout Japan, bankers were restricted to using contrivances and automatic teller machines located in the lobbies of banking institutions. For Liz, the only ATM she could use for her Sanwa Bank operated a gigantic vestibule twenty-four hours on Midosuji Avenue up the ways from Mitsutera Bhuddhist Temple.

Liz withdrew enough cash to pay Radley and then leftover bills for Luzio Silver.

After parting company with Radley, the Retriever, she raced to a nearby phone booth. It was terribly hot and humid with locked heat inside of the glass window cube with little ventilation. Thick, sinewy arachnid webs entrapped menacing-looking mosquitos and moths, and she tried to hurry before one of them freed itself and descended upon her forehead.

She fumbled through her collection of biz cards, Takuto, and Saiko Yamabiko, and then she found and removed the Silver Light Party Supplies insignia, by now battered and wrinkled after frequent usage, crammed inside of her billfold. When she called Luzio Silver, she used a phone booth, or a public phone. She had assiduously figured out that calling from a phone booth relieved her of revealing her own personal cellular phone number to the person she was calling. Although Luzio seemed friendly enough, *he was still a drug dealer*, Liz reckoned, and for that reason he was, to her, potentially pernicious to have as an enemy. She could sleep better knowing that she could contact him, and not the other way around.

This time around, Liz would cop two grams of coke. She rang up Luzio. He sometimes drove his black BMW and delivered the goods to Liz himself, and would generally deliver in a half hour or less. Other times, however, like that particular night, he would dispatch one of his vicious white boys, a rough dude Liz thought she had seen before, a guy called Moose, and another beady-eyed redheaded, goateed Seattle Mariners baseball cap–donning bloke Brad Cooper. She met them a walk off from Yotsubashi Lane near the Daikoku Bridge. If the cops came, they could be seen approaching from a safe distance to ditch contraband if needed. The worst they could get charged for would be littering.

Moose was a grim faced, musclebound, glabrous bald-domed fellow who, judging by his Old Dutch beard, could have been a redhead had he any hair. Tattoos on his chest could be seen through his white T-shirt, but indiscernible markings from Liz's view shot.

Brad was a scrawny, brusque, and sarcastic guy with a witty sense of humor—a guy Liz would probably have liked had he not been such an asshole. He tried to kick it to Liz, but she wasn't having it. He carried himself in such a way he exuded characteristics of a guy who had been inundated with such luck with women—in Japan—that his ego and confidence was skyrocketing into the solar galaxy.

After likening her resemblance to some Finnish porn actress that Liz had never heard of, Brad hit on her: "You seeing anyone? Yer quite the looker, don't see a lotta hot babes like you around."

Liz, always ever diverted by people referencing her to the adult film industry in one way or another, paid money to Moose, and took her dope. She stashed her goods handily in her bra chamber, then said to Brad, "Well, dude, I'm taken."

She then thought of Stephanie mischievously, saying, "But I have a friend . . ."

Brad was like, "Is she Japanese?"

An abruptly annoyed Liz replied, "Ah, no! Why!?"

Brad said, "Well, if she's a foreign chick, I ain't innerested. She's prolly fat too, right?"

"Well . . ." Liz stopped to think about what he had said. Then she had to admit that, yes, Stephanie was quickening toward a plump figure. But what aggravated her about guys like Brad was he proved to be the typical arrogant vain dickhead who actually thought he was the ladies' man, or God's gift to women because a Japanese woman had spread legs for him. Back in Los Angeles, she would see guys like Brad get smacked with their own skateboards on Venice

Beach. Brad was afflicted, and Liz could see how such a sickness had already affected guys like Keefer, Eric, Worm, and somewhat Radley as well.

Before Liz could continue her utterances, Moose cut the shucking and jiving short and was like, "We're outta here," tapping Brad on his shoulder, beckoning him to come along. Business had been transacted; he was ready to go.

Brad shuffled off behind Moose like a yelping sidekick. He shouted back to Liz as distance formed between them in his departure, "Never mind, babe. I just think yer hot, you got yerself a nice bod, take care of it. A lotta you foreign chicks turn to shit after you get in Japan, huh?"

They were gone, vanished, and swallowed by the shadows headed back to their post in American Village in West Shinsaibashi District.

Brimming with contempt, Liz could not bring herself to be too pleased about Brad's backhanded compliment. For certain, she knew however that she had no desire or wish for Eddie to end up keeping company with guys of Brad's caliber. The more she met those types, the more she wanted to ditch Japan altogether and head back to the States.

She strolled quickly down Midosuji Avenue and was careful to not eyeball cops on foot patrol. Arriving at the Sen Nichi Mae Road intersection, she hailed a cab home.

***

Friday rolled around, and Eddie made a surprise, punctual visit to Osaka City. His ongoing spats with Liz had been regular, but less than previously when Eddie felt he was on the brink of giving up on improving things in the relationship, which was showing the strain because of their separation and distance from each other. On this night, he shot a beeline to the city after partaking in his American civic duty and finalizing his absentee ballot vote for the Year 2000 election. At his junior high school, the Japanese faculty—Hiroko Okada included—were having one of their teachers' meetings, which the CHET Program stipulated. Eddie did not have to be present for it, so he was dismissed for the weekend.

Eddie showed up at the Hommachi Bozack School. He just walked in like he was visiting a bank, library, or any public place, without taking into consideration that he was actually trespassing. The Japanese staff gave him skeptical looks, but no one stopped him from walking straight back to the rear of the office to the foreign teachers' breakroom, even though they did not recognize him as one of their instructors. Instead of pressing the issue, they assumed he was a visiting teacher filling in for someone who had called in sick.

Liz had happened to be on her break when Eddie arrived. Surprised to see him, she rushed to embrace him, hopping upon him, wrapping her legs around his waist with exaggerated "Glad to see you!" hugs and kisses smattering his face.

The Japanese staff could not find any records of a teacher at the Hommachi branch who had called in sick, and they came to investigate who Eddie was. They backed off when they realized, based on how he and Liz were carrying on, that the new visitor was Liz's significant other. This, of course, did not sit well with Kayo, who was in charge on that day, but Kayo opted to not give the matter much of her concern, as long as nothing out of the ordinary occurred. For Kayo had other worries nagging her—at work and outside of work. Furthermore, it was almost closing time; she did not want to work unpaid overtime just to write out disciplinary infraction paperwork because of Liz.

Liz said to Eddie, "What are you doin' here?"

Eddie said, "It's the weekend, hon. Don't yew play dumb with me."

They kissed with wet smacking pecks of the lips. Eddie's arms were now a tad beefier, but not with muscle, so he had to let Liz go and allow her to stand on her own two feet because in his arms, she was getting heavy.

Liz methodically broke down the activities she had planned for the evening. She told Eddie about the conclave that was to take place at Sapporo Beer Hall. Eddie had heard of the place but had never been there, so he was stoked and raring to go.

"We're meeting up with teachers from the Higo and Namba branch around ten at Sony Tower," Liz said, busily sharpening a collection of pencils, trying to look busy while Kayo occasionally eyeballed them from up front.

Liz continued, "But sorry, hon, we hafta go back to my place. It won't take long. I need to get changed. Then we'll go to the Beer Hall. It's gonna be great. That place has good food, I heard. Plus, it's all-you-can-drink included in the price! Fucken awesome."

His stomach already growling, having not eaten since lunchtime that day, Eddie's growing gut was craving more satisfaction at the mere thought of barbecued beef. Impatience hacked at his nerves. He said, "Why do we gotta go back to yer place?" Squinting his eyes looking at his Casio, he asked, "What time do you finish here?"

Liz said, "I have only one more lesson after this no-show break. It'll be around nine. We'll take a cab to my place. Gotta get changed. Don't worry, we'll be back in time."

Not only did Liz want to change clothes, she also wanted to pick up her blow. She seldom carried stuff on her to work if she was holding.

After work, she and Eddie flagged down a taxicab on the corner of Hommachi Avenue. Eddie had copped a six-pack of beer for them on the fifteen-minute ride to Liz's Bentencho District. By the time the cab reached the destination, between the two of them, they had consumed four of the cans. Liz shoved money at the elderly driver and told him, in English, to "keep the change."

Seemingly embarrassed by Liz's haughty conduct, Eddie used some Japanese he had been practicing and said to the man, with humility, "*Sumimasen*! Please excuse us." He waited inside of the taxicab to receive the coin change from the driver, then thanked him for delivering him and his companion safely to their location. Pleased with himself and the favorable reception rendered from the driver, Eddie joined Liz on the sidewalk, thinking that his recreational Japanese language and etiquette studies had done him some good.

Liz had already trotted along, several paces ahead of Eddie, who was bumbling along tipsy, stumbling as if the sidewalk was moving like a treadmill. She yelled out to him, "Hurry the fuck up," extremely gruff as Eddie struggled to apply good footing to the concrete path. Eddie had not been drinking much those days, but he didn't drink less when he got the opportunity. That night seemed to be the night, and more was to come.

The avenue was crowded with night people coming home from work, housewives or cheapskates rushing to the closing supermarkets hoping to get marked-down meats; young businesspeople and execs on their way to afterwork dining at festive *izakayas*; and students on their way to or from cram schools. As jammed and loaded at night as it was during the day, the streets of the city were discombobulating Eddie's adjustment mechanisms, what with him having been so used to the country serenity.

Bicycles sped by and dangerously missed hitting pedestrians by narrow space margins. Eddie almost felt culture shocked to the Japanese city life at least. As he checked out Liz ducking and dodging bikes and people with ease, he could see that she had become ingrained to this strange new world.

Liz slowed down as she neared her dormitory apartment building. She saw a familiar face: he was talking on his cellular phone in what looked to be an engaging conversation. He seemed to be in a hurry, walking awfully fast in the opposite direction, toward Liz and Eddie, but so rapidly so it would appear as if the man would walk past and not notice them. The "dimple" on his chin was a dead giveaway.

"Serge!" Liz exclaimed loudly. She pointed at him; her face held an expression of wonderment.

Serge turned, and his face was awash in seeming fright, bewilderment, and shock. His ghastly apprehension was subdued upon recognizing who she was; then he could smile. He clicked off his phone hastily. Liz couldn't tell what language he had been speaking.

By that time, Eddie had caught up with Liz and went to stand beside her as she talked to a man he had never met or seen before. His affable character he tried to hide by poking out his chest and pretending to be a protector, all the while hoping that Liz had not provoked or picked a fight with this guy who stood taller than him a few inches, and with a muscle tone that made his look slightly on the pudgy side.

"What are you doing here?" Liz inquired, not bothering to introduce either Eddie or Serge.

Serge said, "Oh, eet ees nothing, I was thinking to change my apartment, for around here, but I am told by our company I am not for this . . . *eligible?*"

"Eligible?" Liz tried to suss over his French accented speech. "You mean Bozack says you're not eligible for the housing? Why is that?"

"Because they say that I am only part-time worker, and part-time worker cannot get a housing placement. But no problem. I can remain at my now apartment. It's fine. So you live here, yes?"

"We oughta get together sometime, that'll be cool." Liz stopped to hear herself extend an invitation to hang out with another guy right in front of Eddie. She did not see him react, which was somewhat in disbelief, but he stood there silently and cracked another can of beer, trying to not be wobbly on the avenue.

Serge did not appear to have time to shoot the breeze. They exchanged pleasantries, and he said he had to be off. He asked for directions to the Loop Line Bentencho Station. He had to work at the Candy Box and needed to be out. Liz hit him up with instructions, and he was off.

Eddie looked suspiciously at Liz, intimidated by the guy he had just met, and moderately jealous. When he pressed Liz for details about who dude was, Liz blew off his inquisition as if it were unimportant. She explained that the man was her co-worker and he had just started with the company. She also told Eddie that she had also seen him at the club where he worked.

Eddie keyed in on Liz going to clubs. He felt uneasy about her being up in clubs without him. Even though he had known her for years to be a party animal when she wanted to be, and prone to doing things on her own without any explanation to him whatsoever about what she was doing, or who she was doing it with. Still, he shuddered to think that she would think of being unfaithful to him. It may have been selfish of him, he admitted, but he could not control the way he felt.

He decided to not press the issue about the guy with the funny accent. He let it ride. After all, dude didn't appear to be very interested in Liz anyway. He looked as if he had been in a rush; it was Liz who was acting all erratic and overdoing the "Fancy meeting you here" bit.

Having taken a cab, Liz and Eddie beat Denore back to the crib. Liz shucked her clothing while Eddie was making small talk, describing his week in review, voting for Bush while lying and saying he voted for Kerry, and the Hannan countryside scene. Liz wasn't paying him the slightest bit of attention. She was busy locating her dope.

Eddie ceased his babble when the sight of a stark-naked Liz caused a rocky turbulence in his scrotum sack and an expansion in his underwear. She began rummaging inside of the closet space on her side of the room, looking for the fabrics Radley had lifted.

He crept up behind her, pressing his beer-cold lips on the back of her neck. Liz shivered desperately, for at the same time he had wrapped his arm around her torso, his fingers stroking through her golden pudenda shrubbery, flickering her to sudden moisture. Obviously, Eddie was hoping to launch a quickie before Denore came back home, as he usually attempted to do. And just like every time he did, Liz dismissed him, freed herself wiggling out of his grip, and playfully scolded him to forget about it.

Kindly however, she craftily chiseled her hand down the crevasse of his trousers and tended to his pained, stiff organ with gentle, soft strokes, causing him to promptly sweat. He swallowed hard as a lump formed in his throat. After years of being together, he was stupefied at how she could still arouse him the way she did; as if they had just met yesterday.

The radio was on, playing the romantic Yuki Koyanagi and Kashif duet jam "Anata no Kiss." Liz kissed Eddie's lips gently, wet with the yeast sourness of beer remnant on her tongue. Then she said, "Just calm down, we have all night—and maybe tomorrow too. I really think Denore and Chuck're gonna be out all night tonight. We have the place to ourselves after the Yaki-niku thing tonight."

Eddie's face lit up. "Yer shittin' me! Really? That's fucken awesome!" And with that, he was seemingly pacified, in an extremely good mood tonight, despite the minor setback earlier with the tall guy outside that Liz didn't introduce him to.

Liz returned to ignoring him while pretending to be paying attention, as Eddie's rambling talk resumed. She was just happy to have him out of her face because she had located the garments she had been searching for. Her closet was small enough, and getting loaded.

"Go away, go to the kitchen, look at TV, read a magazine, my mom sent some! Shoo! Go!" Liz roughly pushed Eddie toward the outer space and she slid the divider wall between them.

She put on her dress and looked in the full-size mirror both she and Denore inherited from previous Bozack apartment tenants. She chuckled at her figure looking like a human dumbbell, decided not to wear it after all, and made a note to herself to hit the gym more. Not that Eddie's opinion mattered much, but she asked him anyway, and although he was turned on by it, he was quick to claim that what she was wearing was too revealing with the ovular cut-away patterns running down Liz's curvaceous shapely side. Instead, she shucked again and went for the dark miniskirt, regular pink top, and heels and threw on a jacket, pretending as if her California blood made her immune to the creeping nip of autumn.

With all the beer gone, Eddie was insisting on getting more. Liz was tempted to protest but seeing as how Eddie had killed most of the previous six-pack, she agreed. They hit a convenience store and then hopped in a cab. Liz told the driver to go to the Sony Tower in Shinsaibashi, between Nagahori Avenue and Unagi-Dani ("Eel Street"). They managed to arrive slightly before 10:00 p.m.

Many Bozack teachers were gathered in front of the then Sony Tower. Chucky and Eric were the only familiar faces Liz recognized. "Oh, also Jeremy!" Liz noticed Jeremaiah Ng, she thought someone had brought their young child, but realized it was a Hommachi coworker off her radar. Stephanie and Vicky were missing.

Stumbling out of the cab like two contentious urban hipsters, Liz and Eddie fell into the gig. Some teachers there knew who Liz was, had heard of her, and, oddly, held her in somewhat high esteem. Others, who were of Canadian or Australian extraction—UK as well if Vicky were to be counted—were a little avaricious. Whether a fan or foe of hers, their reasons for liking her and disliking her were the same: Because she was carefree, bold, unafraid to speak her mind, and, on top of all that, she was still gorgeous. And like tonight she could assume so many different faces. She and her boyfriend, Eddie, stepped onto the scene carrying master cylinders like soldiers on leave, then throwing the can smack dab on the concrete pavement with a loud clatter of aluminum *ting* when finished drinking.

A small audience formed around Liz as if she was some type of squad leader. She inquired as to the whereabouts of the others, approaching Chucky, blowing beer breath in his face, almost fogging his glasses. He frowned up at her as if the squirrely bitch was half a sandwich short of a picnic. People thought they were about to fight. Chucky had an expression on his face like, *What the fuck did I do?*

Eric said, "Vicky an' Stef'nie 're double datin' elsewhere. It seem z'azif Stef' has found 'erself a boyfriend." He laughed a startling tone as if his breath was being stagnated. Chucky laughed too.

Liz wrinkled her face. "You mean that creepy guy from Worm's house that time?"

"You met'im?" Eric asked, his eyes expanding like eggs with black dots through his lenses.

"Yeah," Liz recalled "I met him that night we went to Worm's house party a while back. Don't you remember? Oh, wait . . . were you even there that night? Sorry, I was all fucked up."

Eric shrugged and said, "I've been t'Worm's zo many times, I don' recall, but he'za Japanese guy, yah."

Now that alcohol was beginning to warp her friendly mind, the malignant side emerged. She said, "Eww . . . what a waste. Yuck, Japanese guy . . . like kissing a roach, if you ask me." Echos of laughter followed her unusually offensive remark. Eddie was a little opposed to such banter but remained silent about it.

Eric said, "Well, whattaya 'spect? She'z lonely. I kin unnerstan' why she'd wunna date somebuddy from Japan. I mean, after all, this is their country."

Liz imagined herself removing her shoes and smashing the heels right betwixt Eric's eerie eyes, severing his thick ridiculous glasses, and dousing his face with an entire canister of pepper spray. Chucky snapped Liz out of her insane momentous daydream by stating how time was flying and that they had better "get a move on."

Somebody said, "But it closes at eleven!"

"Eleven!?" Eddie yelped. "That means we'll only have an our to hang out!"

Jeremy Ng quickly squeezed into the conference. He said, "Yes, the Beer Hall closes at eleven, but we can stay until twelve. We'll all have time to catch the last train. If not, we can do a cab pool, what do you guys think?"

Liz said, "I think Denore had better hurry her Black ass up."

Chucky's head jerked back to glare at Liz. "For your information, Denore told me that she was gonna be late, but she's gonna show. She knows where the place is. Where's Keefer, though?"

For a minute, they joked about how he was more than likely on one of his clandestine rendezvous with Japanese staff member Kayo Terumi. Liz was aware of the rumor that had been floating around the office for as long as she could remember. Some random gossiper even threw Rosiland from HQ's name in the mix.

"This place is never short of drama," Chucky had said.

They began walking east on Eel Street in the direction of the Beer Hall. The conglomerate coterie followed along like a slow parade.

Liz turned to Eddie and said, "Wow, Ed . . . this is what it's gonna be like when you come and work for Bozack. Around our school, it's like one huge soap opera, like an episode of Sarah Jessica Parker's *Sex and the City*." She giggled.

Eric overheard and said, "Wow, Eddie, yer comin'ta work for BOZACK? Cool."

Eddie became tense. He said, "Well, it has been a topic of discussion. I mean, like . . . uh, they have me on a waiting list, they said."

Liz came in with an assist. She said, "Yeah, it's like they wanted him to relocate and teach out at the pilot schools the company is establishing in Tokyo and Nagoya."

"Shit, I wish they'd send me," Chucky inserted. "I been askin' for a transfer to Nagoya when they opened the first pilot school out there, but they rejected the request and put me on a waiting list too. But they 'bout to make three new schools out there, and two more over in Tokyo. So dude . . ." He tapped Eddie on the fat of his shoulder with the back of his bullring–fingered hand, "My dude if you want to take over my position to trade for a slot in Nagoya, I'm down."

Liz said, "What's the big deal about Nagoya? Why do you wanna go there so bad? Are they, like, paying extra money or something?"

Jeremy said, "Actually, they might . . ."

Eric said, "Yah, there'z the relocation bonus, zomethin' like that."

Chucky said, "Nah, that's not my only reason. Anyway, my girl lives out there. She can't quit her job like that. I'd rather go live out there anyway."

Liz was like, "Damn, dude, you are whipped, right? Oh, my gawd." She had now some mixed feelings, as matters had become tantalizingly volatile. On the one hand, she wanted Denore and this Chucky guy to hook up and cure her roommate of her state of melancholy. On the other hand, now he had presented a decent proposal of leaving his position in Osaka for one in Nagoya, and that would leave a slot in the Hommachi office open for Eddie to slide right in!

Eddie, the entire time of the discussion, was quiet. He hoped for the subject to change, and fast. He was having second thoughts about working at the same company with Liz. This, however, would not have been a good or pertinent thing to mention at that particular time.

The caravan of *gaijin* teachers numbered a dozen, including Liz and Eddie. Liz nearly shrieked when she saw the lifelike, three-dimensional eels decorating the tiny posts alongside the narrow footpaths dividing the sidewalk from the street. Arriving at a massively tall store glass window with a series of enormous vats staring through words emblazoned SAPPORO, everybody got chipper and jolly like teens for a school lunch bell.

Liz and Eddie were already halfway drunk by the time they had arrived that night anyway. When the party started at the Beer Hall, they continued to drink like fish. Eddie looked like a kid in a candy store, or better, a happy vampire in a free blood bank. Cramming meat in his mouth, some before even fully cooked on the grill he joined in the festive feast. Each table sat at least four guests and the *gaijin* ensemble had managed to reserve an entire row so that they could all be seated together. The tables were equipped with miniature flame broilers that sizzled raw meat into scrumptious morsels of various barbecue beef viands.

Denore finally arrived twenty minutes into the affair. When she walked in, everyone almost grew quiet for a second, as if they were expecting a surprise gospel singer about to perform a song for the festive occasion. Then most people who knew her, recognized her as Denore without her glasses and with a splendid makeup job.

Stunning she did appear in her fiery-red dress, Chucky's was among the many heads Denore turned when she stepped into the place. Liz could have sworn that she had seen Chucky's jaw drop. For tonight, instead of looking like a masculine, power forward for the Los Angeles Sparks, on this night Denore was an alluring, full-figured glamorous celebrity with a Tempest Bledsoe facial similarity, some would allude. Her lipstick made her Tootsie Roll lips like rose-dipped chocolate chew, and her ebony skin glistening a spellbinding glow reflected off the low-hanging pendant lights of the room. Even Eric had not recognized Denore at first. Her Tina Turner knockout legs were tantalizing his ticker for a quick second or two, because she always kept her gams hidden by atrocious-style slacks.

Liz greeted Denore proudly with a beer glass, which was promptly drained. She ordered another but was told that it was self-service. It didn't matter, though. The Beer Hall staff fetched her one anyway. She thanked the staff person in Japanese, which was as unusual as her drinking.

Chucky watched his friend with gleeful eyes, wondering aloud, "What's gotten into you?" Which Denore overheard as her ordered beer had arrived, and she proceeded to dispose of it in the same swift manner the first had met its fate.

Chucky said, "Slow down, you ain't gotta play catch-up wit'us. At the rate you goin', you gonna drink up the whole entire brew'ry!"

There was a chorus of laughter. Liz magically appeared by Denore's side. She said, "Aw, shut up, Chuck! She's enjoyin'herself."

Liz and Denore hi-fived one another. The assemblage and party were in full swing. The Japanese staff didn't look too thrilled with having to receive and serve such a large group of foreign people and tried to carry on with business as usual. Unfortunately, however, Japanese patrons looked at the *gaijin* collective with awe and subtle contempt as they were very boisterous and unsettled. Once or twice in less than five-minute intervals, someone from the table of teachers was up and about, out of their seats, wandering drunk around the restaurant, either looking for the restroom or refilling their drinks on the self-service tap fixtures.

Liz noticed Eric and Eddie had taken to one another. They were into some type of pseudo-intellectual discussion about why they both had voted for Bush in the absentee ballots that day. This pleased Liz, as it provided a window of opportunity for her to drag Denore away to the powder room.

Denore followed Liz duteously, and they both found the inside of a bathroom stall. Liz had already whipped out her sizzle from a compartment she had craftily sewn into her Peach John bra. The cocaine was inside of an innovative, squeezable capsule with a tiny nozzle that at one time probably contained soy sauce, passed out as a condiment at bento box fast-food joints.

The tube nozzle allowed the coke to spread across Liz's left forearm in a straight line. With a pre-rolled 1G bill into a cylindrical shape, Liz snorted the line and then commanded Denore to do the same.

Denore, who had never done drugs or even partaken in marijuana in sharp contrast to stereotypical references to her Jamaican background, had not ever considered taking any type of narcotic substance before that evening. That night however, her heart was set on trying something new and daring, so she snorted the coke. Immediately, she felt strangely buoyant and astonishingly *relieved*.

At first, she was like, "I don't see what the big deal what this stuff is all about." But a moment later, as she and Liz took another sniff or two, Denore's functioning was like that of a gaga, skittish laughter-prone youngster.

She let out a yelp. "Whoo!" Denore didn't realize how loud she was until she came out of the stall and saw the sudden, disconcerted and shocked face of a fifty something Japanese woman. Liz hopped out the stall behind the beanstalk-tall Denore, and the Japanese woman looked like she was going to have a stroke from fear and incredulous surprise.

Liz appeared at the vanity and sink, ignoring the old J-woman as she scrambled out of the water closet. She was wiping her nose and smacking her lips. She began applying a creamy, peach colored and scented lipstick to her lips. Denore started humming an old Whitney Houston jam. "*Saving all my love for... whoooooooo?*" and started laughing tempestuously.

Liz grabbed Denore's arm and hooked elbows with her, and they strolled back into the dining ballroom. It was clear Denore felt as if a tremendous weight had been lifted from her. When she and Liz reappeared at the party, they were reckless and hysterically loud.

A girl was sitting next to Chucky. Neither Liz nor Denore knew her, but she was a teacher from another Bozack School. Chucky and the girl were chatting, but he couldn't take his eyes off Denore. Seeing that as a good sign, Denore followed Liz as she waltzed over to the girl's seat and abruptly told her, "Move, hun!" like a trump card queen.

The woman complied without argument or fuss. She thought that Denore was Chucky's girlfriend anyway, just like everybody else did. By everyone's logic, they were the only Black male and Black female regularly seen at the branch, so they were *obviously* dating. Chucky didn't seem to object to the new seating arrangement. Denore took her seat next to Chucky.

Liz was feeling herself, hearing the imaginary applause and accolades for yet another successful matchmaking. Thoughts of being a talk show host danced in her dome in delusion of grandeur.

While Chucky and Denore engaged in conversation, Liz bounced back over to where Eddie was and plopped down on his lap like they were at a strip club. Eddie seemed agitated initially, but before he could protest or exude any grievance, she grabbed his head and brought it forward to kiss her lips, thus shutting him up. She had interrupted his and Eric's deep conversation about Japanese culture, the country, and what they liked about it, to put on a gaudy, ostentatious display for everyone—or better, the five other girls there—that she had herself a man. And they didn't. Yes, she admitted that she could be a bitch. It felt better, to her, knowing that she could get away with it.

Before the night was over, several more rounds of drinks were either ordered or haphazardly acquired through treacherous means wading through a hostile Japanese consensus determining their *gaijin* party unfit buffoons not suitable for public dining. Lots of food was wasted over, drinks were spilled, platters of rice and sauce were dropped on the floor.

Liz, on her way to the powder room for another session, inadvertently knocked over a decanter of wine. It didn't break because it was made of plastic. Liz apologized and scrambled for a napkin. A staff member arrived with a towel, and Liz insisted that she take it. She wiped the wine that got spilled on her legs and pretty feet, not wipe up her mess, and threw the towel back at the staff who gave it to her.

Denore was a ball of fire when it was time to leave the Beer Hall. She and Chucky left a little bit before everyone else, as the place was about to close.

Chucky had not been drinking at the same capacity as everyone else, it seemed, and as a result he was a tad more in control of his faculties compared with some of the others, including Denore. Still, however, he invited her to step off with him and hit another place. Both he and Denore were fans of reggae music, and the popular Barry Micron was performing at the Sunsplash Music Hall at midnight. Denore was eagerly excited knowing what she had planned later and thus far appeared it would run its course.

Denore conveyed her information to Liz and dropped her about six thousand yen to cover her and Chucky's tab for the night. Surreptitiously they winked at one another while Liz was still monkey linked to Eddie, stumbling around drunk. This would be the last time Liz, through a clouded, drunken haze, would ever see Denore.

At the Tennoji HQ, Chucky sat distraught, exhausted, and miserable. Earlier, he had been distressed beyond consolation. They had him sitting at a table like he was in an interrogation room. He recounted how he and Denore had been having drinks at a bar on the outskirts of American Village, waiting for the concert to commence. Denore, who had been going through emotional hardships and mood swings—likely due to depression and culture shock—suddenly became upset and stormed out of the establishment where they were dining. Chucky gave chase, but Denore had eluded him by taking a brisk elevator to the streets. He pursued her by taking the stairs in an attempt to race the lift to the ground floor level but failed miserably.

By the time Chucky arrived at the streets, he was greeted by the gravely horrible sight of Denore, his best friend as of recent—albeit platonic—a bloody, hideous mangled corpse. Tragically, she was killed in what was deemed a traffic accident.

According to the information supplied by Chucky and other witnesses, Denore had rushed from the elevator and streaked from the building wailing, hysterical, and out of control. Failure to pay attention to the fact that she was running out into an actual street with no sidewalk which happened to be a thoroughfare for motor vehicles—and sanitation trucks. The garbage truck struck and crunched her immediately. Apparently in shock at the horrific sight, the young sanitation truck driver panicked, put the vehicle in reverse and further disfigured the fresh cadaver, bloody fender dripping like a rich crimson-colored fountain of tomato juice.

42

SHIGERU WATANABE SAT in an exclusive conference room at the Bozack HQ. His wrinkled fingertips in steeples staring at a huge photo image of two Laurel & Hardy, or Abbot & Costello proportioned individuals who were the company's founders of foreign extraction, brothers Boris and Zacharias Smitts from the San Francisco Bay Area of California, Daly City, nearly a decade prior to that very date. Like them, Watanabe had a special love for the youth, especially children, which was how the company was originally formed, when the brothers were unseasonably released from their contracts with a major English school because of excessive fraternization with students outside of the workplace, against company policy. Basically, stealing their former company's clients, they began teaching the children of their previous adult students. Since this was rare, for English conversation schools at the time not catering to younger learners, they carved an early niche in the industry that started an avalanche, which that very day they were reaping the benefits of. Bozack was now growing and expanding. They were, according to some reports, the fifth largest *eikaiwa* in Japan, neck and neck with unrelenting competitor *Berlitz*. With the opening of new schools in the Aichi and Tokyo prefectures, it was their hope to close the gap between their current position and the number one slot. To do that, they had to have a polished machine. They needed elite staff members, who were hardworking, diligent, focused, and dedicated to advancement and betterment—and to some extent, advocates of *neoculture*, which involved adaptation of ideas involving same-sex relationships and pederasty, and charismatic, unique teachers from all over the world.

What they did not need was negative publicity. This was one of those situations where a problem could be immediately identified and attention was paid to it directly, expeditiously to the moment. While other subordinate departments were handling the business of Denore Langston's remains, the morgue, the coroner, legalities, and contacting the family of the deceased, another urgent meeting needed to be held, and it was mostly damage control.

The Bozack procession filed into the conference room and quickly took their chairs at a horseshoe formation set up of fly marble top tables.

Kenjiro Tanimoto spoke. "We have decided that it would be in our best interest to keep the news of this tragic incident confidential."

Watanabe was candid and cold. "No shit!" He said, "How the fuck are we supposed to do that? As soon as it leaks to the public that a Bozack teacher was killed, people are going to talk."

Kenjiro said, "Yes sir. However, if we were to keep the news from the foreign teachers, it would be better for morale. If the teachers who worked with Ms. Langston learn of her death, it might cause them to feel low in spirits, maybe. And also, the students whom Langston taught as well. She has a roommate at one of our company housing locations—who knows what kind of effect it will have on her? If we lose our teaching quality, we will suffer a decline in our enrollment and sales."

There were nods of agreement from the several staff members present. They, like Kenjiro, were nervously hoping that Watanabe would see things their way.

Watanabe said, "OK, then, very well. I'm willing to hear how you propose to keep all of this under wraps."

Kenjiro said, "I yield the floor to Ms. Worth."

Ruth's haggard, barely made morning mug managed a meager, humble smile despite her miserable mood matching everyone else's but could not show. After the Japanese greeting formalities, Ruth said, "So far, sir, Mr. Chilson, or 'Chucky', is the only person who knows of the death of Ms. Langston. There were, as he said, no other teachers from our school. Therefore, as of now, the news of the accident is contained, as long as we can persuade Mr. Chilson to not disclose any information to the other teachers, his coworkers."

Finger puppet–faced Suguru Yamada adjusted his thick black A-Triangle glasses and said, ".And we have protection from the media release of her name until the parents of the deceased are notified. Our correspondence department, of course, sir, is operating on this matter as we speak sir."

"How are we doin' on that?" Watanabe husked in hard, intimidating Kansai dialect, causing the chickenhearted, pussyfoot Yamada to shake, his teeth clattering like African drums were beating inside his mouth.

Yamada said, "Ah . . . ah, from what I gather, there are some time zone issues, and it appears as if this individual, Ms. . . . er, uh . . ." Someone had to help Yamada remember her name. "Ms. L-langston, yes, Ms. Langston seems to have citizenship, or a connection to three different countries, the United Kingdom as well as Canada and Jamaica, so a-all of these emergency contacts must be notified."

Watanabe's irritated look seemed to soften a bit. He rested his elbows on the marbletop, rested his beardless chin on his clasped mitts. He said, "All right. So how can we ensure that this black nigger won't run his mouth about the other nigger's death?"

Kenjiro said, "Sir, I think we should offer him an incentive bonus. Or we could extend his contract, perhaps throw in a raise?"

Watanabe looked at Kenjiro like he wanted to slap him; his nostrils flared apewide in frustration as he gripped his palms together tightly so that he did not lose control. "A . . . bonus?" His tone was icy and strained as if it pained him to speak without screaming or yelling.

Ruth Worth, seated at the far end of the room, was unable to discern or detect the depth of Watanabe's mood, but decided to interject and speak out of place amid her Japanese company superiors. She said, "Sir, Mr. Chilson has been requesting a transfer to our fledgling Nagoya offices and has been on that waiting list for quite some time. I'd propose we grant him the transfer, effective immediately, in addition to the normal relocation bonus, as stipulated by the terms involved with a successful transfer applicant, and maybe . . . a confidentiality incentive bonus, as I believe Mr. Tanimoto—Kenjiro-san--alluded to."

Watanabe widened his plastered smirk so as to not offend the token foreign chief, valuable because of her A-1 top-notch fluency in the Japanese language and an original teacher with the company since its humble beginnings at that very Osaka location. He then addressed her. "So, Ms. Worth, that sounds fine and dandy. It's good to see someone around here does some real due diligence. But might I inquire as to what the reason was for denial of his request to be transferred to Nagoya? We certainly could have used the reliable, experienced teachers there. Has he had any disciplinary notices or infractions?"

Ruth said, "Ah, no, sir, not as far as I am aware of . . ."

She leaned her head facing to the front of the room, enlisting the support of Kenjiro, who quickly added, "Sir, no, Mr. Chilson is one of our better teachers—good attendance, very good overall customer rating."

"So why wasn't he transferred?" Watanabe growled.

Chop chattering Yamada spoke uneasily. "Sir, b-because the Nagoya area managers requested only Caucasians, preferably females, but they w-were apparently operating on our company's contention of being hesitant to hire non-whites because of their tendencies to use basilect dialogue not considered good English."

Watanabe snarled a finish to Yamada's babble and said, "Yeah, yeah, OK. I get it, that was the opinion of the founders, not necessarily mine, but I get the picture. OK, well, for the time being, let's push that to the side. I can override those clowns in Nagoya. They'll get a nigger teacher whether they want one or not. Then, if further down the line, when all this blows over, if they want to get rid of him, they can send him back or get rid of him. Hopefully by then, we will be firmly established.

"For right now, however, we need to ride this wave for as long as we can. The Japanese economy is suffering now, and the bubble burst, but if we freak it right, we can still get this paper and rise to the top. All those other companies can't mess with our ascension right now. Let them other schools have their hangups about not wanting to hire niggers, spics, and third world mongrel Asians. We'll take them in as long as they can speak English and teach it according to our system. So yeah, send that boy to Nagoya. And give him everything he needs to set up. If he keeps his mouth shut, yes, OK, throw in a tasty bonus for him."

Ruth said, "Sir, Ms Langston has a roommate by the name of Elizabeth Amberbush. How do we proceed with matters pertaining to her and dealing with the sudden absence of her flat mate?"

Watanabe said, "We tell her nothing. Simple. We are not bound by any requirement to disclose intimate details of our affairs to subordinates. So long as this Mr. Chilson has no communication with her or anyone else from the Hommachi and/or Namba Schools where this young lady taught, this incident will still be a contained matter.

"What you will do is arrange for all of the late Ms. Langston's belongings to be boxed up, collected, and transported to our storage center. Ms. Worth, I appoint you to oversee this affair. You will put together a team of aides among your foreign deputies and arrange to undertake this task immediately. Make sure it is done at a convenient time, however, and it would be in our best interest to have the roommate present when we remove Ms. Langston's things. We would not want reports or disputes of missing or stolen items.

"If the roommate asks any questions about Ms. Langston's absence, you will instruct your assistants to offer no information, as they will have no information to provide. Only those of us here in this room today are privy to this information. All your aides will know is that they are there to pick up and pack possessions of a former employee. As far as anyone is concerned, Ms. Langston may be, suddenly retired. And, as for the head teacher, that Mr. Swiggler, he needs not know of Ms. Langston's demise either. Until we can handle the blowback from the word getting out, this is going to be a big, ugly secret. It's unfortunate, but that is how we have to proceed. This is a business. We cannot shut down because of the loss of one screw in this big machine. Thank you for your cooperation and patience regarding this matter. So now, this meeting is adjourned, let's get to work."

Everyone stood up promptly and prepared to file out of the conference room, but Watanabe called out to Kenjiro, "Hey, not you. You will stay. I need to speak with you."

Kenjiro obeyed as everyone left him trembling like mouse about to be fed to a boa constrictor. Watanabe had to chew a hole in Kenjiro's ass about the other matters that had been plaguing his mind the entire tumultuous morning and the problems that the Bozack Schools had been rumored to have.

***

So it was done. Instead of Bozack Company breaking the news to its employees about Denore's fate, they chose to keep it a confidential issue. What worked in their favor was that Chucky was not close to any of the other teachers, aside from maybe perhaps Deon Clemente and Tim Valentine. But as for the Hommachi and Namba teachers he worked with, they ran in different social circles generally. Ruth Worth was able to persuade flustered and overwrought Chucky through earnest urging to not convey news about Denore until, as she put it "her family in Canada were notified."

Chucky was reluctant to agree to this, questioning the importance of such a request to not allow Denore's coworkers to properly mourn her passing. He was, however, enticed to comply when Ruth, on behalf of the company, and the authority vested in her, forthwith granted him the request to Nagoya that he had wanted. His relationship with his girlfriend there had, as of recent, graduated to the status of fiancée as he had proposed to her three days prior. He was beside himself for sharing this information with Denore, thinking that she would be happy for him, but knowing all along as well that Denore had developed feelings for him. Somewhat guilt ridden, Chucky felt an emptiness in his heart, but he did not want to refuse the opportunity to leave Osaka behind. Plus, the tasty incentive bonus, an advancement of leave of absence due to hardship, and one month of pay, not to mention relocation expenses and appropriate stipends accompanying the deal made it too sweet an offer to pass up.

Agreeing to comply with the confidentiality agreement, Chucky signed another gang of papers and was finally dismissed. Ruth Worth tried to console him once more, hoping perhaps he would be in the mood to allow her to satisfy his woe-ridden misery by soothing him within the warm campfire of her flesh. Not that she found him particularly attractive, but for the last five years, the only male entity she had been involved with was Mr. D, who was battery operated and was handheld, regrettably unable to hold or caress her back, what she so desperately desired, but could not because in Japan, she couldn't even buy a man's interest. Seeking to take advantage of Chucky's condition, a rare time in which opportunity was presented for her to hug or embrace someone, in this case to mitigate a grieving individual, she pressed her bulky shape to Chucky tightly, pretending to cry along with him.

43

AFTER A NORMAL, wild weekend of carousing activity, Eddie went home to Hannan City. He split late Sunday evening after spending the entire time with Liz and got a chance to stay with her without any sight of Denore, who never returned home after the night of the Beer Hall gathering. They got so incredibly wasted on Friday that both Eddie and Liz came home by cab trashed. The following morning, they both woke up totally naked, no recollection of how the predawn hours were spent. Liz's cute Tinkerbell alarm clock had chimed off at 9:30 a.m. Liz dragged her nude frame out of bed, expecting to see Denore stumble in from her rollicking evening, hearing about the reggae show, and how the night went with Chucky. She thought Denore would be back before she left for work, but she didn't show. Liz decided to let Eddie stick around the crib and stay snoring in the bed on her side of the room, which she closed off with the divider, so as to not offend or startle Denore in the event she eventually did come back. Yet that evening, upon returning home, she was to be informed by Eddie that Denore had not been home at all, and he had been there the entire time Liz was in Umeda, at work. When this was repeated for a second night, Liz gradually became concerned. She called Denore's cellular; her telephone number was written on a memo magnetized to their refrigerator. All Liz's calls were automatically redirected to the voice mail box. From past experiences, Liz recognized this to mean that the receiving party had either shut off their telephone, or the voice box was full. Since Denore did not have a heavy flow of people calling her, Liz assumed the former. Perhaps she had gone to the reggae show and shut off her phone, forgot to turn it back on. While at work in

385

Umeda, she briefly met Taffie as usual. In a conversation with Taffie, she was told by the French darling that she had not seen or heard from Denore since the day they went to Kobe together, a few weeks back, way before the Beer Hall juncture.

Ordinarily, Liz would not have cared about Denore staying out and having fun. However, it had been an entire weekend, and for Denore that was uncommon behavior. The entire time she had known her, half a year, Denore had never stayed out longer than a day. The dormitory was her refuge. It wasn't too much of a worry, though, for Liz thought that this meant that things with Chucky had gone extremely well. The problematic issue was Denore's failure to return Liz phone calls.

Monday morning, Liz sat on her day off at her kitchen table having a bowl of cornflakes and considering another order of C. Then the apartment's landline phone rang. Instead of Denore, it was the Australian-accented voice of Bozack Company official Ruth Worth.

Ruth delivered the news, as per the plan discussed at the emergency meeting held two days earlier, that Denore "would not be returning" and that a team would be by to remove all her items and belongings from the domicile, and they needed access to the room, and for Liz to be present, if at all possible.

Needless to say, Liz was reasonably stunned by the news. As anticipated, Liz immediately demanded more information about Denore's sudden "departure." It was so unexpected, and in her forbearance of life, such was never heard of. Who did things like that? Just up and *leave*? *No good-bye*? No telltale sign of Denore even coming to the conclusion of giving everything up and just abruptly leaving for, assumably back to Canada? It didn't make any sense. Liz's mind frantically troubleshot. Sure, Denore had been depressed, went through some mental and emotional breakdowns, but Liz thought that surely if things became *that* bad, she would have *at least* confided in her, or made her aware that she was going to leave the apartment, or Japan altogether. Still, Ruth was not forthcoming with any information about the matter, and Liz figured it futile to press her any further. As usual, Ruth sounded expedient, gruff and slightly impatient.

Momentarily, Liz wondered if something drastically awry had taken place. Whereas either Chucky or Denore had been caught with illegal contraband like drugs. Yet she had to strike that from her mind. Aside from Liz's forced experimentation episode with white girl, Denore didn't touch drugs, alcohol or even cigarettes. And from what Denore had told her, Chucky didn't do junk either—he drank, but he didn't smoke or do heavy stuff. In any case, Liz dared not ask the company official on the line; the last thing she wanted to do was draw attention to herself or negligently implicate herself.

Of course, Ruth Worth was not going to fulfill Liz's request for more information. She maintained her position and told Liz, "We have no further information to provide you at this time about Ms. Langston. Anywho, we will need to have access to her and your room. Our staff will be along to collect her things, and we need to know from you when a convenient time would be. I see in our records that you are on holiday today and tomorrow. Would either of these days be agreeable for you?"

Reluctantly, Liz agreed and said, "OK, well, then today will be fine."

Ruth sounded happy to hear the news. Both she and Liz agreed that afternoon between three and four would be ideal. Before she hung up the phone, Liz was also hit with another bit of news from Ruth.

She told Liz, "Until further notice, we will be reassigning you to the Namba School on Saturdays and Sundays to fill Denore's shift slot. You will no longer be required to report to the Umeda School on those days. Your hourly schedule will remain the same for the shift."

Liz confirmed receipt of the directive and hung up the phone. She did not much relish the idea of teaching in South Town and being removed from her comfort zone in Umeda School. Now she would no longer get to relax in the laid-back atmosphere, no working with Taffie and easygoing manager Hitomi. From then, she would be more under the scrutiny of Worm and hard-nosed Kenjiro.

On the other hand, convinced that Chucky had something to do with Denore's abrupt exodus, Liz was determined to get to the bottom of what happened when she next saw him. She was aware that the Namba branch was one of Chucky's frequented assignments.

Compliance however, Liz deemed appropriate in the meantime, for she hoped to get back into the good graces of the HQ, in light of her past transgressions and run-ins; the situation with Kwame was still fresh in their minds, she presumed, envisaging them wiping her slate clean, or minus a few abrasions. Mainly, however, she saw the opportunity to facilitate Eddie's hiring, since Denore would no longer be working! Although there was a piece of her that would miss Denore, that feeling would be overridden by Liz's eagerness to have Eddie slide up into a position with the company.

***

Bozack sent four suited company employees, Japanese and foreign, to Bentencho. They were accompanied by a Black Cat *kuro-neko* courier service employee. They came to Liz's and formerly Denore's dormitory equipped with several stacks of cardboard that folded out into ample boxes; also tape guns, labels, markers, wiry kneaded ropes, industrial clips, and other apparatus. The 'Men in Black' CIA agent–resembling quartet of aberrant Bozack suits worked like machines in *the Matrix*. They had Denore's side of the roomy flat stripped and bare in a mind-boggling hour, the only thing amiss was their magic wand or mystical incantations that would induce wonder miracles. Liz finished a long-distance conversation with her mother, Ida, sending her birthday wishes back in

Cali to see that the suits had pertinaciously boxed up all Denore's things and had them ready to roll out with the Black Cats.

Liz returned to the Namba School the following scheduled day and was greeted by slick-haired, shiny jewel sprinkled Deon instead of Chucky. She could have sworn that her heart jumped like on an obstacle course, her voice trembled but frozen, unable to speak but only grasp for air.

Deon, a la mode dapper as usual in lilac amethyst—Taffie liked purple, it was her favorite color—boysenberry suede pants and silver-tipped stomps of unknown maker. Liz caught a whiff of his scent and pretended like she didn't like the primitive tropical, or coconut smell. She assumed incorrectly that he too must occasionally hit up the Retriever Radley for some favors at some high-end Umeda or Kobe City emporium. She did herself a service by not speaking these thoughts as she normally would have done, likely because seeing him startled her in a heartrending way, as if she had run smack dab into a murderer.

Acknowledging Liz by an upward jerk of his head and a ring shiny index air jab in her direction, Deon continued his conversation with Jeremy Ng about sports and or "street shit."

Liz, recovering from her momentary spell of alarm, remembered that Deon was her "fuck buddy's fuck buddy," and since she was the person that made the meeting between them happen, *he owed her*. As such, she needed not be intimidated by him. Interrupting his chat with dwarflike Jeremy, Liz violently tapped Deon on the shoulder with four fingers of her hand, her inched nails clawed into his shirt's silky fabric.

"Hey, have you seen Chucky around?" Liz demanded to know. As if Deon was Chucky's field correspondent.

Deon's notable spiteful oculus trained on Liz, and the stare ripped her to shreds with imaginary bullets of contempt. Liz's propensity to take liberties with how she approached guys like Chucky, Eddie, Eric or some other guys didn't appear to be, by him, welcome.

"I don't know where he is," Deon said a little frosty.

Just that moment, Eric, Keefer, and Radley entered the room with their plastic bag convenience store booty. They greeted everyone and displayed the same startled antics Liz pulled upon Deon, wondering since when had Liz been assigned to work at the Namba School.

Eric said to Liz, "Deon ask'dus 'bout Chucky b'fore you came. He hazn'been t'work at all this week." His breath reeked of grime. She wanted him out of her face. But she needed answers. She tried to move away from Eric, who was all up on her as if she had a hearing problem.

Liz said, "T*his is the weirdest shit*! Denore is gone too, did you guys know?"

The entire room froze, keyed-in to Liz as she held the floor. Keefer said, "The tall, quiet dark girl? Gone? When did she leave, luv?"

"I haven't seen her since the night we all hung out at the Beer Hall. Eric and that guy," she said, pointing to Jeremy Ng, who had a disoriented, innocent look.

"Yes, I remember seeing them both, but if I recall, she and Chucky left earlier than the rest of us," Jeremy said lightly.

"Well, all I know is Denore's gone," Liz said. "That husky chick from the head office called me and told me. They sent people from the Head Office to our apartment, totally cleaned out her side of the room. It's like she was totally erased. I was hoping I would run into Chucky, since he was the last person I know was with her, but now I guess he's gone too. Den' didn't even have the decency to say good-bye! Damn that's weird."

Keefer laughed and shrugged in a mite of exasperation. "That's how it is aye'guess, these lonely *sheilas* can't take it, the pressure of bein' alone in a country like this . . . I guess Jill . . . oh, I mean Vicky is next! Ha!"

From out of nowhere, Radley produced a checkerboard napkin lined Tupperware bowl containing Kayo's famous oven-baked muffins. An uproar of laughter came from most of the guys in the room as they rushed the bowl when Radley set it down on a table.

Eric was like, "Aw, guyz, you weally shouldn't . . ."

"Ah, shut your ratty hole, Eric," Radley snapped, giggling as he, Keefer and Jeremy opened the windows and searched for stray cats in the alley below to firebomb with the rock-hard muffins. Jeremy was the winner of the contest, exploding a cornmeal smash on the noggin of a nabby feline. With the last of the remaining muffins they started playing a makeshift soccer game.

Liz sat upon a table, her feet resting in a chair, as she watched bemused the antics of her fellow teachers. She could hear more Japanese staff and student customers begin to enter the school. This place was definitely a sharp contrast to the practically dismal quietude of the Umeda School on Saturdays. The guys were funny, but she missed Taffie already. She saw Deon retreat to a corner of the room, having removed himself from the shenanigans in which the others had partaken. He was on his cellular phone talking. Liz couldn't overhear because of the commotion lingering, but was quite sure she had heard him speaking Spanish.

Suddenly Keefer could be heard exclaiming, "Hey! Stop! Here she comes!!"

The "soccer" game stopped as Kayo entered the staff lounge, or break area, which was, Liz noted, similar in composition to the Hommachi School. Each of the boys picked the last of the muffins, tore off chunks and pieces, flicked them out the window, and stood at attention when Kayo approached. They each stood with muffins in their hands, moving their jaws in mock chewing motions, squinting their eyes as if enjoying a scrumptious treat. Liz absolutely could not subdue her need to detonate in a fit of laughter, especially when Kayo was the butt of the joke and didn't know it.

Oblivious, Kayo appeared in good spirits, pleased and proud that she had provided the *gaijin* teachers, and Keefer especially, with something that gave them joy. Her contented look disappeared sharply when she focused her attention on Liz. Just like how she was at Hommachi, Kayo was the same at Namba too—very dry and with a lack of charm that made Liz not consider befriending her. All she could do is just be as cordial as she could. Luckily, Keefer was around, so she was a little softer than usual.

Deadpan expression intact, Kayo uttered to Liz, "The head office has assigned you to work here and Hommachi until a further notice." She turned her attention to Deon. "Mr. Clemente?"

In a corner of the room, Deon halted his telephone convo to acknowledge Kayo when she said, "Clemente-san, you will be working here this week, or until Swiggler-san, Mitchell comes back. And to everyone, Mitchell will be in Tennoji Honko this week." She then poised to walk away as if pivoted on a swivel, giving Liz a full view of her back, or her ass to kiss. It was implied that she was not a fan of Liz in the least. Turning then to leave and head up front to the business side of the school, she offered a sweet smile to Keefer before Liz stopped her with a tug on the elbow.

"Hey, wait!" Liz called out to her.

Kayo flung her neck and shoulders around, the choppy, hickory brunette bob hair flew violently in the air as she whirled to face the blonde *gaijin* like she was staring down a bully on a playground. Liz, after all, held an aggressive stance directly in front of Kayo, although she meant no harm, closer to her than she needed to be. A pace or two more, plus give or take the height differential, they would be about to kiss.

Liz said, "I've already been notified about it. That's why I'm here. What I'd like to know is if I'm going to get a new roommate?"

Kayo said, "I don't know anything about that. You have to call your area supervisor. She is Ruth. I am sure that you know her." Hoping that this did not sit well with Liz, she turned once more to leave. Any inconvenience, no matter how great or small, people like Kayo could render upon those they considered unsavory was like a delightful, personal victory for them.

As soon as Kayo left, the boys reopened the transom windows. Radley laughed his goofy chuckle and said "There! There guys!" Liz had never seen him so animated. "I see a cat. Five hundred yen to whoever hits the fucker!" Then he fired a Jeff Musselman, Darren Hall Toronto Blue Jay fastball muffin beam to the torso of a cat in the culvert fare below. He was joined by some of the others.

Liz cursed and was then tapped on the shoulder by a "Long time no see!" shouting Stephanie, who was reporting for work twenty minutes before the start of her first class. Uncharacteristically upbeat at such an early hour on Saturday, she was like "How have you been? Why haven't you called me back?" Embracing Liz with one heavy left arm, pulling her close as if they were friendly cousins.

"Never mind that," Liz said with a sly grin, "Where the hell have *you* been? What've *you* been up to?" As if she didn't already know.

Stephanie said, "Oh, yeah, sorry I missed you guys last Friday. I heard you guys had an amazing time at the Beer Hall. I swear to gawd, I fucking love those places. All you can eat and drink for ninety minutes." She rolled her eyes as if she had taken a brief reverie to utopia. "But I was out with Vicky, her new Japanese boyfriend, and my friend, or my date, Michio. We went to the karaoke. Who'd you vote for by the way?"

"Kerry," Liz said, and before Stephanie could say *Me too!* Liz broke in and said, "You guys have been hanging around a lot." She leaned in close to Stephanie's ear so that their conversation was a little muffled amid a calamitous backdrop of goof-off coworkers.

"You suck his cock yet?" she asked.

In an outburst of giggles likened to chafing imps, Stephanie play-slapped Liz softly on her back. Quickly she pulled herself together, assumed a resolute and sincere composure.

Stephanie then said, "N*ooooo*, but he's so swe*eeet*! He's such a *gentleman*! He's not like American guys or these other foreign assholes!" She shot Deon a wretched look, who had resumed his phone call conversation in the corner of the room. "And definitely not a playboy like *that* creep."

Liz caught wind of to whom she was referencing. "What the fuck's *he* doing here anyway?" Liz whispered as she dragged Stephanie to the sink and canteen area of the break lounge. "And by the way, would you happen to know where Chucky is?"

Stephanie smirked and then sneered. "I don't know what he's doing here, but the last time he came around here to this school, he was trying to hustle his lottery pool bullshit. But I don't usually see him here on Saturdays. It's Chuck."

Liz felt as if she could be one of the Three Stooges, she would be the one at that moment who slapped the living shit out of their comrade. Gritting her teeth and fighting the urge to splash cold water from the sink into Stephanie's grill.

"So where's Chucky?" Liz asked futilely.

Stephanie said, "Gee, I don't know. He's *your* friend."

Liz was slightly put off by Stephanie's low-key snapping back at her. In general, Stephanie held Liz in high regard, despite her time in Japan and duration with the company being twice as vast, she still seemed to look up to the California girl—one she actually believed was a *Bruin*—like a domineering, lordly troop leader. Liz, up until now, had grown accustomed to her arbitrary, oppressive role over her and enjoyed it.

Frigidly Liz said, "Neither are you!"

Stephanie laughed and play-smacked Liz again. "Oh, stop!" Still chuckling, unaware that Liz was dead serious. Figuring she had time for coffee, Liz set to motion preparing a cup for herself while Stephanie rambled on about her new friend Michio. She grew bored with the babble in seconds, sooner than she thought she would. She sipped from her mug and stared at her watch, expecting to start work and her first lesson of the day.

Stephanie said, "You have to hang out with Michio and me, Liz. I know you don't like those types of guys, but I think you'll like him. He's not like all the rest. He has a different sort of character. I don't think he's a chauvinist like most men in Japan are. And best of all, he speaks English really well!"

"I seem to recall that," Liz stated, sipping the coffee, unimpressed by its taste and Stephanie's bragging about her love interest.

Stephanie continued, "Most guys, they take advantage of you. Especially if they find you drunk or incapacitated. But he's not like that. He helped me. I appreciate him for that. And he's so gentle, funny. He's like a good friend. We always have so many things to talk about when he has time to meet. I can't believe I'm saying this, but I think . . . I think . . . he may be . . . the one! The one! My . . . soul mate.

"Can you imagine? I'm like . . . spazzing out, y'know . . . I never thought I would be saying this. I came from a suburban home with the most racist parents you could ever imagine. My dad was a two-timing, cheating truck driver and divorced my mother who's been a lush junky ever since. But even so, if I were to tell either of them that I wanted to marry a Japanese, or Asian, or anything, not . . . American, or 'white' . . . it'd be a disaster, y'know what I mean . . . but, I think he may be the one for me. He's far from the stereotypical tyrannical workhorse Japanese man that we heard about. He's something else!"

Deon's face popped up like a cartoon character from behind a wood-enclosed glass divider, separating the canteen from the rest of the lounge. Stephanie, who had been closest to the divider glass, was visibly startled. Liz never thought she would be as happy to see Deon's playful but tragically malicious face when he interrupted Stephanie's torridly told ode to her Japanese crush. A guy she had yet to be intimate with but with whom she had fallen head over heels for. Liz shifted her beam of focus onto Deon.

He said, "Yo. Either'a you chicks wanna get down with this lottery pool?"

Arrogantly, Stephanie fired, "No thanks, *Leon* . . . like? Why are you always trying to hoodwink everyone with your ghetto scams?"

Deon's eyes narrowed to icy glaring slits. He said, "Yo, I told you my name ain't no damn Leon. It's *Dee* if you too lazy to pronounce the whole thing!"

The commotion had drawn a small gathering to the canteen. Eric and Radley made a move at the same time for the coffeepot and started play-fighting for the right to use it first.

"Yer right, Stef'ny, the lottery'z a hoodwink," Eric said, losing the coffeepot scuffle.

A discussion of the usual poppycock ensued. Nonsense Liz had heard for most of her life from naysayers to playing lottery games. While she still had a smidgen of distrust for Deon, it outweighed her revulsion for Eric. This was essential only at that moment because she knew very well that Eric may have been somewhat correct in his assessment, but it was a fact that her own parents (or father) became fake wealthy overnight because of the hoodwink ranted about.

Keefer appeared and tapped Stephanie's nape over the window divider. He handed her a slip of paper. He said, "This is Ricky's cell phone number. Your boy pal asked fer'it the other night."

"Thanks!" Stephanie tucked the memo in her purse.

Deon said, "So you guys are in or out?"

Liz said, "OK, I got numbers for ya, how many you need? Six? OK, ready? Twelve, twenty-four, six, seventeen, nine, and twenty-nine. Ha ha, that's my birthday, my mom's birthday, and the date I lost my virginity, the night before Christmas! Hahahaha!"

Laughter echoed from everyone like the lounge was a stage for a comedy show. Liz was hoping to get a word in edgewise privately with Deon.

She said, "Hey, do you think I can speak to you about something?"

Before Deon could answer, the Asian Gary Coleman, Jeremy, came over and tried to take the small pad of paper he had been scribbling numbers on. He asked Deon, "How do you play this thing? Is it in Japan? How much money can we win?"

Deon snatched his pad back from Jeremy's childlike grasping paws. He said, "Both Japan and the USA, you dig? Y'see, my brother, in the Apple and my cousin in Carolina are gonna play, but the one I got here is the one we should do here."

Eric said, "It's futile. Th' chances ov'yew winnin'iz az rare az lightnin' strikin' th' same place twice!"

Stephanie added grimly, "And even if you did win, he'd be the only one with the ticket. What makes you think he won't run and take all the winnings for himself?"

Jeremy laughed. "Yeah, who's to say? We all might not be here when the ticket actually wins."

Liz said, "Yeh, with people suddenly disappearing around here, that could happen. How much anyway, dude?"

Deon said, "Two dollars, but you can give me two hundred yen."

"No way!" Liz spat and dumped the rest of her coffee in the sink and started rinsing the cup she used. Then she added, "Too expensive!" But at the same time, she was drying her hands on the side of her grey capris, then dipped in her pockets for coins.

Deon smiled and grumbled, "Yeah, but you ma'fuckaz'll buy beer for five hundred yen all night like it ain't niothin'."

Keefer chimed in, "Well that's the idea, mate!! We'd rather have the beer, brother!"

Everybody laughed except for Deon as Keefer patted him softly on the back and grabbed his folders for classes. The eruption of laughter was deafening. So much so that Kayo had to jog-stride to the rear of the office where the lounge was. She came with the "Shh!" index finger to the lips gesture. Keefer winked at her on the sneak. Kayo blushed as the squad of teachers filing out for classes uttered echoed apologies for being loud.

Liz finally got her moment to talk to Deon. "Here you go," she said as she dropped kopecks of coins into his hand, which she had grabbed and forced to accept the money.

"By the way," she continued, "how's Taffie? You guys got plans tonight?"

Deon's treacherous, hardened face softened at once and melted into a bashful, congenial smile. He avoided looking Liz in the eye, he stared at the floor. He said, "She good. We not hookin' up tonight. She said she hadta go to Tokyo for some shit. She'll be back Monday, she said."

Liz had planned to give Deon the business. She was going to hit him with the spiel about to the tune of 'You better not fuck her over. She's my friend—and lover—and she's a really sweet girl. Don't break my friend's heart!' But she realized she couldn't, because she was quite sure that the reason she was going to Tokyo was to check in with her sugar daddy, the Doc. If she were to admonish Deon in that sort of way, it would be somewhat hypocritical, she guessed. The fact that Deon and Taffie were getting along fine was a good thing, and Liz figured that it would be best to allow things to remain that way, without any of her meddling. She hoped that Taffie was not making a mistake by dealing with two infatuated guys neither of whom she was fully committed to.

The chime of the school's bell sounded. Liz followed everyone out in almost a single file to the classrooms to begin work.

44

THEN THIS HAPPENED... Liz called Eddie the following weekend, but he was already aboard a microbus, courtesy of the PTA and municipal BOE associates, transporting him, other teachers, and school staff who planned on indulging in alcoholic drinks to the fall *nomikai*, or "drinking party" outing. The bus was crowded with mostly dudes—male teachers—or the older ones. Eddie managed to supply this detail to Liz, and it caused her to rest a little easier, although she did not give him any grief overall, she remembered going on such outings when she herself was a participant in the CHET Program. Both she and Eddie enjoyed getting smashed having partaken of bottled beer, fine wines, champagne, and Japanese rice wine *sake* of various distinction, not to mention grub on some of Japan's most exquisite cuisine, sushi, *sashimi*—for free! The program covered everything.

This second term for Eddie was no different. Eddie still got a big kick out of these excursions as they granted him an opportunity to discover and venture into establishments he would otherwise not have access to or even know about. He reminisced over the cock-teasing with possibility of happy endings during times in the previous year when he was taken to, or stumbled upon, the Snack Lounge: Mama-san Yoshiko and other pleasant memories. Everything about his new life was so exotic and more thrilling by the day. He had a creeping notion that he may never tire of Japan, or snap out of his honeymoon stage, and never have desire to return home to America. But Liz? Hell, no . . .

Ten minutes after Eddie finished his abbreviated talk with Liz on the cell phone, the microbus pulled into the parking lot of Shirokiya *izakaya*, where the event of the evening was to be held. Through the bus window, Eddie spotted Hiroko's candy red apple Demio already at the spot. Apparently, she had no plans of drinking, he figured. It didn't matter. He was happy she was there because she was a buffer; a kickstand he often relied upon to translate for him. Although he was frequently commended on how well his Japanese was improving, he was still yet to be released on his own in society with a functioning competence.

Hiroko did not seem to mind translating for Eddie. Even if he was too dense to read the signs that she was craving for him. She too basked in the overwhelming admiration and praise garnished from peers who saw how well she could speak and understand English. It was even hinted to her at some point that she could have enjoyed a more lucrative—and less stressful career—as a legal translator. Gradual to that extent she too would consider it as a future option.

Clear and presently however, she was interested in Eddie. Period. He was her ticket, but a ticket to where? A ticket out of Japan? Out of the Japanese way of life? These were questions she had to ask herself. She still had insatiable wanderlust, but being a teacher, an educator in her home country was putting treacherous ruin upon her dreams. The schedule, duties and hours were potentially exhausting. She sometimes worked on weekends, including some Sundays!

When Eddie fell up into the spot with everyone else, the number of attendees had reached around thirty people. Hiroko saw Eddie and tugged away at his arm after exchanging greetings with her colleagues and the sub director, assistant principal who arrived with him.

The attention heaved upon Eddie from Hiroko was disturbing to her suitors, in particular one science teacher who thought that his nerdy glasses made him adorable, cute, and cuddly to women the same as did his own mother. But he was dead wrong, and it caused him to be bitterly jealous.

When everyone arrived at the dining establishment, they were required to remove their shoes and use the slippers provided. The science teacher silently spied as Eddie peeled his feet out of his black spray painted Vans made to appear like casual but semi-conservative footwear. He waited until the *gaijin* skipped off with Hiroko in tow before he approached the shoe collection on the restaurant supplied shelves. When he was sure no one was watching him, he slipped a small condiment-size packet of mayonnaise inside one of Eddie's shoes.

Hiroko's other suitor was a PE teacher-slash-soccer coach with the true million-dollar physique that should have enabled him to be an international model, for many would have agreed that in their neck of the woods, he also had the handsome looks to match. This Mister Dandy had actually almost received Hiroko's generous blessing to enter her gateway to coition. This union opportunity, however, would be ruined for all eternity as the result of a phone call from his wife. She then would ever hate his guts.

For months he had been hounding her, asking her out, practically begging her for a date. As a relatively new teacher still, her schedule was hectic, her free time limited. She admitted that he was attractive. His black windshield wiper eyebrows always sharply positioned at ten and two, made him appear angry and happy when he smiled. His glistening thin lips beamed a pleasant white toothpaste smile in which you could tell he had orthodontist work in the past. He was always crisp, fresh, and scented well even on hot, brisk summer days and was perennially rugged. Still, he wasn't in Hiroko's league.

By now, Hiroko had been through all sorts of hell and no pretty-boy jock like the ones she encountered in her past was going to dupe her again—she claimed. In high school, people used her for her special ability of English language power, answers to homework problems; in America, they took advantage of her unsettled nature. So the PE teacher soccer coach was like the typical playboy—no more, no less.

Dude begged one day for Hiroko to come outside and check out his brand-new, fancy black Audi 5000. Hiroko hadn't bought her car yet at that time, and she was impressed but tried to hide it. Immediately, her mind made her say to herself since he liked her so much, why not see if he would allow her to drive it. Like a sucker, he did when she asked him. They drove all the way to Sakai City, and he met her mom, Eriko Okada.

Eriko took an instantaneous liking to the man, lavishing him with accolades, offers to stay for dinner, and any effort to make him aware that he had her approval, going so far as to expound upon Hiroko's uxorial availability. Both Hiroko and Dude would laugh, change the subject promptly, and say that they had to get back to Hannan City.

Finally, Hiroko acquiesced to a date with him, having received a wink and a nod from her mother, figuring that if she settled for a Japanese man, it may as well be a striking one. He picked her up, and they had dinner at the famous Spaghetti Factory in Kishiwada City. To impress Hiroko, the PE teacher soccer coach did not indulge in any alcohol. He never drank on the first date because he wanted women to believe the lie that he was trustworthy.

After dinner, they took a drive to *Pitchy-Pitchy Beach* to admire the night view. The area had a famous Lovers' Lane near the shore. Dude wooed her immensely, spinning his sad-sack tales about his life and how hard it was growing up with no mother and assorted bullshit, while a milky-voiced Ken Hirai jam whined a seeping melody from the car stereo speakers. As a youth, Hiroko too had been raised largely in part by her grandparents as well, so that much she found in common with him.

Hiroko was caught off kilter with her guard down by his charm. She didn't trust her gut and dismissed him like the experiences abroad taught her she should have. His charismatic urging convinced her that she could at least give him an F, and not the kind that signified a bad grade. The night had gone relatively well, so it did not seem such a prelude to a relationship was unrealistic. After all, she too had her needs and desires to be intimate with men.

The PE teacher soccer coach leaned into Hiroko's face, and they engaged in a deep, freaky wet kiss that got his juices flowing. True to his assumptions, Hiroko—Miss Chipper and Prissy while at work—was an undercover freak hussy, and he couldn't wait to get it on. He suspected that he was home free.

He would have been, had he not made the mistake of taking Hiroko to the Surf Hotel in Hannan's neighboring city to the north Sennan, which was right across a short bridge from the former. On the Hannan City side of the bridge sat his brother-in-law—his wife's brother—and his family inside of a Gusto Family Restaurant, situated on Highroad 204.

This brother-in-law recognized dude's flashy, inherited Audi as it passed the storefront glass window facing Highroad 204, bound for the Onosato River and bridge. His eyeballs followed the car all the way across the bridge and pull sharply left upon its initial entry to Sennan City, into a service road accommodating the gaudy Love Hotel strip.

Curious as to why his sister and her husband of slightly over a year would need to use a hotel when they had their own home that his family had helped to make the down payment on, the dorky brother called his sister up, only to find that she, of course, was not with the PE teacher soccer coach husband of hers.

Immediately, the wife called up her wayward hubby and jammed a wedge of interruption slashed between him and Hiroko when intercourse was literally about to take place. Eagerly moistened and awaiting the dude's swollen stiff insertion, Hiroko's legs were spread apart like edible, fleshy triangles with a treasure in the center, while he fumbled away, trying to extract a condom from its wrapping.

His phone, he had neglected to place on Silent mode, chimed away on the service table beside the king-sized bed. He scowled in frightful terror, to the point of at the brink of tears in recognition of his home telephone number on the phone device's indicator. Perhaps the wiser thing to do would have been to not answer, but in his reasoning, he could not ignore the unnerving timing of the call and was compelled to answer it. Hiroko frowned and drew the covers over her bare nether region while he took his call.

On the phone, the dude's wife asked, "Where are you now?"

Dude was like "Honey, I . . . I'm still at work. What is it?"

The wife replied, "Really? This time of evening? I thought you said that there was no soccer practice this week?"

While the PE teacher soccer coach was raking his numskull for an excuse, Hiroko was already getting the picture. Anger and resentment festered in her chest, set to boil in a matter of minutes. This man had gone through such great lengths to convince her that he was honest, splendid, and not a cheater, that he was a one-woman man and his grandparents had bestowed upon him all sorts of morals and scruples with bar of soap clean credentials.

In seconds, the PE teacher soccer coach was sweating, and his once enchanting eyes transformed into tear-bulging orbs inflated with panic. On the phone, his wife said, "My brother said that he saw a new Audi 5000 that looks like yours, and it pulled into the Surf Hotel a short while ago. I'm preparing to go there now. Has anyone stolen your car?"

And just like that, consternation set upon him. He leapt to his feet and scrambled to shove his legs inside of his sweatpants. He aimlessly offered Hiroko a hurried excuse that could sound like nothing other than a lie—one that Hiroko refused to even care to hear while he refused to look her in the face while he uttered it. It was painfully clear to her then, for why else would he have chosen to take her to a love hotel instead of his own home? Because his wife was there!

She dragged herself from the bed and started getting dressed, angry more at herself for being gullible to his deception rather than at him for his attempt to trick her. She spared him the agony of waiting for her to get dressed so they could beat a hasty escape and said that she would call a cab. The dude feebly accepted her generous understanding and continued with his half-assed apologies.

Hiroko tightened her lips and strained an angry smile. The PE teacher soccer coach belted away in his car and sped back across the Onosato River Bridge, returning to Hannan City. He ran a red light in haste, in the event his pregnant wife did make good on her threat.

Silently, Hiroko would hate his guts after that night. Although professionally, she would greet him cordially at work, and they both carried on as if the night had never happened. Feeling as if he had dropped the ball in a major way, he elected to not try and mend the relationship in hopes that she would offer him a second chance and become his side piece. This was a pipe dream shattered by the arrival of the American teacher, Eddie, whom he now despised.

Eddie was eagerly awaiting the start of the evening's festivity unaware that he was in the sniper's scope of two enemies. Both men were hungry for the attention that Hiroko was feeding the already-overstuffed foreign teacher.

At the Nomikai affair that evening, to decide the seating arrangement, those in attendance drew numbers out of a decorative *hyotan*, or hollowed gourd. This number on a slip of paper would correspond to a *zabuton* (***16**) at a place by the long rectangular cafeteria-style table.

Knowing ahead of time that this system was going to be utilized, Hiroko had deftly manipulated both her and Eddie's seating by palming the numbers of their arrangements. When Eddie drew his number, quick and furtively she snatched it from him and dropped it back inside the gourd and passed it to the next awaiting person to throw all eyes off what she had just done. She would then pass dumbstruck Eddie the slip of paper which had been in her palm the entire time and had never been inside of the gourd. It read "**17**" and he crawled on the tatami floor beside the table along with others searching for their places as well. Hiroko already had the slip of paper with "**18**" scrawled on it surreptitiously concealed in her hand when it dipped back into the gourd. To everyone around, it appeared like "Wow, what a coincidence!" that numbers in succession which meant they, Eddie and Hiroko, would be sitting next to each other all night.

It looked like a miracle of fate, one that would have seemed to read "destiny brought them together," but in reality, it was Hiroko's cunning and guile. Jealous eyes burned hatred for Eddie in the visual sockets of the PE teacher soccer coach and the science teacher, but to Hiroko's private joy, situated meters away on the other side of the room.

Three hours later, the party was in full swing, but unfortunately, it had to come to a close. The microbus had a meter running and a timed scheduled for departure because there were multiple destinations in which to deliver the staff members returning to their homes or in close proximity of their homes.

Eddie had enjoyed his fill of sashimi, tempura, bottles of beer, wine, and sake. Like many others who had imbibed, he was tore up laughing and singing in gaiety from a special contraption set up for karaoke. Eddie had even grabbed the mike and sang some Neil Diamond and Elton John ditties. The only thing that disappointed him about these types of outings was that they always ended too soon. It was barely even 10:00 p.m.

Stumbling his way to the bus, Eddie was cut off by Hiroko as he neared the exit door. She had ducked the science teacher and dodged the PE teacher soccer coach—whose plan to offer Hiroko a ride home was foiled and thwarted by her decision to not drink that evening—and had hid in a secluded section designated for waiting customers, cigarette machine, and public telephone. Clutching Eddie's arm as he appeared to be limping due to intoxicated impairment, she fretfully asked if he was all right.

Eddie threw his arm around her and very cheerfully stated that he "couldn't be better, Hiroko-san!" And casually he leaned into her ear and nibbled at it before laughing drunken murmurs which translated only to benign sounds. As meaningless they may have been to the ears of discernment, to Hiroko's sensual receptors his utterances sent vibrations pulsing down her spine, triggering a quickened heart pace. She shivered as if it were freezing cold out, but she was anything but frigid. She looked about to see if anyone had noticed them, but luckily, no one had. Everyone was, for the most part, still in postprandial inebriated euphoria. As far as she could tell, everyone else was too engaged in their own individual conversations to have spotted them.

It had been her plan all along to offer Eddie a ride after this gathering. So far, her plan had worked from start to finish essentially, from her handling of the seating arrangements to now this. She then told Eddie, "If you want, I can take you to your home. Or you can ride the bus back with the other teachers, but I don't know . . . what time it will arrive to your home. I think it will be late, because the driver has to take many people, and also, you maybe have to walk home from your station, Hakkotskuri, right? I can take you directly home, if you like. It's no trouble."

Hiroko turned, and a troubled look creased her face. The PE teacher soccer coah was approaching. She tried to lead Eddie outside to the parking lot before they were noticed. Eddie, who had been floundering around trying to slip into his Vans almost fell and pulled Hiroko along with him. Regaining his balance quickly, he complained about his feet feeling squishy as he struggled to keep pace with Hiroko who had speedily trotted ahead in the direction of her Demio.

A lesser drunk, big-mouthed custodial employee threatened to blow Hiroko's cover as she yelled out to her as she pushed Eddie into her ride as if he was an injured athlete escorted to an ambulance. Craftily, Hiroko managed to communicate to the old woman that everything was "fine" and that the English-speaking foreigner in her care was in need of a special medicine that she would take him to get. She managed to shake off the old hag, but not the PE teacher soccer coach, and he watched as Hiroko's car tires burned a dusty trail out of the parking lot, brimming with hatred.

On the drive home, Hiroko took the scenic route using the Kishu Kaido Highway. The starry night sky made Eddie think of the solar system. On Hiroko's CD stereo, Mai Kuraki could be heard chirping harmony about "Love Day After Tomorrow," putting her in a hopeful mood. Eddie appeared to sober up rapidly, as if suddenly realizing that the moment was becoming all too real. The two of them, he and Hiroko were here and now and alone. Only the night could see them, and they were secluded further by the shield of a vehicle.

There had been a long silence aside from the occasional humming and singing Hiroko would do in tune with what she had playing on the stereo. All night they had been talking, seated next to one another at the izakaya. Hiroko had poured glass after glass of beer into his mitts like a dedicated, devoted and loyal companion, the kind of actions Liz would detest.

In Liz's mind, when women tended to men in the ways Japanese women did, she felt that they were being unnecessarily submissive in a chauvinist, male-dominated society. When she saw them engaging Eddie in such treatment, Liz would succinctly demand that Eddie serve himself and that, as a man, he need not be pampered, while Eddie on the other hand, enjoyed it. For him, nothing could top being treated like a royal king. That night had not been any exception. Hiroko had long ago won him over, sealing it when she brought him dinner when she thought he was sick. His dilemma, dormant yet torturing him in constants, was being too averse and overcautious about women due to past rejections and humiliations.

To break the silence, Eddie finally decided to do so by asking an idiotic question like, "Are you taking me home now?"

As if struck by lightning, Hiroko jerked upright as if she had been hastily awakened from a nap. The ridiculousness of the inquiry took a moment to sink in. "Huh? Um . . . Yes? I mean . . . don't you want to go to your home? Did you want to go to someplace else?"

Eddie said, "No, it's just . . . just I didn't recognize this route yer takin' . . . or maybe, shit I dunno where the fuck I'yam . . . hee hee haha!"

Hiroko said, "Sorry, I don't usually go out to such a place like where we enjoyed tonight. I'm not originally from around here either, so I don't know many of the back roads like the other teachers."

"It's not a problem at all," Eddie said, trying to recover himself to normal faculties. "In fact, I think I enjoy ridin' in yer car. I do so much walkin' around it's nice to be driven for a change. Dang it, I miss my old Nova! Aw hell, I couldn't drive it in Japan anyway. You guys drive on the opposite side of the road and all, but I sure do enjoy hitchin' a ride with you, though."

Hiroko said, "I'm happy to hear that, Eddie-san. I am happy you are riding with me too."

As if he had preplanned the night's events anything but accordingly, Eddie remembered that there was nothing to drink in the crib in the event that Hiroko would come up for a nightcap. He asked her to stop at a convenience store, and she obliged. He grabbed a six-pack of Asahi Beer, a big bag of chips, and two soft drinks. Hiroko had followed him into the store and provided him with a basket to place his items inside; loyal companion as ever, she carried it along as he continued shopping.

Coyly she laughed. "I am so envious of you. I wish I could drink as well."

Eddie froze. He said, "I didn't know you were a drinker!"

Hiroko's face seemed alarmed as she replied, "No, of course I like drink. I love wine or *ume-shuu*. I just cannot drink tonight because—"

"You're driving!" Eddie finished. Then he said, "Yeah, I see . . . well, maybe we can drink . . . over at your place?" He did it! Eddie initiated taking things to another level with her. There was no turning back for him now.

To Hiroko, the thought had never occurred to her at all, but it had made perfect sense. So much so she did not question it. She about-faced and selected a cheap, twist-cap bottle of wine and some baby cheese. Eddie was at the counter paying for his stuff, and Hiroko wondered if he was fully aware that he had invited himself to her house, in basics?

When everything was paid for and they were back in Hiroko's Demio, strapped up and ready to roll out, Hiroko felt the need to confirm the destination.

Now it was her turn to ask a seemingly silly question, which was, "So . . . you want to go to my place?"

She had made it seem so casual when she asked it almost threw Eddie off. He said, "Well, yeah, if it's OK with your folks?" Assuming that Hiroko lived with her parents or her family, an aspect of Japanese society and culture he had read about, whereas daughters remain living with parents until married.

Hiroko chuckled. "It's OK, don't worry about that."

She did not bother to mention it to him that she too resided in an affordable housing development for municipal and government employees. Unlike the spying eyes that abounded at Eddie's apartment complex, Hiroko's spot was crawling with an overabundance of denizens, too many faces—like a city within a city—too many people to be noted or remembered. The night was also an inexhaustible cover for clandestine movement.

When they reached Hiroko's place, the long-awaited inevitable happened, and it did not take long for the two of them to get cozy. The mood of the evening was nearly ruined when Hiroko came close to retching at the pungent stench of vinegar and rotten eggs that "noseblind" Eddie didn't detect when removing his shoes to enter her home. He tracked putrid mayonnaise stained footprints on her shiny wood flooring, and it was difficult to mask her disapproval.

"Did you step in something?" she asked him.

Eddie said, "No, no way. Not that I can recall. Why?" Hiroko directed his attention to the oily step tracks on her floor that followed Eddie to where he stood. He looked at the bottom of his socks and found a flattened, empty packet of mayo glue stuck to his sole. "How'd that get there?" he wondered aloud as he handed it to Hiroko.

"Maybe you should remove your socks," Hiroko recommended as she placed the item he had passed her into a garbage bucket.

Eddie took off his socks as Hiroko advised. She watched him shuck his footwear and wondered if he would consider a shower. She decided to wait, collect his socks and placed them inside of a plastic bag from her kitchen. She shifted gears and tried to calm her nerves by having a taste of the wine she had bought and relax for a while.

The apartment was roomy, a two-bedroom spot with a living room that had a soft, quilted futon sofa bed, positioned before a 32-inch Sony color TV. They sat and watched a Disney video *Alladin*. It was the first time Eddie actually sat down and watched it reel to reel. By the time the song "A Whole New World" came on, Hiroko was piqued tipsy from the wine. The mood was interrupted abruptly by serious talk.

"Eddie what's your dream?" Hiroko asked.

"My dream?" He stared at her from the corner of his eye. Right about now, he wished he had a cigarette or a joint. Preferably the latter, but he had neither and his alkie utopia was inching to crash into a writhing queasiness.

Hiroko said, "Do you want to stay here? In Japan, I mean, forever? What is your goal in your life here? Will you be English teacher? What will you do? Are you and Elizabeth-san going to get married? If you get married, will you remain here in Japan?"

The questions rained on Eddie like rapid-fire bullets. Each one ripping to shreds his ability to definitively answer as he was ill prepared to. Not having given it serious thought himself was the glaring culprit, he realized.

With honesty as his only scapegoat, he said, "I guess I never gave it much thought. I mean, I did think about it, but I guess not as seriously as I shoulda', or enough to answer the questions you're asking.

"As for me and Liz . . . well, we, uh . . . we've been together for quite some time. I guess you know this, but I've never told anyone until now, and that someone I'm telling is you.

"Y'see, I never planned to ever even come here to Japan. Weird, huh? Sure, I had some underlyin' interest in Oriental culture, the Far East, and the awesome *anime*, but come here to work? To live? That thought had never crossed my mind. Not in the least. Before we came, I had just recently lost my gig at a video store where I was assistant manager, then I worked a shit job delivering pizzas to shady, wetback neighborhoods of LA and things became dangerous. As a college grad, I'm thinkin' this is what I slaved four and a half years to earn for a career? My options didn't seem plentiful by any means!"

"Plentiful?" Hiroko copied his word. "I forget what it means . . ."

Remembering the need to dumb down his lexicon as to not go too far over Hiroko's head despite her stellar comprehension skills, Eddie explained gently, "*Plentiful* means, lots of options, or choices. For me, I did not have a lot of choices. I was a liberal arts major, y'see."

Hiroko pretended that she fully understood what liberal arts encompassed while she listened to Eddie continue explaining himself to her.

"So one day, I come home and at the same time Liz arrives, and she tells me how she bumped into one of her gay ex-boyfriends. This homo tells her about a lucrative and promising job opportunity working here in Japan. At first, I was like, nah! That can't possibly be the career for me!' But Liz, y'know . . ." He shook his head briskly and sighed. "Liz can be so . . . persuasive."

"Persuasive . . ." Hiroko mimicked him, her highly weaponized brain data checked word definitions as she tuned in to Eddie's every sentence.

Eddie said, "Liz had a very . . . aggressively convincing way about her. She is so persistent and swaying. She's used to getting her way. She's the regular, spoiled, rich, brat—farm girl turned valley princess—she's always got to be in control. And just that's what it was. She decided we should come to Japan, and I agreed.

I basically followed her. Our plan was to save up enough money for a place of our own, gain credentials working here for our resume to find jobs doin' gawd knows what back home, but find jobs nonetheless, not depend on our parents, and eventually get married."

Hiroko choked. She didn't know why she was about to cry. The wine-induced somber mood hovered within the moment in time Hiroko was rescued from by the romantic movie.

"So you followed Elizabeth here, to Japan?" she asked.

"I suppose so," Eddie replied. "I didn't have any intention of comin' here at all. For all I know, I'da stayed working at the pizza shop till I was either hopefully promoted or some spic would murder me when I ventured to the slum deliverin'. Otherwise, the thought of me ever comin' here outside'a long shot of me traveling to Japan for a vacation or somethin' hadn't ever crossed my mind.

"The chance happening, a meeting Liz had with some guy she used to date, filled her head up with the idea that she came and laid on me. Next thing y'know, here we are, thousands of miles away and guess what? I don't regret it all. Not a single bit!"

Hiroko seemed to perk up as if energized. She said, "You don't regret? What, coming to Japan?"

"Not at all," Eddie reaffirmed. "In fact, I'm happy that I came here. Coming to Japan is probably the best decision I ever made. The best thing that has happened for me, I'd bet. The people here are nice, friendly, and welcoming. All the crap I've heard about this country bein' so xenophobic is a pile of poop.

"The culture, the history, and the traditions of this place make it not only exotic but also a fascinating and wonderful place to live. The air is so clean, no smog or air pollution. At least not like LA. I mean, don't get me wrong, I still love my California, but I haven't had a single moment of homesickness. The life here is so . . . healthy, so livable! I never thought I'd hear myself say this, but I can't imagine myself living anywhere else!"

Absorbed and somewhat beguiled by Eddie's talk, Hiroko felt she could understand the way he felt because she shared the same viewpoint about North America, although she secretly acceded that the United States was fabulous, but the terrain was somewhat dangerous, while Canada was beautiful, had nicer people, but horrendously boring and bland compared to the States.

Hiroko said "So you never want to go back to America? Are you serious?"

Eddie replied "Well, I guess eventually I'll have to head back, right? The Program has a two-year maximum stipulation for its participants."

Hiroko said, "You can get a job working at a conversation school, like Elizabeth-san, right? That is what a lot of foreigners do, after they quit their job as an ALT."

All too familiar already, Eddie agreed. "Yeah, I know, but I don't think

I'm as ambitious as Liz." He shook his head, stared at Hiroko's feet. Her toes were painted candy apple red like her Demio. Her legs were blemish-free beige eye stimulants causing his nature to rise by the minute. Seated next to him on the quilted sofa, her skirt had hiked up to mid-thighs during the period of time they had sat watching the movie, chatting, and drinking. As the distance between them gradually became closer, it became clear to Eddie that there was still something on Hiroko's mind, because the green light to intimacy was still being halted by her facial expression bearing a look of caution.

She said, "Elizabeth, she is your girlfriend, or fiancée now, right? Are you planning to marry her?"

It was a serious question. One they both knew needed to be asked, Eddie couldn't deny it. After all, if he were to be married to Liz someday, the current situation in which they found themselves entangled would be considered a sketchy predicament. One that was frowned upon in their established societies.

However, Eddie said momentously, "To be completely honest, I'm not sure about that anymore. Not the way I used to be. A lot has changed between she an' I, and . . . well, my time and her time—our time together might have run its course." Following this statement, the silence was deafening while time seemed to tick slowly as the stroke of midnight approached. Their faces drew close, lips touched, and then it began. The act of corporal intimacy was consummated by the joining of their two bodies. On the sofa, then the shower, and finally in Hiroko's bed. Eddie clocked Z's that night with the taste of his new Japan doll in his jib to sweeten his dreams.

***

The following morning, sunlight wedged aureate beams through cracks of Venetian blinds into Hiroko's room. She and Eddie woke up together in each other's loving embrace. Eddie felt unburdened as if he had slept for a hundred years and was relieved of debilitating fatigue. Hiroko kissed him gently as she rose from the bed, slipped on a silky shawl-collared lace-trimmed lime-green modal kimono robe. Eddie's morning boner stirred curiously in bed as he spied Hiroko's alluring and enticing bareness in the see-through garment. She wasn't the full figure that Liz was, but shapely still in her own way, lesser to tussle with, unlike trysts in bed—when Liz conceded to put out—with Liz, which were more like wrestling matches than love sessions.

As if she could read his mind, Hiroko returned to the bed after putting a teapot on the stove flame. She untied the lace straps of her robe and mounted Eddie like a hobby horse, putting his erection to good use, riding them both to ecstasy once more. By the time the teapot came to boil, so did Eddie. The back of his head collapsed deep into the cotton pillow, feeling like he had died and had ascended to heaven.

Unlike Liz who most often got her extraordinary freakish thrills from playing sex games with him, Hiroko spread her sunshine with no time for delay to brighten his night and day. In turn, Eddie consumed her gracious reward for him like a ravenous beast of burden. Finally. He had got a taste of another flower's nectar and found it instantly gratifying. Not only did he proclaim it "tighter", but the entire affair also seemed more of like what lovemaking was supposed to be—an act of love, not a grappling contest.

Hiroko returned to the kitchen and prepared to make breakfast. She told Eddie he could stay in bed while she went about her "duty." Strangely, Eddie's mind pondered that he could count on one hand, during the four, almost five years they had been together, the times that Liz had ever cooked anything for him resembling breakfast. Most of the time, they either bought it or skipped it altogether.

By early afternoon, Eddie and Hiroko sat inside an out-of-the-way roadside tearoom near Hakotsukuri Genjo Temple. Before parting ways with Eddie, Hiroko too had her own web to spin.

She told him, "Eddie, this might seem strange to you, but I am not the typical Japanese girl. I know I seem like that to you maybe, but I do not share the same mind as most Japanese.

"My country, the people are so traditional, like you mentioned. Maybe they are too conservative? I don't know exactly, but I know myself, and I'm sure that I am not like most people. I consider myself to be more free. I asked you about your dream last night, but I want to tell you my dream. It is to travel again. I want to visit your country once again, but the next time, I want to be with someone, like you to take me around and show me your country.

"But it doesn't have to be just there. I liked Canada too. I want to go to Europe, Hawaii, to anywhere! I just don't want to stay only in Japan for the rest of my life. My point, travel and new things to discover is my life. But as a teacher in Japan, in a public school, we have very little vacation time. In fact, I was supposed to go to work today, but I didn't because I wanted to be with you.

"That's what I dislike tremendously about my country, Eddie. We have unspoken rules. I want to be free of those rules. I thought that my life would never change, that my destiny was to remain here forever with no hope of seeing the outside world other than here, but then I met you . . . and Elizabeth . . . my hope for a dream seemed somehow alive again.

"In Japanese, we have a word—*hitomebore*. It means "love at first sight" in expression. That is how I felt when I saw you that first time. You were so handsome, elegant, and distinguished. Elizabeth was beautiful to us as well, but you . . . you were like a movie star, like an already-famous person. It was difficult for me to stop thinking of you. And now, even though I am happy to finally spend time with you, I cannot help but feel both joyful, yet still a little embarrassed as well."

She reached across the table and clasped Eddie's hands. Then she said "I enjoyed last night with you so much. I never wanted it to end."

Eddie said sharply, "Neither did I! And you can best believe that I enjoyed last night with you too."

Hiroko squinted and exuded a light chuckle. She said, "I'm embarrassed, though. I'm a little ashamed because I don't want you to think I am a slut. I am not a slut, or the type of girl that always sleeps together with a man who is already married to another woman. You and Elizabeth-san are not married . . . yet . . . but it still does not feel right because you are still together, right? She is still your girlfriend, and until now, I had considered Elizabeth to be a friend, but I allowed my own selfish interest in you to destroy that." A tear appeared suddenly in her eye and bombed the table. She sniffed and wiped her face quickly.

She then continued, "And . . . as a . . . because of this, I . . . we cannot see each other anymore like this. You have a girlfriend, and this is a small town. If many people often see us together, especially like this, it cannot mean anything good. We must, see each other"—she sniffed—"only in a professional way, only at school..."

The thought of not being able to be with Hiroko ever again was too disturbing a thought for Eddie to consider now. As like that of a magic wand or enchanted whip, Eddie had in one night been stroked and strapped into a spellbound condition. It was as if Liz's innate witchery had become temporarily stalemated by some extrinsic sorcery wielded by Hiroko. In a mind constructed spiritual realm Hiroko had snatched Eddie's leash away from Liz in a physical world. Her warm flesh had stroked his tender organ until it spewed the Milky Way into her raw galaxy. Twice.

"Please," Eddie pleaded, "Hiroko, don't say that. We . . . should be together. I . . . have feelings for you too."

"But you are still with Elizabteh," Hiroko said, biting her lips. "I cannot be your side partner. I do not want to be your secret lover. I have too much pride to be that. If I cannot have you, and only you, to myself I would rather endure the pain of not having you at all."

"You don't have to say that" Eddie said as he enclosed her tiny hands within his. "Look, maybe you are right. Correct. I shouldn't string you along while I stay with Liz. I think it's you who I want to be in my future."

Hiroko's heart started beating like an uptempo house music rhythm in contrast to the mushy, dreamy soundtrack of a Disney flick that governed Eddie's emotional ticker pattern. Hearing Eddie talk the way he had was in itself music to Hiroko's ears, and as she stared into his baby blue eyes, she believed she saw sincerity. There was no drunken stupor he could have hidden behind at that point.

"Do you really mean that?" she asked him.

After a choked-up pause, Eddie said, "I do mean it. I'm gonna be with you. Me and Liz, that's something I think I'm outgrowing. We've . . . probably outgrown each other." He spoke as if he was under a hypnotic trance.

Hiroko, on the other hand, was growing livelier as his words supplied her with circulations of joy coursing throughout her being. They leaned across the table and kissed. The elderly barmaid smiled and paid them little attention as she removed their cups and dishes quietly from the table.

Hiroko then said, "I believe you, Eddie. But you must tell Elizabeth. In fact, we both should say to her. If we don't, it would not be fair to her."

"You're right," Eddie said solemnly, knowing that it was not going to be an easy thing to do by any means. In fact, with Liz, the threat of physical harm to him was not improbable. "Are you sure you wanna go through with this together? I mean, don't you think it'll be better if I broke it to her myself? You can't blame yourself for what happened between us. If...I was sincere about my relationship with Liz..then, I should never have been with you. So, it isn't your fault. It's my cross to bear, so it might be better if I told her . . . just . . . give me a little time."

Hiroko agreed. "Yes, if you say so, that might be better. Whichever you prefer, but I am just as guilty as you are. I admit, I fell in love with you even while she was announced as your girlfriend. I admit to my feelings for you while you were together. I take responsibility for the blame I am to take."

Eddie stared down at the checkered tablecloth for a moment and returned the eye gazing contest to Hiroko and nodded affirmatively. He had done hard things in his life, but none he felt would be as difficult as what he was planning to do. Elizabeth Candace Amberbush had been a special someone in his life. She had practically made him the man he was, but his mind was telling him that it was now time to let her go and move on. Now his affinity to soak up Japanese culture had him wanting to go to the nearby Genjo Temple and pray for courage to complete what he had to do.

45

EDDIE DIDN'T MAKE good on his word to give Liz the news of his decision, as told to Hiroko. As expected, he could not drudge up enough nerve to go through with it. Instead, he told Hiroko that Liz was "busy" and embellished his story with false details about how neither of them had the time to discuss the matter in the way that they needed to—face-to-face. Eddie too had an upcoming trip to Tokyo that he had to prepare for, and to his credit, he did try to convey at least that information to Liz before their alleged phone tag ensued over the next two weeks after his and Hiroko's evening together. This extended to a month whereas they would be missing each other's phone calls. Or, on the occasions one would answer, conversations would be limited to brief, modicum chats. Frequently, these would be Liz taking the opportunity to impugn Eddie for whatever reason, as always—even before he finally slept with Hiroko—and he wouldn't even bother to argue back at that point. His taciturn character while in her company caused her to believe that she maintained still some sort of upper hand in the relationship. The reality was, Eddie had grown tired of dealing with Liz's scolding and pettish rants. At times, he likened her to a motherly figure, or an older sister he never had, more so than his woman, fiancée, or future life partner. Despite lonesome feelings, however, he leaned toward focusing his energies on things other than her, involving himself more with his job and activities in his local community. Hiroko's submission to him enforced his choice. They continued to see each other at school, but there was no repeat love session because Hiroko was adamant about her own ultimatum to Eddie, which stipulated that Eddie inform Liz about their involvement. Eddie would beat around the bush somewhat cowardly.

In Osaka City, Liz went about her routine as usual. She too tucked Eddie comfortably away in her secondary thoughts as she became more involved with her own living situation and engrossed in her job. In the mail, she received a memo from HQ stating that she would be receiving a new roommate but got no details about who it would be, or when they were due to arrive. This irked her somewhat, but her hands were tied because she did not have the time or energy to try and get an apartment of her own, so she had to go with the flow. Her calls to Ruth Worth were not returned immediately concerning the available positions with the company that Eddie could possibly fill. She even attempted to speak to Worm about it, and he told her that she would have to speak to HQ, for he had little or nothing to do with official biz like that. His job was to be the immediate overseer of the foreign teachers at the local school branches he was selected to preside over.

In the meantime, Liz had decided that it was too much of a tedious process to deal with Tim the Duke and his elaborate system of ordering dope goods. She disliked having to wait for a certain day, usually Fridays, to meet him and often several other teachers and affiliates who had made purchases, and the taking of time to meet in elaborate but clandestine locations throughout the city. As such, she opted to deal with Luzio Silver and his people directly as she did when she ordered coke.

Luzio's delivery boys, Moose, and obnoxious Brad Cooper, would supply the detail to Liz that she could indeed cop other than C—that weed, shrooms, X, and other stuff were also available and with the latter, a twenty-four-hour extra-day notice wasn't needed. When she got hip to that notification, she boldly dealt with the gangster's henchmen directly and relied less on Tim.

Brad would continue to low-key hit on Liz, insisting on accompanying Moose if he had a delivery rendezvous with the ravishing California blonde. Each time they met he would habitually liken her resemblance to the latest Western porn star of his particular delight. This time, it was a new Heather Brooke, someone whom Liz had no idea who she was, as she seldom if ever had watched any X-rated films in the States or Japan. This she did not take much issue with, but his insinuation that Liz appeared to be gaining weight, she did. Not that his opinion mattered to her precisely, but it caused for her to feel a bit self-consciously aware the eyes of others saw her differently than she would herself. Admitting that she had slacked off going to the gym the past month, she vowed to thwart such raillery from guys like Brad and be more diligent about her fitness activity. The last thing she wanted to do was end up looking like Stephanie, who appeared to be blowing up steadily every day like a dirigible.

Liz gave Taffie a tab of X. Like Liz, Taffie too was a little chicken-shit to try it on her own but had a bubbling excitement about doing it eventually. Liz was told by people that if she were to take it, she had better do so on a day when she had no work the following day and drink plenty of water. Stephanie told her about a male teacher at the Kyobashi branch who had gone to work under its influence: He had a bad trip and started being overfamiliar with the Japanese staff there. He was dismissed for sexual harassment, but everyone knew the real reason why and what had caused him to act that way.

Taffie was still with both Deon and her sugar daddy, the Doc in Tokyo, the latter Liz had yet to see or meet but was aware of. Deep in her gut, Liz held a space of pity for Deon. He looked so much happier when he was with Taffie and appeared to her less menacing. He almost seemed normal. He was a person who could smile, laugh, share a joke or two and, simply put, seem down to earth. Although he was still evasive when confronted with Liz's inquisitive pokes into his background, he wasn't exactly the hoodlum in a suit and tie she originally suspected him to be. To her it was such a shame that Taffie was seeing another man still, and in addition, she would be entertaining men nights at the Dream Lounge.

Deon, surprisingly, was cool with Taffie's night gig at the lounge, Liz would later discover. Taffie gave her the details. He apparently knew about the *mizu-shobai* line of work and didn't have any hang-ups with it because his limited privy to that world had him thinking that women did not actually hook up with the male clients outside of work. He was only part right, and Taffie did not care to supply him with the other, darker side nor her major rich benefactor "boyfriend" in Tokyo. She also entrusted Liz, who had grown to be her *meilleur ami*, to let that remain a secret until she was at a comfortable place; so that she could break up with her Tokyo meal-ticket if Deon truly *was* the one for her.

Liz bought into Taffie's reasoning. She could understand, considering Taffie's past. But to her, it was clear that they were both crazy about one another. Their instant chemistry was detectable from day one, when they first met in Umeda at Tocca-Tte. Taffie's dreamy eyes brightened up at the mention of his name. She had to admit they made a splendid couple.

Then there was Liz's affection toward Taffie as well. She was still attracted to Taffie in the intimate way they had interacted once before. They would joke about doing it again, only, in a *menage a trois* situation with some other dude—an idea that didn't sit too well with Liz, as she was a little apprehensive about getting involved with strange men, and she was unwilling to share Eddie anymore like she had years back allowed him the carnal use of friends Becky and Mandy. The first and last time she had been in a threesome herself was in her high school days with Becky and some rival school hunk on a camping sleepover.

There were times when Liz wished that Taffie was, or would be, her roommate. Then she could have Taffie all to herself. Her lesbian feelings and tendencies would come and go like sporadic attacks, triggered by abbreviated meetings with Taffie, curtailed somewhat as of recent because of her schedule change and transfer from the Umeda School. Then it occurred to her that she and Eddie had not had sex since the night of Denore's disappearance a month ago, and prior to that, it had been months!

She had been so enthralled in her own affairs that she had neglected to consider the fact that intimacy was lacking in her and Eddie's relationship. She negligently dismissed the thought, assuming that they had been together so long that coition was not integral to their union. Oftentimes too, when they met up, they would generally be either too tired or smashed to complete the affairs, content with insane 69 acts, which frequently ended with Eddie's muculent erotic deposits prematurely saturating her jaws.

Sticking to her plan in the weeks that followed and the holiday season right around the corner, Liz blew off her coworkers and pals and hit the fitness gym. She had a night membership to Fitness Club situated between her crib spot in Bentencho and one of her work locations, Hommachi.

She still rode her bicycle to work, defying company rules that forbade such but took special care to ensure that she would not be discovered by paying for a bike parking lot, at the damage of one thousand yen a month, near the subway station. She would walk the rest of the way from the station as if she had used the subway, throwing off anyone who would spot her.

After work at Hommachi, she would diligently hit the gym on her way home. On days of inclement weather, she would resume using public transportation. This all went well until one night: Heavy rain pelted the city with intensity before she could complete the odd half-an-hour commute back to her home. With no end to the storm in sight, she resigned to leave her bike parked on the street she was not familiar with but assumed it would be safe because it would be alongside a seeming several hundreds of other bikes along the curbsides and locked it to—whatever it was—a pole, fence, gate, or street side railing. She had done this before, as did a lot of other people, because Japan was a "safe country". She had caught scoundrels in the act of trying to steal her bicycle once or twice but felt largely comfortable leaving it unlocked when she used it for trips to places in the vicinity of her dorm, like to the supermarket, the post office, or to the Thai massage parlor near the Kujo district, an area of town supposedly heavy with crime at the time. This time, however, it was a week before Liz was able to successfully locate where she had left her bike, only to find out that the bike police had snagged it. The cost to retrieve the bike from the impound was about the same price were she to purchase a new one, so she saved herself the trouble and went without a bike for a while, it caused for her to switch her workout days to Saturday and Sunday when she had more afternoon free time, as those days she would work earlier shifts as the Namba branch.

Continuing to dismiss Eddie's phone calls and messages, not giving them attention, they should have required, Liz would go swimming, attend aerobics and yoga classes, walk back to Bentencho from the fitness club, and if she had no plans to meet up with friends or coworkers like Taffie, Stephanie, or others, she would get a full body, oil scented massage at the Thai spot. Dangerous neighborhood or not, they had her feeling so good she would have gladly biked through a cave of hornets to receive the curative chirapsia that parlor provided.

The fitness gym was also an interesting place. There Liz would meet an abundance of Japanese women who were curious about her. They would constantly try to engage Liz in conversation, even though most of them who had the courage to approach her were lacking in astounding English ability, but they were friendly, nonetheless. Liz would receive biz cards, or telephone numbers to various J-chicks who insisted she take them, but Liz would never call and pretty much forget their faces when she left the workout floor. Sometimes, she would show up nights and be greeted by some woman who would have remembered her name, but Liz would have not the slightest clue who that person was. At the end of the night, she would have a collection of three or four names and numbers.

Occasionally she would be graced with the rare sight of foreign people like her at the gym. Mostly males: some of whom she could agree were "hunks". These men, however, did not seem to be interested in Western women like her, and did not shower her with attention in the ways Brad, or even the weirdo Kwame had. These were the guys who had that Brad disease, though, that were also shared by Keefer, Liz determined. The types who were so much into Asian women that they were no longer attracted to Western or non-Asians.

In a bizarre turn of events, some English-speaking Japanese men would try to hit on her subtly, but Liz would snobbishly feign inability to understand their speaking. It was a rude thing to do, but it tremendously reduced the number of unwanted guys like a Takuto who tugged annoyingly at her bra-strap. She momentarily entertained the thought of befriending one or two of the Japanese dudes so that she could introduce them to Stephanie.

Stephanie and Liz had been hanging out less outside of work those days because she had hitched up with Vicky and would be chasing Japanese men around. Liz had no desire to be in such company, nor have repeat episodes of Pink Carnation Bar aftermaths like previously, so she spent more time working on herself.

Liz continued to turn heads at work and outside. Still the epitome of Japanese beauty standards, to an extent, she charmed both coworkers, student customers, and random people on the streets, fitness clubs, and the hangout haunts. Her blonde, quasi-xanthous hair had grown in length, extending down her back, and nearly reaching the distended culmination of her rear bubble that had driven pervs like Kwame into temporary insanity. Takaro, the hairstylist, would essentially beg for Liz to allow him to cut it, but Liz issued him a hollow threat that were he to do so, she would never again grace his shop with her presence, and Takaro bitched up and continued his usual shampoo and treatment operation.

Her chlorine-cleansed swimming-pool-blue eyes were mesmerizing to nearly all Japanese men—school staff included—who were near her. On the occasions she had time to hang out with Stephanie, when her friend Michio—who still wasn't her official boyfriend—stood her up, she tried once or twice to dawdle in chat with some J-dudes, but soon discovered with a degree of disappointment that she was their preferable target above her burly coworker.

Worm pulled Liz to the side one morning at Namba and told her that she was one of the most popular teachers there and at Hommachi. The student customers loved her. Liz added to her lessons by attributing her buoyant personality and vivaciousness despite some days reporting to work with an obvious hangover ailment.

Some daring students of the salaryman business types would even ask her out on dates.

Unlike Vicky who had gone that route of dating her students, Liz stayed cohesive with the Bozack Company policy restricting socialization or fraternizing with student customers outside of work. Although she was just as guilty as everyone else in breaking nearly every other rule or code there was, to an extent, this was one in which Liz steadfast complied. It also gave her a good excuse to turn down suitors, better than pretending to be an arrogant, stuck-up foreign dame as how she came across to J-dudes at the gym.

In contrast, Liz could easily have been the female version of a Keefer, a Brad, or a Radley, or any male foreign teacher in Japan, who clung to their sycophantic female students, continuing to have a ball in their Oriental Paradise. Yet, there was nothing she found enticing or interesting about pursuing affinities with people who she could barely understand and likely didn't understand her either. Additionally, she took cultural differences into account. She had no intention whatsoever in becoming an obedient, passive, or submissive woman like she noted Japanese women to be.

Outside of Brad's goading about her "plumpness" in hourglass figure, Liz was short of taking notice to the effect she had on people. For, somewhere in her multifaceted patterns of ways, there still lurked a tomboy at the core, quickening toward studly, elegantly dressed lesbian inclinations. In addition, she was the commonplace sot and recreational druggie. This could not be ignored. Thankfully, her assiduous workout regimen kept her balanced. But for how long? She wondered while she hit the treadmill for a high-impact run.

46

RING! Liz was awakened by the sound of her dormitory's house phone. This usually meant it was a call from Bozack HQ. Drowsily, Liz slid out of bed and caught the phone on the fourth or fifth ring. "Mushy, Mushy!" Liz tried to answer the phone the way Japanese people did.

"Good morning, Ms Amberbush, I hope we've reached you at a convenient time," went the authoritative, brusque voice of Ruth Worth.

Liz responded in kind with a similar greeting but couldn't mask the atrabilious huskiness of her morning voice. It was fine though. She had wanted to speak with Ruth anyway. Besides, unlike other employees, she was not as intimidated by the commanding area supervisor.

Ruth said, "Ms. Amberbush, this call is to inform you that we would like for you to report back to the Umeda School. There will be a new teacher there that you will be asked to walk through and show him, or her, the basic operation on Saturday and Sunday."

Liz said, "So basically, you want me to train a new guy?"

"More or less," Ruth said. "In essence, he or she will be there to simply observe you while you conduct your lessons as normal. Then you can familiarize him or her with the student customers you teach there. Anything that would help him or her out so that their transition will be a lot smoother. You have been teaching at the Umeda School for quite a while on the Saturday schedule, so you would be best suited for this undertaking, and we would really appreciate it. You will receive a thousand-yen bonus for each class."

Big fucking deal, one thousand yen, Liz said to herself, but she replied that she understood what she was asked to do and acknowledged.

"Do you have any questions about the assignment?" Ruth asked.

"No," Liz responded. "It seems pretty cut and dried, but hey . . . yeah, is this for only Saturday, tomorrow?"

Ruth said, "Tomorrow and Sunday as well, the day after tomorrow, but only for those two days. Like I said, this will be just a walk-through, is all. It's basically to familiarize the new teacher with the weekend schedule operations at that branch. After that, you will report back to the Namba School and resume your shifts."

After that, Liz did not have any questions or concerns, but in the nick of time before terminating the call, remembered to ask about available positions and Eddie being on the waiting list.

Ruth told her, "He would have to call our personnel department. He already has the telephone number. As for your partner's standing on the waiting list for contact, I do not have that information directly, as it is not my department. However, he would have been contacted if his name was in our database. He— and only he—will have to call in and speak with someone. There are so many applicants, many new locations, placements, people desiring to be in certain locations. We try to accommodate all, but can only operate and function in the manner, which is beneficial to the company, as you know."

Liz said, "Sure, I guess, yeah. Well, thanks a lot. I'll be sure to tell you, but just in case. Can I have the hotline number to the personnel?"

Ruth supplied Liz with the information she requested. After she hung up the house phone, she found her Tuka cellular phone on her bedside table. Checking her received calls, she found one or two from Taffie, several from Stephanie, and none from Eddie. This made Liz angry. She felt certain that Eddie had received her recorded messages in his phone's voice box. She tried to calm down, realizing that her phone was over a year old and in Japan, now not considered top of the line. Her Received Call listings had a maximum of only ten names or numbers. Stephanie had called over eight times, taking up most of the slots, so it was possible Eddie might have called, but she wouldn't know because Stephanie had been calling so much in rapid succession. Still, Eddie wasn't answering his phone that moment when she called, so it was getting on her nerves.

Liz went to work that night and saw Stephanie. Liz didn't have to ask the reason for her burning up her line all night. Stephanie was all but too pleased to share her news. Excitedly, she explained to Liz that she and the Michio guy were officially a couple. She told Liz that the dude finally gave her a kiss on the cheek. For her, this was some big, earth-stopping news, but for Liz, it was a yawny, boring detail in Stephanie's life that she shared thinking it would have the big impact on others as it had with her. Liz extended her congratulatory blessings but couldn't reach the level of excitement that Stephanie exuded obviously.

That night after work, she called Eddie again. No answer. Another message of invidious nature was left by her in Eddie's message box. To blow off steam, she went to the gym and worked out intensely. She joined a fitness kickboxing class and in displaced aggression, nearly kayoed a gym staff instructor who attempted to hold her kick and punch gear.

Reasonably exhausted, she returned home by subway. After showering again, she rubbed her legs, arms, and elbows with apricot scented baby butter moisture cream while she checked her celly to see if Eddie had called finally. He had not. Liz felt a spear of rage lance deep into the center of her chest, incurring wrath for her man's impudence and chutzpah to ignore her summoning.

Looking at the clock, if it had not been midnight, she would have gone to where he was, just to give him a piece of her mind. She was thus determined to go see him as soon as possible. To make matters even more upsetting, Liz's phone had been in use the entire day and was then in need of a charge. It shut off.

Liz let out a growling tantrum of whimpers, calming down in time before she hurled the candy bar-sized phone against the wall and instead finding the plug and setting the device to have its battery charged. She wished then that she had not agreed to the task of training the new teacher the following morning. Had she not, she would have called in sick, or tried to use a vacation day, and then gone out to Hannan City. But she decided to go like she normally would, on a Sunday. For whatever reason, Liz felt that her performance from that point on might have reflected positive or negative on the decision to give Eddie a shot, as he was her employment referral as well. According to her last convo with Worm, she was told that she was probably the most popular teacher at the school. This had to be a good thing, she thought. She did not want to ruin Eddie's chances by being a problematic employee herself, then Bozack would be thinking Eddie too was a miscreant of the same ilk.

She knew what would calm her down. Grabbing her "potato chip" bag from a spot underneath the miniature chest of drawers on her bedside table. Her joint making ability was still sloppy, but she had gotten better at rolling, enough to get off a spliff before finally drifting off to sleep.

***

The next day, Liz reported to work in Umeda. Manager Hitomi Hasegawa was so happy to see Liz and greeted her as if she were a long-lost relative. She even gave the blonde Disney princess a light hug usually uncharacteristic of Japanese people.

"Hello, Elizabeth, I am so happy to see you again, we've missed you so much here," Hitomi said with her warm, favorite young grandmother face beaming at Liz like instant sunlight. "The students also missed you too. You were very popular with students in what few classes we've had here on weekends. But, unfortunately, because of the shift in schedules, rotations and teachers leaving the company, you understand, that the main office makes these changes . . ."

Liz reassured her that there was not a problem with her understanding. She said, "It's OK, Hitomi-san, I'm so completely aware. My roommate, Denore, she just up and quit. Then right after that, another guy, one of her friends, he quit too. Nobody has heard from them. So yeah, I know at least two teachers gone."

"Yes," Hitomi's face showed a glum, regretful look. "And there was also a teacher who was fired from Kyobashi. Did you know? He went crazy and started to lick the staff's hands. People think he was maybe on a drug, or drunk . . . but such a shame."

Expecting to see Taffie any moment, Liz was disappointed somewhat to hear that she was not there. She had taken another day off. Even as a part-time worker, she had apparently accrued some paid vacation days, or whatever was stipulated in her contract. As a result, Serge's transfer to the Tokyo office had been put on hold. Liz greeted him as he busily walked past her, clutching papers, folders, and the Bozack French text manual. He was somewhat dapper that day in a check trim dress shirt and silk, olive necktie. His cologne was a little strong, but it was manly and tolerable. Liz did not feel like a lesbian around him.

The new guy was a normal-looking older guy who looked to be in his early thirties. Russel "Call me 'Rusty'" Clark. His auburn-colored hair had the short-layered crew cut, beard, and mustache like a "Hollywoodian." He basically resembled a skinny Chuck Norris in a tangerine-colored shirt, light-brown khakis, knit tie to match and threadbare Pasadena Wide Bucks on his feet. His voice sounded like Paul Simon on some "Call Me Al" song when he informed Liz how she could address him. Otherwise, he was a nice, congenial guy from Tennessee.

The training with Rusty went well; he wasn't really a new teacher. He was just there to be introduced to the students Liz taught. Turned out that Rusty was more of a kid's or children's teacher than adults, and he needed some refresher tutorials. For Liz, it was the easiest money ever made. The unfortunate thing was the rate being so insultingly low for the "bonus".

Around 2:00 p.m., the English lessons slowed down to a halt. Liz and Rusty had a one-hour-and-a-half break before the final lesson at 3:30 p.m. Rusty wanted to grab a bite so he split for a while. Liz had already brought her convenience store booty consisting of apple, yogurt, rice ball, and water, so she was good.

Serge's antsy-paced stampeding around the office had finally slowed down, and he entered the teachers' space—a spoon-shaped smaller room of five sectioned-off dividers for a circular table, forming a communal desk. There weren't many French students, but what few they had took heaps of classes; as such the teacher's job could be trying. No wonder Taffie took a lot of "vacations" and had a yen for pot, Liz thought.

On the other hand, this time, Serge, now on a break, appeared worn and battered. He was tired from working all night at the Candy Box Club. Saturdays were busy nights at the club, and he had to work that night too. He was due for a hard weekend, Liz imagined.

Liz excused herself to make a phone call in private, visiting the corridor outside of the school. She rang up Eddie again. Her call went straight to the voice mail box. Liz didn't even bother leaving another message. Of course, he was going to quibble an excuse, but she was prepared to lambaste him with a verbal trouncing he would not soon forget. He would think twice before he ever avoided her phone calls, she thought, even though there was a tender side of her that wanted to give Eddie the benefit of the doubt. Maybe he went somewhere and had forgotten his phone, or maybe even lost his phone. The jury was still out.

Serge was sleeping when Liz returned. She saw him inside of the waiting room intended for the visiting students or customers. He was "manspreaded" on the huge, plush sofa with his leg hoisted on the backrest and the other leg partially on the floor.

Liz stared at him, started checking him out in the half dark, dimly lit fixture room. He was a handsome stud, Liz thought silently. He was Eddie's opposite. Taller, brawnier, more rugged, a better dresser, and his French accent made him seem even more exotic. Peering at his muscles, she saw how his chest poked out pectoral knolls through the unbuttoned top of his shirt. She surmised him to be the kind of guy who could knock the lesbian in her out of commission for a while. She stood close by fighting a mischievous urge to rub his crotch while he snored lightly, something she would have done to Eddie had it been him snoozing there. She laughed and then turned to leave the room, deciding it best to go have some coffee and a cigarette.

As she stirred about, Serge, who slept lightly, woke up. He rubbed his eyes groggily and said, "Oh! You startle me, Elizabeth!"

"You must've had a hard night?" Liz said attentively.

Serge said, "Almost every night is like this, but in the last night, there was big wedding event, and after they went to there, the Candy Box and we have to stay behind longer to clean up the place.

"Japanese—they cannot drink very well! So much mess, cleaning up their . . . their...how do you say it . . . *vomir, vomir?*" He made gestures with his wide-open mouth, finger almost on his tongue with a grimace.

"Yuck," Liz matched her facial expression to his, as if she guessed the answer to a charades game sequence she responded, "We say puke."

"Yes, they puke! I hate that. Anyway, we have to clean up mess like this," Serge said.

Liz remembered the horrid condition of the ladies' room when she and Taffie had gone there and could understand his disdain for having to clean up such foulness. She said, "Sounds rough. I don't know how you do it. Speaking of that, what exactly do you do there?"

"I am sometimes bartender, but often, usually I work inside of cuisine, but mostly bartending . . . oh." Serge rubbed his eyes again and stretched. He groaned and rubbed his stomach like he needed to use the bathroom.

Liz stated, "I'm goin' out for a coffee and a smoke. Y'wanna come?"

Serge laughed casually and said, "I am not really in a feeling for that kind of smoke. I wish to have *another* smoke."

"So do I," Liz said, if the tacit implication meant marijuana. Unfortunately, what little bit she had left, she had not brought with her that day.

She understood how he felt, though. Ordinarily, she liked to smoke a joint to allay the unpleasantness of hangovers but decidedly avoided doing so whenever visiting the Umeda School. Manager Hitomi may have been facile and kindly, but Liz didn't want to press her luck. Additionally, there were a lot of nosy people in the building that their school shared with other local businesses and firms. She could recount numerous occasions where random Japanese people from neighboring offices would try to start convos with Liz, or another teacher, while inside the smoking vestibule. Just her luck one of them would conceivably happen to recognize the smell of ganja were she to light up.

Curiously, Serge caught on to Liz's response and said, "Do you? Have it? The marijuana?"

In a whispery voice, Liz was like, "Yeah, but I don't have any of it with me now. Shit."

"I was only asking," Serge said. "I do not mean to bother you or anything like this, but I am saying that if you have it, I can buy, or, I would like to buy it from you?" He was making a statement but the way he spoke it sounded like a question in intonation.

Rattled, Liz wondered how it was that a guy like him, working where he worked, couldn't get his hands on some good substance. At the Candy Box, a person like Serge could have access to all the drugs and any nefarious recreational narcotics around.

"Don't you have anyone at the club you can get that stuff from?" she asked.

He responded, "Yes, I know of some people who have that one, but I don't always ask to them. I only like the marijuana, I do not much like the cocaine. I did this before, but it keep me awake too much, it not is good for me. I don't like the speed, or one that use the needle."

Liz said apprehensively, "Oh, heroin, I think . . . I don't do any of that stuff either. But hey, do you know a guy, he's Black, I think he's from . . . some country, I don't know, but he's Black, he has like, this long hair, slicked back in a ponytail..."

"Oh yes, that other teacher, Taffie's boyfriend?" he asked.

"No," Liz replied "you're talkin' about Deon. No, not him. He is American I think, and a little cuter. No, the guy I'm talkin' about, he's from South America, his name is Silver or something like that."

Serge's face changed dramatically at the mention of the name. He said, "Yes, I know him. He is banned from the Candy Box. He cannot enter in there anymore because his reputation. Everyone know of him. Monsieur Najaf, the club owner, he is my boss. He is very strict about bad people. He also keep a watchful eye on staff as well, including me too of course. So no one will do drug because they don't want Monsieur Najaf to find out. But like I said, I don't always use marijuana, but today, I would like because mine *estomac* . . . is pain and also have headache."

Liz sprouted imaginary nimbus of devil horns signifying wicked thoughts dancing in her dome. Promptly, she invited Serge to her apartment after work to have a smoke session. Since Eddie wasn't around, she figured she would see where an evening with Serge would lead.

Serge was like, "Really? Are you sure about this?" He suddenly brightened up and became attentive as if he was no longer in the sleeping or resting mood. "Is your boyfriend OK with that?"

Facetiously, Liz laughed and said, "No worries, my guy—the one you met— he doesn't live with me. No problem, he's fine. He really wouldn't care one way or the other." The latter part was a little on the dishonest side, but she was indifferent because no one was there to check her on it.

"Very well, then," he said, appearing relieved "Thanks you very much. I will finish at five thirty, is OK, yes?"

Liz grunted, "Damn, me and this new guy finish at around four thirty, but I guess I can stick around and wait for you."

47

WHILE SERGE WAS tending to his last two or three students for the day, Liz was free to go. Her "training" with the new Umeda branch teacher Rusty went smoothly, and his transition did not seem that it would be difficult. The manager, Hitomi, was dumbfounded at why she chose to stay around after completing her shift when it was obvious, as far as Hitomi could tell from her experience, that she was exhausted. It would not have been the first time, for Liz. In fact, she knew of all the times Liz had shown up to work hungover. She and countless others under Hitomi's watch would try to mask the fragrances of nightlife exuberance with *84 Spray* and the *Frisk* curiously strong mints, but the underlying scents of musty armpit odor, stale perspiration, and alcohol stains would linger. Perhaps some student customers could detect it as well, but Hitomi did not aggressively enforce rules. As far as she was concerned, she needn't be the *gaijin* teacher watchdog. All she cared about was having them inside of their human aquariums and teaching their lessons to the student customers at the designated times in which they were assigned. Veraciously, that's all Bozack School cared about too.

Compassionate as she was, Hitomi Hasegawa had discovered a method to madness, and that was to remain the gentle and warm person she was and extend that same humanity to others, even if they were senseless foreigners. As such, she would allow them to rest whenever they needed to, or if it was possible, depending on how slow business was on a given day. She was yet to be reprimanded by company higher-ups for the allowances she extended to the foreign teachers, giving them range to break or bend rules. In general, the bureaucratic rigidness she elected to not enforce. For many years she had worked for the company, practically since its inception, had quickly rose through the ranks early on due to her hard work ethic, and maintained a stellar record as employee and manager. She was lauded for her acumen of running every branch to which she was appointed with the type of efficiency that the company desperately needed. Because of this, she was a mainstay, and she pretty much knew it. That all stated, it still did not give cause for her to not feel a slight poke of uneasiness from time to time when she went out on a limb on behalf of her beloved *gaijins*.

Liz was one of her most recent adored pets, and aside from that one time she failed to call in sick the official way, she had a good evaluation. She was disappointed to lose her to the less attractive, scruffy new teacher. Liz's students would be disappointed as well. Hopefully, the HQ would transfer her back to Umeda. Seeing Liz and Taffie together, for her, was like watching a dazzling fantasy show portraying human lily flowers and forget-me-nots dancing happily. They were like the children she never had. She spoiled them too. So when Liz told her that day that she was going to nap out in the customer lounge—where Serge was sleeping earlier—Hitomi, of course, was cool with it.

The Tuka cell phone Liz used let forth an afternoon silence-piercing chime, crepitating throughout the school halls in echo. It was inside the outer breast pocket of her bomber hanging on a hat rack. Liz came from the ladies' room and recognized her phone's ring tone. She rushed to try and catch the call but failed to do so in time.

Arms akimbo in mock anger, Hitomi scolded Liz lightly as the pro-volleyball-endowed teacher lunged past her like a leveler in said game, trying to get to her celly. Dutifully yet not condescendingly, Hitomi reminded Liz of company policy: "Elizabeth-sensei, you must switch your phone to *manner mode* when you come to work. Or turn off phone completely . . ."

Liz apologized ungracefully, "I know, I know! I'm so sorry."

When she finally located her loud phone, she first adjusted the volume lower. She pressed in the code for received calls. It was Eddie! He finally called her back. In an odd way, she was awkwardly pleased that he did. At once, thoughts of how nice it would be for them to make up and go back to being love birds. Having drag-out shouting matches and then reuniting turned her so on.

Tout de suite she went back outside in the hall and tried to call Eddie back. She couldn't. The English-speaking recorded operator informed Liz that she was out of prepaid minutes! Now she was pissed at herself for neglecting to remember topping up her balance, but she was more agitated with Eddie for not calling her back. She pondered waiting a brief, torrid moment.

Curtailing her plan to take a nap, the sudden mission of acquiring a Tuka prepaid card became precedent. She dipped out into the Umeda, Osaka, streets which, even on a Sunday afternoon, was an incalculable human traffic wave in constant succession, tsunami size.

Jampacked stadiums full of Osaka people suddenly released in the Umeda district from portals of grimy subway holes, buildings, train doors, cars, coaches, cabs, and every conceivable crack and crevasse of panorama, like a can spewing swill after hit with buckshot.

Cars, buses, bikes, tricycles, and multitudes of human heads saturated the scenery. Trucks of every shape, size, and design imaginably possible lined the colorful streets like science fiction in excess. Even on quiet days, Umeda was still one of the busiest places in town to be, and Liz hated it. Even when she was with someone, like a Taffie, or a Stephanie, who knew the town well, she still hated clawing her way through the thick patches of people, Japanese and others, and the crisscrossing patterns of ways people walked. It was like a serious jungle. One chaparral that she still had not fully mastered in venturing.

Of all the cellular phone companies in Japan, the J-Phone which became Vodaphone, and that became legendary SoftBank; but in Liz's time, Tuka was one of the lowest, cheapest brands, and as such, it was popular with foreigners and students with visas that were low numbered years. Simultaneously, the problem was that finding their store locations was close to insurmountable. Usually, when Liz needed a card to update her minutes, she would get them from the place in Namba or another place in Den Den Town that Eric Cravens showed her and Denore. Today, however, she was far from there; she was in Umeda, she had no bike, and she did not feel like making the trip.

Enlisting the help of Hitomi, Liz asked her for directions to the nearest Tuka Phone Station Shop. Hitomi supplied her with some imprecise information based on the elder woman's defective knowledge, thus confusing Liz further, having all of her posturing and gesturing to one unfamiliar place after another along with "Turn left at the Maru Building, then cross the street and turn right at the Shin Umeda Hotel, cross under the Hankyu *san ban gai* shopping area. You'll see it next to the Tatsumi Building." Of course, every foreigner in Japan could not understand such impeccable directives on the first shot. And Liz was bound to have walked around all night long based on those rendered by Hitomi, unfortunately.

A kind Samaritan Japanese woman took mercy on Liz, who was nowhere near the destination she desired based on the instructions Hitomi had given, after seeing the theatrically pretty foreigner constantly double-checking a slip of paper and looking about frantically as if lost. The woman was a rare gem of Japan who could speak English and put it to good use by helping people. As luck would shine a luminescent smile upon Liz at times, or whether it was a privilege that other types of *gaijin* were not afforded, those who didn't fit the category of blonde-haired, blue-eyed, and female, she finally found the Phone Station shop for Tuka. It was so small it looked like a toolshed in a sea of skyscrapers.

She planned to buy two or three cards and accrue several hours of talking time. She couldn't. After dipping in her Louis Vuitton wallet, she discovered she was light. No Sanwa Bank in sight, and after the ordeal she underwent trying to find the Tuka shop, she was not about to try hunting for one. Instead, she copped all she could afford, which was the cheapest thirty-minute card for three thousand yen.

Wasting no time, she scratched the number off the back of the card and went through the digit pressing ritual of voice recorded commands involved with registering additional minutes for the celly. She went through all that just to receive the same fury-invoking voice recording of the message box.

Aggravated again, now more so than she had been that morning and the previous night, Liz began the epic trek back to the Umeda School. This time, she deftly retraced her steps and tried to recognize some of the sights as landmarks. When Taffie came back, from wherever she went with Deon this time, she made a note to get her to teach her some more of the back streets and shortcuts.

Miraculously, Liz made it back. Hitomi was smiling as if she had done a splendid job providing directions, but far from it. Liz surmised that the merry old woman would absolutely suck as a tour guide.

The good news was that time had advanced in such a way it was now at the end of Serge's shift. He and Hitomi had been in the school's lobby, waiting for her before the front welcome desk. When she told them where she had been, they could all share a laugh, but it failed to lighten her mood. She was still perturbed.

Serge teased, "You why not this one get, a real phone and not prepaid type?"

"It's cheaper I guess," Liz said as she squeezed herself inside of her taupe Tiffany & Co. bomber jacket.

Hitomi disagreed. "I don't think so . . . really? I think you should get a better phone."

Liz explained her reasoning. "Look, I don't really make a lotta phone calls, to be totally honest with you guys. And if I do, I just limit 'em to just brief conversations. But most of the time, I just call people, let the phone ring off long enough for them—the other party—to recognize my number on their phone, then they can call me back. See how that works?"

Hitomi said, "Oh, now I see . . . and you do not have to pay for the minutes if people call to you, right?"

Serge seemed to be growing impatient. A plaintive look crossed his face as he kept staring at his cheap, knockoff watch and finally said to Liz, "I am now finish. Shall we go?"

Liz shrugged and nodded. They bid Hitomi farewell, Liz's was ceremoniously longer with the hug for after tomorrow, it may be a while until she saw her again, or if ever.

As they were off, Liz expressed to Serge how she loathed having to return to the savage sea of people knee deep in each other's asses. He totally agreed as he seemed to dislike huge crowds of the conglomerate masses Umeda spewed, so they decided to spring for a cab.

Today marked the first time both Liz and Serge could talk at length. So enthralled in conversation they were that they didn't notice the taxi driver, an elderly gentleman in all probability in his sixties, wheeling the vehicle like a retired F-1 racer on main streets, but deliberately getting caught at red lights, hiking up the fare by keeping the passengers longer inside the cab.

Usually, the dirtbag cabdrivers would drive in roundabout circles and side street service roads to scam tourists or unfamiliar foreigners, but since Serge spoke to this cabbie in Japanese, the old dude did not want to risk driving the trickster route and discover that the *gaijin* was hip to his scheme. Instead, he just drove as if he was in a hurry, with impressive turns and honking of his horn, but on purpose would hesitate on the brake at the sight of a green light turning to caution yellow. Ironically, it did not even matter.

Liz and Serge were engrossed in conversation about Japan. It was the usual, a discussion of life before they came to the country, their impressions of the country, what their expectations were being in the country, for how long and why. This, that, and other things.

Only, Serge was not very forthcoming about his past. All he talked about was his plan to leave Japan in the future and relocate to Thailand. He confided in Liz that he was saving money to get an operation of some sort he did not care to divulge. This procedure could only be performed by a medical practitioner who resided in Japan. Liz did not press the issue. She felt he was a mysterious guy anyway, but his sort of intrigue caused him to gain appeal points for Liz and made him even more enchanting. For her, he was a likable guy, but was he likable enough to leave Eddie for?

This was in the back of her mind: could she have a sub rosa affair with a guy, as the jacked-up cab fare shined an amount that made both Liz and Serge scowl savagely.

Reluctantly, Liz dropped her last two bills and dreaded having to go to an ATM machine, which wasn't too far but ostensibly far without a bicycle. Serge waved her hand away and paid for the entire fare. She ruefully thanked him, but in the back of her mind, she was thankful to get a free ride home. *What a gentleman!* she exclaimed in silence.

Moments and a short walk later, they were at Liz's place. As she keyed in, she gave him a glancing look and said, "Please excuse my apartment. The place is a mess."

Serge said, "Do not worry. I believe I have seen place more a worse place. Any case, did you not have a roommate before?"

"Yup, but not anymore," Liz said as she entered her place, then danced out of her Christian Louboutin red-soled heels. "Come on in."

Serge entered the domain. He looked around as if he was impressed, particularly in the empty half side of the ample, broad room. Ignoring the dirty dishes in the sink and a few cans and cups on the round table of the kitchen area Serge was keenly interested in the lonely, bare bed that former roommate Denore used to occupy. He pulled off his size 12 John Lobbs and clunked them sloppily on the floor in the same manner Eddie would. Fortunately, Liz had her place smelling like Apple Pie potpourri and Shaldan Ace fragrance spray so it tended to eclipse his rancid foot sock emission.

He sat down in one of the chairs at the round table while Liz disappeared partially behind the wall she created by pulling the divider along its tracks to seal off the kitchen. "Oh, I wish how I could have an apartment like this," Serge said. "I wish I could live here."

"That can be arranged," Liz joked, but she was temporarily out of earshot. She had stuck herself inside of her closet where her clothes were, hanging up her jacket. She returned to the kitchen area with her bag of "potato chips." At any given time, she could have been holding sizzle ranging from coke, weed, shrooms, and ecstasy, and looking at her, no one would ever have suspected. So when she offered Serge a gold ball-sized collection of bud, his eyeballs could have jumped out of their sockets.

"This . . . is yours?" he asked as if he could not believe what he was seeing was real.

"Of course," Liz said, rolling her eyes humorously. "Like whose else would it be?" Then she sat down and whipped out a pack of zig zags. She tried to roll a pregnant fag but was almost immediately commandeered en mission by Serge, who showed her how it should be done. Of course, she was impressed with the way Serge ensured that the reefer was sealed by running it car wash style sideways through his moistened lips. Finishing the task, he placed the joint in front of Liz on the table and grabbed at the ball of weed.

He said, "How much money do you want for it?"

Liz said, "Gee, I dunno. I hate to part with my stuff. It isn't easy to come by. Plus, it's way more expensive here, as you know. So why don't we just do this . . . we'll smoke a little bit, I'll let you take some with you, and you don't hafta pay me anything, or you can owe me if you like. I'm not really a drug dealer, y'know."

Serge merely made a move for the spliff he had rolled up and took it, saying, "May I?"

Liz was like, "Sure," as she offered him her lighter. They lit up and started inhaling hard. Blowing smoke all over the place like hotboxing in the close confines of the kitchen. A billowing cloud of gray smoke hovered like a scene from a fireman's training course. It didn't take long before Liz's giggling commenced, something that happened a lot when she smoked with other people. Their faces would often seem to become warped, misshapen, and voices always seemed to s l o w d o w n . . . and sound like an old-school 45 record on low speed.

Serge added to the hilarity by performing quaint, unique smoke tricks; French inhaling, blowing smoke out of one nostril, and puffing donuts in the air. His John Travolta chin dimple seemed to pulsate and expand. Liz laughed until her guts almost dry locked.

Continuing the silly antics Serge pretended to eat the donut smoke and said, "Do you have something I can drink?"

Liz said, "Of course!" She went to her fridge and opened it up. Unsurprisingly, among the soy milk, bottled waters, juice, carton of ice coffee, Serge preferred one of the three tall cans of Kirin Beer. Liz took those out and offered him one. She joined him in drink as they cracked their cans open at the same time and performed a tiny toast. The joint had already burned to a crisp roach in the ashtray as Serge upended the can so that its bottom gradually faced the ceiling, quaffing the beer as if his throat suffered chronic xerotic spells.

Alarmed, Liz looked on dumbfounded but decided to respond with laughter in resolve. She had not seen anything like that since her raucous college days.

Serge then released a resounding belch that could have been a noise effect for a revving motorcycle engine in throttle. Liz's fit of laughter intensified to the point where she was tearfully pink faced. When she was able to compose herself, she asked if he wanted the last beer, and he certainly did say, "Sure."

He took the beer and pressed the issue about the weed. He kept reaching for the bag like a sneaky kid. Liz placed a beer in front of him and snatched her weed.

She said, "Just roll me a couple of joints and you can take the rest with you."

Serge was happy and excitedly revived. "You will give me really?"

Liz's head was zonked because the way he rolled the joint must have facilitated a stronger high, compared to how either she or Taffie had done it. In any case, Serge's beggy need for her pot was bringing her down.

"This is just this one time, though," Liz said.

Serge said, "*Merci-i! Oui.* How can I repay you, Elizabeth?"

Liz said, "Well, I really don't like parting with my good stuff. I sometimes get for my friends, but they're all girls. Chicks. Dames. But I'll let you have it since you're afraid of that Silver guy."

"I am not afraid of him. It is just I do not want to have a misunderstanding thing. Monsieur Tabriz Najaf does not like him. That is all. If I met with him, maybe he thinks I am same as my boss who do not like him. And also, in opposite way, my boss Monsieur Najaf, maybe he think I am involve myself with Luzio Silver. I don't need this kind of problem. I need a job. My . . . *un salaire* . . .

compensation, is not so high like is yours, as English teacher . . . so, I also need the club job, I cannot quit right now."

Liz laughed and said, "Aren't you supposed to be shipped out to Tokyo or something? I heard it's harder livin' out there, twice as rough as here in Osaka, or Kansai or whatever."

"Monsieur Najaf also have club there too. He is very wealthy man. My other worry. But not a worry. The Candy Box are all types of people. I never can know who are they. Maybe some can be undercover? Or secret police, something like that? I cannot trust many people, but I think I can trust you."

"Sure you do," Liz said.

She slid the weed bag and the papers and told him to roll the joints. Back returned her dizzy feeling as she drank the beer, smoothly gulping. The creamy aftertaste of the foam reminded her of semen sticking to the back of her tongue.

Thirty minutes later, they were both crazy zooted. Liz, unusually high and euphoric. Serge's appearance hadn't changed much, save for ruddy patches around his cheekbones, rubicund perhaps due to his glutton for the brews. Hoping that Liz had more, he rose from his seat to check her fridge to see. Liz didn't take well to people imposing on her in such a way, but she was in too good a mood to make a fuss. For years, her domineering ways over Eddie brought into existence a bolder and daring, more than average spitfire, and more intractable than typical Japanese women.

Liz got up and floundered over to the fridge where he was and playfully shut its door, informing him that there was no more beer. Serge cursed stiffly in French and then stared into Liz's eyes as she stood before him. There was a momentary pause in time suddenly, and an unexplainable numbness overcame her senses. She did not comprehend how her hand suddenly reached for the hip of his trousers. Her hand rubbed up and down his left hip until it curled around to his left cheek of buttock.

A dubious half smile crossed his face despite his doped-up condition, but before he knew it, he leaned forward and allowed his lips to meet hers. At that moment, Liz's thoughts of Eddie effaced. The deep kiss lasted for what seemed to be a long minute before it intensified. Groping one another in between tight embraces, locking faces before finally arriving at the idea to disrobe.

As each item of clothing was removed, they inched their way walking backward, drawing closer to the empty bed that Denore used to occupy.

Dismally, Liz did not feel much on the side of spic and span immaculate condition, and neither did Serge. After a diurnal schedule as of recent, she felt it necessary to tend to proper cleansing and cleanliness of hygiene. She fell back clumsily on the clean empty mattress, lifted her twinkling toes to pull her legs out of her pants. Serge tried to do the same by lifting his knees to free his legs, movements like someone in an aerobics class sequence. He stood bare save for his boxers, his partial hairy chest sinewy.

His intentions that day had not been geared toward the seduction of Liz, nor to be romantically involved with anyone. His aim had merely been to score some weed for him to smoke and dumb down the nagging headache and sour belly he had sustained from the wedding party held at the club he had worked the previous night, and he had to work again that night. He needed some medicinal relief of some sort for his other problematic conditions too, but until he could afford the prescriptive medicine, the marijuana stuff he felt would do the substitute trick for the time being. All things stated, Liz was never in his line of amorous fire.

To him, Liz was like the typical Western girl, beautiful, yes, but also very audacious, aggressive, and a tad bit unscrupulous. Although he found her sexier and titillating more so than the average woman from outside Japan, it was to no avail. He had an attraction to Asian women that leveled beyond normal, to the extent of psychotic. Nothing, not even Liz's allure, could redirect or distract his obsession.

Still, such a sensuously endowed honey as Liz was too good to pass up, he determined. He decided he might as well go for it. He was impressed by her curvaceousness, subtly muscular, but mouth dropping, buxom breasts, he mused as she wrapped the naked knockout sinister off-peach frame in an abundant, Pinzon heavyweight towel. He was somewhat aroused by how well she could hide and enclose her rack when clothed.

Playfully Liz half taunted when she said, "I'm gonna take a shower . . . why don't you come with?" Intoned incongruously seductive. Officially set to cheat on Eddie for the first time in their long-term relationship, she falteringly ignored that voice inside of her head trying to plead her boyfriend's case. He was too busy, he couldn't call her back because he might have lost his phone . . . no, because he called her back. He didn't leave a message, but he called her back. Still, the other voice stated that it was his mistake, then, if he lost his phone. And besides, here was now, and what was unseen by Eddie may as well not have ever been. In any case, she knew, Eddie owed her one regardless. She always would wield the Mandy and Becky threesome over his head. To shame him at the least. The hot steam of the shower and the smell of the Oriental Dragon Fruit Mist body gel fragrance saturated her noodle.

So, then Serge joined her in the shower, where they continued to fondle, kiss, grope, and caress while pausing at intervals to rinse water off each other after rub-a-dubbing in fragrant soap. Liz finally got a glimpse of his phallic weaponry and thought it to be impressive enough. He clearly had a girth advantage over Eddie, she ascertained after handling the subject. As she felt it become somewhat inflated, her intensified exhale signaled that she was looking forward to seeing how he intended to put his tool to good use. She wasn't quite as tall as he, so she had to stand on her tip toes to kiss his neck while offering his extension the same stroke she would give Eddie that usually launched him to erotic high heaven.

Serge winced as if he were in pain. Liz saw his body jerk and a delicate grimace on his face, so she let go and allowed him to touch on her. They continued to play around for a few minutes before Liz felt she was ready for another kind of heat, steamier than the shower. She excused herself, telling him, "Don't use up all the water!" Then she grabbed up her heavyweight luxury towel and left.

He shot her a sanguine confident look then shut the curtain again so he could pretend that he was washing off the rest of his hairy body. He was trying to will his member to stiff cohesion. In usual circumstances with nude sexy women, he would have already been cemented and firm in his resolutions, but there was something about women of *la race blanche*, and even ones like Liz, who did not arouse the same tension in him! He began undertaking the task of stroking himself, masturbating, in hopes that he could rise to the occasion. Nothing seemed to work.

After an unspecified collection of failed minutes, there was no change in results. He abandoned this mission and had expectations of Liz applying oral administration to his needed area, as his preferred Asian sex partners would, whether he "needed" it or not. When he returned to the room though, Liz was already in her own bed. Sleeping. Snoring like a bee, in fact.

Several minutes earlier, Liz fell onto her bed after perfunctorily drying off and then crawling underneath her cover, as the flimsy room radiator emitted slow-acting heat in the spacious dwelling. For the first time that long day she could lie down again. While Serge could nap earlier, Liz was trudging along on a wild goose chase for a phone card in packed, populous Umeda and teaching lessons with a dorky new guy. To top it off, she was high as a kite from all the smoking. No surprise she was out mere seconds after her head hit the pillow. It gravitated to deep slumber by the time Serge made it to the bed.

Even the indention of the mattress from his sitting next to her didn't disturb her sleep or rouse her awake. All the better, he thought. After all, he could not get his up to snuff, no derivation of stimulation there, so he chose a real cigarette. For, even staring down at Liz's plummy, near coconut sized breasts, no change in condition seemed imminent. His premiere was still a flop. It was not an ordinary thing for him. He was not happy about it, but he tried not to feel disappointed.

His objective that day had been accomplished. He dressed quietly and strode over to the kitchen table; found the potato chip bag he saw Liz stuff her weed in a plastic film. He crumpled the bag and shoved them in one of his pants pockets. Earlier, he had rolled her three skimpy but impeccably wrapped joints, he left them on the table. He grabbed his jacket from the chair and then found his briefcase.

Slipping into his John Lobbs blocks with no socks, he was relieved that Liz was unaware of his erectile dysfunction for the time being. He abhorred the thought of being ridiculed for such a thing. It would cause him a great deal of humiliation. Were such feelings to arise, the chances of him becoming temperamental and/ or violent would be great. He would be a danger to himself and possibly others. His tendency to be hypersensitive had never been fully eradicated from him. It still lingered, however dormant. He needed his prescription meds badly. No one around him had any idea how much. For the time being, he got what he needed from Liz that would help him in the interim. Then his expensive meds. Ultimately, the operation procedure he needed. All in due time.

He eased out of the apartment. Liz would be unaware of his departure until the twilight of the following morn.

48

LIZ WOKE UP around 4:00 a.m. expecting to have found the guy Serge snoring beside her, like Eddie would have been; but such was not to be. She sat up in her bed, still naked, head foggy. She looked around the room, confused and dumbfounded. So groggy was her state she almost called out for Denore instead of the French guy. But he was long gone, and she received no response except for the silence of the room and the window's turbulent broadcast of street sounds five stories below.

Figuring that she must have really been tired, Liz recalled events up until she collapsed into the bed. Her formulation of ideas had her falling asleep, and likely, Serge decided to leave.

Now guessing that he had probably been a little upset, or unimpressed with her, Liz had no idea that it was, in fact, the truth, but with the simple twist of an "unwilling member" for the sexual performance. Thinking, however, that he had gotten pissed with her, maybe finding her asleep caused him to think that she didn't take him seriously, who knows? She thought to call him at once to apologize, but she couldn't. She never got his telephone number, or even his e-mail address.

"Oh well—what the hell . . ." She resigned to lament to herself as she emerged from the bed. Figuring that she would see him later at work, Liz considered going for an early-morning jog but decided against it. She did not want to be too exhausted by the end of her shift. She was planning the dreadful trip to Hannan City after work. She had to get to the bottom of this Eddie business.

One good thing she could determine, or take away, from the previous experience, was that she still had not technically cheated on Eddie. Sure, she made out with the guy, and they almost went through with it, extremely damn close. She couldn't even believe that she had acted that way. Any feelings of guilt that might have existed within her abruptly subsided.

Shivering despite the room radiator finally set in a steady pattern of heat, she found a long T-shirt that belonged to Eddie—once. She slipped inside, and it touched the top of her angel-cake thighs, then followed with some gray satin panties and some puffy, thick socks. She looked at the clock and decided it was too early to wake up for work, so she went back to bed.

Later that morning, it was somewhat haywire at the Umeda School. Serge did not show up to work; he called in sick. This didn't surprise Liz, as she figured dude to have been burning a candle from both ends. Already he had worked yesterday morning till afternoon after an already busy Friday evening. Then he went to her house to hang out until whatever time it was when he left—Liz didn't exactly know—only to work again that same night at the Candy Box. Crazy. Of course, he would probably be worn out.

Hitomi could certainly understand as well, but she almost touched hot water. Because she had entrusted Serge with a spare key, she had presumed the school would be opened by him when she reported for work. Instead, the rollback gate had still been fastened, and there were his French students waiting. She had to apologize to the customers for being inconvenienced.

She had to tell the disappointed French students that their classes that day were canceled and had to be rescheduled, after hearing Serge's recorded message on her office phone. Both she and Serge dodged a bullet because although the students were upset somewhat, they did not register a complaint. This was thanks to the apparent customer satisfaction record of Taffie, who, like Liz, was a crowd pleaser in her own right.

Bummy Rusty showed up for work chipper in the same dusty, wrinkled khakis he wore the day before, same smudgy suede Bucks and today in a green shirt in which he looked as if he had stitched it together with leaves from a poison ivy, top two buttons unfastened so that a hairy patch of chest bush peeked. Liz got through the day together with him, but when it was time to leave, she felt a little sorry for Hitomi. She hoped that her good nature did not lead her to destruction. Rusty was already getting abundantly comfortable, kicking his feet up in the visitor's lounge reading English newspapers when the school was void of student customers. Liz felt good knowing that she herself had always done good by Hitomi, hoping the same likewise.

After work, she didn't go home. She went directly to Namba to take the train to Eddie's place. She induced her anger by thinking, *Who does he think he is to dismiss my call?* A bit unstable in her thinking, and temper increasing rapidly.

Feelings of guilt haunted her subtly, to the extent she suspected Eddie of doing something like what she had almost done with Serge. The fact that he had not picked up his phone triggered her feelings of anxiety.

Around 7:00 p.m., she was at her former living quarters she once shared with Eddie. She no longer used the building or room key because she left it the night of the Hiroko visit while there. In such impetuous haste to attend a house party thrown by Worm, she split without her set of keys that she was supposed to already have returned at completion of her CHET Program contract.

Like clockwork, Liz spotted a cackling member of the resident chicken bevy who also recognized her standing before the outer glass doors of the building and let her in. After a brief and rushed chat consisting of the usual "Long time no sees," Liz was able to blow the middle-aged woman off and rushed to Eddie's room. She banged on the door. No answer!

Placing her ear to the door, she heard no stirring, no sounds of footsteps on floor tiles, nothing. For sure, knowing Eddie, if he were there, the radio or TV would have been on at least. It was safe for her to assume, then, that he was not home. Now where was he? Liz felt herself becoming frantic by the minute. Where could he possibly be on a Sunday evening? Her mind caroused thinking of all the places they used to go, within walking distance, when she lived there. All she could come up with was the local Hayashi supermarket, a coin laundry spot, and a Yamazaki convenience store.

The next moment, all she could remember was stomping back to the building lobby where a small flock of women had formed at a time most would be having dinner with family. Wrath consumed, the look on her face must have frightened the woman she had greeted and spoken with earlier, or the woman could sense by the reddened darkness circling Liz's eyes. Whatever the case, the woman apprehensively broke formation from the two broads she was yucking it up with and approached Liz, who to her looked as if she was about to cry or had already been crying.

In what little privacy the building offered in the form of a tall, plastic lobby plant by the elevator, she grimly managed to communicate with the woman. Liz convinced the woman to give her something to write on and a pencil or writing utensil; she used the easiest gestures even a cavewoman could understand. They went up to the woman's place, and the elevator door shut before her inquisitorial comrades could barge in and get a scoop. Liz was incidentally grateful to the woman for her kindness. She may not have liked Japan much, but people like her would have been the exception.

Liz got a memo and a piece of paper from the woman. She wrote the nastiest letter excoriating Eddie and spared nothing short of every harsh word she could muster, jotted on the paper, leaning on a nearby neighbor's door to write it. She even told Eddie that she never wanted to see him again! Also, that it was over between them. Her anger was a whirlwind type storm about to rampage out of control, with her having assumed the absolute worst and acting out on it. She hadn't noticed that she had made off with the woman's pen and didn't thank her or acknowledge her farewell wishing as she darted down the hall to the stairway. She climbed to Eddie's floor level and slid her bitter, jaundice-drenched letter under his door.

From her memory about the area, she recalled that the stupid, nearby bumpkin supermarket closed at a ridiculously early time of 7:30 p.m. on weeknights, so it was safe to believe that they would obviously be closed earlier on Sundays—if they were even open at all. She ruled out the possibility of him being there. Next she checked the coin laundry. It too was empty. Desolate. No clothes in any washer or dryer. The last place she could check was the Yamazaki convenience store, a brisk walk down the road from there.

***

Meanwhile, 500 kilometers away in the capital city of Tokyo, Eddie prepared to leave town to board the Osaka-bound bullet train *Shinkansen*, roughly a two-hour ride. The big CHET Program meeting he attended had just adjourned and Eddie stayed a short while to have some drinks with some fellow participants before boarding his vessel home. He was reasonably elated because this year, it was announced at that meeting, the program, true to the rumors he had heard, would no longer restrict its contracted employees to two-year commitments. Now they could reapply as many times as they wanted. Indefinitely they could work with the CHET Program, provided that they receive a favorable evaluation by their hosting institution. For Eddie, that seemed like a cinch. Without hesitation, he reapplied to the program! He always figured that he would anyway. He dismissed the idea of working at Bozack, moving to Osaka City, or even moving back to the States. For the time being anyway, at least.

Why would he go back? He was already making what would probably equal thirty thousand American dollars a year—why quit his job now? He was doing so well, saving a lot, earning beyond what he had ever made in his home country. If he could remain working this job for as long as possible, nothing could have been greater. The job wasn't always exactly a cinch, but it was certainly better than being a pizza schlepper waiting for the day he would get popped by a beaner, or embarrassing himself on degrading job interviews.

Furthermore, he had Hiroko. All he could think about while he was in Tokyo was her. Just one night, she rocked his world and had him lingering for her touch, her scent, kiss, and everything that embodied provocation of burning passion. He still couldn't bring his mind to believe that all along, her flirting with him on the job was never a hoax after all. She wasn't one of those video store tricks back in

LA. She was genuine! For as she stated in her own words to him, she loved him at first sight!

As for Liz and the big plan to move to the city, he had to admit that he was never too enthusiastic about the idea of moving there, even if it was more exciting a place to be. Keefer's hot stories may have fired him up in the beginning but scoring a babe like Hiroko proved that he didn't have to necessarily be in the city to find a cure for his lust and longings. He went along with Liz like he always did. That was the reason why he was there in Japan.

Another reason he went along with the plan to move, and probably the most vital one, was because he was in his second contracted year with the program. He would have had nowhere else to go but to a company like Bozack—if he wanted to stay in Japan, at least.

But now he was no longer restricted to two years. He could reapply, and he did. Unaware of the toil and turmoil Liz was preparing for him, Eddie recalled trying to call her the day before. Her constant ringing his phone while he was sitting in a huge meeting was grieving him because he could not answer. On his break, the instant he could catch a free minute, he tried to call her back to remind her that he was in Tokyo. He was sure he told her before he left, but Liz had a habit of brushing people off and not listening to what they had to say if she felt she had something more important to be announced. He had attempted to leave a recorded message in her inbox but couldn't because it was full. Stephanie had been ringing Liz's phone as madly as Liz had rung Eddie's, but he wouldn't know such. To him, it just appeared as though Liz was just as busy as he was. Her calling him constantly he regretted he couldn't answer, but it was hard for him to walk out of a meeting in the rigid atmosphere of a Japanese-influenced company. People who got up to leave during a meeting of such grandiose nature were looked upon as someone who spat in a casket during a wake.

Coincidentally, Eddie too suffered the same woe as Liz, running out of phone minutes for his Tuka phone, having engaged in the phone tag battle again and again. Eddie, however, had neither the time nor the desire to search the streets for a corresponding phone center or shop. While in Tokyo, he was constantly on the go. He had trains to catch, buses to ride, and schedules to keep. He wasn't with lazy, lackadaisical Liz who liked to beat around the bush until the last minute and be forced to take a cab everywhere.

Unable to use his phone to call anyone, Eddie would be in a harsh predicament were he to get in an emergency, so he stuck close to his colleagues. With them, he was able to catch the right train to the meeting, the right bus to the subway, and adhere to the timetables for all the conferences for the two days they were to be in Tokyo.

Plain and simple, he had no time to make or receive calls. Liz's harrowing phone calls constantly bedeviling him was getting played out. He wasn't looking forward to breaking the news to her, but he knew he had to. He closed his eyes and tried to cop some Z's as the bullet train launched from Tokyo Station.

***

Back in Osaka, that very instant, Liz stalked the Yamazaki convenience store. The shelves were so low to the floor Liz thought the shop was for dwarfs or small kids. Soft drinks, candy, and cup noodles galore, but no beer, alcohol, or cigarettes at this one. The bread smelled good, though, so Liz bought what looked like cheese on a huge, thick slice of toasted bread. She wolfed it down outside in the chilly autumn gust with a can of hot coffee. At any rate, Eddie wasn't there either.

It was dark now. She looked around the non-asphalt, gravel-covered parking lot. The convenience stores seemed like the busiest places in the ghost town.

A tall, slender cabbie on break was standing in the opened door of his green countryside taxi having a cigarette and a cup of a drink, talking to some older-looking Japanese bum probably en route to the store. They had been holding a conversation before Liz went in the store and were still there when she came out. She flung her empty coffee can to the distant street and stepped up to the cabbie.

Liz convinced the man to take her to Hannan Junior High School. She thought maybe that the man might have been a local who remembered her from when she lived there a year before, because he was accommodating and didn't seem flustered that his break-time chat was interrupted. She could speak no Japanese at all, so she did her usual charade routine, gesturing the turning of a steering wheel and pointing at the taxicab. It was enough to convey the message, and he knew enough English to recognize the word "school."

Moments later, she was at the junior high school. She paid the cabbie, and it sped off. As expected, Liz could see that the industrious Japanese staff were still at the school, even on a Sunday! For some odd inkling, Liz suspected that there was a chance she would see Eddie—maybe he was at the school today trying to prove to everyone that he was the best thing since sliced bread.

She waited outside of the school gate. Hesitating, she initially thought to boldly waltz up into the place and ask if Eddie was there, but she couldn't bring herself to do it. Feeling desperate but not daring, she waited. She had no cigarettes on her, and she was feeling edgy, along with becoming chillier by the minute. The moment she decided resolutely to go inside of the school, a candy apple–red car, a Demio, pulled out of the parking lot from the rear of the building.

Inside the car, Hiroko's heartbeat intensified seeing Liz's luminescent figure in her headlights, standing trancelike by the school's gate. Tremblingly, she wondered if Eddie had told Liz about the two of them. If so, was she there to exact some type of punishment upon her? Fear gripped her slightly, but she couldn't just let her stand there. She looked as if she may have been a little cold. She wheeled the Demio over to where Liz was standing like a stoic sentry, rolled down her window, and greeted her.

"Hello, Elizabeth-san," she greeted her rival with a timid half-smile edged with a smidgen of genuine concern. "What are you doing here?"

Liz's emotions and feelings were a uniformed mix of startled, relief, and being incensed upon seeing Hiroko. There was something about her, the way she was looking at her, that did not sit well. It was like she was hiding something. Liz couldn't shake the feeling.

Liz tried to be nice to the young woman. She lied, "Nice to see you, Hiroko." Unfortunately, she could not code-switch the overall tone of her voice and appear abundantly joyous. "Have you heard anything from Eddie?"

A tremendous burden was lifted from Hiroko's agonizing thought that Eddie had told Liz, for apparently, he hadn't. She was relieved because the last thing she wanted was to have a scene, or a spectacle because of a love triangle. It would be devastating for her job and career. Conversely, she herself couldn't bring herself to tell Liz either about what happened with her and Eddie. That they were now in the process of beginning a relationship, a love affair.

Liz said, "I . . . I've been trying to reach him. I've been calling and calling and calling . . . he hasn't answered his phone. I went to our old apartment, and he wasn't there, and now I'm worried sick."

Frantic somewhat, Liz rambled on to Hiroko, lucky to an extent, that Hiroko could understand every word that left her trap. Any other Japanese person from Osaka would have been stumped, stuck looking at her like she was a Martian.

Remorsefully, Hiroko said, "He didn't tell you? He went to Tokyo for his meeting. He left Friday, or Saturday, I don't remember. But I think that he will be back tomorrow."

"Tomorrow!? Shit!" Liz stressfully exclaimed as the pieces fell into place. Somewhere within her clouded head, she remembered Eddie mentioning of a trip out to Tokyo. Moreover, she remembered that she too had to go to Tokyo around that time of year previously, like some sort of follow-up training module. She also recounted what it was like as an ALT with the CHET Program after those meetings were over too. It was all about exploring and frolicking around the city—from Roppongi, to Shibuya, to Shinjuku or Harajuku. Now she felt completely foolish; she wanted to cry, but not in front of Hiroko. Her pride had taken enough hits already, plus, this bitch had not even offered her a ride. Liz was certain Hiroko could tell that the frigid fangs of fall were putting a slow freeze on her.

Anyway, Hiroko lied. She didn't know the exact time when Eddie would treturn from Tokyo, but she knew it was not Monday. By all accounts, Eddie would be reporting for work as usual on Monday. Hiroko was feeling acquisitive.

For she now thought Eddie was hers, she did not want Liz to go back to his apartment.

Grudgingly, she offered Liz a ride to the nearest train station, the Ozaki Station. If she did, Liz would be gone, Hiroko thought. It didn't matter, though. She wouldn't be able to keep Liz from seeing him forever. They would eventually have to meet. How else would Eddie be able to break the news to her but face-to-face, like he said he would. But hopefully, when he did, Hiroko wished it would be in the daylight, at a tea shop or a cafe, where the possibility for things leading to intimacy was avoided.

To Hiroko's surprise, Liz declined the ride offer, claiming she needed to walk and "clear my head." She knew where the station was—it was within walking distance—so Hiroko needed not worry about her. With a spec of empathy, she bid Liz farewell for now. Liz responded in kind and made tracks for the battered, derelict-looking Ozaki Station without a second to lose. The quicker she left that locale, the better. As if things could not get worse, she saw the train she needed pull into the opposite platform.

To make the train, she had to ascend and descend a huge wooden stairway that stretched to the sky like a ladder with wide steps. She had to remove her Boden Adelaide Jeweled flats and scamper barefoot. With lithe and graceful strides, she advanced upon the platform and managed to board a partially crowded coach of the train. The doors closed and almost clamped onto her glittery golden blonde coiffure like she was a stunt double in a Harrison Ford adventure flick.

She was sweaty and panting now; the heat was on full blast inside the train car. To make matters worse, hideous Japanese creatures with bulging eyes, missing teeth, deformed lips—ghoulishly unstylish people—stared at her in awe and bafflement. She closed her eyes and reached for a stirrup to hold as the rocky ride commenced, trying to tune the freakish-looking people out. They were probably wondering what a girl like her was doing in their hamlet. She was wondering the same thing.

49

BACK IN OSAKA City, Taffie Jolie was feeling refreshed. She and Deon were cradled inside of her alternate, auxiliary pad, a cozy box room apartment in the catacomb back alleys situated between the Ogimachi and Minami Morimachi Districts. Breathless on Taffie's foldout sponge foam futon, they were moist after another session of ferocious and truculent lovemaking. Deon was still stone solid inside of her as she lay on top of him, panting in post-climax bliss. With splendid dexterity utilized by her long arms, her right hand reached over Deon to the artificial shelf of the recessed window. She clasped the joint there and the lighter beside it, lit it up, took a puff, and then passed it to her lover. Deon took a quick pull and blew out a wisp of cinnamon and ganja breeze in the air. He passed it back to her, she hit the reefer a couple of times, and tried to give it back, but Deon was like "I'm good."

Taffie was impressed. Contrary to her suspicions, Deon was neither heavy boozer nor doper. She ashed the shank in a bedside tray and pecked his Klondike Bar–toned lips. Exhaling in quick desperation, she slid from his impaling rod in a marshy ooze. She wasn't fond of parting company with him, and vice versa as well, it seemed, but they both had responsibilities. Schedules to keep and timetables to adhere to.

Deon rose from the futon and rubbed Taffie's splendorous semicircle backside before beating a hasty path to her washroom. Recklessly, he grabbed a random towel he saw hanging from the shower curtain rail, wet it up in the sink, and started sponging himself down.

Taffie watched him and laughed, saying words in French, like, "Tu es un homme si *sauvage!*"

Deon would render her a charming million-dollar smile and shrug indifference, indicating he didn't understand when she spoke French, but he liked it. He got dressed.

Taffie had to split too. She had to dip into Umeda to hit up her boss and savior, Saiko Yamabiko, to get her cash salary. Some of the proceeds from this month's take would go to buying Deon a gift. Maybe a necktie or some prestigious cologne, something nice. It wasn't his birthday or any special occasion she knew of; it was because he was *un gars incroyale*—an incredible guy.

She never thought she would ever date an American, or a guy like him. He reminded her so much of the singers and dancers she would see on her country's version of MTV. As far as she was concerned, he very well could have been, because the times they went out clubbing, he moved on the dance floor like a platinum-album-selling artist.

Communication between them was a bit shaky at times. Like Taffie had her habit of intertwining her French within her English discussion, Deon too would infuse his urban drenched dialogue uncommon to some mainstream native speakers. They even spoke Japanese to each other, which would baffle the hell out of Japanese people—and practically *anyone* for that matter.

Altogether, they were having a good time and enjoying one another. The relationship had blossomed and grown from a blind date to a passionate pair of lovebirds, taking flight, heating up the frigid nights. But Taffie couldn't lie to herself. True, she liked Deon, but he was "poor." Not in the sense of adverse, bankrupt poverty, but compared to all the heavy hitters and magnate playboys she dealt with on a regular basis, he came nowhere close. Her current advocate sponsor, the Doc, was her most ardent supporter and showed no signs of relenting. Whatever she had done t0 infatuate him so feverishly, she knew not, but he made her feel that high-priced whoring was worth its weight in gold. Literally. For the five minutes it took for the old geezer to reach his erotic apex next to her barbarian nude body, once every other month, and she had an apartment—which was, in fact, her second apartment—exquisite and gorgeous jewelry, elegant and stunning attire, almost anything she had access to. She couldn't give it up so soon.

Taffie had only been half honest with Liz, but she couldn't help it. Her habit of distrusting people had been formed growing up in her later years without parents or true friends. Yes, she wanted to have a boyfriend, and Deon would have been perfect. She would not rule him out, but for the time being, she would have to take it slow. For she could not let go of her bread-and-butter coalition. If she broke up with the Doc, she would have to give up her hideaway and must live in Saiko's dormitory and be subject to the impertinent, officious eyes of other lounge co-staffers. Furthermore, her excursions out of the cramped, stuffy conditions of

Osaka to dreamy retreats to country resorts and *onsen* hot spa visits would end. The shopping sprees, the elegant restaurants, the glamorous nightlife would stop completely. So maybe she was going to buy him gifts, not only because he was such a sweet guy but also because guilt stroked lightly at her heartstrings.

Deon was always so dandy and spiffy, Taffie mused as he put the finishing touches to his silk tie adjustment in front of her tall mirror.

She said, "Tell me, Dee, for how long will you stay here? Japan?"

Deon shrugged serenely and said, "Not that long, baby. But right now, things are good for me. I'm makin' a little scratch. These student loans is a motherfucker, so I'm payin' those back. Work ain't really that hard. This ain't some shit I wanna do for the rest'a my life, hell, nah. I got other plans."

"Other plan? Like?"

He smirked at her charismatically and half joked, "Why you askin' me all these questions all of a sudden? You startin' to sound like your homegirl 'Lizbeth. Shit."

Taffie giggled ardently as she applied her makeup from the bath area. "No, I do not sound like her. You such a crazy boy. No!"

Deon grabbed her up from behind and pressed his lips to the side of her neck, gently biting it like a baby vampire with not-yet developed fangs. Taffie pressed herself back to meet his sudden erection and regretted they had no time for one last futon splash.

She said, "I just thought that you will go back to your country soon. I cannot imagine a guy like you to live in place like here for a long time. Can you?"

"Nah," Deon said as he walked back into the room to scoop up his soft-leather Kenneth Cole jacket. "Like I said, baby, I got plans. If things continue to go smooth, I think I can kick it here for another year or two. When I save up enough loot, then I'll implement the next stage."

Taffie listened warily. In a way, he was somewhat like her, she thought. Just another foreigner who came to Japan by chance, then decided to stick around, seeing the opportunity to come up drastically. After all, back in respective countries, there were no institutions either of them knew readily that would pay them up to fifty dollars or francs per hour to teach English or French, respectively. Unfortunately, alluring females such as Taffie could easily score double, even triple, that of the ordinary, male Deon.

Deon was a unique case, however. It wasn't as if he couldn't make bigger bank by moonlight hustles. He could even work as a male host version of what Taffie did. In fact, when Taffie pressed him on why he didn't choose that option, he flatly refused to consider it, claiming he wasn't a good singer and that he wasn't a "coon"—whatever that meant, Taffie could not understand, but she praised him for avoiding the lifestyle. She knew that the playing field would be evened because there were just as many cougars on the rise in the red-light districts as there were sugar daddies in Taffie's lane. She wasn't sure if she would lose him or not, and she didn't want to; but unfortunately, for the time being, she was stringing him along, and she was starting to hate herself for it. So far, he had shown her complete compromise and trust when she told him about her trips to Tokyo—explaining to him in half-truth that she would make the trip as it was related to work—but she did not know for how long he would remain unsuspecting and unquestioning.

Lastly, by no stretch of the imagination in the least, he was the best lover she had in her entire life, Japan, or gay Paris. She was selfish and she wanted Deon's chocolate "Mr.Goodbar" and creamy "nuts" all to herself. The only partner she had who came even close to making her feel as good as him was Elizabeth, but she had an unfair advantage because being a female, she likely had more insight and experience knowing where the stimulating points were located on a woman's body. More so than the average man anyway, was how she felt.

Taffie and Deon kissed good-bye and parted ways on Ogimachi Avenue. She hopped inside of a cab; Deon dipped back inside of the heavy human traffic arcade to catch the Loop Line train. By happenstance, the spying eyes of a Saiko Yamabiko affiliate note-checked them both.

***

Elsewhere in town, Liz wearily arrived at Nankai Namba Station, returning to Osaka City. Finding a series of phone booths in front of the Takashimaya Department Store, she dipped inside one and made a call to Luzio Silver. A half an hour later, his tinted-windowed black BMW cruised by and scooped her up on Nagahori Street. His ride interior smelled like intense coconut, cologne, and weed smoke; and the cushiony seats had a soothing velvety texture.

For such an "infamous" hard case and baleful underworld figure as the rumors and his reputation would claim, Luzio Silver did not pass on that vibe of perniciousness. Sure, his wardrobe and excessive jewelry might have made him seem or look the part, but otherwise, he was down to earth, generally friendly, and handled the illegal activity as a matter-of-fact daily operation—quick on the uptake like a cashier at a legit drugstore or pharmacy. In short, a lot of prissy young Western women would surely have felt somewhat uneasy with Luzio's sort, but not Liz. Additionally, he wasn't a leering, flirtatious ring-ding like Brad.

She transacted business with him and humorously bemoaned not being able to con Silver to take her farther than Osaka Dome. She playfully jabbed him on his shoulder as if he were her older brother Hal. She was hatched from his ride between the Dome and 'Taisho Station'. This depot and surrounding vicinity were ridiculously crowded, so Liz avoided it and walked uphill in the opposite direction overlooking the Shirinashi River. From there, she took a taxi at Minato (Harbor) Street, and the fare was cheaper.

Something she learned from Tim the Duke was to take cabs and avoid crowded stations if you could afford it; such was worth it if you were "holding." Considering the cost of freedom, a cab fare was relatively cheap.

No sooner had she arrived back at her place she heard the house phone ring. She ditched her jeweled flats and lumbered into the bedroom area where the phone was, picked up the receiver, and heard the morbid, quavering voice of the Retriever, Radley Owens.

A bit alerted, Liz was like, "Wow, hi, Rad, like . . . how'n the freak did you get this number?"

Radley's voice said, "I hope you don't mind, Worm gave it to me. Sorry, I lost yer number, and Steph wasn't around fer me to get it from."

"Worm doesn't know my cell phone number?" she asked somewhat melodramatically.

Radley said haltingly, "I . . . uh . . . don't . . . think so? And I hate to bother you so late, but I have a favor to ask."

Liz sort of knew what was coming, given Radley's track record for impromptu days off and sudden vacations or sick leave. Immediately, she said, "What's in it for me?"

She heard Radley laugh meekly as he said, "I . . . uh, well, tell me what'cha want—clothes, 'lectronics, something realistically attainable, or, uh, *retrievable*, and next time I go on a haul mission, I'll certainly look out for you. I just need a shift swap for tomorrow. I know it's short notice, but you're the only person I know who can help me out. You're the only one I know who's off tomorrow . . ."

There was a long pause of silence before Liz finally said, "What school?"

"Tennoji Honko, the main branch," Radley said hesitantly.

"Aw fuck!" Liz exclaimed. One of the places she dreaded going. Too rigid and too many overseeing chieftains and straw bosses. All the Bozack big cheeses would be about micromanaging and wet blankets seeing to it that the work experience was more rigid and stressful than it needed be. Liz detested the idea of having to work there on a continual basis, and even one day there she knew she would loathe; but at that point, it seemed as if Radley had his hopes up too high for her to disappoint him.

She sighed and said, "OK, damn it, Rad, I'll do it. But fuck, man, you owe me double."

Radley thanked Liz, his voice sounding energetic for once. "Oh, thanks a zillion, Elizabeth. And you got it. I'll hook you up twice. No problem. You work for me tomorrow at Tennoji, and I can work for you at Hommachi. You can pick that day, but it has to be a Friday or Saturday, the only two days I work at Hommachi."

Liz said coolly, "Yeah, OK, whatever. I guess I'll take the Saturday off. I don't like waking up early."

Radley said, "You got it. My shift starts at one thirty. You'll probably get there earlier, so when you do, you report to either Yamada-san or the Aussie chick, Ruth. Just tell her you're reporting for a shift swap with me. Then you'll get the paperwork to fill out. That's when you fill in the day and the date for me to do yer shift in exchange. It hasta'be within the thirty days, though."

"OK, then. You sure do know how to lay on some bad news. What kinda plans do you have anyway?"

"Me and my girlfriend wanna go to . . ."

"Oh great!' Liz rolled her eyes and shook her head, offhandedly thinking, *So this imbecile wants me to work for him so he can spend time with his little Japanese floozy . . . what a bum!* She didn't want to hear him ramble on about how he and his chick were planning to go on some trip with her folks. Also, she was irritated that she had actually agreed to bail him out.

Liz had forgotten about the horrendous letter she left Eddie at his apartment. Preoccupied with thoughts regarding her current situation, thoughts of Eddie escaped her. After a rabbit dinner consisting of garden salad and seaweed rice balls, she took a shower, rolled up, took a smoke, watched some mindless Japanese variety show on television, then retired for bed uncharacteristically early for a Sunday evening.

An hour and a half earlier, Eddie returned to Osaka and Hannan City from his long trip. He also was considerably tired from his bullet train trip back from Tokyo. Dragging his mini suitcase inside of his place, he did not even notice the slip of paper Liz had left. She had slipped it under his door, and he casually, but unknowingly, stepped on the folded A4-to-A5–sized paper. He removed his shoes, entered his place, unpacked, and unwound. He thought about calling Liz, conscientious about how they had been phone tagging, but decided not to. He was too tired and did not feel like going through the motions with her.

***

On the streets of Umeda, Osaka, Taffie hopped out of a cab at the corner of Takagami Strip and Yotsubashi Avenue. She had just terminated a call, not from Liz but from another female admirer, Mikako Swiggler. It was a pleasant, time killing conversation which consisted of the mandatory "Long time, no see" preliminary, and then the bulk, which was an invitation reminder to the pre-Christmas all-night party at her and Worm's mansion. She could only tentatively commit to attending as the date of the event, she checked, conflicted with her night work schedule. The chat was punctuated with half-full promises to keep in touch. And, Mikako added, that should she decide to come, she would teach her the key code to their complex residence security system. That way, she could get inside their locked sentry niche gate. Taffie had so much on her plate it was hard to keep up at times, but she promised Mikako that she would correspond with her about it later in the week.

In other news, another Tokyo trip was planned; she wanted to hit the boutiques of Ginza. The talk with Mikako consumed the entire amount of time it took to deliver her station to station from Ogimachi Avenue where she and Deon parted.

She walked briskly on a crowded bystreet running parallel to the main drag. Storefront posts and neon banners from the sides of scabrous buildings illuminated the dark asphalt path in the Kita Shinchi entertainment district. Hundreds of bars packed the stone mini-towers; a considerable sum of these catered to "well-heeled" Japanese aristocrats, moguls, and tycoons who enjoyed the company of young (or sometimes seemingly so) or younger women—and in some cases, men as well. They did not mind spending plentifully for the company, entertainment, and recreation these dens provided.

Saiko Yamabiko's underworld parlor, the Dream Lounge, was nestled in a maw of urban decadence: garbage-littered streets, the smell of vomit and urine, and creepy mice scurrying vigilantly inside of an older Shimo-Higashi Building. It was an exclusive, members-only spot not heavily advertised and tediously difficult to locate without an invitation. It was amazing that Mama-san Saiko could have such high-paying clients continue to sojourn and patronize for so long, Taffie thought nearly every time she entered the lobby of the tattered building. Yet despite the disreputable exterior, once inside on the fourth floor, the atmosphere magically modified to a polished and stately Shangri-la of nighttime hedonism.

Plucky and munificent Saiko Yamabiko, called "Mama-san Saiko" by her subordinates, sat inside her boudoir, adorned in an ornate Oriental-influenced silk pinafore, on the telephone with her recovering alcoholic sub-lackey, Yutaka. Aside from being Saiko's errand boy at the age of thirty-five, he was also her permanent "friend zone" prisoner. Formally, however, he was building superintendent for the squalid apartment house owned by Saiko, which additionally served as a dormitory for her female employees who had sketchy paperwork and quasi-legal visas. Taffie used to belong in one of such categories, but her paperwork became legit when she bagged a job with the Bozack company.

When Taffie walked in to Saiko's private sitting room adjacent to the barroom area, the still-hot duenna was still on the phone with Yutaka, who had dutifully dry-snitched that he had seen "the black girl" on the north side of Ogimachi Avenue. For months, Taffie had been suspected of having an additional apartment other than the one provided by Saiko, and that was a breach of policy. Furthermore, Yutaka had reported to her that Taffie was rarely, if ever, seen around the dormitory. This was corroborated by various coworkers of Taffie's who also stayed in her building.

Saiko hung up the phone and greeted Taffie with the normal pleasantries and told her to have a seat on a fancy easy chair as she produced a small key. It was for a small, gilded teakwood chest, which had a stack of envelopes, each one with varying gelt sums for employees' salaries. Applying moisture of saliva to a finger, she thumbed through the envelopes until she found the one which had Taffie's name on it. She took it out and handed Taffie her kopeck haul for the month.

After collecting her loot, Taffie's thought was to split and check out Liz to see what she was up to, since she was under the impression that the following day would be her day off. She was momentarily urged by Saiko to postpone and remain for a talk.

Obliging, Taffie returned to her seat to hear what the *mama-san* had to say.

Saiko said loftily, "It has come to my attention, Taffie-san, that you have found yourself a boyfriend. As you know, it is strongly discouraged for you to have a paramour steady, but this is not a mandatory policy—it's just for your personal safety and the sanctity of our business. I can't reiterate the near tragedies we've encountered due to a jealous partner who can't come to grips with the nature of work involved. It is a potentially disastrous situation we would like to avoid."

Taffie nervously said in Japanese, "Yes, it is true. I have been seeing a man. He is a coworker of mine at the language school, introduced to me by the American girl Elizabeth, whom you once met the night of Takuto's birthday party."

Saiko said, "Yes, the beautiful American girl, yes, I remember. Well, OK, I understand that you are a responsible person, and you will be careful in your selection of playmates, but please do realize that I am against it. Also, because he is not Japanese, he may not completely comprehend this business. A hostess must appear available, yet unavailable to the clients.

"Which brings me to another issue. A year ago, one of our elite members, a client that exclusively requested your company, our Dr. Hiro Sarugi, no longer visits our lounge. Do you have any idea why that is?"

Taffie tried to mask her uneasiness, hoping that she was convincing as a liar. She said, "I have not any idea, Mama-san. I only faintly recall this big-hearted man of whom you speak. There are so many clients who come here. There are also many doctors . . ."

Saiko eyed Taffie with attentive, prudent scope. She said, "I do remember, because it is my job, and it also has become my skill to recall my valued clientele. I recount that Dr. Sarugi was so smitten with you that he offered you the largest tip ever in the history of this lounge being in business.

"Now I don't want to know if you have slept with this man or not. Intimate encounters with the customers aren't forbidden, but it is not encouraged. However, you know the rules: If you receive compensation for your services outside of the lounge, you are required to shell off 20 percent back to the house. That's me. And if by chance, you have been keeping company with a client for almost a year without paying your dues, it would really break my heart, Taffie-san.

"I'm not accusing you, but word comes to me that you haven't been around the apartment for days, even weeks on end. That you've been seen about town carrying groceries in an area of Tenma District far from the location of your room, indicating the possibility you may have additional residence . . . You see, this is not a new thing. It is not unusual for the rich clients to maintain a secret secondary abode for their favorite side dames. But it is imperative that you realize that I cannot tolerate this. Though it may seem tyrannical, it is for your safety, my dear, that you stay at the dormitory while you work for me.

"If you can find yourself a full-time job teaching French in this town—and I really doubt you can—and they can guarantee you an apartment of your own, you have my blessings, I wish you the best. But when you work at my lounge, I must have you and the rest of the women housed in a clandestine location. You aren't the only *gaijin*, you know. I have Chinese, Koreans, some Romanians—you know this. Some of them have some immigration issues and woes. For some, this is the only means of income they can have to sustain them until their paperwork issues are resolved. And most importantly, we must protect your location from would-be clingy clients, obsessive, the stalkers . . ."

Taffie gulped hesitantly. She wanted desperately to come clean about her taking advantage of Dr. Sargui's vulnerability the prior year. Having recognized him immediately to be of the same type as deceased Sonny, spellbound by the idiosyncratic allure of dark foreign women, rare but too precious to dismiss, she breached trust and policy to become affectionate and confidential with a Dream Lounge client. Yes, it did cut into the business, but because of having Taffie in his pocket, Doc Sarugi didn't need to go to the Lounge anymore. Furthermore, no, Taffie did not pay her tithes to her *mama-san*, for secretly she had been overly covetous. She wanted everything for herself. The Doc, Deon, money, clothes, and the opportunity to marry a millionaire in the future. With Doc Sarugi, she thought she was at the threshold of achieving that goal, but it was a murky road of uncertainty that could lead her to a bridge she would have to burn once she crossed over. If old dude were to pass away like Sonny did, Taffie would have been, likely, back to where she started when Saiko almost literally pulled her from out of the gutter.

Guilt again tugged at Taffie like how it did when she thought of her relationship with Deon. She did not want to be a liar, but the complexity of her lifestyle compelled her to do it. Then with one lie, it would morph into a burgeoning, entwining web. To untangle it required even more deception. But it did not feel very pleasing for her to use such tactic on people like Saiko, who had helped her invaluably.

Taffie finally said, "I assure to you, Mama-san, I have no relationship with the clients outside of your lounge. And what gifts I receive or tips I get, I always pay the dues. As for my dormitory, I am sorry, but I do not always retire there, it is true, yes. But as I said, I have a boyfriend. I sometimes stay at his place. My friend Elizabeth, I also stay with her. I have another job at the language school,

I have other friends. I apologize for not socializing with the other hostesses who work for you. Unfortunately, we have difference in schedule, or plainly, not much in common. I hope that you believe me, Mama-san. I am indebted to you."

Saiko had a soft spot for Taffie's convincing false conviction. Too wise to be fully gullible to her con, Saiko wanted to believe Taffie and decided to let the issue rest for the time being. One thing was for sure—Yutaka had been doing his homework, and his spy tactics were sharp. Unfortunately, Taffie remained too elusive beyond his pay grade to tail in addition to his other duties and responsibilities that he carried out for his unrequited love and boss. Saiko would still kick him a few extra bills for doing a good job but would forever dangle the tasty carrot of her love garden over his nose like an ass, unattainable.

***

Tennoji and the Abeno districts surrounding the area of the former namesake station, was, in the opinion of Liz, an urban shithole made to appear cosmopolitan because of the massive, aerodynamic-designed overpass at Abiko/ Abeno Avenues intersection. Although it wasn't the multitudinous stampede of human feet area like Umeda, it could hold its own on a day like Monday, at noon, where Liz was, and dreading the evening she had in store. She walked down Abeno Avenue where it seemed to have more people on clanky, rusty bicycles speeding the narrow sidewalk than pedestrians. Narrowly missing Liz by inches and centimeters, she nearly gawked at how skillfully they could steer in such conditions without accident or incident. At times it was nerve-racking. The people down here did not seem to care if she was a *gaijin* or not. The locals looked *holloi polloi*, not too fancy and some within arm's reach of insolvency, despite the strip being lined with modernized architecture and teeming with businesses. Some homeless bums could be spotted pulling drays filled with cardboard while collecting cans. Young miscreant urchins in school uniforms hung around on the hollowed passage Liz used to arrive at the Bozack HQ building. To brighten her day, one of the kids looked at her, flicking a box cutter menacingly. Uttered something vulgar at her in Japanese, the urban urchin, and his team of three similarly dressed boys roared laughter. For the first time in Japan, Liz felt uneasy. She hailed from a city full of crime back in the States, and for the most part, Japan was "safe", but this was one of the times a hint of the dangerous side of Osaka seemed to rear its head.

Annoyed but applying sangfroid finesse to her feelings, she pressed on. Arriving at her building, she growled regretfully. Had Eddie or another one of her friends been with her, she might have had the gumption to approach the little punk and confront him. Not to fight or anything, but to assert enough defiance and make them aware their behavior was unwarranted and rude remarks unwelcome. She felt so entitled.

Liz was so happy to get off the block that she arrived at the Bozack HQ school with a smile of relief. She checked in with the receptionist and was allowed entry. Checking in with the moody Bozack potentate Ruth Worth, Liz filled in the paperwork for the shift swap with Radley. Surprisingly, Ruth did not have any extra discussion in which to engage her, and this was somewhat a relief. She appeared to be busy with something else, and upon closer scrutiny, Liz noticed fatigue bags under the voluminous Aussie woman's eyes. Like she had been crying a river, or not getting enough sleep, or both.

For that, Liz opted to not pester her about the progress of Eddie's situation. There was still also the issue of Liz and Eddie's reconciliation as well. Since it was now Monday, the day that Hiroko said Eddie would return, she would be expecting Eddie to be contacting her soon, especially when he discovered that crude letter she left. Figuring it better to allow Ruth to stay preoccupied with her affairs, Liz hoped it would remain so for the entire time she was there.

Ruth left Liz to fill out some papers and headed back into the greater office. Compared to the other Bozack schools, the Tennoji HQ's layout was like a warehouse.

No sooner did Ruth leave then Worm entered the room with another head teacher named Rosiland Ash, a tall, modish chick who, like Worm, was a *hapa*, but she was Chinese and Scottish Australian Caucasian. Although this was only the second time Liz had met her—the only other time had been at the training she undertook there at HQ—she still remembered her name upon sight and greeted her enthusiastically with a slightly meandering smile.

Worm was all apologetic. "Hi, Lizzie baby, sorry about that. I gave Radley your dorm room line, but I did what I had to do in that situation. Radley was desperate, he needed to contact you. The top brasses might not smile upon me givin' out the cell phone number to another employee, because that might be too private. But the dormitory phone is a legitimate correspondence channel, connected to work, the job, but hey, for what it's worth, I still apologize."

Liz didn't feel like making it a bigger deal than it needed to be. She was already there at work now; she was ready to get it over with. Now she could choose which day she could have a day off in exchange. She sat and thought while Worm and Rosiland made small talk in the background. Asking the other's plans for the upcoming holidays and year-end Celebrations. It was then that Worm reanimated like a wind-up toy afresh with new batteries.

"Hey, you guys, 'Lizabeth, Rosiland! This year, the pre-Christmas party and *bone-nen-kai* is gonna be at my place. It's half catered, half potluck, but if you can't bring anything, you can just make a donation of about three thousand yen." Worm distracted Liz while she was thinking. Since she already knew that neither she nor Eddie would be flying back to the States like they had done the previous year, the subject intrigued her.,

Jokingly, Liz remitted, "You sound like you're hustling like that guy Deon." Worm reacted as if he were offended that anyone could ever make such a comparison. With a look of alarm, he stated, "I have no idea what you mean. Look, I think it's a helluva deal. I've a special connection with the Foreign Buyers Club and International Marketers Club. We're getting some turkey and Cornish hens, scones, beer, and open bar all night, plus theater entertainment, music, all sorts of shit.If you wanna bring somethin' you can, what's the big hustle? I think you can't beat it."

Rosiland said, "I'm sorry, I can't go. I'm flying back to Australia for summertime holidays with the folks."

Liz said, "OK, when is it gonna be?"

Worm provided her the information, time and date, and related matters. He said to Liz, "I can send you some more details by e-mail if you like."

Liz heard Rosiland say, "Wow, Mitchell, I swear, if you get the Regional Head Teacher promotion, you'll be the most popular one of all time with all these events you put together . . ."

Quite certain his wife had much to do with Worm's success, Liz thought about it with disregard because admittedly, she enjoyed visiting Worm's crib. For Japan, it was a cozy spot, especially in a country where living conditions were so cramped due to limited space. She couldn't imagine what her life there would have been like with a place so huge and elaborate. She looked forward to the upcoming event. It happened to be on a Friday, so Liz marked on her shift swap papers that she would take the following Saturday off, so she didn't have to lug herself to the job with a stagnating hangover. Moreover, Eddie would have no next day to work excuse to render either like he did the first invitation to Worm's spot. When she dropped it on him that night after work, he would even have a couple of weeks to effectively clear his calendar.

When all was said and done, Liz submitted her shift-swap paperwork to Ruth Worth. Ruth approved the date, then proceeded to turn her over into the care of Rosiland for the day. Worm bounced after another hour of chewing the fat with people he knew at the branch and spreading the word about his house party coming up.

The Tennoji HQ branch was twice the size of Hommachi and Namba, encompassed two floors of the building it occupied, and had a higher volume of student enrollment. They also had a lot of foreign teachers as well. She saw the familiar faces of Eric Cravens and Jeremy Ng, but the other dozen people she didn't know well, and didn't have much interest in getting more acquainted with. But here at this location, she could finally see the other language teachers of Spanish, German, and Italian. Unlike the other schools Liz had taught at, there were no cancellations, no shows, or free slots blocks on her schedule.

Another thing Liz noticed was how immaculate everyone was dressed. The dress code was adhered, and all the male teachers had on wrinkle-free collared shirts with necktie. Eric, as usual, had a bowtie, vest, and shirt with cuff links. Women were dressed in cropped blazers, jumpsuits, and rompers, basically the same as everywhere else, only here, more neat, less shabby, and no one reeked of booze or unkempt underarms. It was an ideal work environment, or at least one better suited for greeting the Japanese public. Liz was glad she had enough foresight to look standard, white shirt, black multi-pleat skirt. Her suede Neiman Marcus 105-centimeter tora heel pumps accentuated her sturdy athletic, lust-enticing calves when she pranced around the office, to and from the classrooms, as if walking on imported air.

Querulous Bozack *vicegerent*, bed headed Suguru Yamada, couldn't keep his eye-glassed peepers off her. All he could do was stare at her legs and allow her to break his concentration when he was trying to get some work done. Liz's bouncy walk caused her hips to shake, her movements captivated his interest to the point he couldn't stop looking and abnormal vibrations quivered within his lap. The first thing he did was make a bitch complaint about her, stating that her office attire was inappropriate because it was "too revealing."

Even the notoriously disputatious Ruth Worth had to give that grievance the side eye of dubiety. Liz had the kind of physique Ruth would have perhaps sold her soul for and had to admit that she was attractive and alluring but saw nothing that would indicate that she was inappropriately dressed for work. But she had no choice, because Suguru was her office superior, and her compliance was expected. She pulled Liz to the side and issued her a warning about the dress code, but not an official infraction breach.

Liz was baffled beyond capable understanding. Ruth would punctuate with a light admonition about wearing high heels and skirt lengths. To which Liz would silently vow not to abide by, especially if she was forced to wear dowdy, antiquated potato-sack dresses like the female teachers she saw there. Seeing them, old school programs like *Little House on the Prairie* came to Liz's mind.

Aside from the single detraction of Suguru Yamada's nitpicking hissy fit about Liz's appearance, to her wonderment, her day went relatively smooth. It was not as dreadful as she thought it would be. She found that staying busy made the hours seem to pass quickly. Before she knew it, the time had come to clock out.

***

In Hannan City, Eddie would eventually discover the vitriol-seeping note that Liz left him. After reading it, he was provided the fuel he needed to break the news to her that it was over between them.

Meanwhile, Liz was in the city on her way home walking from the Loop Line Bentencho Station. She saw Eddie had called, but once again, she had missed it due to being at work and had to shut her phone off.

Now she was inflated with the excitement and elation of dropping the news on Eddie that there was no better time than now to try and get with Bozack. It was high time he left the sticks and get into the city with her. He may have still been disgruntled or upset with her because of the letter, but when she hit him with the news that there was a sudden opening and that he could be bumped up from the waiting list, she was all too sure that he would spring into action and rush to be by her side, like he always did. The ever-faithful boy toy pet he was, and she couldn't wait to give him the scoop.

When her shift had ended at 9:00 p.m. sharp, the work-wearied Ruth passed Liz on her way out and said, "Area manager Kenjiro will be back in the office tomorrow. If you speak again with your fiancé, the sooner the better. A follow-up meeting can be arranged."

Placing her Tuka phone to her ear, she could hear Eddie's phone ringing. For an odd, perplexing moment she wasn't expecting him to answer, but astonishingly, he did. It was the first time they had spoken to each other in a week.

The proverbial writing was on the wall and had been for some time. Liz, however, had chosen to ignore it for far too long. Or she thought that she was irreplaceable.

As soon as Eddie said "Hello," Liz bombarded him with a cannon blast of speech, instantly overloading his ear canals.

He heard Liz say, "Eddie! Ed! I'm so glad I could finally reach you. Where have you been hiding, you miserable bastard? What the hell happened to your phone? Anyway, don't talk right now, just listen . . . I've got some wonderful news that's going to knock your socks off!

"Right now, the Kansai Region Bozack Schools are in a desperate need of new teachers. Some teachers quit, got fired, or whatever, and that means there're immediate openings. One of my area bosses, that huge Australian chick, she told me you should call up tomorrow, because the Japanese boss is gonna come back, and they said they can get you a follow-up or something like that. You were on the waiting list, so you get first dibs, you know what I mean? Priority selection, get it? Isn't that super?

"Just imagine, we' can probably even work together at the same branch. You met Worm, right? I can talk to him, and he'll put in a good word. It looks like I got pull. All you have to do is call the number I left in your message box. I hope you've heard it by now."

"Liz, I . . ." Eddie tried indecisively to speak, interrupt, or get a word in.

Liz continued, "Now you can finally quit that program, and you can move to the city, and we can be together. I have money saved up, you do too, so I'll move out of the company housing. We'll put our resources together—maybe you can get one of your friends out there to guarantee us, we can get ourselves a place and all that key money expensive deposit stuff won't even be an issue. Oh man, I'm so excited. Isn't that just some spectacular news!?"

The other end of the line was now disturbingly quiet at the end of Liz's tirade. She found it immediately infuriating.

Yelling, Liz spewed, "Well, what do you think, Ed? Say something!"

Her elevated volume of speech caused some Japanese people on the block to look at her like she was some sort of cuckoo nutty as a fruitcake.

Mustering the nerve to speak up for himself, Eddie uttered, "Liz, we . . . we need to talk."

Liz did not appreciate the tone of Eddie's voice or the seriousness of his inflection when he spoke. There was an ominous, prefiguring elocution that did not seem to promise good news following it. In a weird way, she felt like Eddie was ungracefully trying to sound like her father, or shrink, addressing her in a condescending manner, or as if she was mentally unstable.

Impatiently, Liz said, "I'm listening. What the fuck do we need to talk about?"

Eddie said, "Maybe we need to talk face-to-face . . ."

Tears suddenly swelled up in Eddie's eyes; he choked up. Hesitant, he tried to explain himself and how he felt about her. How grateful he was, how he was beholden and indebted to her, but his mind was changing.

Liz shouted, "Just tell me what the fuck it is you want to say, damn you!" She fidgeted in her purse for a cigarette but wished that it was a stick of weed.

Eddie stated, "Look, this isn't going to be easy for me, OK? I . . . I just wish maybe you were a bit calmer, maybe if you sat down somewhere . . . from the sound of it, you sound like yer on the street somewhere. Are you outside? Yer not at home?"

"JUST TELL ME!" Liz found herself bellowing in the night. Passersby on the avenue gaped and glared at the strange *gaijin* woman and mumbled Japanese comments of disbelief and awe at the brief spectacle. Liz didn't care, though.

For when Eddie was to begin by saying, "Liz, I found the note you left me and . . .," and as he continued, it then dawned on Liz what she was to expect—albeit profoundly unimaginable. She knew what Eddie was going to say. And then he said it! When he finally did, Liz froze on the sidewalk before her dormitory building. She went numb. Oblivious to the surrounding sidewalk full of curious Japanese eyes staring viciously at her. Her spirit had sunken to such a lowly state it could be likened to twice the discomfort rendered by a doped-out bad trip. With warm tears burning her cheek, Liz was too exhausted to even argue a case for Eddie to sleep on it and consider a change of heart. She didn't care to listen to Eddie's assurance that they "could always remain close, dear friends" and utter foolish nonsense.

It was over. They were done. The relationship between her and Edward

Roman had come to a dour and melancholy end. Without even realizing it, in a blind rage, she had hurled her phone against the concrete bricks of her housing edifice, smashing it into a network of plastic junk pieces. That was also the end of her Tuka phone.

50

LIZ WAS SO livid she destroyed her cellular phone, so when Taffie called, she was unable to reach her that way. Instead, she phoned her house line. She had run out of weed, and Liz was the only person she knew who could score for her.

Liz was in her apartment, balled up on her bed soaking her pillows with tears of sullen outrage. She had never been in a knock-down drag-out fight in her life aside from minor scraps as an elementary schooler. But for the first time ever, her level of pain and anger was so apoplectic that she was sure if she were to see or meet Eddie, she would have tried to harm him. Violently.

After all the years they had been together, it had to come to an end in Japan. The trump card she held over his head, the threesome with her best friends no longer enslaved him to the guilt trip. In her aching gut and bitter heart, she had a feeling that the Hiroko chick was involved in some sort of way. She could see through her pretend act; she knew that the woman had ulterior motives. She did not stop to consider that her hateful note to Eddie might have also precipitated his decision to end things. Or, like Eddie had told her, that their relationship had run its course and that their "interests" were growing apart. That he was beginning to like Japan and wanted to stay longer, perhaps not ever go back to the States. Liz, of course, would think this to be the most absurd thing she could expect to hear from him. Where did these sudden changes occur? she wondered amid thoughts of crashing his radio repeatedly over his imitation Jude Law face.

Her murderous thoughts were interrupted by the ringing of her room phone, Liz sprang up from her crumpled pose on the bed, alarmed. She raced to the desk where the phone was and answered it, thinking—almost hoping—it would be Eddie. Taffie's canary-shrill French accent resonated through the receiver and brought somewhat of a soothing relief to Liz after realizing it wasn't Eddie.

"What happen your phone? Cell phone?" Taffie squeaked, "I call you many times, but now, I call and the message say this phone number is not in service anymore."

Liz tried to speak, but for the first time in what seemed like an eternity, she was so crushed with overflowing emotional gloom. The unmistakable sound of sniffling and light sobbing made Taffie aware that something was awfully wrong.

"Elizabeth—oh, mon Dieu! Ce qui vous est arrive? What is matter!?" Taffie emotionally inquired, veraciously concerned.

Liz replied somberly, "Eddie and I, we broke up."

"Broke? Up?" Taffie asked, confused. "Do you mean this is that you separate permanente?"

Liz began to whimper lightly before she could respond. She explained the events that had occurred, starting from her trip to Hannan City and up to the current moment.

Taffie said, "You need not to be alone now, so I will go to your place."

Lightheartedly, Liz managed to make a feeble attempt to discourage her from coming, but deep down inside, Taffie was right. Liz really did not want to be in solitude feeling the way she did. She wanted someone to talk to, and Taffie was the best person she could think of. She was fortunate, because her French pal was a sweetheart who wouldn't take no for an answer.

An hour later, Taffie showed up with champagne, ice cream, and some horror movies. Liz cheered up almost immediately upon seeing her as if her appearance was morphine to a gaping heartache wound. Like a true friend, Taffie listened for a half hour to Liz pouring her heart out, explaining her and Eddie's story from start to finish. Taffie did not render her own opinion until they got to smoking the SES and drinking Canard-Duchene bubbly in Styrofoam cups.

Tranquilly numb from the weed smoke, Taffie said, "I am certain that he is with another woman, as you suspected. Men are like that. They always like the Japanese girl. I am so sorry for you, yes, I know, but I wish I could tell you about it sooner. But you cannot trust the Japanese woman with the man who is not from here."

Liz said coldly, "Yeah I know all about these sluts. We teach 'em every day. We see 'em at school and you see how they just drool all over these . . . these fucken geeky ass-turd guys who couldn't score a date in a raisin shop back in their own countries. They just spread their legs for anybody, and they don't even care if the guy is single or married or whatever . . . Gawd, I hate them.

"This happened to another girl I work with. Vicky. Her boyfriend left her too after gettin' seduced by one of those fucken whores! I never thought it'd happen to me, though. This is so fucked, Taf. What am I gonna do?" She paused for a long time to cover her pink flushed face to hide a saddened, weary look.

Taffie squeezed her hand. "You will recover, do not worry about this guy. You are so beautiful, you know it. You will get much better person for you, I know it."

Her talk was encouraging. Liz could find solace in the gentleness of Taffie's light voice and palpable interest in her bearing. Quietly she wanted Taffie to take her and hold her, but this, Liz felt, was not an opportune moment to accelerate or attempt any homoerotic possibility. But she wanted to be held, and at that time, Taffie was the only person available to do anything like that.

Liz initiated contact by offering her good friend a heartfelt hug, thanking her again for coming to her place, bringing all the stuff she brought, and simply plainly being concerned about her. Taffie hugged her back with equal strength and started kissing her on both cheeks in succession until finally completing the action with a long kiss to moist lips. They stared into each other's eyes for a moment, as if paralyzed by indecision, as if they were considering another amorous assembly on bedsheets.

The silence was interrupted by Liz stating, "We don't have any more drink..."

"Don't worry." Taffie broke free from Liz and dipped inside of her knockoff Hermes tote bag and produced a half-pint of Tanqueray.

Liz let out an outburst of laughter, officially cheered up, albeit by all accounts temporary. Glad she had been shopping, she rose up to get some orange juice from the fridge. "No thanks for me," Taffie said she wanted to drink gin straight. She was rolling another joint. Liz frowned up.

Self-conscious, Taffie looked up and said, "Oh, I hope you do not mind? I would like to get from you more cannabis . . . I'm sorry I roll another of yours . . ."

"No, that's not why I made that face." Liz waved off Taffie's worry; the fact that she had been digging in her weed wasn't the issue. "I think I'm about to run out of rolling paper, that's why." She sat down with a cup of ice, pouring gin and juice in her cup.

Toasting cups, Taffie said to Liz, "Oui! I understand now. I always want ask you, why you just not get easy way to smoke, like in a pipe like people usually do it?"

Liz said, "Yeah, I know. Back home we always smoked in the pipes or the bongs, yeah. Eddie used to make em' out of aluminum foil. We can smoke out of the can, but I don't really like that way—sheesh, it burns my throat up."

Taffie started to light up. She said, "You should get it, pipe."

"There's a lot of things I need to get first thing tomorrow, I'd better go see about getting a new phone. In the meantime, I'll have to use e-mail, and hey, don't forget to write down your number, or e-mail it to me. I had everybody's number, including yours, stored on the phone I thrashed. I don't remember anybody's number, and I'm like the only teacher I know who lives in company housing."

Taffie reached in her Grain de Poudre envelope wallet and slid Liz her personal Dream Lounge biz card, complete with her cell phone number as well as the number and address of the Lounge.

Liz collected the card and was like, "Cool." She went to find her own billfold wallet and added Taffie's card to the collection she already acquired. The heaviest one belonged to Candy Box owner Tabriz Najaf, which fell on the table while Liz tried to stuff them all neatly back in her fold's compartment.

Taffie placed a finger on the card, pushed it to Liz, and said in a playful tone "We should go there tonight. We have no work tomorrow morning. We can drink all night again . . . haha!"

Liz said, "Nah, I'm not in that good a mood. Hey . . . we . . . should do that X!"

Taffie got quiet suddenly. Then she said, "Are you serious?"

"I dunno . . . what do you think?" Liz said impishly.

Nervous but enchanted about doing it, Taffie said "Do you think now is good time? We have been drinking a lot . . . is it safe? I mean . . . I never try it before, I worry . . ."

"What's to worry about?" Liz tried to state convincingly, because at the same time, she was trying to coerce herself. All she knew, in the emotional wreck she saw herself in, was that anything adventurous and new would seem to remedy her condition.

Taffie then said, "OK, I know what . . . we will do it together at the night of party. Maybe Dee would like it too, but if he doesn't, we can do it together."

"What party?" Liz asked, "What the hell are you talkin' about, Taf?"

"The party, la fete de Noel, Crees-mas partee, don't you know? At Monsieur Wiggler estate? Mikako-san?"

Liz abruptly remembered. "Oh, yeah, yeah. OK! I remember now. I forgot you guys knew each other. Oh, of course. Worm told me about it today. Yeah, I'm goin', I guess . . . but at first, when Eddie decided to chicken shit out and call it quits between us, I almost wimped out, but if you're goin' I guess it'd be worthwhile. I wouldn't wanna be with all those losers kissin' his ass and Jap bitches sluttin' it up for *gaijin* geeks!"

"Ees good!" Taffie said as she stood up from her chair, kissed Liz on the forehead, and excused herself to the vanity room to change into some lilac silk tank top pajamas. She returned moments later and pulled Liz up out her chair. "Now you change too."

Liz then realized that she had not even changed from her work clothes. Taffie was spinning her around as if she was a store window mannequin and removed her skirt. They play wrestled and giggled childishly before breaking free of one another. Liz found her favorite Tinkerbell long T-shirt and washed her legs in the shower room. Taffie brought all the dope. As they cuddled with limited space on the twinnish sized bed, a torrent of tranquility engulfed Liz's senses. Taffie's scent, warmth, and overall companionship had curative, somewhat invigorating effects on her. Now she knew how Denore must have felt. How Vicky and countless other girls like her had felt. She was crushed, but Taffie was like a rescuing angel. How Liz loved her, but she knew she couldn't have her; she was fooling herself to think she could. Taffie, she knew, was into Deon heavily. But still, she desired to have Taffie stay around and continue to be the bandage to her scarred emotions. Her numbing drug, or maybe the "plugged hole in a dike" to clog impassioned overflow. But it wasn't to be, and for what it was worth, Liz did cherish the time she had spent with her. Eventually, she would have to face the music; she couldn't just succumb to the agony. Thankfully, Taffie had been there to give her that initial boost of vitality that sparked her rekindling. They watched the horror flicks and snuggled all night, and for the last night ever.

51

SOMEWHERE IN BETWEEN losing all contact with Eddie and trying to deal with the fact that she had lost him, dealing with it through cognitive dissonance, working out like a maniac and drowning her sorrows in expensive alcohol, Liz managed to sink even deeper into a devious world of sin, even if she claimed not to have meant to. Her downward spiral into corruption caused others to be entangled, bringing the emergence of malignant contempt.

In the weeks that followed Liz recounted the good fortune she happened upon. Eric Cravens and his wife walked her to a phone station shop they used. There, Liz got herself a new prepaid phone from a 'CELLUAR' company which was cheaper than Tuka and had the added new feature of e-mail. Radley came through with his hook-up and procured for her somehow a two-hour minute card—which was an amazing feat being that these types of data cards needed to be scanned—and a glass hand pipe. The latter was a great gift, as she needed not stress the necessity for making tedious trips to Umeda to cop rolling paper. However, these days, Liz was becoming fonder of cocaine more than ever. Before, she used it to perk herself up when she was feeling sleepy at work, being bored out of her skull by the asinine and gratuitous English conversation lessons she "taught" almost daily. Or she would use it as a turbo boost to an already rocking and rolling mirth gala. Nowadays, these times were more frequent.

Stephanie became her partner in crime. Upon learning that Liz had broken up with Eddie, she too attempted to relieve Liz's discomfort and be her pudgy shoulder to lean on. Initially, Liz was appreciative, but when it became a cavalcade of praise to Japanese men, she pushed back on Stephanie's talk time. By then, Stephanie was explaining to Liz that Michio was shy, and that was the reason why he avoided intimacy, but claimed he was a good kisser. She was no substitute for Taffie, but unfortunately, Taffie became suddenly consumed with her own affairs—working two jobs, shuffling between Deon and rich Doc Sarugi, and bullet train trips to Tokyo.

As for Serge, she finally caught up with him, managing to corner the French guy after work in Umeda, a week after the dreadful separation with Eddie. They didn't speak much about the time he ditched her and split with her weed. Liz thought then that with Eddie out of the mix, she and Serge could experiment with one another to see if they could be a pair, if even temporarily, just so that she could be seen with a man and appear desirable to the public eye, if anything.

Serge did not, for whatever reason, bring himself to explain to Liz that he was attracted almost exclusively to Asian women. Instead, he tried to seem moderately interested in her while remaining platonic. His ulterior motive was to have access to her surreptitious weed connection. So, on a couple of occasions, he would escort Liz to a double date with Stephanie and Michio. One night, things went sourly awry.

Jeremy Ng, who secretly had a crush on Liz for quite some time, crashed a date Liz was having with Serge, Stephanie, Michio, and Deon, who showed up because Taffie had canceled out at the last minute, because she had gone to Tokyo "on business," as he would explain it. After dinner and drinks, they decided to hit a sports bar.

Trying to prove himself to be more than just a short, kid-like companion, Jeremy had seen Serge with Liz, thinking that he was her new boyfriend or love interest. Eyeing the Frenchman with suspicion, he could see the man's wandering eyes following any sexy Japanese girl that came within his perimeter, which made him assume that Serge was either being disrespectful to his date, or simply just not into her. In any case, Jeremy saw it as his opportunity to put his bid in for Liz.

Ready to shoot his best shot to impress her, Jeremy challenged Serge to a game of pool. Serge accepted, thinking that there was no way a half-pint such as Jeremy, who was "barely taller than the pool table itself" could possibly beat him. He was wrong. Jeremy beat the pants off him. Feeling somewhat humiliated because Jeremy broke, then smacked every high ball until the final eight ball call shot, Serge demanded a rematch.

Deon was laughing his ass off because he, like Liz and everyone else who happened to be watching, was impressed. Nobody would ever have imagined that Jeremy had such talent and skill at snookers. Liz did begin to see Jeremy in a different light, but it was little more than a gifted Lilliputian. But Serge, however, was highly pissed. For even though he broke in the next rack up, like his encounter with Liz at her place, he was unable to sink any balls in holes. Jeremy smoked him again, in the same manner. Then, punctuated the victory with a triumphant gloat.

"I guess your pool game has seen better days, eh, Frenchie?" he said.

Suddenly, his eyes narrowed into a scowl of sinister rage. His abnormally pallid face became rosy enthused, and his voice thundered, "You try to humiliate me? You dare to . . . *tu m'as humile* . . . humiliate like this to me? You . . . *scelerat asiatique* . . . !"

Jeremy added fuel to the fire by playing dumb, winking at Liz, who had trouble believing the normally mild-mannered Serge could explode in such a furious outburst.

Jeremy said, "I don't know what ya said, *Frenchie*, but I . . . I . . . I don't think it sounded too nice!"

Liz caught on to Jeremy's malicious attempt to aggravate Serge. Before she could scold Jeremy to quit it, 'Serge' had grabbed a beer bottle from a nearby table in the bar. He smashed it, and the sound of the splitting glass sliced through the cacophonous atmosphere. A brief silence befell the entire bar for an instant, as all eyes looked in the direction of where the crash originated.

Jeremy didn't let up, convinced that he had won Liz's affection and attention, he said to Serge after he made a mess on the floor. "Now what did that poor bottle ever do to you?"

"Aw damn!" Deon laughed gingerly. "Jeremy, chill man . . ."

Serge lunged for Jeremy, but he was restrained by quick acting Michio, who had arrived along with Stephanie when the bottle crashing was heard. Separated from Jeremy by Michio and Deon, Serge chose to just grab his jacket and leave with his scarred pride. He split hastily without saying good-bye to Liz.

Afterward, Jeremy thought he had won Liz over to his affection, mistakenly believing that what he had done to Serge would endear her to reward him. Instead, it had the opposite effect. Liz was torqued with him and reprimanded him for taking digs all night and mercilessly whipping him at pool.

Later, Liz would try to contact Serge to try and console him, but he was not receptive. After seeing the way he exploded, Liz thought it best to give him some time. Usually, it was her who liked to throw and break things when angry, but seeing Serge do it, the shock did not quickly wear away. Being such a hot head, maybe it was for the best he had never hooked up with Taffie, she thought. For there was no telling what an explosive manner like he wielded would do when he discovered that she was two-timing on him with a rich old fogy.

Taffie, who had "forgiven" Liz for stealing his attention from her, compounded with the fact that he was a racist as well, it was a cinch to assure her Serge wasn't the guy she needed. Instead, the foreboding, fury faced Deon was the better option as it later proved.

Seeing more of Deon these days, her impression of him shifted as well. He seemed like a nice enough guy despite the fact he sometimes stared at people so vile, it gave her chills. She wasn't the only one either; also, Stephanie had indicated her discomfort being around him, but she too was a closet bigot herself. Vicky and some Japanese staffers, male and even female, too appeared to give him his space. Until she got to know him, Liz shared their opinions of Deon, but it changed. Especially since he and her now best friend—in Japan—Taffie had hit it off so harmonious.

As far as black people, she could consent to Taffie's biased description of him being exceedingly handsome, but she wasn't buying his story about being Native American. So at times she called him boy just to ruffle his feathers. This, of course, did not win her any favorable points of fondness from him, but he seemed to tolerate her, and it was likely because she was apparently a dear friend to his sweetheart.

To her detriment, spare moments that could have been used to become better acquainted with Deon was marred by Liz's pressing need to access knowledge of his ethnicity. This could cause his trademark, terrifying "Screw you, whitey!" scowl to emerge, followed up with a question like "Why does every conversation with you have somethin' to do with my nationality? If you wanna know 'bout me, I'merican. How 'bout that?"

Liz had glittered with rollicking glee. She said, "See! That's what I mean. Why d'you talk like that? You talk like *them*. You look like *them*, so what the hell kinda *Indian* are you, really? You look like a black, or a negro or Afro-whatever American. I mean, you wear all these feathers and colorful beads . . ." She tried to reach for his *collares elekes*, but he blocked her hand away blandly. "And another thing . . . how can you be a college graduate and you still talk so—ghetto?"

She would then shake her head and say, "What the fuck?" Laughing, she used her index finger circling invisible cones to her ears. "Crazy piffle!" Rolling her eyes casually.

Liz recalled how if looks could kill, Deon's would have murdered her plus one in the afterlife.

Fast forward to the Swiggler pre-Christmas Party, the informal *bonenkai*, year-end party. True to his word, Worm's setup was a bountiful smorgasbord of various dishes—not the usual Japanese stuff but platters that catered to the homesick Westerner. Turkey, poultry, pineapple baked ham, ruby cranberries, airy roll bread, scones, and much more. The affectionately dubbed mansion was transformed into an elaborate, worldly, and sophisticated dining hall. There was also champagne, another drink Liz had taken an extreme liking to as of recent, surpassing beer on her list, which was also in abundance.

Most of the teachers Liz knew who did not have work the following day—and even some who did, like Eric Cravens—showed up. It was also a sleepover event, and some people brought their own sleeping bags. Fun and festivities had begun in the early evening, and by the time Liz showed up, there were at least twenty people gathered.

Deon had planned ahead of time with Worm, and subsequently Mikako, and confirmed that he would sleep over. He had brought his two bottles of Moët, one of which he contributed to the party as a potluck offering and evaded the three-thousand-yen contribution. The other bottle he intended to save for Taffie, who was slated to appear there that night as well, but after midnight when she finished work at the Lounge in Umeda.

Liz almost bailed out again. She had thought for sure that Serge was going to attend, but he refused to take the night off from his gig at the Candy Box. Her diabolical plan had been to bring the seduction to him this time around and make the first move on him if he didn't take the initiative.

On the night of the party, Liz assumed a "devil may care" indifference to her now-blemished attendance record at Bozack and used a vacation day. This so she could get done up and spruced. Her hair was dolled up inconstantly wavy but styled elegantly by low-budget pseudo-homo Takaro in the Shinsaibashi District. As always, Takaro made Liz, as well as his other *gaijin* clients, feel like they received a knockout hairstyle just because they paid him a grip sum of cash compared to his Japanese patrons. Liz had no complaints, though. Takaro's worst was ten times better than what she would have been able to whip up herself.

Afterward, she paid a visit to the Thai sisters, Tok and Vot, at the massage parlor in Kujo. She took her usual oil *chirapsia*, rubbing and stroking. Her feet scrubbed, chiseled smooth with sandpaper brush and toes sweetened by detoxed Helebore leaves and a mint substance mixture, the scent of which pleased her abundantly even though it made her feet feel cold.

Radley, who would work for her the following day, had boosted for her a stunning nectarine-colored Lycra midi dress. Since it was from a downtown Osaka Department Store, the size was a bit off. Thus, for Liz, it turned out to be more like a sexy miniskirt because instead of mid-calf, the garment hiked to her sponge-cake mid-thighs. Her tasty, toned flanks never ceased to cause many ogling orbs oscillating all through town, and that night was no different. This time however, there was no Eddie to dissuade any would-be suitors from approaching her, enticed by her pair of porn-star gams, which were exceedingly rare in Japan. Even foreign guys Liz detested, who were suction-cupped to Japanese significant others, had to stare conscientiously at her while she slipped off her dress-matching-colored saldana pumps, undressing the rest of her in their fiendish imaginations.

Feeling as if she had dolled up for nothing, Liz almost backed out of attending the party because Serge had elected to ditch for work. But she remembered that she had promised Taffie that she would go, and that was the night they would pop the X for the first time.

Earlier, a frustrated and daring Liz decided to postpone her lily-livered apprehension and clipped half of her 200-milligram tablet of X. She chewed it up, washing the powdery excess down with bottled water. Storing the other half of the tab in her medicine cabinet, she split her crib on the upswing of midnight. Outside of her dorm building, she peered languidly at the Loop Line train in the distance, as it coasted its rails admonishingly to last minute dashers and stragglers before it discontinued service for the night. Her light head was beginning to float its way to another space of place and time. Before her mind was totally spin-cycled, she flagged a cab.

"*Way*-Hommachi, *cue-the-sigh*!" she shouted at the driver in one of her first earnest attempts to speak more Japanese by creating pronunciation equivalents in English, falsely foreshadowing a diligent effort to improve her skill to a moderately proficient level.

Along the ride, she was drinking the Nando Asti-Spumante sparkling wine, intended for the party BYOB. But Liz seriously, indeed, thought she had been drinking Sprite or a lemon-lime soda, but in a tall, frosty bottle. She killed it by the time she was dropped off in front of the Kintetsu Department Store. After paying the cab, she took a final zesty swig of the swill and tossed the jeroboam up in the air, and it blinged down on Sen Nichi Mae Street in an exploding blast, she did it as a tribute to her memory of Serge's reaction to his defeat in pool at the hands of Jeremy Ng. To her, this was hilarious; but to the Japanese onlookers, she was an improbable, lunatic pretty girl who was drunk off her rocker.

She couldn't remember the way to Worm's place, so she whipped out her new CELLULAR brand phone and rang up her sidekick Stephanie. Loyal and courteous, the already-tipsy Stephanie obliged to come and scoop her up after successfully guiding her by phone to the huge Pachinko Parlor on the grand intersection.

Finally arriving, Liz was mind foggy and felt as if her brain was rotating, spinning round like a record on a phonograph. It did not affect her balance, but she did not feel in control of her head for it to remain still upon her shoulders. Her neck felt squishy as if it were made of chewed bubblegum. People were partying, drinking, and those Liz thought she knew approached her for small talk, but she was barely coherent in the discussions. She was interested in the whereabouts of Taffie.

Since the party had set off earlier that night around seven, people who had begun indulging in all the wine and alcohol had either drunk their fill, crashed, left, or all of the above. Liz was surprised to hear that Deon was among those who had retired to his guest room provided by the Swigglers. Worm took Liz to the room where Deon was out cold napping. Liz peeked inside and fought the urge to disturb him. Unlike Liz, he had worked that day; and in addition, had also risen early that morning and was bushed. Aware of Taffie's delayed arrival, it was a safe guess for everyone that he was resting up, or just taking a nap. Liz couldn't blame him, and in a weird, concupiscent way, she envied him to be able to kiss Taffie and her body. Worm half-dragged Liz back downstairs to rejoin the festivities.

Nobody at the gathering seemed interested in what was playing on the massive theater-screen television. The attendees, still vibrant, were busy playing some zany, crazy spin-the-bottle-type, truth or dare game. Stephanie, Michio absent tonight, quickly joined the game and urged Liz to join as well.

Mikako wasn't thrilled about having either Liz or Stephanie in her home, but she concealed it well. Popularity, however, with her young husband's friends was a matter of necessary importance to her. To them, knowing and having a decent handful of *gaijin* acquaintances was like being in possession of rare resources. Since Worm intended to someday branch out on his own and create his own English school business, access to an abundant oasis of foreign heads would be beneficial. As such, she did not care to upset the flow and voice her uneasiness around certain types and instead kept the peace. So long as things did not escalate out of control with the drug activity, she could put up with a reasonable amount of craziness and/or youthful exuberance.

She suspected correctly that Liz and Stephanie were heavier into the illicit drug activity than some of the other people Worm hung around. It was bad enough her husband occasionally dabbled with the ganja with his cohorts Keefer, Ricky, and Simon. But after Worm's persistent browbeating her, citing how it was "legal" in North America, he was ultimately able to sway her into allowing him, in a private foyer of the house, to indulge. So Mikako tolerated the weed to a volatile extent, but at the core, she was still Japanese, and one who had a very rigid, stringent view of marijuana. Her view pretty much mirrored the rest of her society about the plant considered a drug—that it was a menace to society and not medicinal as some places in the Western world perceived it. Therefore, she knew all too well that lengthy jail sentences awaited those who dared use it or have it on their person. It was no different, to them, than any other narcotic such as cocaine, heroin, or some other form of controlled substance. As such, she was obviously dreadfully afraid of being caught with any type of dope on her person; she had no choice but to give those high-risk types like Liz the eye of scrutiny.

Around 2:00 p.m., the party had died down to a fraction of what it was at its height. Things got ceremoniously mushy to fit the occasion when ornery Ricky Exmouth and meretricious significant other, Rena Akamatsu announced that they were going to get married. Ricky had popped the question that night. Liz wasn't in any mood to feel happy for anyone; it would remind her of how miserable she was trying not to be, thinking about the fact that Eddie should have been with her that night.

Meanwhile, cigarette waterhole meeting conversations between Japanese-spoused husbands who could sneak away from their women long enough to have a sub rosa daint, went to the tune of "Take a look yonder at that 'Lizabeth chick, damn she's fuckin' hot. If I wasn't married, I'd . . ."

"Give her a go, mate. I heard she just broke up with the guy she was seeing a while ago. I'm sure she's gonna get lonely, man they all do. She'll be dyin' fer a mercy fuck. Like that plump twat Steph . . ."

"Bah! Stephanie's a cow. Her mouth and ass is like . . . everybody's 'break in case of emergency' with yer cock; heard she swallows...but, you hear about Liz and that Black guy Kwame? I heard she got 'im fired or something."

"Shit! Didja hear why?"

"Dunno exactly, but what I gather'd hinted at the big ape tried to grab 'imself a piece of her."

"Can't say I blame him . . . geez . . . she's fucked up tonight too, huh? Anybody could probably give it to her . . . she'd probably like it. She looks like a cunt . . . damn, I brought sand to the beach . . ."

"Me too, oh, speakin' of which, gotta get back, the ole ball and chain beckons . . . thanks fer the fag break!"

Inside the cavernous living room with the fireplace, Liz and Stephanie were giggling like insane asylum patients. Stephanie was drunk, and Liz was something beyond to the point where human faces seemed like rubber masks, voices echoed, the eyes of Eric Cravens coruscated like two giant lightbulbs. Worm looked like he was wearing a balloon suit. Rena's teeth work looked like piano keys. Mikako's body shape was like Mayor McCheese, Liz had endless observations that targeted her funny bone.

A portion of remaining guests were still playing the "Truth or dare"–type game. Things got crazy when people like Stephanie began opening their shirt, revealing nipples on breasts out of drunken dares. Sudden erections began popping up, so Mikako had to quickly split to the kitchen to whip up some iced daiquiris to cool down the tension in the room.

Worm helped his wife make the drinks. He laced them with more vodka than was necessary, and the first to get knocked on their ass from it was Stephanie. Worm started laughing like the whole thing was funny. He too was birdbrained from the pot intake he too had indulged in, and he sneaked away with his boy Ricky to take some hit while Mikako and the girls tended to Stephanie.

Liz did not care to wait around for Stephanie's outcome to be meted, so she roamed about the fantasy mansion in search of discovery. Mikako kept a close eye on her and rushed to gently restrain her as if she were working in a mental institution, guiding her to her straitjacket.

Mikako thought it was good that Stephanie was out cold, Worm and the guys could get her to a guestroom or sofa. Now if she could only reel Elizabeth in, she could rest easy for the rest of the night because she too was tired as hell.

She had forgotten that she had already given Liz the tour of their home, which was nothing remotely akin to any type of architecture the American girl thought she'd ever see in Japan. Simultaneously, Liz was too blitzed in the brain to consider all the babble Mikako was continuously spewing.

Instead of listening to Mikako talk about her home, oil paintings, and artifacts, Liz just threw her arms around her and started kissing her on the cheek as if she were her long-lost auntie, or fake five-dollar Indian sister of her Iowa-native mother, Ida, or her lesbian assistant volleyball coach whose name she never quite remembered. Who would ever have thought? she mulled, never imagining hugging up on a Japanese woman. The daiquiris she and Worm made had been fantastic! Liz thought.

With all the toxins she had taken in the entire night, she was close to having an out-of-body experience. To the extent, at some point, she felt as if she were floating in the air, above toward the ceiling, and watching herself talk to the quadragenarian former felch feature film star fluffer.

Mikako was skeptical, not knowing whether to believe Liz or not, but she welcomed the affection, whether it was genuine or not. She wasn't blind, and because of her own covert past, she could tell that Liz was also a freak. She had her fair shares of lesbian affairs in her rearview time mirror, and was not opposed to any future endeavors, clandestine or otherwise, but she wasn't thrilled about linking up with druggies.

Mikako said in very good English, "Would you like to retire to your guestroom?"

Liz was like, "Sure," and figured she might as well wind down. Or like Deon, "take a nap," since it was billed as an all-night party. Mikako took her to a small room that looked like a walk-in closet, but stripped bare save for a unique adult-sized cushion bag. In her boggled state of mind, it was the most amazing thing she had ever seen. She hopped on it, and as it swallowed her almost whole in a bundle of softness, she recognized Taffie had a similar one—only hers was a bigger, fold-out futon version that could also function as a sofa. She lay there being crushed by cotton, too formless and cushy to be dangerous, and she nearly dozed off. The makeshift bed was immediately "posture-pedic," something a chiropractor would likely approve or recommend, compared to the petrified mattress she slept on every night. She felt the muscles in her back being soothed and the occasional popping kinks like Tok at the Thai parlor.

Mikako returned with bath towel, blanket, and a cute, colorful red peppermint candy–striped dressing gown with a slit on its side that extended suggestively up her prepossessing, goading thighs. Liz had changed into the gown with lightning speed. Mikako checked out Liz's younger, full-figured curves and enviously hoped that she did not come back downstairs and cause more of a ruckus as had the sudden sight of Stephanie's voluptuous boobs.

Approximately an hour later, Liz would awake in a cold sweat. She snapped out of a nightmarish reverie, which had featured herself, Taffie, Stephanie, and Mikako in a bubble bath Jacuzzi. Weird but true. Then, in her still looped and muddled mind state, she realized Taffie was due to arrive at the party that night.

Stuporous, she staggered lightly to the hall outside her room, the mansion had grown sleepily quiet. Bizarrely, the party was pretty much deadened with the departure of Liz, and perhaps Stephanie too. Devious husbands hoping for more ribald antics or manipulating drunken sots like the pair of American broads—the ditzy plus-sized Bitch Curl girl and the classical Dumb Blonde—to strip more so they could have something to fantasize about while sleeping with their Japanese wives and their hackneyed boxes.

Furthermore, although Liz hadn't known about it, Tim the Duke had arrived. He was not welcome at the party or the Swiggler home by order of Mikako, who was hip to his "get down". She didn't even want Worm to associate with him outside of work. Worm did his best to obey, but compromised with his wife, agreeing to never invite him inside their home; but he didn't want to cut him loose completely. He was somewhat a useful person. Like tonight, he had arrived, not to the party but outside in one of his cars. He came to pick up Ricky, Simon, and their girls, Rena and Chikako.

When all those people left, the remaining Japanese wives helped clean things up and had the place stripped like they were ants at a picnic. Stephanie was allowed to crash on the plush acorn-shaped sofa. Others bedded down in their sleeping bags by the fireplace. A dull silence, save for the light snoring, blanketed the space.

Zoned, Liz was creeping about as if she was in a huge haunted mansion. Dimly lit carpeted hallways in the night led her to Deon and Taffie's guestroom. Figuring her honey was there, she entered the pitch-dark quarters; she didn't even bother trying to find a light switch or a lamp. Barely she made out the wide, queen-sized sunken divan and heard some snoring that sounded like a wolf growling its rendition of a light thunder roll. She edged closer to the bed and reached out her hand, and it contacted a thick, furry mane, and ran her fingers through what was like a network of silky cobwebs. Thanks to her heavy intake of vitamin A–rich foods like veggies, squash, broccoli, and such, her eyes could adjust from night blindness somewhat and what little illumination rendered from the double-casement window.

Faintly, she could see the shape of Taffie alongside him in the satin, moon silver licked sheets. Liz giggled like a Satanic gamine. She removed her dressing gown and let it drop to the side of the bed. Standing bare save for her torridly tempting cut out lace panties, which she had worn to initially use as her bargaining weapon to beckon Serge with, but now, the better to feel against Taffie, who, by as far as Liz could ascertain, had not taken the X like she had, but it didn't matter. She climbed inside the bed.

That which she suspected had been Taffie was, in fact, a collection of pillows and a Doraemon plush toy. Removing the stuffed animal, she tossed it and the pillows away and about. Groped in the darkness for Taffie, but she wasn't there! She snuggled quietly, koala-style to Deon's hard, bare muscular back. Compared to Eddie, he was like stone. Warmer too, as if he had been baked in an oven. Liz purred pleasantly as his coconut-and-mango smell teased her nose as if in her dreams she could taste a cookie of the same aroma. Her near-sandpaper-rough tongue blindly and dreamily flickered like that of a serpent for a "cookie," tasting the sweet back of Deon.

All of a sudden, the snoring stopped. Deon shifted position and reversed himself toward her. A beguiling erection poked at Liz's inner thigh, arousing her instantly; but in a lethargic, and slumberous drug-induced sort of way. Without realizing it, she clung tighter to him, their faces so close together, their lips literally touched. Her sleepwalking reverie turned hallucination drifted her off into a deep sleep. And that was it. Nothing happened.

This was unlike a decade earlier, back in California, at Crystal Lake Camp in Angeles National Park. She ditched Carver Burk so that she could go camping with Becky and some other volleyball teammates. She crashed the tent of Becky and a football jock she was with. Becky didn't get upset about it because they were kooky cohorts in promiscuity. However, it was not like that this time.

Liz and Deon fell asleep in each other's arms. Simplistically, an innocent thing, but Taffie was not able to determine as much when she discovered the two of them in such position when she arrived there in the wee hours of the morning.

Earlier, Mikako had taught Taffie the security code to their intricate house gate. It was for her to use in the event things became too festive at the party, she could just enter as she pleased. Problem was, Taffie's conflict with Saiko, her apartment mates, and coworkers had intensified. She believed that she was being followed around but couldn't prove it. Her work had finished later than expected. Saiko requested her presence again to accost her with inquisition, while Taffie defiantly remonstrated. The ensuing discussion caused her tardiness to deliver her at the Swiggler estate at around 4:00 a.m. when everyone had long since retired. Having been on good terms with the Swigglers, it hadn't been Taffie's first time there at the mansion, and she knew where *her* guestroom with Deon (and her *Doraemon*) would be; but she never expected to see the sight she saw that twilight dawn.

Imprudently, Liz had some aberrant determination she was to have a repeat experience as she had with Becky back in the day. She and Taffie had joked about it before—a threesome, where she would conceivably offer up her Eddie, or do the "Eddie thing" and go double up on Serge or some random guys at the Candy Box or Pink Carnation or Sun Splash where Chucky and Denore used to go. Ironically, however, she would fall asleep. Mistakenly thinking that Taffie was also in the bed, Liz had no functioning idea that it was Deon with whom she was cuddling.

Likewise, Deon too was oblivious. Normally, he was neither a smoker nor a drinker, but earlier that previous day, he had risen early to shop for a gift to present to his other friends across town. They too were having a get-together; he drank and smoked with them before arriving at Worm's spot to consume another load of champagne that kayoed his low tolerance for substance. Feeling the warm embrace of who he thought was Taffie, but was actually Liz, he cradled her lovingly. Delirious.

Taffie was shocked, forthwith heartbroken. She felt betrayed by both Deon and Liz. She may have joked about *menage a'trois* with Liz, but she never intended for it to include her own Deon, if she even agreed to it at all. And Deon, all his talk about how he "despised *le diable blanc*" and "white devils" and not being attracted to white women—it was all talk! Lies! He had definitely fooled her, she thought.

Deciding to leave as quickly as she came, Taffie did just that, but not before snapping photos, with her digicam, of the scene she saw. The camera's flash streaked phosphorescently in the room like lightning but failed to awaken the ostensible love couple in bed. What a bitch! Taffie muttered to herself. She left. Liz would never see her again. Ever.

***

At 10:00 a.m., rays of the morning sun glinted brightness to the chamber in which Liz and Deon had slept. Yawning, Liz crawled out of bed and casually slipped into her peppermint gown. She exited the room to tinkle at the lavatory in the outside hall.

Deon woke shortly after Liz's evacuation with her saliva all over his cheeks like ectoplasm, exacerbating his eerie, gnawing feeling as if he had slept with a ghost. He regretted drinking tequila with his homeboys the night before, then later arriving at Worm's and drinking more champagne with the *diablos blancos*. Looking at the empty space beside him on the bed, it was clear to him, or so he thought, that Taffie hadn't shown. She had blown him off again. He was no idiot. All those trips to Tokyo couldn't be only for business, he deduced. He correctly suspected Taffie was double-clutching another dude. So he too was a little distraught. Because although he was crazy about the exotic French Rae Dawn looker, he would have to eventually cut her loose. Checking his phone, she hadn't even called him. To even have the decency to call and inform him, leave a message—something, anything just to let him know that she wasn't coming. Nothing. So he didn't bother to call her back either.

Instead of returning to Deon and Taffie's guestroom, Liz opted to return to her own quarters and plopped down on the cushion bag. It was so fluffy and enveloping that it induced her to snooze again for another half hour before she was awakened by the knock of Mikako.

The lady of the house politely requested Liz's presence for late breakfast. Liz obliged and got dressed pell-mell quickly, joined the others downstairs where the smell of coffee, silver dollar pancakes, and popcorn greeted her pleasingly. The battered faces of the morning, motley collection of hungover foreign and Japanese at the long banquet table looked like an offbeat reenactment of the Thanksgiving Dinner at Plymouth Rock and Pilgrims.

Loquacious Stephanie machine-gunned Liz's ears with gabble as soon as she appeared, proceeding to ravenously slam down morning feed. Around this time, a massive headache bombed Liz's skull not long after she enjoyed a return to a state of normalcy with ingestion of the aromatic black coffee.

Finally, around noon, all party attendees—Liz and Stephanie included—had dispatched into the directions of their dutiful paths of existence. Deon had taken his time and utilized the home's shower, so he missed the breakfast gathering, wasn't there to say good-bye to Liz and tell her that Taffie—to his knowledge—hadn't shown up.

Liz, on the other hand, was convinced Taffie had been there but wanted to get back to her own dorm bed, even if it was stone hard compared to her choices of where to rest at Worm's. She had to nurse her aching dome with an extended spell of rest and left, splendidly satisfied she had requested that day off from work. She would get in touch with Taffie later. Or so she thought. But it was not to be. She was neglectfully unaware at the time that she had severely damaged her relationship with Taffie to critical, irreversible proportions.

52

WITH THE CHRISTMAS parties and year-end celebrations coming to a pass, Liz would be poised to endure perhaps the worst holidays ever experienced. For the first time in her life, there were no Christmas trees, elaborate shopping sprees on Rodeo Drive, no stockings by the fireplace, singing carols, sipping egg nog, opening presents, and, overall, spending time with loved ones. If not Eddie, then at least her family. Her brother, Halbert just got married. She received pictures of the wedding. She spoke to her mother Ida.

Mother, Ida wanted Liz to come home. Especially when she heard the news of Liz and Eddie's breakup. She practically begged.

Liz had said, "Mom, I thought about it, but . . . I can't . . . not right now . . . Besides, it's too late. It'll cost a fortune to get one of those last-minute flights for the holidays."

Ida said, "But, honey-y-y, since when does money really matter? That country is nowhere for you to be at a time of year like this! Especially if you're alone . . ."

Somewhat nagged, Liz said, "Not true, Mother-r, I'm not *alone*. I have my friends here. It's just that asshole Ed . . ." She sobbed, her voice starting to crack. "I...can't believe he would do this to me! Why? And why now!?"

Ida said intently "People change, honey...it's inevitable. It's par the course of life. Anyway, you don't need him. We never really thought he was good for you anyway, me or your father. We always thought you could do better. I mean, what ever happened with you and Carver? He calls from time to time. He even wrote you a letter, y'know?"

Sniffling, Liz said in disbelief, "He did? What in Gawd's name for ?"

"Well, I never opened your mail. Whatever comes here for you, we keep and put in your old room," Ida said soothingly "But I'm sure he merely wishes you well and maybe he just wanted to see how you were doing. He doesn't have your number there, does he?"

"Of course not, Mother," Liz said, drying her eyes, loading up her favorite new "toy" as of recent, her hand pipe with some ambrosial "hydro" bud. "Even if he had it, he wouldn't have it now, because I changed my number a few weeks ago. Right, after me and Ed broke up."

Ida continued to low-key plead Carver's case. "He's such a nice, sweet guy. He's the kind of man you need in your life. I heard he is doing well. He's out in Pasadena now, and he had a good career, he's some kind of social worker teacher, something like that, I heard through the grape vine, you know..."

"Pasadena, *where the grass is greener*. Well, that figures," Liz said, toying with her pipe. "The job he put us on to was teaching."

"I don't think that was a bad decision for you to make. I was proud of you, actually, when I heard you were a teacher just like me!" Ida said cheerfully.

"That's why I don't wanna come back home just yet. I don't want to give up. Not like this. I don't want it to seem like Ed broke me because of what he did to me. I'm not a quitter. Besides, things are going well for me. I'm doing fine with my current job, the money's pretty freakin' awesome, and the work itself is a piece of cake, can almost do it in my sleep. The only thing I hate is just all the craziness in this country with politics, and the people . . . people like the women. You just can't keep a man here if you're a foreign girl like I am . . ."

"Dear, you should really consider coming home soon, however. I understand you are doing fine with your job now, and your father and I support you 100 percent. I want you to know that. But I am absolutely certain you can find work just as rewarding and beneficial right here in the U.S., in California. Or anywhere, your home will always be waiting."

"Thanks, Mother," Liz said, somewhat upbeat, feeling the love and support emanate from her mother's vocal transmission to her ears. She maintained her stability to not succumb to tears, then said, "Thanks for always supporting and encouraging me. I won't let you down. I won't let myself down. I . . . I'm gonna get through this."

Ida sighed peacefully, for she was relieved that her daughter was showing signs of fortitude. She could not perceive, however, that Liz was also a drug user and booze fiend. From start to finish, Liz had championed the art of concealing her vice from her folks.

She said, "What if Carver calls again? What do you want me to tell him? Do you want me to give him your number there?"

"No, it'll probably be better just to give him my e-mail address. Electronic mail is the new standard now, Mother. It's quicker and easier and free most often."

"If you say so," Ida said comically. "I still am trying to get up to date with all of these new gadgets and technology. I mean, over there in Japan, it must be mind-boggling. All those rapid fast trains, the computerized robots and motorcycles—it must be bananas!"

"Sure is," Liz said, eyeing her pipe, wanting to take a hit, but fearful her mother might catch on to what she was doing by the long pauses and clicks of the cigarette lighter to flame the bud. She could care less about Japan and its technology to a large extent. Only that which she could use and understand was all she concerned herself with, and what she didn't know, she could have computer wonks like Eric or Radley on hand to explain.

The conversation would continue for almost an hour. Liz used an international phone card purchased at a convenience store to have the 90-minute conversation via house phone. She also got a chance to shout out to her father and brother Halbert before his honeymoon to Las Vegas.

As for the job, Liz worked on Christmas Eve, as this day in Japan was not the sacred, grandiose holiday it was represented as in Western society. Kayo Terumi and a distraught-eyed senior sub-manager, Mayumi Kazegawa, threw a makeshift party with grab-bag presents for all the teachers. There was food and drink (non-alcoholic), but the boorishly rude goof-off guys used Kayo's Christmas tree cookies as *shuriken* for alley cats.

Fortunately, the pangs of heartbreak and melancholy feelings did not prevail over her during her shift. She was also joined by other teachers stuck with having to work through the holidays because they either couldn't take the vacation days off, or simply didn't have any vacation days to use. In Liz's case, she had to play the back and allow teachers with seniority to take leave before she could, as she was a new employee of less than a year.

Liz could not have imagined that she would be so happy to see and meet Stephanie. Taffie had suddenly gone AWOL, and so did Deon. Worm had taken yet another two-week vacation, and pretty much everyone else she knew had either gone away or had plans other than remaining in the Osaka area.

Jeremy Ng, who still had eyes for Liz, was relentless in his campaign to try to score her to his harem. He insisted upon being a part of any outing that she and Stephanie had planned. He too was stuck in Japan for the holidays.

Stephanie too believed Liz needn't be alone during the new year, so she called a kangaroo court meeting consisting of herself, Liz, Keefer, Radley and Jeremy after work, Sunday Christmas Eve. Bozack School was going to close on December 28 until Wednesday, the third of the following year. During that time, Stephanie figured that they should all do things together during this time of the winter recess. This was more for her benefit—and subsequently Liz's as well—so they could stave off piercing pricks of empty solitude. For Stephanie's Michio was busy working his job and claimed he had to visit his mother in the faraway Japanese location of Hamamatsu, some three and a half hours east of Osaka.

Jeremy came up with the brilliant idea of going snowboarding. He had eavesdropped on Liz's conversations during her lessons and discovered that among her many athletic hobbies, they shared a common interest in winter sports like skiing and such. There were several affordable and economical getaway package tours in the prefecture of Nagano that looked interesting and tempting—so much so, that even Liz was brimming with a little excitement at the thought of going.

As it were, Keefer was out. A busybody such as himself had plenty of options on how to spend his holidays, and for him, a standard, grimy pub in the Osaka atmosphere was all he would need. Loneliness, like how it struck foreign girls such as those around him, was never an option he had to consider. Radley's story was similar, but he also had a girlfriend with whom to spend time.

Vicky and her Japanese boyfriend almost went, but they backed out at the last minute because they were going through some relationship turmoil. Liz didn't get the entire gist of Vicky's situation, but it had to do with a possible love triangle involving not only her J-dude, but also the estranged fiancé Jack, and still yet another English teacher whom neither Stephanie nor Liz knew. Regardless, Vicky had been busy in her days and time off, and considerably lots on her own plate to deal with. They could understand why she opted out of the trip.

Leaving only three people: Stephanie, Liz, and Jeremy. The former and the latter tried to contact other teachers, even Deon; but everyone either had plans, or couldn't be reached. Eric Cravens and Radley were spending times with wife and future wife, respectively.

Determined not to allow the absence of a crowd to discourage them in any way, Stephanie and Liz resigned to take the trip, and Jeremy eagerly tagged along, appearing with them like an adopted kid brother from an exchange family. They even shared the hotel room. This worked against Jeremy's fiendish plot to crawl up onto Liz after getting her drunk, because Stephanie was always around to cock-block. Until the final evening of the three-day two-night package tour.

In the daytime, they endured yawn evoking sightseeing tours of Azumino City's wasabi farms, the latter of the afternoon hitting snowy slopes of Hakuba. At night, they partied hard with some Yamazaki 18-year whiskey. Liz, of course, had snuck her precious pipe and smoked up the party with the latest batch of hydro copped from Mr. Silver, as well as a gram of C, pure and white like the milky banks they had enjoyed the previous two days.

Like Deon, Jeremy was a little weak for smoking marijuana, but considered himself a bullfrog when it came to drinking games. He tried to con the ladies into a strip poker game, but neither Liz nor Stephanie was familiar with the game, so they played crazy eights instead, and loser—or losers—had to either take a drink or remove their clothing. Having seen how blitzed Stephanie could get, it was a cinch to get her fucked up and see her pass out, so Jeremy figured Liz would be much the same.

To his chagrin, however, it was not to be. Liz could hang with the best of drink champs, and Jeremy would find that out as the night progressed on past midnight.

Jeremy kept losing. He was a pool hall prodigy perhaps, but a card shark he wasn't on that night. Stephanie and Liz would practically take turns winning, literally beating the pants off Jeremy, who would have to take heaping glass drinks to the head, as was the agreement. Although he too had the option of removing an item of clothing, the outcome he had hoped for did not end quite as planned. Stephanie did eventually drop like a ton of bricks, but so did Jeremy; both, relieved of their pants due to their losses at the game. The last remaining was Liz, who polished off the last of the whiskey and sealed it with a mega-blast of the THC Poltergeist to the brain. She was so entranced she had to go for a walk outside.

She ventured out of the hotel lobby and stood in the icy-cold climate of the Nagano Prefecture, one of Japan's most popular destinations for winter sports and activities. The mountains of Azumino were bewitching. She was taken by the rich, beautiful scenery, but the place seemed void of life, like Hannan, only covered with snow. When creeping thoughts of Eddie emerged, and how she should have been spending such time with him and enjoying the view together, it alerted her that it was time to return to her quarters and rejoin her party.

When she got back to the hotel room, she beheld the comical sight of partially clothed Jeremy and Stephanie stretched out on the same bed of two in the hotel room, knocked out, flush faced, and snoring. Liz wasn't exactly wise to the fact that Jeremy had the hots for her, and even if she did, she wouldn't have taken him seriously. To her, he was like an imitation Japanese lookalike, only shorter, who just happened to have been born in the United States and could call himself American, but she didn't find him attractive or desirable in terms of what she'd look for in a bedtime stud. Jeremy, in her opinion, would have had a better chance with Stephanie, as she was hard up and desperate. On the bed together, they looked like they had just finished a sexual act, and Liz couldn't stop giggling about it.

Relieved that she could crash in the vacant bed intended to be for Jeremy as it had been the previous night, Liz laughed herself to sleep. It turned out to be a therapeutic getaway after all.

***

Approximately two hundred miles away to the west, a heartbroken Taffie Jolie walked the chilly late night, streets of Osaka, having just returned from a self-imposed exile in Tokyo. Still disheartened by the sight of Liz and her newest, and favorite paramour Deon, hugged up and naked in bed, after what she had apparently taken to be a hot sexual tryst. The funny thing, she accepted, was that she had expected it to happen. She really wanted to like Liz. She was the only foreigner at the language school who had ever tried to be her friend, besides Worm; but for him, it seemed he wanted her to have a female friend more so than he had taken interest in being common with her in the same capacity he was with others like Liz, Stephanie, and those he worked closely among. However, all along she had a feeling that she would not be able to put her trust in *les Americains*—the Americans—for a lengthy period.

It was inevitable. Because their mindsets were so different, it would be impossible for harmony. For in her native France, extramarital affairs were not uncommon occurrences, but the lengths to which Americans felt they needed to go to hide, lie to and deceive people—some of whom their friends or loved ones even—was befuddling, difficult to grasp. Liz was not the only one to blame— Deon was too. Supposedly, he had loved her, Taffie mused solemnly; but he must have been a superb liar. He hadn't even called her again! Perhaps, he and Liz became "official". At this point, how could she trust anyone?

Life in Osaka, for her, had been turmoil from the jump. First Sonny had to up and die. In the aftermath of his passing, she received no inheritance, allowance, or bequeathing of any sort from his estate. In Japan, engagement did not officially count as almost married, especially to a non-citizen and foreigner. She didn't even have the scratch to return to France, as she had given up everything to make the Japan move in the first place. Even if she did return to Paris, a homeless shelter was her likely destination. All because her sugar daddy meal ticket for life had ticker issues, he had never discussed with her before he asked for her hand in marriage and flew her out.

So fortunate she was to have met Mama-san Saiko Yamabiko. She had been, at one point earlier in life, Sonny's hostess, friend, and confidante. Taffie was weeping her beautiful, darkened eyes at a ceremonial hall where Sonny's funeral was held, and where she hadn't been welcomed. Pitying her, she took the dethroned young French princess under her protective wing. She gave her a job right away, seeing her value and what a prize she would make for the Dream Lounge. The rare sight of *kokujin*—or black people in Japan—would make her appeal even more exotic. And she was right.

When Taffie was fed the idea of working as a hostess, she did not understand completely what the job entailed. But she was a quick study. She learned the ropes, and the art of fleecing and gold digging emerged from her character as if it was a dormant attribute that had existed all along. She would make quick money, but she would still be indebted to Mama-san Saiko because of her "loan" and expenses covered for the one-room shack in the roach- and mice-infested building she owned, where Taffie and other hostesses at the Dream Lounge were *required* to reside.

Initially, the deal was that Taffie would work for Saiko, for however long it took for her to get her money up and save enough to pay the *mama-san* back. Problematic, however, would be Taffie's ad interim need to pay rent, utilities, cell phone, and its bill. In addition, she had to eat, buy clothes (that fit), use public transportation, and a minutia of various expenses. If matters couldn't worsen, Saiko had to add "interest" to what Taffie owed to the tune of "half itchy-man" monthly.

Fortune again befell her because she was quite the attraction for the Lounge. She stole attention and clients from some of the wrecked Romanian chicks and cock-teasing Korean girls. In so doing, she collected lots of tips, and it complemented her salary well, so she could earn a franc. Also, she enjoyed her work, but this had a drawback because it turned her into an alcoholic. This was the last thing she wanted to be as she didn't want to go the route of her deceased mother, who had become a depressed alkie before her untimely freak-accident demise.

Working in her favor for popularity was her diligence in studying Japanese. While with Sonny, she had studied and practiced a lot; now with the job as a hostess, talking was an integral part of the job she embraced and got on-the-job training, abundantly sufficient. Again, this made her popular in a good way with the Japanese clientele, but in a bad way with her foreign colleagues. Hollow threats of violence and whispering campaigns ensued, making life at the Saiko-owned dwelling borderline miserable, and creating more distance between the coworkers even though they hid this while at work.

Before too long, Taffie came to understand the debacle in which she was immersed, and there was no way around it, because Saiko would take her cut from her salary prior to Taffie even touching it. To just have the money to purchase a return flight to France would not be enough, she would also need a sizable cushion of money to land in stability until she could attain employment, hopefully—however dismally—back as a domestic or in an exclusive hotel. To do this, she needed another job, it seemed. Otherwise, she would be like a slave to Saiko for an extended time frame. She wasn't sure about this. Although she liked drinking, dancing, and enjoying the benefits of the nightlife, she didn't imagine it to be healthy in the long run.

She caught wind of teaching opportunities to earn cash, but few schools were hiring French teachers as the demand for learning the language was not as high as English. At that time, Taffie's English was not impressive enough to any small-time school for them to hire her. She almost got a job at a transient school called Special K, but her procrastination due to considering the measly sum of pay they were offering resulted in the place hiring a male French teacher in her stead; and for a while, her hopes of a side hustle making loot had to be shelved.

One fateful night, a hiring scout for a relatively newly established language school paid the Dream Lounge a visit after being tipped off about certain night lounges and "snack" bars in the Kita-Shinchi District having foreign hostesses. The scout struck gold at Saiko's lounge, but also almost got himself "struck" by the blackjack of henchman-like errand boy Yutaka, who thought the guy was an undercover immigration agent. Nervously the scout individual explained that even if immigration issues were precarious, he assured that they could be legitimized.

The Japanese man was a representative of Bozack Corporation. He was combing the streets within Japan's borders for foreign staff to cut costs compared to hiring from abroad. These successful candidates would be teachers for their schools. To compete with the big dogs, this company had to come up with something that differentiated them from the other schools in a unique way. So they hired lots of "non-white" teachers and offered more languages than just English. French happened to be one for which they were in desperate need. Thus, it was understandable for the scout's elation upon discovering two birds with one stone fortune in Taffie. Likewise, the man's proposition to Taffie caused a brief glimmer of delight.

The Bozack scout was then able to work out an under-the-table deal during the "human traffic" negotiation with Saiko. She was paid a nominal fee for her "introduction" of a client and said individual's subsequent signing of a yellow-dog contract of sorts. Taffie had no knowledge of this, or the negotiation made; all she knew was that the man offered her a job working as a teacher at a nearby school in Umeda teaching French.

Taffie thought that Saiko was going to give her grief, but she didn't. Saiko had already worked things out behind the scenes. On the other end of the scope, Bozack doctored Taffie's paperwork to change her visa from Entertainment to Humanities/Services, but still sponsored by Saiko.

Work nights for Taffie, Saiko agreed to reduce her hours to three or four evenings a week instead of six. With the combined income of both places, Taffie was able to stack her paper rapidly. Things were looking up, even though relations with her colleagues had not improved. Furthermore, she got a strange, uneasy feeling about the hinky Yutaka, also the superintendent of the housing. One of the Korean hostesses had accused him of covertly supplanting a hidden spy camera in their bathroom and warned other women that it's possible he may have done the same to them.

There was no amount of money Taffie could spend to make Saiko's housing abode any more appealing or pleasant. The only window the room had offered a view of practically nothing, save for a boarded barbed wire fence, a backyard to a factory of some type. Generally, the room was oppressively dark, dinky; and the peeling paint color was a dismal light blue; and no matter how much she sprayed insecticide and placed traps, the occasional sight of flight-enabled, cigarette lighter–sized cockroaches occurred.

Aside from this, Taffie saw her bag increase steadily to a point where she had enough money to return to France. The considerable amount she needed for her safety net back home was steady on the rise. In a matter of mere months, even; she was that close! Only, now, for what purpose was there to even return to France? What was the hurry? she thought. She was having fun, a good time, and making easy money.

That was then.

Nowadays, Osaka was losing its charm for her. It was running out of nice people, or in some cases, the niceness was running out of people in Osaka. Whatever the case, she had her sights set on Tokyo. Ever since she met Doc Sarugi, who copped her another apartment so she wouldn't have to sleep with roaches, the idea of moving to the big city permanently had always been her emergency evacuation plan.

Maybe it was the change she needed. Perhaps it was time for Osaka to be the past tense chapter of her Japan experience, she thought. She was tired of being treated badly, used, and emotionally abused. She was tired of the superficial, fake relationships. She had endured her fill of those back in Paris. Tokyo reminded her somewhat of Paris, maybe a tad bit cleaner and easier on the nose; but generally, the atmosphere was quite different. She got less "repulsive" stares and glares there, as her appearance seemed more marvelous than the oddity it often caused her to feel walking around Osaka, riding the trains, visiting the various supermarkets, shopping centers, and commercial areas. Bottom line: Tokyo may or may not have been any better for her, but she was ready to take the chance and find out.

She would miss Takuto. He was a bit saddened to hear when Taffie broke the news to him that she was splitting town. Still, he understood because of the transient nature of *gaijin* in his country. All he could do was wish her the best and honor her request to keep their conversation a solemn oath secret. She had the feeling that she was being followed around, and she was right. She had caught on to Yutaka's spying on her, and she was unsure whether he had discovered her other pad, but she was certain that he was on to her, and so was Saiko. It was an uneasy feeling. But she was going to cut Saiko loose soon. All she had to do was commit to Doc Sarugi and be his one and only, and then pay off Saiko. There was nothing she could do. She didn't even need Bozack anymore. But she couldn't just leave . . . not like that. No, not this time.

"Non pas, cette fois!" she said as she neared her safety pad after checking and double-checking for weirdo spies. All clear, she keyed into her place, embraced by the comfort and warmth from the outside cold and the harsh elements of the weather.

She couldn't just leave without exacting some sort of revenge. Maybe it was her calling to teach her contemporaries, former acquaintances at Bozack, a valuable lesson on the sanctity of friendship. Two people, she felt, would value heavily from what her lesson taught. Deon, well, he was just a regular guy—she wouldn't have expected his loyalty to withstand the test of time. It was Liz and Serge who had caused her to feel less than human—again. Just like her father who lewdly lavished her with saliva-coated licks from the time she was six until he relieved her of her virginity at the tender age of twelve and then rejected her a year later.

Serge, although he was a lady-killer of a tomcat himself, Taffie fell head over heels for him similar to how she was soaking wet seeing Deon for the first time. It was innate in her composition possibly. All sorts of men turned her on. In retrospect, Taffie would reflect that she had indeed been lovesick. She was feeling the razor-sharp incisions of infelicity, recalling his remarks regarding her racial-ethnic component. But she did admit to having a wild side, a savage within her. This was what she would show to Serge.

The biggest disappointment was Liz, who she thought was her friend. In fact, they had become more than friends. But apparently, it must have all been an act. It was hard to believe. Taffie had blessed her with a shoulder to lean on, to cry on in her desperate times of need. Then after already steering Serge away from her, inducing him to make his offensive remark, she would then seduce her new lover, Deon, the guy she introduced to her! She vowed she would do something to even the score. For once in her life, she would fight back. She needed to break the cycle of people abusing her before it grew to be a lifetime thing, and because of her kindness, she would forever be taken advantage of by people who saw opportunity to feather their nests. She contemplated the many ways to go about it, but it would be done. Remembering the nightmare photo, she took of Deon and Liz in the bed, her brain bulb lit up with a scheme . . . or two.

53

New Year's Eve 2000

LIZ READIED HERSELF for a function Stephanie and Jeremy got her into. Her winter recess turned out to be not as miserable as she thought it would be. She would have to be grateful to Stephanie for that mostly, but the Bozack School provided her with a community of *gaijin,* in the same boat usually, whereas if she was still with the program like Eddie, she would be isolated and more alone. She had hoped to get in touch with Taffie, but she was still missing in action, no return phone calls. Since no one had heard from Deon either, Liz assumed that they were doing their lovebird bit. So she decided not to bother them.

Meanwhile, Jeremy Ng's side hustle was teaching kids independently, or freelance teaching. Being the *gaijin* bar raker that he was, Jeremy made the acquaintance of a pseudo-gangster Osaka patrician one night. The man was in his mid-fifties, he could barely speak English, but he was more interested in his two elementary school-aged children learning. Jeremy agreed to teach the man Mr. Sakamaki's kids and eventually became friends with him. As a result, he would get perks such as invitations to outings like the New Year's bash they were celebrating at a gaudy palatial spot in Azuchi-Bingo Town (***17**). Of course, Jeremy didn't want to be the only foreigner there, so he asked Mr. Sakamaki if he could bring his friends. Sakamaki was amply cool with it, for not surprisingly, he had ulterior motives.

Jeremy and Stephanie showed up at Liz's place around 7:00 p.m., dressed up like they were going to work, only considerably prim and neater. Liz was in a pine-juniper long-sleeved V-neck dress, trying to slip into some clover suede Christian Louboutin pumps when they arrived. Jeremy was salivating seeing Liz struggling her bare feet into the shoe and her calf muscle tensing as she half stumbled.

Stephanie was like, "Hold up, wait, can we get a smoke? I'll pay if you want."

Jeremy started beefing. He said, "Aw geez, Steph, we don't have time. We gotta go..."

Liz and Stephanie ignored him checking his watch. Liz had already taken her hit from the pipe and doused her eyes with a Japanese equivalent of eyedrop medicine, which made her look more like she had just finished crying more than clear away the redness.

She complained to Jeremy, "Why can't I bring it with me?"

Jeremy said somewhat impatiently, "I explained to you, I don't wanna take any chances. These clients of mine are really affluent people. I don't wanna take the chance and have you guys get caught smoking that shit and it comes back on me. Not only *you* might get in trouble, but I could lose them, and quite honestly, I don't wanna do that. With what they pay me to teach their kids privately once a week, I can basically live off of it. You guys should really think about doing that yourselves. Mr. Sakamaki owns a few daycare centers."

Stephanie said, "I'd think about it. Some of the kids are simply adorable, but I don't really like tryin' to teach them. Ugh!"

Liz said, "Yeah, I don't think I'd want to do that either. Worm approached me and asked if I was interested, and I was like, 'Nope.'"

Stephanie said, "They drool, cry, and shit all over the place, I heard. Then the smell gets into your clothes, especially on the hot days. And some of the schools don't use the air-conditioner. I think they do it just to be assholes. By the end of the day, your clothes are reeking!"

Jeremy said, "Well, that's why you get paid extra for teaching them. Now can we please go? We have to be at the place soon, and it's rude to be fashionably late in Japanese society!"

"Oh brother," Liz stated flatly.

Stephanie flicked flame to the grass pipe hole and sucked in a huge hit. Her chest inflated like two spheres on the front of her shirt before she exhaled with a raging series of coughs. She stumbled around as if someone had turned off the lights.

Liz snatched the pipe and lighter from her. She said, "OK, that's enough. Let's get outta here before Jer' pees on himself." She burned off the remaining pot, blew it out, and popped a curiously strong mint in her jib. Then she went to conceal her prized tool in a stash hideaway.

Stephanie said, "That was some good shit!" Still trying to walk as if she had blurred vision, approaching Jeremy, who still waiting by the door.

"There's gonna be plenty of booze at the banquet," he said.

Liz grabbed her pebble-gray silky-textured anorak and threw it on as they left hurriedly. A gust of her sweet-scented perfume, overshadowing the sharp marijuana oodor, tickled Jeremy's nose as she did, like minty blossoms, disarming his uptight mood briefly, replacing it with amor.

Moments later, they all were curbside. They had a brief spat about catching a cab. Jeremy's restiveness returned and he was like, "What the hell are you guys doing? The subway is right here!"

Liz replied, "Stop acting like such a pauper! Come on!"

A cab was hailed, and Jeremy instructed the driver to deliver them to the Hommachi Station on Midosuji Avenue. The rendezvous spot was supposed to be a block from where they arrived on Chuo Boulevard (*18). Luckily, because of flamboyantly alluring Liz and fleshly endowed Stephanie flanking a Jeremy who looked like a Japanese sixth-grader dressed up, they stood out on the bustling intersection. Mr. Sakamaki's portly driver and sidekick, Mr. Goro, spotted them from a mile away. He had Mr. Sakamaki's Lexus parked on the service road curbside.

Sakamaki was Japanese, for sure, but Liz and some Americans could have also taken him to be a Mexican or Hawaiian with a Moe from Three Stooges–bowl cut and red Howdy Doody puppet-like lips, with pop-out eyes to match, especially when they were laid upon the Disney Princess come-to-life introduced to him as "Elizabeth." Immediately, Liz caught Takuto vibes from him. Being that he was another one of those high-society guys, Liz was flattered and tolerated the excessive attention.

Stephanie too was getting her fair share of assiduity. Her robust rack cleavage overshadowed her burgeoning stuffed-potato belly in a red A-line midi dress, drawing the fanfare of Mr. Goro. Unfortunately, he was cross-eyed and creepy like a Japanese version of Stephen King, with protruding pelican lips that could dispense not even a spec of English. Stephanie was into Japanese men, but apparently, Goro was subpar of her subzero standards.

Sakamaki was only the second person in Japan Liz had seen have a cigar; the only other had been Tim, but Sakamaki's wasn't lit. He was gnawing on the tip but used it in his hands when he spoke. When he was introduced to Stephanie and Liz, he placed it in his trap before they shook hands. Shorter than Liz and Stephanie but taller than Jeremy, he squeezed himself between the women and tried to speak to them in cringeworthy English, and tobacco- and whiskey-laced breath.

Jeremy, who had been bounced off the curb into the street by Sakamaki's rump, called out to him and spoke in Japanese, "Mr. Sakamaki, sir, they don't understand Japanese."

Somewhat offended, Sakamaki thought he had been speaking English, he said, "I sorry, I nice meet to you!"

Liz and Stephanie were still potheaded and giggling fanatically. Earlier, they exchanged jokes about how the two men, Sakamaki and Goro, had Humpty Dumpty bodies, looked like Tweedledum and Tweedledee, the "Frog and the Toad" references were many. Then, when he began talking, Stephanie really thought he did say, "I want to give meat to you."

When Stephanie replied in an innocently shrill tone, "You want to give meat to me?," Liz couldn't maintain her composure. She started to laugh hysterically. Both Liz and Stephanie laughed and held on to Sakamaki for support as they could barely stand from their antics.

Jeremy stood by nervously thinking that they were screwing things up for him. He tried to grin, but his forehead was forming beads of sweat, hoping that Sakamaki wouldn't get annoyed with the girls acting silly and childish. *God forbid Liz defied me and brought her pot*, he struggled under his breath.

Sakamaki wasn't offended at all. He thought he had said something to make the women laugh and go crazy for him, that he still had the big-city country-boy charm—even on foreign women. Enjoying the close company and half embraces of the foreign lovelies while his wife wasn't around, Sakamaki also fought the urge to allow his hand to slip down the arch of the back to caress the sponge rump quartet.

With introductions quickly out of the way and Jeremy's jitters having subsided, Sakamaki said, "Please, come, my wife, family, wait . . ." He reluctantly disengaged from the peach-scented *gaijin* to aggressively gesture, pointing fingers in the direction across the wide avenue Midosuji. He beckoned everyone to get inside of his Lexus. Goro drove.

The actual location was not far away; athletic types like Liz and Jeremy could have walked it easily. Though near, the maneuvers on one-way streets caused a ten-minute drive to arrive at a parking lot walking distance of the Bingo Town posh establishment Hijo ni Goka.

The entrance was a small, carpeted room with a series of compartments that looked like small square lock boxes or kitchen cabinets. Everyone not Japanese was instructed to remove their shoes and place them inside one of the available compartments. Liz took off her pumps, placed them inside one of the boxes. When it closed fully, it activated a lock, which slid out of its opening a thin piece of grooved wood the size of a business card. The wood chip had the corresponding number of the locker. Liz wiggled her unpolished toes upon the carpeted floor but grimaced slightly, thinking she should have worn socks or leggings like Stephanie had, who disliked her feet getting cold.

Sensing Liz's discomfort, Stephanie mentioned as she deftly oozed her pro-wrestler female leg out of the gray Peter Pan boots, "Don't worry, they have slippers." ·

Liz saw everyone grabbing the slippers from inside of the box, so she opened hers back up and took the set provided inside, which she initially ignored or hadn't noticed. They were a one-size-fits-all generic type and were a little tight, very uncomfortable.

She said, "I hate taking off my shoes. I'll be glad to get back home to the States!"

Stephanie said, "Me too, I hate taking off fuc-kin' shoes every gowdamn place, ugh! Gets on my nerves, but I'm glad, and you should be too, that they have these storage boxes. At least nobody can steal your shoes."

Liz was repulsed. She said, "Ew! Gross. They actually do that here?"

"Are you kidding?" Stephanie said dramatically. "Vicky and I were out one night with our buds, and we went to one of these type places where we hadta take off our shoes'n stuff'n when we came back, Vicky's shoes were gone, because she screwed herself for leavin' the key thingy in the slot, of course, but she's a 'gai-jane' like the rest of us. Bottom line, they'll steal anything in this fucken' country."

"I believe that"—Liz nodded ardently—"especially your boyfriend, fiancé, husband, whatever!"

Jeremy overheard, and being the kibitzer he was, he injected himself into their gabble. "Aw, come on, you guys, you can't possibly compare crime of theft here to the States."

The conversation continued as they entered the remarkable grand court behind a huge set of heavy wooden double doors. Upon piercing the Orpheum spatial terrace, the lights were considerably brighter. Liz among her party, approached a ledge that circled the miniature auditorium-sized room and saw that they were on the second level. She looked down at the floor below. Its interior was aqua blue; in fact, at first glance, Liz thought that they had walked into an indoor pool because the collection of water there was an aquarium with exotic fish swimming around along with squids and octopuses. Exotic decorative plants surrounded the pool at random locations to create an outdoor type atmosphere, but the splashing of water echoed off the stadium-like walls.

Animated, Sakamaki used his finger gestures, scooping imaginary food into his tobacco-stained chops, saying, "You . . . like . . . sushi-i?" When everyone nodded cautiously, Sakamaki continued "Here . . . sushi . . . very, very fresh!" He was practically screaming.

Goro was patting Sakamaki on the back, congratulating him for such "amazing" English ability. It was almost as if he was some kind of hero for such an accomplishment.

Stephanie and Jeremy were still arguing about crime in Japan, Stephanie mentioning, "Well, when I first moved here to the city, the first apartment I stayed, I had all my panties stolen from the laundry room! They steal stuff like weirdos!"

Liz was admiring the almost-breathtaking sight. She couldn't believe Stephanie and Jeremy's discussion was so important that they could miss the beauty and uniqueness of the indoor aquatic palace. They were as soon greeted by a young woman in a turquoise-aqua mermaid bathing top piece with her toned belly button revealed. With a very welcoming smile, she took the heap collection of Liz's, Stephanie's, and Jeremy's jackets, coats, and hats and dashed off with them like a thief on tabi-footed toes.

Jeremy cracked to Stephanie, "Don't worry she works here!"

Several hurried paces ahead of the trio of *gaijin*, Sakamaki yelled something in Japanese at them over his hunched Quasimoto-esque shoulders. Only Jeremy, however, could comprehend.

"He says hurry up, guys'" Jeremy said.

Liz mumbled, "We're tryin', but it's hard to walk in these friggin' slippers, dude!"

They finally arrived at a suite, like a box seat at a ballpark stadium. A long, banquet table was sunken into the floor, and it stretched to the huge window overlooking the aquarium below like a handle to a great magnifying glass.

A young boy of about five years old jumped up joyously at the sight of Jeremy and ran to greet him with a hug. The boy, Hayato, was followed by his sister, Shichi, who was three years older. Seated at the table were Sakamaki's and Goro's wives. Sakamaki did his best to introduce everyone, including his son and daughter, but it was clear that Jeremy was going to have his hands full translating for the greater part of the night.

The Japanese wives' English ability was not any better than their husbands', but they were extremely friendly, delighted to have the foreigners as their guests. Both women appeared to be similar in age, carbon copies of the "chickens" Liz met in Hannan City; young women who became "old" too quick because of childbirth. Nape length, but voluminous, slightly disheveled hairstyles, not strikingly beautiful but not ugly either. Pretty she could describe them at the least, Liz safely assumed that Sakamaki's wife was considerably younger than him but wouldn't have guessed that she was in her mid-thirties. Being a mother of two and married to a rich, older man offered her the luxury of looking tacky in expensive clothes.

Liz and the others took their seats at either side of the table after kicking off the slippers. Jeremy sat opposite Liz as she marveled at how their legs disappeared into the floor, carpeted beneath their soles.

"So, this is how they spend their New Year's, huh?" Liz mused.

"Oh no, there's no Dick Clark or any ball dropping here!" Stephanie laughed humorously.

"Not always," Jeremy injected as the playful and energetic young Hayato danced around and jumped in and out of his lap. "Many Japanese spend time with their families and visit temples and shrines. Which is what we have planned for tomorrow. You guys free?"

Considering she did not have anything planned or something better to do, Liz told him that she was game, as he hoped she would. It was his covert way of asking her out on a date. She monkey-wrenched his plan, however, by inviting Stephanie to tag along; but it was his mistake extending the invitation in speech to them both.

Liz said absentmindedly, "So, Jer, I guess *they* see you as one of *them* because you sorta look like Japanese people and you speak the language too."

Jeremy's face flushed for an instant, as if he had been embarrassed or suddenly angered. He liked Liz, but he wasn't fond of the way she took digs at him and at times derided him. He was beginning to wonder if she was worth his efforts.

He said, "Absolutely not. I mean, I'm not like them . . . I . . . I'm an American. I look Asian, but I . . . I'm just like you guys. You know I grew up in San Francisco . . ."

"Oh, Chinatown?" Liz blurted.

Frustration growing, Jeremy said, "Um . . . no, I grew up in Nob Hill. My parents are white like you. I was adopted. I speak Japanese because it's advantageous for me living here, that's all. I don't think they treat me any different than you guys. In fact, I think they treat women like you better than me here in this country."

Sakamaki's daughter Shichi was pretty and, luckily, didn't have the orangutan features of her pops but the remnant beauty of her mom. She hadn't been able to avert her starry eyes from the two *gaijin* females, especially Liz. She urged her mother to "scoot over" in Japanese so that she could wedge her tiny little body in the *zabuton* space next to Liz, whom she viewed as a glass-slipper-wearing princess from animation come to life.

The host of the gathering, Sakamaki, stood up and addressed the congregation, then turned to the foreign faction and commenced his karate kung-fu gesturing. This time, his technique displayed the invisible cups to the lips.

He said, "You . . . like . . . drink?" Then he was joined by the Japanese adults in an outburst of laughter, which he led like a choir conductor.

Although his speech was somewhat primitive, the Japanese language study novices like Liz and Stephanie could make out what he had wanted to say. Stephanie was like, "Definitely!" Liz agreed. Her throat was dry from all the weed smoke earlier.

"How about we start with beer?" Stephanie suggested.

Jeremy joked, "Geez, you chicks drink like dudes!"

Liz remonstrated, "Oh, that's chauvinistic! Who's to say which gender drinks like whom? I've always enjoyed the taste of a good beer."

Jeremy's eyes widened in disbelief. He had hoped his remark would resonate with them in a complimentary sort of way, insinuating that they were strong drinkers like men, not weak or prissy. He then started to feel as if he had put his foot in his mouth yet again. Stephanie guffawed like a happy giant, concurring with Liz as if she had a "Come to think of it, that's right!" epiphany.

Drinks arrived in tall bottles. The mermaid-clad restaurant girl delivered them and commenced to pour the drink in every single glass. The non-alcohol drinker Goro and the children received soft drinks like tea and orange juice. After the initial drink-pouring ritual was completed, they all raised their glasses and shouted out the toast chant, "*Kampai!*"

Exemplifying Jeremy's earlier jocose observation regarding the drinking prowess of the ladies, Liz and Stephanie upended and emptied their *Sasaki* highball glasses, practically draining them of the beer in two or three gulps. The Japanese people gazed at the American women in wonderment. They would never have expected a pumpkin chariot princess like Liz to guzzle like that, a wicked stepsister like Stephanie, maybe. However, had they not been under inquisitive scrutiny, neither Liz nor Stephanie would have covered their mouths to conceal their belch the way they did that night before their Japanese hosts. They instinctively must have taken Jeremy's feelings into consideration and did not want to embarrass him too much. Otherwise, they were there to have a good time. After all, it was New Year's Eve!

Reaching for one of the many bottles on the table, Liz attempted to refill her glass. At the head of the table, Sakamaki witnessed this and yelled out to Jeremy. He uttered in Japanese a frowning command followed by his trademark Cheshire cat from Wonderland grin.

Jeremy jumped into action. "Ah, er . . . um, hey, Elizabeth, I . . . I'll pour it for you."

"No, thanks," Liz snapped, "I can handle it, move . . ." She swatted his hand away. She filled her Sasaki glass to the rim then passed the bottle to Stephanie.

"In Japan, at dinner engagements like this, it's often appropriate for other guests to pour glasses for you," Jeremy stated informally.

"Yeah, yeah," Liz said after taking another hearty sip of her drink, halfway finishing it. "I know already. I was with the CHET Program, remember? We had these types of 'formal' extravagant outings all the time. I know the routine."

"Me too," Stephanie said. "I was with the Porkpie Program, and it was the same. I didn't mind pouring drinks for other people, it's just . . . what's the need when my hands are free and the bottle's right in front of me?"

Liz tended to agree with the things Stephanie said when it came to complaints about Japan and its customs, formal or informal. Jeremy tried to explain these

Japanese nuances, but Liz wasn't as open-minded about receiving the information as Stephanie, who took somewhat of an interest, probably because she was seriously pursuing a meaningful relationship with her Japanese "boyfriend" Michio. Liz, on the other hand, was determined to be unimpressed. Such zealous enthusiasm about being so Japan knowledgeable reminded her of Eddie and rang heavily to her as being a bootlick.

When it was time to start the evening grub fest, the ice-breaking conversations were interrupted by the appearance of a Japanese staff member clad in all white digs except for a black apron. He also had on white rubber boots and a white paper hat. He greeted everyone cordially but tended mainly to Sakamaki, who stood up by the window. There was a panel that could be opened on the glass. Sakamaki's kid Hayato was excited and ran to the window. Shichi, the daughter, also sharing the same spirit as her brother, tugged at Liz's arm as if she wanted her to come along to see what was happening at the window.

Morbid curiosity motivated Liz to join the little girl, who didn't seem to be shy meeting new foreign people. She escorted the little girl to the window. Everybody thought it was cute. Soon nearly everyone was standing by the window.

Stephanie was like, "What's goin' on?"

Sakamaki pointed to the aquarium, exchanged dialogue with the Japanese staffer in white, then they did some sort of hand-gesture communication with a member of the staff down by the poolside with all the exotic fish. The dude had a long pole with a sealed net attached. Sakamaki gave him a nod, and the dude with the net inserted the net pole, extracted it, and there was a drawn-out punctured-tire sound accompanying the squirmy squid in the snare.

Liz felt as if her heart had dropped to a lower depth in her chest. She had seen people catch fish before, but never a creature like that. The kids were jumping with amused furor, the Japanese guests were making sounds like, "Oooh! Ahhh!" Wonderment. Awed and intrigued as usual.

Jeremy was like, "I think that's gonna be our dinner."

Liz tried not to think about it, being that it was so crude. The same squid they had seen taken from the pool was delivered to their dining suite minutes later. The man with the white garb whipped out his impressive set of *Ginsu* blades and began grating his metal in both hands, producing sparks. The entire scene looked brutal and menacing. Even Liz had to admit that it was intimidating and gripping to watch.

The doomed squid was merely a foot or two from her, squirming and tentacles wriggling as it struggled to free itself from the long platter in which it had been placed. Its long serpent-like arms had slithered away from its body and crept out onto the table, almost as if it were reaching for the seated inhabitants. It was like a horror flick excerpt, and the "strong" American women couldn't conceal their frightened screams. Stephanie went overboard and nearly pushed little boy Hayato out of Jeremy's lap so she could replace him there to get away. Sakamaki and his crew were having a ball laughing at the sight.

Jeremy was pretending to be calm and understanding. "Relax, relax, you guys. It's not gonna hurt you."

"The damn thing is still alive!" Liz nearly shouted. The squid's eyes were very much focused. It even looked as if it were blinking. Staring at her.

Suddenly, the man in white took his blades and commenced slicing and dicing in an artistic manner, suggesting it may have originated from a time-honored method in culinary craft. Next, he doused some dark soy sauce on the now-diced tentacles, still writhing and crawling about like a colony of worms.

Sakamaki, Goro, and the wives grabbed up their chopsticks and moved in on the ill-fated sea creature with a look on their face that spelled out, *Dig in!* Then they started plucking at the "worms" and devouring them piece by piece.

Liz exchanged a mouth-agape look of exasperation with Stephanie as they beheld the sight of people ghoulishly feeding on the living animal like fiends in a zombie blockbuster. Even the little kids, Hayato and Shichi, were chopsticking little white pieces of the sea creature into their mouths.

Jeremy had already gotten his taste of the feed. He encouraged Liz and Stephanie. "Come on, guys. Get over it. You like *sashimi*—it doesn't get any fresher than this, huh?"

Liz gulped and decided it was her time to be daring. She picked up her chopsticks and tried to grab a slippery morsel, but it was difficult. Complex as it may have been, both she and Stephanie received rave reviews on how well they could use the Orient-based utensils. Finally, Liz was able to grab a piece and put it on her saucer. With a *Here goes nothing* look, she tried it. It was chewy. A little gritty and salty, but for the most part, it was soft. Since she wasn't dishonest when she said that she liked sushi, the taste was not an agony-inducing phenomenon. She liked it!

Stephanie, as if encouraged by Liz's spunk, followed suit. She said, "I guess when in Rome, do as the Romans . . ." Then she tried it and liked it as well.

"Glad we got that out the way," Jeremy laughed.

"Isn't bad at all," Liz stated. "But I guess the way it was presented . . . that kinda threw me off . . . I mean, we just don't ever get to see shit like that where we come from. But you guys are used to it."

Jeremy was like, "Aw, jeez, there you go again, what do you mean *you guys* . . . I'm from California like you. I'm not used to this kinda stuff. If they were to do this in the States, they'd get shut down for cruelty to animals or something."

Liz let the subject rest, and the gaiety continued. Various other seafood dishes arrived, some cooked, others were raw; but everything was fresh from the aquarium below the terrace. The drink selection changed gradually from beer to rice wine, a favorite of Sakamaki's apparently. Poor Goro looked miserable as he chain-smoked and sipped on rusty-colored Oolong tea. He must have been on the wagon, or better, he took his job as a driver very seriously.

The cute mermaid server appeared again with a gigantic bottle of *Nada Kenbishi Shuzo* Sake. It looked like a huge fire extinguisher in the girl's arms when she poured its contents into shot glass–sized porcelain cups. These sake cups were situated in small wooden boxes, like miniature crates for Barbie's doll house. The poured sake overflowed the cup, and the box retained the spilled portion.

Sakamaki was orchestrating. "*Masu*, no . . . blah blah blah . . ."

Jeremy said, "You hafta drink all the excess from the *masu* before you sip from the cup."

Stephanie said, "What 'muscle'?"

"The box! The box is called a *masu*, not a muscle! You're supposed to drink all the wine that spilled over first before you taste from the cup! That's how it's traditionally done."

Liz was like, "Oh, jeez fucken' cryin' out loud! So many damn rules and steps and fucking around, taking off shoes here and pouring drinks there, now you have to have a special routine just for having a jazzed-up shot of booze. What's this stuff made of anyway, huh? Unicorn piss!?"

Stephanie burst out laughing as if she was the number one fan of Liz's comedic routine. Still, she was a fan of sake rice wine, so she was the first to down hers in the scripted manner. Everyone mimicked afterward, and Liz eventually downed her share. A few more of these, and all rhyme or reason was disengaged. Liz almost passed out. If it weren't for the elated, lively, and vigorous "HAPPY NEW YEAR!" chants, she would have. A couple of blackout spells had Liz regaining consciousness, and more Japanese people had joined them in the suite. She didn't know where the music came from, but somebody, she recognized, was playing some tune from the Spice Girls. She tried to get to her feet, but she was on Bambi legs. Jeremy rushed to support her from out of nowhere. People thought they were trying to dance.

Retarded-drunk Liz spoke to Jeremy. "Let . . . gowamee!" Thinking Jeremy was trying to wrestle with her, she tried to push him away, mistaking him for young Hayato because of the height similarity.

True to rumors, however, Jeremy was quite strong and managed to sit Liz down on a pile of cushions the playful Hayato kid had arranged with the *zabuton* like a beaver dam. He knelt beside her and urged her to listen to him.

He said, "Hey, listen, I think we oughta get outta here. You're really wasted. If you want, you can crash at my place. I live near here in Namba . . ."

Liz may have won the drinking battle with Jeremy in Nagano, but on this night, she had met her match. Japanese rice wine was her Achilles' heel, it seemed. Still, she had been in such a situation many times before in her life, dating back to college days and nights at Harbor. She knew when guys were trying to get the best of an intoxicated, vulnerable girl situation.

Coherently astute, Liz said, "Where's Steph?"

"Over there." Jeremy pointed to a section of the room where fallen Stephanie had long ago succumbed to the bold richness of the wine, unconscious and collapsed like a beached whale. Even the peppy vigor of the music, laughter, drinking, and actively playing kids didn't awake her.

"I think we should leave her," Jeremy said.

"We can't . . . leave her!" Liz tried to stand. "I'll take her . . . to my place!"

She got to her feet with Jeremy's assistance. Jeremy said, "You can't be serious? Why go so far? My place is pretty big—it's literally five minutes away by cab. You live way out by the harbor, right?"

Liz wasn't in the mood to argue, and in the back of her soaked mind, she knew she would need the relief from her weed pipe, and there was no way she was going to Jeremy's house. Even if she had to lug Stephanie's portage.

Ignoring Jeremy's unrelenting coercive attempts to get her to dip back to his crib, Liz knelt beside Stephanie, slapped her to semiconsciousness. As if a nursing assistant, the Liz-curious young Shichi appeared by her side. Liz looked at her and didn't bother trying to speak Japanese. In English, she told the girl to fetch her a glass of water from the table. The attentive quick study of English she was, Shichi made the correlation with the word she knew "water" and the direction in which Liz was pointing to on the table. The little girl went and got the glass and brought it back to Liz, who then doused the water on Stephanie's face. Stephanie woke up promptly, terrified, like, "Who? What?! Where . . . !?" and shaking herself off like a wet dog.

All the while, Sakamaki and his wife, Kazuko, had witnessed the entire scenario. They giggled. Sakamaki was impressed with Liz more than ever now. Not only was she the most gorgeous young sexpot he had seen in years—and he was a heavy visitor to "snack bars" and *soaplands*—but also, his wife Kazuko had taken a liking to her. Not only because she was lovely to their eyes, but because it seemed that a rapport between her and their daughter, Shichi, was evident. Shichi was the more reluctant of the two children to learn English, but after seeing Liz give her commands in English, to which she responded as if she understood completely, the Sakamakis grew to believe that Liz had some sort of special powers over children that compelled them to become better students.

Before Jeremy, Liz, and Stephanie bid their farewells for the evening, Sakamaki reconfirmed the meeting and excursion plans for later that New Year's Day. He really wanted to see Liz again, but obviously, because of her inebriated condition, trying to make conversation with her in such a state would be futile. He even offered to allow them all to stay at his place in Tanimachi Towns, but

Jeremy politely refused. He was still hoping to get Liz back to *his* crib, even if they did have to bring Stephanie along.

Prior to departure, the mermaid-clad server and Sakamaki presented to each in the trio a takeout tray consisting of traditional *osechi ryori* New Year's food boxes. They were filled with morsels of seafood from the restaurant itself, plus the customary *datemaki*, *kazunoko*, pickled vegetables, and so on. The combined value of all three boxes were well over three hundred American dollars if they were purchased conventionally. After thanking them profusely for the wonderful night and New Year's celebration, Jeremy, Liz, and Stephanie left, practically using each other for support. The cute mermaid waitress returned their jackets, coats, and hats. It took a few moments to locate the card-sized wooden chip keys for their footwear in the compartments, then sit Stephanie down and help her get her boots on; but with the help of Liz and Jeremy, it was accomplished, and they took the elevator down to the streets.

The cold rush of the new year of 2001's first morning air had sobering effects on Liz for the most part as they hit the street. She half-lugged Stephanie to Hommachi Avenue and Sankyubashi Street, and there they hailed a cab.

Jeremy was almost begging now for them to go to his place, but Liz wasn't having it. "Not this time, kid. Anyway, what time . . . tomorrow are we meetin'?"

Giving up and settling for at least one more chance to get his bid in with Liz, he said, "Not tomorrow, Liz. Technically, that's today! At noon. We're supposed to meet up at his place, but you guys don't know where he lives. That's why I said you should stay at my place. We could sleep it all off, then go over there together."

A taxi pulled up to the curb after Liz's active flailing of her hands to get the driver's attention. She then turned to the deflated Jeremy after shoving Stephanie inside the back seat of the cab. "Look, Jer . . . just come an' get us like you did tonight. You're such a . . . gentleman and all . . . what's the big deal. Anyway"—she leaned over and kissed him on the cheek—"we'll see ya later, OK?" Then she got in the cab, and it sped off.

Jeremy rubbed the sticky deposit on his cheek left from Liz's slimy peck and licked his fingers, stimulating his blue-balled pecker. He could have taken a cab or an all-night train home himself, as the trains operated throughout the night on New Year's Eve, but he decided to walk, reflecting on the night, the past week, and his progress in winning Liz's heart. He passed an all-night convenience store along the way. He found a trash can and dumped inside of it the three *osechi ryori* gift lunch boxes, then pressed onward to his apartment.

54

EDDIE SPENT CHRISTMAS and New Year's with his new honey, Hiroko. He literally became the host student like Hiroko was in North America, only minus the tragic turmoil she endured there. In contrast, Eddie's experience was fascinating and rewarding in his own words. He was invited to stay at the Okada home, or rather, the maiden family of the Hashimotos, who Hiroko's mother, Eriko was before she married and gave birth to her only daughter.

Eddie expected the experience to be a difficult one. His Japanese wasn't up to par, and as he was informed by Hiroko, her family couldn't speak an iota of English, especially her grandparents, the Hashimotos. Hiroko however, assured him that he needn't worry. As always, she would be available to translate for him.

Meeting the mother for the first time, Eddie had flashbacks of the women he met at the "snack bar" and Mama-san Yoshiko's lounge. His impression of Eriko was that she didn't appear to be the woman in her early fifties she happened to be. She had no gray hair, barely any facial wrinkles or telltale signs of age, she was the same height as her daughter, but a little more robust in body framework. Compared to Hiroko, Eriko the mother was, of course, slightly heavier due to age, but she was neither chubby nor fat. She was well endowed, with bigger, wholesome breasts, and quite frankly, she fit his description of a MILF; and in terms of facial features, if the proverbial apple didn't fall far from the tree was anything to go by, a future with Hiroko didn't forecast much disappointment for looks.

Eriko, as well as the elderly grandparents, pretty much welcomed Eddie with open arms. Given Hiroko's past experiences overseas, her background abundant with interactions with people from abroad, and skill set in the English language, no one was surprised that she would, at some point, be socially or romantically involved with a non-Japanese individual.

Being that Eddie was, in the opinion of Eriko, a dashingly handsome man, she was enthusiastically supportive of him seeing her daughter. The grandparents may have had some reservations initially, but their satisfaction in knowing that their offspring had an eligible suitor outweighed any hang-ups they had about him not being Japanese. Besides, he had a good job, he did honest work, and, being a teacher, he was looked at as being an upstanding, status-holding citizen, not run of the mill.

While staying in the Okada-Hashimoto home, Eddie was the perfect house guest. He tried his best to speak Japanese, even though he sounded like a baby executing it, but in so doing, he won their hearts. He was appreciative of their hospitality, thanked them generously and even helped wash dishes, clean up chores, and, most of all, his attentiveness to Hiroko made her family aware that she was special to him.

What they didn't know was, after so long being with a hard master like Liz, Eddie's catering to the whims of new significant other female came somewhat easy to him. Hiroko made it all simpler. She was easygoing, agreeable, compromising, and didn't share the same argumentative tendencies as Liz. She was open to hear his ideas, thoughts, and respected his feelings and was far less fastidious than who she replaced. When it came to intimacy, Hiroko didn't hold back. She gave Eddie everything she had to offer, and he was overwhelmingly receptive. Every time they slept together Eddie felt as if he had been whisked away on a magic carpet ride into the starry heavens—so high he felt he didn't ever need to smoke another joint. Likewise, Eddie was Hiroko's knight in shining gold armor. Her compassion for Liz had lessened because she slowly came to the notion that one person's trash was another's treasure, and as such, she had no intention of letting such a gem like Eddie go. They were so infatuated with one another they began to get sloppy. People at work were noticing.

***

In Osaka City, Liz wondered how Eddie was occupying his time on New Year's Day. She couldn't help it. It was natural, she thought. And she also wondered if he was thinking about her, and if he was having any regrets like she had always expected he would. For the longest time, she had thought that allowing him to have a threesome with her friends would compel him to stay with her and see the exorbitant length she would go to prove how serious she was about her "love" for him. Now that she could no longer hold this trump card—her gambit—over him, she began to see how utterly foolish she was!

Now she was stuck with Jeremy, Stephanie, and some kooky Japanese family, the Sakamakis, whom she barely knew, and visiting a shrine with a horrendous hangover that a morning "wake and bake" smoke couldn't smooth out. Luckily, the day's activity did not include any hard drinking of rice wine as the night before entailed.

On this day, they took a lot of pictures. In fact, this was the most Liz had ever used her digicam at one time. Selfies, group photos, photos with the kids Shichi and Hayato, and random Japanese people thrilled and fascinated seeing foreigners. Liz posed for pictures with piteous smiles masking the miserable melancholy she felt inside, but she lumbered on through the day, determined to make the most of her Japanese experience and not let a breakup be the cause of her ultimate life ruin.

After rinsing hands at the shrine with ornate ladles, a pilgrimage to the shrine's foreground amid a seeming mile-long line of people, shaking a rope ringing a bell, and receiving a good luck charm called *Omikuji* (*19), Liz and Stephanie were pooped. The ever-generous Sakamaki patriarch treated everyone to an early-afternoon dinner at a Skylark Diner. This pleased Liz because this place seemed to have food more agreeable with her Western taste buds as opposed to having all Japanese dishes. So when she could order a spinach omelet and toast, she was practically ecstatic.

Jeremy still had his heart set on trying to hook up with Liz. She wasn't making it easy for him, but he wasn't giving up. It was simply going to be more of a challenge than he had expected. He had overcome great obstacles before.

Liz may not have taken Jeremy's bait or hints that he was into her, but his alternate plan had worked rather smoothly. Anticipating that Liz would make a good impression with the Sakamakis, his next move was getting her interested in freelance teaching like he did. The Sakamakis would be her testing ground. From there, they could spend more time together, if not actually dating. If he asked her out on a date, she could flat refuse and turn him down. That would end him and potentially put him in the friend zone. He figured if he trapped her into a situation where they would meet constantly, he could eventually win her over with his charm. So far so good. Liz appeared to have a natural way with kids. Shichi had taken a liking to her; she was glued to her the entire day. Question was, would Liz be interested in part-time work?

While Stephanie was distracted talking "kids talk" with Shichi and Hayato at the dinner, Jeremy managed to get an isolated moment with Liz to spring his trap.

He said, "So, Liz, have you given any thought to that freelance teaching thing I talked to you guys about?"

Liz said, "Not really, Jer. I'm not really into kids that much, especially Japanese. I mean, I used to babysit back in the States . . ."

Jeremy said enthusiastically, "Oh! Maybe that's why you seem so great with these kids, especially Shichi. She really likes you. They really like you, in fact."

"*They* who?" Liz said sharply.

"The Sakamakis, can't you tell?" His voice lowered when he had said their name. He then said, "They absolutely adore you. *So do I, by the way.* I've never seen Shichi take to anyone the way she did to you. Usually, teachin' her is like pulling teeth, lemme tell ya!"

Liz said, "Oh, don't get me wrong. When I say I'm not into kids, what I really meant was, I'm not into the idea of teaching them. Otherwise, I don't mind kids. These kids are so cute, I like them. Shichi is such a sweetie! But when I was with the program, I taught a bunch of elementary school kids. It was easy, but at the same time, it wasn't easy . . . hard to explain."

"No, I get it," Jeremy stated. "But let's be realistic here, there isn't so much you can teach kids, right? I mean, I've been teaching these guys the same thing since September. All you really need are a few toys and flash cards. It's not like they're expecting their kids to have a full-blown, drawn-out conversation with a panel at Harvard or Yale." He laughed comically.

Liz started to get a funny feeling from Jeremy's insistence. She said, "OK, Jer, why do you want us to teach kids on the side like you? You're sounding like Worm. He's always talkin' about how he wants to create his own English school and stuff."

Jeremy said, "That's because he lives here. He plans on living here for good. I'm just here for the short ride. I'm gonna move back to the States. Hopefully, I can open my own bodybuilding gym. Japan is a good way for me to stack up a lot of money. These side jobs teaching kids, I'm tellin'ya, this is the future!"

"Well, I'm not planning to be here for much longer either. As a matter of fact, I'm probably gonna ship out when my contract is up," Liz said.

"When is that gonna be?" Jeremy asked, looking worried.

"In a few months," Liz said certainly. "Around spring, I guess. I ain't gonna be here another year, that's for sure."

Jeremy said, "Well, here's the situation. I would like to ask you a favor. It's just a temporary thing. I'm up for a vacation soon. I'm going to Thailand with some buddies. And, well, while I'm gone, I was kind of hoping that you would take over my English lessons with Shichi and Hayato, just for two or three weeks while I'm away. When I come back, I'll resume."

Liz was outraged. She said, "What the holy fuck!? Why does everybody always come to me with these oddball requests and shift swaps . . ." Her mind was referencing the most recent favor-asking pain in the neck, Radley.

Jeremy said resolutely, "I'm telling you, Elizabeth, it's the easiest money you'll ever make. Seriously, all you have to do is just play games with them. Card games, anything . . . you can get a pack of casino cards in the 100-yen store (**20**), or some flash cards in the toy section. When you're done, they'll pay you an itchy man for just an hour! What's that? Think about it. What kind of job back in the States would pay you that kind of money? A hundred bucks an hour!?"

Money was not a big issue to Liz. She came from a rich, well-to-do background. At the same time however, the times when her parents held back with their financial support, she remembered how she and Eddie "struggled" back in California when they were job hunting. Now that she was no longer with Eddie, she figured that she would need to occupy her time and mind with other activities. If teaching kids was a cinch as Jeremy claimed, she thought, then it was easy money.

Liz said, "Why me, though? Why don't you ask Stephanie?"

Jeremy said wryly, "No, that's what I've been trying to explain to you. The Sakamakis, they like you. His wife likes you. They're so happy because Shichi is crazy about you. C'mon, Elizabeth, you'll be doing me a real big favor. Hey, you never know, you might like it. When I come back, we might be able to teach freelance together. We can hang out with all these rich Japanese, high-society folks. You see how generous they are, right? That spot we went to last night—you didn't have to shell out a red cent, did you?"

Liz shook her head. "Good point."

"So what do ya'say?" Jeremy asked desperately. "We got a deal or what? You can pick the day. They'll work with you, flexibility wise."

Half reluctantly, Liz agreed. "OK," she said. "I'll take over for you. Just till you get back. Where do you teach them? And are they gonna pay me each time I show up, or are they gonna pay once a month like those Bozack bastards?"

Jeremy laughed, genuinely happy now because Liz followed through and committed to the temporary job. He was sure that Liz would like the Sakamakis just as much as they liked her, and that their generosity would make her stick around.

He said, "You'll teach them at their home in Tanimachi. They have a big three-story house. It's amazing. Sort of like Worm's but a little less elaborate. And as for pay, shucks, they'll pay you in advance if you like. Money doesn't seem to be an issue with them."

"No way!" Liz said theatrically "So if I were to tell them to pay me the bread right after the lesson, they'll just fork it over?"

Jeremy said, "Sure! That's how I used to get mine. But now, since I'm not strapped for money like I was before, I can just collect it at the end of the month."

It was settled, then. Jeremy shared the news with the Sakamakis. Of course, they, along with Shichi, were overjoyed. Mr. Sakamaki rambled off his Japanese mixed with broken English, and Liz immediately began to feel stress because she remembered that she couldn't speak much Japanese. She wondered how she would be able to communicate. This was the part Jeremy had not planned on explaining away. Instead of supplying Liz with some useful sentences and phrases to help her with the dilemma she was due to face, he tried to assure her that communication with the parents would be minimal. All she had to do was show up; the Sakamakis would know why she was there. She would be escorted to the kids' playroom, and that would be where the lesson was conducted. The mom and the dad usually left the teacher alone and reappeared at the end of the hour. Punctually and with an envelope of money. It sounded good enough to Liz at the time, and she fell for it.

With everyone basically satisfied, the day ended on a good note. Jeremy was thinking it would only be a matter of time before Liz was his. It almost never failed. He had scored with several lonely *gaijin* females in Japan who were pure babes, which he could never have pulled off in the States.

Jeremy examined Liz's *omikuji* fortune slip. His eyes brightened up. "Wow, cool, check it out, Liz," and unraveled her rice paper scroll decorated with mystical snakes and a myriad of Japanese (Chinese) *kanji* characters. Liz had no idea what it meant until Jeremy explained to her. "You got the big *dai* symbol just like me— that means you'll be incredibly lucky in 2001!"

"Yeah, right!" Liz said, rolling her eyes as if she didn't care to believe in such Oriental fantasy, but deep down inside, she was hoping for it to be true.

Stephanie overheard the conversation, and she passed Jeremy her fortune slip. "What does mine say?"

Jeremy made a face of mock displeasure. With a blunt smile, he said, "Doesn't look too good for you, Steph . . . You got the lowest rung of luck. You got the *Daikyo*, which means you're cursed."

"Oh well," she said sardonically, then ripped the fortune slip into shreds.

Liz laughed with her and said, "Looks like you're doomed, Stephanie! Hahaha . . ."

"What would you expect, huh?" she said, making a goofy face. "It's the year of the snake! I hate snakes . . ."

55

ON THE SECOND day of the new year, Liz came home mid-afternoon from the gym and received a heart-attack-provoking shock. She keyed into her place and heard voices coming from the interior chamber of the room beyond the kitchen. She peered down and saw a big pair of green suede zip-up ankle boots with thick platform heels, and another pair of peanut brown Chelsea boots. At first, she thought she was at the wrong apartment, but that would have been impossible, because she used her key to get inside. Her next thought was that Denore had returned! Quickly, she shucked her athletic shoes and ran into the room. The chattering she heard had come to an abrupt halt.

Liz breached the dividers and stared not at Denore but at glaring, unfamiliar faces who appeared just as surprised to see her as she was them. Sitting on the bed in the section of the room where Denore used to occupy were two Asian females, but they didn't strike Liz immediately as being Japanese. In fact, the chubbier one wearing glasses, Liz could have sworn she had seen before but couldn't straightaway place.

When Liz entered, both females stood up after wearing off the initial surprise at her sudden appearance. The chubby Asian girl with glasses and fluffy green sweater smiled vibrantly as if she were happy to see Liz.

"Hi, Elizabeth Amberbush, right!?" the girl said, and then Liz remembered where and when she had seen this girl, just before she introduced herself again. "I'm Ingrid Avecedo. Do you remember me?"

Liz certainly did. She was the loudmouth cover blower who ran up on her one day in Hommachi and almost got her busted by Kayo for riding her bike to work. In Liz's mind, she was screaming, *oh, puh-leez don't tell me this bowl of corn lardass is my new roommate!* But as Ingrid commenced to show Liz paperwork she had received from Bozack, it was painfully true. Liz's straining to smile literally needed the assistance of her fingers to stretch her lips to create one.

The Ingrid girl said, "I was, like, supposed to, like, move in, like, last month, but, like . . . I kept putting it off because I, like, wanted to come back from the Philippines first, because I knew I was goin' home for the holidays . . . Sorry! I know it's all of a sudden . . ."

Liz gave up trying to seem cordial and welcoming. Even though she had enjoyed the company of Denore, she had grown accustomed to living alone and enjoying her privacy. Moreover, she knew Denore better than this new Ingrid girl; she and Denore started at Bozack at the same time.

Ingrid said, "This is my friend Marcia. She, like, helped me move." Marcia was slender and taller; she had a face full of what appeared to be acne and wasn't very attractive in Liz's opinion, but extremely nice. It was hard for Liz to be mean to them.

"Do you work for Bozack too, Marcia?" Liz asked.

"No, I don't," Marcia said. Her voice was squeaky like she could sing for Alvin and the Chipmunks. "I work for Special K."

"Oh yeah, OK," Liz said, trying not to laugh. She then said, "I've heard of that place." *But not good things.* That's why she laughed whenever she met people who worked there.

As if she could read Liz's thoughts, Ingrid chimed in, "Special K is like the loser's last hope in this town!" She laughed and took a playful jab from Marcia.

"Shut up!" Marcia squeaked.

"But it's true," Ingrid said as they sat back down on Denore's bed, now made up again with a cute Winnie the Pooh spread. "Special K is the place you go to work when you've got, like, nowhere left to go! They'll hire, like, anybody. If we're the McDonald's of English schools, then they've definitely, like, gotta be the hot dog stand of English schools!"

They all laughed. Even Liz had to yuck it up because that was the same thing she had heard about the place. One of the lowest-paying English schools in town, Liz wondered how someone could even make a living teaching there full-time, if such were even an option.

"Why don't you work for Bozack?" Liz inquired.

When Liz asked that, their smiles disappeared into dismal, almost-saddened faces. Ingrid squinted and said, "Well, because . . . I hope you don't take this the wrong way, but these schools are really . . . like, um, discriminatory . . ." Her intonation rose slightly.

Liz said, "Um, are you asking me, or are you telling me? What, that they discriminate?"

Marcia said, "I applied to your company, but they never hired me. I think they prefer people from your country. You are American, so they want people like you. I think they think it is better."

Liz sat down on her bed and massaged her feet, then addressed Ingrid. "So how did you get a job with the company, then?"

Ingrid said, "Well, I spent, like, a few years in the States. I lived in Wisconsin. And after getting rejected by Nova and Aeon and all the other big names, Bozack popped up. I applied from overseas, took an interview in Madison. I was on the waiting list for a while, but then a position opened, and I became a field runner. Exhausting sometimes, but it's a job. I finally got in. Marcia, you see, she's straight from the Philippines, though. Usually, these companies think we don't teach good English, because technically, the Philippines isn't an English-speaking country."

Liz looked confounded. "This is weird, because before I started working with the company, a friend of mine told me, at that time, I didn't know her, that Americans were the rarest people at Bozack."

Ingrid shrugged. She said, "Maybe, but I think it's, like, changing now. I believe they hired me because I lived, like, in the States, though. But I came at, like, a complicated time, I guess. They wanted me to do the jobs all the other, like, um . . . *white teachers* didn't want to do."

Liz didn't care and stretched her lips wide in a blank expression, not offended in the least. But curious, she asked, "What exactly did you do as a 'road runner' or whatever it is they had you doing?"

Ingrid said, "As a field runner, I have to start early, like, I have to be on standby every day at 10:00 a.m., sometimes 8:00 a.m. Then I get a call, and I'm dispatched to, like, anywhere they need me to be. Like, if one of you guys call in sick, the field runners go to your school and basically fill in for you. Usually, it's like, within Osaka. Hyogo branches are like, dispatched from like Amagasaki and so on."

"No shit," Liz said, amused and grinning. "So you actually go all over? No way! Do people really get that sick so often?"

Ingrid clasped her inflated bosom and said, "Oh! You wouldn't believe how many people either use, like, the sick leave or like emergency leave . . . and short notice too, and we go far . . . it's crazy. One teacher, like, actually went all the way to Nagoya!"

"Nagoya!?" Liz snarled. "Isn't that, like, five hours away or something?"

Both Marcia and Ingrid shook their heads rapidly. "Oh, no not that far. In fact, you can, like, take the Urb and get there in about an hour, I think."

"Where is the farthest place you went to?" Liz asked.

"Kakogawa," Ingrid said, dropping her tongue from her face in fake exhaust. "If you only knew . . ."

Liz had never heard of the place, but she judged by the name that it sounded dreadfully far away. She was struggling to get over the depressing reality that she was now to be burdened with a new person with whom to share space.

Ingrid did not move in everything on that day, as it was what she described as "the preliminary move." In the later days, she brought more things: luggage, boxes, and more cruddy clothes. She even wanted to tack posters of idol Japanese singers like T.M. Revolution, L'arc en Ciel and Da Pump.

Their days off conflicted somewhat. Ingrid's nonworking days were Wednesday and Thursday. So, on those days, Liz would come home from work, or maybe a night out, and be greeted by a mixed coterie of male and female Filipinos sitting at the kitchen table having a community gathering of sorts.

Liz would be like, "What kind of tribal *balderda-sh*it is this!?" And to top it off, Ingrid and her people would have some funky, smelly dishes that made her bowels curl. It was as if they had created a dish from ingredients—dairy butter, eggs, milk, and cheese—which were all spoiled or rotten, then sprinkled over with garlic, rice, and ketchup.

Ingrid would be like, "Oh, hello, Elizabeth. These are all my Filipino friends. Would you like some tomato *sinigang*?"

Liz would refrain from shouting, "Hell, no! Get that shit out of my face before I gag!" Then she would politely refuse. This was some crap that she was not looking forward to, having Ingrid as a roommate. Even though she was nice enough and well within her rights to have guests, Liz was the moody type and tended to not tolerate people she considered irritating for a lengthy period of time. Eventually, she would have to sit down and talk with Ingrid one on one.

As she shut herself off into her side of the room by using the sectional dividers, she was now considering the move to get her own place more than ever. But if she was sincere about what she told Jeremy, that she would be returning to America, she thought she could tough it out for a few months.

Next, she had decided that the day in which she would teach young Hayato Sakamaki would be Fridays and Shichi on Mondays. That was when the clever idea popped into her head! Mr. Sakamaki! Since he "liked" her so much, maybe he could be her guarantor! In fact, the more she pondered, she came to believe that he would. Then Liz could escape that crummy dormitory. Even if for only a few months, it would probably be worth it. She didn't know if she would be able to put up with the bizarre, exotic, otherworldly dish aromas Ingrid and Marcia and others drudged up. They dirtied up the kitchen, and additionally, the Filipino community congregating there weekly would eventually wear on her nerves. With Jeremy set to leave on his trip to Thailand in mid-January, Liz planned to run the idea by him on the first day she showed up to teach Shichi.

Back on the job, Liz saw Jeremy, and he gave her a bunch of last-minute information like the Sakamaki residence address, what trains to take, buses, alternate routes, emergency numbers, and the like. He even supplied her with teaching materials: colorful flashcards with easy vocabulary like fruits, vegetables, days of the week, and ABCs.

Deon showed up finally, and it was the first time Liz had seen him that year. This time, there was something strangely different about him, Liz noticed. He was still dressed nice, his Stacey Adams were polished, he cordially greeted everyone with "Happy New Year" all around, but there appeared to be a subtle sadness in his otherwise furious eyelids. A pleading dreariness seemed to lurk underneath the terrifying exterior he exuded to all. Liz was ready to blow off Jeremy's empty talk so that she could harass him. She planned on grilling him about Taffie. He beat her to it, though.

Using the back of his left palm, he moved Jeremy aside with a motion that looked as if he was opening a shower curtain. Jeremy stumbled, hobbled on one foot before regaining traction. Embarrassed and startled, he was like, "Hey! Excuse you . . ."

"You seen your girl?" Deon asked Liz with an icy smirk, one eyebrow raised.

Liz was still laughing at the way he had just dismissed Jeremy, who was still standing there with a manic expression and mouth agape, like he was sucking an invisible golf ball. Meanwhile, Deon was asking her about Taffie, while Jeremy was still babbling in an abbreviated voice growing lower in volume: "And one of these days, yer gonna push me a little too f-a-a-r-r-r . . ."

"What do you mean, Dee?" Liz asked. "Seen what girl? You mean Taf?"

"Yeah," Deon said, checking his fly G-Shock. "I ain't seen her. We broke up."

"Huh!?" Liz practically yelled.

A startled Worm ran into the teachers' room. His saucer-like eyes scanned the room for trouble as if he were a Keystone toy cop. "What'sgoin'on?"

"Deon is causing a lot of visceral reactions from people today," Jeremy spat out somewhat bitterly, as if his feelings had been assaulted.

Worm said, "Well, if you don't mind, would you guys keep it down. Kenji is gonna come and start bitchin' . . ."

Liz couldn't believe her ears. But then again, why shouldn't she? Even though Taffie and Deon seemed perfect for each other at face value, it was only a matter of time before it imploded. Liz wondered if Deon had found out about the Tokyo "Doc". Had Taffie come clean?

Grabbing Deon by his elbow, digging her nails into his shirt, Liz shout-whispered, "Hey, let's talk after work tonight—are you free for a minute?"

Deon couldn't concentrate on what she was saying. He was staring death blows at her fingers clawing his arm. He said icily "Get . . . your . . . damn hands . . ."

Worm interrupted the teachers' lounge again, this time followed by Eric Cravens and some other teachers. "Hey guys," he said as he centered himself among a semicircle gathering of the several odd foreign staff members. "My friend and Keefer's friend Ricky Exmouth, as you guys know, is gonna get married. So, he's gonna move back to Australia. We're planning to have a *sayonara* party for him in February. If any of you guys wan' to go, you're all invited. Hey, there's actually going to be some live entertainment and some kind of magical show. Gonna be a blast!"

"Count me in!" a random voice from the crowd echoed.

"Damn, I can't go," Jeremy said dismally. "I'll still be in on my vacay at that time."

Deon said, "I don't even know that muh'fucker that well. Why the fuck would I care?"

Worm tried to throw his arm around Deon's shoulder, but the New Yorker had had his fill of being touched for one day, and he escaped to the coffeemaker in the canteen. "Aw, lighten up, Deon. Why don'cha hang out more with us for a change? Don't be such a loner, guy. Bring Taffie, I'm sure she'll have a good time watching the live show."

Liz spoke methodically, "They broke up, Worm. Sucks, huh? A lot of these breakups are going around. Next, it's gonna be you and your wife, Worm." There was a minor laughter outburst.

The school's chime sounded off. Worm then said, "No, next, it's time to go teach these classes. Let's move, guys!"

The teachers filed out of the teachers' lounge. Liz lagged so that she could get a final word with Deon. She said, "Hey, are you free tonight or not?"

Deon said, "Probably not, Liz. Anyway, what're we talkin' bout? She won't answer her phone. I called and called, fuckit . . . I can take a hint. Fuck that bitch, then."

Liz could empathize with Deon's feelings, and she even wanted so badly to tell him that Taffie did indeed have another guy in Tokyo, but she didn't want to violate her trust and loyalty. Furthermore, she didn't like Deon referring to Taffie as a bitch, even if he had a right to feel the way he did—to Liz, Taffie was *still her* girlfriend.

"Hey!" Liz almost shouted again. "She's not a bitch, OK?"

Her flare-up once again attracted the attention of Worm, who had almost disappeared inside the inner sanctum of the office before doing an about-face. "Hey, what is it with you two?" he asked nervously. Considering some roundabout rumors, he had heard about Liz and how she got Kwame transferred and basically fired, he thought it was an obvious wise decision to keep a close eye on her.

"Nothing," Liz answered casually, but annoyed. "I'm just keeping Dee on his toes. He's bummed out, I'm just trying to cheer him up. Isn't that right, Dee?"

"Yeah, whatever," Deon said sleepily, somewhat beyond annoyed.

"Just wait for me after work tonight, I just wanna talk for a few minutes," Liz said finally as they dispersed into different classrooms for their lessons and the student customers who awaited them.

Unfortunately, Liz would be disappointed. When the 9:00 p.m. chime sounded, signaling the finish to another workday, Liz returned to the teachers' lounge only to find that Deon had bounced. The only thing he left behind was the memory that he had been there. Liz was boiling with anger. His impudence and arrogant manner was rubbing her the wrong way. She had to get to the bottom of the situation between him and Taffie. Plus, she wanted to know why Taffie hadn't returned his, or *her*, phone calls. Something was up! She knew it. At that moment, through her outrage, an odd tingling crept down her spine as she thought of how she seemed to make Black people disappear—Denore, Chucky, Kwame, and now Taffie too? The thought was almost unbearable. For, she would have lost a boyfriend and a girlfriend within the same time frame. How depressing! She shuddered silently.

Remembering the "good-luck charm" fortune slip she got at the Shrine, Liz wondered, *How can this be my lucky year?* For it was also the Year of the Snake. Just like that creature, Liz had an inkling that there was something afoul slithering about in the shadows of her life. Her subtle, growing fear was being lost in the dark, devoured by those shadows.

56

Elizabeth!

Hi, It's Carver.

> *Long time no hear, your mother tells me that you're still in Japan, she gave me your e-mail address, I hope you didn't mind me reaching out to you.*
>
> *Something tells me that you're doing well, I can't wait to hear all your details.*
>
> *I'm working and living out in Pasadena now. My job is challenging, but it's rewarding work. I think this is what I was meant to do, help people. But enough about me, I'm looking forward to hearing from you soon.*
>
> *Contact me at this e-mail address whenever you're free!*

–C.B.

LIZ WAS SURPRISED to get an e-mail message from Carver, but then again, per her conversation with her mother, she should have expected to hear from him sooner or later. Liz wondered if her mother had spilled the news to Carver that she and Eddie had broken up. Had he contacted her because he was interested in rekindling what flicker of flame their masquerade relationship was before? If that were true, then it was obvious that he either had a fetish for abuse, or he was utterly devoted to her. Bearing those thoughts, Liz chuckled softly at the idea of going back with him. Maybe she could clean up her act, clear her dope head, and go easy on the booze, go to church more like him, and just square up L7-style. Or better still, perhaps Carver was just being a good friend like he always said he would be. Liz didn't ponder these thoughts for long. She suddenly had a lot on her plate.

Since the appearance of Ingrid, her lifestyle had been abruptly interrupted. Ingrid was three times more talkative than Denore was, and the topics she wanted to discuss were folderol nerd junk that kept her awake. She was heavily into J-Pop; although she was twenty-four, she acted like a teenybopper for idol music groups in Japan that Liz had never heard of and had no interest in whatsoever. Also, she was a part of some Filipino clique that pooled all their money and food and got together weekly like a soup kitchen. Often, they chose to have their meetings on Wednesdays and extended until almost midnight. Liz was coming close to putting her foot down but chose better to bide her time, feeling she may be moving out soon and needed not create bad blood. Still, Ingrid and she didn't seem to be destined to form a bond or chemistry. Liz couldn't even smoke or do her dope when Ingrid was around.

If that weren't enough, work was starting to get busier. In the earlier days, Liz could expect one or two cancellations or no-shows, giving her extra break or down time, but Bozack experienced an increase of customers at the start of 2001. That meant Liz would have a full schedule from start of work till finish. It didn't become exhausting until Ingrid popped up. After an all-day shift of talking to empty heads and calling it a lesson, she would come home and dwell with another airhead with airheaded conversations.

Then there were the weekly lessons with the Sakamakis, which turned out to be not as big of a drag as Liz thought it would be, in the beginning.

Everything Jeremy said about the gig ended up being accurate. The Sakamaki kids were relatively easy to teach, and time seemed to pass quickly. It seemed more like a one-hour babysitting job than instruction of any kind. Hayato was a bit more of an active busybody, hard to control or get to concentrate at times, but generally, he, like Shichi, could look at pictures on flash cards that Jeremy left, and could tell Liz what the object was in English. Good students. That was basically the extent of an English lesson given by Liz. The rest of the time was playing with toys and talking to the kids in English.

At the end of the hour, just as Jeremy said, Liz would receive from either Mr. Sakamaki or his wife, Kazuko, an envelope with money equal to a C note in her country. Of course, Liz was pleasingly aghast comparing it to what she was making while babysitting back home, and for just one hour! She was so surprised at their generosity she forgot to ask, or attempt to ask, Mr. Sakamaki if he could be her guarantor.

She got Worm to help her construct a script in Japanese to communicate the request to Mr. Sakamaki the following week. When she hit him with the question via this script, Mr. Sakamaki's reaction was the vigorous equivalent of "Hell yes, of course!" But in his mind, he was thinking that this *also* meant Liz was signing on to be his daughter Shichi's permanent tutor/teacher *in the process*. This, however, was not communicated to Liz at the time she received her good news. Mr. Sakamaki's attempts at English were pretty much at the same level as Shichi's, and Liz understood the bare minimum of what he said, but clearly not enough.

To avoid going home and enduring an ear beating from Ingrid, Liz would stay out later. She would either go to the gym or hang out with coworkers. In the recent days of the new year, Stephanie had become Liz's tight bosom buddy. There was still no word from Taffie, and she was too busy to try tracking down Deon, but the situation had her spooked. She couldn't understand for the life of her why Taffie had suddenly become a disappearing act.

She would receive gut-stomping news finally when one Sunday she paid a visit to the Umeda School after work. Thinking she would bump into Taffie or get information from the manager Hitomi, she instead received word from her that Taffie had quit! She had submitted her thirty days' notice and used the rest of her sick leave and vacation days.

Now Liz was totally in the dark. She returned home with an empty, eerie feeling coursing inside. She thought she and Taffie were better friends than that. Why would she quit without telling her? Why hadn't she returned her phone calls? Why hadn't she visited? Wished her Happy New Year? There were so many questions that she needed answered. She wanted to find out and was determined she would as soon as her busy schedule eased up. Since Mr. Sakamaki had agreed to be her guarantor, her search for an apartment was officially in progress.

In the meantime, she would occasionally sleep over at Stephanie's cramped one-room dump in the Taisho area. She had a nice view of Osaka Dome from her spot, but that was about it. Had Stephanie not been so much of a slob, the pad could have been comfy, but Liz preferred her dormitory to the living conditions of Stephanie. Still, it was good to escape blabbermouth Ingrid and the Wednesday-night Filipino congregation.

One night Liz was at Stephanie's, and they were smoking weed, getting high, and watching rented videos, having a "Fuck Japan" bitch session. Stephanie's love, Michio, rang her up, returning her phone call. When Stephanie told him what she and Liz were doing, he got excited and said that he was coming over. This sort of pissed Liz off because she wasn't in the mood to entertain any Japanese people, and Stephanie was so lovestruck that she would be willing to forget all the complaints she had about Japan and Japanese people and make room for Michio to come over. She apologized for making it seem like she was kicking Liz out, but since it was late, she was hoping for some intimacy with Michio. Liz didn't care about that; she just hated having her night intruded upon again. So she took a cab home. Stephanie asked her to leave her a little grass, but Liz was like, "Hell no!" In a playful but dead serious way.

When she got home, Ingrid was still awake, of course. On her side of the room, she was watching a music video of some Japanese group called Kinki Kids. She was amiable and cordial as always, but promptly became unusually quiet. Liz noticed she kept staring at her while she was changing clothes. Liz's first thought was maybe Ingrid had some bi-curious interest forming, but it was something else.

Cautiously, Ingrid said, "Um . . . Elizabeth, can I, like, ask you a question?"

"Sure, what?" Liz responded, minimally suspicious.

"Please don't get angry with me for asking but, like, um do you . . . do you, like, smoke pot?"

Liz laughed and shrugged. "Well, sometimes. But . . ." She decided to not be completely forthcoming with information. "You see, some of my friends get the stuff from time to time, and I know it's illegal and we can get fired, but . . ."

Surprisingly, Ingrid wasn't the square that Liz took her for. She became animated and then said to Liz, "Oh, wow! I did it once when I was in Wisconsin. We had such a blast. I remember, like, I couldn't stop laughing for an hour. Hey, do you, like, think I could, like . . . um, try it the next time you get it?"

Liz thought for a moment that Ingrid had gained cool points in her book, albeit not very many. Her impression of Ingrid was that she was a nerdy, church-infatuated girl who didn't drink or do vice. On the contrary, Ingrid was a social wannabe who desired the acceptance and camaraderie of her peers. Just like any other young chick, she had a wild side tendency, but it was far from ever being shown while in Liz's presence. That night, though, Liz let her guard down and decided to trust Ingrid, that she wasn't so dense to squeal or broadcast to everyone that she smoked the illegal pot and that she had given it to her.

Liz said "Well, as a matter of fact, I have a little bit left, you want it?"

Ingrid got excited and sat upright on her bed. "Oh my gosh, really? Like . . . sure! Do I have to pay you or something?"

"No, it's on the house," Liz said. She was only going to give Ingrid what she had packed in her trusty pipe before leaving Stephanie's anyway. She wasn't about to give away the rest of her stash by any means. "It's only a little bit anyway."

Ingrid took the pipe, and Liz showed her how to apply the lighter and what to do after that. A smidgen it may have been, but for Ingrid, it may as well have been an entire ounce of THC straight to the head. Moments after taking the hit, true to her recounted tale of doing it in Wisconsin, when the weed hit her brain, she started laughing uncontrollably. So much so that Liz had to take her pipe back and get Ingrid a glass of water. When the fit of humor finally ceased, Ingrid started up her cavalcade of conversation chatter boxing, but Liz wasn't having it. She gave Ingrid a half valid excuse that weed smoke made her sleepy, and that night was no exception. She switched off her lamp and closed off her section of the room with the divider.

The next morning, with stamina renewed, Liz woke earlier than usual because it was Monday, her day off at Bozack but a decided workday to teach young Shichi Sakamaki. Ingrid was already awake, in the kitchen, and preparing to leave for her standby post at Tennoji HQ. Her puffy-cheeked face beamed upon the sight of Liz, and she greeted her splendidly, even offered to make her some breakfast.

The questionable aroma of some of Ingrid's dishes caused Liz to decline the breakfast offer, but she accepted the coffee. Ingrid's cheerful face chirped gratitude once again for the previous night's "peace pipe" of sorts. She had a look in her eyes that made Liz predict what was coming next.

Ingrid asked, "Hey, like, do you know where I can, like, buy that stuff?"

Liz sipped the coffee then said, "You mean, all this time you've been with the company, same time as me, right? You haven't heard of *the Duke*?"

Ingrid's gleeful face shrank into one of disturbed innocence as she said, "Oh no . . . Duke? You mean . . . like the university?"

Liz tried not to get aggravated. Obviously, Ingrid had not been privy to the secret system a lot of the teachers used to get drugs. No one had pulled her coat. Liz said, "Do you know a guy named Tim?"

Ingrid said, "I'm . . . not . . . sure." She looked genuinely confounded, deep in thought, searching her brain. Her eyes were wandering about.

Liz proceeded to spill the entire operation as far as she knew it. Basically, she explained how people could place an order for dope once a week through the intercession of one guy, who they nicknamed the Duke. Then when it got complicated in terms of placing orders at certain times and meeting at odd places for pickup, Ingrid got lost and seemed deflated about the possibility of scoring some pot. In addition, because of her job details as a field runner, meeting Tim or adhering to his ordering system would have been too complicated.

"You see," Ingrid said, "like, I was hoping for soon, maybe, like, before this Wednesday."

Liz figured she knew why. She was probably planning to smoke out her Filipino crew. She had two ways to look at the situation. On the one hand, she could do Ingrid a favor and pick up for her since she had a direct hotline to a dealer. On the other, she had to consider the possibility that her doing Ingrid the favor of picking up could turn into a habit and she'd become dependent on her to cop sizzle. This she didn't mind doing for Taffie, but Ingrid wasn't Taffie. Taffie was her babe. In addition, she already had weird feelings about Ingrid's Filipino posse, subject to worsen if they started having blaze sessions in the apartment and one of their members got to wilding out. Or if one of them got careless and alerted the attention of cops. A lot of things could go wrong.

Still, the cat was already out of the bag: Ingrid knew that Liz had weed. She was also aware that Liz knew how to get the weed. So just like with Serge, Liz told Ingrid that she would cop her a "dime bag" at the rate of an itchy-man, but it was a one-time-only thing, reiterating that she was not a drug dealer. The only reason she was doing it was because she wanted to re-up anyway.

Ingrid barked at the price but reluctantly accepted it. Liz told her she could understand the reaction, but it wasn't her decision. Ingrid apologized like a brown nose and grinned humbly as she forked over exactly ten crisp one-thousand-yen bills into Liz's pink palms. After that, she checked her watch and then jumped up from the table.

She said, "Like, when do you think you'll get it?"

Liz said, "Today, probably by the time you come home tonight."

Ingrid's face was alight again; her eyeglass lenses seemed to be flashing. Grinning, she said, "Wow, cool! Like, I gotta run, I'll be back before ten, I hope." She threw on a linty wintergreen wool toggle coat and snug-fit her bowling pin legs inside suede-green boots. "See ya!" The door slammed shut behind her.

57

LIZ BOUGHT HERSELF an0ther bike. She thought it would help her get around quicker while searching for apartments. Since she had a little extra loot to spend because of the freelance teaching gig, she decided to purchase a cycle she saw on Yotsubashi Lane after work one Saturday while in the Namba District. It was a used, recycled bike, but the price was low, it had a decent-sized cargo case, and the brakes worked well. Almost too good compared to her previous bicycle. She vowed to take better care of this one.

The transaction with Ingrid went smoothly. Liz copped some sizzle for herself and her new roommate. Ingrid was highly appreciative and promised to keep the affair top secret. The next dilemma she had, which Liz couldn't readily help her with, was how she would smoke it. Liz had no intention of lending out her one and only pipe, and it was a pain in the neck to visit the shop in Umeda where she once bought rolling papers, let alone try explaining to Ingrid where it was. Still, however, Ingrid was so content with the purchase, the matter of how she could come across apparatus enabling her—and perhaps friends also—to enjoy the smoke became an issue she would deal with another day. Graciously, though, Liz shared her pipe usage sparingly, and it was mainly because it was Ingrid's stash that they were burning at nights before they turned in.

***

The fateful night of "Sand Groper" Ricky Exmouth's farewell sayonara party slash engagement party for him and his newly appointed fiancée, Rena, fell upon a Saturday. It was originally slated to take place at Worm's mansion, but due to his wife Mikako's constant scolding and warning him of the dangers of drug activity—citing his growing joy of occasionally smoking joints—both he and secret smoke buddy Ricky agreed that finding somewhere else to hold the event was better.

Worm's Japanese friend, whom he met through the influence of his former smut celluloid star wife, allowed him the use of a multipurpose room located on the top floor of a high-rise apartment building in a Tempozan District complex. This worked out well because in this area of Osaka City, loud parties and music was the norm as the location was near the harbor. There was also a festive, noisy amusement park, concert hall, and a famous aquarium in the vicinity. Scores of bars and unique restaurants catering to non-Japanese immigrants and miscellaneous *gaijin* of all sorts lined the blocks and situated in the center of this was the apartment building, seemingly the ideal place for a party.

Ricky couldn't be happier. He finally got himself a nice chick to settle down with, Rena, even though she was one of his cobber's throwaways. Rena, being the undercover strumpet she was, would never bring herself to admit that she resorted to involvement with Ricky because she had been unable to keep track of Keefer, who she really had liked in the beginning. The same with Chikako.

Keefer was constantly out and about gallivanting, never the faithful or one-woman-man type. Regular, plain chicks like Rena and Chikako couldn't hold his interest for long, if at all. Distraught and clueless, Rena thought to get even with the Aussie by sleeping with one of his pals. Ricky was the first target in her line of revenge fire. Her plan boomeranged in an unexpected pattern after hooking up with him—she fell in "love."

She fell in love with the fact that Ricky had a job and a small house waiting for him back in his hometown of Karratha, Western Australia. His father ran a small scuba gear shop, and this company was going to produce some new kangaroo oil product for surfboards. The way Ricky had run it down to Rena, she was led to believe that she would be marrying an affluent man, even though in Japan he lived and looked the part of a bum supplicant. Yet this was no deterrent, for Rena was comfortable with the idea of having a dual-life residence in both Australia and her homeland. Even better, she was crazy about the beach, scuba diving, and the Great Barrier Reef. Naturally, she accepted his proposal, even though she had confirmed cases of his infidelities with other Japanese women; but counting on there not being Japanese women in Australia for her to compete with, this fault of Ricky's was outweighed by the value of what Rena thought she was to gain by marrying him.

Ricky's friendship with Keefer did not change in the least. Keefer granted Ricky his full blessing upon hearing of his pal's engagement. In fact, Keefer had always believed Ricky had helped him out a tremendous deal by taking Rena off his hands. As contemptible as it may have seemed, it was something they deemed comparable to teammates passing a ball in a game of Aussie Rules.

Simon, Ricky's closest cousin, like a brother in essence, began dating Chikako, Rena's closest friend. Because she was so much like Rena character wise—passionate, persistent, and often relentless in tracking and hunting a potential *gaijin* pet down if need be. But Simon did not appear to be having any marriage plans in mind for the near future.

Chikako and Rena were known to be notorious *gaijin* bar fixtures. The type of women Liz detested the most would be personified in their likeness. Once they locked in on a foreigner they were fond of, they would zero in, attacking other suitors or competition like a swarm of bees would. They would stalk *gaijin* prey even if they had to sit and wait outside of their target's apartment doors all night. Shucking all sorts of pride and dignity in many cases. Simon had seen these antics when Rena chased Keefer around, and then his cousin, Ricky, so he was treading carefully with Chikako, and for good reason. Tonight, he was feeling uneasy, however. Hot-tempered Ricky was unusually hyper and energetic like a bouncing superball. Simon hoped his cousin and Rena weren't going to have one of their chainsaw-screeching, screaming quarrels.

Ricky was so high-strung on this night, not only because he was happy to have bagged and impregnated a swell Japanese broad to take back home to flaunt, but also because he was a cokehead. He liked to get stoned out of his mind and enjoy life to the fullest, not unlike scores of other young adults, mid to late twenties! Before leaving Japan, he thought, why not go out in style? Nothing would be better than going out with a bang. So he invited everyone he knew to come to his function; even Liz was on the list.

Ricky and Simon didn't work for Bozack, but they knew Keefer and Worm, and Worm ended up being instrumental in putting the entire thing together. As a result, more people from Bozack came to the jam than those from Ricky and Simon's company. Furthermore, Ricky had quit his company that same day of the party.

Liz wasn't too close or connected with guys like Ricky and Simon, but she tolerated these coeval cousins because they were Keefer's buddies. Liz had long ago decided that Keefer was an asshole, but at heart, he too was tolerable because he was fun loving and wasn't a drag to hang out with. Still, she was a bit surprised to be invited to Ricky's party, albeit by way of Worm. For Liz it was a way to take her mind off losing Eddie, and now Taffie, and not being in a rush to spend a boring night at home entertaining talkative Ingrid.

Stephanie had taken the day off the Saturday of the party. Liz finished work in the afternoon, went to the gym, and after she finished, she got a call on her cellular.

Stephanie's jolly voice boomed, "You're goin' to the party tonight, right? Ricky's party!?"

Liz growled, "Yeah, I'm going, but I might be a little late. I've got some things to do." She pedaled her bike, one hand on the handlebar, the other holding her phone, riding on narrow sidewalks, potentially barreling down Japanese women and children. "It's in Tempozan, right?"

"Yes!" Stephanie sounded as if she was screaming. "It's in 'Tempozan'. You take the green subway—I think that's the nearest subway to your house. Didn't Worm or Rick give you directions?"

"Don't worry, I'll find it," Liz said. Her bicycle dipped in and out of human traffic. People on the sidewalk glared at her in utter disbelief. There was an itchy feeling in the left chamber of her bra. It was her sizzle stash hideout, but she could not adjust it while riding the bike and talking on the phone.

Stephanie said, "I'm so excited, Liz. I think tonight's the night. Michio . . . he might propose to me!"

At that moment, Liz thought her ears had gone numb. That, or she was hearing things. Before she could respond in any kind of way reacting to what she thought she heard, Stephanie continued talking.

"We've been together a lot recently," she said to Liz, "and the other night, when I told him that we were going to Ricky's engagement party, he almost cried. Then he asked me if I too thought about marriage . . ."

Liz seriously wanted to hang up the phone—she almost did, but she wanted to ask Stephanie some questions about who would attend the party; Stephanie always seemed to have the inside information about everything. That moment, however, she felt Stephanie was becoming delusional. The dope she planned on bringing to the jam probably wasn't going to help either.

Stephanie's voice rendered, "I . . . told Michio that, yes, I was interested in marriage. And well, he said that he was too! And, when he said it, Liz, he looked into my eyes!!"

Liz had better things to do and a plentitude of other worries than hearing Stephanie's prattle about her oddball relationship with the Japanese weirdo. She barely knew the man and felt Stephanie was in the same boat. She had known this Michio guy less than a year and in the back of her mind felt that it was too soon for either of them to be thinking about tying the knot. Her bicycle bumped along and barely avoided being hit and smashed by a speeding motorist in a junk truck. This winter was colder than the previous year, Liz realized. Icy-cold winds were intensified by the speed at which she traveled, her gloveless fingers were beginning to go numb, so she gripped the handlebars tighter.

She said to Stephanie, "Hey, Steph, I'll call you back in, like . . . ten minutes!"

Stephanie said persistently, "OK, but . . . oh, gawd . . . Liz, pray for me. I'm so nervous. Wish me luck!" Her voice was a bizarre, unearthly intonation a fine line between ecstatic and psychotic. Liz presumed that she was already hitting the hooch heavy.

Reassuringly, Liz quickly stated, "Yeah, yeah sure. I wish you all the luck." Stephanie could not see Liz rolling her eyes and bike-crossing the street during a red signal. The crumpled bag of SES was irritatingly unsettled inside of her left bra chamber. She squeezed strongly upon her brake, as she was arriving at the street corner of an intersection. A cluster of people on the sidewalk, waiting for the crosswalk street signal to change, refused to move despite Liz frantically ringing her bike's bell to alert them of her approach. Her tire skidded on moisture and crankcase oil smearing the avenue. She managed to bring the bike to a halt using her left leg for extra leverage to stop the momentum, but her rear tire swung forward and smashed into the shin of a businessman strolling along. Which wasn't the only bad news.

Her sizzle slipped out of her cleavage and, as bad luck would have it, dropped and rolled into a nearby curbside catch basin sewer! It was gone.

Now seething with indescribable rage and disbelief, Liz shot the Japanese man a quick "Sorry, sorry, *gomen-ne*" done-deal apology. She sucked up her anger and loss and as the man she hit pasted her with the shittiest look, she urged him to do the same, like, *That's life, pal!* Suck it up! As she sped off. Now she was mad. It was her own fault for bringing her stash with her, but it had been a habit of hers recently, having suspicious worries about Ingrid "accidentally" discovering her hiding place at the dormitory.

Miraculously, during the entire ordeal, Stephanie was still on the line. Liz heard her talking and asking, "What happened?"

Then Liz remembered the party. She asked about the Duke.

Stephanie said, "Who, Tim? Definitely, he's coming tonight."

As opposed to calling Luzio Silver, delaying time further, Liz then hoped that she could cop some weed from Tim, even though it was too late to make the order the conventional way they had set up the system for. She told Stephanie what had just happened.

"Oh, bummer!" Stephanie whined. "But don't worry, Ricky already took care of it."

Aggravated, Liz said, "Ricky took care of what?"

Stephanie said, "Ricky arranged to have Tim supply all the orders and deliver to the party. I'm told by Ricky that he's gonna bring a little extra. He apparently has a surplus of undelivered orders from the New Year's! So don't worry about what you lost—you can get it from him when you get there."

Liz was a little bit relieved. She said, "Really? That's cool."

Stephanie said, "There's gonna be all kinda shit, coke, pills, pot, you name it. You might better call-in sick tomorrow." She boomed laughter.

"Good," Liz said maneuvering her bike along slower now. "I don't want to have any arguments with anybody about being late making an order or whatever."

Stephanie said ardently, "Like I said, don't worry-y-y! Michio is gonna buy some shit too. He already told Ricky. Tim is gonna be in drug dealer mode tonight as a favor to Ricky, I guess, bein' that it's his farewell party and all. So if you want anything, you should be fine."

Liz said, "So your guy likes to get wasted, huh?"

Stephanie replied, "No, I never saw him get high, but he said he was interested in trying it for the first time since he came back to Japan from New Zealand. I think maybe he might be doing it to fit in, or help him build up the courage to propose . . ."

Liz had heard enough. She said, "OK, yeah sure. Listen, I really gotta go. I have to change clothes, and I'm thinking of going to see the masseuse too."

Stephanie blurted, "Hey! If you can't find the place, just gimme a call when you reach the station. I'll come by and pick you up . . ."

The call was terminated. At long last, she arrived at her apartment/dormitory. She parked her bike and auto locked it. She shot upstairs to find out that Ingrid was not at home yet. So relieved to have the room to herself again, she bypassed the visit to the Thai massage parlor and took a shower, then a nap.

***

Later that evening, the party was in full swing around 10:00 p.m. People who finished work past the hour of nine came straight to the jam at the penthouse multipurpose room arranged by Worm's friend. The low-tier local live band slated to perform that night cancelled at the last minute, so music was supplied by a mix-tape CD which played from a Sony stereo system connecting speakers in strategic locations. Lively voices from the mixed crowd of foreigners and Japanese echoed throughout the tennis court–sized penthouse room. The only thing missing was Tim and the delivery. Shortly before 10:30 p.m., Ricky received a call from Tim, and everybody in the place seemed happy to hear the news he was soon to arrive.

The room with a crowd of people that numbered thirty or more had, up until then, enjoyed the beer, wine, corn pizza, and various snacks; but the folks who had placed their orders for sizzle were ready to up their thrills for the night. Ricky included.

Liz had yet to arrive, but she was, at that time, on her way. Ricky had collected all the money for the orders and prepared to meet Tim out in the parking lot of the apartment complex. In his mitts he had several slips of paper with secret codes that corresponded with different illicit drugs.

Just as Ricky walked out the door, Stephanie remembered Liz had wanted a dime bag of weed and a gram of coke; if Tim had one of those packages left over in his surplus, she would get it for her. She gave chase and snatched up Michio in the process like he was an inflated doll. Michio stumbled along excitedly, people chuckled at how heavyset Stephanie was manhandling him.

Ricky had taken a quicker elevator to the ground floor and had already greeted Tim in the parking lot. Before leaving the party, he had given Rena a long, wet smacking kiss that had everyone there watching, shouting cheers and whistles of approval. "Be right back, pet!" he exclaimed in a coke-induced outburst and then dashed out, shooting a wink at Simon as he split.

The exemplary paragon of style, Tim the Duke stood tall like a shadowy black shroud in new fedora hat, silk black blazer, matching trousers, pointed Italian stomps with gaudy but unique vamps of sharp edges that perched upward almost like shark fins. An unlit panatela jerked to the right side of his jib as he shook hands greeting Ricky. A classy Jaguar coupe in the cut, nestled in the night shadows provided by decorative trees tributary to Tempozan Park, ensconced Tim's felicitous and seductive Catwoman companion.

That instant, Stephanie jogged out into the parking lot with Michio in tow. Tim, who was usually expressionless, had at that moment an alarmed look that matched Ricky's as Stephanie and her guy approached. Rightfully so, because Stephanie was noticeably dizzy from her liquor intake, and she was screaming out their names. "Hey Tim! Hey, Rick!"

Tim remained cool and sheathed his wrath when he realized who she was. Ricky too let out breath of respire and grinned. Relieved to see Stephanie and their now mutual friend Michio, who Ricky had become buddy-buddy with too as of late.

Ricky greeted them appropriately. He said, "Hiya, Michi-ol' mate. Oh yeah, I remember you said you wanted to pick up some X too, right?"

Stephanie said, "Tim, this is my boyfriend—"

Tim's voice almost trembled with stormy umbrage. He didn't normally deal with Japanese nationals. It was for his own protection. His business depended on his coworkers and those who utilized his services to know that. If he dealt with foreigners such as himself, he knew without a shadow of a doubt they wouldn't be undercover cops, with the intentions of making a bust like how they did in the United States. However, since Ricky approved of his Japanese friend, he relented just that once, because it was the Aussie's farewell and engagement party.

"Michio. He wants to buy somethin' from you, and from now on . . ." Stephanie's voice rendered as Tim eyed her with hostility. Ricky read the look and slapped Tim playfully on his stone muscular arm. Tim's incensed eyes locked onto the face of Ricky without a single twitch. The chills raced up and down Ricky's spine. His usual bravado and tough guy act were out to lunch.

Ricky said, "S'all right, mate, Michi here is cool. Yanno, I-I'd vouch fer'im, he's a good true-blue guy, a bit of a dag, but he's a cool nerd. Hahaha." He tried to lighten the mood.

Michio stood pokerfaced before asking, "Ricky, is everything all right? Are you all right?" Sounding off now in an off-color, dainty way, almost effeminate. He separated himself from Stephanie and placed his right arm gently around Ricky's shoulder and then lower back.

Tim lightened up and chuckled softly. The marshy thick tension was dispersed as Tim nodded and waved his silk-gloved hand through the air like he was lackadaisically clearing away imaginary smoke. He smacked his sugar-puff lips and said "OK, just this one time, but you know the rules, Ricky."

Ricky was like, "Oh, of course, mate, absolutely." He then shot Stephanie a hot look that implied his disdain for her being there, and her boisterous conduct drawing unneeded attention to them. He then said, "Heya, Steph, why don'cha run'long, tell Rena I'll be along in a minute. Might make another beer run after this."

Stephanie said, "Yeah, OK, sure." She glanced lovingly at Michio, who smiled at her with an accommodating and deferential expression.

He said, "I'll meet with you later."

Stephanie grinned exultantly and skipped off, delighted. She caught the elevator and went back upstairs to the party at the penthouse. She was still thinking that tonight was her night, and soon a party like this one would be thrown for her after Michio popped the question. Unable to contain her excitement, she gouged on cold pizza greedily and washed it down with a swig of ice-cold *Yebisu*. She looked at her watch and then checked her phone. Liz had called, but she missed it while she was dallying around with the others in the parking lot.

Worm and Simon approached Stephanie and asked about Ricky and Tim. Worm was ready to get blazed, and people who had placed orders were getting antsy about receiving their goods. The two-bit, prosaic magician hired to do some tricks was unimpressive to the impatient addicts among the gathered audience and was practically booed. Stephanie was still chewing but managed to explain to the dope fiends that the transaction was still going down in the parking lot. She herself was on her way to receive Liz as soon as she placed a call to her.

Worm was like, "Why didn't Tim come up? Damn . . . he's grown accustomed to not being able to come inside my home. Maybe I should go down and tell him to come on up."

Simon said, "Yeah, and what's takin'em so long?"

Stephanie downed her beer and said after a sick belch, "Oh, probably Michio, and Liz. Y'know how Tim gets when people don't order the regular way, intraoffice mail or whatever how it goes. Plus, he had a lot of extra stuff because people who put in orders over the holidays didn't pick them up. You know how it goes, guys. You've done this a zillion times already. The process takes longer, I guess . . ." She crushed her beer can like a she-hulk and burped again.

Worm said, "Fuck it, he can just bring the shit up here. I'll go down . . ."

Before Worm could grab his jacket, Stephanie said, "Oh, they might be gone. Ricky said they were gonna make a beer run."

Simon got pissed. He said angrily, "But we've already got plenty of beer, mate! I'm ready to get inta somethin' heavy!" He began pacing impatiently, feeling uneasy anticipating his cocaine fix.

Stephanie rang up Liz and had a brief conversation. A moment later, she was ready to be off again.

This time Worm said, "Now where are you off to?"

Stephanie said, "I'm going to the station to pick up Liz. You assholes didn't give her directions."

Worm shrugged meekly then said, "Oh well, if you take the rear exit in the lobby, the back way is quicker. It'll let you out on the avenue side. But you can't come back in through that way, though. It locks automatically. You'll have to use the front entrance when you come back."

Clumsily, Stephanie staggered and said, "I knew that . . . already."

Worm said, "Just take a sharp right after you get off the elevator and you'll see the side door." He was almost shouting over the Backstreet Boys' hit at Stephanie's back, hoping she would throw up when she got outside and not inside, at the party spot.

Following Worm's instruction, Stephanie discovered the rear door he had referred to. He was right. This exit spared her from walking the entire length of the building and its gated lot to arrive at a narrow service road leading to the main street. True indeed, she could arrive at the station quicker. This was good, Stephanie's befuddled brain deduced, because Liz didn't like to wait, and she could be something of a hellion at times. Still, she respected and admired her a great deal. She hadn't a friend like Liz ever in her life, and when she and Michio finally walked the aisle, Liz would be her matron of honor without debate.

Five minutes later, she was at the station hugging Liz. As if an unconventional nouveau ritual, they embraced like they were long-lost relatives.

Her eyes darting sideways rapidly, Liz giggled with all the attention bestowed upon her. She was pleased to see Stephanie but more interested in getting lit up and in a drunken frenzy before too long. She hadn't let loose in a while, as she had been trying to keep herself busy. She even found time to send Carver a response e-mail. Tonight, she was well rested from the nap she took, but still reeling from the freakish bad luck of losing her sizzle to a manhole maw. Again, she was reassured that her dope package was already taken care of. Stephanie had left instructions with Michio before arriving to meet her.

On their way back to the party spot, they passed a Lawson's all-night convenience store. Figuring she'd get the ball rolling, Liz wanted to stop and grab a few *chu-hais* to slam, just to see how buzzed she could get before reaching the jam.

Stephanie found it odd she hadn't bumped into Ricky or Michio when she passed the convenience store on the way to pick up Liz; now on the way back, still no sign of their purported beer run. Unless they had decided to go to another store, which seemed unlikely as that one was the closest around. On that note, she joined Liz in the alcohol purchase.

Remembering that she couldn't use the same door she exited from of the building, she took an alternate route. They walked along the service road extending the length of the gated parking lot and the sidewalk accommodating the building's front entrance. It took a bit longer, but tonight Liz was wearing comfortable "docksides."

Just as they rounded the corner, the silence of the once-empty side street throughway was pierced by loud, angry yelling. The commotion was like the sound of distressed and dismayed sports fans seeing their team lose in the wake of a sudden death outcome. The closer Liz and Stephanie came to this brouhaha, the louder and more intense the furor grew, until they were close enough to witness the harrowing sight: Tim and Ricky handcuffed before a nondescript dark-colored cruiser with flashing blue lights on the dash. It was the all-too-familiar light that represented law enforcement. Ricky's terror-stricken wails had drawn a crowd of locals as two regular-looking police cars rolled up.

Liz shrewdly analyzed the situation and quickly tugged Stephanie with all her might to get her to retreat to the corner of the building, shielded from sight. Her voice was almost a whisper. "Oh. My. God. Steph, stay back!"

Stephanie seemed on the brink of panic. She began to whine and then whimpered, "Oh my God, what's happening? What are they doing!?" Her frantic voice was steadily rising, making Liz nervous and slightly fearful.

In horror, they watched as Ricky jumped around with hands cuffed behind his back, screaming, yelling, and kicking like a crazed savage animal in restraint. "YOU CAN'T DO THIS TO ME!!" He writhed and squirmed while undercover narc "Michio" and another, a uniformed police officer, struggled to restrain him.

Tim, also handcuffed, silk gloves and hat now removed, the latter on the pavement nearby, stood with his tragically dismal face staring down. He wasn't carrying on in the same frenzy as Ricky, but he was visibly uncomfortable and on the verge of emotional anguish. Until that moment, he could have been described as the coolest, calmest, and most collected of players around, but his imperturbability was dissolving like a sandcastle on the beach; the tide came in the form of tears from his eyes. Lips trembling, he peered up to the sky as if he was praying to the night, wishing upon a star for divine, supernatural intervention that wasn't to come.

Ricky broke himself away from the uniformed cop and tried to charge his way through a newly formed barrier of assembled police. After a failed attempt at what looked to be a game of Red Rover, Ricky sobbed, realizing that there was no escape for him. All his ranting and screaming was to be of no avail. The undercover narc formerly known as Michio, grabbed Ricky in a loving embrace.

In his exceptionally polished New Zealand–influenced English, Michio tried to console Ricky. He said, "Please, Ricky, please stop. I will help you all I can. I'm sorry about this. Please let me help you."

From the distance, Stephanie continued to watch in horrified shock. Her hands unconsciously clasped the sides of her temples as her heart leaked profusely to the seat of her pants. In the next moment, she would come close to hysterical, seeing the person she knew as Michio, who was improbably supposed to have proposed marriage to her that night, who had led her on for so many weeks and months, having her believe that he was into her; her brain did not seem to want to accept it. She started for the cluster of commotion, but Liz grabbed her arm.

Whispering loudly, Liz said, "Steph, don't be fucking stupid! If you go over there, they might arrest you too! That guy was an undercover! Who knows what you might've leaked to him all that time you two were supposedly dating? It's too late. It looks like they already busted Tim and the other guy!"

Stephanie jerked away with her girth and neurotic might. Determined to get to the bottom of the mystery destroying her, she stormed over to the crowd of onlookers and the police. She froze as she drew nearer. She made out Michio's face clearly.

The cop they knew as Michio held the howling and quavering Ricky in an embrace that looked like a bear hug, but from the front, and they were face-to-face. "Yes," the man said, "yes, I am a policeman. I was working undercover. But I got to know you, and I think you are good person. I want to help you because you have drug problem. You have bad addiction." His snaky voice was quickly urgent, and his face was so close to Ricky's they could smell each other's breath and probably describe the last thing their mouths consumed.

Ricky was inconsolable. He wasn't trying to hear anything Michio had to say. All he could ascertain was that life, as he knew it, was set to come to a screeching halt, and he was helpless to change it. In a surge of utmost contempt, he drew back gunk in his throat and spat in the narc's face. The deposit hung from dude's nose like a grotesque dripping stalactite before he wiped it away on his sleeve.

"Aw, fuck me *dead*, you bloody, *drongo* yellow wanker!!" Ricky bellowed. "I don't wan'cher bloody fuckin' help. Just let me go! Please mate, be a *larrikin* and let me go, man . . . I mean, for gosh sake, mate, I . . . I'm gonna get married . . . oh, Jeez-us . . ." His voice trailed off into a piteous sob fit.

Michio said with a fatherly sigh, "Ricky, you would need to consider that before you were involved with drugs and narcotics. You knew that drugs are illegal here in Japan. But thanks to you and your friends, we have apprehended a drug supplier, a dealer," motioning toward Tim who was out of earshot and being led away that instant to the back seat of one of the squad cars.

The narc continued, "Your involvement was minimal, but you are still guilty of possession, and it is an offense that warrants an arrest. But I still think there is a chance that the court will be lenient to you in sentencing. You won't get as much time as that other man."

Stephanie could not make out what Michio was saying to Ricky as he held him close. Ricky could hear the narc spew what he deemed nonsense, but he was angrily and defiantly still trying to liberate himself from Michio's restraining hug.

Stephanie had chiseled her way through the gathered onlookers and got close enough to the scene where she thought she could be heard. She called out, "Michio!" But the cop who had assumed that name no longer responded to it.

From the cover of decorative bushes aligning the side of the building, Liz could hear Stephanie crying out Michio's name and knew that nothing good would come of her actions. Just then, an additional wave of cops appeared on the scene, from out of nowhere seemingly, and dutifully restrained the onlooking crowd, ordering them to disperse, or step back. Amused Japanese people beheld twisted entertainment seeing the real-life drama unfold and how erratic foreigners behaved when they got arrested. Stephanie was blocked from Liz's view. Suddenly she thought that this would be the ideal moment for her to dip out, exit stage. She would have to leave stubborn Stephanie behind to fend for herself.

Liz was also glad for the "accident" of her weed bag loss to the gutter. Hastily, she retreated to the avenue. When she reached the corner of "Seafront" (*21) and Minato Street, she managed to catch a cab.

Back at the scene of the arrest, "Michio" barked orders to his subordinates in Japanese. "Have that party upstairs discontinued and have everyone restrained for questioning." As for Stephanie, who had moments before caught his attention with her vexatious yelling of his narc pseudonym, he ordered, "Please take into custody that loudmouth tippler also!" Pointing her out in the crowd and coldly dismissing her as if he had nothing to say in the form of the same comfort he offered Ricky, still in his macabre clutches.

Energy expunged, Ricky's struggling by then had died down. "Michio" stroked his dirty-blond hair and cradled his head as he wept. He said, "Is there someone I can have called for you in Australia, Ricky? I promise, I will see to it you are helped."

Although his words seemed kindly, considerate, and caring within hearing range, Stephanie being cuffed nearby felt an odd, churning uneasiness seeing "Michio's" embrace of Ricky. Aghast, she would then scope with revulsion and, pummeled into a state of dreadful consternation, witness the "Michio" narc dry-humping Ricky. In full view of everyone not distracted by the ruckus, he pretended to be talking while, in actuality, he was holding Ricky tightly, firmly, securely.

Stephanie stood gaping at the sight. A cop gently tugged at her arm, urging her to move, but she stood like a petrified stone as if she had just seen Medusa.

"Michio's" corduroy pants–clad hips rubbed friction as his crotch brushed the front of Ricky's jeans. His pointless talk to Ricky was accompanied by heavy breathing that picked up rapid pace until he cried out with a swift, unforeseen jerk of exigence. Beads of sweat even in the crisp, cold air of the night could be seen tinkling his forehead. They stood there for what had seemed to be an eternity. Ricky was still weeping in "Michio's arms, but finally, it seemed as if he was willing and able to make his perp walk to a squad car.

Stephanie took one last, thunderstruck look at Michio, the so-called love of her life; then she retched, hurling violently in the bushes after having seen the cum discharge stain imprinted like a wet circle soaked around his zipper.

58

SCANDAL EMERGED IN the days that followed the cataclysmic saga of Ricky Exmouth and Timothy "Tim the Duke" Valentine. Bozack took a major hit because Tim was still employed at the time of his arrest, while Ricky no longer worked for his former company, and therefore that school's name was left out of the news!

Liz had done the wise thing and hauled ass, but she had only temporarily dodged a bullet. She *and* everyone at the penthouse, which was raided. Fortunately,—or better, miraculously—no arrests were made, and no illegal drugs were discovered. Still, Worm was present and questioned by the police. The cops could not connect him to Tim other than the fact that they worked at the same company.

Stephanie was released because she was not in possession of drugs. The police kept her overnight and searched her place and came up with nothing. Since the narc had never seen her or any of the other teachers partaking of drugs—but only the aftereffects—there was no concrete evidence to arrest them. But Stephanie was not out of hot water.

Eventually, word reached the Bozack Head Office soon after news of the drug bust leaked to the media. Tim was effectively terminated. In the days circa Y2K, it wasn't uncommon for a foreigner's employer to be listed on their *gaijin* cards, and Tim's ID was such. The police contacted Bozack immediately. It didn't take long for him to get the axe. Worm and other Bozack teachers who were at the party were not fired, but they were reprimanded; some were punished for breach of company rules regarding interaction with students outside of the school classroom. Worm faced demotion of rank. Stephanie's fate, however, was in the hands of Kenjiro Tanimoto and, ultimately, Shigeru Watanabe of Bozack HQ.

At the police station, Tim was crying and sweating like ice cubes in a sauna. His cool had cracked, and the jig was up. Hoping to be granted some sort of clemency or an option to be deported as opposed to being locked up, Tim was down to snitch, rat, double-cross, or tattle—anything to go home to his mama in Gary, Indiana. The narcs knew he was a low guy on the totem pole in the grand scheme, but he was in possession of an extremely large amount of illegal dope, a literal walking pharmacy. Among the names the songbird sang on the stool was Luzio Silver. The fact he had so much weight was because he was delivering it to Worm and others at the party.

All Worm had to do was deny the claim, and he did. Just like that, he severed ties with Tim, denying any involvement with him whatsoever. Unbeknownst to Simon, Worm distanced himself from Ricky as well, stating to the fuzz that Tim's presence at the party was only because he was meeting with Ricky. This he emphasized as being a natural fact, because that was the reason he wasn't busted in the parking lot making the drug deal. Furthermore, he challenged anyone to honestly state that they had ever seen Tim at his home. Bozack elected to support his story but did proceed to demote him from his rank and title of head teacher. Worm was humiliated by this.

Clemency did not seem imminent for Tim and Ricky. They both faced ten-year and five-year bids, respectively, and deportation upon completion of sentence.

Ricky was beside himself, and Rena was said to be constantly weeping in a manner of hysteria. In custody, Ricky refused to eat and was placed on a suicide watch. The wedding was obviously called off. Rena didn't want to bring shame on her family name to be involved with someone dealing in drugs—and got caught. Unlike Ricky, she felt she could survive; she'd just have to wait for the next empty seat at a *gaijin* bar to be filled with another blue-eyed stranger.

Simon did all he could to help his cousin. True to his word, the Michio narc did his part to help Ricky by finding him a pellucid translator for English to Japanese, as well as an opportunity to phone his family back in Australia, which was unprecedented and extremely rare. The grim news was that all his family's fancy money and influence in their country was of no consequence to the stern policies regarding Japanese law and order. Japanese guards, officials, and diplomats on every link in the chain of command proudly refused bribes; they were said to gladly eat globefish raw before accepting foreign money at that.

Stephanie had to face the music at Bozack as well. Although she was not arrested and released on her own recognizance, she had to be escorted home—or out of the police station—by company reps Ruth Worth and Mayumi Kazegawa. In a queer turn of events, to save her skin and job, Stephanie threw Liz—her best "friend"—under the bus. Knowing her job was on the line, Stephanie let herself off the hook by telling the desk pro tem and the cops that she had got all her drugs from Liz.

Students of Bozack who attended the party had seen Stephanie leave in a police car along with Tim and Ricky. Even though Stephanie was released, the student customers talked and reported what they had seen to other people, friends, or acquaintances, who were also Bozak student-customers. Then it was reported in the newspapers and TV news. The bombshell discovery of a popular teacher employee busted for dealing drugs was a crushing blow to sales. Parents would no longer feel comfortable sending their children to so-called learning centers, conversation, and cram schools that dealt drugs in the back rooms.

***

The usual consortium of Bozack big wigs got together for an emergency meeting to discuss their next moves. Shigeru Watanabe, still fresh off a voracious chunk chewed from the ass of Kenjiro Tanimoto for the previous Chucky Chilson–Denore Langston incident, had his angry fangs bared and ready to rip into him and everyone else who didn't see this disaster coming. Kenjiro had assured him that he would take care of the situation with the alleged drug dealing and usage, but apparently, he was unable to accomplish such detail. Expressionless, he sat at the head of the marbletop boardroom table with fingers steeled in deadly silence. Finally, he cleared his throat and addressed his grim-faced cortege.

"Now let me get this straight." His voice sounded cold like he had ice cubes in his throat. "This black nigger Mr. Valentine was selling drugs at Bozack and delivering it to other teachers like a pizza man. Ms. Pritchard gets arrested along with Valentine and some other buckethead fucker, then there's another familiar controversial name we've heard before, Ms. Elizabeth Amberbush, also suspected—according to the statement Ms.Pritchard gave to the police—of supplying drugs to staff behind the scene. I thought we went over this. You assured me that you would get this gobbledygook straightened out."

Ruth Worth spoke out of turn, causing saucer eyes to point her way from everyone in the room. "In all fairness, sir, Ms. Amberbush wasn't seen by anyone at the party that night. We know not whether the alleged statement Ms. Pritchard gave to the police was accurate."

There was a moment of silence. It was almost as if the roomful of Japanese people had to process the only foreigner in the room speaking their language.

"Thanks," Shigeru addressed Ruth with a gratuitous smirk. "OK, so what are we going to do about this Stephanie Pritchard?"

Nervously, Kenjiro spoke. "At this time, we don't feel as if she should be terminated, sir. We still are in need of female teachers. It's very unfortunate that she was taken into police custody and suspected of drug involvement, but it reflects negatively on our company."

Shigeru wiped his eyes and smacked the table. "Dammit, man! Tell me some shit I don't already know. I want to know: what do you propose to be done?"

"Yes, sir," Kenjiro said, trying to keep his voice from trembling. "We . . . have decided to offer her a transfer option to our newest office in the Tokyo area. We pay for half of her moving costs, and she will remain on probation . . ."

Shigeru sliced into his explaining. "Oh, and speaking of probation, Mr. Swiggler will not be considered for promotion, I take it, and he is to be demoted from current corporal status as South Town head teacher?"

The three Japanese heads turned like dominoes to face Ruth at the far end of the table. Alarmed by the sudden attention, she stated, "Yes, sir. Effective as of—"

"South Town schools are our most problematic—Hommachi, Higobashi, and Namba especially. Who the hell is going to replace that brown-nosing pipsqueak half-breed!?"

Ruth said, "Sir, Rosiland Ash we feel could . . ."

Shigeru covered his eyes with a wrinkled palm. Shaking his head he was like "Aw, hell no. That pair of leggy little hot pants doesn't have enough experience. She can barely handle the HQ hotspot. Surely, you have somebody else. Otherwise, you're inviting disaster. Who else you got? Name some names."

Ruth calmly opened a manila folder, and with one eyebrow raised, she began running off names of potential replacements. "There's Eric Cravens, Ellen McDowd of Amagasaki, Laura Violi Kyobashi, Rusty Clark formerly of Kyobashi now Umeda, Darcy Blake . . ."

Shigeru rubbed his temples as if he was having a migraine. He started waving his hands frantically to get Ruth to stop talking. He said, "OK, OK . . . OK! Damn it . . . for right now, put Rosiland at the South Town schools, let's give her a shot. As for Mr. Swiggler, I don't think he should be demoted for long."

Kenjiro said, "Sir, what would be the best way to proceed?"

Shigeru looked at Kenjiro as if he wanted to slice his neck with a *muramasa* blade. He said, "What do I pay you fools for anyway? I'm supposed to tell you? You demote him for a while and give him a chance to earn his position back. He may be an ass-kisser, but he's done some good work for us these past few years."

The room responded with a collective chorusing of "Yes, sir. Absolutely, sir".

Shigeru seemed moderately pleased with the answer, which came as a relief to all present. Then he said, "And if this Ms.Pritchard refuses the offer, she will be terminated, is that correct?"

Kenjiro said, "Yes, sir. Actually, her option is to be transferred to a remote branch office in the rural area of Saitama. Her only other option would be to submit resignation forms."

Shigeru said, "Why can't we transfer her to some schools in this area?"

Kenjiro said, "We have a functional number of female teachers here in the Kansai Western region, but our newer offices in the Kanto Eastern region are in dire need. We feel that Ms. Pritchard would be better put to use in that region. She has experience teaching children too. She is a seasoned, well-trained employee so this, we feel, would be the best way to proceed."

"OK, then," Shigeru said. "Get that done."

***

Stephanie, of course, took the offer. She shipped out in practical immediacy. Given a small window of time as she was, she had only a week to get her things packed up, have her apartment walked through, and other sorts of bureaucratic red tape; odds and ends (electricity, water bills, and such); then make it out to Saitama, not too far from Tokyo, but in an area far from urban. It was back to the countrified life like Shiga . . . like Arizona . . .

Nobody missed Stephanie much. Many, including Worm and Simon, saw her as the catalyst for everything that happened. It was Stephanie who brought the Michio guy around, and ultimately led to Tim and Ricky getting busted.

Worm was livid to realize that he once had the narc in his very home as a guest and thanked his lucky stars he hadn't done any dirt when he was around. Still, it was Stephanie who was the airhead who took the undercover straight to Tim in the parking lot. Ricky was just at the wrong place at the wrong time. Worm didn't stop to think that Stephanie had also inadvertently saved his skin as well. When he was about to go to the parking lot to tell Tim to come up, he would probably have been busted too. Or, if Tim had come upstairs to the penthouse party like he had wanted him to, then he would really be in hot water. Not only him, but a lot of other dopehead co-workers and teachers at the party too. Indeed, he had his lucky stars to thank. As for Stephanie, he was no longer privy to news regarding her fate, as he was not the head teacher anymore. But the fact that she was not at any of the schools, Worm figured that she was transferred away or canned. Still, as much as secrecy and confidentiality tried to reign around the Bozack offices, snippets of gossip and news always leaked. Worm's advantage over other *gaijin* was his half-Japanese ability to understand the language. Because of this, he heard that Stephanie had dropped Liz's name while she was being questioned by the police.

Otherwise, Worm was relieved he was spared Ricky and Tim's fate and vowed to listen to his wife, Mikako, and follow her advice by keeping folks like Stephanie at arm's length. Now, however, he was holding a grudge because he was back to being a normal teacher again, among his former subordinates. Every day before work, he would fight back tears, and sometimes after work too. He resumed his talk of quitting the company and embarking on his mission to create his own school business. Mikako immediately told him to forget it and would not allow him to quit. She wasn't ready for him to live off her money while he chased his dream. She made him earn it on his own.

Around the office, the schism was formed when people began looking at Liz in a similar light as Stephanie, even though she hadn't shown at the party. Still, most people at work were of the idea that Liz and Stephanie were close, and maybe they were, but Liz was a little ticked off with Stephanie as well. Determined not to be bullied, Liz pulled Keefer and Worm to the side and tried to plead her case. She came short of even detailing how now she was suffering because of Stephanie's blunder, subsequently getting Tim the Duke busted. She no longer had access to him or Luzio Silver. In the nights following the bust, Luzio Silver had no longer answered the number on his biz card she had.

Keefer might have tried to forgive Liz if she had any involvement with Ricky getting arrested, but he was highly sympathetic to his countrymen. Furthermore, he was consoling Ricky's cousin Simon. He had a high degree of disdain for Stephanie, and because she was close with Liz, he wasn't trying to be too social with Liz as he once was.

The same seemed to echo throughout the former group with whom Liz was the most familiar. Eric, Radley, and Worm distanced themselves. Vicky had finally decided to call it quits, dump her Japanese boyfriend, and rumor had it she left Japan pregnant, so she was nowhere to be found at that point. The only people Liz had left to be on good terms with was, ironically, her roommate, Ingrid. The jury was still out on Jeremy, for he had yet to return from his vacation.

Now workdays would drag along. The once-bubbling and spirited atmosphere of the Hommachi and Namba branches died down to dismal when Liz was around. She could feel her head reeling like a revolving door which had swallowed up a person at each revolution from her world: Denore, Chucky, Taffie, now Stephanie . . . Eddie . . . She was about to lose her noodles.

She was going through a withdrawal of sorts because she had not smoked or snorted anything for several days and nights after the big bust. Feeling sick a lot more, she had to use some vacation days once hoped she would use for traveling somewhere, together with Eddie. She was feeling as if her life scenario was becoming a weird TV drama series in jeopardy of being canceled. She would shut herself off in her side of the room, and on some days, she even paid extra money to sleep at a hotel just to have peace and quiet away from Ingrid. The Sakamakis were even so generous to actually allow Liz the use of one of their guestrooms.

Anomalistic chain of events reached the peak of peculiarity one night as Liz lugged along after her last class and headed for home. En route to the doorway that led to the downstairs exit, she passed by the Japanese office staff area. Kayo, Mayumi, and Kenjiro were working late as usual, busy as bees. There was an additional staff member on this night, a little sleek and slender. Liz had to do a double-take on the woman, she hated when she couldn't place a face.

Squinting her eyes, she shook her head. It was hard, but her Western mind was deprogramming from the thought that all Asian or Japanese faces appear similar or identical. Still, she could have sworn she had seen the woman before. Just not at work. Not at the office.

Liz didn't notice her own actions, but Kayo did. Liz stared at the woman curiously, entranced and immobile, forgetting that it was time to go home for a moment.

In her usual dry, uninterested manner Kayo snapped Liz out of her trance, saying, "Do you know Nishinari-san?"

That instant, upon hearing her name called, Sachi Nishinari turned to also see a familiar face when she and Liz locked eyes. It was also then Liz understood, with alarming clarity, who this woman was and where she had seen her before. It took a moment for her to put the identifying pieces together, for this night was the first time she had seen the attractive woman dressed so "conservatively," like a flight attendant immaculate. At least, more so than her "catwoman" style when out on the town with Tim Valentine.

The otherwise-furtive former companion of Tim, Sachi, played dumb with secret agent–level aptitude as she too squinted her eyes looking at Liz. She said to Kayo serenely in Japanese, "She looks familiar, but I cannot say for certain that I know her. These people come and go, as you know." She could breathe a sigh of relief, because only Liz had ever seen her and Tim together. The night of the bust, Sachi sped off undetected and absconded in the Jag when she saw the flashing cop lights.

Liz knew her only through facial recognition. Choosing to not give any indication she had any close ties with Tim, Liz pretended she had never seen Sachi before. She said, "I thought I met her before, but I guess I was wrong. Sorry . . . hahah, I didn't mean to stare."

In reality, Liz didn't know what to think, seeing this woman. Was she a snitch? What would be *her* fate were it ever known she was Tim's assistant and companion? Practically his accomplice. With Tim being in big trouble, was he going to drop her name to the cops? Or yet, was she still in the life, and if so, could she help Liz score some bang in the future?

Sachi resumed her work and her masked exterior, hoping that Liz would go away. Her mission there at this Bozack location was near completion, and meddlesome distractions like Liz jeopardized it. She engaged Kenjiro in an impromptu, meaningless conversation to ignore Liz and Kayo, deflecting herself from their focus of interest.

Kayo said reassuringly to Liz, "Maybe you know her. Have you ever worked at any Bozack branch in Nara? She's the Nara area sub-manager."

Liz replied emphatically that she had not ever worked in a Bozack branch that far away, and then she left. The whole thing was too strange and vexing for her to make sense of now. Nara Branch? Manager? What was she doing there at Hommachi, then? And how did she ever have time to be with Tim every weekend, driving him around, making deliveries and pick-ups? Things did not add up. She hopped on a train for a change, wondering how long it would be before she wore out her welcome at the company.

***

Less than a week later, the living drama would intensify in madness. With Jeremy Ng due to arrive back in Japan in a few days, Liz went to the Sakamakis' home for what she thought was to be her last scheduled lesson teaching Shichi before his return. She still had no clue that Mr.Sakamaki was under the impression that she was going to stay on as Shichi's private tutor. Liz thought about his agreement to be her guarantor and hoped he would keep his end of the deal. This verbal contract was problematic though, because up until then, their communication was through broken English, shattered Japanese, and archaic, kung fu sign language gestures. Liz was thinking that Jeremy would return and continue teaching Shichi. Then her schedule would be freer to conduct apartment searches.

On the same day of Shichi's last lesson, it also happened to be the birthday of Mr. Sakamaki's septuagenarian mother. After the lesson, Liz was invited to a lavish home dinner and birthday bash. Liz, of course, didn't have anything better to do, so she did. In a span of time riddled with ghostlike faces reappearing, Liz met the handsome Japanese guy Yoh, who used to date Vicky before she dumped him cold. He was a friend of the Sakamakis and had played an instrumental role in Jeremy's meeting the Osaka slumlord.

Liz had only met Yoh once or twice. He had made an impression on her with how amazing his English ability was, and he was probably the most handsome Japanese as well, because he looked more Cuban than Asian. While he was with Vicky, he stood tall and spoke with confidence. Now that she had canceled him, he was broken, depressed, and sleepy looking. He livened up somewhat upon meeting Liz again, but it was, for him, a bittersweet reminder of his lost love. Still, he didn't mind translating for her if she needed him.

The birthday party wasn't too big; only a few friends and family of the Sakamakis came. They ate, they drank, and they had cake, ice cream, and cream puffs from France. Then, of course, Mr. Sakamaki, in his ceremonious fashion as always, whipped out a gargantuan-sized bottle of Chogin Junmai sake. People started drinking. Heavy.

Liz remembered the hangover she had the last time she had tried to do the Japanese sake challenge, and it wasn't anything she cared to experience again. Furthermore, she didn't have any weed to chase the queasy side effects away in its wake. She said to herself that she wouldn't drink much, but she got peer-pressured into drinking more than she should have. The stuff was warm, it tasted sweet, and it had somewhat of a calming effect, but simultaneously caused her to liven up and be merry.

Things got better before taking a turn for the worst. Yoh pulled Liz to the side as if he had a big secret to share. Liz was hoping he wasn't getting any ideas about getting with her just because he had managed to score with another foreign chick like Vicky. Her attitude would soon change, however.

Yoh said, "I am sorry about what happened to your friends. I heard about Stephanie and Tim's arrest. But I can trust you because you were a friend of Jill."

"Jill?" Liz sounded confused, but then she remembered that Vicky took on an alias, like she had led a mysterious, double life. Liz said, "Trust me? What do you mean?"

Yoh said nothing, but he reached inside of his pocket, pulled out a box of Mild Seven cigarettes. He shot a quick look around to make sure all the party guests were still preoccupied in the festivities. He pulled out a baseball bat spliff, ran it quickly under his nose, then Liz's.

Liz smelled the weed, and her eyes flicked open wide; she shook with a quick tremor of excitement. Just as she made a grab for it, Yoh's face looked startled, and he tucked it safely away back in his cigarette box before Mr. Sakamaki and his driver pal, Mr. Goro, approached them in the hallway. Yoh also worked for Mr. Sakamaki, but Liz was unsure of exactly what he did for him. They exchanged Japanese with each other, then Yoh explained to Liz that the two gentlemen had to leave but would return shortly. They asked if Liz could stay longer, and of course, Liz was cool with it. Especially now since Yoh had suddenly become a person of interest to her.

When the two men left, Yoh said, "Jill . . . I mean, Vicky, used to do this thing, together, and if you like, I can share together with you?"

Liz was hoping more along the lines of him giving it to her for free, or allowing her to purchase it from him. Regardless, she intended on cutting into him to find out where he got his stuff from. But since she didn't know the dude all that well, she decided to accept his generous offer. A little buzz was better than nothing.

Yoh said, "OK, we can do it later. The guests will be leaving soon. It's getting late, the children Shichi and Hayato will be sleeping soon, I think."

Liz and Yoh went back to the kitchen and the dining room. The women were already cleaning up and preparing take-home boxes for guests. Hayato was playing with toy robots and cars, and Shichi was entertaining two of her friends of similar age. A Disney animation flick of some sort was playing for them on a living room TV set. When people finally began to disperse, Kazuko, Sakamaki's wife, told Yoh that she would be back and forth out the door seeing people off.

They slipped off to the veranda through some sliding screen doors and pretended to be having a cigarette smoke, but instead blazed the weed spliff. In full view of the children and the old folks remaining, but neither knew what the smell of marijuana was and went about their playing and drinking as normal. Liz laughed at how freedom danced in the clutches of danger like an outlandish game. For like Tim and Ricky, she and Yoh could get arrested for their act, but at the same time, nobody knew that they were doing something illegal so freely and under their noses.

Liz got around to asking Yoh, "Where did you get this from?"

"From black man, I think, maybe your friend, Vicky's friend," Yoh replied.

Liz was stumped. "I don't have any black friends . . . oh, Deon? He had, like, a little ponytail thingy in the back of his head?"

Yoh laughed excitedly as he passed her the spliff. He said, "Yes! That's him . . . very good dancer, handsome guy"

Liz took a deep inhale of the SES, tried to hold it in her chest before exhaling with a coughing fit. "I don't know about handsome, but"—she coughed—"yeah I know him. Never really seen him dance. In fact, I haven't seen him much at all recently. You got his number? I think I lost it."

Yoh said, "Sure, I will look for it." As he took the spliff back, he flipped through his phone. Delighted, Liz took Deon's number and programmed it into her phone's database like how Eric Cravens, the digital computer whiz, had instructed her to. So, Deon was to be her new light at the end of the tunnel, especially if he was holding stuff. Liz imagined she should have thought of him before, considering how much Taffie enjoyed getting high. The problem with Deon was that he seemed mighty arrogant, more than usual these days, and continually blew her off if she tried to meet with him.

When the spliff was all done and burnt to a crisp, Yoh flicked the useless roach over the banister. They went back inside. By then, Mr. Sakamaki and Mr. Goro had returned. Mr. Sakamaki was drunk as hell, cracking jokes and making people laugh like he was a comedian doing stand-up. Despite his condition, he was astoundingly able to function normally in terms of maintaining his balance and his ability to walk without a drunken stagger.

People began filing out of the Sakamaki home, including the wife and the elderly mother. In a pleading tone, the Sakamakis had a conversation with Yoh pertaining to Liz. She could tell because Kazuko kept swiveling her head back and forth at him and her with a worried look.

Yoh turned to Liz and explained, "They would like to know if you could stay awhile. You can even sleep over in the guestroom you have used before. The reason is because they must take Mr. Sakamaki's mother home. They will be back late, so they need a babysitter, I guess. Sorry about this. Can you do it? They said they will pay you extra, of course."

Liz didn't really see any problem with it. She was already lightheaded and had a mellow buzz. Hayato was already sleepy, and Shichi didn't seem too far behind him. Chances were they would be sleep within the hour, and once again, Liz would score easy money for doing practically nothing. She had work the following day at Bozack in Namba, but from the Sakamaki residence, that would be a five- or ten-minute taxi ride away, so she agreed to stay for the evening.

After Shichi and Hayato had been tucked away in bed, Liz retired to her guestroom located in the same hallway of the house as the children's shared room. The guestroom was equipped with a desk, a TV, laptop computer, and a futon foldout bed. Liz sat down at the desk and started sending e-mails to friends and family back home in the United States. She got another e-mail from Carver that caused her to erupt in a brief fit of laughter. From what she could piece together from his latest message, it appeared that her mother had informed Carver that she and Eddie had broken up.

A stressful irritation began to fester while thinking of Eddie, and Liz was suddenly in the mood for another drink. She went to the Sakamaki kitchen. Nobody was around, so she checked their refrigerator for something of a beverage. The huge fridge was fully stocked, something Liz hadn't seen for a while as hers and Ingrid's was generally bare. She shifted items around—juice, milk, tea, and finally found beer cans and *chu-hais* in the back. She chose the latter and returned to her guestroom.

She probably drank the alcoholic beverage too fast, for it wasn't her intention to fall asleep, but after a long day, she sat upon the futon bed, trying to read Japanese comics, surrendered to fatigue and intoxication. Because of her sizzled brain, her dreams were infused with colorful and aberrant images on this night. She was now Alice or one of the characters she had glanced at briefly on the TV downstairs earlier, when the Disney videotape was played for the kids. She was surrounded by "Thumpers" or cute, adorable little rabbits. They were so soft. She reached out for them, but she couldn't reach them, in her dream. They just cuddled against her legs, her feet, and her toes. The softness around her toes soothed her. So much so she started to laugh in her sleep. The rabbits licked her toes, but it was a different type of tongue—it was more like that of a dog's. In fact, the one white rabbit made canine yelps. The dream continued as the tickling sensation intensified. Liz could be seen chuckling in her sleep as her hands moved to the hairy mound between her legs. She found her treasured flesh through the fabric of her dress. She could feel a rising sensitivity, causing her passion to increase, she bit her bottom lip. Her fingers began doing a walk to her moistened clitoris. The dream was so steamy, she began to sweat. That's when her eyes flared open wide. Awakened, she saw a digital clock on the room's desk reading 4:29 a.m. The heat at footside of the futon upon which Liz reclined was very real. Only, it had not been a White Rabbit applying moisture to Liz's white gel-pedicured toes. Moon and streetlight rays glinted through the window and revealed the mysterious figure in the night to be Mr. Sakamaki!

The dream was, then, for Liz, a wig-flipping nightmare as she felt goosebumps spring to life on her skin. Mr. Sakamaki, obviously bombed-out-of-his-skull drunk, had one of Liz's anklet bearing pods raised to his jib, and he was lavishing her digits with licks deserving of an ice cream cone or lollipop. His right hand was stuck inside of his trousers, pumping up and down like a reverse trampoline. It was also he who was making the howling, doggish groans.

In stark revulsion, Liz let out an agonized shriek. The foot Mr. Sakamaki held she used to kick him in his face. He fell back and hit the floor on his rump. She scooted her buttocks backward and folded her knees. In lithe form, she rolled sideways off the bed and jumped over him like she was a live version of Mario Brothers. With speed, she hurried her way downstairs and found the "front door" and escaped to the cold streets without even bothering to take her shoes. She was like, "Damn the money!" too. Barefoot, she didn't stop running until she found the Tanimachi strip. A passing cab finally rescued her and her freezing, blistered toes, and she escaped back to her home.

59

STEPHANIE PRITCHARD WAS delusional at times, but she could rapidly wrap herself around the fact that she had been played by Michio the undercover narc. She was more distraught in discovering that on top of him being a deceiver, he was also a clandestine homo who had the hots for Ricky Exmouth all along! And he had used her to get next to him. Juggling a nightmarish turn of events in her dizzy brain, she was trying yet to recover from humiliation and stupefaction endured. Numerous times since the incident, she had succumbed to fits of sobbing pukes by the toilet. Calls to coworkers went ignored and vice versa. For starters, Keefer, Worm, and then Radley straight up blocked her number. Stephanie, in turn, also grudgingly blocked Liz. Of course, she didn't really want to, but she was ashamed of herself for trying to shift the blame away from her and telling the cops that Liz was responsible for supplying her with drugs. Even though it was true most of the time—Liz did give Stephanie some of her weed or coke on occasions—but she had nothing to do with Ricky and Tim getting busted. Stephanie was a moocher who just didn't have the mature, responsible wherewithal to accept her own culpability alone. For fear of losing her job, or even worse, she tried to drag Liz's name into it. She knew she was wrong for that, but she did it anyway; and in feeling guilty about it, she didn't have the guts to speak to or face Liz. For her, it was about survival and always saving her own skin. She would make new friends like she always did.

Arriving in Tokyo, Stephanie tried to put all thoughts of Osaka temporarily behind and mentally prepare herself for another transition. Having not been set up yet in her new living quarters, she holed up at a mediocre business hotel in the Ikebukuro District. She spent much time e-mailing long-winded sob stories to family and what friends she might have had left who gave a damn about her before the arrival of a Bozack company representative who would escort her to her new place and get her situated.

Alex, a clean-cut Australian Bozack rep for the Kanto Eastern Japan offices met her inside of the business hotel lobby. He was decked out in a gray suit, had freckles that spattered his milky-white face, which looked as if it had been cut from a child's magazine about "friendly people in your neighborhood." Alex arrived punctually at 1:00 p.m., just like Ruth Worth and Osaka affiliates stated he would. He was all energetic and bubbly compared to the dismal, methodical, and rigid reps Stephanie was used to dealing with prior. Subtle reminders of Eric Cravens caused Stephanie to think Alex was an abnormal, but functioning, societal dweeb who discovered he was a hunk ladies' man the minute he arrived in Asia or Japan.

He was nice enough, though, and he kept Stephanie company with incessant chatter and a seeming inexhaustible energy, as if his only job for the entire day was just to meet people at hotels and train stations. As they jumped on the Yamanote Loop Line, Alex breathed a sigh of relief. He had helped carry Stephanie's bulking heap of suitcases all the way to a convenience store from the lobby of her hotel, and the strain appeared as if it would have killed him were he to have attempted to lug the clam shells several yards any further. His face was red and sweaty, but his happy-go-lucky disposition remained constant.

He said, "Don't worry, the Black Cat courier service in Japan is most reliable. Your bags will be at your residence by the early evening, if not sooner. They will pick up your bags from this hotel."

For Stephanie, this was a definite succor. Having heaved her things from Osaka had her feeling like a beast of burden. They left the Ikebukuro proximity of Tokyo and transferred for trains bound for a bucolic area of Saitama. Stephanie couldn't believe it. There were so many trees around that she thought she was riding through a safari or a wildlife animal reserve.

When they finally arrived at the dormitory, it was a clean-looking, somewhat-modern building nestled in what appeared to be the more "citified" area of the town near a Lawson's convenience store, a coin-operated Laundromat, and what looked like a Post Office next to a Chinese restaurant of some sort. Her room here was more spacious than her place back in Osaka, and that it was already semi-furnished with a folding cot bed, TV, dining, and kitchen table with microwave made her adore the place immediately.

Stephanie met her landlord, building superintendent, and some of her neighbors on the second floor of four edifice. Everyone seemed so nice and welcoming, countering what she would have expected in the Tokyo area. Prior to coming she had heard Kanto, or Eastern Japan folks were colder and distant in comparison to Kansai in the West. So far, she had heard wrong.

The Bozack dude Alex showed Stephanie where all the bus stops were and provided her with schedules and timetables for buses and trains to and from the offices that she would be working. He even arranged for a taxicab to shuttle them around, and it was almost like a pastoral tour. At first, Stephanie thought she was going to die of boredom, but then decided wisely to count her blessings that she still had a job and freedom. Despite some bureaucratic bullshit, she thought, Bozack was still a good company to work for. Besides, she never wanted to return to Arizona. For she there was the female version of the same type of loser she claimed guys like Eric Cravens were. At least in Japan, she had a chance to pull the wool over the eyes of some unsuspecting guy and cause him to not see that she was a love-starved, somewhat-overweight, emotional, whiny train wreck and borderline alcoholic drug abuser.

Upon completion of the Saitama preparatory guide and tour, the animated Bozack rep bid Stephanie a fond farewell. Before he left, there were a slew of papers for Stephanie to fill out and sign. Forms for her room keys, forms for receipt of her room keys, forms for receipt of her spare keys, and numerous nugatory papers apparently necessary in fustian complex Japanese society. These were all tucked neatly away in the rep's briefcase; then he whipped out Stephanie's advance money of 500,000 yen, for which she had to sign for as well. She couldn't get over how such a shrimp of a man could carry around such a huge sum of cash all day long as if it were play money for a boardgame and not feel any type of angst or apprehension. Japan was a wonderful place, she thought, notwithstanding her recent woes, but at least she felt safe.

The rep informed Stephanie, "Usually, these matters are handled by the accounting staff, and your bank account would be provided for you, but yours is a special case. As you've been briefed, this area of Saitama chooses for its employees to use the Post Office postal accounts as it is more convenient for them for transactions with the local businesses and this includes this dormitory in which you will reside.

"You are to immediately start an account at the Post Office down the street—we passed it while coming here—first thing Monday morning. A Bozack representative—not I unfortunately—will assist you at that time. She or he shall be arriving around 9:00 a.m. when the Post Office opens.

"In the meantime, your advance is free to use at your disposal. You will find that your expenses have been reimbursed in the receipt portion of one of the documents you signed earlier. Your salary will from now on be transferred into your postal account from Monday, and if you choose, your rent can be deducted automatically from your salary. Are there any questions?"

There were none. Stephanie knew the drill. Finally, as the perky Aussie chap made his exit, she was happy to get him out of her face. It had been a long, exhausting day. Aside from the frugal, "pinch fist" late lunch she had with the rep earlier at a diet noodle shop he chose in the city, Stephanie's inflating gut felt empty. As the day suddenly transformed to night, from her third-floor window, Stephanie could see the remarkable city lights of Tokyo from a distance. It beckoned her to come out and play. She decided what the hell and opted to give it a go. Her bags had arrived from Tokyo like the rep had said they would. The Black Cat courier even brought the heavy suitcases the entire way to Stephanie's door.

With all that out of the way, she ripped into one of her clam shells and dug out something different to wear. She couldn't wait to hit the city and run wild in the night. Funny thing was, as soon as she stepped outside of her room and the elevator emptied her out into the areaway of the building, all the busses and cars seemed to disappear. Almost as if she was living in a ghost town. Occasionally, a local individual would ride by on a bicycle, eyes would open to massive width upon sight of a pale-faced *gaijin*, some kids would point and stare at her. She was used to it. What she wasn't used to was the need to use or catch a bus. Back in Osaka, her life was centered around the subway or the commuter trains. After looking at her bus schedule provided by the rep earlier, it appeared that the busses weren't going to be frequent on Saturdays and weekends, so she decided to walk to the train station.

In a taxi, the distance seemed close from Stephanie's place to the train station, thus she figured she could make the walk instead of catch a bus. She would quickly discover that the trek, coupled with the terrain of uphill inclines and "Don't walk" signs on some streets, took nearly a half hour. She looked at her watch, and it was already 8:30 p.m. Around the station, there was a McDonald's, and she elected to hit the Golden Arches instead of taking a discovery tour to the city at such a late time. Judging by the ride from town earlier when she left the hotel, she knew it would take an hour or more to reach Tokyo. She decided to wait. In the interim, it was time for her to allow her fatigue from walking and sorrows to disappear and be devoured like the large fries and teriyaki burgers she was about to consume.

An hour later, Stephanie tottered out of the fast-food spot with astounded faces in her wake. People behind the counter were amazed to see a female put away burgers and apple pies like a hippo and still order cheeseburgers for takeout. There was no way Stephanie was going to walk all the way back home, and she missed the bus. The next one wouldn't come for another hour. Since she was near the train station, she took a cab. Around train stations, there never seemed to be a shortage of taxicabs. Here was another reason Stephanie loved Japan.

About ten minutes later, she was back in the familiar area of her new residence. Her Japanese ability was minimal, but good enough to direct the driver who couldn't understand a word of English other than "Hello," "Good-bye," "Thank you," and "Pay money." She got out of the cab near the Lawson's Convenience

Store. Next to the Chinese restaurant nearby, there was a video store. She went inside before it closed and managed to create an account by showing her *gaijin* card, along with another card showing her recent change of address. Now, she didn't have to be totally bored. She rented some "Usual Suspects" type videos, afterwards hit the Lawson's for some beer. She wished Liz and/or Tim or her Osaka friends were around because they'd have more of the heavy stuff like coke or weed—especially Liz. How she missed her!

Stephanie returned to her apartment, unpacked her other suitcases, and found her banged-up miniature VCR. Luckily, she was able to still get it to work when she plugged it up to the furnished TV set. The place where she lived might have been an ass crack in the middle of nowhere, but at least it was better than Arizona, and the apartment was roomy, and she felt less compressed than her place back in Osaka. She sat down at her kitchen table, cracked a beer, and smoked a cigarette. Afterward, she decided to take a shower and wind down. It had been a long day. The walk to the station was the most exercise she had done in the recent times.

Thirty minutes later, the once-cello mass of Stephanie, which had bloated into an overweight "apple" figure hopped out of the shower and dabbed a towel to her ample nakedness. The doorbell chime to her apartment sounded like two keys of a child's toy xylophone. It was followed by a heavy knock on the metallic door. Somewhat irked by the timing, Stephanie scrambled for one of the elaborate, sumptuous and voluminous silk oriental robes Radley had scored for her in their better days, nestled in her suitcase. Haphazardly, she put it on and raced around the room looking for her towel. The persistent knocking continued.

"Just a moment!" she called out, somewhat frustrated, while patting the wet towel she found to her still wet hair, annoyed that anyone would be making house calls at such an hour. Having been in Japan for almost five years, she figured the would-be visitor to be one of her new neighbors, there to either introduce themselves while welcoming her to the building—offering some sort of gift like dishwashing liquid, garbage bag or symbolic beneficence—or worst-case scenario, to complain already about the noise from her TV.

Unfortunately, due to weight gain, Stephanie was unable to conceal herself completely with the robe without one hand holding the waistline fastened at her midsection. Her inflated cleavage threatened to expose her busty rack through the garment should any careless movement on her part cause her grip to release the fabric. Had she not been in a rush to open the door, she would have found one of her T-shirts; but thinking that the visitor was an elderly person and likely a female, she assumed they would excuse her deshabille state—perhaps they would opt to come again later at a more convenient time.

As the door swung violently open due to it being kicked once it was ajar, Stephanie had no time to react as a leather-gloved fist struck her dead in the face, jerking her head back and dropping her on her plump rump. Momentarily dazed, she was ushered back into reality by the sting of her hair being pulled upward by one of the two balaclava-masked and eye-goggled figures who had stormed into her room. The larger of the two had been the one who had punched her, now grabbing a fistful of her shoulder-length bob and leading her to her bedroom's unfolded cot. The smaller intruder had already shut the apartment's door, placed a towel under the door at the lintel crack and increased the volume of Stephanie's TV set, which was still switched on, effectively drowning out her screams for help.

Stephanie struggled hopelessly against the looming assailant, but it was no use, for this massive bugbear had already pounced upon her and thrown her on the quasi bed. Her legs were astride, and she was pinned beneath a heavy individual she knew for certain by then was a male due to the bulging erection attempting to force its way out of the black denim jeans he wore. She froze in mortification. Never would she have expected something like this to happen—not in Japan! Until that very moment, she thought Japan was the safest country in the world. Nothing like this was ever supposed to happen here! How could it be happening? Why her? Her thoughts rattled as she maundered, "Please don't hurt me!"

The smaller intruder did not appear to have rape on his mind. Instead, he was rummaging through Stephanie's drawers and desks adjoining the mini-kitchen dining area. He was looking or something, as if he knew what he was searching for and Stephanie was hiding it. She pretty much knew what it was as it dawned on her, she knew of no other place other than the kitchen drawers to store the bulk of money, in the interim, until she deposited it the following day. How was she to know or expect that she would be robbed in such a safe country. The intruder then eventually found her stash of currency along with the gamut of paperwork that accompanied it. She became terrifyingly aware of the possibility that the "friendly" and sprightly Alex from Bozack might have set her up! Who else would have known of her having all that cash?

The hulking beefcake who had Stephanie pressed down on the bed was now panting and wheezing, either due to the exhaustive measures it required to keep his victim pinned and motionless or unbridled arousal. His goggled specs kept trading stares at Stephanie's massive breasts and the wad of cash now in his partner's mitts a few feet away in the kitchen diner. They hadn't spoken to each other the entire time they had been there, having communicated only through a series of head movements and hand signals. The TV set's volume was still set at its highest, loudest setting.

The smaller invader sliced his index finger slowly across his neck and then pointed it at Stephanie. The hulk figure atop Stephanie grunted and nodded but held up his gloved hand as if to communicate *Wait!* as a command. He then unzipped his fly to free his agonized reproductive tool.

Stephanie saw what he was doing and screamed at the top of her lungs, as loud as her voice would allow. The hulk and his smaller accomplice wrestled as the former seemed to be trying to stop the rape about to take place, but the larger criminal shoved the smaller away, sending him stumbling several feet away back to the kitchen.

Stephanie squirmed beneath the heavy man, who, from what she could tell, was a black man due to the pigmentation of the penis as he slid it inside of her. They both exhaled deeply, as if crying in pain. To the length of her underbelly, she could feel his rod impale her; a second or two later, after two or three strokes he withdrew himself, with muffled whimpers underneath his mask, discharging heavily, forming gushy white "archipelago" islands all over the fleshy hillocks of her belly and torso.

The unwelcome sight of the violator's seminal release infuriated Stephanie to enable her one last attempt to fight back against her intruders. She managed to kick off the temporarily distracted oaf who had just mounted her, knocking him away while he was recovering from his quickie rapine. But as she tried to escape, the sting of her hair fibers violently yanked would jerk her head back and cause her to collapse back on the bed. A thick feather-filled pillow covered her face. The last thing she would hear before her eternal blackout was the smaller individual's reprimand to his huge partner: "You can't do that, you fucking idiot! They'll find your DNA . . . Now you'd better clean all this up on her!" It was a familiar-sounding voice, but it wouldn't matter much at that point . . .

60

TAFFIE'S OSAKA EXODUS was already set in motion. She had just returned from Tokyo and had before then decided that Osaka was no longer the place for her to be. She was moving to the capital city, and from there, who knew? Maybe she would one day have enough courage to visit the United States. Though she had been disappointed by the only Americans she had met—Liz and then Deon—it still didn't kill her curiosity about the place. For Deon, she was nothing more than a jump-off equivalent, she thought; guys like him, she imagined, were playboys, and there was no way around it. But Liz—she was the real disappointment.

For a fleeting moment, Taffie thought she had found a genuine friend in Liz. Japanese people, like Takuto—probably the only "friend" she had left in Osaka—were OK, but sometimes she wanted to have friends who weren't from Japan. She desired the company of another foreigner who understood what it was like to be a *gaijin* and/or a female in the country.

However, Liz betrayed her. Not once but, Taffie felt, twice. First, it was the incident with Serge that she willingly forgave her for. But then next, she came for Deon. She slept with him, and at a time in their relationship when Taffie had grown fondest of him. In essence, ruining her Christmas and New Year's as well, because her discovery of the wrongdoing she perceived had destroyed her merry mood and served as the final straw to her already broken spirit.

Taffie wasn't the violent type. She avoided confrontational situations for the most part and had a tendency to retreat from circumstances that could possibly lead to such. Still, there was a vengeful side to her character that had an eagerness for getting even or settling the score in a way that gave her closure. The aspect of her character, for which she was most ashamed, was being attracted to people who despised her or looked down on her. Throughout most of her late teen and young adult life, Taffie knew she was white just as much as she was of Caribbean descent, but people in society always judged her on how she appeared to look. In Japan, it wasn't as bad as France. In Japan, her faults, as so decreed by a race-obsessed society, became charm points. There was no struggle between being "more French" or "more Caribbean" there—she was simply Taffie from Paris, and that was it. She had found her peace. But people like Liz and Serge would come along and disrupt the joy in her placid oasis world, and it was only fair, in her resolve, that she take a swipe back at them in her own subtle way.

***

Umeda school manager Hitomi Hasegawa was taken highly aback and disheartened to hear about Taffie's sudden resignation. Taffie was one of the few *gaijin* that she would sincerely miss having, much like Elizabeth "Liz" Amberbush. The difference was that Liz was still around and made an appearance from time to time, whereas Taffie indicated that she was leaving the city altogether and had no intentions of returning. Also, she knew of Taffie's night occupation. She knew what that life entailed, and as such, she sympathized with Taffie as well as Serge and plenty of other "freejack" foreigners throughout her lengthy time with the company. All she could do was wish Taffie the best. Taffie had only one more day to work coming back from using her remaining vacation days. The French department had pretty much been taken care of at that point, as Serge had been successfully broken in; but since it was Taffie's final day, she received an abbreviated schedule. This was one reason she elected to get a jump on the early, chilly Sunday and beat the crowd headed to Osaka's Umeda District—that and the fact she had to awaken the likely-to-be-snoring Serge, whom she had venturesomely entrusted with the school key. So far, he had been responsible and that was a good thing.

In the earlier hours of that morning, within a remote isolated chamber of the Umeda Bozack School, the exhausted French teacher snoozed comfortably on one of the several colorful, gossamer love seats intended for awaiting student customers. Hitomi was an absolute sweetheart for allowing him to rest there for a spell, he mused, especially during the predawn hours, like tonight, after his shift at the Candy Box club. He was so lucky to have landed that job teaching French. No one had discovered him yet, and in a few months, he would have saved up enough money to pay for the operation he needed to alter his appearance and subsequent counterfeit paperwork.

Problem was, there were times when sleep did not come easily for him. For there wasn't a day that went by he didn't think of his friend, and how he ended up in the country of Japan. He and Serge were the best of friends. Back in the Quebec days, they chased and pillaged Asian chicks from sunup to sundown, and it was such an easy and joyous time. In those days, the girls were mostly Chinese, Vietnamese, or from other countries in the Pacific Rim. Why did it all have to end? His deep thoughts would plunge him into a slumber only to wake up again in a cold sweat. His heart raced as if something had caused him to be deathly afraid. He stretched his long arms to lift his jacket from his chest, which he had been using as a makeshift blanket.

From his jacket pocket, he retrieved a tiny vial containing powerful drug tablets used to treat psychopaths, and *haloperidol* used to treat paranoia. Obtained illegally, of course, from friends whom he dealt with secretly, but on a frequent basis, at the Candy Box. These associates had ties with Luzio Silver, but in the recent week or so, no one had been able to reach Silver. He had no idea why, but as a result, some of the illegal pharmaceuticals had become difficult to score. Approaching panic mode, he washed the tablet down with a swig of dangerous Scotch from his flask and dozed back into a more serene slumber. Not to worry, for human alarm clock, Hitomi, would assuredly wake him up when she came along later to officially open the school.

The sheer darkness invaded his groggy mind as it did the room. Twilight shadows gave birth to a distinct silhouette, in the form of vague outlines, for a master seductress. Dreamily, he saw as she slid her nakedness across him. He grinned. The Asian women he had encountered, here or abroad, had absolutely nothing on her, body-wise. Her breasts were an elliptic round pair, like a sightly inflated softball set, yet wobbly, and her chocolate nipples his mind made appear as goofy eyes staring as she peeled his pants down his legs. His trousers then formed manacles at his ankles as she crawled over them to a straddling seat upon his aroused and upright flesh.

She kissed his face; the smell of her sweet, ambrosial *odeur mysterieuse* alone made the boiling pressure of his meat escape the slot in his boxers. Her goddess locks dangled from her like curly mythological serpents, turned him to stone in a way that hadn't occurred the time in the shower with Liz. Thick-set lips were soft as marshmallows that smashed into his. He opened his mouth to welcome the intrusion and the stale taste of gin, lime, and lust lapped his tongue like a lizard. Her soft hands caressed his careless-whiskered chin at the same time her coarse, woolly pubic mound rubbed against the tip of his organ. Her eyes widened suddenly in a flash of titillation as his pink mushroom sloshed against her sodden vulva, and her abrupt gasp could be heard fracturing the erotic silence. He too shrieked, feeling the succinct sensation of warm ecstasy briefly inside of her.

Medium-length-manicured glittery-nailed fingers gripped his cheeks tightly. The sharp edges of her pinky broke his skin on the right cheek, but he didn't care.

They were lost in the moment as they glared into the eyes of one another, as if they could see clearly in the opaque of the room. Her eyes seemed to have formed tears, pleading in expression.

"Serge!" she cried out as if she had just then climaxed. He felt the proof as her essence trickled down his shaft in an ooze, moistening his boiling sack.

He arched up into a reclining position with his head to rest upon the arm chaise of the love seat while his visitor inched her way to his personal "Eiffel Tower" that had arisen. Her copious maw descended upon it and electrified every nerve from his loins to his belly button like direct currents. Asian women had never been able to make him feel like this. They hadn't the slightest clue about what to do, yet she did it so well, and so naturally, to dispatch him to a comfort zone in bawdy heaven.

Within seconds short of a minute, his testicles pleaded for mercy, and he surrendered his troops. Fluffy white gushed furiously from him into Taffie's mouth. She continued to stroke him leaking, even as froth leaped from her top lip, splashing his boxers, sternum, and even sprinkled as far as his face until he had released all drops in finality. She giggled an amused little chortle, wiped her lips and hands on his boxers, then rose from the love seat.

Dazed, but in a state of euphoria and rhapsody, he sat up, still erect and showing no signs of deflation. His next thought was to take advantage of the moment and express his desire to return feelings of passion with a quick probe of her *Africain* womb. It wasn't about to happen. Taffie gripped the bundle of her clothes and left the room. He stood up and attempted to give chase, but he tripped over his pants, tangled at his ankles because of how Taffie had left them when she undressed him earlier. She laughed, hearing him smack the floor in the dim light, giving her time she needed to make her way up the long corridor of the school leading to the lobby. She made her way to the staff's ladies' room and water closet, dipped inside, and locked the door behind her. Of course, he had followed her, then approached the door. In a cold sweat, he turned the knob, pleading for her to open it.

In French, their exchange went as follows: "Taffie! Wait, darling . . . Please open up! Mustn't we finish this affair?"

Inside the ladies' room, Taffie's voice uttered, "For what, Serge? I'm just a monkey race to people like you, remember?"

He was at a loss for words or reaction. Dumbstruck for the fact that he had no ready recollection of referring to her as such, although he couldn't completely deny it. When Taffie reminded him of said incident, he could only but barely recall it, but he most certainly regretted it at that moment. He commenced to beg for forgiveness via animated cackles, explaining away what happened as a "misunderstanding."

"No, Serge," Taffie said viciously. "I don't think so."

As his banging on the door intensified, inside the closet, Taffie got dressed and found it satisfyingly entertaining to hear his voice crack in frantic trepidation. For this instance, she would have Liz to thank for sharing information about how tender Serge's pride was, at how he "hated to be humiliated," and his outrageous short temper tantrum outbursts if he couldn't have his way. She knew that to tease him and lead him along, in the way she had, would work in her favor to produce the desired effects. She had timed it perfectly too.

For no sooner had he raised his voice in a crazed, passionate plea to get Taffie to come out or open the closet's door, he turned awkwardly to face a horror-struck Hitomi, who had just walked into the school. Her already-stunned face upon entering the school to see the front entrance wide open and unattended was accelerated into utter aghast. She saw the new French teacher banging on the women's staff ladies' room door with his torso revealed through unbuttoned shirt and wearing only boxers that appeared to be stained in the front.

Hitomi flushed pinkish red in the face, literally resembling a peach in a wig as she gasped and quickly turned her head away before something emerged from the slit in his boxers. Up until then, she had thought of him to be a well-mannered, astute European gentleman. All of a sudden, her mind wouldn't allow her brain to supply her with words that could adequately describe how she felt in that moment. All she could do was shout at him in her native Japanese language.

"Serge!" she cried. "What on earth has gotten into you? What's going on here!?"

His first impulse was to grab her by her old throat, strangle her, and tear the door down to the ladies' room. Then he would run Taffie through with his inflamed lust sword, impaling her womb while his hands choked out her last breath. But by now his raging bulge had died down once again, and instead he apologized profusely to his manager and rushed quickly to the back room where he had been lounging prior to Taffie's interruption. In the meantime, he had tried to explain his case, but it was benign babble as far as the heated Hitomi was concerned.

The rarely flustered Hitomi was then stuck between a rock and a hard place. She knew that Taffie was leaving the company. Reporting the new French teacher to the Head Office for inappropriate behavior, especially an infraction of that magnitude, could possibly lead to his dismissal, even though he was fresh off probation as new employee. Not only that, but she had also stuck her neck out for him and broken the rules for even allowing him—as well as other teachers—to squat and bunk on the school floor. If written up, he could conceivably rat her out in the process.

Frustrated, Hitomi gritted her teeth nervously as she thought of how foreigners in Japan seemed to display very little knowledge about duty, honor, or obligation. If they did, they didn't hold these in high regard. She saw herself as helping them all out and at the same time helping herself, one hand washing the other; but constantly, she was repaid in outlandish ways, such as this, by them.

Why couldn't they understand? Hitomi wondered. Just because she had a streak of kindness, it didn't mean she intended for people to trample over her. Allowing them to squat at the school was so that they could be at work and be on time, after they recklessly roundabout the nights in exuberance; a privilege, not a consent for them throwing private, wild parties there!

Wisely she decided—however difficult it may have been—to turn a blind eye to the fiasco she walked in on. But not without consequences.

Hitomi said to the French teacher when he had made himself presentable. "Serge, please do not let me discover you in this way again. Lucky we are that there were no students here! If so, I would have had no other choice but to write you up."

He understood Japanese very well at this point and diligently affirmed his intention to obey. Hitomi continued, "And I'm afraid that I must now ask that you return the school's key, Serge. I can no longer allow you to arrive early here. I'm not going to write you up for disciplinary action, but I cannot take a chance after what I saw this morning."

He heard and was disappointed. He knew that he had made a serious blunder. Inside, he was boiling and almost surrendered to an emotional breakdown. Instead, he mustered enough strength to hold himself together as he obliged Hitomi's request. He unfastened the school's key from his pocketed others and reluctantly gave it to Hitomi. He had no choice; he wanted desperately to keep his job first and foremost. After all, he was so close to getting the money he needed to set himself free. The combined take from the French lessons at Bozack and the Candy Box Club gig would catapult him into within range of the financial requirement needed to get his operation under way. As such, his fight to maintain his composure would eat at him like acidic corrosion throughout the day, because he had to keep his cool and forget about continuing his unfinished business with Taffie.

Ten minutes later, Taffie had emerged from the water closet. Though she was generally perky and vibrant, she chose to overplay her innocence in that morning's shenanigans. Otherwise tidy, made up, and immaculately attired as always for work—even if for her final day—sharply contrasting her replacement French teacher, who was mussed up, poorly shaven, disheveled, and visibly wired. She made brief eye contact with the raging French teacher, as if nothing had happened, when she greeted everyone "Good morning" both in French and Japanese.

Hitomi poured on the elaborate good-byes appropriate for a resigning teacher. She even went so far as to present Taffie with a small bouquet of flowers. She really poured on the affection, embraced Taffie, and carried on with her as if she could never have fathomed in the least what she had just done inside the school that morning with the other teacher.

The morning would sludge along, and soon the first students of the day would enter. Then the English teacher, Rusty, showed up chipper and authoritative but unimpressive. More students came in the form of kids, and the school day was busily under way, and in full throttle. The French class schedule wasn't overwhelming, but it was steady; very little time for breaks in between the classes, which was usually about five minutes. Taffie and her ex-facto paramour would bump into one another, or pass each other in the school hall, where she would shoot him a seductive glance for a second, then look away while he stage-whispered to her in French, urging and pleading for him to meet him after work.

Taffie, who had an abbreviated schedule because it was her last day, said, "I'm sorry, Serge but I finish work early today."

"What time is this!?" Frantically, he almost shouted and broke his composed demeanor. Hitomi eyed him suspiciously from her desk across the room. He was still in hot water with her, and she was slightly on edge because she had never witnessed such erratic behavior from him.

Back to work they all went. The male French teacher's student showed up at 11:30am on schedule, no cancellation. Taffie paused and looked innocently at the time on her Cartier Tank Francaise.

"I will finish today *une heure*. I am sorry." She made sure to speak so that Rusty could hear it in English as best she could before she laughed and vanished inside of her cubicle.

The heated voice of Hitomi stabbed at him. "Serge, your student is waiting." Gritting his teeth in frustration, he plastered a smile on his haggard face and greeted his elderly student.

Two hours later, he raced from his cubicle and barely bade farewell to the old woman as he dashed into the lobby of the school in search of Taffie. True to her word, she had vacated the premises according to the schedule she had given him, and the faint smell of her essence was the only trace left. He could still feel her sticky saliva pasting his thighs. His lusty anxiety was at a peak level. He urgently sought from Hitomi Taffie's whereabouts; he even asked for her address as if he were searching for a fugitive convict and he a desperate sheriff.

Hitomi shrugged sadly, but then with a spurning tilt of her semicolon eyes said, "Even if I *was* authorized to provide you such information, it doesn't matter. Didn't you know? She will not be back. She will leave and take up residence in—Tokyo, I believe. That's why you are the new teacher of French here, and you take over her shift from tomorrow. Surely, you received the memo have you not?"

He had no idea what she was talking about.

That instant, a half city distance away from that location, Taffie was packing the rest of her things, which wasn't going to be much. The stuff that remained in the squalid room that Saiko set aside for her she didn't need, and the apartment that belonged to Doc Sarugi, *still* belonged to him, so there was no need to remove much from there. Saiko wasn't happy with her decision to leave, but there was nothing she could do to keep Taffie around. She had repaid her debt with interest, but for selfish reasons, Saiko was drumming up some kind of hidden fees and/or questionable surcharges to apply to her moving out of the apartment. Taffie had no intention of waiting around for all of that.

With the help of her only friend left in Osaka, Takuto, who drove her around in his Mitsubishi Diamante during the day or in the early morning hours after working at his kitchen bar joint, she packed what she needed and split. Taffie's other unwanted items were claimed by Takuto's friends and workers. Finally, she unzipped her schoolbag that she used for when she worked at Bozack. From it, she pulled out memorandum papers and documents giving notice to all other teachers at the Umeda School, about shift changes. She had lifted them from the mail slots earlier before the action on the love seat that morning. She ripped up the papers and tossed the shreds to be thrown away.

61

LIZ WAS STILL reeling from the shocking ordeal she encountered at the Sakamakis when she received a call from Jeremy Ng, who had returned to Japan from his long vacation abroad.

"Hello, Liz, this is Jeremy, did I catch you at a good time?"

"Not really," she said. "I'm on my way home from the gym. I'm on my bike, and I'm freezing. You mind calling me back later?"

"I've got an envelope with your money," Jeremy said, as if he hadn't heard what Liz told him.

Liz pumped her brake then said, "Hey, those creepy people! I swear to gawd, Jeremy, I oughta kick your ass for introducing me to them!"

Jeremy sounded as if he was laughing; he seemed so calm. He said, "What happened over there while I was gone? Did you like . . . get high? Please don't tell me you did!"

Liz said, "Ah, fuck no. But even if I did, I wouldn't have been so messed up that I could've mistaken what happened. That fucking creep, Mr. Sakamaki, he tried to . . . get . . . freaky while I was sleeping! I woke up, and there he was, like . . . licking all over my foot and . . . ugh! It was so gross! I swear, I'm never going back there!"

Jeremy said, "Oh, I . . . um . . . are you sure?"

"What do you mean, am I sure?! Look, I don't care if you don't believe me. I'm never going back there. So I'm sorry if that ruins your reputation or your good standing with those folks, but I'm not gonna subject myself to some weird asshole perverts. I'm not one of these Japanese sluts!"

"Just take it easy, Liz. I'm just trying to understand what went awry. I mean, I get back to Japan, I've got this shitload of voice messages from Mr. Sakamaki. I go there, then he gives me this story about how he was drunk, thought he entered your guestroom by accident, and then you became suddenly violent, like you were having a bad dream. He tried to calm you down, but then you became uncontrollably erratic, and then you ran out screaming. You even left your shoes."

Liz was growing impatient. She said, "That's the short, edited version. I ran out of there when I found him being obscene while he was feasting on my cruddy feet—that's why I was acting 'erratic,' as you put it."

Jeremy said, "Well, you do know that if you sever ties now, you'll completely ruin your chances of getting Mr. Sakamaki to be your guarantor, right?"

"Big fucking deal," Liz said, resuming her biking trek home after the long-pause break to rant her side of the story. She then said, "I don't ever want to see him again, let alone have some predator like him be my 'guarantor' or whatever. For Chrissake, he might feel he has the authority to come inside my apartment, because he helped me get it, while I'm sleeping and try to rape me or something. Anyway, you have my pay?"

"Um, yeah," Jeremy said deflated. "Your shoes too. You want to stop by my place and pick it up?"

It was a nice try, Jeremy's ploy to get Liz to come over to his house, so he could pour on his charms and hope to whisper sweet nothings in her ear. He even added, "Oh, and I've got a souvenir for you too, from Thailand."

Liz, however, wasn't taking the bait at all. She said, "Nah, no big rush. Just put my shoes in a plastic bag or something. I'll pick it up when we see each other next at the Namba School. Look, I gotta go."

She hung up amid Jeremy's desperate voice calling out for her to "hold up, wait!" About twenty minutes later, she arrived back at her dormitory. Ingrid wasn't at home, but the place smelled strongly of garlic, soy sauce, and yeast. The conversation with Jeremy had irritated her because she was trying to get the lewd encounter with Mr. Sakamaki out of her mind. She wanted to get a little stoned. She grabbed her phone and tried to call Deon. She had tried to call him ever since the guy Yoh had provided her his number, but he had yet to call her back. But this time he finally answered.

"Dee!" Liz almost screamed. "Where the hell have you been? I've been trying to reach you!"

There was a long pause. On the other end of the line, Deon was trying to place the voice before finally rendering, "Oh, this is Elizabeth? The blonde girl? Oh . . ."

"Yeah, it's me, dude, don't pretend you don't know who I am, you dick!" She was subtly appalled, but since she suddenly depended on him for the favor she was about to ask, she decided to play nice. "Yeah, it's me, the blonde, white girl, the one who set you up with Taffie, the love of your life . . ."

"Whatever," he said, exuding a long sigh like he was annoyed or bored. Then he said, "What do you want anyway?"

Liz didn't like how gruff he always was with her, especially since Taffie was no longer around. Word around the office had it that he didn't like white people very much, but Liz could pretty much vouch that there were some white people in the company that didn't like him either. Still, Liz was indifferent. After hearing Taffie speak about how much of a sweetheart he really was, her mind changed a little bit about him. Now she had to struggle to keep from losing her temper, because he was giving her attitude when he should have been grateful to her, as far as she was concerned. She didn't share for him the same contempt as those like Stephanie or some others, but now he was starting to test her patience.

She said, "Hey, I thought we were cool, but if every time I reach out to you, and you always have to act like I'm getting on your goddam nerves, then just forget it!"

Deon said, "Yo! Chill. OK, my bad. It's not like that, though."

"What!?" she almost yelled.

"Nothing. You cool. We cool. No problem. My bad." His voice sounded resolute, not shaky. Liz didn't know if he was being serious or sarcastic.

She said, "I'm sorry too, I guess. I shouldn't have brought up Taffie. I mean . . . maybe you're still thinking about her, huh?"

Deon said, "Yeah, a little bit. But nah, I don't care that you brought her up. Just, with *you people*, I don't understand when you're jokin' or when you're serious. Especially seein' how crazy and goofy y'all be actin' around the office."

Liz laughed and said, "That's those other assholes, not me!"

They had a meaningful conversation for the first time in a while, if ever they had one in the first place. It lasted short of three minutes before Liz got to the point of why she rang him up. She wanted to score some weed or speed or anything that did the deed to fulfill her needs.

"Hey, Dee," Liz said, "I'm looking to try to get something . . . a little high grade, if you know what I mean?"

***

The chat with Deon hadn't been too long. Liz had absorbed a lot of colloquialisms and code speak banter from her dealings by now that she could communicate her request without stating it blatantly. Deon was a little more than hesitant, especially in lieu of the recent events stemming from that bust. By now everyone had heard of it. However, sensing a bit of desperation in her voice, he took pity on her and used his influence, or street cred, to grab hold of Luzio Silver affiliates on her behalf. Ever since Tim the Duke name-dropped Silver in hopes of being granted leniency, the Brazilian drug lord was the target of an investigation, so he was laying extra low. Only those who had specific credentials could get in contact with him. Deon happened to be connected within that network, albeit unintentionally.

An overjoyed Liz met Deon in Umeda, as instructed by him, at the same saloon bar she introduced Taffie to him, Tocca-Tte on Shin Midosuji Boulevard. Liz showed up around 10:00 p.m. The spot was moderately crowded and picking up. In a black Ann Taylor wrap coat, camel scarf, tapered denim jeans, and matching pumps, Liz looked like a Hollywood damsel as she turned heads strolling through the smoke-filled dive. Deon showed up exactly ten minutes later. She almost didn't recognize him as this night, he wasn't suited and booted as usual. He was casual with loose fitting jeans, gray hoodie, black leather jacket, and some Jordans. He told her they were going to another place, so they split.

They crossed the street at the Picadilly Theater and hit Doyama, a village on the outskirts of the Umeda District abound with labyrinths of bars, lounges, eateries, queer and lesbian clubs, and vice dens. Liz had vaguely remembered traipsing through this dense area of town before with Taffie but would never have known how to discover it on her own. Deon mentioned during the small talk along the way that he told her to meet him at the place they both knew instead of trying to explain to her how to get to the place that they were headed to. Liz was grateful for that decision he made; otherwise, she would have been helplessly lost.

Walking inside the indoor arcade known as Higashi Dori, they came upon the Park Avenue by-street. Arriving finally at an alley, they halted at a strip with three small buildings—the Tatsumi, the Marugame, and the Takeda. Deon led her inside of the dark, quieter of the three, the Takeda, and went to the fourth floor by a tight compartment elevator.

They approached an atypical black-painted, arch-shaped door immediately to the left of the opening elevator; a seasick aqua-green-colored sign read "FELL LOW Kitchen Bar." Music coming from inside was muffled, but when Deon pulled the handle on the door, the sound thrashed their eardrums like a minor explosion. They walked through a narrow thoroughfare, like a small tunnel, and there was a counter with a thick-lipped Japanese girl, wearing a rosy-red dress with bateau neckline. She was wearing some long-fitted silky red gloves, as her hand formed two fingers representing the number of people for which she would apply to seating in the dusty place. Liz was amazed at how cavernous this spot was; from the outside of the building looking in, she would never have guessed it.

In actuality, the place was made to seem bigger as its design was like a cave with holes in its plastered "walls" that formed makeshift windows. The patrons were mostly Japanese, but there were sprinkles of foreign faces here and there, the types that did not look like the typical clean-cut English teachers. They looked more like pirates or sailors with bandanna-tied heads, patches over eyes, and ring-studded fingers. Although the smell permeating the air had the pleasant aroma of something good cooking from the kitchen, Liz didn't think she would feel very comfortable in this spot were she alone.

Deon was having what appeared to be an exchange quickening toward a heated one with the rosy-red-dressed hostess, in Japanese. With a tired look on his face, Deon shot Liz a quick glance and said, "Yo, give this chick five hundred yen."

Liz made a funny face at first, but she didn't argue. She just took out her expensive purse and happened to have the exact amount of coin. She gave it to the hostess; then her entire demeanor changed. She almost blushed red as if she was embarrassed. She apologized in Japanese and showed Deon and Liz to a table in the back, a quieter spot tucked away in a corner. Before leaving, the woman sucked in her lips and stared at Deon amorously, as if she had a craving for caramel-coated flesh. Liz watched as she recognized that look. It was the same way Taffie looked at Deon too.

"What was that all about?" Liz asked as she sat down at the rounded-edged square table.

Deon said, "She was givin' me a hard time because I asked her for one of these tables in the back. So I told you to give her a tip. I guess because you're white, she made it her business to accommodate you, more so than me."

Liz responded sharply "Aw, bullshit! It wasn't because I'm white—it's because I gave her a tip, dude. I don't get treated any better than you do here. Are you kidding me?"

Deon sneered lightly. He said, "Whatever, if you say so."

"I thought Japanese people didn't take tips," Liz said, but the two-bit DJ selections drowned out her voice at that moment. Besides, Deon's wicked frown was scanning the misty cave interior, as if he was looking for someone. When he squinted, then leaned his colorful beaded neck out in the direction of visual target, it was clear he had spotted the intended party sought.

He said to Liz, "Order us some drinks. I'll be back." Then he got up and walked away, leaving Liz alone at the table. She caught the attention of another female staff server dressed less extravagantly than the hostess who had showed her and Deon to their table. From her she ordered a gin tonic for herself and a beer for Deon. Shortly thereafter, when the drinks arrived, so had Deon returned to the table.

Deon took a sip of the beer, then said to Liz, "Yo, you got that loot?"

Liz said nothing; she just fumbled through her purse for her wallet. She fished out a series of bills, counted out about thirty-five thousand yen and handed it to him. Deon glanced at the scratch, did a quick count, and folded the bills into one of his jacket pockets. Under the table, Liz felt a tap on her right knee. Her hands sank beneath the tabletop and contacted a small, lime-sized bundle wrapped in plastic Deon was trying to pass her. She took it and clumsily managed to stuff it inside the pocket of her Fashion Avenue wrap coat. No eyes seemed to be on her, but the place was relatively dimly lit.

Deon said, "That's two dimes of the 'dro and two grams of the yeyo. My advice is you get the hell up outta here before that shit starts to stink. A lotta Japanese people might not know what that shit smells like, but around here, don't get too comfortable thinkin' so."

Liz was so happy she threw her arms around his neck as she stood up to leave. She said, "How do I get out of here? This area makes me feel a little creeped out."

Deon said, "When you leave out this building, turn right, keep walkin' till you reach the avenue. You can catch a cab from there, in front of the smoke shop on the corner."

Profusely, Liz thanked him again. Deon gave her the similar spiel Liz gave people like Serge and Ingrid, that he would only do that favor for her once. He claimed to not be a drug user, and not a dealer. Liz didn't take it too seriously as she planned the same sweet-talking tactics of diplomacy, she used this time to coerce him again should the need arise. She was sure it would, but that was a thought reserved for another time. She split the grimy spot.

***

Moments earlier, Deon had received the bundle of sizzle he would later pass off to Liz from Moose, accompanied by Brad Cooper. Deon and Luzio Silver were neither friends nor associates, but they had mutual friends who vouched for the former. Such was the reason Deon was able to contact Silver, who while still in hiding, dispatched his white boys, less likely than he to be randomly stopped by creeping cops.

Brad watched Deon from a distance and spied him getting hugged by Liz. He got a double dose of incensed reactions. First, he was surprised to see Liz, one of the chicks who reportedly had dropped dime on Silver. Next, he was heated, for even back in the United States, he had a deep-seated hatred in seeing white women interacting with blacks; Deon, being what he deemed a "fancy-shmancy slick-talkin' greaseball spic nigger from New York," made it all the worse. At once, all desire he might have had for her was abruptly dissolved and erased, replaced with contempt.

Excitedly, he said to the grim-faced Moose, "Hey, man, that bitch his here! She's here!"

Moose tucked the money he got from Deon away in his fanny pack, looked at Brad like he was an annoying pup, then upturned a beer mug to his bearded lips. Finishing with a loud burp that sliced into the ear-torturing drum'n'bass tune on deck, Moose said, "What bitch?"

Brad practically screamed, "The blonde bitch, the Liz chick. The boss wants to have that bitch cut up for singing his name to the pigs!"

Moose frowned. He stared in the direction Brad pointed, focused his ferocious bulldog eyes in Liz's direction, and ascertained that it was indeed her.

Brad slapped Moose's beefy muscled arm. "Hurry up, let's go. She's getting' away! We can take her in the back of one of these alleys and slice her! This place is perfect—what're we waitin' for!?"

Moose shook his head. "Naw," he said. "B'fore we do all thet, we gotta make shure she's the one. B'cuz the broad the cops pick'dup wuz a fat gurl named Stephanie or sumthin."

Brad said "Maybe not now, man, but eventually she'll talk, man, they all do. We'd better take advantage of where we are, man, and get her. C'mon, man, she's leavin'!"

Moose dismissed Brad with a wave of his hand, shook his head again. "Lissen, ya turd, we ain't got no specific orders t'ice that chick. Yew kin dew what you wanna, I'm gonna get this score loot back t'th'boss. If we need t' get her, Luzio's gonna say."

Brad knew Moose was right. Luzio was aware that Liz was close with the girl Stephanie. It made logical sense because they all worked at the same company as Tim. But when Tim snitched on Luzio, Stephanie was also present at the station for interrogation. Luzio received word through the infinite grasp of the street vine that Liz's name had also emerged, connecting him through Stephanie as well, inducing him to cease contact with her, disposing of the telephone number supplied on her biz card. His business suffered tremendously as a result, as many valued customers were unable to reach him because he had to "dead" that number. Liz was a person of interest to him, but he didn't want her wiped out just yet.

Brad, however, was acting off of emotions. He was pissed off seeing the gorgeous blonde hugging up on "niggers," even though technically, he worked for one as his main side hustle. In his twisted mind, he was thinking that Luzio had ceased dealing with Liz for a reason. Only certified people were able to contact Luzio nowadays, she wasn't one of them—Deon was. But him dealing with her on the side couldn't be a good thing as this scenario played out in Brad's dome.

Outside, Liz remembered Deon telling her to turn right upon leaving the building. Unfortunately, the building was situated on a corner side of the Park Avenue Doyama and the arcade street. As such, the edifice had two entrances and exits. Liz couldn't recall from which one she and Deon had entered from. Her sense of direction was thrust into a state of confusion.

Of course, she exited from the wrong door from which Deon would have accurately guided her to Shin Midosuji Boulevard. Instead, she walked the length of the arcade before she retraced her steps, frustrated. At the far end of the indoor tunnel, she could vaguely make out a street where cars and trucks passed. She headed in that direction. As she closed in on what she assumed was to be her destination, she felt a violent tug on her left elbow, causing her to lose balance and stumble in her pumps.

Behind her, Brad's right arm closed around her waist and with his left hand still controlling Liz by her elbow, pushed her roughly into an alleyway behind the Kinki Hotel. Liz screamed and yelled at the top of her lungs, but her cries were drowned out by the loud sounds of activity in the urban setting; car and truck horns blowing, loud storefront jingles of music, pitter patter of pedestrian traffic dominated the air. For those who did pay any attention to Brad and Liz, wrapped up like wrestling ballroom dancers, Japanese people thought them to be drunken foreigners having a love quarrel outside of a fleabag hotel. Nobody seemed to care, as if this was the section of town where such a sight was not uncommon.

In a secluded cul-de-sac of the alley, Brad threw Liz up against a wall; then he pulled out a butterfly knife. Liz recognized Brad's face immediately: she was about to put up the best fight she could give and make a run for it, until she saw the gleaming blade in his fist.

Trembling with both fear and outrage, Liz shouted, "WHAT THE FUCK ARE YOU DOING!? YOU FUCKING ASSHOLE!!"

Brad matched her rage. Gritting his yellowish teeth, he said, "Fucking cunt. On top of bein' a rat, yo're also a nigger lover too, huh? Bitch." He unzipped his fly and looked around. "Yo're gonna give me something for my trouble.."

Liz felt like she was going to puke. She was terrified now; she had never been in such a potentially dangerous situation as this in her entire life. She usually had someone else, like an older brother, other friends, or an Eddie to hide behind. Now she was alone. If matters couldn't have been worse, she now seemed to understand why it was she hadn't been able to reach Luzio Silver herself. Apparently, he and his faction must have thought that Liz had snitched on them to the police. She knew she hadn't done that, but Brad was now blind with his contempt and a jealous anger. She didn't want to suck him off there in that pissy alley, but her composure was breaking as she thought of doing whatever she had to do, to not get cut. She clenched her fists to her chin and stared fearfully at the asphalt.

The next instant, she would hear a harsh *thud*, a heaving gasp, and a sound reminiscent of one losing breath in a tackle on a football or rugby field. Liz looked up to see the knife several feet away from Brad's rolling body on the concrete. He stumbled to his feet, but Liz saw the familiar Air Jordan sneakers step between him and his blade.

Deon's head jerked toward Liz briefly and said, "You better get the hell outta here, now!" Then he trained his fierce eyes back on Brad.

Obeying her implausible instant hero, Liz jumped out of her pumps and beat it back down the alley. She wanted to wait around and make sure that Deon was

OK, and to thank him for helping her, but she remembered that she was loaded. The last thing she needed was to bring the heat down on herself and Deon, however cruel it may have seemed. Self-preservation had to kick in unfortunately.

Back in the alley, Brad was pissed that Deon had dared to blind side him with what he would have considered a sucker punch. The side of his temple was still tingling from the broad strike he had absorbed, which had caused him to lose his equalizing butterfly blade. As he squared up with Deon, as if he was prepared to fight him, subtle apprehension gripped him as he wished Moose was around. Compared to Deon, Brad looked like a bantam trying to box with a light heavyweight. His mind was raking over combat techniques he picked up while serving in the navy, trying to put his mind to the task of beating Deon up.

He tried to inject fear into a conversation in some absurd thought that it would cause his would-be opponent to stand down. "You done fucked up now, Deon. You hangin' 'round with that rattin' blonde bitch. And now, yo're interfeerin' in Luzio Silver's business. He don't play that shit, nigga!"

In the next second or two, after a blackout that reeked in his mind of an indeterminable span of time, Brad regained his faculties with his nose touching the crotch of Deon's jeans. Having dropped to his knees, his recollection of losing his legs suddenly returned. For with his final utterance, Deon had no sooner plugged the index of his knuckles straight and hard into Brad's solar plexus, directly beneath the sternum.

Deon heard the voice of a Japanese girl from a window above in the hotel shout "Come, Yuki! A white foreigner is giving a dark man fellatio!"

Disgusted, Deon mushed Brad in the face, causing him to fall on his back with both legs rocking upward in the air. He checked out of the alleyway and split the scene. Now Liz owed him big time as he thought to himself; he didn't sign on for this. If what Brad had said was true, when he reported back to Luzio Silver what had happened in the alleyway, Deon estimated that he too was going to be on bad terms the underworld figure, a complication he didn't feel good about in any way, shape, or form.

62

FOLLOWING THE INCIDENT in Doyama Village, frightened out of her mind by Brad, Liz decided it best to lie low for a while. After work, she went straight home; no gym, no drinks with what co-workers still tolerated her, and she took the train to and from work. She didn't ride her bike much at all, save for local neighborhood trips to the supermarket or drugstore. Now that she knew Luzio Silver and his crew were salty with her and meant to do her harm—exemplified by Brad's near assault—she was glad she had never told where she lived. She always met with her drug deliveries in places like Namba or Shinsaibashi. It was a bummer that she had to work in those areas, but she still felt safe because those were crowded places and, in the unlikely event any thugs jumped out to snatch her up, like Brad did, in the grimy mazes of Doyama streets, that would cause a huge scene. People would probably help her. The last thing the goons would want would be for the cops to show.

Liz's search for an apartment was put on temporary hold—maybe indefinitely. Her contract with Bozack was near completion. She was not sure if she wanted to renew it or extend it, but strangely, she was now not in a rush to head back to the United States either. Even though she didn't like Japan, she was not excited anymore about returning to America. She no longer had Eddie, her friends Mandy and Becky seemed to have moved on and experienced their own complications involved with life; nothing would be the same anyway. The issue was juggling around in her brain. Late-night chats with Ingrid had got her thinking in a different directional pattern unexpectedly. For once she considered, returning to

America, but then she would have to look for a job again, but already, she had a job where she was making money effortlessly in all practicality. The Sakamaki experience had finished nightmarish, but until that time, it was surreal. The easiest "babysitting" gig ever. How would she top that back home?

Now, however, with goons after her, life in Japan wouldn't be enjoyable in the least. Somehow she had to find a way to get through to Silver that she had nothing to do with Stephanie ratting him out to the cops. If only they would listen, she would convey to Silver and his hooligans that Stephanie betrayed her too.

For the time being, Liz stayed at her apartment and made the best of company with Ingrid. She even hung around the Filipino "pow wow" on Thursday, but when it came time to eat one of the greasy dishes Ingrid scrounged up, she claimed to be vegetarian and only dug in on the spinach salad.

When the conclave died down to three or four people, including Liz, after squares like Marcia had split, it was finally discovered how Ingrid got high. One of Ingrid's two male friends, Janz, had a fancy little weed pipe of his own. Ingrid was a miser with her stash, because she still had the weed she had bought sometime ago with the help of Liz. Her tolerance was obviously lower than Liz's, and a lesser dosage of THC could make Ingrid bonkers. The same seemed could be said for her Filipinio comrades Janz and Francisco.

To stave off boredom, Liz added her own inventory and smoked up the party. She ended up having a decent time, and they enjoyed themselves too; but around midnight, Janz and Francisco started acting like they wanted to stay all night. Francisco was high as a kite and staring at Liz as if he wanted to peel her out of her Tinkerbell T-shirt and slurp on her nipples. He kept licking his lips and talking incoherently in both English and Tagalog. Janz and Ingrid found him to be hilarious, but Liz was edgy around strangers and let loose her bossy spirit. She told the guys to leave, and rather gruffly.

Initially, Ingrid had a confused, lost-puppy look on her mug, but Liz was comically ushering the smaller of the two guys, Janz, in the direction of the door. She was making jokes and singing the song "Closing Time" by Semisonic to lighten the mood. That's when Ingrid got behind her and agreed that it was time to bring that night's session to a close.

Before Janz and Francisco finally departed, the inevitable happened. Janz asked Liz if she could score some dope for him the same as she had for Ingrid. Liz had to break the news to him bluntly that she was unable to do that because she lost contact with the dealer and, truth was, she had only been able to cop because it was through the help of a third party. She didn't say who it was—Deon—because there was a chance Ingrid knew him; and if the recent experience had taught her anything, she knew better than to drop names.

Janz didn't seem to believe Liz, and he frowned scornfully, shook his head, and mumbled something in his native language to a brain-zapped Francisco. In

Liz's mind, she was shouting *Fuck you!* to Janz and almost did. He had the nerve to cop such a reaction to her, after she had generously shared her bud with him and his pervy pal for free.

Feeling like she was in hiding, Liz took delight now in going to work; otherwise she would feel as if she needed to watch her back if she was out on the streets. Saturday, she went back to the Namba Branch. There she met up with Jeremy for the first time since his return for vacation.

Jeremy gave Liz a paper bag containing her shoes she left at the Sakamaki home the night when she ran like a bat out of hell from there. He also gave her two envelopes—one square, one rectangular. The latter had some bills equaling the sum of a Japanese grand. The square envelope had a Hallmark-type card in it. Crudely inscribed messages in English, written by Shichi and Hayato: "We miss you!" and "Please come back again!" threatened to tug at her sympathetic heart levers. The poor kids, she thought. Liz actually grew somewhat fond of Shichi, and in some ways, even Hayato too. But she didn't savor the idea of being a veritable walking menu to a hungry toe stalker in the midst. Although the money was impressive indeed, she didn't want to be in that type of volatile situation.

Jeremy wanted to press the issue and continued pestering her about teaching freelance with him as a side hustle. Liz entertained him briefly, but she smelled Deon's familiar Fahrenheit cologne. She switched off all communication with Jeremy like an old television set, turned and rushed to Deon to give him a big hug as if she was having a reunion with her brother Hal. Jeremy froze in ecliptic shock and dismay, his eyes like glaring, teary moons.

Deon looked embarrassed to be hugged up, so he patted her lightly on the back and slid to the side, moving away from Jeremy and other people around. Liz was chatting the regulatory thank-yous and such, Deon jerked his head mildly, beckoning her to convene with him to a secluded corner of the room near the pantry.

He said, "Yeah, so what happened was, that dude Brad saw you at the bar. He was there that night with Moose. When you split, Brad followed you. I just happened to be going that way. I don't know why you was over there. I told you to turn right when you left the buildin'."

Liz whined and stomped one of her D'Orsays on the floor. "Sorry! I get confused like that. I get so lost, and this place is so crazy. There's Chinese and Japanese writing everywhere and no street signs and . . ."

"Shh! Damn, chill," Deon said with an ice-cold scowl that froze Liz's rant. "Look, anyway, it doesn't matter. That rat bastard thought you and Stephanie were responsible for the cops raiding Luzio's warehouse. He's hiding out, but he's still in business for an elite circle of people."

"And . . . you're a part of this big bad elite whatever circle?" Liz was growing upset but managed to reel herself in. "Look, I've had enough of this code shit talking, you get my drift? So you're in an elite circle that can get to Luzio Silver?"

"Nah, but my pal Cyclone and Paz Lucha, those're my peeps. They score occasionally. But now it's fucked up because Brad thought he was doin' a job for Luzio, I guess he was gonna take you out. When I showed up, it jammed him up. I didn't wanna see you get hurt up, or worse. So I took dude out. Now, them motherfuckaz might be comin' after me in retaliation."

Liz was legitimately concerned now. She remembered how paralyzed with fear she was at seeing the blade Brad wielded. "You can't be serious. I mean, he wasn't serious, was he? I mean, was he really, gonna . . . try to actually kill me?"

Deon could see that Liz was about to lose her composure. He didn't want to create more of a scene than had already been made, so reluctantly, he told her, "Lissen, let's talk about this a l'il later, y'know, like after work. I'll walk you to the train or sumthin' . . ."

Liz cleared her throat relieved. She said, "OK, cool. And don't sneak out on me like you always do, really!"

"A'ite, a'ite!" Deon said, easing away from her and commencing to extract his work texts for the day. Elsewhere in the teacher lounge, several teachers had gathered and engaged in small talk. Now that Stephanie was gone, there were no regular females she had to chitchat with. The recently demoted Worm would make cameo appearances as a regular teacher in the lounge, carrying on as if nothing was bothering him and that he was taking his forfeiture in stride. In actuality, he was hiding out, sulking in a seldom-used but spacey broom closet down the hall from everyone—pretending he was still working on duty as a head teacher. In his stead was Rosiland Ash. Liz had met her before in Tennoji at the Bozack HQ. But she didn't seem like the hang-out type. She was all about business and on her way to being another Ruth Worth with the company, only— she was more stylish and conceivably sexier. She called Deon into her office.

Jeremy crept back into Liz's attention span. He and Deon used to be somewhat closer, but in recent times, it didn't seem so, Liz didn't know why and didn't really care. Jeremy, on the other hand, was a little jealous; and seeing Liz hug Deon shattered his bubble somewhat because he had hoped she would show him the same type of affection.

He said, "So what's with you and Deon? You guys dating now or what?"

Liz was appalled. "Hell no! Why'n the fuck would you think that, Jer?"

Jeremy's ray of hope once again beamed like sunshine at the end of a summer squall. He started stammering. "Well, I, um, er . . . ah, I just, ah . . . saw you guys, uh, hugging and talking over there in the corner,,,"

Liz squinted as if she had bitten a fresh raw lemon. She said, "Fuck no, Jer, we're just friends. He helped me out, and I was just thanking him."

Jeremy asked nosily, "Helped you out how?"

"And another thing," Liz talked over him as if using her vociferous authority to stampede his words. "Even if we were dating, so the fuck what? I mean, gee whiz, dude, talking to someone doesn't mean they're dating." Neglecting to mention that they had shared a bed once in what would have appeared to be a pseudo-intimate affair, but both Liz and Deon were genuinely oblivious to the event due to their burdened conditions health wise at that time.

Jeremy said, "No, I . . . um, didn't mean it like that . . . I mean, I just know what kind of guy he is."

The school bell chimed away, like a proverbial save, rescuing Liz from a woo attempt on her by Jeremy. It was time to be whisked away for work duties; students were waiting. By now she was on to the fact that Jeremy was trying to get at her, but she wasn't about to entertain that idea at all. The mere thought of going out with him had her thinking she'd look like someone dating a short *Fantasy Island* TV cast member, and how ridiculous *she would look*. She figured she would let him down easy if it ever came to that.

In the meantime, she would have at that point cut Jeremy off altogether, if it weren't for the fact that he had proven himself effective in hipping her to some lucrative side-hustle gigs. Otherwise, he was just another talking head, unimpressive—didn't do pot and smoke cigarettes or drugs, a bit of a kiss-ass to the Japanese and whites except for Serge that time at the sports bar, but simply put, he literally came *short* of what she was looking for in a significant other.

After work that night, Liz rushed out of her classroom after timing her lesson's end perfectly to the minute of the chime so that she would have already bid her students a cordial farewell before she split. She was expecting Deon to cut out on her like he usually did, then claim later that she took too long. This time he couldn't because she was already packed up and waiting for him in the teachers' lounge.

It seemed that she wasn't the only one who wanted a piece of Deon's time. Worm also indicated that he too wanted to speak with Deon about something, but to Liz's surprise, Deon rain-checked him, citing that he already had plans after work; he hadn't forgotten about his deal to meet up with Liz, and she was relatively grateful. He zipped up his leather jacket and said to Liz, "Come on, let's break out."

With no argument, Liz followed Deon out before the flood of bodies splashed out of the classrooms and crowded the path to the school's exit. Beating the rush, Liz and Deon bounced, but not before Jeremy caught them leaving.

Urgently, Jeremy called out to them, "Hey, where're you guys headed? Hold up!"

"We're in a bit of a rush, Jeremy," Deon spat over his shoulder and pushed through the exit door, Liz followed closely behind him.

She said, "Yeah, I'll call you later, Jer!"

Disappointed to the point of near tears, Jeremy vengefully stated, "I'm not feelin' the love, Deon!" But by then, he and Liz were gone. He couldn't give chase because he had to return to the teachers' lounge to pack up, write student reports, and grab his coat.

Outside, Liz and Deon dipped into a cab; there were plenty in front of the Ichiei Hotel nearby. The car dropped them off in the Chuo Ward and curbside to a building bearing the name Tanimachi. They went inside and took the elevator to the eighth floor.

There was a lounge called Paradise that encompassed the entire level, accessible almost immediately outside of the elevator. Liz accompanied Deon inside, where she saw him greet and shake hands with some lanky older Japanese dude he called by the name Hiromasa, who appeared glad to see him. Hiromasa showed Liz and Deon to a nice table for two by the huge window with a scenic view of the neon-lit avenue and Tani-Shikigo Park. The lounge was sparsely crowded with mature-looking, semi-formally dressed Japanese people. A mixed jazz quartet, comprised of two Japanese and two Americans called Neckbone was performing. It's leader, Tony Spruill, was blasting some smooth tunes from the sax that soothed Liz's nerves like the scotch that Deon had ordered brought to their table.

Liz didn't often go for that type of music and had very little exposure to it; but on this night, it was a welcome change from the usual eardrum-battering trip hop she would otherwise be subject to were she to visit another night club or similar type of lounge.

Deon said, "Anyway, I don't wanna keep you too long. I brought you here because I didn't feel like sittin' up in no smoky coffee shop."

Liz responded in slight jest, "So you brought me to a smoky jazz bar? Great!" When Deon eyed her questioningly, quickly she added "I'm just joking, dude. Calm down. I like it. It's not often I get to hear live music that sounds halfway decent."

Deon relaxed and sipped his Chivas Regal on the rocks. He said, "Well, from now on, I'd suggest you stay out of American Village. At least until everything blows over. It ain't like those goons can go to the cops. I already talked to my dudes. Silver ain't salty because I smacked up Brad, I heard. That's a relief. But that don't mean they still ain't up to no good. So like I said, if you want to stay out of harm's way, to be on the safe side, I'd recommend you hang out somewhere else at nights."

"What a bummer," Liz said. "Now I feel like a prisoner! This is such bullshit. I didn't tell the cops anything. Hell, I didn't even talk to police at all!"

Deon shook his head. He said, "That's how shit goes sometimes. People talk, they gossip, spread rumors, and then when the word gets passed along, the truth gets distorted. Too bad you got tangled up in it, and even worse, I did too.

"And yo . . . you asked me earlier, was he serious about killin' you—that Brad sucker—and the answer is hell yeah. You damn right. Over here, you might be the white queen, the high exalted 'princess' or whatever, but at the same time, you're just a vulnerable foreigner too. Especially if you don't know Japanese. Or even if you know Japanese . . . you heard'a what happened to that *Lucie Blackman* chick?"

Liz hadn't.

"Well, one of these days, you'd better check out her story. Or, another chick I think she was from Australia, Carla Ridgway back in '92. I'd run it down to you, but I don't wanna give you the chills. But a cutthroat sucka'll try to ice you if they had enough reason to. Next thing you know, you're dead in an alley somewhere, nobody knows your name, it'll take months before they find out who you are or who your family is . . . and mothafuckaz can get away with that shit too. It's been goin' on here for a while. So, yeah this is a safe country an'all, but it has its dangers, it's perils, as you now see, I bet."

Liz was forced then to acknowledge her involvement of Deon in her predicament. She had called Deon to meet her and transact the drug exchange on her behalf, and in so doing, alerted Silver's thugs to her presence that brought about the chain of events in which they were currently snared. She was compelled to offer a weak apology again, but adamantly applied her claim of innocence.

They stayed at the lounge for the duration of the jazz performance and then left before midnight, around the time of the last train. Warily, Liz took the subway home. The Saturday evening rush of passengers had smatterings of foreign faces, some of whom made her a little on edge, thinking they may have been Luzio Silver affiliates, but she dismissed the thought, fearing she was being too paranoid. She arrived home via the Bentencho Subway station without incident and was relieved. Checking her phone, she saw that Jeremy had called her several times, but she hadn't noticed because the live music and conversation with Deon consumed all of her attention. It didn't matter, though. She would call him later, if at all. There were more pressing issues on her mind that took precedence over her dealings with him and his growing obsession with her.

63

ARLIER IN THE week, yet another emergency meeting was held at Tennoji HQ and once again hotheaded hebephile/ephebophile Shigeru Watanabe presided over his subjects from both the Osaka and Tokyo regions. On this occasion, the latter office reps had to make a special, but official, trip to the Kansai area, discussing the grim details of Stephanie's murder in Tokyo's neighboring prefecture of Saitama. Bozack dodged a bullet, for they were able to keep their name out of the news, already reeling still following the media exposé of the drug bust involving several of their teachers in Osaka. The Saitama School, fortunately, had not yet been registered as a Bozack subsidiary. It was a newly acquired school, now defunct; it was formerly known as the International Language Lab. Its prior owners, an international couple comprised of a foreign white man and a Japanese spouse, divorced and decided to shut the school down. Bozack saw the opportunity to expand their growing enterprise and swooped in to buy out the spot, ushering in their campaign to win the rural Wild West side. So when word of Stephanie's demise hit the news, ILL School took the hit. It was a big deal, but people from the Osaka area who knew Stephanie would not be aware that she had been the victim of a break-in murder until months later. Due to the delinquent behavior of the deceased Arizonian's mother, it was difficult to locate her as she was the emergency contact.

Shigeru assailed his Tokyo manager. "So, Asano, lay it on me *pretty boy*. You're telling me that this young lady got raped, robbed, and killed? And on top of that, there're no suspects and no motives other than it being a robbery? No witnesses at all? Are you kidding me? And we're supposed to be opening a new school there?! How are we supposed to keep our teachers safe if you have them situated in such cantankerous and danger-trap locations!?"

Koki Asano, in navy-striped tailored suit, adjusted his Clark Kent eyeglasses and cleared his throat, concealing his apprehension addressing his boss with a cooler exterior, more so than his Osaka region counterparts. He said, "Sir, fortunately, we were able to liquidate our assets. Representatives from our Tokyo office were able to consolidate a deal, acquiring us another real estate space at another location, several kilometers away, same size as the ILL School, same potential customer base. The good news is, when Bozack opens the office there, no one will make the correlation between us and the ILL School. The public will likely associate the recent tragedy to them, not us."

Shigeru gritted his teeth, more annoyed that Asano seemed so calm and carried on with aplomb in the face of this crisis than of his quibbling. Lightly karate-chopping the marble meeting room table, Shigeru growled hoarsely "That's all well and good, 'Romeo', but tell me what's the point of opening up a school in a crime-infested neighborhood of . . . of thieves, and . . . and serial killers!?"

Asano broke from his placid and collected character to doggedly claim that such an incident was unheard of. "Sir, we have word from the local authorities that this type of crime was completely unheard of in that vale. In fact, the area was void of crime prior to this horrific incident, save for the occasional speeding tickets. We are assured that this is an isolated crime, or that the victim knew her assailants, or likewise."

Shigeru said, "But . . . didn't somebody tell me there weren't any suspects? What about that charming little freckle-faced whippersnapper that took her out there? You think he had anything to do with it?"

Asano dabbed a slight finger to the perspiration on his forehead, pretending to again adjust his contemporary specs. He said, "Alex Lachlan is beside himself with grief now at the moment, sir. He is not a suspect in the least. His whereabouts are accounted for by his Japanese wife the entire evening, encompassing the time in which the murder was committed."

"How do we know that?" Shigeru barked.

"Because the deceased instructor, this, Ms. Pritchard, was seen leaving a local fast food restaurant in the latter of the evening, and a taxi driver issued a statement claiming to have dropped her off at the address where the break-in occurred."

There was a moment of silence, which was deafening, until broken by hard saliva swallowing, sniffing, chattering teeth, and rumbling stomachs of the several people in the room. Shigeru shook his head and crumpled his face into a familiar, depraved sneer. No one dared make eye contact with him, all including Ruth Worth at the farthest end, stared at the tabletop.

Shigeru said, "This stinks to high heaven, I don't like this shit one bit. We have drug-dealing teachers, drug-using teachers, alcoholics that like to play in traffic and get snapped like crab legs, and now teachers found naked and raped, robbing us at the same time. Something just doesn't sound quite right. Who the hell else besides that Alex nincompoop knew she was carrying all that cash?"

Asano appeared stumped a bit. He said, "Sir, I'm afraid that was information privy only to our Tokyo and Osaka regions . . . sir. Due to the sensitive nature of the situation . . . the delicate process required to open the postal account needed because . . . of the red tape involved with the ILL School, the tangible issue of currency was necessary . . . this is not unusual, sir. We've done this on numerous occasions without incident."

Shigeru cut him off. "So you're insinuating that it's an inside job? Since the only people who knew the woman was holding cash money were the people in this room, am I to assume that someone in here is a rapist and a murderer?"

Everyone in the room looked suddenly startled and stared at one another like they were suspects in an Agatha Christie tale. Shigeru found it a bit amusing, and the mood lightened up a tad.

"Relax," Shigeru said. "I know none of you wimps are killers. Besides, as hard as you all work, I'm sure you can account for your whereabouts with credibility."

Asano punctuated with his assertion, "Sir, we cannot rule out the possibility of Alex . . . possibly flashing the cache accidentally, or inadvertently—we don't know for sure, sir. Alex, of course, adamantly denies this, but as I said, we cannot rule out the possibility. But I assure you, sir, we were the only parties aware that Ms. Pritchard would be in possession of that sum of money. I believe that we should allow the local authorities to handle the investigation and we cooperate when necessary. In our best interests, we have to find a replacement for her in the new location."

Shigeru said, "I figured that already. Luckily—but unluckily—our grand opening is gonna get pushed back a month, right?" He saw Asano nodding in concurrence, then continued, "Because the new location we bought has to be constructed, since due to this incident, we had to move from that former ILL School hole-in-the-wall. I guess you have that Rosiland Ash chippy in mind, eh, Kenji?"

Kenjiro, Kenji to his superiors, Tanimoto had been silently wincing at the tabletop, relieved up until that moment he hadn't been in his boss Shigeru's firing range for most of the meeting. Now he nervously took his place at the altar to receive his verbal lashings.

"N-no, sir," Kenji said, clearing his throat as if swallowing dry rice. "Ms. Worth and our managerial team had considered Russel Clark."

"What!? Wait . . . you mean *that* bearded *walnut*? Looks like a skinny wolf man? Hell no. No way! We don't need any hairy, scary muppet monster like him scaring those country bumkin kids. I thought you said we needed FEMALES! Stick to the plan. I know you despise women, I do too sometimes, but we all agreed that the women are less likely to scare the wits out of Japanese people. We can't send that man. Besides, he's married. All these ball-and-chained foreign employees bitch too much about being relocated! Nope. No way. I don't approve of that candidate."

Ruth Worth found a moment of intermittent courage and spoke up. "Sir, we didn't feel as if Rosiland Ash was up to the task right now. She's better suited here, where her services are needed due to the recent demotion of Mitch Swiggler."

Shigeru smirked quickly like he was making faces at a nursery window trying to make a baby laugh. Then his stern grimace returned, addressing Kenji. "What about that other local troublemaker in making the Amberbush darling?"

Mention of her name had Shigeru Takeda tighten his legs and an involuntary response by his right hand to suddenly fall upon his sudden perched lap. He was thinking about how her legs and back looked when she had come to Tennoji the day he wrote her up for inappropriate attire. When talk of transferring Liz to the Saitama office came up, he didn't notice himself shaking his head in staunch opposition.

Ruth Worth followed his lead and said, "Sir, we aren't sure if Ms. Amberbush will be up to the task either, sir. She doesn't have any experience teaching children that we know of. Her only experience with children, if I remember correctly . . ." She fumbled with her wrinkled manila folder, applying moisture to a finger before fishing out Liz's bio-data sheet. "Yes, she has experience babysitting, but we would prefer to have someone with more experience with younger learners."

"Enough!" Shigeru exclaimed, causing a rumbling in the room like an earthquake's aftershock waves. "Everybody out! You, pretty boy, get your ass back to Tokyo, asap. Get that Saitama issue squared away, and I don't want to see you again. You, *bum*, you sit your funny ass down." He pointed a finger at Kenji like a wicked pirate's hook for a hand, clipping a chunk from his subordinate's shoulder and slumping him back down in his office chair. Others filed out nervously, except for Kayo Terumi, who carried a troubled expression on her face as if she was in deep thought about something. She tried to speak to Kenji, who she low-key despised and pitied at the same time, but he blew her off coldly, explaining to her that he would discuss whatever she had to talk about later, when he stopped by the Hommachi office, where she presided mostly. Shigeru too shooed Kayo off and cared not to pay any regard to her apparent insistence.

After everyone left, five-foot-five Shigeru jumped up from his oval back office boardroom chair. He tottered gleefully to a glass top nook table in the corner of the vast room and opened up a silver-rim crystal Waterford whiskey decanter and poured himself a stiff one. He downed it and pranced back to his seat at the royal table as if he was a king lion of an animation classic.

Shigeru turned his attention to Kenji seated close to him, calmly commencing to lambaste him with breath blowing his face steeped heavily of bourbon and sweat from teenage balls. "I don't know what you think you're doing, bum, but I'm putting a stop to this freak show. I want to get rid of all this riff raff. Get rid of them all. We'll start fresh. We'll do more recruiting overseas—only this time, we'll go to more populated areas on the East Coast of America, not those flunky Midwest towns or kooky Canadian towns offering only creeps with petty theft records. We've got to do better than this. And, my bummy boy, it starts with a well-polished engine that gets its oil changed every once and while. And in me saying this, if you don't get your act together, you are going to very well be among the gunk that we get cleansed of.

"Another thing, you have to put that Swiggler prick back as head teacher. I've given this some serious thought. We can't lose an employee like that. He's practically a permanent resident. He is married, he has a stable residence, speaks Japanese, and he's put in tremendous work to get where he is, and with good 'results too, aside from this blunder he was recently involved in. Since he was exonerated, he should serve out his probationary punishment measures and be reinstated so that we can get the best work output from him. It will trickle down to us restoring the quality service provided, which made us one of the fastest-growing language schools in Japan. Good businesses start with good people. We have to keep him, but a lot of these other sketchy scum posing as teachers have got to go!"

Kenji's troubled voice responded faintly but audibly, "Understood, sir. However, the dilemma we face is terminating employment without cause or reason, sir. Although we might suspect some teachers of being unsavory, we can't use that as a viable reason to release them from their contracts, sir, then, there's the issue of replacing them . . ."

Shigeru barked, "Why? Why's that an issue? You don't get rid of them all at once, you stupid fucking idiot. It's a gradual process. You replace them over periods of time. Even I'm aware of the fact that we have a waiting list that stretches longer than the Yamato River, you fuckhead. That's who we replace them with!

"As for the reason to fire fools, that's where that Swiggler twerp is going to come into play. He will be your eyes-and-ears double agent, spying on the foreigners, and reporting back to us. Then when we've successfully rid ourselves of the bad apples, we can replace them with fresh ones. He will think he earned his position back; we'll let him think that, and he'll continue to do an even better job watch-dogging for us. We could then send Rosiland or some capable female out there to Saitama in a month, and we'll be on our road to recovery. Unless you got a better plan?"

"I . . . I couldn't have orchestrated a better course of action at all, sir," Kenji stated in top-grade, blue-ribbon-award-winning, brown-nose fashion, bowing his head in the Japanese norm. "I can only hope to be half as wise as are you, sir. I'll get to work on the matter of rectifying this situation."

"Yeah, you do that." Shigeru waved him away as if to say, "Be gone!" Then he stood up from his chair to make a return trip down the expanse of the boardroom to the nook table for a refill, wondering briefly about what the hell it was that the Hommachi submanager, Kayo Terumi had wanted to discuss.

64

WORM WAS WORKING a brief overtime shift at the Namba branch of the Bozack School—one he enthusiastically volunteered for. Reason being Kenjiro, the regional manager, or Mr. Kenji had been spending a lot of time there as of recent. The South Town schools—Namba, Hommachi, and Higobashi—had a lot of truancy issues with teachers, frequent no-shows, and plenty people calling in sick. Until his demotion, Worm was a part of the staff that could be called upon to take up the slack, for a little extra pay, of course, but that was the job of a head teacher. No longer in that position because of his alleged involvement with the drug bust party that got Tim Valentine and Ricky Exmouth arrested, in the process smearing the company's name in the news too.

Kenji had been so reluctant to demote Worm. He was the most dedicated brown-noser and reliable foreign teacher he ever had working under him. Plus, he was half-Japanese and could speak the language of his mother's side of the family, which made him all the more favorable. But Shigeru Watanabe, the big Bozack Boss in chief was right, Kenji had to be tougher on his subjects. He had to discipline his subordinates. Things were getting out of control; examples had to be made in order to be taken seriously. Teachers were constantly showing up late; some didn't even show up at all from time to time. They weren't abiding by dress codes, students had complained about hygiene and body odor issues, and of course, the rumors of rampant drug use and abuse on and off the clock couldn't be ignored. Tim Valentine's arrest, plus one teacher at a Kyobashi location had decided to get so stoned that he got naked, whipped out his privates, and offered them as "fruits and nuts" for visiting guests, potential clients, scaring some unsuspecting Japanese people clean and clear out of their socks.

Of course Kenji had no time to do a thorough investigation himself, as Shigeru Watanabe apparently assumed he did. He was swamped already with his day-to-day duties as the Osaka regional manager at Bozack. He needed workers like Worm to do that sort of dirty work. When Worm was the head teacher, he seemed to have done a good job, in Kenji's view, but not good enough to keep his own nose clean as apparent by his connection to Tim Valentine, who was another vast disappointment to the company's reputation.

After the latest big meeting with Shigeru Watanabe, Kenji hinted furtively to Worm that he could indeed earn his position back—not only that, but also gain another promotion in the process. He could move up to the HQ level, subordinate to Ruth Worth at the head office. Worm was resuscitated from his coma of melancholy hearing this. He jumped at the opportunity to redeem himself. Thus, wherever Kenji was, Worm tried to be sticking to him like glue, so that all the efforts he was making to prove himself worthy could be seen. At the same time, he would keep a watchful eye on the foreign staff suspected of committing infractions. He'd be Kenji's extra set of specs.

Worm felt like a lowlife spying on his coworkers, some of whom he had considered friends. He had hoped one day he could quit Bozack, start his own English school and hire the teachers to work for him who were his former colleagues. But stabbing them in the back to keep his job or regain his esteemed position or title at the company, threatened to make his hope of lifelong friendships dismal.

It didn't matter, because his aspirations about going into business for himself had taken a back seat. His sudden demotion had crushed his pride and shattered his confidence. He had briefly considered quitting the company, but discordant wife Mikako wasn't having it.

Sure, Mikako was rich: she had her inheritance and a stash tucked away from her days of sucking and dildo-fucking on the porn set but mulishly opposed having a home-bodied husband. Especially one such as young as Worm was. In her opinion, he should work or have some type of prestigious position in society. She had no desire to be a porn fluffer turned cougar, and although she loved her tenderfoot hubby, she wasn't about to allow him to be a slacker or "freeter."

Instead of quitting then, Worm decided to stay longer and learn the inner workings of the company so that it would better benefit him in the future when he did make his own school, his own business. In the meantime, however, he would have to do some dirty work that would require him to backbite and betray his comrades. The "good" thing was, at least he could hide his wicked hand in the deed, and his replacement, Rosiland Ash, would take the blame. He, on the other hand, would continue to throw lavish parties at his mansion to throw suspicion off his name. While his guests from the job would gripe about Rosiland's hard-nosed authoritative and oppressive overseeing at work, he would play dumb, low-key strengthening his case for returning to his former rank and title. It was a dirty business—what could he say? Dog-eat-dog world it was, and he wanted to be more than just a watchdog. He wanted to be top dog.

After the most recent meeting, Kenji pulled Worm to the side and had an informative conversation with him, conveying mostly what had been discussed, only with a spin to it that caused the underling to be on a power trip he had no official right to. But when Kenji insinuated that "certain people had to go," instinctively, Worm knew exactly what to do.

Such was the exact reason why he so feverishly volunteered to substitute at the Namba school on that very day. On the weekends, especially Saturdays and Sundays, a lot of teachers called in sick. At the South Town schools, centered in one of Osaka's largest recreation and party zones, it was almost a certainty one of the three: Namba, Hommachi, or Higobashi would need substitutes, or "field runners," on duty. Those in the latter group were comprised mostly of Filipinos, or people from countries where English was considered the second language. And finally, Blacks from Caribbean extractions. Although these teacher employees were considered reliable and extremely necessary, Worm's brilliant idea was to get rid of those first and have them replaced by clean-cut, fresh new faces that were a little "brighter." Those who, in his idea, would be least likely to make the Japanese students—the customer base—feel that they weren't being taught English by "native" or "authentic" speakers of the language. Usually, this meant white people, or Caucasians, from countries like the United Kingdom, Australia, Canada, New Zealand, and the United States of America.

The USA and Canada sometimes came with complications, as these two places often rendered a multitude of races and or ethnics other than the target community desired. Tim Valentine, Denore Langston, Chucky Chilson, Kwame Chwaku and some random others, exemplified this. Most of these instructors were no longer with the company, Worm considered, but there were a few who still remained. If he could, he would do what he could to tarnish their work performance records or nitpick some breach of company rules and report this to Kenji. Then, he would earn his stripes back when it was discovered how good of a job he was doing. Sure, he was aware that these "minorities" had served their purpose, they were recruited at a time when Japan had a thirsty curiosity about non-whites and their pop culture. Now that they had served their purpose in getting the students to come through the door, their future necessity seemed to gradually dissipate. In the beginning, Bozack had led the race and was among the first in the English conversation school world to feature and maintain a language lounge with a variety of nationalities, faces, and accents from all around the world. Now this no longer seemed to be the pattern they followed.

Worm, in his broom closet "office," used the edge of a wide bucket sink for a desk chair and one of the shelves on the wall used for storing bleach, cleaning agents, air freshener and the like, for a flat surface—serving as a tabletop. When Kenji was on duty at Namba, he allowed Worm to use this walk-in storage unit as his private quarter so he could better plot and scheme. At the same time, he did not have to endure the humiliation of facing his former subordinates constantly in the teachers' breakroom.

Conveniently, Worm chose to ignore Radley Owens's tattered history of delinquency. His fellow Canadian held the title at the South Town schools for the most "out sick" calls. Still, Radley's invaluable shoplifting skills made him a keeper in Worm's book. Instead, he focused his attention on his fake friend, Deon Clemente.

Despite an appearance that would otherwise make people like Kenji nervous and apprehensive, Deon was, surprisingly, neither a troublemaker nor a nuisance around the company or schools. He was often misconstrued as being a pugnacious type, for his face seemed predisposed to having that hateful frown permanently painted. But this angry look and demeanor with others was due to habitual idiosyncrasy which originated from an apparent tumultuous childhood. His manner of staring at people became somewhat an indefinite squint which could be off-putting to certain people, especially if they didn't know him well. For furthermore, he hadn't been much of a mingle type with his coworkers anyway.

That being stated, otherwise, Deon had a stellar record. He always came to work on time; seldom, if ever, called in sick; adhered to the dress code; and had no student customer complaints. None at all.

Deon, in all probability, should have been the polar opposite to the type of employee that Bozack would be looking to get rid of. He was hardworking—if such could be said about work carried out at an environment such as theirs—and his attendance record spelled out that he was generally reliable. The only thing negative that could be stated about him was his occasionally annoying people around the office, badgering them to go in with him on some lottery pool or some other fast-money, get-rich-quick scheme like Amway or a pyramid angle. Still, he was expendable, as far as Worm was concerned. Especially when he considered his own future; if it came down to him or Deon, of course, it was Deon who had to go.

As Worm clocked out using a time card signifying the end of his shift, he spoke briefly to Kenji as his manager had stepped out of his own office. He was carrying papers and other apparatus to make it appear to his Japanese boss as if he had been working his fingers to the bone, even with lessened responsibilities from no longer being Head Teacher.

Kenji praised Worm "Thank you, Mitchell-san, for working today. We really needed the extra help."

Worm said "Don't mention it, Mr. Kenji. Is Deon around?"

Almost as if on cue, Deon appeared. His lessons had ended and he had descended from the upstairs classroom to grab his suit jacket. He looked as if he was preparing to leave the office like Worm.

Worm spotted him and called out "Hey, 'D-man' how are ya, buddy? You got time for me today?" As he approached and threw his arms around the shorter, muscular American's shoulder in an exaggerated display of familiarity fellowship. Kenji sheepishly disappeared back inside his office, not caring to partake in any *gaijin* small-talk banter.

Worm gabbled away in Deon's ears, telling him that he was finished and headed to lunch. Deon indicated that he was about to do the same, only, he would be returning to work to finish out the entire afternoon for his shift, whereas Worm had only volunteered to work the early-morning shift, and he would be done for the rest of the day. As such, he presented Deon an invitation to dine with him at the eat spot he was headed to.

At first, Deon was going to decline the offer. However, due to his exorable nature, he would be easily coerced when Worm stated that lunch was his treat. So, he waited for Worm downstairs while the Canadian cleaned up his broom closet station and grabbed his jacket.

Off they went. Worm and Deon left their decrepit, derelict building sandwiched between the Shin Nankai and Ichiei Hotels, nestled among several rows of sex dens, massage parlors, love hotels and hot noodle stands. They exchanged small talk and lewd jokes about the environment, the job, and various aspects of Japan. All the while, Worm was hoping that Deon would state something bizarre and outlandish so that he could use it against him later as being unprofessional, but Deon kept the conversation politically correct, choosing not to say much that would reveal his true feelings or character, code switching his vernacular to that which was mainstream friendly.

Worm had a peculiar penchant for being jovially facetious one moment, then impalpably serious the next. Deon and some others found this aspect of his character troubling at times, but it never raised their antennas that he would do anything to wrong them.

As a head teacher, they saw Worm as a subtle brown-noser. Yes, he was strict when he needed to be, but otherwise he ran a loose ship, and most found the work experience with him to be jocular and sprightly. In stark contrast to places like the head office in Tennoji, where the top brasses hovered over teachers, ever ready to critique and scold every slight mistake an employee made, and generally they would do this to feather their own nests and make them appear on top of their jobs. So, until his demotion, working with Worm had been far from stressful or tortuous, but his flippant tendencies and angular manner of trying to be suddenly bossy irked people at times, Deon included.

Not the biggest fan of whites, Deon decidedly had no beef or anything against Worm. According to the flimsy Canadian in the blow-up balloon suit, him being "half Japanese" afforded him the right to claim—albeit privately—that he too could relate to the struggles of a minority, or colored, person. This, he thought, would gain him affinity with people like Deon in ways that the other standard white couldn't.

A farcical nature prevented Deon from fully accepting the accuracy of Worm's notion. From his vantage point, Worm's whiteness and non-whiteness was something he could turn on and off like a light switch and use in his favor depending on the company he was among. Yet rather than be confused, he elected to accept him at face value, seeing him as neither white nor a *hapa*; he was just another English teacher.

Deon didn't hang out with other teachers much. He wasn't too enthused about the way they partied and the outrageous antics they engaged in. He did, however, accept party invites to Worm's mansion every once in a while, which were fun, he had to admit. Free champagne, free food, sleazy girls in the days before he got introduced to Taffie Jolie, and a free hotel room in the event he scored with one. It was great, so he had no immediate reason to dislike Worm. New Jack richy folks knew how to party, he reckoned.

As they walked, Worm jabbered on and on to Deon about how cool he was, overdoing the obsequious so much so, one would have thought he was being disingenuous. He said, "You're one of the best dressers at our schools, you're so stylish. I know you must have a lotta women. Sorry to hear about you 'n' Taff, but a guy like you shouldn't have no problem getting a replacement, huh?"

Deon shrugged, laughed uneasily as if he had wished Worm hadn't brought up Taffie. He said, "Yeah, but I really dug her."

Worm guffawed "Ha! Dude, you're in Japan. Go grab you a Japanese girl like your friend Chucky. I heard he's gonna marry that Japanese girl he was with. What the hell man? I'm surprised to see a guy like you down in the dumps over a chick, man. You're the coolest guy at our school. I wanna be like you, man!" He stopped for a minute and started patting Deon's arms and hardened shoulders. "Geez! Lookit all that—you must work out constantly! You're a bit stocky, but gawdamn, you're all fuckin' muscle! How can I ever get like that?"

Deon looked at the Gomer Pile stick man's frame and was at a loss for words. He merely chuckled lightly, shrugged again, and tried to take Worm's compliments in stride. Truth was, he knew not how to react to such a pouring on of adulation. Especially when he was sure he had gained all but too much weight since coming to Japan, and didn't see himself as the musclebound, "hip hop" heartthrob others viewed him as. One thing for sure, he was on guard, hoping Worm wasn't on some homo shit, as he would put it. The sun was shining brightly despite the late winter chill still in the air, and Deon wanted to make it through this lovely day without incident.

Although a relatively short walk, arrival to their destination took about ten minutes due to traffic, both human and vehicular. They took the Hanshin Highway underpass, finding them at yet another score of small streets crowded with lunchtime local regulars and tourists of every shape, size, color, and extraction. Worm sidestepped onto a tributary drive extending from Sen Nichi Mae Road, and Deon followed him to the Thick Land Building and vanished inside. There was a college-classroom-sized cafe on the second floor.

Deon turned up his nose at this place, as it didn't seem too impressive, with decorum resembling a shooting gallery in a soon-to-be condemned building in the Bronx. He had his mind set on a fast-food, beef-over-rice joint like Yoshinoya's or Matsuya, closer to the job, cheap and filling. But since Worm was paying, Deon dummied up and bared his teeth in silent protest.

Worm had apparently been there before and insisted that although the place appeared old and dilapidated, he could rest assured that the food was good. Deon expressed no further qualms.

They entered the retro, rinky-dink cafe, which was exceptionally crowded despite being off the beaten path of commercial Osaka shops that had more flare and attraction power for tourists and keen diners. In all likelihood, Deon mused, it catered to local area people who worked around there and the adjoining Nakatani Building on the other side.

Some cafe employees knew Worm by his real name, Mitchell, and one portly old man with a gigantic inflated Chef Boyardee hat on greeted him as such. This fluffy old man Worm referred to as Mr. Saito, or Saito-san, had approached Worm and Deon, stepping out from behind a huge counter that doubled as a seating place with stools on one side and a prep table on the other kitchen side. A partition with glass enclosure had plastic model dishes displaying examples of the food served there along with the prices, appearing like oversized old props for a giant's doll house. These didn't do much to entice the appetite, but Deon was used to these sorts of establishments. He shrugged off the less-than-impressive surroundings and reminded himself that Worm was footing the bill, as the old man Saito showed them to two stools at the bartop with two menus already spread on the counter.

A petite, young but unattractive waitress (server) scampered along and placed two small glasses of water before them. Deon took a sip immediately, appearing thirsty as he drained the glass in seconds, already prompting the long-faced girl to refill it.

Worm opened up the menu in front of Deon and told him, "Order whatever you want."

Deviously, Deon showed a rare grin. "Anything?" he asked like a conniving trickster.

Then Worm's unpalatable humor kicked in. Seriously, he stated, "Not anything. I'll pay, because I'm rich, but not that rich today. Something within reason."

Deon laughed and assured Worm that he wasn't out to break his bank. He said, "I know, I know!" He ordered a reasonable chicken instead of pork dish. Worm followed up with a rice omelet and fruity parfait.

Worm said, "Don't you want anything to drink?"

Deon said, "Nah, I'm good. This water is fine, I guess."

"Bullshit!" Worm blurted out in a harsh, skeptical tone. He called out to the old Mr. Saito and told him in Japanese, "Bring this man a beer, please. One!" He then turned to Deon and said, "Yeah, you need a man's drink. Besides, buddy, you owe me one. You didn't even come to my wedding party a while back!"

Deon wrinkled his forehead, bewildered. "Man, I don't remember you even invitin' me to any weddin' party, let alone even knowin' when it was!" His beer arrived quick as a whistle, in a miniature flute glass. Deon stared at it then said to Worm, "Where's yours?"

"Don't worry about me, man." Worm shook his head rapidly. "You go ahead and enjoy yourself. It's on me, dammit. I may not be the head teacher anymore, but I'm still telling you, enjoy! That's an order."

Service was speedier than Deon had expected. Both of their dishes had arrived, hot and ready for consumption. They dug in.

Despite his skeletal, gaunt frame, Worm gobbled his feed like a gluttonous gourmand but had a disgusting habit of trying to speak with his mouth crammed full. This disturbed people, and Deon was no exception, as the sight of him threatened to ruin his appetite. He turned away as Worm continued to blabber away about nothing too important.

In a matter of minutes, the meal was finished. Deon had cleaned his plate, and so did Worm. He slurped down his parfait and licked the whipped cream off of his spoon like his wife used to do when her nose was buried deep in a porn lead's anus crack. He saw Deon impatiently checking his watch.

Deon said, "Well, I guess I'd better be headed back to the school. Lunch break is almost over."

Playing extra dumb, Worm reacted, like, "What? You have to go back to work today?"

Deon was like, *Duh.* Exigently, he said, "You knew that."

Worm's demeanor suddenly flipped back to a serious, hard-nosed disposition he would hold when he was a head teacher when trying to keep his subordinate coworkers in line.

Somewhat sententiously Worm said, "Are you telling me that you drank alcohol while on duty as a Bozack teacher? Don't you know that's a serious company code violation? What kind of example are you setting?"

For a moment, Deon couldn't believe what he was hearing. He said, "You've gotta be kiddin' . . . you can't be serious, right?"

Worm snapped back into jest mode. His laughing countenance returned, and he slapped Deon playfully on his shoulder with the back of his palm. He said, "I'm just kiddin' with ya, man. Don't worry, I'm not even a head teacher anymore. Even if I reported you, I couldn't get you in trouble, relax. Besides, man, you're an asset to our company. They would never get rid of a teacher like you. You're probably one of the most dependable guys we have around."

This was not far from the truth. What wasn't quite accurate was Worm's sincerity. Deon, at the time though, had no reason to doubt him. Still, the fact that Worm would joke with him like that had him on his toes. His street survival instincts were kicking in like an old TV set needing time to warm up for maximum performance and output.

If Worm's lauding of him was true, then Deon felt he had nothing to worry about. Although he wasn't the type to beg to keep his job, he wasn't ready to ditch an easy career like the one he held. It paid good money; all he had to do was show up, read a book in front of some Japanese people like a human tape recorder, then ask and answer questions about what he read in the book. Easy as pie! It would be such a shame to lose such an easy gig as that before he was actually ready. He prided himself on his commitment in maintaining standards, which would prevent his untimely dismissal from the job.

Deon and Worm parted ways. Worm didn't return to the Namba School on that particular day, but he returned on the following. He shot a bee line to Kenji's office to rat on Deon, like he all but swore he wouldn't do.

Kenji seemed almost pleased to hear the news Worm reported, to the point of impish glee. It was short-lived as reality sobered him to the fact that Worm's mere accusation alone was insufficient indictment. There was no concrete evidence of whether or not Worm had stated the truth. He might have been embellishing a tale to endear himself to his superiors to take his word at face value and credit him for notable work.

Thus, as if he could hear what Kenji was thinking inside his head, Worm volunteered, practically insisted, that he escort him to the same cafe he and Deon had dined at the day before. Duplicitous Kenji then scooped up his factotum, Suguru Yamada, and followed Worm to the cafe in the Thick Land Building.

There, the same blimp-chef-hat-sporting Mr, Saito greeted Worm and company happily. He showed them to a nicer, cleaner table away from the counter, pleased to have Worm's patronage two days in a row.

The trio ordered coffees and an orange juice, even though they had no intentions of staying long. Their purpose for being there was to have Worm's story substantiated and verified by the old man, Mr. Saito, satisfactorily for Kenji and his assistant, Yamada.

As expected, when asked by Worm about the previous day, the old man told Kenji that the man who had accompanied his "favorite Canadian customer" was "a person who resembles a black man" (Kokujin mitai hito), a clean-shaven, almost-girlish "pretty" face, coffee-colored skin two creams tainted maybe, and shiny, slick hair in a braided ponytail. And so on. Mr. Saito's graphic descriptions were more than enough to establish in Kenji's and Yamada's heads it was Deon. Moreover, Kenji saw Worm and Deon leave together the previous day before he dipped into his office.

Still, the proof had to be beyond a shadow of a doubt, so Kenji gave Yamada a wide-nosed head nod. The nerdy-glassed underboss produced a picture of Deon from his Bozack bio-data folder. Mr. Saito immediately confirmed that the face on its passport-sized photo was of the same man who accompanied Worm the day before, and yes, he had ordered and consumed a beer along with some chicken-katsu.

For Kenji, this was all the proof he needed. He and Yamada began talking too rapidly and quietly for Worm to pick up, but he knew for certain that Kenji was pleased. His apparent distaste for Deon wasn't masked or hidden, and on this occasion especially, he seemed to be reveling in the moment. He and Yamada were almost laughing, as if they had gained hold of something they had long been yearning for.

Not everyone at Bozack was as open-minded as their hiring practices would claim. Sure, there were plenty on the executive board stretching back to its founders, Boris and Zacharias Smitts, who wanted to push the idea of them operating a multicultural, multifaceted, "rainbow room" of inclusion; but the core decision makers were mercilessly unhinged from the idea that white faces make the company seem legit. Especially the scholastic academia, or institutions, that claimed to be such. In such regard, there were people like Kenji, who loathed ilk such as "smooth" drug dealers like Tim Valentine, who dated and used Japanese women freely as a rotation of endless toilet paper and disposed of the same way.

It was always the black employees Kenji had the most problems with, but it was displaced anger. While teachers like Chucky, Deon, and a previously fired teacher named Taylor, refused to cut their hair pissed Kenji off and threatened his authoritative swag around the office, it was these same guys who also came to work on time, rarely called in sick, and had good customer reviews. Other teachers like Keefer came to work so often smelling of booze that it was now considered his after shave. Radley would call in sick so much he seemed to be vacationing weekly. Stephanie would commit all the above offenses and showed more cleavage than sympathy for struggling students, sometimes yelled at the children in the kids' lessons, and received a complaint of some sort once or twice a month. Jeremy, although astute in his own right, had a rude tendency to fall asleep during his lessons. And Liz Amberbush, although recently she had improved, used to come to work with subtle traces of ganja smell, but masked abundantly with expensive perfume. The list went on when it came to the disciplinary reports about the teachers. Yet there were those in the company, like Kenji, who overlooked all other infractions to focus on minute details of a disliked target bunch. Unfortunately, Deon fell within that categorical group.

Unquestionably, Deon didn't take the news very well, then, when he was called into Kenji's office the following Tuesday and presented his walking papers. After an extended disquisition adorned with rebuke and tender scolding, Kenji apprised Deon of the thirty-day notice of his termination with Bozack School Company. The reason was for violation of company code prohibiting intake or being under the influence of alcohol while on duty.

Both Deon and Kenji knew, damn well, that even if true, he wasn't the only teacher around there who ever drank alcohol while on the clock. Teachers all over the Bozack circuit, from Himeji to Nara, came to work intoxicated, high on drugs ranging from cocaine to freebase, marijuana, shrooms and a litany of other amphetamines. Furthermore, the amount of beer Deon had taken wasn't nearly enough to inebriate him and incapacitate his work performance. He alluded to how he had returned to work that afternoon and Kenji not mentioning anything to him, which caused for suspicion as proof. But Kenji had already made up his mind that he wasn't buying it. For him, proving that Deon was drunk was unnecessary. Ingestion of alcohol alone was sufficient-enough ammo for dismissal in his eyes. He was hell-bent on dragging a body back to his boss, Shigeru Watanabe. Like Worm, Kenji too was on a redemption path for his superiors.

65

Hello Elizabeth!

> *Just hitting you back. Things have been so busy for me lately.*
> *My new gig is demanding. I rarely even have time for myself.*
> *But it's still rewarding work. How's Japan? Are you still enjoying it?*
>
> *I was surprised when I read in your e-mail that you were planning to return to the U.S.*
>
> *Have you given any thought about what you plan to do when you come back?*
>
> *Like what kind of work will you get into upon return? If I can help, don't hesitate to reach out. I'm always here for you, you know that.*

Take Care,

Carver

LIZ WAS NOW corresponding with Carver on the regular—not every day but at least once or twice a week. They were almost having regular but brief conversations. When he inquired about the type of work Liz planned on getting into when she returned to the United States, he had her a bit stumped. She obviously hadn't given it too much thought. Her first thought was to take it easy, maybe go skiing, or go on a simple, long retreat in the comfort of her estate, snuggling up to Mother. But on the other hand, that didn't fit in with her feminist, independent woman dogma, so she considered a career that would enable her to use her skills and experience gained having lived in Japan for the past two or three years. Right away, she could think of nothing except being some type of schoolteacher, and that wasn't anything she was interested in. Sure, her mother had been a schoolteacher, but had she never accepted a job as one while in Japan, such a career would have never been her primary choice.

Liz's pondering of her future was interrupted by her cellular phone ringing. She went for it, grabbed it up off her service table in the main chamber.

Serge's voice on the line went, "Hello, Elizabeth, I am sorry to bother to with you, now, but I must need know from you to where is Taffie? Where is she, I cannot find to her . . ." His speech was speedy and frantic.

Liz said, "Slow down, slow down, Serge. You're trying to reach Taffie, right?"

Distressed, Serge said, "Yes, I am try to reach her now for about a week, two weeks. I know she have retire from company, I know, *oui*, yes, but I call to her phone, this number is no working. I have not any information, where is she, so I thought maybe you can know about her?"

Liz was a bit surprised to hear Serge sound so troubled and excited about anyone, especially given his opinion of Taffie based on the conversation she had with him. Now all of a sudden, he was fit to be tied seemingly in quest of her whereabouts. Unfortunately, Liz would be of no help to him as her situation regarding Taffie would mirror his.

Clueless, Liz said, "I really don't know, Serge. What do you want her for?" This was somewhat a serious question. As far as Liz was concerned, she and he had some possible unfinished business. The afternoon in the shower was never allowed to progress further than the stage of tender caressing and fondling. Liz hadn't been intimate with anyone, since Taffie, but with a man—Eddie—it had been a few months now! Serge was a person of interest to her now. She didn't want to reduce herself to succumbing to Jeremy Ng's attempts or, God Forbid, the horny Mr. Sakamaki.

Serge, however, didn't seem to be receptive. As usual, his abrupt pattern of communication ended almost as promptly as he began. He said, "Nothing, I must contact with her it is all. Very, important, but . . . if you do not know, it is fine. I am sorry to interrupt you. Good-bye!"

Liz tried to get him to wait, but dude already had hung up. She didn't waste time even calling him back. She looked at the clock and prepared her gym bag for a visit to the fitness club after work that evening.

In another section of town, Kenji's time to gloat over the successful ejection of an unwanted element was short lived. His assistant "second" in command, Suguru Yamada brought it to his attention via abbreviated phone conversation that there was still no new information about the death of Stephanie Pritchard. This was not good news. Not only for Shigeru Watanabe, the head honcho, but also Watanabe's vice squad exec board members, also Kenji's superiors, of course, were shitting bricks about yet another death. This time, it was more serious than the last, as Stephanie's death was an actual murder, whereas Denore Langston's could be written off as a freak accident, which was more her fault than Bozack's, or even the garbage truck operator who mangled her.

Two deaths in almost the same year, or several months within a year's time frame, and the news had also surfaced to the public about Tim Valentine and "other Bozack employees who had been involved in a drug bust. It didn't look good for the company; there was a growing consensus emerging among those who felt that Bozack was drifting away from its image of being a safe haven and comfortable environment for teachers or students. Something had to be done, and since Kenji was the whipping boy, he was the one who had to make the trail of tears to Tokyo—alone—to face the music and get more of his ass grinded by another company of wolves, while Yamada remained in Osaka poised to take the helm.

After the nerve spasmodic bullet train ride riddled with frequent trips to the toilet for unsettled bowels, Kenji met again with Shigeru Watanabe, and this time with his three other exec board members who had been down with him from day one. They all pounced on Kenji and thrashed him with soft-kill criticism and scolding, which, in the end, had Kenji feeling as if he should commit suicide by jumping clean out of the boardroom window from the twentieth floor of that building.

Throughout the entire homily, Kenji was on the brink of tears, and he resolved to break down and apologize for his lack of leadership and the mistakes and errors in official judgment which had led the company to its current crisis in the Osaka area. Taking full blame, he got down on his hands and knees in a Japanese ritualistic type of way to express sorrow, grief, and hope for atonement. When the committee of old fogeys had decided that he had suffered enough, they allowed him to rise and issued him the same basic admonishing Shigeru Watanabe had given Kenji the previous week, and it was basically, "We're going to give you one more chance, but get your act together, or kiss your job good-bye, cretin!" Then they shifted gears and tried to figure out how to catapult back from all of the madness.

So far, Stephanie Pritchard's name or her murder was still not connected to Bozack. Her emergency contact had been notified, but little could be done until that individual came to Japan to claim the body. It was a rigorous detail, and Bozack managed to stay out of it and let the local Tokyo office people who could speak English deal with that end. Until that time, Kenji and his crew could do very little. The important thing, they decided, was to keep the news from the people who might have worked closely with Stephanie, those employees from the South Town schools, especially Namba and Hommachi, where she was based. It was fairly simple, because Stephanie had been transferred away to Saitama where the fatality occurred, and it was far. In essence, she was out of sight and out of mind, and that was how they wanted it to be.

Denore Langston's death, by now, had been kept so far under wraps she was almost completely forgotten. The only person still around who might have possibly even thought of her still was likely her former roommate, Liz. It couldn't be confirmed now since Liz had received a new flatmate, but Denore's passing seemed to conjure less urgency because of the manner in which she met her doom compared to Stephanie. This was because of the board committee considering the disquieting death of Lucie Blackmon at the hands of notorious serial killer Joji Obara, which was big news at the time. Their biggest fear was creating another controversial disturbance of such magnitude to shock the populous.

Kenji was able to keep the bloodthirsty gang of old fogeys satiated with his campaign to rid the company of bad worms and replace them with fresh apples and pledged to spend more time doing more in-depth investigations into hiring better and more qualified applicants and potential employees. He planned on keeping Mitchell "Worm" Swiggler close by and eventually promote him back to head teacher.

He trembled in his oversized Elitous Oxford shoes all the way back to Osaka, hoping that there would be no more events such as these, no more deaths, drug involvements, or nefarious situations that needed to be dealt with anytime soon. Checking his messages, he saw that the persistent Kayo Terumi was still bugging him about something she had wanted to discuss a week earlier in the Tennoji HQ, but he still hadn't gotten back to her; and at this rate, he didn't know when he would. One thing was for sure—he didn't consider it to be of the utmost importance.

66

D EON HAD ONLY been in Japan for
three and a half years. He had arrived
shortly before Liz and Edie and for most of that time, he had worked for the
Bozack Language School Company. His hiring came about during a season when
the company's personnel division—consisting primarily of Japanese and Caucasians
from mostly Australia—preferred that prospective staff be people like them. But
during that moment in time also, which was the late 1990s, within the English
language school business circles, there was a particular acknowledgment that
American pop and the fascinating hip hop culture was rising in huge popularity.
As such, the rising stardom of artists like Maraiah Carey and TLC as well as a
colorful assortment of others would cause some companies to use performers
like the former to grace their national ad campaigns. Yet these endorsements
from popular foreign singers alone wasn't enough to coerce multitudes of student
customers through their businesses' doors. The inclusion of, or decision to hire
more, "people of color" became a short-term agenda.

Bozack was started in the Osaka (Kansai) Western Region of Japan, whereas
established rival companies already had footholds throughout the entire country.
Although a growing entity, they still had to stay competitive, so they hired (or
wanted to hire) people who were more in tune with the latest trends and more
closely associated with the burgeoning genre taking the country and world by
storm. The teachers they already managed to acquire were rejects and throwaways
from other companies whom they gave jobs in acts of desperation to get suitable
teachers. For a while, it worked, but with the emergence of hip hop and pop

culture's slow domination, they would discover that those they already had hired knew very little to "not a damn thing" about soul music or R&B. Moreover, whatever little knowledge of rap music these teachers had was delegated only to comical anecdotes and stereotypical images, and overall carried a negative impression of the arts in question, and their opinions filtered out among the student populous. Thus Bozack circumvented this by a campaign to hire non-whites, and in particular "black people"—those who were associated with the faddish culture, something many of the English language schools were not popular for. They broke new ground in this experiment.

Unlike others who were hired overseas, Deon was hired from within Japan. He had arrived in the country beforehand without any intention at all whatsoever of becoming an English teacher. His reason for traveling abroad had been to participate in mogul club owner Tabriz Najaf's cultural arts program, set to kick off in the city of Osaka, where he opened up his biggest and most provocative nightspot, the Candy Box.

Deon and a score of others like him—recruited from the inner cities of the United States, the Caribbean, and Brazil—were scouted, hired, and brought to Japan in order to be live performers of the new hip hop, reggae, and break dancing arts at Najaf's Candy Box, which was not only to be a disco or dance club, but also a live house offering nightly performances with these artists. It was to be unlike anything Japan had ever seen.

Unfortunately, this project never reached fruition. The Japanese financial supporters and musical affiliations Tabriz Najaf worked in conjunction with to get this project up and running were a kooky bunch of hauteur upstarts who had more of an idea to use the recruited foreign performers to train or teach their arts, dance moves, fighting styles, and the like to up-and-coming Japanese performers. These Japanese would eventually replace the foreigners when their skill sets became impressive enough. The only reason given for this suggestion was because the Japanese organizers felt it would be less costly to train imitators than to afford the costly recruitment of talent from overseas.

Tabriz Najaf immediately had a problem with this idea, as did many others within his faction. For he felt that having authentic performers from the artform's origin countries was the best. Unable to reach common ground with the Japanese section of the planning board, he came to see that the project was doomed.

The icing on the cake resulted when several foreign background dancers from Najaf s squad began hooking up with Japanese female dancers, singers, and up-and-coming artists. Word got back to a music exec who was linked to popular music producers like famous Tetsuo Komuro, that there was a subcommunity on the rise of black men coupling up with Japanese women. This made the Japanese board members antsy and inimical. Finally, when Tabriz didn't agree to the terms board members rendered—get rid of the foreigners after they trained Japanese performers to execute at the same or similar aptitude, then carry on with his plans to make the club, the Candy Box, a live house—the cultural arts program was suddenly canceled. This left a number of people without jobs and little other recourse save for returning to their places of origin, which several did, but not Deon.

Deon, who had been recruited as a type of "dancer," decided that he didn't feel the excessive need to return to his hometown of the Bronx, New York, so quickly. His life back home hadn't been the greatest story to tell anyone, and the trip to Japan had been his first time outside of the United States.

Facing the dismal option of returning to New York and possibly spending time wasting away in a Manhattan business office mailroom basement, his mind steered toward staying in Japan. Especially when persuaded by a set of fellow ensemble group members of Tabriz Najaf who had also decided to remain in Japan to pursue other employment options. His pals, Preston Ciclon and Paz Lucha, were also from the same city; and although they didn't know each other back home, they became good friends in Japan.

Paz Lucha was the first to venture out on his own, hooked up with a nabob gangster and formed his own small English language school. Paz hired Preston to work for him part-time; then Preston found another job at an Umeda transient dump school called Special K. Preston's combined income from both part-time jobs was so impressive he shared his news with Deon, who in turn elected to also "milk the cow" teaching English in Japan. Fate redirected his steps, however, when he responded to a classified ad in the *Kinki Newsletter* regarding Bozack's hiring with a starting salary of three thousand American dollars' equivalent a month, with a thirty-hour work week! He applied for the job, and the rest was history.

During his interview, Ruth Worth was among those who were in favor of not hiring Deon. The consensus seemed to be that due to his eccentric appearance, flashy jewelry, unique hairstyle, and swagger, his type would be outlandish within the company walls and potentially frighten away student customers. The Japanese portion of the hiring decision committee were of mixed feelings that ran the gamut of "Yes," "No," and "Maybe." A sole Canadian member at the time—not Worm—saw no problem with Deon's inclusion among staff. In fact, this person argued successfully on his behalf that Deon would make a good, almost-perfect fit for the diversity campaign that Bozack was trying at that stage to implement. Thus, Deon was placed on the notorious Waiting List to be hired, if none better could be acquired.

Eventually, Deon got the job. At the time, Bozack was one of the only growing, but still considered a major, company in big cities where a black teacher could be seen—even if only in small numbers. As a result, a considerable contingent of Japanese people were willing and interested in spending money to see, sit, and talk with unique foreigners. He received a call about a month after being interviewed and supplied the good news of his hire. Prior to this, he was hanging on by a thread, making small beans working for his pal Paz Lucha part-time and staying at daily hotels that resembled elevated, horizontal coffins called capsules.

Nowadays, he was well into his Japan life, adjusted for the most part, despite the country being astoundingly different than his own. In fact, he liked living in Japan. Sure, it had its ups and downs, but the quality of life he enjoyed, which was being able to walk the streets and not worry about the need to watch his back. He gloated to his people back home about how strict gun laws were in Japan, so he didn't have to worry about walking the blocks at any time of night for fear of his life or getting stuck up for his jewelry.

As for love life, he had his share of women but didn't share with many of his comrades the feverish desire to be with Japanese women. Sure, he liked some of them and found a lot to be attractive, sexy, and appealing; but for the most part, he found that they weren't his type, as he held a stronger desire for women who were more endowed body-wise, whereas his image of the Japanese females was they were too slender for his tastes.

While working for Bozack, he befriended Chicago native Chucky Chilson, who had immense "yellow fever." Chucky tried to influence Deon into sharing his affliction, but Deon was still trapped in an American state of mind, which allowed him to remain attracted to women of all shapes, sizes, and colors. He would party with his crew every now and then and have one-night stands, but never professed to liking solely Japanese women like Chucky, Keefer, Radley, and other coworkers who swore by the country's women being the end-all objects of desire. Having been so close to financial ruin in the days prior to his miracle hiring at Bozack, Deon's main intention became to stack his paper, as he felt such an easy job came rather once in a lifetime, and he intended to make the most of it while trying to hustle on the side, having an astute gambling background of throwing bones, blackjack, and lottery pools.

Finally, the coworker he casually referred to as a "white witch," Elizabeth "Liz" Amberbush, had struck a chord on his good side by introducing him to the stunning and effervescent French teacher Taffie Jolie. Almost immediately, he was enchanted by her, pleasing and surprising him at the same time as barely any young female had been able to do prior in his twenty-eight years of life, even coming out of a large cosmopolitan area such as where he grew up.

Simultaneously, Deon would change his mind about Liz. After hooking up with Taffie and she turned out to be the girl for him—of his dreams, practically—he felt maybe Liz wasn't such a witch after all. At times, he pegged her to be like any other uppity whitey or yuppy, lame, obnoxious, talkative, and an overall drag to be around. Although he could have considered her alluring and glamorous in her own right, he didn't go for her type either. At times she got on his nerves with her antics that he fought the urge to slap her.

He would never have imagined that down toward his last days of working with Bozack that he and Liz would be on friendlier terms. What he didn't like however, was to be dragged onto the molehill she made into a mountain by her involvement with the street smart lacking imbeciles dealing and using illegal drugs; activities that eventually got some of them busted. The one time favor he called himself doing for Liz exploded into something more serious when he interrupted slimy Brad Cooper's attempted assault upon her in that Doyama Village back alley. Now, it was up to him, he felt, to smooth things out, clear his name and make things right as he wanted no smoke with gangster Luzio Silver and his faction.

Luckily, his name was still connected with Tabriz Najaf, who was influential, in his own circle of prominent, wealthy figureheads around town. As such, certain types as Luzio Silver were hesitant to muscle in on Najaf and stayed clear of his establishments, and in Osaka, the Candy Box was one of those places. In the beginning, Najaf had trouble with the riff-raff, but he cleaned up the image, instituted a "dress code" on most nights, and Luzio's ilk stayed clear, but Deon and his "homeboys" were still welcome.

Paz Lucha was originally a street guy who hailed from Brooklyn, New York—Brownsville to be precise—and he indulged heavily in the pot, even in Japan where it was banned. This did not prevent him from dealing weed from time to time as a side hustle while operating his own small English School in the "Suminoe Park" district on Osaka City's extreme south side. Like scores of others, he got his goods from Luzio Silver, but recently, he had struck gold when another pal, Preston "Cyclone" hit him up with a "pillow" of grass. How Cyclone had come upon this heap of contraband was a shady side-story in itself, but he had connections with folks in the real estate business in another part of town. When other drug dealers got busted, their unconfiscated sizzle was at times abandoned in mailbox slots of their apartments. Cyclone somehow got his hands on one of these bundles from a third party and would then turn this over to Paz, and at a good time too. With the disappearance of Luzio Silver, the dope fiend streets were desperate in his absence. Paz would prosper for a while doing his weed selling side gig, his profits tripled. It wouldn't last forever though, and he had to score some new connects if Luzio was permanently out of the picture.

Coming from a gritty background himself, Paz and Silver became good, on amicable terms, similar to how the Brazilian had been with Tim 'the Duke" Valentine. When his pal Deon debriefed him about what had gone down in Doyama Village, Paz felt it necessary to intervene. He was able to convince Luzio that Deon had no involvement with any of the snitches who caused him to go into hiding.

Deon was still uneasy. Not to mention, his recent dismissal from Bozack had him even more edgy. Somewhat fuming with outrage that Worm would sink to such a low level and report his having a beer while scheduled to work, he was seriously considering evening the score. For, clearly now he was in a bad situation. Jobless, he had a little scratch saved up, but with rent due, he knew he was on borrowed time before the hard times would once again come knocking. He had to think of something quick. He didn't want to do it, but if he had to, he too would deal dope if it kept him from being homeless in a foreign country.

Preston "Cyclone" offered to introduce him to the places around town he worked; various small-time English Schools, host clubs in Umeda, roving gigolo, and such. Deon almost took a job at transient trap school Special K, but he was interrupted by a series of phone calls. One was from Liz. He had no intention of calling her back, at least not right away. He figured she desired for him to score some coke or weed for her again, and he wasn't having it. The other phone calls were from Paz Lucha. With him, Deon did return the call.

Paz's husky voice on the line told Deon to shoot by his place when he was done. Paz lived in Suminoe, where his English school was located. Deon took the dark-blue subway line Yotsubashi, to the last stop. Paz scooped him up at the bus station outside the subway hole underneath the new tram underpass. They greeted each other with a pleasant, intricate handshake dap as Deon hopped into the front seat of Paz's Suzuki wagon car.

Paz was a buff, muscular-built individual with pecan-brown gingerbread complexion. His dreadlocks were now touching the tips of his broad shoulders, as opposed to the shorter length it was when he and Deon met a couple years earlier. Many people in the know likened his facial features to those of R&B sensation Maxwell, or implied that he could be a close relative in resemblance; but when he was recruited by Tabriz Najaf, he was supposed to have been one of the rappers, not a sultry love ballad singer.

Paz and Deon made small talk as Paz cruised his marijuana-and-sandalwood-incense-infused ride along Suminoe Street. Paz had been smoking a pinky-finger-sized spliff that he offered to Deon for a hit, but he politely declined. They turned down a side street before reaching the huge police precinct and drove until arriving at Yamatogawa Street where Paz's building was. He deaded the spliff and parked his ride in the lot of his building residence.

When they disembarked the ride, Paz said, "Yeah man, we're gonna put this Luzio Silver issue to bed tonight. This whole shit's been a misunderstandin', and I don't want none of my boys mixed up in no unnecessary bullshit."

Up inside Paz's spacious two-bedroom apartment, a small party was in progress. Deon and Paz joined the already-present Preston "Cyclone" who greeted the former with a similar decorative, elaborate handshake, followed by a one-arm embrace. He was followed by two other black guys of similar age and stature, one named Curtis Allgood and another named Lester. Three dizzy, ostentatiously-fashioned Japanese girls were there too, drinking various alcoholic beverages, smoking cigarettes and weed, with Jay-Z rap music playing in the background, yammering, "Can I get a . . ."

Less than a half hour into the festivity, Paz got a phone call. It was Luzio Silver. Then Paz cleared out his apartment and told everyone except Preston to basically beat it. By the time Luzio made his appearance, Curtis, Lester, and the three girls had bounced.

Tonight, Luzio wasn't with his entourage of menacing, musclebound redneck white boys and rolled solo. Everyone repeated their ritualistic, de rigueur daps and greetings with Luzio, and they sat down at the 40" x 72" rectangular, glazed pewter–finished dining room table. Paz poured everyone, including himself, a glass of Maker's Mark Bourbon.

Deon was the first to complain. "Aw, man!"

"Aw, quit actin' so square, mother fucker," Paz teased as he screwed the cap back on the bottle of whiskey. "Anyways, we know you be drinkin' with all your damn white coworkers."

Preston chimed in, "He don't work there no more. He came on board with me at my school, G. Ain't 'at right, D?"

"Yeah, sort of." Deon said, squinting as he took a sip of the bourbon. "But I ain't always tryna get lit up like you, motherfuckaz. You just like them—y'all get fucked up every day. Damn, that ain't my style."

Paz laughed. "As dizzy as these Japs are, I need some heavy drugs to get me through these lessons I gotta teach these motherfuckaz every day."

Preston agreed. "Hell yeah, sometimes it's like I gotta smoke a 'eL' before I teach a class, otherwise, these non-interesting clowns gonna put me to sleep. Plus, I only get mostly dude students!"

Deon said emphatically, "Hell yeah, I noticed that. Me too! Who does the schedule over there at Special K?"

Preston said, "I dunno, *familia*, but all's I know is, alla'the white boys be getting' the superhot Japanese *chiquita*s, man—younger ones too! But I get stuck with all these borin'ass, business men in suits, or nerdy fuckers in raincoats that don't talk about shit!"

Luzio had remained relatively quiet during this exchange, but he stared intently at the congregation gathered. His English ability was better than average, but he still struggled with pronunciation and grammatical issues. In appearance, his hairstyle resembled Deon's—slick, lustrous, and relatively long, almost shoulder length. Facially, he had a thicker set of lips, wider nostrils, and darker complexion. Contrary to Deon, Luzio seldom appeared to be frowning and mostly wore a pair of shades, even in the dark lounges of nightclubs. Tonight, was no different. He gulped his glass of whiskey and set his glass back down on the table. A gold bracelet watch glistened on his wrist as he moved his glass toward Paz for a refill.

Taking that as a cue, Paz said, "Let's get down to business, folks."

Luzio said, "Yeah, brothers, I wan' to apologize to jyu, about that fokin' guy Brad. Actually, that motherfoker, he don' work for me. That guy, he's Moose's friend. Moose, that guy he work for me, but not that Brad. He's just a motherfoker likes to hang around Moose and pretend like he is gangster. He want to make a name for himself around town, but everybody know him, he's an asshole. Sometime, he try to cut side deals, jyu know, he try to sell drugs and fake like he big drug dealer. Foreign people, they trust him, since if they don't know me, they can go to him. He sell higher price, of course."

Paz poured Luzio another tall glass of the bourbon. He had heard tidbits about the Brad character. Word was he was selling parsley and basil with maybe a smidgen of real marijuana and passing it off to people as legit.

Therewith Paz said, "Cool, I'm glad we could get this situation cleared up. My man Deon here, ain't in no way had your name mixed up with no cops, bro. That ain't how us New York cats get down. Now, that brother Tim . . . well, it's fucked up he didn't uphold the code, but—"

Luzio said, "That was because Tim brought *menina branca*—the white girl—to my attention. He int'oroduce her to me. Don't none of the other white people ever contacted me—only Tim and only that white girl. That's why Brad got suspicious. He think he doing me a favor, but I got some even more crazy, fucked-up news."

All grew quiet as Luzio's statement warranted their close consideration. Paz, who was doing most of the talking while Deon and Preston sat in awed presence of the underworld figure, pried Luzio for the information he was to purge.

"So what's happenin'?" Paz inquired.

Luzio finished his drink and said, "That other girl, the fat one . . . she get killed. I hear she is dead now. Somebody wasted her. Over in Tokyo somewhere."

His words sent shockwaves through the veins of his audience at the table. Deon reacted with his confused look intensified.

Slightly taken aback, Deon said, "Who's that? What fat girl?" Initially, he assumed the girl Luzio was talking about was Stephanie, as she would have been the only person who fit the description; however, he was unaware that Stephanie had been transferred out of Osaka and relocated to the Tokyo area.

Luzio confirmed her identity, stating, "The girl who went to the station when Tim got arrest. She is die."

Deon was like, "Are you fuckin' serious? C'mon man, you gotta be bullshittin' me . . . That bitch can't be dead! Who mirked her?"

Luzio shrugged indifferently. "I don' know. But it was no me, my brother. And I don' know who kill her, but my connection people over there give word back to me here that she is dead. Nobody know who did it. They rob her too, take her money, and kill her. I think choke to her. So I think jyu maybe should be careful. Maybe she have more enemy than jyu know about."

Deon said, "Well, that motherfucker Brad pulled a knife out on Liz when I stopped him that time. I think he was plannin' on doin' her. You think that fool might have done it?"

Luzio shook his head. "No, ees impossible. He always is here in Osaka, following Moose or one of my other boys around, tryin' to hang with the big dogs. Besides, he don' know his way around Tokyo at all. A sloppy guy like him? No . . . the police would already have catch him. No, this was somebody else. Like I say, maybe she have more enemy than jyu know about. Maybe the white girl, the 'Lizabeth chick, she might have same enemies, I don' know for sure, but I think because they were good friend, from what I gather."

Struggling to recover from the newsflash, Deon said, "Damn, that's some heavy shit you layin' on me, partner."

Luzio continued, "I'm still on the run. The cops are lookin' for me, but they don't have no hard evidence against me. They raided one of my spots, but they not able to pin nothin' on me as of yet. I'm gonna blow town for a while. I going to lay low down in Mie Prefecture for a while. I got a secret spot down there. I'll be back in a few months when all this blows over. Until then, ain't nobody gon' be able to contact me. But I just want jyu to know, everything is cool. Jyu an' me don't got no problem. Jyu ain't never fucked me over, an' I trust jyu and jour boys. Tim is a rat motherfoker, but I'll deal with him some other day. Jyu guys is different. I don't like your boss, though, the *Iran* motherfoker, he own that club in Kyobashi . . ."

Paz said, "Who? You mean Tabriz? Is he from Iran or Iraq? Don't remember, but anyway man, we don't deal with that low-life scumbag no more. He fucked us over."

Deon had a different take on the issue. He said, "Nah, not really, Paz. I still fucks wit' Tabriz every now an' then. What happened wasn't really his fault."

Preston said, "Word, Tabriz is cool. He still calls me every now and then to see how I'm doin'. He always let us in his club for free too."

Deon said, "Yeah, Tabriz don't control who signs the papers for our visas in Japan. The Japanese motherfuckaz do. Those was the people he was doin' business with, and they was the ones who pulled the plug on our entire gig."

Paz said bitterly, "And leavin' us stranded here in Japan with no place else to go, jobless, and almost homeless. Luckily, we all found some hustles."

Preston said, "Word, *claro*, homeboy, and you ain't doin' bad for yourself either. It's almost like a blessing in disguise."

Paz said amicably, "Well, whatever, I don't fuck with Tabriz Najaf, man, but as you can see, these cats still do. So whateva beef you got with Tabriz, I can dig it."

Luzio concluded his preliminary business of correspondence geared toward absolving Deon of any problematic issues with him and his faction. He slid his chair back and rose up from the table as if he was preparing to leave. At that moment, he and Paz exchanged secretive glances with one another, then excused themselves to another sector of the apartment, leaving Preston and Deon alone in the dining room area.

Paz said, "Dee, Cyclone, y'all hang tight right here for a minute. Me 'n boss man got some business to take care of." He dipped out of the room. Luzio was behind him, but not before extending a spell of farewell pleasantries to Deon and Preston.

"Damn man," Deon said, feeling as if perhaps another drink would do him some good after all in light of what he had just heard from Luzio. "That's some cold shit. I wonder who in the hell woulda offed Stephanie like that? Yeah, she was an obnoxious, drunkard bitch, but she was relatively harmless!"

Preston, who actually knew Stephanie, had met Liz before briefly perhaps once or twice, and was rumored to have had an illicit affair with Vicky, knew the type of person Stephanie was. He said, "Well, she did have a big fuckin' mouth."

Deon said, "Yeah, no argument there. She's worthy of a punch in the face every now and then, but I couldn't imagine anyone getting' so riled up from her shit enough t'wanna kill her. That shit so close to home, just don't sit right wit' me. Cyclone . . . it's fucked up."

Preston said, "I thought dude said Tokyo? What the fuck was she doin' way the hell out there? She was workin' here in Osaka wit'y'all, right?"

"Yeah, that's why I was stumped at first when Luzio said chubby girl because the only chick around us like that is Stephanie." Deon decided to gulp down some whiskey and pour himself another glass. "Stephanie is plump. All the rest of the bitches around the schools I work at look a little thick, but in all the good places."

Preston started simpering, laughing as if he cradled a big secret in his mind he didn't want to share. But he hinted at his attraction toward certain women they had mentioned in their earlier conversations. He said, "Yeah, white girls are skinny back home, but I think if they come to Japan and gain a bunch'a weight, they look better, huh?"

Deon looked at Preston, like, *"What is this nigga talkin'about?"* But it didn't come out because he abhorred dropping the N-bomb home or abroad. Instead, his mind flashed to think about Liz, at Preston's mention of white girls. In lieu of Stephanie's death—by murder at that— he wondered if he should give her a heads-up. After all, they had at one time been close, she and Stephanie; whoever had got to Stephanie all the way out in Tokyo could have surely done the same to Liz as well.

Now he was stuck with some heavy considerations. Should he get involved? After all, he had never snitched on anyone; he barely did drugs at all and was, for the most part, like Paz had alluded, a square who kept his nose clean—literally too. Luzio tonight gave him his word that there was no beef he had with him. Nobody was trying to cut him with a blade in city slums, so why get involved with Liz's affairs? Since he no longer worked at Bozack, they were not even coworkers anymore. His only tie to her was merely for the fact that she had set him up on a blind date with Taffie, which turned out to be temporarily satisfactory, but now Taffie too had hit the wind without a trace, and he wasn't any more improved in well-being as a result.

Deon's network of thought had its program interrupted by the pattering sounds of footsteps. He turned abruptly while his heart revved like a turbo race engine, thinking the cops had raided Paz's spot. He was relieved when he saw Paz grinning a gold tooth cap at him, ushering along two buffed redneck-looking individuals inside the apartment. Each were carrying shoebox-sized parcels underneath both of their arms.

Paz was saying to the white guys, "This way, last door on the left. Set them down in there."

Luzio appeared at the apartment door, still wearing his sunglasses at night. It seemed then that he had brought his entourage after all, but they had been waiting downstairs by his ride the whole entire time, doing the lookout thing. Although Deon was glad the cops hadn't raided the place, he wasn't too thrilled about being present there too much longer. He may have been straying toward the L7, but it didn't take a genius to get wise to the fact they all knew what those white boys had in those bundles. Deon figured there was no way of reasoning with Brooklyn people; he never could and probably never would. He liked Paz, but he wasn't fond of how he danced in the shadows of danger.

Almost a half hour later, Luzio and his boys had dispersed. Deon and Preston too prepared to file out homeward bound. Of course, Paz was volunteering to whisk them away to their destinations in his ride, but Deon adamantly refused and talked his whiskey-breathing homeboy down.

He said, "C'mon, Paz, man, hell no! You been drinkin' an' smokin' all night. Cops catch you drivin' around, you gonna lose your license and your business! Plus, no tellin' what kinda shit they might find up in your car!"

'Yeah a'ite," Paz said huskily, seemingly convinced by the fact he loved having a car and being able to drive around the city, one of the few foreigners lucky enough to have a driver's license in Japan. "So how you gonna get home, taxi?"

Preston said, "Dude I live in Shinkitajima . . . I can walk. Peace out, you guys.

Lucha, I'll see you tomorrow afternoon!" They dapped on farewell, and seconds later, Preston was off.

Paz said, "I forgot that nigga live around here. Where you stayin' at these days?"

"Miyakojima," Deon said flatly, rolling his eyes as if he dreaded going back to the place he mentioned, but he surely wasn't going to crash at Paz's place.

"Where the fuck's that?" Paz asked quizzically.

Deon said, "North side, way north side. Polar opposite of here."

"Gonna cost you some paper to get back there by cab, son." Paz shook his head. He lit up a menthol cigarette and told Deon, "Yo, hang back for a second, my dude. Let me holla't you 'bout some shit."

Deon shrugged, slightly annoyed, but figured he might as well because he was in no absolute hurry. He watched as Paz disappeared back into the hallway, blowing out smoke. Deon closed the apartment door and instinctively locked it. In a moment, Paz returned with one of the shoeboxes. Deon started laughing because now he knew where this conversation was headed. He could almost script it in his head like a cheap, blacksploitation movie plot, but one formulated in the 1990s.

Paz was like, "So I heard you lost your job with that white boy company. I guess now that white boy salary ain't gonna be comin' in like it used to. You workin' over there at that English school wit' Cyclone ain't gonna scrape you enough beans to support whatever rent you got, bills, plus all the fancy clothes, brother. Tell me I'm lyin'."

Deon couldn't disagree. He knew he was a stronger person, but for whatever reason, he felt compelled to continue listening to Paz even though his gut told him the dialogue was leading to nowhere good imminently.

"Cyclone thinks he got it figured out. He swears he's a ladies' man, a pimp, player. He wants to sing at Ambush, or some bitch-made host job at night with a bunch of old cougar broads uptown. Then work two legit jobs in the daytime— one for me and one over there with you. He swear by that, he's gonna get rich. Bro, I got a different idea." Paz revealed the contents of the shoebox parcel to Deon.

No surprise, there was a collection of plastic bags, wraps, and containers filled with what looked to be a third of grassy marijuana, caplets, pills, and glassine bags of off-white powder. In a macabre, offbeat way, within the dim cerise shade of the room, the contents appeared like candy and confections, sparkling like magic in the night. Eerie reflections settled upon the glow in Deon's eyes.

Paz said, "An' I got four more of these. Bro, I think one of these weed batches alone gonna keep my rent paid for the whole year." He started laughing like a madman."

Not unimpressed, Deon's curiosity got the better of him. He asked, "So what's up wit'you an' Silver? Now you gonna be his new 'Duke'? Or you tryna be the new Silver or some shit?"

Paz smirked as if he were offended. "Sheesh . . . nigga, look, I ain't tryna be the new nobody. This all about me, my brother. I'm just sayin', you can be down. This is what I know I can do. This shit is in my blood. Easy as pie, I could do it back home, it's even more easy here!!"

Deon said, "Yeah, but riskier . . . I mean, you heard about what happened to Tim."

Paz said, "Man, Tim had to'a been a punk, man. I'm sorry. I don't think he was a real one, man, but fuck Tim. This ain't about him. It's about here and now, my brother, and takin' advantage of an opportunity.

"Silver is gonna lay low for a minute. He ain't gonna be on the scene. That means, there's gonna be a lotta undercover junkies out there flakin'. It's gonna be thirsty hour 24/7 out in them streets. People gonna be buyin' and sellin' from this-that-here-n'there-ass dealers around town, and for a higher price too!" Paz paused and set his parcel down on the coffee table in the living room.

He continued, "And you already know you have a built-in customer base." He gripped a plastic-sealed bundle of grass the size of three crackerjack boxes taped together, placed it forcefully in Deon's grip.

Deon couldn't believe he was taking it. He laughed as the scenario played itself out, scripted in his mind beforehand prognosticated.

"You don't owe me nothin', brother," Paz said. "You owe it to yourself. I don't know about you, but I came here because of my God-given talent, not to slave my life away working for no white man or no yellow man tryna disguise himself as a white man. Fuck that. I can rap, I can do graffiti, I can DJ and I can sell drugs, *and I'm good at it*! Don't miss out on the gravy train if you can too, ya dig?"

"Yeah, man, maybe you're right." Deon couldn't believe he was agreeing with Paz. It was almost as if he was existing outside of himself and watching his life flash before him on a screen, and he silently tried to warn himself to not make utterly ruinous decisions. Only, this time the voice of reason was snuffed out.

Roughly an hour later, Deon would receive a phone call on his cellular. The incoming call had numerous digits that surpassed the normal eleven digits of a national call from within Japan. Deon had seen this before and enough times to know that it was a call from overseas; upon closer observation, he saw it was the familiar number of his former residence in the Bronx. He halted his steps en route to his apartment in the Daito-cho section of Miyakojima, North Osaka, to immediately take the call. It wasnt very often he got calls from home, so naturally, his first impulse was to be worried.

Deon clicked on the Talk feature and heard the frantic voice of his younger brother, seventeen-year-old Aguila Clemente. "Yo, Dee! Yo Dee!" His voice was so charged with emotion he sounded as if he was crying.

Indescribably jittery, Deon, replied "What's good, *hermanito*? You sound *frenetico* as hell, calm down. Whats up?"

"Dee! Dee!" Aguila practically screamed. "You did it, man! We got it! You gotta come home right away! Oh, *Dios mio* . . . damn, bro . . . we got it! Please, come home as soon as you can!"

Deon was able to listen with patience to the rest of the conversation spewed by his younger brother and, before it was all over, understood the reason for his sibling's jubilant demeanor. Indeed, the news he received gave him cause to immediately cancel his schedule, promptly book a flight, and return he did to the United States.

67

LIZ WAS AT the sweaty kickboxing sub-unit gym at her exercise club, training under the tutelage of a sham fitness club instructor. She vowed to use the techniques and intensity of her punches on Brad or anyone else who tried to assault her should she bump into them in the near future. She felt strangely relieved after throwing haymaker punches at inflated airbags and, in general, refreshed after the workout. Skipping the shower, she elected to hit her favorite massage parlor, the Thai spot in Kujo. Tok and Vot, the sister team who operated the joint, were Liz's undeniable heroines. For the entire time she had lived in Osaka City, and in that neighborhood, their Thai massage parlor was never closed when she went. They operated until late and always were able to fit Liz in on their schedule. While under their care, Liz was convinced that their hands could work wonders unlike any Midas-touch magician the world had to offer. After the kickboxing charade exhibition at the gym, Liz hit the Thai massage spot before going home.

As usual, the experience relaxed and soothed her. The shower she skipped at the gym was better at the Thai spot, as the water was hotter and with more force from the faucet. Exotic lilac-and-balsam-infused soap from the Orient served to add more of a tingle to the cleansing process. Her aching muscles were kneaded like dough on the padded cot where she lay naked. Tok or Vot would then use one of many soothing special unguent ointments from their native Thailand's jungles. Oftentimes, this alone was enough to send her head into an orbital course through a higher galaxy of consciousness; on other such occasions, she would climax herself.

Tonight it would hit her: her new aspiration in life, for the future. It was this! She would learn the art of massage. Not only that, she also could take the time to seriously study all the techniques Tok and Vot used. She thought she could learn about all the quaint, demulcent oils they used, the topical ointments, and their paregoric effects. Even the calming effects of the music in the background and the subtle but brash fragrance of jasmine, sandalwood, and myrrh of the air was the sudden subject of her interest.

Finally, it hit her: how she could fit her study of ways to improve human functioning in a career that interested her. She wouldn't just be another aromatherapist, fake faith healer, or massage spa operator—no, she would apply the Secrets of the Orient, which she picked up authentically from Tok and Vot, two Thai women living in Japan. She needed not take a course; she needed only to take a photo or two, should anyone question her credentials. No one could accuse her of lying. All she had to do was get the Thai sisters to pull her coat about the oils, ointments, and herbal concoctions they used and learn the functions for which they were applied. The salutary effects would be the difference between her place, her salon, and the others.

She pictured it all in her mind. Liz would have her own aesthetic salon, or health spa. Focusing on mental and emotional issues while at the same time improving health and beauty through a colorful and unusual lens. She would deck the place out to look like a resort in Asia, like something she had seen in Japan, or a scenic locale on the Pacific Rim, or maybe even like Hawaii. It didn't matter. She would have her own thing, and maybe she would have a love interest.

Oddly, the comical idea of Carver coming back into the picture caused a moment's injection of humor in Liz's fantasy muse. Then she considered it seriously the next minute, but still with a devilish smirk. What if she did get back together with Carver? At least give him an opportunity to buy her dinner, or take her out, assuming he didn't have anyone, or if he was still single and unattached. When they went out, spent time together, Liz imagined, she would then see where his head was after all of these years. It was obvious, in his e-mails, he still had a zealous interest in her and her well-being. If he hadn't changed, Liz suspected that he would still be the piteous pushover he always was and would be. Still, he would be just another one of Liz's boy toys, as was Eddie; but unlike him, she humored herself, Carver wouldn't run away! He wouldn't stray like Eddie did. In fact, after all that time, and in the wake of the abuse suffered at her doing, Carver had yet to banish Liz from his thoughts. Not even close. Now what began as a thought in jest had grown to a considerable option.

Liz was awakened from her reverie absorption to be made aware her servicing for that evening had concluded. Tok, who had been undertaking the procedural operation of finger-working Liz's muscles into blissfully revived bodily components, gently helped raise the pendulant-breasted American girl up from the cot. Liz thanked her immediately and exchanged small, cordial talk with the elder Asian woman, in both English and some Japanese. How she loved that massage parlor, and she would miss the place, especially when she returned to America. Before she left that night, however, she made good on her secret mission to get a tutorial on the herb- and apothecary-type demulcents and oils their shop used. She got an abbreviated lesson that particular night but gravely intended to continue where she left off upon future visits.

Liz arrived home slightly before midnight. The clutter of shoes at the entrance of her apartment's door reminded her that tonight was the Thursday Night Filipino Fiesta. Only, like before, the party had died down to Ingrid and her obnoxious guy pals Janz and Francisco. In fact, Janz appeared to be Ingrid's love interest. Liz heard her hint around it, but due to some Roman Catholic–type restrictions, they were "taking it slow." Francisco, on the other hand, Liz could see, had wandering eyes that often landed upon her so heavily she could feel them creeping upon her when her head was turned. After the experience with Mr. Sakamaki, guys like Francisco she didn't want anywhere near her when she was about to sleep.

Thinking she was going to have to open a can of whoop-ass and throw everyone out, Liz stepped out of her sneaks and threw them down aggressively on the floor. All eyes, including additional eyewear goggles worn by Ingrid, fell on Liz as if she was Mama Bear coming home from a hard day's work and they were naughty children, smiling as if they had concealed a broken vase or tumultuous household disaster. Their expressions were gleeful and beaming with hope.

Ingrid rose from her chair and went into the kitchen area, but not before greeting Liz with a heartfelt, warm welcome. She then said, "Hey, if you're hungry, we have a lot of *sinigang* and stew left. Here, I'll fix you a bowl."

Janz muttered, "It's really good. Marcia and the girls made it."

Usually, Liz would take a whiff of the air and pass, but tonight seemed a bit more normal. She was uncommonly hungry tonight and decided to take a bite of Ingrid's concoction. She saw her fix a bowl and apply it to rice, and Liz figured that it couldn't be too terrible. She placed her books and gym bag down in her section of the quarters before returning to the kitchen party of sorts. Janz and Francisco were drinking beers, laughing and talking in Tagalog before Liz joined them at the table. She tasted the stew and found it to be much too sour for her taste, but she elected to scoff it down quickly and drown the taste with a beer she claimed from a collection of cans on the table. Ingrid offered her more, and of course, Liz declined. She cited that she had eaten earlier and felt it was a sufficient-enough lie. Now her pressing thoughts pertained to the time when Janz and Francisco would be leaving.

Liz hated to be selfish, but at the same time, she did not think so much of it as being such; instead, she felt that she was entitled to having her way. Were it the other way around, she felt she would be the same way. If Janz wanted to spend some time with Ingrid, he should take her to his place, or a hotel. If he couldn't afford it, this wasn't Liz's fault, she reasoned.

Furthermore, she had but only a little bit of grass left, and she had intended to enjoy it all for herself. Now that she was completely dry of sources from which to get stuff, she didn't feel as if she could extend enough kindness to share hers with them like she did before. She knew it was coming. She knew one of them would eventually ask her. They were looking at Liz like she was a Christmas elf about to bestow gifts upon them ever since she had arrived home. She also disliked being the bearer of bad news, but it was imminent that she would deliver it if they were hanging around with the expectation she would whip out her magic pipe.

Then it came. Ingrid said, "Liz . . . like, we were like . . . um, thinking . . . well, we were like wondering if like, we can . . ."

Janz cut her off and finished her fumbling. "What she's tryna say is, we want to buy some of your ganja. I . . . I'll even pay you extra."

Liz laughed she said, "Sorry, dude, but I really am assed totally out. I have no more. I'm completely barren."

Janz's and Francisco grimaced as if they had been punched in their guts with a spiked fist. They began a trio's torrent of Tagalog conversation. Ingrid angrily raised her voice and appeared to be reprimanding Janz as if he had said something offensive. He looked down at the floor and avoided eye contact with Liz, which made Liz think he had been saying something about her that was less than polite in the foreign tongue they used. To Liz, it all sounded like someone gargling mouthwash. It was the same as Japanese spoken around her on a day-to-day basis. The sentiment, however, wasn't lost on Liz though. She could see that Ingrid's friends were visibly upset. Still, Ingrid appeared to have taken Liz's word for the truth and had defended her apparently.

Ingrid said, "It's totally fine, Liz, like . . . really, we understand. It's just, like, well, we like to get stuff like that. Or, well, like Janz and Francisco like to get high when they DJ at the clubs sometimes. It's all . . . I mean, like, it's no big deal, really . . ."

Liz felt somewhat like a heel. She didn't mind sharing what little she had with Ingrid if it came down to it, but she felt no obligation to smoke out her boys. Additionally, she wasn't a dealer and had no desire to be one, and was growing to detest people treating her like one. Even if she had enough to share, she wouldn't want to sell it off. She almost regretted admitting to Ingrid that she even used the stuff. Now she was feeling a bit sorry for her, so Liz decided she would see if she could help her out, unsure, however, to what avail it would arrive.

Checking her sports watch, which had the time to be at precise midnight, she picked up her cell phone and said to the three's company, "Look, I'm gonna make a couple of calls, but I can't promise you anything."

Janz and Francisco looked at each other as if spontaneously cheered up. A glimmer of hope festered in their sharp oval eyes. Tagolog talk continued quietly while Liz rose up from the table to go for her phone call. She rang up Deon, of course.

Deon's phone call resulted in a Japanese recording. Not surprisingly, Liz couldn't understand it. She asked, "Anyone here understand Japanese? What does this mean, Ingrid?"

She passed Ingrid her cell phone. Ingrid had studied Japanese and spoke it reasonably well. Her comprehension skills were put to the test when she took the phone to her ear to hear the recording. After a collection of seconds, she handed the phone back to Liz.

Ingrid said, "Oh, the person you called, is, like, in a place where the signal can't reach it . . . the person is like, out of range, or something."

With that, Liz was all out of ideas, exhausted of options. She spat out harshly, "And just where the total fuck could he be?" Had she still been on good terms with Luzio Silver, copping sizzle would be as simple as ordering a pizza. Reliable service, and twenty-four hours too. But now the only person she knew who had access to that world, the only person she could trust was Deon. And he couldn't be reached. She redialed him and received the same recording.

Tim was gone, Stephanie was gone, Jeremy wasn't a pot smoker at all, Keefer and Radley were more into booze and shrooms, and these days they weren't on the best of terms. Her mind flashed back to shine light on all the individuals she knew who enjoyed getting high and drew a blank until she absentmindedly flicked her phone tab. This new phone could store more numbers than her previous Tuka Phone. She came across her device's registered record of the previous twenty-some calls she had placed. Toward the end of that list, dating back to several weeks prior, she saw the name she misspelled "Yo" for Yoh, or Yoshiyo Wamushi. That handsome Japanese boy she bumped into at the Sakamakis' residence, the same night Mr. Sakamaki flipped his lid and got freaky with her polished pods.

She remembered Yoh's generosity at Mr. Sakamaki's mother's birthday party, sharing his "mother milk" weed stick with her then. It was a long shot, she realized, but it was worth an attempt. So despite the late hour, she contacted him.

After a series of persistent chiming, a sleepy voice answered the phone. Liz made sure that she woke Yoh up further by greeting him with a louder-than-usual animated voice while apologizing for waking him up.

She said, "This is Elizabeth. You remember me, right? Jill's friend—last time we met was at Mr. Sakamaki's place a while ago."

Yoh's slumber-soaked voice oozed into the receiver. "Yes . . . yes, of course, I remember you. What's wrong? What happened? Are you OK?"

Liz was pleased and relieved that Yoh remembered her. It seemed he wasn't outraged with her calling him so late. Without wasting precious time, Liz got to the point of why she called. Using leverage of what she knew about him and his relationship with Vicky—or Jill as she became known by some by her alter-ego—she pressed him like she intended to lead him on.

Liz said, "Hey, I'm really sorry to bother you, but Jill used to tell me how you were such a sweet guy . . ."

Yoh was like, "What!? She did? You . . . you spoke to her recently?" His voice sounded so elated Liz could almost envision him springing up in his bed, now fully awake.

With that momentum, Liz said, "I did, yeah, we had a nice long talk about you. I'd like to tell you everything, but it's really important that I see you tonight. Do you, by chance, have any of that stuff . . . you remember? That stuff we smoked at Mr. Sakamaki's house that time? Do you have any of it, Yoh?"

Yoh said, "You mean . . . like . . . the marijuana? Um, yes, I don't have, but I can get some of it. Do . . . do you want?"

"Yes! Yes!" Liz cried, practically screaming in the dude's phone ear. She said, "I need it tonight, Yoh. I'm really sorry to bother you. I promise I will never ask you anything like this ever again. Look, I'll even pay you for it."

There was a moment of silence and pause, but not because Yoh was speechless. It was because he was putting on his pants and getting dressed. He then said, "No, it's OK . . . you don't have to do that. I'm really surprised . . . I want to know about Jill . . ."

Liz felt pangs of shame having fibbed about talking to Vicky (Jill). She and the British girl had fallen out of communication so long ago Liz was unaware that she had even left the country. It didn't matter, though; she could fabricate a conversation she had just to placate Yoh and achieve her goal of getting some dope, and simultaneously get the Ingrid and crew off her back. So far so good; it looked as if he would.

Liz said, "Yeah, um, do you have a lot of that stuff?"

Yoh said, "Not so much, but I can give you all of it. I can get more later, anytime. For you, I will because you are Jill's best friend."

Liz took her celly and cradled it against her chest as if she was silencing noise intake. She gave Ingrid and the intently staring audience a thumbs-up wink of hope. She got back on the phone with Yoh, who was still talking.

Liz interrupted and asked, "So where should we meet? Shall I come over to your place?"

Yoh's voice sounded troubled. He said, "No . . . well, you see, it's complicated. I don't keep that here. It's at another place. It will take me some time to get it. If you like, maybe I can give it to you tomorrow . . ."

"No," Liz almost shouted. "Tonight is fine. I mean, we—I can wait, take all the time you need. As a matter of fact, let's meet at . . . geez . . ." Liz didn't know right away of any place she could meet him. It was enough trouble trying to meet foreigners like herself in Japan by listing any discernable landmarks or spots familiar to most, but with Japanese people, it could be considerably more complex. She remembered how Hitomi's directions to the Tuka phone station had her wandering all over Umeda in a wild-goose chase. Because it was after midnight, many of the fast-food, tea and coffee shops were closed; options were slim. Then she remembered—the Candy Box! She knew he knew that place. Everybody did. In fact, what little she did remember of his and Vicky's affair, their first date was in the Kyobashi District where the club was. She remembered that night like a blur as if faded memories were returning. She, Eddie, Deon, and his friends met Stephanie, Vicky, and, for the first time, Yoh at a clamorous bar in Umeda. She almost took him for a soft-spoken, "dweebish" Latino, but recalled seeing him around the Higobashi Bozack School once or twice prior. As the pieces fell further into place, Liz's data on Yoh had him being a wuss who could be easily used and abused.

Liz asked Yoh if he could meet her at the Candy Box Club. Yoh seemed servile, almost pleased to do so. Possibly, as if he was expecting to meet Liz like it was a date. He ended the call and tended to his business, preparing to leave. He stashed his goods in a locked mail slot at one of the janky slum apartments owned by Mr. Sakamaki where he worked as a head handyman.

When Liz put away her phone, she returned to the kitchen area where Ingrid and the others awaited. She delivered the sobering good news.

"You might be in luck," Liz said. "I just talked to a guy. He said he'll meet us in Kyobashi. I don't know how much he has, but—"

Janz said, "How much does he want for it?"

Liz didn't mention anything to Yoh about the price; she only stated that she offered to pay for it. She hadn't expected for Yoh to tell her that he was going to bless her with it for free. Deciding to play it by ear, Liz simply stated, "Just pay whatever when you finally get it. In the meantime,"—she went to her closet space and started moving garments on the rack—"you guys feel like hittin' a club?"

Ingrid was like, "Now?!"

Liz looked at Ingrid like she was a child on the level of a Hayato or Shichi Sakamaki, in the wake of asking a crazy question. "Why, yes," Liz said kittenishly, "this is the time when most clubs are in full swing, dearie!"

Janz didn't appear to be against the idea of going out, and neither did Francisco. Ingrid was the square of the bunch, but it didn't take much to sway her. Especially when Liz made it clear that to get the package that they desired, and bugged her about, they would have to go, or else they were shit out of luck. With that, she received no more questionable attitudes denoting reluctance. Everyone seemed game.

Ingrid said, "So we're, like, . . . gonna meet somebody . . . at a club and they're, like, . . . gonna sell us some stuff?"

Liz said, "Yeah, something like that." She stopped her search for something to wear and said, "Yeah, and you guys, you're gonna have to excuse me, I'm gonna get dressed, and I don't feel like moving this wall thingy around so, why don't you all go downstairs, wait in the lobby."

Janz and Francisco shared a laugh and a gargling throat conversation with one another as they rose up from the table. Without protest, they made their way to the door.

"What club are we going to?" Francisco asked.

"The Candy Box," Liz stated. At once, everyone's face dropped, mouths agape and wide-eyed in a startled manner.

"Damn! That place is expensive as fuck!!" Janz protested. "That place is like four thousand yen a person."

Liz frowned. "Are you nuts? What are you talking about? It's the Candy Box. I thought all foreigners get in for free. You mean to tell me that you've been paying all this time?" She laughed and resumed pulling out clothes from her closet.

Ingrid said with a little excitement in her voice, "Like, I'm just stoked now . . . I've always wanted to go there. I heard the place is huge, the sound is like . . . awesome, and the design is freaked out."

Janz said, "Yeah, I told you we went a long time ago. But that was the only time. There're so many other places to go cheaper."

Francisco said, "When I find out the admission price, we decided not to go there. Four-thousand yen cover, and just one free drink? Not worth'eet, man."

Liz said, "OK, guys, trust me, it's free. And even if it's not free, I'll just meet the guy and get the stuff for you, OK? Now, if you'll excuse me, time is ticking. We gotta move, and I gotta get dressed. Go ahead and wait for me in the lobby downstairs."

Ingrid stayed behind and decided to touch herself up with makeup and a change of attire as well. She wasn't insufficient or skimpy with her gratitude to Liz for taking the time after her busy day to undertake such a tedious-seeming mission. She was unaware, however, that Liz too had her own motives. For one, Yoh might have had a surplus of grass, some of which she could "sell" to Ingrid's friends, the rest she could take for herself, or get connected to whoever Yoh got his sizzle from.

The other reason was Liz could get to see Serge, as she was quite sure he would be working tonight. After coming from the gym and then hitting the massage parlor, Liz thought she would have been exhausted and ready to hit the sack for the rest of the night. On the contrary, the effervescent bath and massage had served to energize her and heightened her carnal urges, exacerbating an erotic craving inside of her in need of penetration. She knew he was the only one capable of accomplishing the goal of satisfying her need, so there was her other good reason to go out, and it invigorated her.

Ordinarily, they would have taken the Loop Line to Kyobashi Station from Bentencho, but due to the late hour, no trains were in operation, so they had to take a cab. All four of them crammed inside of a taxicab, whose driver agreed to take them with three people in the back seat, and Liz electing to ride in the front passenger seat next to the driver. The way Janz and Francisco had eyeballed her when she approached them in the building lobby, there was no way she was going to squeeze in between them in the back seat like one of them had suggested.

For the night out, Liz had slipped into a black wrap dress with sleeveless bodice and subtle surplice neckline pleating above a fitted skirt. Displayed were her sculpted body parts, upper thighs and sleek peachy legs into stiletto heels and enticingly seductive cleavage. She wrapped up in her silky anorak to thwart the night seasonal chill, but was still enticing nonetheless. Janz figured he could coerce Ingrid to ride up front because she was "heavier set" while Liz rode in the back seat of the cab, thinking he or Francisco was going to rub up against her during the ride. He was to be dismayed, though. Liz was hip somewhat to the scheme and volunteered to ride shotgun.

About fifteen minutes later, they were in the Kyobashi District. They made their way to the Candy Box Club. In minutes, they entered the ostensibly diminutive building and stood in a line leading to the hideous Candy Box clown figure, behind a queue of late-night partygoers.

An astute admission staffer, name tag reading "Ando," spotted the breathtaking blonde *gaijin* who stepped onto the scene, appearing as if she had arrived directly from a photoshoot with a major fashion magazine. He waved Liz forward to the front of the line.

As if she had expected such treatment beforehand, Liz pranced to the head of the line, as she had before when accompanied by Taffie. Unfortunate, waiting patrons had no other recourse but to watch as the privileged foreigner skipped ahead of them in line to approach the admission staff at the double-door entry. Liz was greeted politely in Japanese and, like before, inoculated with the translucent invisible-ink stamp of the Candy Box Clown, which could only be seen in a certain type of black- bulb light. She also received not one but two free drink tickets. It was what she came to expect.

When Liz turned around to tell Ingrid and company to follow her inside, she expected them to be right behind her, but not so. They still remained at the rear of the line, peering away at her from afar like lost and abandoned puppies at the pound. Liz became a little frustrated with them and wondered why they were acting so scared. Her cell phone in her purse started buzzing. She complimented herself for remembering to put her phone on vibration manner mode; otherwise, with all the noisy competition of music inside the club, she would have never heard the phone's chime and missed Yoh's call.

Yoh said, "Hello . . . Elizabeth? Are you here yet? I'm inside."

Liz stood to the side of the admission door lectern. She said to Yoh on the phone, "I'm right outside. I'm on my way in. Hey, meet me by the big bright bar counter—you know which one I'm talking about? The one with all the bright little lights on the underside." She frowned up as she waved Ingrid, Janz, and Francisco forward violently, urging them to join her there. Hesitantly, they appeared to comply.

Yoh said, "I . . . I think I know what you're talking about. Please, hurry . . . I . . . I'm a little nervous."

"Yeah, yeah, I got it," Liz said. Then she hung up. She was focused on getting Ingrid and the guys to pick up the pace. To them, she said, "Let's go, these guys are going to give you all stamps."

One of the staff attendants, the medium-built thin-moustache-wearing Japanese man who, to Liz, had been exceedingly polite, was in turn gruff to Ingrid and her group. To them, he mustered enough English to explain in a gruff tone, "Only foreigners for free."

In unison, they all chorused, "We are foreigners!"

"We're not Japanese, we're Filipinos," they said.

Liz quickly pieced together the situation. Because Ingrid and her friends were Asian, had features similar to Japanese in appearance, the staff mistook them for Japanese. And as such, they were subject to the regular admission charged for Japanese and nationals. She, of course, could vouch for them not being Japanese, so she asserted her influence on the happenstance.

She said to the doorman, "They're foreigners. She's my roommate, these are her friends—they're all with me." She turned to Ingrid, "You have your *gaijin* card on you, right? Show them your IDs."

While they fished out their identification cards and disgruntled waiting would-be clubgoers in the line grumbled irritated beefs, the doorman Liz spoke to had a Japanese exchange with one of the two other assistants. When three ID cards were produced and poised at his eyesight, the door man threw up his hands with palms facing them like he was in a stick-up. Liz whipped out her very own blue United States passport, and the man's Japanese eyes flew open wide as if he was a vampire staring at a garlic-scented crucifix.

With a plaintive head nod, he said, "OK, two thousand yen for *sangokujin* and one free drink."

Liz didn't understand what was meant by the term the man used, but presumed it had something to do with them being Asian. Still, in her mind, charging them admission didn't seem fair. She thought to stand up for them, but they didn't do so for themselves. Instead, they appeared to accept the differential treatment. She watched as Ingrid, Janz, and Francisco shrugged as if to say that two thousand yen was a good deal compared to the normal price, despite the apparent fact that foreign people were granted free admission.

Liz sheathed her passport in her pocketbook and said, "Hey, wait!" She placed her hand over Ingrid's wallet when she tried to take out fee money for her and Janz. Liz complained, "But they are foreigners, *gaijin*, like me! Why do they have to pay anything?"

The doorman didn't reply. Either his English ability was only but so good, or he was not in the mood to explain his logic or job duties. Instead, he told her to wait a moment while he assisted his coworkers in moving the growing line along.

Liz was growing moody, because she didn't want to keep Yoh waiting. Also, she was steadily rising in excitement to see Serge. She said, "Is the owner here tonight?" She remembered that she had his fancy business card on her person. She opened up a compartment in her hand purse and produced it. She showed it to the doorman. "Is he here?"

The doorman's eyes darted across the card and then into Liz's cold stare. Humbly, the man nodded to Liz, told her, "Just one moment," then grabbed a shiny metallic, candy-bar-sized cell phone from his black blazer pocket. He spoke in Japanese to the party on the other end of the line. He then leaned toward Liz and crew, then asked for her name. When Liz told her who she was, the door man spoke the information into the phone, then he hung up.

Less than two minutes later, the eccentric, glossy-attired Tabriz Najaf appeared at the double doors. His jolly Groucho Marx–face greeted Liz with a bountiful and hearty smile. Wearing a satiny, golden material blazer with the sleeves rolled up to his hairy-forearmed elbows, he cupped Liz's hand like she was a royal queen from England bearing the same name, then brought it to his lips.

"Elizabeth!" he exalted, "Elizabeth Amberbush, if my memory serves me right. It is such an honor to meet you again."

Liz was absorbed with awe and delight seeing him again as well. More shocked she was that he even remembered her name, who she was, and what she looked like. She didn't know if she should be honored or unnerved. For the time being, she basked in the royal and dignified treatment. She complimented Tabriz and mirrored his sentiments when she initially spoke to the gracious club owner and host. Therewith, she came to the defense of her companions.

"Tabriz, why do my friends have to pay for admission if they're foreigners like you and me?" she asked.

A troubled expression covered Tabriz's thick eyebrow-coated forehead, altering the position of his circle sphere-lens glasses. He looked at the three Filipinos with Liz and asked her "Are they with you?"

Liz said, "Yes," and went on to introduce them to Tarbriz in the same manner she had done with the doorman. Tabriz nodded his head calmly and then ran down some Japanese instructions to the doorman, smiled, and then told Liz and her crew to follow him inside. Problem solved. In the next minute, Ingrid, Janz, and Francisco were happy like kids in a candy store to be allowed inside the Candy Box for free.

Upon entry, the sound of an unidentifiable genre of club music invaded their dome heads and vibrated their skulls. The bowl-shaped dance floor tonight looked like a sunken empty swimming pool. Within it, flailing arms, shaking bodies, and frolicking movement to the beat of the music made the party people appear like they were boiling in a soup of flashing orange lights. A young staffer grabbed up Liz's anorak like a servant, placed a hanger inside, and made away with it.

Tabriz said, "Don't worry, I can assure you that your coat check is safe. In the meantime, can I interest you and your party in champagne in the VIP lounge?"

He must be really into me! Liz thought in amusement. What was the catch? she also wondered. Finally, she remembered Yoh. She said, "That sounds fabulous, Tabriz. It really does." She didn't turn him down. Quickly, she managed to say, "Actually, I'm meeting a friend of mine. He's . . . a student . . . and, well, I told him I'd meet him here tonight because I'm . . . I'm too busy because of my schedule. So after I meet him, maybe, sure, I'd like to take you up on that."

Tabriz didn't seem the least bit disappointed or flustered. His attitude was matter of fact and cavalier, but always polite. He said, "As you wish, my good lady. Well, you have a good time, and should you need anything from me, you can alert me through any one of my staff here. Just like the doorman Ando outside. OK?"

Liz's eyes roamed about the huge ballroom as she accepted a kiss on the cheek from Tabriz. She thought she had spotted Yoh, but she couldn't be too sure. The activity in the room was festive like rush hour, but only with loud music as a backdrop. Liz tugged Tabriz's sleeve before he walked away.

She said, "Hey, Tabriz, is Serge here tonight?"

Tabriz's normally placid and agreeable expression disappeared. For the first time, Liz saw what his possible angry face looked like when she mentioned his name. Tabriz shook his head.

He said, "He no longer works here. He is gone. I don't know where he is. Just like that, he quits one night. He's gone crazy. Lately, he had been really . . . bad temper, arguing, fighting with the kitchen staff. He was a nightmare. Is he your friend?"

Liz was reeling from the impact of the shocking new developments. This was hard to recover from if what Tabriz said was true. But from what she already knew about Serge, it wouldn't be hard to believe. He worked a hellish schedule, if she thought about it. He would work at the club from its opening time until the wee hours of the morning, then go to work in Umeda and had very little sleeping times in between. Who wouldn't eventually go apeshit over that schedule, Liz pondered.

Noticeably chagrined, Liz said to Tabriz, "He was something like a friend, I guess, but he was my coworker at the language school. I guess he got overworked, huh?"

Tabriz shook his head again. He said, "I suggest you might better stay away from him. I don't think he is mentally stable any longer. He was seen talking to himself, he is in a cold sweat all the time, despite the weather out now is very cold sometimes. It doesn't make any sense. Maybe his departure is for the better. I don't need that kind of person working for me here. I don't like him quitting so soon or abruptly, but I'm glad for it than to deal with any problems. I would like to keep the Candy Box . . . sweet!"

"I . . . I understand Tabriz." Liz was deflated now because like the proverbial adage, she was all dressed up with nowhere to go afterward. Serge was the only guy she had mustered up enough like points to award access to her body, prior to and in the wake of her split with Eddie. The thought of sleeping with a random Japanese guy turned her off completely, but for a fleeting moment, she considered Yoh.

All the while, when Liz was holding conversation with Tabriz Najaf, Ingrid, Janz, and Francisco had instinctively made their way to the bright oval-shaped bar with the bright lights to get their complimentary drinks. As Liz approached, they actively waved her over.

Slope faded, feminine sashaying bar staffer Katsuo astonishingly remembered Liz as well, inflating her pristine ego further. He had a Band-Aid over his left eye. He greeted Liz with a limp-wristed wave.

"Hello again, will you have your usual gin and tonic?" Katsuo asked her in a stridulating voice that laser-beamed through the obstreperous music to her ears.

"Sure!" Liz yelled out to him with a smile. Then she pointed at his Band-Aid over the eye, using her face as a model. She squinted her face sympathetically and asked, "What happened?"

Katsuo pouted and released an aggravated sigh, then said, "Your friend . . . punched me! It's much better now, but it was so painful!" His English seemed to have improved a bit. Liz felt bad for him. She assumed that when he said friend of hers, he meant Serge. She wondered what the poor little flaming soul could have done to set him off so to bring him to strike. Recalling the pool night and the defeat at the hands of Jeremy, Serge's action in the realm of violence wasn't too far-fetched to believe.

When she received her drink, Liz, Ingrid, and the rest raised their glasses to toast. They were so happy to be inside the club they became lost in the occasion, almost forgetting why they had actually come there. Janz came back to reality when his rum and Coke was near gone as he was hungrily crunching down the cup's ice cubes too.

He said, "So, where is this person we're supposed to meet?"

No sooner had he mentioned this than Liz felt a light, cool sensation graze her arm. Somebody's cold drink glass was pressing against her flesh. She turned to face Yoh. He was sporting a newsboy cap, looked more Cuban or Latino than

Japanese with rounder eyes and industry standard pencil facial hair, grown in thick since the last time they met, with a hint of a widow's peak.

"Hello again," Yoh said.

Liz greeted him with a cheerful hug. Yoh embraced her back the best he could while still holding his drink and trying to maintain her weight. She was the same height as him, but, strength-wise, seemed more rugged.

"Sorry to keep you waiting for so long," Liz practically yelled. She said, "I'm here with my friends." She motioned her hands toward Ingrid and the guys who stood by with watchful faces.

Timidly, Yoh said to Liz, leaning toward her to more or less whisper in her ear, "Shall we go to another place? I would like to just give this to you, and we can talk later."

Liz said, "Cool, that would be fine. Just gimme a sec to shake these three." She turned and grabbed Ingrid and pulled her close. "I'll be back in a minute. When I come back, we'll be ready to leave."

Ingrid seemed surprised. She was like, "Oh . . . OK. Leaving here so soon? We just got here!"

Liz wasn't listening, however. She was already off. She didn't know where she and Yoh should go, but the expansive club didn't have a shortage of dark corners here and there in which shady characters could successfully operate. Too bad Yoh was a male; otherwise they could have done the deal inside of the ladies' room quick and easy.

After a few minutes of walking around and carving a path through wacky, wild frantic-shaking dancers and drunk floor pacers, Liz found an uninhabited space near what appeared to be steps leading to a stage. She sat down on one of the steps and beckoned Yoh to join her.

Yoh complied and took a seat not next to her but a level below and back-arched away as if he were shy or afraid of her. Even though he was charming and good-looking, his bashful and diffident manner of acting was not attractive and turned Liz off. She didn't like egomaniac beefcake jocks—to date—but she wasn't into sissy-acting cake boys either; it was so much like Carver in her memory, and he came dreadfully inadequate in satisfying her. In all probability, Yoh would be much the same if she allowed him the opportunity. Guaranteeing her a regret, waste of time, and a possible love-obsessed stalker. Yet another problem she didn't need. As a result, she struck him from the list of a quick screw candidate and elected to let their dealings remain in the realm of sizzle exchange, and if needed, she would have to conjure a spell of falsehood to placate his tender feelings and emotional clinging to Vicky (Jill).

In a classy, surreptitious manner, Yoh passed her a loaded cigarette box emptied of its smokes. A bubblegum machine jawbreaker sized bundle of ganja was inside, probably a little bit over two dimes when uncompressed. They sat there frozen like two performers in an offbeat stage play stuck in a scene where neither could remember their scripts. They just played roles, like they were lovers holding hands in a romantic interlude that excluded a kiss. When the imaginary episode was cut, Liz had the cigarette box safely tucked away in her purse. At which time she decided that not only was the scene finished, it was "To be continued."

"Thank you for meeting me tonight, Yoh," Liz said as she stood up and leaned into his side in order to be clearly heard. They were somewhat secluded, but not entirely alone. Clubgoers wandered about and interfered with their ability to hold a conversation. This was to Liz's advantage, because now that she had gotten what she came there for, she didn't feel like following up with the make-believe convo she supposedly had with Vicky (Jill), which she used as bait to coerce Yoh out of his comfortable bed that night. Obediently, he met her there and surrendered all of his weed to her stone-cold gratis.

One of the tackily dressed club patrons who had interrupted Liz and Yoh's moment of bonding suddenly felt it necessary to vomit in close proximity to them. Splashes of tummy gunk splattered the cuffs of Yoh's jeans and the side of his Doc Martens shoes. He jumped away from the steps just in time to not wear any more of the rotten mess. With amazing grace, Liz leaped over the nasty puddle, heels and all, landing on her toes.

"We have to get out of here," she said.

Yoh agreed, and they merged into the thick chili bowl of dance floor bodies to carve a path back to the illuminated bar spot, where Liz had last seen Ingrid and the guys. She, Janz, and Francisco were still seated there looking like stranded travelers, cradling their drinks like they were prized possessions. When Liz and her friend reappeared, their hopeful looks returned too.

Yoh turned to Liz and said, "I must go. It's late now, and I must go to my work in a few hours. Can we . . . meet again? I really would like to talk to you about—"

Liz said, "Yeah, Yoh, I know . . . I'll call you, I promise, thank you." She leaned into him and kissed him on the cheek. He was so happy, but instead, he blushed. The darkness of the surroundings shielded his bashful reaction. He tipped his newsboy cap and left. Liz was both relieved and pleased that the transaction had been successfully carried out. To Ingrid, Liz ordered to follow her to the ladies' room. Compliantly she did.

The dank and balmy women's restroom was crowded with inebriated nightmare beauties fixing their makeup, powdering their noses, and those waiting their turn to use one of the three toilet facilities available. When one of the doors to the stalls opened to release an occupant, Liz rudely ignored the order of the cue and went straight for it. There was slight protest, angry voices from the line of women awaiting a turn to tinkle didn't deter Liz in the slightest; basically she was oblivious to the slight commotion she caused.

Indifferently, Liz slammed the door, informing Ingrid that she was to wait outside and keep watch. Nervously, Ingrid tried to explain to the complaining Japanese contingent that her blonde American friend was "very sick" and imperatively needed to use the facility.

Inside, Liz managed to break the weed apart, separating the bud in half and placing one portion back inside the cigarette box to pass to Ingrid when she left the stall. For the other portion, which was for her, she took the cellophane wrap from the cigarette box and placed it inside, then crammed it safely inside of the coin compartment of her purse.

When she exited the toilet booth, she was greeted by angry Japanese faces, but she ignored them casually and pushed her way through the patch of bodies and advanced to the vanity area to check her face. Amazingly, no one seemed to have any desire or need to pursue any argument or confrontation with her. She was taller and "rugged" in appearance more so than most of the Japanese females present. Ingrid, also tall and chunkier and somewhat intimidating, assuming that she was a bully type, stood beside Liz at the vanity. Liz was applying some moisture to her lips. Upon seeing Ingrid, she placed the cigarette box on the sink counter. Nobody seemed suspicious as she told Ingrid to take it, as it looked like a normal box of Lucky Strike.

"It's in there," Liz said. "Just take it. Put it away, it's inside the box."

Ingrid said, "Oh wow! Thanks!" She grabbed the cigarette box and stuffed it inside of her strap purse. Then she grabbed her wallet and said, "How much did it cost?"

Liz said, "Just gimme an itchy-man," knowing full well that amount was way too much but decided that she had to be compensated for her assistance. It wasn't a nice thing to do, and she did acknowledge taking advantage of Ingrid's kindness and naivete, but at the same time, it wasn't her problem. If she and her friends wanted some dope that bad, they were thus subject to paying the price, be it good or bad. Ingrid didn't complain, so Liz felt free of guilt. When they felt secure in leaving, they split the restroom.

Ingrid then said, "We're like . . . um . . . gonna stick around. What are you gonna do?"

Liz said, "I think I'm gonna head back. I have work tomorrow. Don't you?"

Ingrid sighed and let out a weary utterance of grief. She said, "Actually, yeah, but . . . it's OK. I have to give this to Janz, because technically, like . . . this is his stuff. I just, like, bought it with my money because he's like, low on cash until his next payday, so he'll pay me back. Plus, we have to stick around because there's no more trains running now."

Liz scowled. "Just ride home with me. We'll split the cab costs. It'll only be about a thousand yen. That's not too bad, right?"

Sadly, Ingrid said, "I could do that maybe, but then Janz and Francisco would be stranded here. I couldn't do that. And, like, I couldn't, like, inconvenience you by bringing them back to our place. I would never want to disturb you."

Liz couldn't argue with that logic. As fatigue gradually began to set in, Liz didn't have the inkling to give Ingrid dating or relationship advice dealing with Janz. She didn't know the extent of their liaison, or what cultural elements presided over their coition or intimacy, and at that time had no desire to delve deeper. Instead, they gave each other a friendly hug and parted company.

"Oh, and Elizabeth." Ingrid turned quickly and said, "Thanks for, like, sticking up for us back there, earlier tonight. At the door, with the doorman. That really meant a lot to us."

Liz walked off after that heartwarming moment and grabbed the attention of the first Candy Box staff member ambling about. With her fledgling Japanese ability, she communicated to the person, "Tabriz? Where?"

The short Japanese servant seemed to understand, then quickly extracted a cell phone. He spoke to someone briefly, likely Tabriz. When the phone conversation ended, the staffer said to Liz, "Please, come." He sped off, Liz almost had to struggle to keep pace with him as he could dip in, out, and through clusters of people congregating in the crowded club. The short trek ended at a side room near the entrance, the coat check. There, Tabriz joined them. This time, on his arm was a tall, slender Japanese girl in a pink dress. The woman was cute, Liz could admit. At least it seemed that Tabriz had found someone to take his attention away from her, but still he kissed Liz's hand again like she was royalty.

Tabriz said, "I take it that you are leaving now, Elizabeth? Are you sure I cannot interest you in a drink before you depart this time?"

Liz said, "I'd really like to, Tabriz, but I really have a busy day ahead. But I do want you to know that I really enjoy this place. This is by far the most impressive club I've ever been to in Japan—maybe even better than some places I've been to in California. It's so amazing. I'll definitely be back."

Tabriz said, "And I'll be waiting. You will always be my guest here. You will never pay for another drink or admission here. This I guarantee to you. Take care, until next time, and, oh, remember, if you see that guy Serge, I recommend you best avoid him if you can." His round glasses twitched on his face as he spotted his trusty servant, who had returned with Liz's anorak. Tabriz helped Liz fit her arms into the silky garment. The pink-dress-wearing Japanese girl watched with a tinge of envy but dared not stray far from Tabriz as he showered Liz with attention stolen from her.

When all of the pageantry had run its course, Liz could finally leave, but not before drawing a small crowd of awed spectators who thought she was actually a famous person, or at the least one of Tabriz's "wives." The way Tabriz's servants were holding the door for Liz and making a hole for her to pass through thickets of people standing around caused people to take notice. It was so hypnagogic even

Liz herself started to imagine she actually was some sort of fabulous elite royal princess. If only Eddie could see her now, she thought. People were practically kissing her pretty feet, and wealthy "nawabs" or "A-rabs" like Tabriz were apparently fawning over her—and Eddie left her for some two-bit garden-variety Japanese chick. She suspected, never confirmed, but suspected he had—and she probably could have slept with him too!

Liz was glad, however, mollified that Tabriz had found an object of desire to occupy him and it wasn't her. She also felt secure because Deon assured her that she wasn't in trouble with Luzio Silver; his thugs weren't going to accost her, and while at Tabriz's Candy Box, she was safe.

Not that he wasn't her type, but there was something about Tabriz that didn't make her feel relaxed enough to have a go with. Like any sheltered individual, she had suspicions about Middle Eastern people, and some political views that didn't align with hers. Particularly thinking that she would be subject to being dominated by a religious stipulation of her wearing a headdress, cover her face, and share him with a harem of multiple partners.

Liz escaped the hideous clown's maw image of the Candy Box and made it to the littered-up, pissy streets of Kyobashi. The back alley tributaries burned with the glow of neon signs and glittery arrows pointing to red-light establishments and pleasure parlors. Liz looked like a Western version of the elegant, polished, and stately high-priced courtesans who emerged from those dusky dens. Japanese businessmen in black suits and wrinkled neckties stumbled by drunk and stared at Liz in such great numbers she almost felt compelled to sing or make a speech. The eyes were so wide she thought she must have carried sunshine in the crevasse of her cleavage breast lines. She started to get nervous, but jittery feelings subsided when she came across the Police Box. Then, she remembered she was loaded.

Luckily, in Japan, a taxi or a hired car was never far away or too difficult to hail, especially in the big cities. This Liz would always praise the country for, despite her so-called "dislike" of the place. She hopped inside one and headed home. Watching the city lights glide by in the night windows, she leaned her head back and celebrated her entire day in review. She thought about Serge. Maybe it was for the best she never went through with getting involved with him, she thought. Too bad, now she would have to find a way to please herself in the absence of a suitable partner as her lonely craving for companionship steadily boiled. She knew she was too picky for her own good, though. Whereas Luzio Silver wasn't after her, and she initially feared his crew, one of his henchmen, like Moose, for example, would be a welcome sight in her room on solitary nights. Especially, she mused, for a one-night thing. Maybe it was time she lowered her standards, Liz chortled, and then shuddered at the thought.

68

LIZ MADE IT home and hit the sack pretty much right away. At noon the following day, she woke up well rested. She eased out of bed and prepared for work. Peering across the room, she could see that Ingrid had not returned home. *Good for her*, Liz thought. Ingrid decided to party all night and head into work like a "trooper," whereas somebody like Liz might have opted to call in sick, especially if she were to have had a monster hangover to accompany feelings of exhaustion. Liz brushed her teeth and took a quick splash inside the shower before getting dressed and leaving the apartment. She had no idea what she was in for that day.

Upon arrival at work, reporting for duty at the Bozack Hommachi branch, she was greeted by dry-faced Kayo Terumi. Kayo told Liz that she had been removed from the schedule that day and was to immediately dispatch and appear at Tennoji HQ. When Liz asked why, Kayo conveyed to her that she had no idea, but all she knew was that Ruth Worth had ordered that she be taken off the schedule for that day and had been requested to go to the Headquarters, and spared the news that a problem had brewed. Hell had already broken loose. Upon arrival at Tennoji, the tension in the air was so thick Liz felt she could rub it on her skin like balm.

Ingrid had indeed decided to go to work that morning, but not after indulging in excess of the previous night's haul. It seemed that Ingrid and her companions had stayed out partying until the crack of dawn, around 5:00 a.m, when the city's trains resumed operation. Instead of returning home, she went to Higashi (East) Osaka where Janz and Francisco resided and crashed at the former's place. She got some experience points in the oral sex department and an hour or two of sleep before waking up extra groggy. Refusing to use a sick-leave day and determined to have a perfect work record, which she felt would endear her to her company to render her positive reviews, Ingrid decided to report to Tennoji HQ for stand-by on field runner status.

Janz too had to work at a job in Nara, which required for him to rise early much the same as Ingrid, so they left his place together. The morning coffee available at Janz's dinky one-room hovel of a pad came from a vending machine outside of the building. This was insufficient in perking Ingrid up, as she was used to the hard and strong taste of the java she consumed from the instant maker she and Liz had at their place.

Janz suggested that they hit the weed pipe once more, and according to him, such would liven her up and replenish her state of alacrity. Poor Ingrid had no idea that the effects would be the near complete opposite. Initially, she believed Janz was right, for after she took a hearty session of indulgence, she went into her normal fit of laughter. Everything was funny to her—Janz's morning face, his bummy clothes, people walking up and down the streets, children dressed in funny uniforms reporting for school, the way people looked rushing for trains filled to capacity from Yaeno Sato Station; anything triggered her belly-cramping fits of giggling, so much so she almost had to close her eyes for the majority of her commute to the job. So at first, she did believe that the weed had livened her up.

When she arrived at work, however, creeping paranoia side effects set in. This was set in motion by a sentient, pettifogging brown-nosing Worm, who was also at Tennoji HQ that morning, and took notice of an all-too-familiar malodor of marijuana lingering upon Ingrid's person. While Worm didn't know Ingrid entirely too well, he generally took her for a mousy, soft-spoken chick who seemed more like a church, religious zealot than a party girl who would indulge in reefer. Japanese people and other straight-and-narrow squares around the office might not be hip to the marijuana smell, but wanting to appear like the sapient staff wise man, Worm spared not the opportunity to tattle and, hopefully, win back his company stripes.

Kenji wasn't available as he was at the Namba branch that morning. Suguru Yamada was in an important meeting; the other Japanese managers were also too busy. Worm had no recourse but to shoot a bee line to Ruth Worth. He spilled his guts about what he suspected of Ingrid, that she was under the influence of function-impairing substances.

Ruth had to take Worm's accusation seriously. Even though he was no longer the head teacher, he had still manifested the instincts and know-how associated with the job. His quid-nunc niggling could be annoying, but unwise to ignore.

Sure enough, when Ingrid was called into Ruth's office, the insipid and timid offender broke down in tears and admitted the truth! No sooner did she snitch on herself in hopes that she would be granted some mercy for being honest, spared from any punishment or termination of employment than she also inadvertently implicated Liz. Worm was quick to add some dirt on Liz's name as well, not failing to remind Ruth that she too had been a person of interest since the night of the drug bust.

Ruth did not have the authority to dismiss or terminate anyone, but the authority she wielded in the company was great enough to suspend or enact such disciplinary measures if provided probable cause. Ingrid's admitting her culpability was reason enough, and she did dismiss Ingrid from duty that day. She was told to return home and await a decision to be made by the higher-ups when Ruth made out a report and submitted it to her superiors. She immediately sent word to the Hommachi branch that Liz too was to be struck from the scheduled list and replaced by another field runner substitute teacher. When Liz arrived at Tennoji to face the music, Ingrid had already been sent home.

This was not the end of the kerfuffle. For instead of Worm receiving praise for his in-depth second sight, spotting potential troublemakers, he was told that he would be transferred to the Umeda School until further notice! This was because Serge had suddenly quit. Or better, he had failed to report for work, causing his termination to be enacted. As such, they were suddenly in dire need of French teachers. Worm, being from Quebec, was also fluent in French and was dispatched at once to Umeda to cover for him.

That wasn't the end of it. Another female employee, a Laura Violi, had also resigned by not renewing her contract with the company. It was a lethal blow as her decision to leave the company had come at a time when Bozack was facing an immense inner turmoil, and she was a highly favored candidate to become a much-needed female head teacher. This, in turn, became a catalyst leading to an impromptu decision to remove newbie Umeda branch staffer Rusty Clark and subsequently offer him Worm's old position as head teacher of the South Town branches! Shifting Rosiland back to Tennoji and lessen her workload. Worm was livid. His attempt at pious fraud and calling others to the carpet had backfired on him in a twisted way, beyond the pale. Now he was a shaky mess, fit to be tied and on the brink of crybaby tears.

When Liz showed up for her meeting with Ruth, she could tell by the look daggers received that she was sitting on the razor's edge. Ruth shut the door to her tiny office, not much larger than the cubicles Liz and other teachers taught students in. She didn't beat around the bush or keep Liz on tenterhooks. The crotchety Ruth Worth seemed to be in a dither as she fumbled with desk paperwork before addressing the usually blithe American girl.

"Ms. Amberbush—you mind if I call you Elizabeth?" Ruth didn't wait for affirmation. She sighed heavily and continued, "Elizabeth, it's been brought to our attention that you have been involved in the usage and possibly the possession of illegal substances. This is yet another instance where your name has been implicated in activity that Bozack Corporation does not tolerate. I'm afraid we have to take these situations very seriously."

Undoubtedly, Liz was struck by an invisible hand of fear, which left its mark on her face in the form of a flush of red. Uneasiness tightened its grip on her within her chest as she struggled to maintain her composure, not wanting Ruth to see her sweat; but it was a battle she was losing. She managed to question the accusation.

"I . . . I don't understand what you mean," Liz said, rubbing her palms together to alleviate the moisture the sudden tension had brought about. "What illegal substances? And why has my name been implicated or whatever?"

Ruth said, "I must bring it to your attention that your flatmate, Ingrid Avecedo, was discovered this morning to have been under the influence of marijuana. A drug, as you are well aware, is illegal in Japan and punishable by incarceration here and unquestionably grounds for dismissal from this company should you be found guilty of partaking of it. Now at this time, it is likely that in lieu of Ms. Avecedo's admission of using the substance, she will face termination procedures, unfortunately."

Liz clasped her hands together as if she was timorously praying. Not that she could keep her job, for that was the lesser of her worries. She was hoping that Ruth hadn't decided upon anything drastic like call the cops and have them search her apartment, which Bozack had every right to do, as that was officially their dormitory in which she resided.

Trying to maintain a stoic but unsettled pokerface, Liz said, "So am I to then assume that the same termination procedures are to be carried out on me too? I'm gonna get fired?" She didn't care about her job at this point. She had enough money saved and didn't have to grovel in hopes to remain employed. All she wanted was to get the entire affair over with so that she could at least cover her ass and not be caught with possession.

Ruth, however, wasn't quick to drop the ax as Liz had figured she would. Instead, she voiced a different resolution. Liz was gravely unaware that she was still an invaluable asset to the company, regardless of her seeming transgression.

Ruth said, "Not entirely so, Elizabeth. You see, Ingrid's implication of you was considered . . . a mere accusation. We have no tangible evidence that you were involved in any drug activity. My reason for calling you here today is to alert you to the situation we have at hand here. The fact that you are flatmates with Ms. Avecedo and your connection to . . . Stephanie Pritchard . . . and Tim Valentine and others who were involved in that dreadful drug bust calls for you to be investigated according to company policy. While we don't require our employees to be vade mecum totes or Bible thumpers, we do expect for you to be well versed in the rules and policies of our company handbook."

This handbook mentioned was a thick, magazine-sized manual that Liz and Denore too had chucked seemingly ages ago. They received it when they were first hired and used it only during the orientation. Liz nodded as if she completely understood, but that was not entirely true. What she really wanted was for Ruth to get to the point so she could get back to her place, grab up her stash—maybe give it back to Yoh—and then unleash a verbal trouncing upon Ingrid.

Ruth continued to disseminate a blue streak of company babble, then at long last arrived to a point where she told Liz, "And we do have to take these matters seriously. And as such, you will be temporarily suspended without pay for one week. You are to then report back here at Tennoji HQ, where you will be required to undergo a drug test—one which you agreed to upon your hire. Should your tests return with negative results, this will not necessarily deem your termination.

"If your tests come back positive, you will be required to report to a confidential treatment facility called the Center for Rehabilitation for users of drugs located in the East Yodogawa ward of north Osaka. There will be an eighty-hour program that you will be required to complete satisfactorily in ten days, and should you be absent one day, you will be immediately disqualified and subsequently terminated of employment. Also, failure to comply with completing this program will also unfortunately be grounds for dismissal.

"The good news is, if you are not guilty at all, this will all go away, and everything will be back to normal. I, for one, will do everything within my power to extricate any blemish on your company record that this big to-do might have caused. But all in all, Elizabeth, I've done what I could to extend you an olive branch. You have a week to reflect on your actions and everything we've talked about today and consider your future. Now, unless you have any questions, that'll be all for now. See Rosiland Ash on your way out. She will provide you with the paperwork you're to bring back here a week from now. Good-bye."

The judo-practitioner-statured Ruth stood up from her desk wearing a *militaresque* skirt-and-jacket ensemble and pointed Liz out the door like a drill sergeant. Liz wasted no time leaving. Although Ruth could at times be a hard-nosed, "female dick", she seemed to maintain enough compassion that could deem her a tolerable human. For within a week's time, Liz was confident she could beat any drug test that didn't require a hair follicle. All she had to do was refrain from smoking, work out, and glaze in a sauna if she had to. Then if she came back positive for drugs, claim she got a contact high. Too simple, she thought. But then again, such measures had not helped her in the past back home in the United States, where, on a few job searches, she had failed tests. She shrugged, for anyway, she had no intention not getting high or completing some ten-day rehab program at CRUD. All she cared about suddenly was just getting home.

69

LIZ RACED BACK to her dormitory after receiving the paperwork from Rosiland Ash at the Bozack HQ in Tennoji. Basically, it was a printed transcript of what Ruth Worth had discussed with her inside of her office. In addition, there was more information about the CRUD treatment center, which she would be expected to report to should her drug test have negative results the following week. She thought no more of it as soon as she reached her place.

Grim, long-faced Ingrid was there, sitting lonely upon her bunk. She had been crying her eyeballs out. When Liz made her presence known, she quickly hopped up to apologize lavishly to the point where she almost fell to her knees to bow at Liz's feet. Although Liz was upset and disappointed with Ingrid, she couldn't help but pity her in a way. Before Ingrid could descend totally to the floor, bowing down to Liz, Liz helped her to stand up.

Loosely compassionate, Liz stated, "Ingrid, oh, come on, get to your feet. You don't have to be so over the top, OK? I can't believe you told them about me even though it was you who got busted. I mean, what the hell happened? Did you take it to work and the shit fall out of your pocket or something?"

Ingrid's face became blanched and dusky as she shook her head furiously. She said, "Absolutely not! I . . . I didn't even have any pot or anything on me. I . . . gave everything to Janz last night. He . . . and I, like, smoked this morning before we left his place."

While Ingrid was talking, Liz remembered to grab hold of her stash of weed she had hidden in her favorite place in the space underneath her service table's drawer. Once she regained possession of her sizzle, she held it secretly on her person, poised to chuck it or flush it down the toilet should the rollers come knocking down her door. It was obvious the paranoia bug had bitten her as well.

Ingrid rattled on, "I . . . I don't even know how they even knew I was high. Like, I know I wasn't acting strange. Like, I'm always quiet when I go to work. I mean, like, nobody ever really speaks to me anyway. It's not like I'm the most popular person around the office. I mean, like, the only coworker I really ever talk to on a frequent basis is you—and that's more than likely because we live together."

Liz listened to her ramble on and realized that albeit sad and a pity, what Ingrid stated was quite the truth. Being that she was non-white, a lot of the other teachers around Bozack had the tendency to tune people like her out. Only exceptionally outspoken types like Jeremy Ng could infiltrate the silent wall of non-inclusion, and even Jeremy wasn't a core member of the clique Liz used to run with. Unlike Jeremy, however, people like Ingrid didn't have the luxury of adopted Americanized parents. She was an anomaly who grabbed a diploma while residing in America and conned the Japanese into believing she was a naturalized American. Lacking the bold charisma, she didn't juxtapose herself within certain groups of people so candidly. That she knew to be true. Liz didn't have difficulty believing what Ingrid had said. But there had to be more to it, Liz thought.

Ingrid continued, and finally, it became clear. She said, "I just reported for stand-by as usual. The only person who actually, like, spoke to me this morning was Mitchell—the former head teacher."

"Worm!" Liz said. She was unsure if Ingrid knew him by that name, but Liz certainly did.

Ingrid said, "He was so nice. He said, 'Good morning', we chatted for a few minutes, we talked about last night because he mentioned that I appeared to be tired. I didn't lie, I was tired. I got, like, maybe two or three hours of sleep before I came in. But I swear, I didn't tell him that I had smoked any marijuana. It wasn't until later, when Ruth Worth called me into her office. Then she . . . she . . ." Ingrid started to break down and cry again "It was like she could see right through me. She had this, like, serious expression on her face. I . . . I thought she knew . . . and . . . and . . . I just came clean. I admitted that I had smoked marijuana with a friend."

Liz rolled her eyes. Now she was really ticked off at Ingrid. How could she be so weak and fold under pressure like that? she wondered under her breath. If only she had stuck to her guns, stood strong on her square, neither of them would have been in the predicament. As for the run-in with Worm, Liz figured that out right away. She was sure that it was Worm who had spilled the beans. Worm wasn't the fair-haired clean-cut choir boy he fooled everyone into thinking he was at the top brass level. Liz knew he was low-key into weed himself and more than likely, he had caught on to the fact that Ingrid was still high when she came to the job. Then he had ratted to Ruth Worth.

Liz said, "So after that is when you told Ruth what? That I gave you the stuff?"

Ingrid tightened her lips, wiped away tears underneath her fogged lens glasses, then nodded affirmatively. She said, "Well, I . . . didn't like, volunteer, your name. Ms. Worth mentioned your name. I don't know why. I just said that I was with you when I got it. I...I didn't mean to make it sound like you gave it to me. I'm so sorry! I could kill myself," she whimpered and sobbed amply and sat back down on her bunk.

"All I could think about was my job. I . . . I so don't want to lose this job. In a moment of desperation, I thought if I, like, came clean and honest about what happened, they would give me a second chance or something . . . I mean, like, I . . . it wasn't like I was drunk or anything . . ." Ingrid paused to blow her nose with some tissue.

"I don't think it's really going to matter," Liz said somewhat solemnly. She already received a foreshadowing of Ingrid's fate based on her discussion with Ruth earlier. She asked Ingrid, "What did the old hag Ruth tell you was going to happen about your job?"

"Ms. Worth?" Ingrid sniffed betwixt tearful tirades "Sh-she said that there's, like, gonna be a meeting sometime this weekend. Like a jury, they're gonna vote or decide if they're gonna keep me. Right now, I'm suspended from work until next Monday . . . when the decision is supposed to be, like, the verdict . . ."

"Yeah, yeah," Liz said, "I got it, I got it. They told me the same thing—only I'm suspended for a week. So I'm guessing you'll learn of your fate come Monday, huh?"

Ingrid nodded. "Yeah, and I'm, like, so nervous now that I could just die. My mother will shame me! My family back in Cebu City will look at me as a failure. This was my big shot. No other large company will ever hire me now if I lose this job! Most of my fellow Filipino *kasama*—my comrades, they work shit jobs here for less money. I understand why, but I don't understand why . . . some have to wake up before sunrise to make, like, two-hour commutes to jobs that treat us like the shit they pay . . . it's just so fucked up. It has to do with the reason why they wanted us to pay at the club last night and you could get in for free, and like, with no problems. It's different for us here. So that's why I hope they'll, like, see it in their hearts to take us back."

Liz relaxed a bit, then allowed herself to recline and rest her head on her soft pillow. She said, "It's better you save that sort of speech for them, if you're begging for your job back."

Ingrid said, "It's not that simple. Like, even if they don't agree to fire me, I have to attend a ten-day rehab program."

Liz saw the familiar yellow brochure detailing the CRUD treatment center in north Osaka. She sat upright on her bed again, fit to be tied or on the brink of such condition. She said, "They're sending you there too?"

Ingrid had by now stopped crying. Quizzically asking, "You too? Yeah—we . . . we'd be like, classmates, I guess? It's like an eighty-hour thing, what I read, we'll, like, watch films, take tests and stuff, sounds, like, rigid as hell, but I'll definitely do it. I'll do anything to keep this job."

Ingrid's groveling disposition had grown to be something Liz had a distaste for. She was genuinely getting on her nerves again, and she dreaded the thought of having to attend such a program at some drab, dinky rehab spot with her. It was bad enough the program would be so intense and stringent, but to also have a garrulous gorilla like Ingrid clinging to her all day, then come home and still have to share a room—the thought was putting her on the brink of saving them all the trouble and simply quitting!

Just as soon, Liz dismissed the idea. She would still be in a jam, because she would have nowhere to live. Growing somewhat restless, she decided to change clothes and head to the fitness gym. Maybe she would calm down after practicing kickboxing and pretending the inflated balloon bag she punched was Ingrid. Or Worm, or Stephanie . . . Eddie! Anybody. She left abruptly and didn't say much to Ingrid on her way out. She hoped Ingrid wasn't sincere in her thoughts she had conveyed wanting to off herself. But if so, Liz hoped she did it somewhere else and not at the dormitory. She hated to be so torpid in her own thoughts, but she had exhausted herself of sympathy for Ingrid.

A few hours later, Liz felt better as she thought she would. She beat up the balloon bag so viciously she had drawn a crowd of old Japanese women who thought she was actually the studio instructor. As usual, a comely gym male staff member, or random gentleman working out tried to *nampa* her, give her their biz cards; but Liz had yet to consider what kind of Japanese guy she would get involved with or sleep with. God forbid he be another narc like the one Stephanie fell for, and then she would be in deeper dire straits.

After showering at the gym and squawking about how weak the water pressure was compared to that at the Thai massage spot, Liz toweled off and sat on a bench in the locker room. Japanese women were staring at her, some waving and grinning, treating her as if she was a Hollywood movie star. Her hair was so long it looked like a stringy golden towel trailing from her head, and curious ladies wanted to touch it. It became so excessive she rushed to get dressed. Of course, her lengthy mane took a while to blow-dry, so inadvertently, she took longer than expected. As a result, she missed a phone call from Yoh. She had forgotten to call him that day as she promised she would. With everything that had been going on with her that day, it was no wonder.

When she came home in the early evening, Ingrid was not at the apartment.

Jokingly she hoped that Ingrid didn't make good on her threat to commit suicide. She looked around the place, checked the bathtub for floating corpses. There were none, nor was there a hanging effigy from the ceiling. She looked out of the window and saw no watermelon splatter five stories below. It was safe to assume she hadn't killed herself, Liz reasoned with gallows humor. Probably she had gone to cry her woes on someone willing to listen, like her friend Marcia or Janz.

In that regard, she was lucky, Liz thought. At least she had someone whom she could talk to when things fell apart. Liz sat for a moment and thought about it. How she no longer had anyone she could really lean on. Denore was long gone. Taffie had disappeared. Stephanie vanished, and there was no Vicky (Jill), or any other female she had camaraderie with. She thought of vanishing too. Just like that. Quit. Leave. Go back to America. It wasn't as if there were any shackles on her that caused her to remain in Japan. She could leave anytime she wanted.

On the bright side, she thought, if she were to quit, she would be under no obligation to report to the CRUD treatment center. As she could tell, by her already loading her pipe to smoke some weed, and maybe later sniff a little coke, there was no way she was going to pass any drug test. But failure to complete the program, she would lose her job anyway; but should that happen, she would be evicted.

Stuck now between a rock and hard place, she knew it. Her Japanese ability had never really come to be at all, and quite frankly, she never needed it. With the assistance of everyone around her like adulators and fan groupies, she practically got everything done for her. Still however, despite all of this, she had not managed to amass a considerable number of Japanese friends outside of the company—or within it, for that matter. Most of the Japanese women she worked with day in and day out at Bozack she had contempt for, with Kayo Terumi leading the pack. What scant number of Japanese people she had opportunities to develop meaningful relationships with had ended in disasters like the incident with Mr. Sakamaki. People who she knew while living in Hannan City were forlorn memories.

Even calling Eddie now was no longer an option. Secretly she had, but from a desolate phone booth, not from her cell phone. That way, Eddie wouldn't have ignored her call seeing her number displayed on the digital screen of his celly. Also, she was spared the shame of seeming beggarly and desperate. It hadn't mattered either way. Eddie too had since changed his number, and were she to have ventured out to see him in Hannan City, she would have discovered that he had changed addresses as well. Fortunately, Liz had maintained a grandiose level of pride. She was determined to tough her situation out. Probably this was the reason she wasn't quite ready to leave Japan—not just yet. She felt she still had something to prove. Prior to this latest disaster, she had decided her future goal and intended to embark upon that mission heuristically.

Liz found her lighter and lit the flame to the bud in her pipe. She inhaled deep and then exhaled ghostly white contours shrouded in spectral mist. Yoh had passed along to her some strong shit. No wonder Ingrid had bugged out that morning. Within moments, a gradual stoned delirium borne of high-grade indulgence heightened her desperate thoughts to locate the elusive Taffie. She felt like a famous Scotland detective with the pipe in her hand, pondering evidence. Something about the way she lost all communication with Taffie still didn't sit well with her. She had nothing but time on her hands now, as she didn't have to go to work for the next week. It was almost as if she was on vacation. The downside was, she had no one to share it with. She changed clothes again.

Later that night, she hit up the Can of Pee restaurant bar in Umeda's Kita-Shinchi outskirt. It was Friday night, the weekend opener, and the place was crowded as could be expected in Japan's second largest city. Surprisingly, there were vacant spaces at the bar counter, which only one foreign girl sat at. The rest of the seats were empty, so Liz decided to take a seat there. As she made her way through a chaparral of occupied tables and chairs, tangling her path to the bar counter, she caught sight of Takuto. He hadn't changed much; his head was still clean shaven, or coated with "pepper," and he was still rocking his greasy "don ho" shirt as if he had just flown in from Hawaii.

Takuto was busy because the place was crowded, and he was steadily barking out orders to his kitchen staff and a foreign girl working with him behind the counter. She was a new face, and Liz saw her talking to the lone foreign chick seated at the opposite end of the counter. Liz also took a seat.

Finally, Takuto took notice of Liz and greeted her—at first with a surprised look, but then greeted her less enthusiastically than what she would have expected. It was a dry acknowledgment from a guy who would have gladly consumed her used bathwater with a straw less than a few months earlier. The night of his birthday party, he was so drunk Liz recalled having to pry his clinging arms from wrapping around mostly her—and Taffie—trying to get her to kiss him. What a wild night it was. They had some memories to have a laugh about. But this night, Takuto didn't really appear to be in any type of laughing mood.

As Takuto seemingly blew Liz off to rush to another section of the establishment, tending to customers or assisting a staff in clearing a table to make room for new customers, Liz checked out the new foreign girl. She then thought, with her current situation, she ought to take Takuto up on the offer he once made to her about working there. It was obvious he needed the help, especially on a night like tonight. The foreign girl he had hired should have been helping him with the work he was doing in the dining area, clearing tables, wiping up messes, taking orders, and other duties. Instead, she was talking up a storm with the foreign girl customer. Liz and the other foreign woman's eyes met briefly. Liz gave her a quick, smug grin and then waved the foreign barkeep girl over.

Somewhat arrogant and slow to respond, the foreign girl dragged her way to

Liz's end of the counter. She stood before her and was like, "Yes?" Eyes blinking impatiently as if she was annoyed that someone had dared to waste her precious time and interrupt the conversation she was having.

Liz said, "You work here, right?" Equally smug in execution.

"Yeah," the girl said, not smiling and approaching abrasive in attitude.

"Well, how about you get me a drink. I'll take a gin and tonic, dear, and you can go easy on the ice and hard with the gin, you get my drift?" Then she averted her eyes to look at her cell phone to see how many calls she had missed.

The foreign barkeep rolled her eyes as if she didn't feel like working, but she went about the task she was ordered to do. She told the girl she was talking to that she would return to her company as soon as she "got the American her swill." Liz heard the snide remark and chose to ignore it. She had her fill of the American haters she tended to come across already while working at Bozack and knew how to tune them out. Were she to work there, Takuto would probably fire her in a week, Liz thought.

She got her drink. It was weak. The girl didn't know what she was doing, and as soon as Takuto made his way back to the counter, Liz would let him know. Knowing him, she thought, he would start making her drinks himself. In the meantime, she considered working at a bar like that. Sure, the money might not be as good at the English school, but she wasn't desperate and on the brink of destitution like Ingrid seemed to be. Ever since she had come to Japan, she had been doing the same type of work. Something different wouldn't hurt. Experience was experience, she gathered, as she toyed with the thought gradually becoming a serious consideration. Especially the rates Takuto said he would pay.

Takuto, however, would hit Liz with a bombshell. His whole attitude and demeanor toward her had changed in almost a three-sixty degree. As he greeted her upon his return to the counter, Liz felt a shivery, polar opposite readout of his character that differed from any other time she had met him. He wasn't bubbly, not cheerful to see her, and carried on almost as if they barely even knew each other. Sure, Liz hadn't been a frequent customer of his place, but the way he was when she was with him and Taffie would have suggested they would be friends for life. Now he was cold, distant, and not very animated with her presence at his place that night. Before, he would supply her and Taffie with all the free drinks they could put away, and strong ones too. Not like the watered-down lime juice his new girl had supplied. She barely felt inclined to even pay for it. It was obvious, though, tonight wasn't going to be a repeat of past experiences at the Can of Pee.

The petite, waif, skinny unnatural blonde girl tending the counter, still enmeshed in conversation with the other foreign girl customer, Takuto referred to as Sadie when he called her over. When she spoke to Takuto, her attitude had taken a congenial, more humble turn as opposed to the surly demeanor she presented Liz with. Her accent when talking was like that of Keefer, Ricky, and Simon, so she figured Sadie was Australian. She also did what Taffie used to do—mix and interject random words in her native language when trying to communicate in a foreign one, this time speaking Japanese to Takuto while using English words to fill the gap when there was a word she knew not how to say or explain.

Regardless of how she executed it, Liz could quickly see that this girl Sadie's Japanese was at a level that was still superior to hers, so she could see how her services wouldn't likely be needed were she to ask Takuto if his job offer still stood. It became apparent to her what had happened. She almost had to laugh, for she wasn't even bitter. In fact, she was happy for him.

Takuto had finally found a Disney princess of his own for the time being. Liz imagined that however Sadie became introduced to him, Takuto had probably fawned and ingratiated himself to her in the same way he had to her when Taffie had first brought her around. It had to be the case, Liz reasoned, because Sadie appeared to be a lazy, trifling "whiffet". Despite all of this notwithstanding, Takuto's finding himself a *gaijin* pet didn't seem to account for the reason he was acting like he was practically a stranger to her now, when before he had been so enthralled with her. It didn't compute in her brain.

After his quick cold shoulder when Liz inferred about her working there at the Can of Pee, Takuto raced off to clean up and clear another table. Sadie was now acting a little busier than she had been previously by washing a glass or two, albeit at a snail's pace, and she was still shouting conversation pieces at the girl at the counter's end section.

When Takuto came back around, he spoke to the girl Sadie had been kicking it with the entire night. A torrent of rejection needles stung away at Liz's fragile feelings seeing Takuto greet the woman with a smile absent when he had spoken to Liz that night. He hadn't even volunteered to make her a stronger drink. He took the other woman's glass and commenced to fix her a cocktail. He ignored Liz. She got fed up.

Liz said, "Hey, Tak'-san, if you're not gonna give me a job, I can understand, but what's the reason for you acting so strange? I thought we were cool, dude? I went to your birthday party, remember? What's your problem?" She edged her seat away from the counter as if she was preparing to leave. She forgot to ask Takuto about Taffie, but the way he had been carrying on, it didn't seem likely he would offer up anything useful for her quest.

There was an underlying feeling of guilt Takuto had tried to conceal. It was true what Liz had said. He really did like her. Still. But at the same time, he had deeper feelings—on a fellowship level—for Taffie Jolie.

Taffie had been his friend, acquaintance, and confidant for a longer time than the beauty queen candidate Elizabeth Amberbush. He tried and succeeded, to an extent, to understand Taffie's pain. Thus, when he had learned of—or better, heard of—the things that Liz had done, as told to him by Taffie, on the frosty evenings following the Christmas party where she saw the girl she thought was her best friend in bed with her boyfriend at that time, Takuto's opinion of Liz plummeted like a failed parachute.

It was hard for Takuto to accept the fact that Liz was that sort of person, but he had never known Taffie to be a liar. Secretly, he was also jealous that Liz had chosen to sleep with one of Taffie's boyfriends and not him. He had campaigned heavily for her affection since the first time he had met her. He showered her with free drinks, offered her the same sucker job Sadie seemed to be enjoying, and would have given her so much more too, if she had been his girl. All those nights carousing the streets of Osaka after hours together in hopes that Liz would allow him to devour her pristine, angelic anatomy from head to toe, had evaporated in smoke. Although he would never reveal any of these reasons for being the tumid factor in why his attitude toward her had changed, Liz could sense it in a cerebral, subjective sort of way.

Takuto couldn't hide or submerge his stigma too much after Liz had reminded him of their better times. Still, he tried to maintain poise as if he was contented with his new Australian cutie, Sadie. Although she was nowhere near the sexy, alluring "snack" as was Liz, Sadie abated his yearning for foreign flesh at least, and satiated his Disney girl fetish.

Unfortunately, Liz wielded an enchanting and beguiling form of magic that unsuspecting men such as Takuto were unable to resist for too long. Sure, he was strong and had seen scores of *gaijin* come and go. Sadie probably did much to keep him reeled into reality with enough of her own endearing qualities, but she was no Liz by any stretch of the imagination. As Liz grabbed her purse and stood up from her chair, Takuto, as if released from a spell preventing him from interacting cordially with Liz, gritted his teeth and spoke earnestly with her for the first time that evening.

Without betraying Taffie by giving away her location, for he knew where she was—he remained loyal to her—but he had enough feelings for Liz to throw her a bone. He told Liz that she ought to check out the place where Taffie used to work, the Dream Lounge. He referred Liz to a woman she knew about, but only in drunken passing, Saiko Yamabiko. Liz still had the woman's card in her collection of others too vast to even keep in her wallet any longer.

Takuto said, "Maybe Saiko will have some answers for you about Taffie."

That Liz decided to do: she was going to pay a visit to the Dream Lounge. But that would have to wait for another night. She didn't have the biz card on her person. The card with the name and address of the Dream Lounge was in a pile at her pad, in a conglomerate mass mixed up with the myriad of other cards she would get from people at the fitness club, random *gaijin* bars, and assorted other places.

Liz didn't even bother to finish the drink Sadie made, which ran concurrent with the name of the bar in terms of its appeal, but dropped a 1G bill on the counter, overpaying for the drink. When she left, Sadie called out for her, explaining that she had some change coming. Arrogant with pride, Liz pretended to not hear her and subtly made it known the chump change wasn't needed. As far as Liz was concerned, Sadie could keep it and save up to buy a better attitude.

Takuto watched the ambrosial American angel Liz leave his sight, and a tear almost trickled down his eye. When he called out her name, Liz didn't hear him, but someone else did. The woman seated at the end of the counter, the side that was perpendicularly closest to the streetside curb situated at the outside portion of the "canopied" bar, looked up suddenly. As Liz walked away outside the restaurant, on the sidewalk, the woman called out to her.

"Hey, Elizabeth?" she called out to Liz with a loud, melodic voice.

Liz turned to face the girl. She squinted, for the first time staring at the woman's face with intent. Now she seemed familiar, an occurrence Liz found to happen quite often. But Liz didn't feel the need to try to draw a composite in her mind as to who the girl was. She thought that she was trying to help Sadie alert her about the change she had coming. It wasn't so.

The woman said, "Oh wow! Y'know, I kinda thought that I knew you, but I wasn't completely sure until they just screamed your name out."

Now Liz was completely in the dark. Now she had to know where she had seen this woman before and where she knew her from. "How do you know my name? Where did we meet before? Do I, like . . . know you?" She tried to not seem rude, but it was sometimes a bit unsettling to meet strange people who knew her and she couldn't recall how they became acquainted. It was OK, because the woman seemed harmless, nonthreatening, and amiable.

"We work—well, *we used to work* at the same company. You work for Bozack, right? The English school? You worked at the Hommachi Branch I think it was, right?"

Liz confirmed with halfhearted repose upon realizing that the woman was a Bozack teacher. She said, "Yeah, I guess you can say I work with Bozack. I'm on my way out, as we speak, I think. How about you? What branch do you work at?"

The woman said with an arbitrary laugh, "Oh, no, I don't work there anymore. But I used to work mainly at the Kyobashi branch. My secondary school was here in Umeda, and every once in a while, I was at Higobashi. Hey, do you have a minute? I was just about to leave here." She got up from her chair.

Liz thought for a minute and decided why not. After all, the woman seemed affable, she too was a foreigner, and Liz could use a friend, or a semblance of one, right about that time. A minute later, the woman was standing next to her outside the Can of Pee, leaving behind a sour-faced Sadie, who appeared pouty because her chat "mate" had vacated the outfit.

"My name is Laura," the woman said. "Laura Violi." She was a bit tawdry in her duds, but she had a cute face. Thick eyebrows over an upturned set of eyes, somewhat full lips, and a small Roman nose. Her chestnut-auburn hair was collarbone length, with curls full around her shoulders and balanced with her forehead's width. She was a basic cute broad, Liz determined, standing almost the same height as Liz, but more on the frailer side in terms of figure and composition. "I know a better place than that anyway," she said. "I only go there from time to time because they have happy hour. Otherwise, they suck. That new girl they have working there sucks! She couldn't make a drink even with step-by-step instructions a kindergartner would understand, but she certainly had stories!"

They shared a laugh. Liz was basking in the joy of having someone around her who had a sense of humor, and one who also shared the same opinion.

Liz's eyes swept Laura as they walked along the brightly lit Takagami Broadway. "I still can't remember where we've met. I mean, like, I don't mean to sound like a stuck-up bitch, but people are always coming up to me and telling me they know me, and I can't ever seem to remember where I saw them or met them. It's sometimes a little freaky, y'know what I mean?"

"Oh, sorry about that. You were quite popular, you have a boyfriend, right? The last time we met you, it was at the Sapporo Beer Hall, last October, I think. You, your boyfriend, and some black girl came." Laura laughed "You practically came and threw me out of the chair so that she could sit next to Chucky Chilson. How is old Chuck, by the way? I never see him much these days. He used to hang out in American Village a lot, at the Moon Slice Club or the Cellar."

It was becoming somewhat clear to Liz now about who Laura was albeit vague still. Just like a lot of other times when Liz had been out and about, painting the town alongside her friends and Eddie, she was "zooted" or drunk out of her mind. On the night of the Sapporo Beer Hall gathering, she had been heavily snorting cane, so a blur in her memory's time frame came with the territory.

"Where's Chuck?" Liz responded to Laura's inquiry rhetorically. "That's the zillion-dollar question I've been asking for months. He just up and disappeared. So did that black girl, Denore, you must've seen me with that night. She used to be my roommate. Gosh, what a bundle of nerves she was . . . but she up and split too. One day, I showed up to our room, the next thing I know, a bunch of suits from Bozack HQ show up and squeaky-cleaned up her side, leaving it vacant. I haven't seen or heard of her ever since."

Laura's face went from jocose to troubled. She uttered, "That's creepy. But there's no shortage of that kind of thing with Bozack. Face it, we worked with a bunch of weirdos. I wish you the best of luck if you stay there. Me? I've had enough of it. I can get a job somewhere else with less stress and strife. Hey, let's go here." She pointed to a glittery bar Liz had seen before but never visited in the area. It looked like a wooden shack from a rustic, outback setting that had been cemented and pushed inside of a modern stone building and had a kangaroo cartoon image above its transparent plastic-glass-windowed doors.

They went inside. The place was dark, but illuminated by neon signs advertising various alcoholic beverages like Zima, Miller Lite, Budweiser, Foster's, and others. There were also streams of Christmas decorative fairy lights situated all over the room, which was about the same size as Liz's apartment in terms of space. Loud music played, Eagle-Eye Cherry's "Save Tonight" infusing the sound of bar room mirth and that of darts banging electronic targets in the recreation section in the rear. Even though this was Japan, Liz felt like she was in a regular country Western–style bar and grill back home in California.

Laura and Liz sat at a makeshift wooden table that looked like an empty, side-turned industrial spool, which must have once supported lengths of factory cable on a harbor dockside. A husky and friendly Japanese staffer in a black T-shirt bearing the same kangaroo emblem seen outside the place's entrance greeted Laura with a half hug. She ordered something like a screwdriver while Liz stuck with her gin and tonic. Moments later, the drinks arrived, and Liz was more satisfied with the efforts made there as opposed to the disaster Sadie had prepared for her at the previous joint. Liz and Laura made a small toast, and the theme may as well have been to new friendships.

Minutes into the conversation with Laura, Liz regretted not being acquainted with her sooner. She was more interesting than other female coworkers like Stephanie. She was from Canada, she grew up not too far from Montreal, in a town called Mirabel, and the daughter of Italian immigrants. She could speak Italian, French, as well as English, and due to being in Japan for the last five years, she was well on her way to being able to brag about a fourth language she spoke. Bozack had her doubling as a part-time Italian teacher as well as an English teacher.

Laura said, "I would teach Italian lessons once or twice a month. And just now, the French teacher suddenly quit. So they asked me to cover the French lessons there. In fact, they even asked me to be the head teacher of the North Town schools—Kyobashi and Umeda. I was, like, hell no! I've had too much on my plate for too long, and—"

Liz was still reeling from the news of Serge. "Wait, that French guy, the one with the curly blond hair, chin dimple, always looks like he could shave a little better . . ."

Laura said, "Um, yeah, the guy who took over for the black French girl . . . Tiffiany?"

"Taffie!" Liz blurted. "Like that candy, sticks to your teeth. Oh that's fucken' crazy! He just suddenly quit? That's what the guy said at the club where he works at too. That he just quit. Oh wow, now he's quit Bozack too?"

Laura laughed and sipped her drink. "There's a lot of that goin' around, then.

After the last few outlandish months at Kyobashi, I think I've seen it all and don't care to see any more. Like I said, I don't care how much they pay—which, believe me, isn't much more—I'm through working these long hours, sitting with these Japanese zombies and their children in kids' lessons, and . . . ugh! I'm so free now!"

Liz said, "So who's gonna teach French now since you turned the position down?"

Laura said, "Worm!"

Liz laughed. "Oh, you call him that too? I thought only the people who knew him at the South Town schools called him that."

Laura said, "Yeah, well, his real name should be Maggot, or Slimeball. Everybody knows he threw Tim under the bus, but word around the office has it he got ol' Dee fired too."

"'Dee'?" Liz asked with a worried face.

"You know Deon? We used to call him Dee. He doesn't work at one school—they kinda have him floatin' around to different schools. I hadn't seen much of him these days, after Chucky and some of the other guys quit, but—"

A confounded Liz could barely find the words to speak. "Oh, my fucken' gawd! Are you serious? They fucken' fired Deon?"

Laura said, "Yeah. And I take it that Worm had a lot to do with it too."

"How so?" Liz asked.

"Well, I'm not exactly sure, but it's no secret that ever since the drug bust and Worm's demotion, he's been trying to kiss ass and brown-nose all over the place to get his spot back. So when Deon got drunk on his lunch break or somethin', Worm ratted him out to the management for brownie points. Then Deon got fired. It sucks, but I guess he took the risk."

Liz listened with suspicion. "That just doesn't sound like him. He's not really a drinker."

Laura's face was painted in dubiety. "Really? I've seen him get wasted a couple of times. Not recently, but—"

"No, don't get me wrong," Liz added quickly. "I mean, he does booze out every now and then, but generally, he doesn't drink all that much. I've never known him to drink while at work. Hell, he's probably one of the best employees they've got—or had—fuck! That doesn't sound right. If Worm did that, then he's a piece of shit."

"Trust me, he is," Laura said. "I mean, his wife is all right, I guess. They throw these lavish parties at his place. Have you been to their house?"

Liz said, "Yeah, several times. They know how to throw a party, I'll give 'em credit for that."

Laura said, "I stopped going to those parties. It's nothin' but a popularity contest. It stopped being my cup of tea. Too many groupie Japanese sluts hangin' around trying to sleep around with any dorky foreign guy, making them feel like they're gallant, manful studs. I had to take my hat off to you for having a boyfriend and bringing him around. Are you still with him?"

Liz had hoped she wouldn't ask that, but since she shared the same opinion as Laura about how Japanese women fawned over foreign guys, she felt less pressure. "We broke up. In the worst way too . . ." She fought back a creeping lump in her throat. "He broke up with me right before Christmas!" Then a tear finally fell from her eye; it came from nowhere as she reminisced about her past. Meeting Laura had dredged up memories at an odd time for her. Quickly, she dispersed her eye moisture to the air. "Sorry!"

Compassionately, Laura lightly rubbed Liz on her shoulder. "Hey, it's OK. It happens to the best of us. It's happened to a lot of us girls. Let me guess, he left you for a Jap girl too, huh?"

Liz sniffed slightly, her nose and eyes flushed a little bit red; but the dim maroon-sangria lighting of the barroom shaded her sockets. "I'm pretty sure he did. I'm thinking that it was some bitch he teaches with at the junior high school he works at. Fucking bastard!"

"Oh, wow! He's an ALT?" Laura finished her drink then looked about in search of the same staff guy who had served her and Liz.

"Yeah, we came here with the CHET Program," Liz said.

"Good grief! That program is just a scam. They all are. I mean, don't get me wrong, good for you, but tell the truth—you barely did any work, did you?" Laura laughed, and Liz did too. "But everyone I ever met—guys, I mean—who did any of those programs, they seem to always meet their wives doing that job."

The friendly burly server returned so Laura could order another drink. She asked Liz if she needed another. Liz quaffed hers down as if she were a sot like Stephanie.

Liz said, "Yeah, make me a strong one, same thing!"

Laura spoke Japanese to the man; he seemed to understand, and then he laughed and offered Liz a thumbs-up before scuttling back to the bar and kitchen. Liz praised Laura for her Japanese.

Laura said, "Yeah, I still feel like I have a long way to go, though. Japanese is a language that feels so difficult to ever conquer. But hey, don't they have free Japanese classes when you're with the CHET Program?"

Liz bit her lip, then shrugged with indifference. "They do, I mean, they did, but—it's a long story. Yeah, I didn't take advantage of it, I know. I tried in the beginning, but then it just became too much of a drag, and I never really bothered. Like I said, it's a long story. Y'see, we never—or, I never planned on staying here in Japan for so long. Me and Eddie, we thought we were going to come here for a year or two, work, save money, then go back to the States and live happily ever after, you know how that story goes. Didn't you have a boyfriend too?"

Laura said, "Well, I dated some guys, but when I came to Japan, I was single.

I mean, I had just graduated, so . . ." Drinks arrived, so she had to pause to receive hers. The friendly staff guy gave Liz another thumbs-up when delivering her drink. He waited to watch her sip it as if to seek approval for his efforts to make the drink strong as she requested. Liz took a sip and felt as if she was drinking Tanqueray straight with only a lime. She laughed and made an "OK" sign with her fingers. Dude guffawed like a goofy giant and retreated to the kitchen.

Liz said, "Can't believe I never came to this place before. It's pretty cool."

Laura said, "I work around here sometimes, so when I hang out with the Umeda teachers, we usually do this strip and Shin-Midosuji, Tocca-Tte, and Bar-Isn't Shit . . ." She kept naming popular bars and clubs.

Liz redirected the conversation back to her epic story of how she came to Japan. She said, "It's funny, you say most of the guys you met who did those programs like CHET met their wives, but the guy who told me about the program, the guy who *really* got us interested in coming here, he didn't marry a Japanese girl."

Laura was busy drinking. "I'm sorry, a guy you knew told you about what?"

"I used to date this guy back in the States. He was a real pushover, but he was a nice guy. Anyway, me and Eddie were job hunting, I bump into him at our alma mater, and he tells me about how he just came back from Japan, he's got a new job, he saved his money, and Japan was so wonderful—all that gobbledygook. So he filled us in about the CHET Program. He did two years and yeah, he came back, no wife."

Laura paused to take a break from her sipping straw to tighten her thick lips. She said, "Maybe he was gay, or not into Japanese women."

That caused for an eruption of laughter from Liz, for she often wondered the same about Carver. Questioning his sexuality was a given, but in the initial stages of their dating, it was only to pacify her mother, who feared Liz would be a full-fledged lesbian if left to her own devices. Liz was hesitant and reluctant to share too much of her past with complete strangers, even though Laura seemed nice enough. She had hit her with some heavy news that night.

Liz said, "I still can't believe it . . . Serge gone, now Deon . . ."

Laura said, "So they're gonna bring Worm to Umeda, because he speaks French too. The American guy, Russel, he's the new South Town head teacher. Rosiland is back at Tennoji HQ, and, I believe, Ellen McDowd is gonna stay at Amagasaki. They wanted me to be here in Umeda and Kyobashi, but I said no, so Elaine Fleckler is going to be there."

Liz said, "I heard of some of those people but don't know them personally. How do you know all the scoop on everything?"

Laura said, "I think the Tennoji chick, the big bossy Ruth Worth is an undercover dyke, and she occasionally gets down with this blatant, monster-sized lesbian Darcy Blake. She's at Kyobashi too, but she's sweet, though. Yeah, she kinda spills it if you get her drunk enough."

"It's crazy how so much has been goin' on. All this time, I should have been hanging out with you." They laughed.

Laura then said, "Are you kidding? Your schools were the most popular. We wanted to hang out with you guys. Plus, I heard you're one of the best teachers in South Town. Because of you, the wacky school image bumped up a notch."

Liz took the complimentary info in stride. She asked, "So what are you gonna do now that you've quit?"

Laura said, "I'm thinking. A friend of mine works in Shikoku. It's a small island south of this Honshu island. She says she can get me a job as an ALT, but with a legit Japanese company, not any of those 'programs'. Or, I dunno . . . you do know you can work part-time jobs and get the same if not more money than you can working for one company, like Bozack—which bans you from moonlightin' another gig on the side."

Liz squinted in deep thought. "Yeah, seems to me somebody else told me that." She thought about Jeremy. Suddenly his idea of freelance teaching became appealing once again. She told Laura about her recent adventures in teaching children on the side, sparing her the details of the obscene run-in with their father, Mr. Sakamaki.

Laura was like, "Oh, absolutely! Teaching kids on the side? Excellent. Especially if you have your own students. If you go through a middleman or a smaller school, you know they'll take their cut. But if you find your own students, you can negotiate your own price, keep all the profit. They even pay your transportation too."

Liz said, "You got me thinking. I know a guy, Jeremy. He has these private lessons he teaches, maybe I'll get him to introduce me to some of his clients."

Laura said, "The biggest challenge will probably be arranging your schedule. If you get too many gigs, your time slots might overlap. Whoa! Are you thinkin' about quitting or something?"

Liz explained her situation. She ran down to Laura about the weed-and-Ingrid situation as well and how she became entangled in her current predicament. Laura listened intently. She came across as a more worldly sort than Liz, and was also calm and mild-mannered even though becoming noticeably drunk. Still, she didn't act wild and savage like others Liz had partied with while in Japan—herself included.

The night stretched on, and the more they talked, the more Liz debated whether or not she would stay with Bozack. One thing was certain, and that was Liz's overall mood was lifted after meeting Laura. Meeting her came in a timely fashion. They remained at the bar until a little after midnight before parting company. They exchanged contact information and made a pledge to stay in contact like people usually do. Too bad she wasn't really attracted to Laura in the way she sometimes was to other females; otherwise, she could escape and spend a night with her. She dreaded the return home and facing the moping Ingrid, but she also had a weighty load on her own mind. Besides, there was an itch Liz had that no female could effectively scratch for her at that point. As a result, she had an uncanny yearning to see Serge, but from what she had heard, he too had been erased from her life's picture.

70

BORN SAEKO YAMAUCHI and originally from a countryside town in the Yamanashi prefecture of Japan, the woman who would come to be known as Mama-san Saiko Yamabiko grew up a stone's throw from the majestic and picturesque Mt. Fuji. In her nineteenth year, she left her hometown behind for Osaka with aspirations of meeting a wealthy urban upper-cruster and living happily ever after with this fancy magnate. She often wondered about how her life would have been different had she not chosen Osaka over Tokyo. It was a decision she made because her paternal grandparents were from there, and visiting the city as a child gave her a feeling that Osaka was her second home.

The erstwhile Saeko's story was so similar to Taffie's that it seemed eerie. She met a sugar daddy while working *mizu-shobai*, or "night life" (water business because it involved the serving of alcohol). She was a hostess, a high-priced hooker. Eventually, she caught the eye of a rich but married fuddy-duddy twice her age. As his sidepiece mistress, her recently declared "adult" flesh proved to be too much for the old gent to handle, and he too perished from a heart seizure while sticking her stuff. The only difference between her story and Taffie's tragic turn of events was Saeko/Saiko's love daddy actually bequeathed upon her a grip of long dough and some property. Apparently, the old man who kicked the bucket didn't give a damn about what his wife thought, and they never had any kids during their marriage.

With her newly acquired fortune, Saeko/Saiko didn't have any particular business skill or talent. All she knew was how to be a hostess. So with her granted money, she established her own lounge, one which she would also operate. This would be a success for many years until she decided to change her name and relocate to Osaka City's Kita-Shinchi area. This was a district that could be otherwise considered the red light for "richy folks," with a high concentration of bars, exclusive clubs, secret sex dens, and extravagant restaurants.

The name change to "Saiko" came as a result of her desire to distance herself from her past and relinquishing connection to her benefactor. She also wanted to control her image. She wanted people to think that she was a hardworking showbiz chick who made her fortune on her own and not because she had received an inheritance handout from a sugar daddy contributor. It was a simple formula, and it worked.

Along the way, she met a guy—Yutaka Morimoto. He was a divorced truck driver at that time and didn't mind spending his extra bucks at Saiko's lounge, before she relocated. He never had a snowball's chance in hell of hooking up with Saiko, but he didn't know it, and she made sure he didn't. Yet she made sure to call him and cry her woes on him, and he would soak up her tears like a sponge hearing about her failed romances with other men. Finally, dude pleaded his case, practically begged for her to be his woman; but she turned him down, albeit tenderly, and masterfully manipulated his emotions. She shaped him like a clay object, basically, to be like one of her shelf ornaments. Yutaka accepted his rejection, but not before he fell into a brief depression that resulted in him drinking heavily and losing his job as a trucker. Pitying him, Saiko gave him a job as a handyman in the property—the apartment building—imparted upon her by her deceased benefactor. He had been following her around ever since like a blind, hypnotized footman, a devoted gofer.

With her plentiful income, Saiko could afford to splurge on things ordinary women her age didn't have easy access to. As a hobby and interest, she learned English and French. She received private lessons from astute tutors. She even attended major English conversation schools, and eventually, the newly formed Bozack School. As a result, her English communication skills became remarkably good, and she acquired clientele on the corporate level from these schools where she studied.

Because her apartment property was a dumpy building in a slummy section of town, it was difficult for her to acquire tenants. To solve this "problem," she delved into the illegal side of the game and employed struggling immigrants and people of foreign nationalities to work for her, but she registered their names under Japanese people. She would take the rent money from their salaries directly once a month. Plus, they had to pay a "service fee" for the legit Japanese person's name on the registry. The idea behind that reasoning was explained as it was a small price to pay to evade the oppressive entanglement of red tape from the government.

The successful formula worked for Saiko. Her lounge, which she named the

Dream, became popular. While most other similar establishments offered only Japanese—or Korean women pretending to be Japanese—Saiko's Dream Lounge would offer not only these but also Chinese, Romanians, a Russian, and every once in a while North American Canadians. Taffie, of course, was her first two birds with one stone—French and Black. Since she could speak English and French, she didn't have communication problems with the foreigners she employed. The uniqueness of her lounge lineup brought her a mountain of business. As a result, her women were well paid, and she was paid even better. She required her women to reside at her apartment, and she took rent money, plus tip contributions from their intricate system of payments and exchanges.

Now she was forty-nine and having regrets that she never settled down at a time in her life when she was youthful and plummy. Although she named her lounge Dream, like the big ones she had, she witnessed them fade like her once-beautiful features, which were these days ghosted by heavy dabs of makeup and enough powder to bake a cake. Hiding wrinkles and damage associated with many a drunken night frolicking after hours became daily maintenance and tiring rituals.

True to her intentions, Liz toughed out a night with Ingrid and abated it by drawing her divider to separate the rooms and fall asleep. Luckily, she had downed enough gin to feel tranquilized.

The following night, she was able to locate the Shimo-Higahsi building because she showed a taxi driver the business card Saiko gave her a while back. The cabdriver skillfully eased his vehicle between the slim alleyways and backstreet lanes of Kita-Shinchi. When she arrived at the building, Liz could hardly believe that the decrepit, derelict building was even a place considered suitable for occupancy. At first glance, the building looked like one that would be marked for demolition. She dared to enter, however, and took the elevator to the fourth floor as the biz card indicated.

When she arrived at the Dream Lounge, there was a huge wooden door with a horizontal handle she pulled open like that of a refrigerator. Inside, she felt as if she had stepped into a portal that had transported her to another place and time, betraying the haunted-mansion appearance of the building outside. Several sectional sofas lined the expansive room, exotic plants in strategic locations, dim beige lighting, and a huge wall with a realistic-looking mock photo of the Umeda skyline, as if they were on the rooftop of a skyscraper. In addition to the decorum, there was the traditional Japanese ornaments on *etagere,* ceramic vases, silk tapestries, and a quaint, unique bamboo rocking water garden with an actual indoor stream that flowed into a small rocky aquatic pool in the center of the room and had real goldfish. Music in the background was that of some traditional *hogaku* sound—rich with the bold strokes of the Japanese *koto,* a stringed instrument. The place smelled like whiskey and perfume. Liz's mind was blown.

It was early evening, though officially open for business, the nightly calamity had yet to kick off and reach its peak as it did around and after midnight. As such, the Dream Lounge wasn't very crowded. She saw two foreign chicks flanking a grinning Japanese man who looked to be in his fifties, short, stubby, and the unlikely sort to be mistaken as a lady-killer. Yet the two Caucasian women petting and stroking his head like he was an adorable pet probably made him feel like he was a Japanese Ultra Man. Meanwhile, Liz checked out the women: their frames were bony, arms appeared flimsy and in a state of desuetude perhaps, and were decked out in gaudy red and burgundy shoestring dresses. With their disheveled hairstyles, the only thing that saved their appearances was some dangling earpiece jewelry that made a semblance of elegance for them. Maybe the Japanese man that paid for their time couldn't tell they were cheap broads, but Liz surely could. Had she seen them in Los Angeles, she would have thought them to be streetwalking prostitutes like the ones on La Cienega Boulevard.

One of the Romanian hostesses entertaining the happy runt Japanese customer spotted Liz, and her eyes narrowed in jealousy and outrage. Her stare spoke as if to say, *What are you doing in here?*

It was not necessary. Almost startlingly, Liz remembered the poised and swanky Saiko Yamabiko when she emerged from her luxurious sitting room boudoir that doubled as her private office. Likewise, with uncanny coincidence, Saiko faintly remembered Liz. At once, they took to one another like long-lost friends. For Saiko, the pieces fell into place about who exactly she was when Liz made mention of Taffie and her desire to learn of her whereabouts.

Liz filled Saiko in on the events that had taken place. She told her about how she lost contact with Taffie and was unable to reach her. Saiko had listened curiously, for she too was looking for Taffie.

Taffie broke out on Saiko too. She had split town, left Saiko's apartment, and provided no information as to her whereabouts. This incensed Saiko because she felt betrayed. She had helped Taffie and, in so doing, felt that she was obligated to obey her like she was her actual mother, as her panjandrum *mama-san* suggested.

Saiko listened to Liz with objectivity and determined her to not be a liar. Especially since she indicated to Saiko that her need to see Taffie was important because there was a possibility that she would leave Japan soon. This, in turn, caused Saiko to inquire as to why she was leaving. Then, Liz would go on to explain her current situation with Bozack at the time, again however, sparing the details of her drug habit and what lead to her job being in jeopardy.

Upon hearing Liz's candid talk, Saiko felt as if she had struck gold yet again. She checked Liz out and viewed how lovely she was. The way she was dressed that night in a high-waist, belted pencil skirt, textured-seam tank blouse, and slingback pumps with peeptoes, she looked like she could make an excellent hostess. The Dream Lounge's loss of Taffie caused it to suffer somewhat a blow and impacted business, but were she to acquire another foreign girl, especially an authentic United States American girl, she would once again rise to the top of underworld late-night entertainment dens.

In this bizarre twist of fate, Liz's meeting Saiko Yamabiko formally, without being stagnantly intoxicated, would be a stroke of good luck as well as a life-altering event. Saiko had decided she would harbor no ill will for Liz being friends with Taffie, as Liz had no idea about the inner conflict that existed between her and the estranged French girl. What transpired between Taffie and Saiko remained a secret, and to Liz's disappointment, Saiko was unable to provide her with any information she sought regarding where Taffie was.

Instead, Saiko shifted gears, and on the flip, offered Liz a job working in her lounge. Hearing the young American girl's job woes and fear of eviction from her company housing, Saiko felt that she could end it all with basically a snap of her finger. She conveyed to Liz that there was no need to worry about being evicted or homeless, because she could move into one of the vacant apartments in Saiko's building where her other hostesses and Taffie resided.

The idea was intriguing, Liz had to admit. She had played with the thought of being a porn star in her prior days, back in California when she felt desperate at times for quick, easy money. Now, propositioned to be a type of "prostitute," she still had some reservations.

In reality, even though Taffie spoke about her work at the lounge sparingly, Liz had very scant knowledge about what *mizu-shobai*, or a hostess's job, actually was. Furthermore, she had a deep-down subtle disdain for Japanese women—Japanese society in general—that trickled down from uneasiness and distrust for some of the more unsavory types of people she had met in the country. She expressed her feelings to Saiko in a way that she hoped would be understood, so that she could politely communicate "Thanks, but no thanks" to the job offer without offending.

Saiko, however, dressed the job up to make it seem appealing. In a manner much the same as the convincing way Carver had steered Liz toward the CHET Program and living and working in Japan, Saiko made the Dream Lounge job seem like it was a gateway to heaven. Having attended English conversation schools like Bozack in her time, Saiko likened Liz's job there to the work in the lounge. Instead of having controlled conversations and fake dialogues with people crammed in forty-five- or fifty-minute session intervals like at the schools, at the lounge she could have relaxed conversations on comfortable recliners, enjoy alcohol, and have the freedom to move about—even be taken on dates outside the lounge. Clubs, expensive dinners, vacations, shopping sprees, and other such benefits awaited should she take the job. Of course, she neglected to mention would-be stalkers, possible rapists, and other degenerates; but fortunately, with her high-level clientele, such was rare. Liz remembered how Taffie would go shopping at expensive boutiques in Kobe and Tokyo every other month. It was worth a thought. Taffie also never seemed short of money either.

Eventually, Saiko somehow gained Liz's trust. In an odd way, Saiko reminded Liz faintly of Hitomi, her former manager at the Umeda School. Although not quite as aged as Hitomi, there was a warm, "grandmotherly" spirit Saiko exuded, which wasn't lost upon her. Additionally, what would ultimately work in Saiko's favor was her offer to assist Liz with a place to stay. Everyone else had pretty much abandoned her, and she had too much pride to go begging people like Worm, or her ex Eddie for help. Maybe, she thought, she would try her hand at the hostess job. As long as it didn't entail her sleeping with strange Japanese men for sex and money, she was game. From what she recalled hearing Taffie speak about her work, never did she mention anything of the sort. For Taffie, the only difficulty she seemed to encounter, as reported moderately to Liz, was the excessive drinking involved with the job.

Saiko assured Liz, however, that she needed not worry about such things as sex or going to bed with clients. It was considered, as Saiko put it, "rare," and something she personally advised against. The final kicker was Saiko's promise to have Liz paid anywhere from the Japanese equivalent of two to five hundred US dollars per night. Hearing this, Liz was convinced that it was worth a go. Aligning with the previous night's discussion with Laura Violi, Liz figured she would hook up with Jeremy Ng, have him introduce some of his private students, and maybe do that sort of gig in the daytime, then at night work for Saiko. It would be fun and interesting, she thought. Even though she had hit a dead end on her search for Taffie for the time being, Saiko made it seem to her that Taffie's disappearance was "temporary," and that she sometimes did such things. Often being absent for weeks or months at a time. It was a lie, of course, but Liz fell for it. She was gullible because Saiko had a deeper history with Taffie and knew her longer.

Punctuating with a declaration that reeked of a homiletic mission statement, Saiko rendered, "Our clients are lonely, hardworking wealthy gentlemen who merely require conversation, fun companionship with classy, charming women to pour them drinks and drink together with them. That's all. We are here to fulfill their wildest dreams. That's why this is the Dream Lounge."

With an offer that promised in excess of five hundred dollars a night, if she worked five days a week, Liz saw herself making far more money than she was making at Bozack, and lesser hours too even though it was to be in the evenings from 10:00 p.m. or 11:00 p.m. until the early morning, around 5:30 a.m., when most public city transportation resumed daily operations.

Graciously, Liz accepted the job! Albeit with her slight discomfiture not quelled completely, she still decided to be audaciously daring; she would embark upon a new life experience to sit back and joke about in her later years.

71

LIZ'S SUDDEN DECISION to quit Bozack might have fortuitously saved Ingrid's job in the process. Needless to say, her choice to abruptly resign came as a shock. Ruth Worth had not anticipated her making such an announcement bright and early on Monday morning, just when she was about to drop the hammer on Ingrid. Liz had arrived an hour before Ingrid's scheduled verdict was to be levied. At which time, she managed to gain an impromptu minute of Ruth's time and delivered her news inside of the micro-office room, which resembled an expanded phone booth. While Ruth was trying to enjoy her morning coffee, she also struggled to remain impassive, but it was a difficult task as Liz's departure would cause yet another wrinkle in the company's fabric to be smoothed out. Her name had been floating about during council meetings and had been considered for promotion. Ruth felt it pertinent to mention such to Liz in hopes that it would sway her from making the hasty move. It didn't work. Liz had made up her mind. The talk she had with Saiko two nights earlier had convinced her. She was sold. She even spent time in the Dream Lounge that same night, "training" just to get the feel of what the new hostess job would be like. So far, Saiko was right. The hostess job was just like working at Bozack, only, there were no draconic, oppressive micromanaging rats and snitches watching over her shoulder waiting for her to make a mistake so they could run to the Japanese management to tattle and gain brownie points, feathering their own nest at the expense of the poor, lowly-level teacher employee.

Dangling the carrot of a promotion before Liz like they did with Laura and a few others was a useless tactic. She had no interest in holding a higher position or title. If it meant that she would have to work even a slight amount of longer hours as well as an extension of job duties, these factors alone would have dissuaded Liz from assuming the position as head teacher. Then there was the possibility that she would have to try to "police" fellow teachers in not only one school but possibly two or three. It wasn't something she thought she was cut out for anyway. And after talking to Laura Violi, she was convinced that it wouldn't do much for her to have higher aspirations working with Bozack. Only heightened stress levels. For Liz, that would have been both at work and at her living quarters.

At the dormitory, although it was livable, it wasn't the ideal setting in which she wanted to reside anymore. Although a certain degree of privacy could be attained, with the use of the hospital room–like dividers—like ceiling-to-floor curtains—she was still subject to companionship, be it welcome or not. And in the case of Ingrid, that package seemed to include her friends and small Filipino commune as well. So when Ruth Worth tried to portend and threaten the loss of Liz's eligibility to reside at the company dormitory, Liz was unmoved. She was ready to leave. She had *been* ready to leave.

Ruth did everything in her power to get Liz to stay, to remain with the company. Even to the extent of enticing her with the possibility of her being able to pull strings so that she would need not undergo the CRUD treatment center sanction. She tried to stall, make dummy phone calls with dummy (no party on the other end of the line) conversations, and tried to maintain her composure while she desperately tried to contact her superiors Kenji or Suguru Yamada. Neither was available, as it was still early in the morning. Yamada usually arrived closer to noon as he remained at the HQ until late hours of the night. Kenji often worked in between shifts and was more often than not situated at the Namba school when not at the HQ. Ruth vigorously attempted to contact her supervisors to report the news. She couldn't enact a decision to nix the rehab program. She hadn't the authority. At the same time, nor did she have the right to detain a person against their will. If Liz wanted to leave, she had no legal authority to keep her.

Just like that, Liz was out.

There was a heap of paperwork, as she expected there would be, and some of the forms were yet another stall tactic Ruth deployed, hoping that one of her bosses would call in. As people gradually began filing into the HQ office, Ruth Worth stopped Rosiland and broke the news to her that Liz had resigned. She spoke as if she was delivering somber funeral condolences; you could actually see the urgent disappointment on Rosiland's face, almost as if to convey that Liz's loss would impact them greatly. It could also have been an exaggeration too, Liz thought. By now she was hip that this company had too many two-faced snakes for her taste. Meeting and talking with Laura was eye-opening and a conscientious awakening, or at least Liz seemed to think at that time. Additionally, she felt empowered by the support she felt she had from Saiko Yamabiko.

Liz didn't wait around to see or hear about what happened with Ingrid. After she submitted her forms, she split afterward. Among the stack of papers, Liz used all her vacation days, sick leave days, and then accepted penalties for unworked days during teaching periods. It was chump change. Then there was the move out, return of her dorm room key—basically, forms for this and forms for that. In Japan, there was a form, a slip of paper to be filled out, stamped, ripped off, ran copies of, and in general aggravate a Westerner like Liz, who on days like this did so much writing and filling out of forms she felt she was catching arthritis.

By noon that day, Saiko contacted Liz like she said she would and wanted to know if Liz was ready to see her "new place." Liz was eagerly awaiting Saiko's call, as she spent the morning packing and trying to contact Jeremy Ng.

Saiko swung by within an hour later and picked up Liz in a milky white chocolate Infiniti whip, Yutaka behind the wheel. Yutaka had a hairstyle like Bruce Lee's in *Enter the Dragon* and liked to wear mirror-lens aviator sunglasses. He was slim built and acted like a rugged chauffer. He opened the door for Liz to get in the car and did the same when he arrived at the apartment building spot, slightly askew of Nakazaki-cho, which neighbored the notorious Doyama Village—where Brad almost had his way with Liz, but she was unaware at the time how close in proximity the area was. Locales she had not done much to familiarize herself with outside normal, routine travels.

The gloomy, almost sunlight-deprived corner of a tenement conglomerate on a small street, Saiko's apartment building stood five stories and close to a commuter train "ell" but not near any station. It housed a storefront coin-operated laundry open to the public, not just the building tenants. There was also a vending machine and *takoyaki* stand vendor's small, shabby eatery.

In addition to Saiko's hostesses, she also rented out her apartments to people who lived and worked in the Umeda area like low-rung dishwashers, chefs, students, or people with extractions outside of Japan. Liz was given the room that formerly belonged to Taffie.

At first, Liz was happy about having a room on the first floor. No steps to lumber up or an elevator to wait for. But the size of the room was a huge disappointment. She tried to hide it but failed. "I was hoping for something a little bigger," she told Saiko. The domicile reminded Liz of a dinky college dormitory room, but at least she didn't have to share it with anyone, and it was a reassurance she could live with for the time being. Saiko also embellished a possibility of her having Liz moved to a larger place. "In due time," she said.

Saiko also said, "For now, let's just get you moved in and situated. We'll take care of the other things later."

Liz could agree with her on that and went along with the program. She had no reason to distrust Saiko, she thought. After all, she seemed to be going out on a limb to assist her. She even offered to have Liz's things delivered by professional movers and have the fee taken from her first month's earnings.

"Let me get back to you on that." Liz told her.

Jeremy returned Liz's phone call. He was on the other end of the line, flabbergasted with the news that she had quit Bozack. She curtailed his tirade of concern-laced comments and queries and asked if he could help her move stuff to her new place. Without the slightest hesitation, Jeremy jumped to be at her service; he would have volunteered to assist her anyway. During that time, Liz planned to fill Jeremy in on everything that had happened, then cut into him about the freelance private-lesson circuit.

Finally, Liz made a phone call to Yoh Wamushi, the call she said she would make some time ago but didn't. When she was eventually able to touch base with him, Yoh didn't appear to have harbored any grudges or shade against her. Most people might have had feelings of ire toward a person that woke them up from a peaceful night's sleep, and to have them deliver an illegal substance to a nightclub, only to be brushed off a day or two later by that person—but Yoh was devoid of ill will. He was pleased to hear from Liz regardless of when she called.

Liz told Yoh that she was moving to another area of town. Somehow, she recalled hearing that he had a car, so she asked Yoh if he could help her move. Not surprisingly, Yoh too obsequiously proffered his service. Ingeniously, she got Jeremy and Yoh to show up at the dormitory around the same time.

Jeremy and Yoh actually knew each other, and neither of them suspected that they both were vying for Liz's affections. Jeremy and Yoh would meet occasionally, as they both had a mutual employer, Mr. Sakamaki. On infrequent chats here and there with each other, Jeremy had never heard Yoh make mention of Liz being a person of his interest. As far as he knew, Yoh was still hung up on Vicky (Jill). Vice versa, Yoh thought Liz and Jeremy were just friends and, as of that moment in time, former coworkers. Had Jeremy known that Yoh had developed some feeling that Liz had taken an interest in him much the same as how Vicky had, the dwarf-sized Jeremy with a giant's heart might have come off with a bit of animosity.

The situation never rose to such a level of excitement or disjointed proportions. The only problem, if any, arose, was from the fact that Yoh's tiny Suzuki Swift coupe was simply unable to carry all of Liz's things, plus additional people, without making exactly two trips. Rather than dismiss Jeremy, she urged him to stick around for she would need to kick it to him about the freelance teaching bit. Yoh's services would no longer be needed once he had transported the things to the address on the slip of paper—her rental agreement with Saiko.

Since Liz had gone to the apartment for the first time with Saiko by car as well, she didn't remember how to get there. She was so caught up in all the movement and excitement she neglected to search out the nearest subway, bus, or train. She barely even knew the name of the new section of town she was to live in. Therefore, she also needed to yank the coat of Yoh to translate and locate the Japanese address on the agreement form. Yes, Liz admitted, it was sneaky and low, but if Yoh wanted to really be her friend, she reasoned he would have to complete and endure tasks such as these. So far so good—he was excelling with flying colors.

Problem solved. Liz instructed Yoh to write the address on a separate sheet of paper, and when he did, she gave it to Jeremy. She said to him, "You jump in a cab, tell the driver to go to that address on the paper. If you get there before we do, just wait. Don't go anywhere. Here's some dough." She dropped a 1G bill on the table for Jeremy to grab.

With an angry smirk on his face, Jeremy took the money and said, "Hey! It's probably gonna cost more than this . . ."

Liz wasn't in the mood to argue. She had solved the issue's complexity concerning the size constraints of luggage and people. She wanted to exit, leave, and be gone before ever having to see Ingrid again.

Liz said to Jeremy as she was leaving the apartment, "Just pay the difference, Jer. Now come on, stop trying to be a wiseass. Yoh! Let's leave now."

With that, they were gone. Even though her new spot was a one-bedroom, something she would have considered to be a slight upgrade from a prison cell, it received rave reviews from Yoh and Jeremy. For the mere price of roughly five hundred dollars and near the heart of the city, it was a reasonably good price. In addition, there was a coin laundry on the ground floor, eateries, and the best of all, her room situated on the first floor. Maybe, Liz thought, it was because they were men and didn't mind cramped, squalid shelters. Still, considering the rent would be less than what she planned to take home in a day—should things work out with Jeremy's work proposition—she decided to go for it, for the time being. After all, Saiko had said she would see about moving her into a bigger place. Ultimately, neither mattered because she was headed back to the States before the end of the year anyway—if not then, before the expiration of her work visa the following year.

Yoh delivered Liz to the address on the paper copy. Along the way, Liz got a visual lay of the land. Yoh assisted her with the Japanese terms and name recognition of landmarks to help her. She saw that her nearest subway station was either Nakazaki-cho or the inordinately named Tenjinbashisuji Roku-chome, both on the purple line. She could choose either one because she was in the precise middle in terms of distance. The latter station, shortened by many to "Ten-Roku", was a bigger station that connected to other train lines; and the main drag was Ogimachi Avenue, so it was a big hub. The best thing of all, for Yoh at least, was that Liz's place was near one of Mr. Sakamaki's apartments where Yoh spent a decent amount of time.

What made Liz's neighborhood at least minimally attractive was its closer proximity to the bustling metro area of Umeda. A trip to her new job was only a five- or ten-minute ride by taxi, depending on traffic; and from what she could tell, there were more stores and food shops to choose from in contrast to where she was in Bentencho. The only thing she would miss about Bentencho, or where she had lived, was the close distance to that Thai massage parlor she adored.

Yoh informed Liz that her place was situated between Umeda and the district along Ogimachi Avenue known as Tenma. This was a lively Osaka neighborhood steeped in history, but Liz wouldn't have known had Yoh not explained it to her. By day it was an energetic shopping district, and by night a backstreet maze of quirky bars. She had regrets thinking her appreciation for Japan might have been significantly increased had she someone to describe and expound on the place as would a tour guide. A Japanese guy like Yoh would have been perfect. She was starting to see Stephanie's, Vicky/Jill's—or even Eddie's—point of view. Japan, explained to her through the eyes of a real Japanese live and in-person would have made a world of difference to how her impression of the place became. Still, there was an air of mystery surrounding this Yoh guy, as far as Liz was concerned. For as nice and congenial as he was, there was nothing so irresistible about him that caused for Vicky to remain in Japan and with him! In the days preceding Vicky's departure from Japan, they had communicated very little, but all she knew about her backstory, a guy like Yoh should have been a reasonable cure for loneliness and lost love. Liz was looking for something like that herself, but unfortunately, she wasn't attracted to Japanese men the same way. Yoh had a slight advantage because his facial features, through perhaps a freak accident of DNA; she wouldn't immediately peg him as Japanese were he in the United States.

The clanky little red Suzuki Swift vessel swerved off onto a side street from Ogimachi Avenue underneath a train overpass. He felt it his duty to help Liz get familiar with the neighboring hub. Meanwhile, Liz was fascinated by the area, feeling stoked to discover new territory.

In the weeks that followed, Liz had broken into the night life, and Saiko led her along with baby steps. First, Liz was introduced to her coworker "sisters" and given the run-down of do's and don'ts. Then Saiko sent Liz to get her hair done. Liz insisted upon seeing Takaro in Nishi-Shinsaibashi. She paid a visit to the Thai massage parlor and vowed that she would continue to patronize even though she lived farther away. After getting prettied up and refreshed at the Thai spot, she would get her nails and feet done at an exclusive salon in Ashiya, near Kobe City, a place Saiko herself frequented. She also had stressed to Liz the importance of keeping her feet clean and beautified as many of the clients had weird fetishes that involved feet, toes, and "shrimping" was not an uncommon thing. She didn't profess to knowing the exact reason for this but supplied her own theory being it had something to do with Western white women and glass slipper fantasies.

Regardless, Liz routinely managed her hygiene matters in resolute fashion and would have had a pedicure done anyway, as well as other things.

The drinking on the job wasn't a detraction, at least not for Liz. She had a reasonably high tolerance, so at times she could water her whiskey or gin or whatever drink down. The problem would be the customers themselves, who drank beyond their capacities to function normally. Otherwise, getting tipsy only served to make Liz's conversation attempts flow more freely. For many of the clients spoke no English, only Japanese! Gradually, Liz found herself using more and more Japanese. It didn't take long for the compliments to start pouring in.

Some of her coworker sisters were a little jealous of Liz. For the Romanian cousins that saw Liz the first day she walked in, their disdain for her was immediate and straight out the gate. Liz wasn't dense and could sense friction by their narrowed eyes when they were in her presence. Because of them, Liz wasn't very motivated to meet with or associate heavily with any of the other hostess girls. Luckily, they often operated independently, much like teaching at Bozack, and interacted with clientele separately. Most girls had their own exclusive and regular customers. The Romanian family set was like a "special order" Liz just happened to walk in on.

The big bucks really started rolling in when Jeremy followed through with his pledge to get Liz some private students. He was a shrewd-type individual who would haunt *gaijin* bars and pounce upon unsuspecting Japanese people who thought he was also of Japan because of his Asian features. He would then surprise his would-be victims with his incredible English and instantly become a success story to model oneself after. Upon further probing, he would find out whether or not they had kids, grandchildren, nephews, nieces, or any little children who were interested in having private lessons taught to kids. He had met Mr. Sakamaki that way, and he continued to be a success. He managed to snag a three-day-a-week circuit for Liz; and just like that, Liz had an extra $150 a week to add to her purse, with more available if she wanted. But for the beginning, to see if she could hack the day-and-night schedule, she decided wisely to embark upon it slowly, so as to not get burned out.

Needless to say, Jeremy still had his ulterior motives for helping out Liz. He still was secretly in love with her and had hopes that she would eventually fall for him. In his mind, all he had to do was just be there, be around her, and wait for the magic moment, the right place and the right time, and allow her to naturally gravitate to him, attracted by the magnetism of adoration he would bestow upon her. If that didn't work, he was prepared to take more drastic measures.

Brad Cooper, the low-life Luzio Silver wannabe affiliate and part-time English teacher, also hung out at the popular *gaijin* bars. In addition to being a squeaky sidekick to Moose, a budding MMA fighter, and henchman of Silver's, Brad also delved in side-dealing drugs and mind-altering substances, in particular the recent and popular sex/rape drug Rohypnol. These he copped himself from Luzio Silver quite some time ago and sought to charge customers double the price. This he could do with ease because most of his customers would be white foreigners like him and too chickenshit to look up or do dealings with shady characters like Luzio Silver. He became somewhat known around town because the foreign community often congregated in gregarious-type settings that induced familiarity. As such, when names came up in association with goods and/or services, certain ones were invoked, and Brad happened to be the one Jeremy became familiar with while he was in the *gaijin* bars hunting for client prey.

In the days following Luzio Silver's absence from the street scene, not to mention also Tim the Duke and Ricky Exmouth, Brad's reputation would gain a higher level of infamy. Oftentimes, when he was seen around town, it was with Moose, who himself was very intimidating and formidable in appearance. As a result, Brad too would be associated with such to a degree because he kept company with Moose, and some people *actually believed* that he ran with Luzio Silver. Now that Luzio Silver was out of town and temporarily "out of business," Moose was off the street and now concentrating on training for his MMA career and "off duty" as one of Silver's security and delivery operators. Thus, leaving Brad with no big homie to follow around. With Moose training to be a professional fighter, he didn't have time to run the streets with Brad and cut him off.

It didn't matter, Brad thought, because he could hide behind Luzio Silver's reputation. If people connected Brad to the big boss, he didn't feel as if he would have any problems out on the streets. As long as he followed the basic guideline— deal drugs only to foreigners—there would be no problems with the Japanese police, or the Japanese mobsters. For a while, this worked out fine.

Over a period of time, Brad had used his ability to get close to Luzio Silver by way of Moose and, in so doing, managed to pilfer some product and sizzle for his personal use. Other times, he made purchases on his own. In addition, he experimented with growing marijuana himself, which turned out to be a failure, but most of the square *gaijin* in Japan would hardly ever know the difference between good stuff and bad homegrown grass. That, as well as mixing it with a blend of "shake" that could be purchased legally in head shops in American Village, basil, parsley and paprika could be bought from any supermarket, he created his little profitable side hustle for a while.

The shady business took a hit, however, when Luzio took a break from the scene. Brad's connections went dry. Sometimes he had to travel as far as Kobe or Kyoto in order to find someone who had product he could buy, then return to Osaka and sell for a higher price. When he sold the last of his X tabs, mickeys, and other mind-altering hallucinogens, he began mixing his weak homegrown microwaved plant weed with "shake" from the head shop. Although these batches would initially sell like hotcakes, people were disappointed with the potency, and Brad would be thus considered a fraud and a trickster. People were upset by his deception, deeming his batch of sizzle to be hocus-pocus, but he didn't care. He partied like he was a superstar, enjoyed women, and still accomplished, on occasion, to sell his garbage pot to unsuspecting goobers. Late one night, as he was leaving a taco restaurant in Doyama Village, he was jumped and dragged into an alley near the Tsunashiki Shrine by two masked individuals dressed in black. There, he was issued a severe beatdown that was interrupted only because of the yelling and screaming from the Japanese girl that he had been with. The two assailants then robbed that woman and Brad of all their loot and made off on foot before the cops arrived. Brad was taken to nearby Kitano Hospital, where he was treated for fractured ribs, shattered eye sockets, broken fingers, and multiple bruises and abrasions. No suspects were arrested.

72

CANDACE WAS LIZ'S middle name. It was a name hardly ever used in her life. It was only invoked during her childhood, when she did something to make her mother upset or angry, Ida would call out her entire name. Otherwise, it was just an additional title she sometimes saw on documents like her diploma from Harbor College, her passport or an identification paper here and there, but in general, the name was a dormant description of who she was. And this was the reason why Saiko suggested Liz be known by that moniker when she started working at the Dream Lounge. Saiko too had changed her name, to disconnect from her past, and advised all her girls, not just Liz, to have derivative names.

At first, Liz wanted a cute name like Betty (as in Betty-Boop) and a play on her name in short, or her favorite Disney character, Tinker or Bella. It was Saiko who suggested Liz use her middle name, Candace, after learning her entire name for identification purposes, having her name unofficially registered as a tenant in her apartment housing. When Liz pronounced the name for her, Saiko and most Japanese people heard "Candy", or perhaps its plural form. It was a bit garish, but Liz decided to go along with it anyway. At least now she would have a good excuse to ignore someone on the street who recognized her, like an Ingrid, if they called her by the name she formerly went by while working at Bozack. Luckily, this didn't happen, though.

Liz/Candy's first month's salary take from the Dream Lounge, Saiko paid her in cash, as she did all hostesses. Saiko took her rent and tip, or house fee cut, straightaways like government taxing. Liz wasn't impressed by her net sum, but she quickly realized why. She was working only four days a week, and every night wouldn't be busy. That was the catch, but Saiko never lied about that. On some nights, they would receive less visitors than others. A regular night with minimal activity would net about two hundred dollars, and the busiest nights would be in excess of five hundred dollars, and those nights were almost guaranteed to be on the weekends, particularly Fridays and Saturdays.

Liz/Candy's schedule was almost the same as it was when she was with Bozack, only now she worked four days a week. Her three days off were Sunday, Monday, and Tuesday. Conveniently, she was able to arrange her private kids' lessons via "the Jeremy Network" on those days. Her students were two girls and one little boy—not related, but their families were friends. They were well mannered fifth- and sixth-graders; and teaching them was a breeze, because Liz received tutorials from Jeremy, who had been doing his gig for quite some time by this point. He would school Liz on the tricks of the trade, how to stall for time by making kids do brainless paperwork games like mazes or connect-the-dots, play redundant card and board games such as UNO, Candy Land, or Snakes and Ladders, which absorbed the child's mind in fun rather than learning English. In no time at all, Liz was getting paid for hourly sessions just playing games with kids. Her cake walk was on Easy Street.

In another section of town, Yoh was still a person of interest to Liz. Occasionally, she would enlist his vehicular services to drive all over town to get stuff for her new apartment. Basically, all she brought from her former residence was mostly stacks of clothes and her bicycle strapped on the back of Yoh's Suzuki coupe. All the appliances belonged to Bozack in the furnished abode, so Liz, with her own stash saved up, got herself a microwave, coffeemaker, TV, a new VCR that played the new DVDs on the scene at the time, and, additionally, a midget-sized refrigerator.

She wasn't happy with the size of her new place but found that when she jazzed the room up with a plush sleeper sofa, fluffy pillows, the right cutesy furniture, and sleek floor lamps, the place was pleasurably livable. She was able to get most of her goods, even wall posters and decorations, from a department store Yoh recommended called Tokyu Hands.

Yoh wheeled Liz around town from place to place, transporting and delivering furniture and doing favors for her. Occasionally, he smoked her out when he got his hands on some excess weed he would cop from some Chinese or Mexican cooks he knew who resided in some of his boss Mr. Sakamaki's tenements.

In return, Liz offered Yoh no compensation whatsoever—not even for gas— in the form of money currency. Instead, she would have lunch or dinner with him when her schedule permitted. Also, Yoh asked that Liz teach him English, since he no longer attended Bozack school ever since Vicky (Jill) left.

Liz agreed that she would teach Yoh English, but these sessions with him gradually became Japanese lessons for her. What she learned came in handy when Liz became "Candy" and worked at the Dream Lounge.

To no one's surprise, it didn't take long for Liz's popularity to grow. She was still the same vivacious, sprightly person she always was, and now she was in an element where she felt relaxed and free. Sometimes she was having so much fun drinking, talking, and playing English games with clients that her job didn't even feel like work. Time would fly like speed rockets. All she received was praise from Saiko.

Now fully settled at her new apartment, Liz established an updated routine for her everyday life that flowed smoothly. She joined a different gym, one closer to her new pad. After work in the morning, if she wasn't too drunk or hungover, she would take a quick nap, wake up, and hit the gym. Afterward, if she was up to it, she would ride her bike all the way to Kujo and get a Thai massage, while also getting schooled in the massage techniques either Tok or Vot employed. They were also teaching her about herbs and apothecary-type medicines. On her days off at the lounge, she taught kids' lessons, and on other spare moments, have lunch or early dinner with Jeremy.

Laura Violi had decided to remain in Osaka, so when either of their schedules could jibe, Liz and she would hang out, grab drinks, chitchat, and break bread. Liz preferred Laura's company, obviously, more than the shuddersome coworkers she encountered at her new job and inside the building where they lived. She barely even talked to them outside of work.

Once, Liz had a run-in with one of the Romanian sisters. The apartment doors auto-locked when shut. Liz made a mistake once by propping her door open with one of her gym shoes, so that it would remain ajar while she dipped out for a moment to grab a juice or two from the vending machine in front of the building. Or she would jog over to the Laundromat first to get coin change to use for the vending machine when it didn't take her bills.

The Romanian girl Daniella was on her way back to her own apartment on the second floor after leaving the ground floor coin laundry center. She passed Liz's door, saw the shoe Liz used to prop her door, then kicked it away to allow the door to close. She was calling herself a "good Samaritan" by doing so, for when Liz returned, she took it upon herself to give Liz a newbie's lecture on the dangers of propping one's door. Liz was fuming because she was locked out. The sanctimonious Romanian was off and on her way before Liz found the composure to scream at her. Luckily, Yutaka was almost always available in the afternoons and late nights. Despite his hard, grungy look, he was a reasonably kind man, and although he couldn't speak English very well, he didn't seem to mind taking his time with Liz, explaining to her as best he could how to use the remote control for the heating/air-conditioning unit in her room, or tending to her claims that her shower water wasn't hot enough. He showed her how to also adjust water temperature levels. Generally, he was the only friendly person in the building Liz associated with. Thus, should Liz have been locked out again, Yutaka's room and board was on the first floor as well, and his service was to be enlisted. As for the Romanian Daniella or her sister, friendship didn't appear imminent.

Pertinent also to mention would be the budding of a renewed relationship between Liz and Carver, who had been intermittently corresponding with each other via e-mail. Their contact had shifted from one or twice a month to once or twice a week. This came about as a result of Liz candidly suggesting that she and Carver "get together and discuss old times" when she made her return to the United States. Thereupon which Carver excitedly concurred and began making dates and plans, seemingly eager awaiting the day.

Liz toyed with the idea at first, but the more she thought about it, getting back together with Carver seemed like a safe move. Plus, in periodical conversations with her mother, Ida, the pressure increased urging her to "come home, settle down with a nice guy, and be happy for the rest of your life!" Though aggravating at times, it remained persuasive. Liz couldn't deny it.

Another wake-up call came when Liz went for her physical health checkup. Saiko enrolled her in an offshore insurance company and accompanied Liz to one of her female clinics. Basically, Liz was healthy, but according to the female doctor, her vaginal area had appeared swollen, her cervical mucus was thinning, her cervix softened. When asked if she had experienced cramps or uneasiness, Liz replied that she indeed had but had mistaken it for the result of intense workouts and unhealthy diet. The doctor claimed, however, that she was ovulating at the particular time. Then Liz started considering her future, about seriously settling down eventually with someone. She always had thought it was to be Eddie, but that didn't happen. If she could go back to America and make a man out of Carver, he would be almost perfect.

Meanwhile, Liz's former employer, Bozack, was dealing with the stench that resulted from the shit hitting the fan. Kenji's big plan to fire or expurgate the company of undesirables and replace them with *jake* clean-cut types wasn't successful at all. Basically, he sacked teachers and replaced them with the trash employees discarded from other similar companies. If one was fired from Nova, ECC, or Berlitz, they would stumble over to Bozack and get hired. Because they were newer faces, the façade of the school getting an upgrade worked for a short time, but not for long. For soon after, the complaints of teachers smelling horrible, giving tacky lessons, being late or truant from work, and other issues related to drug use would resume, and, in the South Town schools, with increased capacity. It wasn't a good look. The promotions and appointing of various teachers to new titles did very little to turn things around for the company as they had anticipated.

The lessened quality of lessons and un-improved conditions of the schools' classes alone wasn't the sole reason for the decline in sales and mass exodus of students. Japan's economy at the time, as everyone knew, had taken a turn for the worst. Many companies were either folding or merging with larger entities in order to survive. In light of this, Bozack wasn't the only English conversation school who was feeling the hit. Other major companies were facing the same dilemma.

This crisis in turn gave rise to the independent, non-corporate, and private English schools. Smaller, private enterprises began springing up everywhere, becoming the rage because compared to the larger outfits, these were cheaper, affordable, and reasonable. And if not so, they were in better condition, or willing to negotiate rates that were suitable. They could arrange payment plans that could be worked out, whereas the larger schools like Bozack required student customers to pay exorbitant fees up front and unbreakable contracts that couldn't be renegotiated or arbitrated whatsoever. Thus, during this time, private schools like Special K and Paz Lucha's Suminoe Park English School, would get a steep rise in business. Even Jeremy was finding more gigs on his side hustle outside of work. He too began considering leaving Bozack like Liz did and going into business for himself, unwittingly undermining Worm.

Worm was now on revenge mode. His transfer to the Umeda School to teach French was the last straw his damaged pride allowed him to endure. He was never restored to his former title as head teacher, nor was he given a promotion as he was illicitly promised by Kenji. It was as if their scheme had backfired on them. They had not expected the loss of so many good teachers, or reliable ones at the least coupled with the firing and dismissal of others. First, Stephanie's murder, then Laura Violi's resignation, the French teacher Serge, and then Liz. Kenji had no time to consider Worm's hurt feelings or pride. He had his own ass to cover and a company to try to get back on its feet. If Worm didn't like it, he too could quit. Of course, no one thought he would, but he did. Worm bided his time and quit.

When the small English schools began sprouting up like weeds everywhere, Worm took advantage of the opportunity to do the same. After all, he had been low-key planning to do so all along, and if the moment was ever right, this was the opportune time to establish his own English conversation school. He had successfully snatched and stolen away many students from Bozack, especially in the days preceding his resignation.

He was in the process of having his English school built and located in his wife's mansion. The classrooms would be the remodeled guest quarters, made over to resemble learning environments. His wife, Mikako, supported him and praised his ambition. Worm's efforts were impressive. He had gotten his new business off the ground with a comfortable number of students to keep him quite busy, so much so the expanse of his project was highly promising. There was no stopping him now. Years of hard work, being a social toady accumulating contacts and acquaintances had finally paid off, and he saw himself being the next best thing to a Bozack. All he needed now was a bigger staff to accommodate a larger, excess influx of student customers he was bound to get. Good news traveled fast around the city, and when Osaka people caught wind of a good bargain, they often jumped on it.

Radley Owens and Worm's good buddy Eric Cravens were sometimes recruited to appear at his school as guest-appearance teachers, to the delight of those students who knew them at Bozack, having been former customers there. Radley still made Worm a little nervous because of his tendency to have sticky fingers, dredging up apprehension of household items coming up missing. Worm preferred Keefer, a longstanding Bozack company favorite, but the Aussie sybarite was profoundly opposed to working on days he was scheduled to be on holiday, so his appearances at Worm's school were very rare. Mikako suggested to Worm that he hire a female. Women teachers, in her opinion, gave the school a nurturing, safe, and wholesome image and one that would attract more students than a beckoning *maneki-neko*—a good luck cat figurine believed to draw commerce.

Subtly, Worm regretted his decision to stab Liz in the back the way he did, because she became a person of interest to him now that there was no longer a Stephanie or Vicky for him to call upon and ask a favor. This favor would be to work for him and be the female teacher his wife recommended he acquire. He was unaware that Laura Violi had less-than-flattering comments about him that she delivered to Liz. Thinking that Liz didn't know about his underhanded dealings, he sought to contact her with the remote possibility she would be receptive to him and maybe get her to come and work for him. His initial attempt to connect with her failed, because Liz had long since changed her cell phone number, and she no longer accessed the landline phone that was connected at the Bozack Bentencho dormitory where she no longer lived.

Remembering only one other person from the Namba School he recalled Liz being on friendly terms with, Worm contacted Jeremy to find out if he knew Liz's number, as Eric didn't have it, and because of sore feelings; neither did Radley nor Keefer—they erased and blocked her numbers for safety measures in wake of the big drug bust.

With Jeremy, Worm hit pay dirt, because he supplied him not only with Liz's new number, but also her new apartment address. For some reason, Jeremy assumed that Worm was propositioning him to go into business together. He heard of Worm's fledgling school in operation and wondered why Worm had asked all the other guys to work there and not him. When he finally got the call, Jeremy was ready to discuss his business plan on how to combine all the kids from his private lesson circuit with Worm's budding project. Instead, all he received was a heartfelt expression of gratitude for supplying him with Liz's contact info and a clicking sound of a terminated cell phone call.

73

STRANGELY, WORM DIDN'T contact Liz right away. It wasn't until several weeks later he was finally able to catch up with her. Before that, Liz was made aware by Jeremy that Worm was trying to get in touch. This didn't sit well with Liz because she had some ill feelings for him due to what she heard about him by way of her conversation with Laura Violi. She avoided him for a while. In the meantime, she continued her routine: going to work at nights, some part-time kids teaching on the side, and occasional dates with Yoh or Jeremy.

Yoh would pay Liz for English lessons with some pot whenever he was able to get his hands on some. But the so-called English lessons was more like a language exchange session because he found himself teaching more Japanese phrases to her than she was teaching him any new English. Also, she enlisted Yoh to be her occasional car service, and when Laura decided to finally pack up and leave town for Shikoku like she said she would, Liz got him to drive her around, assisting her to take care of odds and ends involved with moving.

One day, Yoh summoned his available courage and put his cards on the table. He came clean with Liz about his feelings for her. They were at a café where they usually had their meetings for lessons. At the end of the session, Yoh spilled his heart.

He said to her, "Elizabeth, the past weeks, I have really enjoyed the time that . . . we have been together. I really enjoy being with you. I never thought I would love another foreign girl the way that I liked Jill' but after I met with you, it is changed."

In Liz's mind, she was like, *Oh no . . . I knew this was coming.* She fretted, because now she would have to find a way to let him down easy. Laura hipped Liz that a "mercy fuck" was for desperate foreign chicks who were horny and had to settle for some less-than-stellar foreign dude they would never date back in their respective extractions but settle for them due to lack of better options or selections. A courtesy fuck was a simple shag—emotionless sex requiring no commitment, almost like a handshake between friends—Liz considered Yoh a candidate for, albeit reluctantly. But the way Yoh was carrying on, elaborating about his sudden love for her that had materialized, Liz was unsure if her making the offer would suffice.

Yoh rallied on, stating his case, "Before Jill, I was with a girl, she broke my heart. She was Japanese. But Jill was able to make me feel better. I think a foreign girl is better for me. Because I met you, and I felt better too. The night we first met, in Umeda, with Jill at the bar, I thought you were like . . . a movie star actress! I don't know how to explain this very well . . . but, Elizabeth, I . . . I think . . . I think I love y—"

"Yoh, wait . . ." Liz sighed heavily and tried to hold back a laugh by biting her bottom lip and squeezing her eyelids tightly closed. She placed her hand on his palm, tapped it as if to signal for Yoh to stop speaking. She said, "Yoh, listen, you're a great guy. I like you. A lot. You're so sweet, and I enjoy talking and hanging out with you too. But I don't love you. I don't think we could ever be in love like how you think."

Noticeably, Yoh was instantly punctured; his deflated look appeared promptly when Liz's rejection stabbed his heart. It was as if he was accustomed to hearing such news. The damage caused his eyes to bleed tears. He tried to avert his gaze from Liz's, but it was hard because he was sitting across from her at the table. Shades of pink blushed his eye sockets as he wiped away moisture and sniffed. Liz wanted to pass him one of the table's service napkins, but she didn't want to insult him or damage his pride any further.

Liz had been hoping to avoid situations like this. She was well aware that Yoh had caught feelings for her, but wished in her heart that she would be able to keep his excitement at bay. It took her off guard. She tried to allay his anguish by assuring him that he was still a handsome gentleman and that he would meet a wonderful, lucky girl in the future. Guaranteed, she added. But it did little good. Yoh's spirit seemed genuinely amiss.

Liz said, "Truth is, Yoh . . . I have someone in my life. I never told you about it, I'm sorry. But you see, I'm headed back to the States in a couple of months. He's a guy I used to see before I ever came to Japan. We're getting engaged. It wouldn't be fair to him if I got involved with another guy . . . you can understand that, can't you?"

She hoped he would. Liz could use the continued benefits of his sporadic car rides and weed freebies, not to mention the catch phrases of Osaka dialect Japanese he taught her during these lesson sessions. Be that as it was, she was prepared also to give it all up if she had to. She dangled the possibility of them sleeping together, but Yoh appeared to be so distraught that he didn't recognize the bait.

Stroking his hand lightly, Liz said, "Is there anything I can do to make you feel better? How can I make it up to you?"

Yoh got quiet. He stared at the table for a moment or two; then a serious look covered his face. He shook his head and drew back his chair from the table. He said, "No, you are right. I was selfish for telling you my feeling." He stood up as if preparing to leave. "I'm very sorry."

Liz remained quiet too. She let the situation play out. Without complicating matters further, she watched him grab the bill slip and walk up to the counter. He paid the bill and walked out of the café. Uncharacteristically not even saying good-bye. Just like that, Liz would never see or meet him ever again. A server waitress came by and asked if she was staying, as the tab had been paid. Liz had time to kill, so she told the woman that she would hang out for a while, then asked for another cup of coffee and a slice of cake.

Maybe it was for the best anyway, Liz decided. What she told Yoh wasn't exactly a lie. She was planning on leaving for the States in the near future. She was heavily considering a reunion with Carver—what that escalated to in the future, she didn't know. One thing was for sure: with her susceptibility now to get pregnant easily, she might have dodged a bullet by avoiding sleeping with Yoh, even as a courtesy. Who knew? He might have not been able to handle it and become obsessive. Well, this didn't matter. He was gone.

She thought about the following night. She would go back to work at the lounge and meet some classy, rich dudes who also had cars. They weren't all just older gents either; there were some in their mid- and late thirties too. What she also liked was that in contrast to the businessmen who were her English students at Bozack, they were all shy and reserved. But when they came to the lounge, they were the opposite: they were aggressive, confident, and unabashed. At least once a week, some distinguished don or polished man would ask for Liz to go on dates outside the lounge on *dohan* transactions, like escort or rent-a-date. For this, Saiko had her reservations because she was around during the time when the Australian girl Carita Ridgway was drugged and poisoned in Tokyo back in 1992. Little did she know, a Lucie Blackman of the United Kingdom would suffer a similar fate.

Such an arrangement paid big bucks but also could be a little unsafe, and as such, it was something both Saiko and Liz discussed. They would split the proceeds fifty-fifty for what the client paid for the date, which sounded a little crazy to Liz, but when she found out that she could earn up to almost one thousand dollars, she was eagerly game. Sure, there were perils involved in going out with complete strangers, but her assurance had risen a notch in recent times. She was taller than a lot of the older men customers, and others she felt she stood a reasonable chance to escape or overpower if in a tense situation. Her wild swinging at inflated bubble balls and hyperactive pitty-pat punches on padded pillow dummies garnered her undeserved praise at the fitness club's kickboxing classes. Unsurprisingly, this blew up her head with confidence in fighting skills. She regarded her cowering out to Brad because he had a scary knife, and it did a number on her psyche.

They came up with a plan. Liz figured it out: she would only go to the Candy Box Club. There, she was safe, she estimated. Tabriz all but seemed to promise that. He always treated her like she was grand. She really liked the place anyway, so aside from dinner at a nice restaurant, the only club she would go on a date would be to the Candy Box. Saiko was cool with that idea and added that she should not accept rides in a client's personal car. She should always ride in the cabs. That way, she wouldn't be at the mercy of anyone else should she become too incapacitated due to overindulgence of alcohol or whatever. Having claimed to understand, Liz was approved to go with clients on dates outside the lounge. Soon she would be making enormous tips, if she went out with two dudes in one night—dinner with one guy, to the club with another. Just like that! About a thousand dollars. It was crazy. She really didn't need Yoh's car service, really. She could afford her own. The downside was Yoh was a good tour guide who could speak English and supplied her with some free smoke. It didn't matter. She was quitting anyway. If she were to have a baby, she didn't want the child to be affected; it was bad enough she herself was an addict in denial.

While Liz sat and thought about how insane the new job was, she couldn't help but be amused at the turn of events that had taken place in her life up until then. She came to Japan as a so-called teacher, but she would leave as a sort of prostitute; but with the latter job, she had the opportunity to rapidly accrue a huge sum of dough. It almost didn't even seem real. Just to think, if it were possible, she could earn that much a day and work at the rate of four to five thousand dollars a week! In a few months, she would leave Japan with a whopping fortune. Her mother and her father would be beyond impressed. Liz would have some bargaining power when she opened up her own health spa or whatever she would decide to create. It was good that she could salvage the disaster that happened as a result of her separation from Eddie, and she would leave Japan on a high note. It was wonderful the way things worked out, Liz thought. She sipped her coffee and checked her watch, wondering how she could spend the rest of her night off.

That was when her cell phone rang. It was Worm. Liz didn't recognize his number; if she had, she probably wouldn't have answered. She did anyway and was a little startled to hear his pompous boy-like voice trying to sound manly.

Worm was like, "Hey, 'Lizabeth, long time no see. I hope you don't mind me callin' you out of the blue like this. Our friend Jeremy gave me your number, just thought I'd reach out to you, see how yer doin' and all . . ."

Liz wasted no time impugning Worm with every ounce of fury, displeasure, and indignation she could muster on short notice. She also had choice words for him in regard to the part he played in getting Deon fired. She almost hung up on him altogether but, curiously, delayed such action just to hear his rebuttal and see how he would react.

Surprisingly, or maybe even deceitfully, Worm was amazingly humble. He very well could have assumed the "Screw you too" attitude, but he chose a different approach. His tact was solid, and his voice was made to sound sincere when he tried to explain to Liz his side of the story.

Assessing her mood while she lambasted him, he thought quickly and had a premeditated excuse ready. First, he apologized adamantly for if there had been a "misunderstanding," in hopes that he could cleverly maunder his way back into her good graces, he supplied her with compliments about herself and her work performance, and how he had never betrayed her in any way.

He thought of a canard that she could possibly go for. "I really didn't mean to implicate you, Liz—honest! Actually, it was Deon. His termination wasn't my fault. I didn't tell him to drink; in fact, I tried to tell him he shouldn't. He was like 'You ain't my boss no mo.' You know how he talks . . .

"But anywho, somehow it got around to Kenji. Kenji wasn't goin' for it, so he fired Deon. It was out of my hands. But he begged and pleaded for his job, and in the process, he offered up some names of other employees in the company who were involved with dope and all that shit. Please, you've got to believe me. Hell, he even put my name in it all this shit. Why do you think I don't even work at Bozack anymore!?"

Liz's ears began tingling. This information she hadn't heard about. What he had said about Deon sounded like some bullshit to her, but Worm's no longer working at Bozack came as somewhat of a shock. She thought he would be there forever and all the big talk he used to spew about him starting his own English school was hot air. But the more she allowed him to ramble on, the more she would discover that he had made good on his proclamation and did make his own school. He even asked her if she would like to come and be one of his teachers.

Naturally, Liz flat out refused, but her mind eased up a bit on Worm, against her better judgment. The sincere tone of his voice played a factor, a boyish cajole. Still, Laura didn't have any reason to lie either. Her opinion of Worm being a maggot still weighed heavily on her mind, but she filed it away for the time being and chose to listen to him while proceeding with caution.

Worm continued, "I think you'd make a perfect fit at my new school, 'Lizabeth. You were one of the best teachers I've had the experience of workin' with, and that's sayin' a lot because I knew a lotta other teachers before you. Gosh,

I've told you about that many times. I've never had anything bad to say about you. If your name came up to the top brass or Ruth or anybody like that, it was not my doing alone. Listen, everybody thinks I'm the rat? Hell, the company is crawling with those! Everybody bites everyone's back. They stab each other just for pats on the head from the Japanese staff. So, they can get praise, promotions, raises, considerations for transfers to their favorite places—all sorts of shit. You think it was just me? Hell no!

"When Deon put my name in it, thinking he could save his job, Kenji and the higher-ups were still sore and pissed about the dope bust incident with Tim and Rick. For whatever reason, your name came up again, and it was Deon who squealed on you. There was nothing I could do about it. So you see, I didn't really implicate you. At all. But I guess my biggest error in judgment was just not defending you enough, and for that, I'm sincerely sorry. You've got to believe me, 'Lizabeth. I would never do anything like that to you."

Liz started thinking to herself. Was Worm telling the truth about Deon? Worm's spiel about how any or everybody in the company had potential to be backstabbing rats sounded all but too true. She had Stephanie as a huge example of this. To save one's skin or to save their jobs or practicing deceit in hopes for a reward *did* seem like a regular, normal thing. She thought about Deon and pondered whether or not he was that type? If he lost his job at Bozack, would he be in the same boat as someone like Ingrid? Ingrid cried and bawled her eyes out when she was in fear of losing her job and constantly highlighted the fact that she would never get another job like that in Japan. Implying that because she wasn't white was the reason; and Deon was probably in the same boat too, making it remotely plausible that Worm might have been telling the truth. True or false, Liz silently acknowledged, as the elephant in the room was a glaring shame; exceptional employees like the Deons and Ingrids had to stress not finding a job so easily in Japan, yet meanwhile, she practically walked into a job at the Dream Lounge. Before that, Takuto had offered her an easy job without her even asking. Jeremy promised her a rose garden of employment, now here was Worm with yet another offer. Like Japan or detest it, Liz had to admit—the opportunities for her seemed nothing short of abundant.

"Maybe I was wrong then." Liz eased up a bit. Worm could hear her voice lose its caustic tone. She said, "With all that's happened over the last few months, it's been hard to trust people. You hear things, you know? Things you don't know what to believe or find hard to believe . . . I didn't mean to come off like that to you."

Worm said, "Oh no, it's all right. It's OK. Hey, look, I'll make it up to you. Lemme throw you a farewell party . . ."

Liz was practically lurid with alarm. She said, "No way! I don't want any more trouble, no more undercover cops looking to make a bust—"

Worm laughed. "No, no! Ha ha ha, it's not gonna be that kind of party, I promise you that. Trust me, my wife Mikako won't allow any more wild and crazy parties like that anymore. She'll have my head. No, what I meant to say, I'm throwing a school opening bash, and at the same time, announce your farewell and make it like a dual function. Whaddayasay?"

Liz calmed down and considered the idea. She said, "Yeah, but who would be there that knew me well enough to wish me a fond farewell? Stephanie's gone, Denore, Vicky . . . Keefer and Radley don't even like me anymore."

Worm lied "That's not true. Radley talks about you from time to time. Keefer? He doesn't have ill will toward anybody. Plus, you got other people who remember you, don't forget Eric and his wife, Rosiland and a few other girls. Plus, I'm sure Jeremy would drop in. Come on, it'll be fun."

"I don't know," Liz said, still seriously debating and taking everything in mind. "Where are you holding the party? At your place?"

Worm said, "I thought about that, even talked about it with the wife, and we decided against that. The classrooms are still under construction, and we felt that holding it at a nice rented space would be better."

Then Liz came up with the idea of her favorite place. "How about the Candy Box? That place is huge, and they have plenty of party rooms, right?"

Worm's voice sounded invigorated at the mention of her idea, as if to imply, *Why didn't I think of that?* He then said, "Yeah, great idea. I know the guy who runs the place. He's like a Middle Eastern dude, dresses real fancy like a gangster, but he's really cool. They also have good food there too. Awesome idea. So are you in?"

"I guess so," Liz said. "Sure, why not. When is this gonna be? I work at nights, so I gotta make sure it doesn't interfere with my schedule, or I can take a night off. Luckily, it's really flexible."

"Well, since it'll be a private, invitation-only affair, we'll probably need one of the antechambers or lounges you were just talkin' about. What say we meet there next week, at the Candy Box, get together and discuss it with the owner?" Worm said. "Maybe we can take a look at a few rooms, see what's available and what would be best for our function."

"Sounds good, but why do you need me to go?" Liz asked.

Worm said, "My wife is comin'. She remembers you and wants to see you. Plus, Eric and Radley too. I think even Keefer is comin', but not sure yet. It'll be like a little reunion. None of us have seen much of each other these days. It'll be fun. Plus, it's gonna be your party too, so you should have some say in what kinda atmosphere it should be, right?"

She thought for a minute and guessed that it should be fine. Maybe Worm was right. It perhaps would be refreshing to see and meet some of her old coworkers again. After all, they did have some good times. Liz appreciated the calamitous but entertaining work environment she once shared with them; oftentimes the fun and enjoyment of everyone's upbeat attitudes and convivial personalities overshadowed the humdrum of teaching zombie-like students. In recent times, the only company she was subject to enjoy was a drab experience with a new roommate who nearly dragged her to the dumps as misery's company.

The call ended. Liz would have to ask Saiko for Saturday night off. Not to worry, the *mama-san* allowed for flexible schedules and nights off as long as she received advance notice. But Saturday night at the Candy Box was guaranteed to be crowded. That was the hip-hop night. When asked why he chose Saturday night, Worm insisted that everyone's schedules conflicted so much that this would be the only day they could all gather and meet at the same time. Liz could offer little to no argument about the reason, so she agreed to the date. Unaware that all hell was about to break loose.

74

LIZ CLEARED HER schedule for Saturday night's so she could attend the conclave at the Candy Box, arranged by Worm. The night before this so-called event, she worked at the Dream Lounge, got Saiko's approval, her impressive monthly salary—in cash, and met a handsome, upbeat young Japanese businessman who could speak English, a little. His skills weren't as high level as, say, a guy like Yoh Wamushi, but he was more communicable, to an extent, than most of the clients that the Dream Lounge welcomed. Liz figured him to be another upstart salary man and one that came from a well-to-do family at that. Anyway, he was one of the Japanese people who had spent time overseas, a short stay in Australia, and he had a heavy interest in foreign women. Because he was so interested in Liz, he tried to arrange to have a date with Liz anyway, "renting" her from the Dream Lounge. Saiko asked Liz if she was OK with that idea, as in essence, she would still be working even though she had technically asked for the day off. Liz assessed the dude to be harmless. He wasn't very tall; in heels, she would probably surpass him. Also, he didn't appear very rugged or beefy. He was a standard sack of bones, and if she could level a stationary cotton dummy at the fitness gym's kickboxing lab, she certainly could do the same to him. So then she agreed to the *dohan* arrangement and ended up scoring an extra three hundred dollars. Liz didn't even remember the dude's name; she just came to work as usual on Saturday, waited for the man to arrive, then they both left together around 9:00 p.m. As instructed for safety, they took a cab together to the Candy Box.

Though early for a Saturday, there was still a long line leading up to the building that housed the notorious club. The people waiting in the queue were mostly, if not entirely, Japanese. It was mind-boggling to Liz, throughout her time in Japan, to witness Japanese people's seeming fascination for waiting in long lines. It was remarkable that so many people shared her agnate curiosity and enchantment for this place. For her, the free admission was her main reason. Furthermore, as always, Tabriz Najaf treated her like an honored guest, even if she had come with a Japanese "date," who still paid the hefty admission price. Apparently, money was no object to him. He ordered a bottle of champagne right away, a drink of choice Liz had enjoyed as of recent, as soon as she and the guy skipped past the line of disgruntled waiting clubgoers and allowed entry. Ando, the doorman, scoffed at Liz, reaching for her passport again, as he remembered her—how could he forget her? And he even greeted her by her new moniker: "Good evening, Candy-san! Please, right this way."

The music, as usual, was boisterously loud. Darker than usual, rainbow streaks of light would flash at intervals, in intermittent pattern, lighting across the already-flooded dance floor, occupied by human bodies enjoying the relatively new genre of music known as hip-hop. Liz wasn't much of a fan of the music, but she always had a good time on nights out on the town with it as the backdrop. She wasn't much of a dancer, either, but she liked to dance, even though tonight she was dressed more for a prom than a nightclub disco. She was wearing a sleeveless, draped sequined tulle gown of a blush rose gold, sculpturally draped with a cowl neckline, showing off her toned frame, enticing cleavage, and, because of the gathering of shimmering folds at her side, curvaceous waist and hips. She seemed taller than she actually was. *Aquazzura* purist leather-heeled sandals were on her feet, prettied up from that afternoon's visit to the Thai massage parlor and painted in a like blush that blended perfectly with her pink-peachy skin tone. Her hair was dolled up half up and half down partially braided in the back. She was able to arrange it by herself. She looked like a prom queen and had come a long way since her earlier, all-jeans tomboy days. From estranged bestie Taffie, she had inherited an extensive wardrobe collection.

The Japanese dude for whom she was an escort was talking incessantly about random topics that ranged from music, movies, sports, and other hobbies he had that interested him more than Liz. In his mind, however, he was thinking that he could eventually get her drunk and have her at his mercy by the end of the night. All he had to do was keep her glasses filled with the Moét, and everything would go according to plan, or so he thought. He didn't know Liz's drinking prowess. To the naked eye, she appeared angelic, pristine, and fairy-tale innocent. In reality, she had probably seen more of the streets than this man ever would. In Japan or the United States. And, like Japan or hate it, for the first time she felt a little sad—as if she would miss the place, knowing that she would be leaving the country soon.

When the time gradually progressed beyond 10:00 p.m., Liz began to get a little restless. Her old "friends" were unusually late. Worm had said they would all meet at the Candy Box around 9:00 p.m., or between the hour and 9:30 p.m. Now the time was dragging toward ten thirty, and she saw signs of no one she knew. She was aware that it might have been a tedious affair to arrange for everyone to meet because of conflicting schedules, but Worm assured her that there would be no problems if they were to have met on this particular night.

Worm also stated that he was acquainted with Tabriz. Liz informed Tabriz upon entering that she was awaiting a group of foreign friends, she name-dropped Worm by his real name Mitchell, or Mitch. The name didn't seem to ring a bell with Tabriz at the moment, but he mentioned to Liz that he would have his trusted doorman, Ando, keep a look out for her expected group. Liz was in a VIP lounge with her escort "date," so she would be easy for him to find. So far, however, she received no notifications that any of them—Worm, his wife, Eric, or Radley—had shown.

Liz looked at her cell phone in between champagne sips and her escort date's circuitous rambling appearing as if his plan to get her drunk was backfiring on him and he was the one gradually becoming plastered. She had received no calls, and according to the indicator on her cellular, no new messages had arrived.

She said to the Japanese guy "Excuse me, I- have- to- make- a- phone- call!" Making sure she spoke loudly and slowly so that he could fully understand her English over the noisy rap tunes playing in the background.

The man seemed to understand and remained jolly as he continued drinking and excused Liz so that she could go for her call. Outside the VIP Lounge, Liz approached the first staff member she saw and asked if he could contact Tabriz for her. Obliging, the staffer got hold of his boss; and in minutes, he appeared.

"Hello, Elizabeth—or, should I say, Candy? I think this name suits you very well. You are so sweet, and you are a good fit for this club, don't you think? Perhaps if you marry me, this will be your club too, eh?" Tabriz let out a hearty laugh. Liz joined him laughing, albeit somewhat impertinently. She didn't know if he was serious or not.

Liz asked, "Hey, did any of my friends show up?"

Tabriz's smile disappeared, and he said, "Ah, no, not to my knowledge."

"Gee, Tabriz, how would you know? There're so many people here. How can you keep an eye on every single foreigner that comes in?" Liz looked around and pointed to the packed dance floor and steady ant line of people still filing into the place. "Besides, you're so busy doing what you do—maybe they came in and you didn't notice?"

"Not likely, my dear." Tabriz shook his head. "I gave specific instruction to Ando. He was to ask all of the foreign guests tonight if they are here for your party. Ando knows your name."

Then it hit Liz that maybe Worm and the others didn't know Liz by her new pseudonym Candy. Could that have been it?

She then said to Tabriz, "Hey, is there anywhere in here I can make a phone call? It's so loud in here."

"Oh, certainly," Tabriz said. "Please follow me!"

Tabriz lead Liz to another section of the club as if he was headed back to the entrance. Behind the coat-check booth, there was a small stage with a curtain and an antechamber on downstage right. This windowless room was completely bare save for a single fold-up chair, and Liz hadn't the faintest clue as to what this room was used for. Yet while there, music from the greater part of the club seemed muffled. Tabriz allowed her the use of this room so she could make a call to Worm.

After several ring chimes, just when Liz was about to hang up, Worm finally answered. His voice didn't sound enthusiastic to hear Liz's voice. In fact, his demeanor seemed to denote an indifferent annoyance. Right away, Liz too was irked.

She was like, "Um, where are you? Where's everybody? I'm here at the Candy Box. Didn't you say we were gonna meet here tonight? Nine thirty-ish? Remember?"

Worm sighed and said, "Sorry. Forgot to tell you. It has been called off."

"What?!" Liz was promptly outraged and miffed. "Are . . . you fuckin' serious? You mean to tell me you got me to take a night off from my work just to meet you for a goddamn party for your school that you said . . . y'know what? Screw you, you fucking shithead. I hope your fucking school gets fucked up by an earthquake!"

She had been practically screaming when she ended the call. Tabriz heard the commotion, as he had been standing close by. He dipped his head around the corner. "Is everything OK?" he asked her.

Liz was furious. Livid. Visibly upset and the sudden terra cotta shade her face had flushed to exemplified this. She replied in a somewhat curt fashion to Tabriz, "No, I'm not OK. I'm really pissed off now. As a matter of fact . . . look, can I have my coat? I've gotta go . . . I can't be here!"

"Yes, yes, absolutely, Candy," Tabriz uttered some Japanese orders to a coat-check staffer, and he turned to Liz with a worried expression. He removed his round, mirror-lens eyewear, and Liz could see the concern on his face without glasses for the first time.

"Is there anything I can do for you?" he asked. "And what about the gentleman whom you came with tonight? Has he given you a problem?"

"No, it's not that," Liz said, just as the coat-check staffer had arrived with her lightweight top. "It's just . . . I'm suddenly not feeling well. Plus I'm a little pissed off. I just can't be here now. I've got to go. Please apologize to that Japanese guy for me. I think he'll understand."

"Absolutely," Tabriz said. "Please take care of yourself . . ." His words trailed off as an incensed Liz made tracks for the exit. The way she felt, she could give less than a damn about the English bungling escort date she had come there with that night. All that was on her mind was how right Laura was when she so accurately described Worm as a maggot scumbag, plus a few more invective descriptions. Too bad she wasn't a guy, for if she was a badass like a Moose, or Luzio Silver thug, she would eagerly kick his ass. She flagged down a cab and headed for her neck of the woods.

Not yet familiar with her exact or precise location, she simply told the driver to drop her off at the Ten-Roku subway station. From there, she used landmarks to guide her as she walked home. As soon as she arrived, she unstrapped her sandals and looked in her fridge, and it was bare. She needed something to clear her throat, so she decided to get some bottled water from the vending machine outside. Barefooted, she went, but not before propping her door. Her key was new, as was the door's lock, and Liz considered it cumbersome to always deal with it. This time, however, instead of using a shoe at the threshold saddle, she used a crunched-up envelope between the hinge stile and jamb, creating the image that the door was closed. That way, nosy chicks like the Romanian Daniella wouldn't come by and bitch about it or get her locked out of her room. Liz was in no mood for a sanctimonious lecture. The mood she was in, a catfight might ensue.

Upon returning to her room, she sat down on her fluffy futon bed and tried to relax. She took her water and turned on her radio. In her purse, she had her last joint and a capsule gram of coke that she had been saving and sitting on for a long time. She had been trying to kick actually. Now, she thought, it was a good time to reconvene with an old habit. The radio was playing a Britney Spears tune, and Liz's brain took a trip down memory lane hearing the pop star grouse, "*Oh, baby, baby, how was I supposed to know / I shouldn't'a let you goooooooooooo / My loneliness is killing me now.*" She tried not to think of Eddie. She tried to force her mind into seeing Carver in her future. "*Don'cha know I still believe / that you will be there / I regret / my loneliness is killing me nowwwwwww!*" She found herself singing along. She forgot all about the prop in the doorjamb.

The door swung open with a powerful bang, explosive like a discharge of gunfire. Liz's eyes flicked open in savage horror as she looked up to see two dark figures in black clothing and balaclava masks enter her dwelling. The icy thrust of fear jammed a lance through her chest. She issued an ear-splitting scream that sounded like a shrill, antiquated fire alarm. It did nothing to stop the approach of the invaders. The taller of the two grabbed her immediately, and they began tussling. Liz struggled with the formidable huge figure, but his strength was too immense. The smaller home invader was kicking over the table and throwing things all over the apartment. He spoke in what seemed to be an exaggerated, urban American voice.

"We been a'lookin fo' yo' white ass, bitch!"

Liz had no earthly clue as to who these frightful individuals were; their faces were concealed by masks and goggles. But there was something dreadfully familiar about the voice of one of them. The tone she vaguely recognized, but as fear's frigid fingers forced a fiery grip around her heart, so did the night attacker's around her throat. She couldn't try to figure out identities. All she could do was let out a pathetic whine, now slightly husky. The man's grip was so tight she felt he could snap her throat with just a slight movement of his powerful shoulders. He was breathing so heavily he sounded like a wounded bear, as he had her wrapped up from behind like one. She felt his erection upon her lower back and knew right away that he was hung like a dinosaur.

Just when all hope seemed lost and Liz was slowly blacking out due to the lack of blood and oxygen, the door to her room again opened, but slowly. A bewildered-looking Yutaka stuck his head inside the door. Apparently alerted by the commotion, the Japanese handyman and superintendent of the building had investigated and astutely assessed the situation. He viewed upturned furniture, two masked men, and a damsel in distress after having responded to a scream in the middle of the night. He knew trouble was afoot.

Yutaka began yelling and screaming in Japanese, demanding to know what was going on and the release of Liz. He had hoped that his stentorian outburst had riled the attention of other building tenants who would in turn alert the authorities. Whether or not his attempt was effective was uncertain. Courageously, however, he attempted to thwart the actions of the intruders, whatever they may have been, by entering the room himself and coming to the aid of Liz.

Without missing a beat, the invaders pounced on Yutaka, who didn't know karate or kung fu, even if he did bear somewhat of a resemblance to a famous Hong Kong film star that did. Be that as it may, he managed to throw one or two punches that landed, connecting well enough to the smaller assailant and drop him. But the larger man, who had been holding Liz, threw her down violently and aided his companion. Lucky for Liz, the softness of her futon's cushion saved her from a potentially broken bone impact with the floor the way she was discarded. Unlucky for Yutaka, he had to tangle with the beast who had done it to her.

As they all began to brawl like a free-for-all and the room became ransacked in disarray, Liz's fear and state of horror got the better of her. She grabbed her purse and made a break for the door. The smaller invader tried to grab her as she brushed by him. Liz used her fitness gym haymaker move and connected with the side of his head. Wasting needed time, she managed to free herself and grab her sandals by the straps and streak away from the building, screaming and yelling. Poor Yutaka was left to his fate as Liz ran outside and hustled as fast as she could to the nearest convenience store.

In that particular neighborhood on a Saturday night, the nearby convenience store was crowded with late-night drunks, party hoppers, late-night socialites, and urban country bumpkins. When Liz came in with smeared makeup, disheveled hair, barefoot but wearing an expensive-looking dress and yelling "Police!," everybody laughed and thought that she was just another drunk *gaijin* that had more booze or drugs than she could handle and was off her rocker, in their country acting a damn fool. Nobody made a move to help her; they just stood around and watched her as if she was a spectacle putting on an infantile, pathetic live performance. She gave up trying to get through to anyone and cursed, "Fuck you, Japanese assholes!"

She grabbed her phone from inside her purse, which she instinctively knew to take when she bolted from her place. For not only did it hold her last bit of sizzle and celly, it also had her wallet, passport, ID, and the cash she got from Saiko. She tried to dial 911, like she would if she were back home, but then forgot that she wasn't back home. She called Yoh in hopes that he wasn't still bitter with her. No answer. The next number on her directory was Jeremy. She dialed him up, and *he* did pick up.

Jeremy's sleepy voice responded, "Hiya, Liz. What's up with you? I thought you'd be working tonight . . ."

Frantically, Liz cried, "Jeremy, Jeremy! You've gotta help . . . how do I call the police? These two guys broke into my place tonight. I think they tried to kill me. Omigod! Omigod! What the fuck!?"

Jeremy was genuinely startled. Although he had slept early for a Saturday night, the way Liz was talking had fully woken him. The sound of her voice was steeped in a seriousness he had never before heard. Now he too was curiously concerned.

He said, "Liz, calm down, calm down . . . where are you? Are you at your place?"

Liz started to cry. Her resilient, tough-tomboy exterior qualities were in shambles like her room now was. She said, "No, I ran. The guy who works in the building saved me, but those guys they might still be around. I . . . I've gotta call the police. I can't go back there. Omigod! I'm so scared now, Jeremy!"

Jeremy sprang up from his floor mattress. "Where are you now?"

Liz said, "I don't really fuckin' know. I just ran from the apartment. I'm still not familiar with this neighborhood. I just ran to the nearest convenience store. I tried to get some help, but none of these fucking people want to help . . . DAMMIT!"

Jeremy said, "OK, try to calm down, Liz. Look, OK, the number to the police, or emergency number here is 1-1-0. What's the nearest subway station around you now?"

"I don't have a fuckin' clue, Jeremy. And even if I spotted one, they wouldn't be running now at this hour, would they?"

"Yeah, OK, you have a point, but listen, I was just trying to get an idea, so I could come and meet you somewhere." Jeremy thought and then said, "Hey, just get in the cab and call the police. Or tell 'em to bring you over to my place. We'll call the cops together."

Liz decided it was tentatively a good idea to follow Jeremy's instruction. She retraced her steps to the convenience store and waited along the main drag. Even if those bad guys were still in the vicinity, it wasn't likely they would seize her out in the open. But to be on the safer side, putting some distance between her and that neighborhood seemed like the best idea.

Like clockwork, a taxi arrived. Liz got Jeremy to explain to the driver where he should go. She got inside and was on her way. Jeremy hung up so that Liz could call the police. She punched the three keys that Jeremy taught her. She contacted the police, but only to be frustrated by them not being able to understand English of any sort. Nor had they anyone within reach who could speak the international language of communication. At least, not at that hour of the night. So Liz couldn't explain to them what had just happened to her. In anger, she clicked off her phone and cursed Japan, but didn't fault herself for not being more diligent in her Japanese language study. As if matters couldn't get worse, she hadn't charged her phone at all the entire night. Her battery was on its last two bars of power out of a maximum of four.

Almost twenty minutes later, she arrived at the address Jeremy had supplied the driver. He was outside his apartment building waiting in jeans, slippers, and a jacket draped over his bare chest like he just threw something on. Liz flew a 5G bill at the driver and told him to keep the change. He tried to refuse, but Jeremy ushered Liz away before a big deal could be made about the generous tip she laid on the old man.

Liz hugged Jeremy and cried. Her fear had dissipated somewhat, and she had never been so relieved by the sight of someone than at that moment. Jeremy was her second unlikely hero of the night. She hoped Yutaka was all right and wondered if she should contact Mama-san Saiko.

For Jeremy, on the other hand, tonight was like a dream come true. For not only did he finally get the hug and embrace from Liz that he had been longing for, he also had her where he wanted her, in his place. He had no idea if what she had been telling him was true or not, as it sounded to him like a tall tale. Considering what he already knew about Liz, she very well could have been high out of her mind on dope or some other hallucinogen. Thing was, she was visibly shaken. Something had happened to her—that much was clear. Either that, or Liz had dabbled with the wrong drug and it resulted in some haywire side effects. For the time being, he treated her like a sensitive hospital patient, gently, carefully and attentive to her needs. He sat her down in his spacious kitchen.

"What the hell happened?" he asked her.

"I . . . I don't know, Jer. I was at home, then these two creeps broke down my door and tried to attack me. My building manager guy, he heard the commotion. He tried to help me, but I dashed out. I tried to call the police, but they . . . they don't understand fuckin' English!"

"Just calm down, Liz," Jeremy said. "Please, just try. Can you do that for me? You're safe now. Let me make you some coffee, or tea?"

"Coffee, yeah." Liz nodded. Then she continued, "This entire night was fucked up. First, Worm sends me on a wild-goose chase, tellin' me to meet him at the Candy Box Club. He decides to no-show, and he's like nonchalant as hell about it. I go back to my apartment, next thing I know, these scary masked men barge in, and like I said, I got away." She continued to recount events from that evening and then thanked Jeremy as he placed a heaping mug of instant coffee before her.

"Here's cream and sugar," Jeremy said as he placed condiment packages beside the mug on the table. "So you don't know who these men were? The ones who tried to attack you?"

Liz took only one of the creams and stirred it into the coffee, before taking sips of the drink. She then said, "No. They wore these masks. One was tall, the other was shorter, but I didn't see their faces. They wore all black clothes and looked like ninjas, or power rangers." She drank the coffee and wished for a cigarette that she didn't have. "You need to stir this coffee a little more, Jer. Gee whiz, this is chalky as fuck."

Jeremy folded his arms and tried to keep his perturbed look of concern genuine. He said, "This sounds crazy as hell. I wonder if Worm has anything to do with all of this?"

Eyelids gradually feeling heavy, Liz said, "Maybe, but . . . fuck . . . who knows? I think we should call the police . . . You know Japanese. Maybe I can explain to you what happened, and you can tell them . . ." She felt sleepy, like she wanted to yawn, but one would never formulate.

Jeremy said, "Yeah, we'll do that. In the morning might be better. Right now, you need some rest. You've been through a lot tonight. The best thing for you to do is crash here. I'll take care of you, and you can just get some sleep . . ."

Liz was already knocked out. She may have had a high tolerance for some alcohol, but for the Rohypnol drug, she was vulnerable, and only a small dosage was needed to sap her into a slumberous state. Sometime earlier, Jeremy had copped two tablets of the date rape drug from Brad Cooper at the price of about three hundred American dollars. True to his inclinations, all he had to do was bide his time and be at the right place. The magic moment had now arrived, and nowhere could be more right than his own place. She may or may not have gravitated to him naturally, but the fact of the matter was, she was there! Good or bad, she was now his. Nothing could stop him from getting what he wanted from her, and what he wanted more than anything, was to be one with her. To be inside of her. To make love with her, even if it was against her free will, it wouldn't exactly be a crime as far as he was concerned. He lifted Liz's mass from the chair. Then with his improbable upper body strength, he carried his sweet love interest to his bedroom and laid her down gently on his mattress bed.

75

JEREMY RANG UP Worm. The time was almost 1:00 a.m., but Worm answered the phone, sounding relatively upbeat and not sleepy.

"Hey, Mitchell, it's me Jeremy!"

Worm said, "Oh, hi'ya, Jer'. What're you up to this hour, man? You hangin' out somewhere?"

"Actually, I'm not hangin' out," Jeremy said with a coy chuckle. "I'm at home. I'm sorry to be callin' you so late, but you'd never guess who stopped by my place. Yeah, and in the middle of the night too."

Worm got quiet. Then he said, "Who?"

Jeremy laughed and said, "Elizabeth! I mean, you should've seen her. She was crying, hysterical. She said she wanted to call the police because two guys broke into her house. She was really freakin' out, and she had mentioned your name, so I was just wondering if you guys had partied tonight or what . . ."

Worm sighed deeply. He started talking faster after that. "Aw, fuckin' great. Maybe she got so pissed with me that she drunk herself crazy. What happened was, we were supposed to meet at that club in Kyboashi, you know, the gigantic, huge place owned by that Arab guy . . ."

"Candy, something . . . the Candy Box! Yeah, that's what she said." Jeremy stirred about, keeping a watchful eye on Liz, who was sleeping soundly on the mattress in his bedroom. "She said you stood her up, you didn't show?"

Worm said, "It wasn't my fault. Me and the wife got into a little argument. She doesn't want me to be involved with people like 'Lizabeth. I, uh . . . didn't know how to tell her. See, yeah, we were supposed to meet over there, I told her that. So around a quarter till eleven, she calls me up, she curses me out. She sounded drunk even then."

Jeremy stated honestly, "Yeah, well, she did smell a little bit of alcohol when she came."

Worm said, "Well you know how those girls get. They're all emotional. They get angry really quick because they're lonely and half-crazy anyway. Then they get to drinkin' out of control, plus with 'Lizabeth, we all know she likes to do *extra* stuff too, if you know what I mean? That's why Mikako doesn't want me to hang out with people like her anymore. That drug bust got her all spooked."

Jeremy listened carefully, but he wasn't buying the fact that Liz being drunk was the only reason for her bizarre behavior. He could bear witness that Liz was a solid, capable drinker, exemplified by how she outlasted both he and Stephanie at the closing of the previous year when they went to Nagano.

Jeremy said, "Yeah, maybe she just drank too much and probably just got carried away and took some other med, and it made her go loony."

Worm sounded analytical. "But she was coherent enough to make it over to your place, eh? She still there?"

Jeremy said, "Well yeah, she's sleeping. That's why I'm talkin' in such a low voice now. I figured I'd just let her crash and later, like in the real morning, not now, just have a talk and figure out just what the hell is goin' on, because the way she was, you should've seen her. I mean, she arrives here with a real . . . elaborate dress, barefooted, hair and face all messed up. She really went through somethin', I'm sure. So she mentioned you, I just figured I'd call to see if you had any idea about what went on."

Worm said, "Where the hell do you live anyway, Jer? You still live in that shithole neighborhood in Namba somewhere?"

Jeremy exuded a sarcastic laugh. "Haha, very funny, ya Canadian prick! I live in the building down the street from Tominaga Hospital. You and the Aussie guys helped me bring my furniture last year. You tellin' me you forgot already? I guess Elizabeth isn't the only one who's lost her mind."

Worm laughed. "Screw you, ya dwarf. Anyway, thanks for callin'. If you talk to Lizzy, just tell her I'm sorry about last night. Shit happens, y'know."

"Yeah, yeah OK. How's your school comin'?" Jeremy shucked his jeans.

"Coming along just fine," Worm said quickly. "Stop by sometime."

Jeremy said, "I'm still waiting on you to get with me so we can discuss some business. I have a lot of privates right now. More than I can handle, to be completely honest. Maybe we can put our heads together and come up with somethin'. One hand washes the other, right?"

"Right," Worm said. His answers became short and abbreviated as Jeremy went on elaborating on how the two of them should go into business together, merging students. "Yeah, yeah, just stop by sometime, Jer. We'll talk. I've gotta go now. The wife is gonna start bitchin' in a minute."

"OK, fine. See you later!" Jeremy ended the call.

Now undressed save for his white Fruit of the Loom briefs, he took his folded jeans into his bedroom and placed them aside. Liz was knocked out on his mattress. He pressed his lips together, smearing his excitement drool evenly to moisturize them. He joined Liz on the bed, still in her dressy gown. He took a moment to stare at her in sleeping form. She looked so peaceful, tranquil, and in a suspended state of beauty for him to behold. He kissed her face. First, on the cheek, then gradually moved to her lips. A wicked tumescence abruptly formed in his underwear briefs. He ran his hands the length of her body, starting from her breasts to her waist, and then stopping at her hips and thighs before repeating the action.

Next, it was time for him to relieve her of the elaborate dress. It would prove to be a delicate affair. He had to lift her back easily, for his hope was to not have her wake up. He had never tried or tested such a rape drug like this before, so he was unsure about how effective it actually was. So far, Liz seemed to be deadweight as he lifted her gently from the mattress, appearing as if she was sitting up in bed. Her head fell limply, so Jeremy guided it to his shoulders for support as he groped the rear of her dress, looking for some sort of zipper. Finding it, he unzipped the length of it until it ended at her lower back. When this was done, the rest wasn't as difficult as he had expected it to be; all he needed to do was slide her torso out of the sleeveless top portion. Once that was done, the garment was slid from the waist down, carefully and lightly, lifting her buttocks until he could drag the entire length of the material off her legs.

Jeremy moved to the foot of the mattress and pulled the dress clean from Liz's body. He briefly stared, amused, at the greyish soot that had accumulated on the soles of her feet resulting from the barefoot running around she had done earlier. This being no deterrent to his gradient passion rising, for Liz was undressed save for her flesh-colored bra and panties. He tossed the raiment aside and knelt before her, marveling at her sensationally sculpted features. Compared to him, she may as well have been an Amazon-like Wonder Woman or a Grecian goddess. He buried his face between her legs, his chin wedged them wider as his nose grazed the surface of her panties, feeling her pubic mound underneath. He caught a whiff of her sweaty odor, but this too was no distraction to his feverish desire; it only heightened it.

"It's all mine!" he whispered loudly to himself as he shifted his position and reclined beside her.

His hands were still stroking and rubbing her soft, tender skin and halted his palms on her inflated breasts. He slid the left strap down her muscular shoulder, then freed one of her orbiculate infant feeders. He wasted no time applying his mouth to her sweaty pink nipples. In the blink of an eye, he had both breasts exposed, her bra moved to the center of her torso. He continued lavishing his lip attention to her twin peaks, his hands still cradling both in either of his palms while his chin lightly poked her sternum. His heavy breathing intensified.

Liz's eyes opened ever so slightly, but just as soon she closed them again. This repeated every so often, but Jeremy didn't notice until she shifted her body. She moved to rest on her side, her back to Jeremy now. This only served to assist him in removing her bra in entirety as the strap hook was exposed. He unclasped it and removed the bra from her top portion, threw it to the foot of the mattress, where he had discarded her dress. From there, he snuggled against her, Koala-style, he wrapped his right arm around her from the back, basking in the ecstasy of feeling her warm flesh against his own. His solidly erect penis poked eagerly through his briefs and made contact with her rear side. Because of the height differential between them, Jeremy's head only reached to the middle of Liz's back. He kissed her spinal path, occasionally using his tongue; his hand was still cupping her breasts. As he did this, he heard Liz suddenly release a slumberous moan. One of her nipples became erect, Jeremy noticed, as he kept rubbing them.

Liz moaned like she was having a dream in which she was trying to speak but couldn't. Jeremy continued his molestation, readjusting his position to the upper section of her body and mattress. He mildly grabbed a handful of her voluminous blonde locks and strands as if it were a thick golden stringy curtain and draped it over her body. Her nape now exposed, he brought his lips there. Liz, despite her comatose-type state, apparently felt a sort of tingle from Jeremy's actions. Again, her eyes would open, then close. She tried to talk but couldn't. It was like she was stricken with catalepsy.

In and out of the state of rapid eye movement, Liz would awaken briefly but succumb to a burdening drowsiness. On one such interval of her being conscious, she felt Jeremy's caress, the heat from his body, the kisses on her neck. She was immediately turned on, but then she would doze off. In her mind, or dreams, she may have envisioned Jeremy to be someone that she was attracted to. But as she continually fought through the effects of the drug she had consumed, the more her brain's natural instincts of self-preservation seemed to be warning her of danger or an unsavory predicament.

Jeremy couldn't take it anymore. He stood up from the mattress and damn near ripped his own underwear off. He had to have her now. Returning to the bed, he tried to reposition Liz from her side to her back on the mattress, so he could mount her. His moving her shoulders served as an agent to awaken her somewhat. For as soon as he could get her on her back, Liz's eyes opened to a lethargic squint. She looked into Jeremy's eyes for a brief second but closed them again, perhaps due to the brightness of the light emitted throughout the room.

"Jer!" Liz mumbled angrily. Then she turned back on her side and fell asleep again. Briefly. A second later, she was stirring. Rubbing her head, then groaning.

Not wanting her to wake up just yet, Jeremy thought it a good idea to dim the lights. He got up and switched off the overhead lighting of the room and clicked on a desk lamp. The room was converted to a sandy ochre shade of brown dimness; and for the most part, Jeremy was right, doing this did seem to cause the relaxation of Liz's apparent defense mode. She dug her face deeper into the pillow Jeremy had her head resting upon and looked as if she was falling back into a heavy sleep.

Jeremy had to remove her panties. He eased his fingers through her waistline straps and tried to peel them off. He was only able to remove them partially; her dirty-blonde mound of vulva bush sprang out like instant germinated golden grass. He tried to lift her hips, viewing the revealed top crack of her rear end. This movement and shifting stirred Liz again to awaken, briefly but long enough to let out a moan that sounded tinged with annoyance.

"Jer . . . quit . . . it," she growled in a soft murmur. With her back and rear, she bumped against him, as if to move him away with what little strength her weakened state could summon.

"It's OK, Liz, it's OK," Jeremy whispered in a voice so loaded with lust he sounded as if he was short of breath. "I . . . I'm with you, it's gonna be OK, you'll see . . ." He haphazardly yanked the panties down her thighs. He didn't care if she woke up now. Even if she did, she would be virtually unable to stop him from doing what he wanted to do. Still, he tried to not be too rough as he turned her over on her back again, waited, then continued removing her panties until his efforts successfully completed the act of dragging them to her lower legs, and off, over her blackened-soled feet. She was now totally nude.

Jeremy's heart machine-gunned a drum solo within his chest. He was so consumed with desire and longing he nearly dry-retched. He trembled, even whimpered, as he knelt between her legs, parting them with gentle ease. Her matted crotch area tickled his belly as he prepared to crawl upon her and enter. He was set to attach himself to her and his moment of truth!

"Oh, Elizabeth . . . I've wanted you for so long . . . I'd do anything to be with you. I love you so much, babe." He took hold of his male operative tool and readied himself to be launched into heavenly bliss. His heart banged in his chest as if it were trying to escape. He could feel himself touch her as the initial contact with her flesh took place. He was going in . . . then . . .

BANG! BANG! BANG!

The resounding noise heard was loud enough to rouse Liz, but ever so slightly. She would have returned to her inanimate state had the sound not been repeated. The banging on Jeremy's apartment room door startled him just as much as it might have Liz.

Jeremy, close to panic, was unsure about what to do. For now, Liz was awake more so than she had been earlier. She was stirring, wiping her groggy eyes, mumbling particles of sentences more intelligible like, "What the hell? What time is it? What's the noise?" She was looking around the room, frowning and squinting, struggling to attain her faculties and questioning her whereabouts.

Elsewhere, the banging on the apartment door didn't stop. "Who the hell would be paying a visit this godforsaken time of the night!?" Jeremy wondered aloud in jittery alarm. He had hoped that his not answering the door would cause whoever it was to go away, but when the persistent banging continued, it was clear that was not to be.

Deciding it best to go to the door and see whoever it was off, Jeremy sprang to his feet and found his jeans. He jumped in them uncomfortably without underwear and still aroused below the belt. He scurried over to the door without saying anything to Liz. The banging on the door had yet to cease.

Liz was now awake, albeit groggy. Because she had only ingested a small amount of drug within the coffee she drank, she suffered only minimal effects, to her positive kismet. When able to regain considerable-enough coherency, she realized that she was naked. She looked about and saw that she was in unfamiliar surroundings. Immediately, she sought her clothing to cover her nudeness; her creeping feelings of anger and disgust began floating. She located her undergarments and dress.

Outside the room, Jeremy went to the door and opened it without standing on a milk crate to look through the peephole or ask who was slamming a fist on his door like a sledgehammer. The two masked men who accosted Liz earlier muscled their way inside of the apartment. Bowling Jeremy over. A ruckus then commenced.

From Jeremy's bedroom, Liz had barely just got inside of her bra and panties before she heard the loud pandemonium. Her heart switched instantly back to panic mode, and whatever feelings of woozy unsteadiness she suffered earlier magically snapped her alert, although with slower movements than she would otherwise be capable.

Jeremy put up a good fight, and had there been only one assailant, he might have prevailed as he was able to lift the larger of the two and wrestle him to a standstill on the ground. Had he been an insect, he would have had the prowess of a praying mantis, as his upper body strength and forearms had sufficient power to lock the huge intruder in a choke the man couldn't escape. His feet kicked wildly as Jeremy applied more pressure to the choke. The giant assailant was subject to losing consciousness. Meanwhile, the shorter of the invaders, discovered one of Jeremy's lightweight dumbbells conveniently lying around.

The hulking giant invader was able to push Jeremy away as the grip on his neck had been lessened. Jeremy tried to evade the descent of the dumbbell wielded by the shorter masked man. He was distracted long enough for the giant to grab him and lift him off his feet in a crushing bear hug. Jeremy head-butted the front of his assailant's face, but only halfway knocked off the man's thick motorcycle goggles.

The melee found its way gradually to the bedroom, where Liz was on the mattress trying to get inside of her dress. When the three bodies came crashing into the room, Liz had already located her purse. She fumbled through it, looking for her phone. By this time, the giant attacker had immobilized Jeremy long enough for the smaller partner to whack his head with the metallic gym tool, leaving an immediate whelp dent. Blood sprayed from the crack like a garden hose's sudden leak on full blast. Jeremy fell to the mattress, face-side prone between Liz's knees with his eyes open as if staring listlessly at her. Liz shook with ineffable fright and sobbed pitifully for Jeremy. She forgot about her phone as the two looming figures descended upon her.

Although somewhat winded, the bigger masked man pounced upon Liz and held her down with his weight. The smaller man snatched Liz's purse, rummaged through it, and found her envelope thick with her cash salary received from Mama-san Saiko. His gloved hand did a quick count of the bills, and he let out an amused exaltation.

"Fuckin' ay!" he said. Then his voice switched back to a mock so-called African American voice reminiscent of the stereotypical rap or hip hop reference. He knelt beside the mattress and leaned into Liz's distressed face.

He said, "Now youz had betta git yo' white ass up, bitch. You be a-comin' wit us! And if you give me and my homey boy here any trouble, bitch, we gonna cut yo' throat! You undastan' me, BITCH!?"

"Y-y-yes, yes, oh yes!" Liz squeaked and quailed as if she were a shrill canary surrounded by the grimy alley cats who they used to throw Kayo's muffins at.

"P-please . . . d-don't hurt me." She shivered, fear-frozen. "P-please, just take all of the money. Y-you can have it . . . just please don't hurt me . . . oh God!"

The large man on top of her began breathing heavy and out of control. He had mounted Liz on the bed, between her thighs, dry-humping her. His gloved fingers were trying to move the stirrup of her panties aside so he could wiggle himself inside once freed from his zipper. Liz fought hysterically underneath him, but she was short of energy still. She may as well have been trapped underneath a fallen tree or a building. The attempted rape was interrupted by the aggravated smaller mystery man, who slapped his large partner hard on the back.

The smaller creep said, "What you is gonna do, gurl, you is gonna take us to yo'r bank. Your ATM, and you gonna teach us your PIN number. And youz betta not tell me no liez, bitch. Now git yo'self up and git dressed!"

He slapped the large intruder on the back again. He clenched his fists, then communicated with the man in argot sign language–type gestures. It was as if they didn't want to use their voices, or true voice, within earshot of Liz.

Meanwhile, Liz frightfully chose to comply with the men in hopes that the ordeal would be over with. Trying to piece together in her mind who these dreadful individuals were took a back burner. She got to her feet and put herself in her dress as properly as she could. When she was done, the two men led her away, leaving Jeremy behind, his head dead center in a bloody afro print upon the mattress.

Outside the apartment, each dark man flanked Liz on each side tightly, holding her arms and walking her along. There were few people stirring about at this time of night, and astonishingly, the commotion that had erupted in Jeremy's domicile had not disturbed neighbors to the extent that police had to be summoned. If anyone were to see them, they appeared like two men assisting a drunk or incapacitated companion when they exited the elevator. The masks were a little outre, but no one was about, so they were unseen all the way to the vehicle they entered. Its color was gray, a four-door hatchback ride Liz was unfamiliar with, so she knew it wasn't Yoh or anyone else she knew with a car.

The larger dark man loaded Liz in the back seat with himself. In the front seat, poised to drive, the smaller man reached into a bag and produced a set of wrap-tie shackles. He tossed them to the man in the back holding Liz as if his partner cohesively knew what to do with them. The man forced Liz's wrists together and tightly strapped the wrap ties around them like handcuffs. Next, he did the same to her feet. He discovered the white-gold anklet Eddie had given her seemingly ages ago, yanked it off, and pocketed it as he applied the shackles to immobilize her legs as well.

"You really don't have to do this," Liz pleaded piteously. "I'll cooperate. I'll tell you my PIN. Just please, let me go after I do."

"Just you tell me dat PIN, white bitch!" the smaller dark man shouted. He had her purse and sandals in the front seat with him. He found her bank card in her wallet. He stared at it and said, "Yo', bitch, dis bank done changed its name! You kin still use dis card?"

Liz assured the scary man that he could use it the same despite the name of the bank being different than the former name inscribed on the ATM card. She taught the man her personal identification number, and he drove around until he found her bank.

"Cover that bitch face," he ordered to his partner.

The large dark man covered Liz's eyes and face with a black bandana and his gloved hand long enough for his partner to unmask and enter the ATM vestibule. Sure enough, the number Liz supplied him was correct. Unfortunately, the ATM stipulated that only a maximum of two thousand dollars could be withdrawn per transaction, and in addition, only two of these could be done at the same vestibule. So after jacking Liz for four thousand dollars at that one ATM visit, they drove around and hit at least two more branches before finally cleaning her account, or almost doing so.

When the final ATM raid was complete, a gleeful bandit returned to the car, pleased with the bundle he had acquired. Of course, he would be obligated to split it with his partner, but altogether, the cash amount had amassed to over ten thousand US dollars. The entirety of Liz's savings since coming to Japan!

Through muffled ears, Liz heard the man say, "You was loaded there, bitch. I think you gots some more, but we'll get that later. We got another deal to do." Then his voice softened. It changed back to his normal elocution. He spoke to the man in back with Liz with a more natural-sounding Aussie twang.

"Let 'er go, mate," Simon said. "It doesn't matter now. We got all the cash. Let's get back to the warehouse. We'll take care of her later." He gunned the engine of the car and sped off.

The gloved iron gripped hands were removed from Liz's jaws, as was the bandana from her eyelids. Liz would then see Kwame Chwaku take off his mask and suck in a semblance of fresh air. He said, "Phew! I'm glad. Let's get the fuck out of here. I can't wait to stick it to this bitch! Remember me, bitch? You got me fired, you fucking bitch! Remember? You didn't have to report me to the staff! We could have worked that whole ting out!"

Reeling from consternation borne of utter shock seeing Kwame's hideous face again, then Simon, Liz shrieked in horror. She tried to cringe into an upright fetal position. "Omigod! What are you two guys doing? Why are you doing this?"

Although Liz somewhat understood Kwame's reasoning, she never thought that Simon hated her enough to harm her in this sort of way. Regardless, she thought that they were taking an act of revenge excessively far.

Simon said, "Because of you, bitch, my cousin is locked up. You and that fat cunt Stephanie! You fucking cunts bringing your undercover cop boyfriends an'all. Now word of his arrest brought shame on the folks back home. My uncle had to damn sure sell half of their family business, ya CUNT!" His anger was steadily rising. His mouth began dripping.

"You know it costs a fortune for his folks to fly back and forth from 'Stralia to here, y'know, and they have to pay for their lawyers too, hon! You have no fuckin' idea! And it's all because of you, and you think you're gonna just prance about with your Hollywood slutty charm and big talk? After Kwame here's done with you, we're gonna dump ya in the bay for the sharks. By the time they find you, you'll be chicken of the sea!"

"Noooo!" Liz cried. She tried to twist her wrists to break free of the wrap ties, but it was a futile endeavor. Useless. They were so tight they were already cutting into her skin. Her yelping grew irritating to Kwame, so he slapped her face with an ashy, hard-textured palm. Liz's teeth clacked together loudly, dangerously short of cracking. Kwame's bandana then was wrapped around her jib and inside of her mouth.

"Shut up, bitch," Kwame said. "We don't wanna hear anything from you. I wanna piece of your ass too. You know how hard it is for a Black man to get a job like that in Japan? You got me fired. All you had to do was accept my apology, but you had to take it too far and get me fired! I'm gonna give it to you for real now, girl, and then we gonna throw you in the harbor!"

Liz could do nothing as the car drifted the midnight streets. She thought for a moment that she could escape the car by wrestling with the door and the lock, but at the speed Simon was driving, she assessed that such action too would be unwise or fatal. She was still bound, and now gagged. She couldn't relax; seeing what they had done to Jeremy, she understood what they were capable of doing to her. She had no reason to believe that they wouldn't make good on their threats to kill her, to indeed throw her in the bay. But for the time being, they hadn't. She heard them mention something to the effect of having "another deal to do," getting "back to a warehouse" and meeting someone. Something of that sort. As such being the case, they were keeping her alive until that matter was resolved, apparently. For that much of a chance, Liz tried to hold on and remain hopeful that her possibility for escape or survival would remain. She looked outside the vehicle in the direction the car was headed. Liz saw a sign that read "Nanko" Road," but she had no earthly clue or idea where it was. Or, even if that was the place where they were headed. But many road signs that pointed the way along the car's course seemed to indicate that they were en route to that destination. Liz shuddered and prayed silently for this nightmare to end.

76

ABOUT A WEEK earlier, a fresh-dressed happy-smiling Deon Clemente stepped off a Japan Airline flight that flew into Osaka's Kansai International Airport. Dipped in a fly, dark-gray Italian Napoli suit, not the least bit wrinkled despite a fifteen-hour trip in first class, he didn't appear to be sapped of energy or jet lagged. Baffled customs agents searched his one piece of luggage desperately thinking or hoping that they would find some hidden contraband or illegal substances, but had their feelings deflated after discovering nothing. All they could do was feel good about themselves for rummaging through his bag just to leave his various expensive items of clothing and silk underwear in a disorganized muddle. Nothing could dull his mood. For the first time in a while, Deon had good reason to smile. His salient wry face and gloomy countenance was on pause, at least temporarily.

Paz Lucha greeted him when he exited the customs barrier. There was a ceremonious reunion consisting of celebratory hugging and congratulatory wishes, like two people who had just won a World Series Championship. It had to be curtailed somewhat because Paz was markedly parked illegally outside.

On the ride back to Osaka City, Paz was telling Deon, "You lucky motherfucker. You da man! When you left so quick like that, you had us all worried. We thought there was a death in the family, so you split back to New York. We didn't even think you was coming back. In fact, nigga, why *did* you come back?"

Deon said, "Why not come back? Ain't shit happenin' in the Big Apple like that anyway. I had somethin' like an interesting life here in Japan. My family is taken care of, shit is good back home. So, I'm good. In fact, I got to thinkin' maybe I can get together with that Candy Box Tabriz guy. Maybe we can revive that cultural arts program, who knows? A lot of brothers can get work, fancy careers, y'know, positive shine."

Paz shrugged expectantly. "Maybe. We'll have to see about that. So . . . I guess now you gonna be returnin' that pack I let you hold, huh?"

Deon got quiet but answered with a wide grin. He said, "Nah, a deal's a deal. I already took it, so amma make good. You'll get the proceeds. Gonna make you whole."

Paz laughed. "I know you gonna break your man off with a piece ain't you? Don't forget who it was took you under their wing when you was assed out. Long-faced, bitchin' because you didn't wanna go back to the boogie down and workin' at a mailroom for them Jews downtown. That was me, homeboy."

Deon said, "Man, you don't need to remind me. Respect, fam, I always give you your credit. You'a hustler on two continents. You know how to kick it with the gangsters even on foreign land. You used your street knowledge to put you on the next level. That's some real shit. I take my hat off to you, bro, You know I always told you that."

"I'm just fuckin' wit you, man, chill." He lit up a hand-rolled cig. "Even if you did break me off, son, I'd almost feel greedy. Shit is goin' so well for me now I don't even know how I can go broke. Now that I made that Luzio Silver investment, my money keeps rollin' in. Shit, not only has business been boomin', I'm getting several new students a week, itchy-man a head—I'm getting' money from customers, and the foreign white boys and bitches who work for me." His roaring guffaw of mirth echoed through the car, and Deon could've sworn it vibrated the windows.

"Hell, I damn near take the cash out of my teacher's salary every month. My best customers! They bring their friends too."

"Man, tell me that ain't weed you smokin'," Deon said. "I ain't tryna have my suit smell like Bob Marley. I get enough stares as is."

"Relax," Paz said, exhaling in Deon's direction before turning on the air conditioner system to ventilate the air. "This just a loose square. If anybody needs to smoke, it's you. Maybe you'll calm down. You always so uptight."

Deon said, "In the meantime, you be careful too. A lot of these foreign white people are just as shady as anybody else. They some sneaky motherfuckers. No street smarts, no damn sense of loyalty whatsoever—at least not with us. No need for you to be another Luzio Silver, or Tim Valentine. They'll just throw us under the bus."

No worries, fam." Paz tried to give Deon a smirk of reassurance. "I got all my bases covered. But all bullshit aside, I ain't trippin' about that pack fam. If you wanna gimme that back, ain't no shame in the game. Do you. Everybody ain't cut out for that type of life. And now, you got a brand-new chance, an opportunity to make somethin' of yourself . . . you don't need to mess it up getting' yourself in trouble. Especially over here in Japan. It'll be all for nothin'. So just drop it off sometime next Sunday."

Deon shook his head. "Nah, my bro. A deal's a deal. If I didn't have the intention of takin' care of it, I shouldn't have accepted it. Anyway, I got somebody lined up to drop that off on. I'll hip you to the details later. Don't sweat it, we good, my dude."

"Whatever, man," Paz said as he hit the city via Hanshin Expressway. "Where you live at again? Miyakojima? Damn, you right that shit is far as hell." They laughed and joked all the way until their destination was reached. For the time being, they parted ways after Deon was dropped off.

A week later into the present, Simon Bunderburg parked his ride at a nondescript parking lot of a low-income apartment building. At the wee hours of the morning, it was less likely for parking police to discover illegally stationed vehicles. He and Kwame Chwaku noiselessly hustled a petrified Liz into a hideaway in the Hirabayashi area of the Osaka City's Suminoe District. Seagull and albatross feces covered the streets and hoods on some cars as the locale was coterminous to the murky Nanko Harbor, nestled between the Yamato and Kizu Rivers. The so-called warehouse destination was actually a low-budget small-time two-bit English school where Simon found some occasional part-time work. This gig was a hookup he got, thanks to acquaintances of his girlfriend, Chikako. He conned these folks who were the school's owners into believing he was reliable and dependable enough to open up the school on Saturdays for early-morning lessons and entrust him with a school key. Without permission, however, he would at times use the key to the school and gain access for purposes that didn't fall within the description of language instruction. Confident he wouldn't get caught, he chose this place for the location to follow through with his nefarious deeds and evildoings. His mental stability had always been a questionable thing, but no one ever picked up on this aspect of his character. Although he seemed to be soft-spoken, run-of-the-mill clean-cut on the surface, beneath it was a contemptable "schmegge"; and the arrest of his beloved cousin Ricky Exmouth had driven him over the edge. To the point where he didn't think twice about committing murder and robbery as an act of revenge.

Inside of the English school, Simon ordered Kwame to lower the blinds, close the shades, and draw in all curtains. They used the dim light of a sole classroom's lamp to illuminate the place instead of the overhead lights, to make the one-story building appear uninhabited, or at least as much as possible.

Simon pointed to a storage closet. He said to Kwame, "Put her in there for now."

Kwame did as instructed. Still gagged with Kwame's bandana, Liz's face was smeared with tears of fright, pinkish red. She whimpered as Kwame opened the storage closet and threw her inside upon a collection of stuffed animals, kids' toys, and cushions. When he shut the door, the closet was almost completely dark save for the little bit of light that crept underneath at the threshold.

Outside, murder accomplice Kwame sat on the edge of the sole desk in the wide, furniture-bare schoolroom. Seated at the desk, Simon counted out all the money they took. He was dividing his cut with Kwame.

"So we're going to . . . end her too?" Kwame asked.

Simon glanced up and looked as if he didn't like being distracted. Then he sighed and stopped what he was doing. He said, "Look, mate, I know you wanna have your way with her, and that's fine. Just remember why we're here and why we're doin' this. I really need this money. Ricky needs this money. His family needs this money. I'm givin' you your cut, but if the cops find out your DNA . . . I'm just worried they can catch up with us. I mean, we're lucky because the cops don't really investigate *gaijin* murders, an' that's great an'all, mate, but if they get a'hold of yer DNA, you could be done for!"

Kwame said, "What about if we dump her in the bay, it's right there under the overpass. I saw it on the way here."

Simon said, "Now that's a thought, mate." His cell phone rang. He had a brief conversation, punctuated with "Just tell them to drop you off at the convenience store down the street from the Highway 4 bridge. You'll see it after you pass the bridge. It'll be the only store there. I'll send Kwame out to meet ya." He ended the call. "The first guest is here, he's on time. This shit is gonna be funny as fuck all, mate. Go grab up our friend at that Family Mart. Try not to make too much noise."

Ten minutes later, Kwame returned to the hideout English school with Worm. He was all buoyant, chipper and cordial, dressed in casual jeans and a white T-shirt that looked oversized on him as if he was wearing the clothes of an obese sibling. The first thing that caught his eye was the stack of Japanese money on the table. His eyes glistened with excitement and anxiety. A greedy grin grabbed his grill as he clasped his bony fingers and rubbed them together.

"What a score!" Worm said. "So some of this is mine, right? Cool. Just let me get my cut, I gotta be back. I hadta sneak out the house as is. Mikako's gonna flip."

Simon looked at Kwame, and they exchanged ill, sneaky grins. "There's been a change of plans, Wormy."

Before Worm could respond, he barely had time to react with a look of shock and disbelief before being dropped with a single sock to the face by Kwame's powerful fist. One of his mandible bicuspids was loosened and he spit blood on the floor.

"What the fuck!?" Worm cried. Kwame lifted him up from off the floor, shook him like a rag doll, then slapped him so hard the sound resembled the popping of a balloon. Worm fell to the floor again. Kwame then whipped out a shiny, menacing Japanese *santoku* knife, held it to Worm's throat. Simon tossed Kwame a set of wrap-tie handcuffs.

Kwame sat upon Worm, threatening to crush his bones with his weight. "You wet noodle piece of shit! You could've saved me from getting fired too. Why didn't you speak up for me, huh? All those times I shift swapped with you, came in on days I didn't have to work...Fuck you. And why didn't you ever invite me to your parties!?"

There was no way Worm could move or go anywhere as Kwame fastened his hands together, then did the same to his ankles as he had to Liz earlier. He was now so petrified he could hardly concentrate on Kwame's imposing interrogation.

Worm pleaded, "Come on, Simon! Why? Why're you doin' this? I mean, we . . . we had a deal. The deal was I tell you where she was. I . . . I found her address for you. I told you where she was. Keep the money, keep the weed man. I . . . I don't need it. Forget about it."

Simon said with a wicked smirk "Yeah, sure. We'll forget about it won't we, Kwame?" They laughed. "Don't worry about the dope. The weed. It's on the way. In fact, you're the guest of honor."

Worm said with disgust, "Dude . . . I don't understand . . ."

Simon's demeanor changed. He switched to his insane mode. He sprang up from the desk and threw himself on the floor, leaned into Worm's face. "As far as I'm concerned, mate, you're just as responsible for Ricky getting locked up as Stephanie. That's why we offed her, mate! We should do the same to you, now eh? You didn't try an' lift a finger to help Ricky, you wanker! All you cared about was coverin' yo'r own arse!"

Worm was now scared stiff. He said, "Oh . . . dear God! So, it is true . . . Steph is really . . . dead! It was you!?"

Kwame said, "Fuck that, you stupid son of a bitch. Why didn't you call me to work for your shitty school? Why you never invited me to any of your parties!?" He slapped Worm again hard on the back of his head. Worm felt like his skull was pulsating.

When he was able to regain his senses, Worm asked, "But how did you know she was in Tokyo? Or, wherever she was? You never worked for Bozack, K-kwame was long gone. How did you . . ."

Simon said, "We got our ways. Might as well tell ya it was Tim's old broad, you know, one of the managers, the sexy little piece that liked to wear spandex— Sachi Nishinari. She made a special trip to Osaka to get the intel. It was her idea, in fact, for us to go on our little fundraiser. She was tryin' to help her man Tim until he got desperate and pissy and started tellin' and runnin' his mouth. She told us where and when the money drop would be, how much we could get, and we ninja'd our way to Tokyo and back, didn't we, Kwame?"

Kwame nodded with a vile grin that quickly disappeared and his grim face returned beaming down on Worm. Just then, Simon's phone rang again. He looked at the incoming phone call number on his receiver. "It's him!" Simon said excitedly to Kwame, who also straightened up and stood at alert attention waiting for the next move.

Kwame asked, "You want me to go out and meet him?"

"No," Simon said. "It's better he come here directly so we can get this over with. Take this clown and put him in the closet with that bitch over there." Kwame lifted and dumped Worm in the store closet like a sack of potatoes, practically atop Liz. Their fearful faces reacted with bulged eyes upon contact with one another, then Liz's and Worm's muffled murmurs could be heard before the door closed again.

Simon gave the party on the line the address to the school. An instant later, a taxi arrived across the street from the English school. Deon got out of the cab, and it sped off.

The warehouse-based English school was on the second floor of the building. Access to this upstair space was gained by a single flight of steps leading to a small alcove and outside door. Deon approached this door as he had already passed the enclosed parking lot in the front of the edifice.

Simon went down to greet Deon at the door and surreptitiously let him inside. They exchanged pleasantries and small talk about Deon's recent trip abroad. Deon was dressed casually: hoodie, sneakers, loose-fitting baggy jeans, and was carrying a backpack. Simon guided Deon upstairs to the spacious classroom level where Kwame waited.

Deon and Kwame acknowledged one another, but dryly. There was no hint of camaraderie, fraternal cordiality, or the eccentric handshake often employed as when Deon would meet his kindred pals like Paz, Chucky, or Preston Ciclon. Simon saw Deon eyeing the money on the desktop and then started hand sweeping it in Liz's purse he still had.

Deon stared at the floor and frowned up, looking at a sudden stain on his fresh new kicks. "Somebody bleedin'?" he asked. "And what you doin' with a chick's pocketbook?"

Simon laughed uneasily then said, "Oh, that . . . Before I get into that, me and Kwame have a little surprise for ya mate."

Deon's trouble antenna went up, and his suspicion level was rising. He didn't want Simon or Kwame to get wise to his feeling of uneasiness, so he maintained a cool and calm exterior. He then said, "Damn all the surprises. It's late as hell.

Let's just get down to business." Deon opened his backpack and pulled out the bundle of weed totaling multiple ounces, consolidated into a package the size of two standard bricks. "Here's the gangster. That'll be the price we agreed upon a week ago."

Simon said, "Sure, sure, Dee. But first, I gotta insist you come take a look at this." He nodded to Kwame, who opened the door to the broom closet. Simon pointed in that direction for Deon to take a look.

Cautiously, Deon approached the store closet. Breath left his chest in a mighty heave of horror as he saw Worm and Liz gagged and tied up inside. At first, he thought it was some sort of joke, but he witnessed the frightful looks on their faces and the blood trickling from Worm's gagged jib. Liz's normally cute face was now hideously shadow-eyed by failed makeup and blackened tears. They made terrified mumbling tremors.

"There he is, Dee!" Simon exalted. "That's him, dude. Worm. That's the swine who got you sacked, mate. We know all about it. Sachi spilled the *vegemite*! As a present, a surprise, we thought we'd hold 'im for ya. Hell, I don't even like the guy either. You know what he wanted to do? He wanted to get this weed from you, then go into business for 'imself, yah? Then get me and Kwame to do his grunt work, takin' all the risks while he gets all the money and the glory. Meanwhile, my cousin Ricky is rottin' in a Japanese jail cell. We figured we'd save him here for ya, so you can get first licks, eh?" He laughed like the diabolical villain he was.

Deon froze. Fear wasn't a factor; indecision was coursing through his head. While it was true, Worm was an abhorrent, loathsome ring-ding, one who deserved Deon's vengeful trouncing, he had no ultimate desire or need to punish him to the extent they had ventured. He had some feelings of ill will towards Worm absolutely. He knew that Worm had set him up just to rat on him to Kenji, which led to his firing. He had also considered doing a "187" attack on Worm too but was so occupied with his own life situation that thoughts of revenge had taken a back seat. Then when his life had suddenly taken a turn for the better, his outlook changed. Worm was the last thing on his mind and had escaped his radar.

Upon his return to Japan, his intention was to make a deal with Liz, or maybe even give the weed pack to her as a gift, knowing she was such a fiend for sizzle. He saw that she had tried to call him while he was away. However, before he could catch up with Liz, Simon called him from out of the blue, supplied his number from Worm, and made Deon an offer he decided to take. As per his conversation with Paz, he would sell the pack because he made his friend a promise that he would, even though he really didn't have to. The proceeds he claimed he would have donated to Paz's legit school business.

Now Deon was in a precarious situation. The way Worm and Liz were muzzled and bound reeked heavily of crime that went beyond drug dealing and wandered into the territory of assault and kidnapping as well. Dealing drugs was a bad-enough offense, and Deon wanted none of even that. For, as Paz admonished, he now had an opportunity to "make something of yourself," and need not get into trouble. It was as if his slate was wiped clean and he had a chance to restart his life and career. The thought of the cops running up on them then and there started to weigh heavy on his mind, and he was fighting not to let it show. He was a little shook and timorously thinking of calling everything off and making a dash. He looked at the heartrending expression on the faces of the closeted captives, especially Liz. For whatever reason he couldn't unravel, he pitied her. Deon had, through unfortunate circumstances, seen and come into contact with killers in his day. On several occasions throughout his troubled life and upbringing, some people he knew had gotten locked up for it. Heinous, brutal ones too. When he looked into the demented eyes of Simon, he knew he was staring at another killer—a murderer.

Poised with uncanny calmness, Deon said, "I understand why you'd wanna fuck up that Worm punk. But what did Elizabeth do?"

Kwame then shut the door to the closet, imprisoning the two hostages once again. Simon spoke. "Never mind her. She's collateral damage. She's just as much to blame as Stephanie or anybody else. Stephanie, Liz, and Vicky and all these sluts date these Japs who turn out to be undercover coppers, mate. Then they squeak out everybody's name when they get in trouble t'save their sweet cunts from the slammer. Well, she's gonna pay the price, you can betcha."

Deon said, "Nah, man. I think you're wrong about her man. What do you plan to do with them? You got them all tied up. What if they go run to the cops on you?"

"Oh, we ain't worried about that'a'tall, mate." Simon's face reverted to that of a sick, demented angry man. He toyed around with his own little jackknife, touching lightly on its bladed edge. His austere expression and manner couldn't be dismissed.

Deon said, "You gonna waste them? You crazy?"

"Never mind that, mate, like I said," He stood up from the desk again, holding the knife to his side. Kwame stood ready as well. Simon continued, "So we were thinkin', Dee. You, me, and Kwame here, you and us, we'd make a good team. We'll go into business. You bein' our new connect and all. That wanker Brad, I'm sure you know him. We broke a few of his bones too, mate. He's been sellin' the fake bud 'n all. He had a bundle of cash on him. I still gotta raise money for Ricky. His folks are checkin' into the poorhouse mate. We're all sufferin' here. Whaddaya say?"

Deon backed up. Kwame and Simon closed in on him in slow, deliberate steps. As if, were he to render them an answer that didn't strike their fancy, things would result in catastrophic consequences for him. Courageously and defiantly, though, Deon stood his ground.

He said, "If you mean to go along with offin' somebody, or bein' an accomplice to murder, you motherfuckers can best forget that shit!" The level of his voice raised in volume to the length it resonated like a battle cry. His last stand.

Meanwhile, that instant inside of the closet, within the dimly lit space, Worm had managed to manipulate his clammy, osseous wrists out of the tie wrap, freeing his hands. Kwame hadn't anticipated that the skeletal Canadian's limbs were not only wiry but also flexible and double-jointed, almost like a contortionist. Just when a thunderous crash erupted outside the door, the sound of a fracas signifying a brawl of some sort had ensued, Worm used this as an opportunity to plan his escape. Thus liberated of hand constraints, he used the reserves of his lightweight strength to twist and tug on the heavy duty plastic to no avail until he miraculously spotted a school supply box among other stored items on a textbook shelf. He rummaged through it and found a pair of scissors. He cut himself free and removed the rag from his mouth.

Liz tried to arch her back, leaning into the back wall shelf to hoist herself to her feet. She moaned muffled pleas for Worm to cut her loose as well, but she seemed to be of no concern to him. All he thought about was his own path to safety. He discarded the scissors into the pile of stuffed animals and toys, and it fell to the bottom of the box. Liz scrambled frantically trying to dig them out, but the light in the closet was too dim to see clearly. Worm cracked the door and witnessed Deon fending off the knife-wielding pair of Kwame and Simon. The desk had been overturned, and Deon was fending off his attackers with the chair Simon had sat upon.

Using a moment of distraction while the trio tussled, Worm made a decision to bolt and scram from the storage closet. He shot a killer bee line to the exit as the storage closet door swung open with a slamming bang. Simon spotted him immediately.

"Kwame! Go after him!" Simon yelled. "Don't let that wanker get away!"

Adrenaline-rushed Kwame obeyed and gave chase. He rushed out after Worm, who had made it down the single flight of stairs and run into the streets screaming and yelling. Unfortunately, Worm hadn't the athleticism of a soccer field sprinter like Kwame, who closed in on him with muscular calves propelling his race. Grabbing the back of Worm's T-shirt neckline, Kwame yanked him backward, easily controlling his movement as if he were a life-sized action figure toy or a crash test dummy.

Kwame's *santoku* blade plunged into Worm's side with the ease of puncturing a ripened tomato. Worm released a guttural heave as Kwame repeatedly stabbed him in his midsection. The white T-shirt was gradually becoming crimson laden accompanied by rips and tears from the knife. He then allowed Worm's mass to slump onto the streets and bleed out. Kwame looked around and saw that there were no people around. It was late, and the neighborhood was quiet and secluded for the most part. Occasional cars would pass along the main drag, but at that time of the pre-dawn, no one seemed to pay much attention or notice late-night stragglers. Homeless drunks along the Yamato River basin, which they were in close proximity to, were not uncommon. As such, the sight of Worm prone on the concrete near the huge highway underpass wouldn't cause alarm, perhaps until the broad daylight crept its way in hours from then.

Back inside the English school, Simon had tried to gut Deon with his jackknife. He thrust and stabbed at Deon, but finally, the New Yorker used the legs of the chair and rushed the Aussie. Simon evaded the rush like Deon was a charging bull and he a matador. He sliced Deon's left shoulder with his blade. Deon's thick Fubu hoodie's material absorbed most of the slash, but the blade was sharp enough to leave a slight rill on the flesh.

"Come on, ya black wanker!" Simon goaded Deon with rage. "You're makin' it hard on yourself. You're gonna go inside the bay with the bitch and that Worm wanker!" He swung the knife again, dangerously close to Deon's face.

The chair was a little heavy, as it was a standard office piece with the revolving base and made of metal. Deon's arms were getting tired of holding it outright. But he felt his life was on the line, and with that, he forced an extra rush of energy to surge within his capable effort to survive. On a whim, he decided to toss the chair at Simon. Again, Simon evaded, but the projectile chair went sailing through the window with a loud crash. This didn't sit well with Simon. He hadn't planned for this. The noise from the broken window was guaranteed to attract some sort of attention in the stillness of the night, the sound of shattered glass was sure to arouse some nosy people. He had to hurry and finish the job, hoping that Kwame would soon return.

While Simon stood momentarily disoriented because of the chair going out the window, Deon seized the opportunity to swing his left leg upward in a motion resembling a tae kwon do or karate practitioner's axe kick, aiming his foot at the hand in which Simon held the knife. When it made contact, the knife went flying through the air and landed several feet away. Before Simon could scramble over to retrieve it, Deon pounced upon him with an NFL-type tackle. They both hit the floor with a loud *thud*.

Deon commenced pummeling Simon. He rained blows mercilessly upon Simon's face; jaws and teeth cracked underneath his mounted flurry. He finished him off with some elbow smashes to the Aussie's temple to ensure that he would be out cold and in no condition to trouble him anymore. When satisfied that this was the case, he stared down at the motionless, unconscious Simon; breathed a sigh of relief; then turned his attention to the storage closet. He saw Liz inside; she was cringing and still squealing through her gag with fright.

Deon found the knife Simon had and picked it up. He entered the closet and used the knife to free Liz from her bounds. She removed the gag as Deon helped her to stand up. With a cry of utmost relief and gratitude Liz threw her arms around Deon and thanked him abundantly. Tears of desperation from her face stained his hoodie. He shook her loose, anxious and nervous.

"We gotta get outta here," he told her. Liz spotted her sandals and tried to strap them on, while Deon crammed her purse inside of his backpack. The overturned desk had also spilled the brick of weed on the floor. Deon punctured the plastic sealing the grass with the knife and took a handful of marijuana in his fisted palm. He went over to Simon, still out cold, and stuffed the weed inside of his cargo pants's compartment pockets.

No sooner had they tried to split, descending the stairs, than Deon and Liz run smack dab into a raging Kwame with a bloody, katana-like Japanese kitchen knife.

"Liz, run!" Deon yelled, hoping she could evade Kwame as he had them somewhat cornered in the enclosed lot that had bordering walls too high for normal people to scale.

Instead, Kwame blocked her passage and stuck out his left leg and tripped her. Liz fell and hit her head on the wall. She lay stunned on the asphalt.

"Come on, motherfucker!" Deon said, averting Kwame's attention from Liz to him. Kwame did shift his target from Liz to Deon. A searing expression of hatred materialized on his face. Kwame gripped the knife like he was hunting for food in a jungle and he was a hungry tribesman. He stepped toward Deon slowly and methodically.

"You slave nigger! I never liked you or your kind anyway, *akata*!" Kwame said, his voice tinged with wrath and acrimonious contempt. "I am a real African! You're a disgusting slave! I hate you, fucking *akata*—you black American cotton picker!"

Deon started humming a peculiar, harmonious medley with his voice as he began bouncing his body, like he was dancing. His feet shifted from side to side, like he was practicing a basketball move, but without a ball. The humming grew louder, until he started mumbling words that were deemed incoherent by Kwame, for he didn't understand the language.

"*Voce me trau!*" Combining renditions in both Portuguese and Spanish. "*Me traicionaste!*" Deon's voice slashed Kwame's nerves.

As he continued to move his legs from side to side, in deceptive movements, Kwame watched him closely but continued his approach, still gripping the menacing knife. However, the song that Deon was chiming while he was doing his "dance" was seeping into his brain like slow-acting invisible poison or nerve gas, which intensified his anger.

"Shut up, you slave nigger!" Kwame yelled. "I'm going to cut out your vile tongue!"

Deon sang, *"Oi quem mandou levar! Oi quem mandou levar! Me traiconaste! Me traiconaste! Ya no eres mi hermano!"*

He stood facing Kwame, stretched his left foot backward, then quickly brought it forward, aligning it with his other leg at shoulder width. His right foot swerved backward and repeated the rhythmic movement, still shifting from side to side.

Deon's chanting intensified; it was if he was possessed by an unseen spiritual entity. He chimed, *"A cobra mordeu caicara! Me traiconaste! Ya no eres mi hermano!"*

"SHUT UP! SHUT UP! Damn you!" Kwame screamed as if either the sound of Deon's voice or the words he uttered was destroying him internally. With a brash, wild swing of the knife, he made a slashing attempt for Deon's eyes.

As if he had seen it coming in slow motion, Deon dropped himself to the ground, his palms touched the pavement, supporting his weight. He then kicked out his leg, upward and struck the wrist of Kwame's blade-wielding hand. Briefly unbalanced, Kwame still maintained the weapon in his grasp but suffered a stinging blow to his face. Deon decked him suddenly with a quick right hook as he gracefully returned to a standing position.

In a fit of rage, Kwame lashed out with a backslash movement holding the blade. Deon moved swiftly to the side in a counterclockwise motion; then he cartwheeled, tricking Kwame into thinking that he could rush him before he landed on both feet substantially. Instead, he was hit with a spinning roundhouse kick that came from seemingly nowhere—first the right sneaker, then the left followed through, both hitting Kwame's jaw with ferocious impact. It didn't appear to be enough to knock out the African, but he was staggering as if he was on Bambi legs. The knife dropped to the concrete with a clang. Kwame's hands covered his wounded face and staggered about like he was dizzy or sloppy drunk.

Deon dropped to his side again; his hands supported him as he then threw one arm over his own head. With a straight leg, he kicked and swung his leg at Kwame, just when the African had let loose a haymaker-type overhand right punch. Kwame took the full brunt of the attack and was sent to the ground, landing on his rump and then falling back. Wasting no time, Deon ran over to the fallen Kwame and kicked him in the head a couple of times to ensure that he was out cold. Careful not to touch the knife Kwame had, Deon ran back to the school's entrance. He found the fire alarm, broke the emergency glass, and pulled its lever. A shrill, screeching sound emerged, and an obstreperous bell began chiming away.

Liz was now stirring at this point. Deon quickly tended to her, once again lifting her to her feet. "We gotta get outta here," he told her. "We shouldn't be here when the cops arrive. It's gonna be a big mess. This shit is ugly out here tonight, trust me!"

Liz was in no mood to argue. She was thankful that peril was at bay temporarily, but was still apprehensive, so she followed Deon. Once again, she unstrapped her heeled sandals and decided she could move faster without them, even if uncomfortable. Within minutes, they both could hear the sound of police sirens. Skillfully, Deon mapped out a course of flight that enabled him and Liz to escape undetected from the immediate vicinity of the English school, by cutting across a wide courtyard that belonged to the Hirabayashi neighborhood elementary school. Arriving at Yamatogawa Street, one of the main drag vessels of the area, Deon and Liz hid in a service alley between two residential abodes as they watched cop cruisers speed by. When satisfied that they were unseen, Deon urged Liz to press on until they could arrive at the more well-lit section of the street, where all-night diners and convenience stores were in abundance.

Taking a look at Liz's face, he saw she was a far cry from the glamorous *Baywatch* beauty or Hollywood starlet everyone proclaimed her to be, Deon noticed. Her makeup was nonexistent, and her facial features were shot to hell due to the stress and discord the night had brought to her. Keeping her out of the public eye, even at that time of the twilight hours, he felt would be a good idea. Nosy people would surely be asking questions. At the time, he was unaware of how Worm had met his fate but didn't expect for the outcome to have been good. The knife that Kwame had attacked him with was quite bloody, and so was its wielder. When the cops showed up to respond to the fire alarm, along with the fire engines, they would no doubt discover Kwame, the bloody knife, and, inside the school, the broken window, the place in disarray, and Simon with a heaping batch of weed on his person.

"What are we gonna do, Dee?" Liz asked in a shivering fit. "I . . . I can't really go home. My place is a wreck. I'm so scared! What if more scary fuckin' creeps are out there coming after me? Luzio Silver—"

"Liz, shut up, I'm thinkin'. Look, there's a park over there, let's hit it. It's dark." Thinking quickly, Deon hit a small patch of trees and open area designed for recreation for small children between two tall building complexes. They lay low on a bench there and watched as fire engines sped by along with another set of police cars.

Deon whipped out his cell phone. He rang up Paz Lucha. In a stretch of time that seemed like an eternity, Paz finally answered the phone.

"What the hell you want this time of night, nigga?" Paz's groggy, post-intercourse voice seeped through the line. "You tryna interrupt my fuck session, or what? This better be good."

Agitated, Deon gruffly stated, "Yo, man, I need your help. ASAP. It's a matter of near life and death. I need you out here. I need a ride!"

Paz cursed in a mood denoting agitation and turmoil, but he wasn't about to leave Deon stranded. Especially upon detecting that his fellow New York City pal was in serious trouble as his voice sounded over the line. He rose up from the bed. The Japanese girl who had been caressing him had her hands roughly removed from his chest.

"Where you at, bro?" Paz asked, slipping into a tight sweater, standing up to extend his legs inside of some sweatpants.

"Over here in Suminoe, around your way," Deon said uneasily, still standing guard and looking out for stray rollers on the avenue. "I just don't know exactly where I'm at."

"That's good news, look around . . . what do you see?" Paz said roughly. He was now dressed and grabbed his car keys. "Is there a store around you or somethin'?"

Deon said, "I'm not sure . . . wait, oh, there's a Yamato Bank, a Family Mart convenience store, a video store . . . shit . . . man, I don't know. We on a big street. It looks familiar . . . but . . . ."

"Say no more, homie, I got you. In about five or ten minutes, I'm gonna pull up in front of the Yamato Bank ATM. I know where that's at. Don't fuck around, bro. I'm out." He hung up. True to his word, he arrived on the schedule he laid out. When Deon spotted Paz's familiar Suzuki wagon pull up on the side street adjacent to the small bank, he ushered Liz across the wide street, defying the green light and walk signal. Because there wasn't much traffic, they made it to Paz's car.

Paz jumped out of the car from the right side driver's seat. He saw Deon bringing Liz along like she was a rescued victim from a burning building, halfway supporting her, as she was limping due to her feet having somewhat blistered soles now.

"Who dis?" Paz asked as he opened the rear car door and helped Deon place Liz inside. Half-jokingly, he uttered "I know snow bunny ain't your girl?"

Deon shut the door once Liz was securely inside. He said, "No time for jokes, my man. Just get us the fuck out of here." He ran around to the passenger side on the left shotgun. Another cop car sped by with the sirens blasting. They stayed motionless before Paz started up the engine. On pins and needles, they remained still and quiet in hopes that the police didn't notice them in the illegally parked car on the wrong side of the road. Luck seemed to be on their side as the light changed to green. Paz turned left on Yamatogawa Street and drove in the opposite direction the cop cars headed, en route to Roadway 29 alit with a cavalcade of all-night diners, gas stations, and a lively flow of traffic. Paz's Suzuki blended in obscured and undetected among a convoy of trucks, taxis, and other passenger cars.

Triumphant in escape, Paz asked, "Where to playboy?"

"Head downtown," Deon said. "Things might be hot for a couple of days. Thinkin' I might need to lay low, me and this broad. Amma check into one of those fancy hotels. Maybe the Dai-Ichi one on the outskirts. I'll show you the way. Let's hit that one."

Liz breathed a sigh of relief at long last. She was usually talkative, but on this occasion, she was uncharacteristically silent. Rightfully so.

77

*K*WAME HELD LIZ *down, Simon jumped on top of her, held a massive blade to her tender neck. She tried to scream, but no sound would escape her, only fragments of noise, pieces of a shriek as her attacker's hand clamped down like a slab of iron over her mouth. Simon's psychotic gaze transfixed upon her as he came down with his blade! Liz screamed . . .*

"Noooooo!" she yelled and then arched her back as she jerked her body upward. She woke up in a cold sweat. She was in a different place now. The smell of fresh linen hit her nose; her surroundings were sterilized, almost like that of a hospital, only the bed seemed larger, wider, softer, and more comfortable. Nearby to her left, a large weatherproof window with an open, grayish curtain displayed a pleasant, breathtaking view of the Osaka City skyline, from a view scoped from maybe the twentieth floor. Rays of the late-morning sun glinted off the collection of buildings and skyscrapers that made up the Umeda composite. Liz didn't recognize her exact location but remembered vaguely the early morning when Deon and his friend accompanied her into the lobby of some large ornamented hotel that had a marble-tiled pool with a fountain spraying up weeping-willow formations of water.

She remembered walking sore, barefoot over the shiny black floor before resting upon a soft, plush couch, while Deon left to somehow pull some sort of strings or make some sort of transaction with the front desk lobby staff. Before that, she recalled riding in the back seat of a marijuana-scented car and then dozing off. Fatigue continued and caused for words to trail off into an incoherent jumble that she could no longer piece together. The fact of the matter was, she was now comfortably situated in a luxury hotel. As Liz looked about, she could also tell that this place was also at least a 4-star. Fresh linen, shiny floors, partially carpeted, extraordinary view, not to mention amenities. The hair dryer an expensive type, silver polished, top-of-the line shampoo, conditioners, body lotions, and several herbal-fragrant cleansing wash. Everything imaginable was available, including feminine items, miniature shavers, makeup applicators and other apparatus. Instead of a tiny box for a shower, she had what appeared to be an entire room in itself, as if at least three or four girls her size could fit inside the glass enclosure. The bath looked more like a miniature pool, sunken into the floor, equipped with what appeared to be a controller panel that could activate a whirlpool function.

This, Liz could no longer wait to try. For if she was dreaming, she might as well take advantage of this luxury. And she knew as well as anyone else she was badly in need of cleansing. She took a quick walk through the roomy, penthouse-like suite to ensure that she was alone, because after the night she just had, it felt more comfortable to explore first. The room was shaped like a cross, and Liz found herself standing in the center or an X. In the top right of the room was the cozy and satisfying bed from which she had awakened. Next to it was a service table with a lamp, a telephone with a series of menus. With a clockwise turn, she faced the shower and washroom facilities. Next she saw closet spaces, hangers, and compartments for shoe or accessory storage. Then there was the entrance alcove, and finally, in the top left chamber of the configuration was yet another window with a different view of the skyscraper city outline. This one had a brilliant sight of the HEP 5 Ferris' wheel, which by day was a splendid bright red, contrasting with the grayish-black mosaic of the horizon. There was a fold-out bed that was, at that moment, a plush white chenille-fabric-cushioned sofa, on top of a matching, colored carpet flanked on each side by service drawer tables atop which sat fancy one-tier lamps. Where Liz stood in the center, there was a small buffet table that came to around her waistline; nothing too fancy about it, but it was above the grade of what she would pay for if not for her parents' money. There were two chairs for the table, and in the center of it was a set of tumbler glasses underneath them, thin napkin coasters bearing the hotel's name: Shin-Dai-Ichi Osaka. The name rang bells as she had loosely heard of it from random conversations with former Bozack students and a probable few she met at the Dream Lounge. From such information sources she understood that she was in one of the fancier hotels in the city,

After her search of the room, she noticed Deon's and her belongings. Deon's partially ripped, blood stained, dark-gray hoodie sweater and his backpack in one pile. Next to it were her purse and her sandals, which by now were one heel broken and straps as well. Recovering her purse, she also reclaimed her entire sum of bills and cash that had been stolen from her. Other items like her wallet, gaijin card, passport, make-up kit and miscellaneous items were still in her possession. She found her phone too. She attempted to flip through its directory to call Deon and find out where he was, but she couldn't. Her cell phone had been depleted of its battery power. It didn't matter, she figured. It was safe enough and seeing that Deon had his things there, she knew he would be back around sooner or later.

She went to the closet area, as a thick cotton terry robe caught her eye. At first, she thought a previous guest had left it, but such idea was removed when she saw the hotel's name also stenciled into the heart side of the fabric. Liz was still wearing the dress from the previous night, now tattered horrendously at the lower end, stained, and anything but glamorous, prom like, or something befitting a princess. It was as if she actually had transformed from someone regal back to a pauper pumpkin chariot-riding, rag-wearing chick no longer with glass slippers. She shucked the ragged garment and would have trashed it altogether had she not had anything else to wear besides the hotel robe. However, she was eager to get clean, and even more so keen on using the fragrant soaps.

After about an hour of soaking in the whirlpool bath, muscles relaxed, and relief to her aching sole blisters and ankle was achieved, she also shampooed and conditioned her Rapunzel-length hair. This, along with the blow-drying, consumed another half hour, and with hair not completely dry, she blotted out the rest with one of the thick, absorbent bath towels that were almost like miniature blankets. She could only then appreciate the skill and artistry of Takaro, for only but he could tangle with Liz's multitudinous mane on a continual basis and have her leaving looking like a regular human female. Otherwise, were she to deal with her own hair she would have taken his advice and cut it all off.

Combined with the super softness of the bamboo terry robe, she felt like she was walking in a silky, viscose-fibered second skin. Now refreshed and enlivened, but with stomach growling, she could eat a horse. She thought of room service— since she was in such an extravagant hotel, she might as well splurge. She had no idea of the cost, but she could afford it, whatever it was. She took a look at one of the menus beside the room phone, finding the one with the hotel's name. There were pictures displaying what was available, and translations in English too! She picked up the phone, hoping she would be lucky enough to speak with someone who could speak or understand English.

The receptionist sounded like a young Japanese girl, with a friendly and lively voice. She couldn't speak English extremely well but combined with Liz's minimal Japanese speaking efforts and slow execution of her English words, communication was achieved. Only, Liz made the mistake of ordering two of the largest breakfast platters offered. For some odd reason, she was unsure if the actual portions matched what had been displayed on the menu illustration.

After hanging up, Liz heard a knock on the door. She almost grew anxious and uptight, due to the lingering trauma, but the feelings subsided when she saw Deon enter the room. He had a sliding card key. He was carrying a bundle bag under his arm and appeared to have changed clothes. Now he had on a large black T-shirt bearing the name of the city he came from with a Statue of Liberty image staring with ominous eyes. He was still wearing black jeans and a pair of white sneakers. Liz didn't know if they were the same ones he had worn earlier, but if so, they were now touched up and wiped clean of blood and street sludge. He was also wearing dark shades and a water sport hat with wide brim and straps, like he wanted to be disguised. He greeted Liz tenderly, with a weak smile as if he felt sorry for her.

"How you doing?" he asked as he approached the table and set down the bundle bag he carried. It was a collection of individual plastic bags within a larger one that had the name of the store *Jeans Mate* on it. "I picked you up some duds."

Liz thanked him as they rummaged through the collection of clothes: A large yellow T-shirt that might be tight on her but still wearable; some pink and orange sweatpants that Liz would never consider wearing unless they were for pajamas; three pairs of shorts of varying sizes and of darker colors; and, finally, a pair of cheap, no-name brand canvas sneakers that looked like low-cut *Chuck Taylor* knockoffs.

Deon tried to hide an innocent smirk. He said, "Sorry if it ain't your style, but you can go out and get some more stuff you like later."

"How did you know my shoe size?" Liz examined the sneakers, gratified because at least Deon had got one thing right. His sense of fashion for her was off, though.

"Oh, I checked your shoe size. I put all your things over there." Deon pointed to the bundle of clothes Liz had already seen.

"I must've been out like a rock. I barely remember even checking in here." Liz took the clothes and laid them on the bed and examined them as if she was having a difficult decision trying to select what to wear.

Deon shook his head. He did feel bad for Liz. Even though she was a white chick he would have otherwise never given a damn about, his mind was a wreck thinking of how he had stuck his neck out for her and she now was casually cavorting about like she didn't almost lose her damn life the previous evening. Those crazed lunatics, Simon and Kwame, had really meant business, obviously, as he discovered they were the ones who must have iced Stephanie.

"Yo, listen, this might seem a little weird," Deon said, "but I think it would be best if we cool out here in the hotel for a couple of days. I don't know what you plan to do, but that shit we got into last night was a deep, fucked-up situation. I think some people were seriously injured. Kwame had a bloody knife when he came back after chasin' Worm."

Liz said, "Yeah, and you should see what they did to Jeremy. I was at his place before they crashed in and pretty much kidnapped me from there. They bashed his head in. I think . . . oh God, it was so horrible!" She tried not to cry. "But don't I need to go to the police?"

Deon said, "You could, but me, personally, I don't wanna have anything to do with the cops. The truth of the matter is, I was in there to deal drugs. That weed, that was supposed to be a legit drug deal between me and Simon. But then he had some other plans. Him and Worm was supposed to be doin' a bunch of side dealin', but he crossed Worm too. Thought I wanted to get back at him because he set me up at Bozack."

Liz said, "Yeah, that much I was able to make out. Plus, that they also murdered Stephanie! That was crazy."

"Exactly," Deon said. "Plus, check this out." He took out a Japanese newspaper. They couldn't understand the Japanese language headline, but the photos were blurred face images of Simon and Kwame in cuffs, escorted by police.

"I don't know many Japanese characters, but I know this one." He pointed to one of the bright onomatopoeia-type headline prints. "This one means murder!"

Liz said, "I want to go home . . ."

Deon said, "You could do that too, but I don't recommend that either right now. We don't know if your name is mixed up in this thing right now. The cops might be at your spot."

Sharply, Liz uttered, "No, I mean . . . I wanna go *home* . . . back to the States! Home! California. Beautiful beaches, clean streets, palm trees, and normal people."

Deon sat down at the table and shrugged. He lifted his shirt sleeve to play around with the cut wound Simon's knife had left, covered with a crude Band-Aid and absorbent pad. Liz walked over to him and acted as if she knew how to apply first aid. She ended up going to the bathroom and collecting cotton balls and swabs. She came back and tried to clean up excess blood. "Hold still," she said as if she was performing a major surgical operation. Then she walked over to her purse and dug out her handkerchief, returned to Deon at the table, and wrapped it around his arm and tied it.

"There!" she said. "I guess I owe you my life, Dee. I can't thank you enough. And just to think, all this time, I had always thought you hated my guts."

"Still do," Deon said, griping, but with a hint of sarcasm. At least, Liz hoped that he was. She resumed staring at the newspaper. "Yeah, you might be right. I'm sure my apartment will be crawling with cops now. Seeing what they did to Jeremy, no telling what happened to Mr. Yutaka, who came and tried to save me."

Deon said, "What?! They tried to get you at your crib too? Oh shit!"

Liz said, "Yes, and I figured out now how they found out where I lived. I told Jeremy, and he told Worm. Worm told those fucking goons, and I'll bet your ass that that whole entire bit about the farewell party he told me about was just another setup too. And you know what? On top of all that, would you know, that bastard Worm managed to wiggle out of those plastic cuffs, and he didn't even bother to help me get free! I don't know what happened to him, but I think that asshole pretty much deserved what he got."

Deon said, "I don't know, but I think, honestly . . . if you did want to go home, yeah, this would be a good time to do it. That's what I'm gonna do. I've had it for a while."

Liz said, "But you . . . just came back from America, didn't you? Seems like a waste of money to me. Does your new job pay that kind of big bucks that you can afford to fly back-to-back to the States? And at short notice, to boot?"

Deon smiled contentedly. A look of comfortable reassurance appeared on his face. No frowns or scary looks detected. He said, "I ain't never got to worry about money ever again. At least if I'm smart. And I don't plan to turn stupid anytime soon."

"What's that supposed to mean?" Liz asked curiously. Deon didn't appear to be in a rush to elaborate. He took some drinks out of the plastic bags and placed them on the table. Liz immediately grabbed up a bottled water, opened it, and gulped it down like she had been a desert-stranded vagabond.

Deon said, "I don't know about you, but I'm famished. I'll go out and pick us up something from somewhere. I think you should stick around here."

Liz said, "It's OK, I ordered room service right before you arrived. Sorry! Maybe you can get something for yourself. And why do I need to stay in this room? Am I a prisoner now?"

Deon said, "Hell no! In fact, you can leave anytime you want, but if the cops pick you up for questioning, please don't put me in it! Like I said, I don't want no involvement. No tellin' what Simon and Kwame are tellin' the cops now. All I know, I don't want to be part of it, or mixed up in it in any way. We was lucky enough to get away, basically unharmed, and not apprehended. And no, you ain't a prisoner. What I was sayin' was it's probably better if you go out at night if you go out. Less chance for you to be recognized, I think. I don't know. We foreigners stick out like sore thumbs here, know what I'm sayng?"

"Well, for how long, then?" Liz asked somewhat apprehensively "I'll have to go back there eventually. I mean, Mama-san Saiko is probably going to be looking for me—plus, I have to salvage my things if possible . . ."

Deon gazed blankly toward the window view. He said, "Yeah, plus, you'd have to get your passport if you need to travel."

"No, I have my it," Liz said in a perky voice. She went for her purse and brought it back. She unzipped a panel within its chamber lining and produced her credential. Deon was astonished.

"You carry that around in your purse!?" he exclaimed.

"Yeah, of course," she said as she tucked it away, returning it to the same compartment from which she had exhumed it. "I always do, don't you?"

"Hell no," Deon said with his recognizable scary-faced look of bewilderment making a cameo return appearance. "I might lose that shit. Besides, that's what we have *gaijin* cards for."

Vainly, Liz said, "Yeah, but I hate the picture on that ID card. Yuck! It was two and a half years ago when me and my ex-boyfriend had arrived. It was the middle of the hot, humid summer, and my makeup and skin at that time weren't prepared for the weather conditions here." And she went on and on, expatiating about her life and reasoning. Deon found himself not listening much, just waiting for her to stop talking.

Finally, Deon said, "Well, to answer your question, I think we should stay up in here for a couple of days. Don't worry, I've already put the cash down. If you feel brave and bold and you wanna leave, I'll stay here. Otherwise, I'll get another room. Hopefully, I can get one close to this one. I've already moved out of my crib."

Liz opened her purse and flashed the foolscap resembling stack of money bills. "I can obviously reimburse you for the room."

"I don't need your money, rich girl," Deon said as he backed his chair from the table to stand up and move toward the living room area to grab his backpack. "I paid with my own credit card, and I would've got separate rooms, but it was late, and I didn't feel like goin' through the hassle. These 4-stars always give people a bunch of crap if they don't have reservations. I hadta tell 'em you was my pregnant wife, and we desperately needed a high-class facility to suit our needs. I guess my Japanese and persuasive looks won 'em over. Even though they tried to recommend some smoky-ass fleabag down the street. Told me the only thing they had left was these exclusive penthouse joints, and they looked spooked as hell when they saw I could pay for it. Life is good, baby!"

"Anyway," Deon continued, "sometime tomorrow, I'll get another room. Until we find out what's goin' on, or until you decide what you wanna do." He was foraging through his backpack like a small bear searching for hidden morsels.

"Well, if we're gonna be stuck here, don't we at least have some type of entertainment?" Liz stomped about and stared out of the bed area's window that had a view of Osaka Station.

Deon said, "You mean to tell me you didn't see this huge-screen TV?" He pointed to a console that encompassed a recessed niche above his head as he knelt, tending to his bag. Liz had ignored the cabinet previously, thinking it was yet another feature of the suite designed for more storage. When she witnessed Deon open it up, she saw a huge television set, at least 40 inches in width and over 20 in height. There was also a set of remote controls, one for the TV and another for cable. Also, one of the controllers could activate a radio intercom system, which

Liz accidentally triggered on when she grabbed hold of it. Instantly, hidden Dolby speakers broadcast music all over the apartment. Had she not happened to like the '80s tune that played, an old Bangles hit, "Manic Monday," she would have clicked it off altogether; but instead, she figured out how to reduce the volume and sing along.

In between cheerfully singing as if she had been cleansed of all her troubles, Liz returned to the bed and examined the set of clothes she had laid out. She said, "I guess you'll be crashing on the sofa couch, then, right?"

"Hell yeah," Deon said. "Where the hell else? This thing folds out into a bed, I think."

"It does. I already checked it out." Liz vocal pitch had dipped into subtle crotchety envy. She deviously recalled how she was once able to buffalo Denore and get the better side of the dormitory which had the window and a little more space. This time, the side of the hotel room with a "bed" in front of the TV set was appealing. She wondered if Deon would be as obliging.

"Gosh, I'm so hungry. I wish they would hurry up." Liz returned to the table and made a grab for another bottled drink that Deon had brought.

"Oh, almost forgot!" Deon said excitedly as he took one more item out of his plastic bag bundle. It was a laptop computer folder. "This hotel rents out these. You have internet access. You can plug it up over there. That small closet doubles as a miniature foyer."

Liz took a quick look at the spot Deon was pointing to and compared it to the size of an old-school phone booth, equipped with a small stool on a revolving base. "Awesome!" she belted. "You mind if I check it out?"

"Sure, of course," he said as he made a move to plug it up and turn it on. "That's why I got it. Because neither of us understands Japanese at a hundred percent, right? We need to click on to the internet if you wanna get some up-to-the-minute, breakin' news."

When the setup maneuvers were complete, Deon left Liz to play around with the console. "I'm gonna go for a shower," he said.

Sure enough, the *Daily Mainichi* and Japan Times news sites reported in English the grim details of the crime that had occurred the night before. It was a short article, although it confirmed that there was a murder, but the victim's name wasn't released. Liz assumed it was Worm, though. Simon and Kwame were arrested for drug possession and homicide, breaking and entering, assault and more charges pending. Thinking to herself, if she added her kidnapping to the equation, the list of offenses would expand. But Deon was right. Liz didn't want to be mixed up in all of that madness. With rotten luck, she might have been arrested too. Thoughts of going back to America grew enormous on her mind. Get out. Now. While she still could. *Go home*, she was thinking.

She stepped up to Deon while he was in the bathroom area, barged in. Deon stared at her sudden intrusion like she was a few cents short of a dollar. His shirt had been removed, and he was picking at the handkerchief she had wrapped around his scarred arm.

Somewhat angrily, he almost shouted at her, "Do you mind!?"

Ignoring his outrage casually, Liz said, "So you're heading back to America too, huh? You really moved out of your apartment?"

"Yeah," Deon snapped. "But check it out, I'll rap to you a taste on that when I get out of here. Now just—"

Liz stopped him from shutting the door on her. "How do you suddenly now have so much money like that? You had all that grass—what? You a drug dealer now?"

"Yo, Liz, can I please take my shower?" Deon made an exaggerated plea. "I'll talk to you about it when I get out."

Obligingly, Liz left Deon to his affairs. During the time she was in the shower, a hotel staffer had showed up to the room with a pushcart carrying two huge silver-covered platters. The friendly young man greeted Liz in English with "Haloo" and rolled his cart into the quarters, placed the platters on the table, and split. Had he been American, he would have expected a G-tip, Liz mused.

Starving, she opened up one of the two identical platters and unveiled a smorgasbord of culinary breakfast delight. Pancakes, French toast, sausages, bacon, muffins, soup, salad, the works. Liz wasted no time and dug in. By the time she felt herself getting full, she discovered that she had barely put a dent on the amount of food delivered. She covered the platter back and decided she could leave it for later or have Deon polish it off so that he didn't have to go out and get anything for himself.

Returning to the computer, she decided to have a look at her e-mail. When she logged in, she examined her inbox. Most, if not all of her correspondence records, displayed exchanges with Carver. She laughed, seeing his name encompass the entire page. It was hard for her to believe that they had been back and forth so much the past few months. She opened his latest, most recent mail, sent a couple of days prior. It detailed the usual—inquiries of how things were going and a short passage about his day-to-day routine, then his punctuation ending with how he couldn't wait to see her again. That he too was hopeful of a rekindling of their relationship. By the time Liz had finished reading, it had her thinking that Carver had finally manned up. She had always had his telephone number but had refrained from trying to call internationally with her cell phone, as it was a tedious and meticulous affair requiring registration of phone cards and a litany of access code numbers to input on the keypad. Eric Cravens had once showed her how to do it, but she had never bothered with it much. Her mother, Ida, would generally call her and relieve her of the need to post international calls. Now, since she was in a fancy hotel, she figured it to be easier and simpler to try it that way.

She found the hotel stationery and pen inside of the drawer to the service table underneath the room phone. On it, she scribbled Carver's number as listed on one of his e-mails. Ignoring the time zone difference, she decided to place a call and speak to Carver as opposed to replying to the e-mail. She got the hotel front desk to assist with the call.

Overseas, at an undisclosed location outside of Pasadena, California, in a secluded subdivision of the Sierra Madre outskirts, a sweaty Carver Burk was interrupted from his activity having heard his landline telephone ringing. He checked his water-resistant watch and the time read to the effect of slightly past 6:00 p.m. He removed his bloody gloves and like-stained apron and rushed to the phone. The sound of Elizabeth's sweet voice greeted him. Needless to say, he was exceedingly stunned hearing from her out of the blue.

"Elizabeth!" His high-pitched voice sounded like it was cracking. "What a surprise! I never expected to receive a call from you, how are you? Still in Japan?"

"Yeah," she said, "but I'm ready to come home. I've had enough. I'm leaving here soon."

Carver sounded dumbfounded. "What? What do you mean by soon? Soon, as in really soon?"

"Really soon," Liz stated in an almost melodramatic way, followed up with a likewise exhale of breath. "I'm talkin' . . . in a week or so. Two at the most."

They talked on for a while. Deon came out of the bathroom with a towel wrapped around his waist. He saw Liz chatting happily reclining on the bed, and he frowned up with suspicions, wondering who the hell she was speaking to. His purpose seemed to have been to look for an extra robe like the one Liz had been wearing. Successfully finding one, he retreated back to the bathroom. Liz continued her jovial conversation with Carver, ignoring Deon's evil glare, even going so far as sticking her tongue out at him like an impish brat before he shut the bathroom door harshly, vanishing inside.

Toward the end of the almost-twenty-minute phone conversation, it gradually came to what both Liz and Carver would deem a positive close. Carver seemed to have been in the middle of something when Liz had rung him up, and he was low-key eager to get back to it. He was pleasant enough, however, to break Liz off a piece of time, for to him, she was that important. This, Liz had also reasoned.

Carver said to Liz before they ended the call, "Be sure you contact me the first thing when you arrive. In fact, I can come pick you up myself!"

Carver was so sweet. Still a gentleman. No matter what he was doing, he took the time out to be patient, caring, and proved that he was the good listener he had always been. It was a good thing to know. These were characteristics that would solidify him as a good future husband and father of her children. When they exchanged "goodbyes" for now and hung up, Liz felt sanguine and full of hope.

As soon as he hung up the phone, Carver's eyes narrowed to ghoulish slits. In his delicate, near-feminine movement and gait, he put on a fresh pair of surgical rubber gloves drawn from a pocket of his bloody apron. Thoughts of Liz both excited him and inflamed him at the same time. One thing was for sure: he had never forgiven her for her sublevel indecent treatment of him back in the days. He had difficulty forgiving any women, even the former woman in his basement whom he was at that moment in the midst of dismembering, before Liz's call interrupted his cumbersome task. He was battling demons of some kind his entire life. He had grown up in the church and was told to forgive like his Holy Book taught, but after being molested so much by the elder clergy and his chorus club retreat roommates, the act of forgiving and forgetting was a constant inner struggle. He was used, abused, and even sodomized; and just when he thought he had reached his breaking point, Liz had come along. Showed interest in him as a real male. She did, and he thought he had hope to be a "normal" person.

Little did he suspect in the beginning, however, that she really hadn't liked him. She just needed someone to use for alibis to cover her ass when she was defying her parents and hanging out with people, the unsavory types that her folks didn't want her hanging around with. Still, he took his treatment with grace. Because at least it could have been said that he was "needed." If only for the purpose of being her sucker. Eventually, he caught on to her and what she was doing. But he was still too weak-willed to remonstrate her powerfully persuasive personality. Japan changed him for the worse.

There, he studied karate, and then the sword art of *Iaido*, and learned of ways to unleash his anger. Learning the intricacies of the blade arts helped him to understand the surgical tactics with which to slice into flesh and bone. He may have not become an expert or master of the craft, but he had definitely been a good learner. As could be exemplified by the precisely cut limbs of a doomed former courtesan, stacked up beside his makeshift operating table. Like Liz, she too liked to make up lies to cover up her seeing other men. He had learned to be a master stalker. She learned the hard way, and at stark midnight, Carver was going to bury her parts in nearby Angeles Forest. He couldn't wait until he saw Liz again . . .

78

DEON HAD BEEN in the bathroom for a long time. While there, Liz enjoyed the music of the room's intercom system at peak level. The radio station was playing 80s music, a type of retro program. The idea hit her to get high on her last pieces of sizzle that she had lingering in her purse. Finding it, she placed her Ziploc bag containing the items of her one now wrinkled fat spliffs and the gram of coke. In fact, this was from the bundle Deon had copped from Moose and Brad some time ago. The wrinkled joint was not suitable to smoke now because of the rigorous activity in which she had been involved the night before; it was damaged and now leaking its grass content. With the last of her rolling papers, she sloppily tried to create a new one but had never managed to become adept at the skill. Wanting also to be rid of the coke as well, she combined a large portion of it upon the long green line of weed, making a coolie. She was still trying unsuccessfully to roll it up by the time Deon came out of the shower room, clad in the same bountiful terry-cloth bathrobe as her. His face beheld Liz's, and from his troubled look, Liz felt like she was in a flashback to their old Bozack workdays, and Deon would stare at people like he was an angry hater. Today he was reacting in such a way because he was agitated seeing that Liz had yet to get dressed and was also curious about who she had been speaking to on the hotel phone.

With casual indifference, Liz was like, "That? On the phone? Oh, I was speaking with a guy I know from back home. It's a guy I used to see. His name is Carver. When I get back to the States, he and I are gonna, like, start seeing each other again."

For the first time since their sudden reunion the previous nightmare of an evening, Liz caught sight of Deon's lustrous mane. Last night he was wearing a bandanna, or doo rag, and today he had been wearing a ridiculous hat. Now that he was out of the shower, he let his hair flow freely, until finally wrapping up his shiny, licorice-streaky hair into what she would have considered to be a bun but on him looked like a meatball, or one of Mickey Mouse's ears, on the rear of his head. She giggled, thinking it was cute, but uncharacteristic for a guy as vicious as him, in her mind. "How do you wash your hair?" she asked.

"With shampoo," Deon replied and impassively grabbed a bundle of clothes from his backpack, getting for himself another T-shirt and change of clothes, perhaps jeans or pants. Changing the subject, he asked "You getting' married when you go back?"

Liz shrugged, still trying to make a joint, fitting paper between her fingers; her somewhat longish nails kept interfering with the even positioning of the contents. Distressed, she replied, "Maybe, possible . . . who knows what the future holds? What about you? What are you gonna do back in New York? And, hey, you never answered my question. Did you, like . . . suddenly come into some money or something? What happened—did you and your 'secret group' or whatever start dealing major shit?"

Deon shook his head comically, annoyed at her assumption. Finally, unceremoniously, he tapped her shoulder and told her, "Get up, move!" Using sweeping motion of his hands as if to gesture to Liz to leave her chair so he could sit in her place at the table. Then she realized that the reason was because he was taking pity on her and commandeering the task of rolling a nice, even standard smoke-able joint.

Liz's heart raced as she saw him complete, within seconds, a perfectly sculpted "submarine." Four beautiful inches, thickness of a sharpie marker. Then he flicked it quietly in front of her. "Guess I might as well tell you. I mean, when it comes down to it, I really oughta thank you. You're right. I got money. Lotsa money. I never have to worry about it ever again."

"And you ought to thank me for that?" Liz asked, totally in the dark.

"When it comes down to it," Deon repeated. "To be completely honest, you would be due a degree of gratitude." His charming smile creased his cinnamon-cigar-colored lips. Liz squinted and stared at him as if he were the one high on drugs. He stared beyond Liz, facing the view offered by the window at Liz's bedside. Liz waved her palm in his face to interrupt his temporary daydream.

She said, "I don't get it, Dee. Maybe you can elaborate!?"

Deon snapped out of a self-induced trance, thinking about his sudden introduction to wealth, how he enjoyed the first-class section of the planes now, the quick access to car service, and the luxuries—including that same hotel—that were now at a touch of his fingertips. For all intents and purposes, neither he nor any of his family members would ever go hungry again. Of course, he was hungry now, though.

He said, "I'm surprised you haven't got dressed. What's wrong, you don't like the clothes?"

Liz laughed and nodded, choosing to be frank and up front. "If that's how you like for women to look, you have really low standards. I mean, you used to see Taffie. You know how glamorously stylish she was! Oh dude, I wouldn't be caught dead, but thank you, though. The shoes, I can maybe wear, but those sweatpants, that yellow, ugh! Doesn't go well . . ." She kept babbling. Deon was unsure if he would be able to tolerate her for two or three days while laying low and hoping the dust would clear.

"So maybe you can go out later, and if you find a store like GAP or something similar, you can grab me it and bring it back here. I can show you on the internet," Liz had been saying. Deon was gradually tuning her out because he was hungry, smelled food, and was curious about the gigantic "Hershey's Kisses" on the table.

Liz said, "Hey, oh, the room service cart came while you were in there showering for a long time like a girl." She laughed and lifted the breakfast platters. "Take a look at that. Isn't it great? You can have it. I ordered two. I didn't know they would send up so much. The menu picture looked small. Never can tell here in Japan—they always have these smallest portions but make them look big on the menu picture."

She was funny, Deon mused. He found it extraordinary how she could endure a hellish night like the one before and the following day snap back into her old, energetic, fun-loving self. He envied her seeming ability to detach herself from reality and enjoy living in the moment. It was as if she never had a care in the world. His thoughts of her took a detour when his sights zeroed in on the breakfast platter. Curtailing climbing into his clothes, he put the task on hold to dig in. Liz had jumped up from the table to leave him to his feasting. She went to play around with the large television.

"How do we watch cable?" she asked, playfully dancing to the 80s' tune broadcast aloud like a miniature party within the hotel room walls.

"Beats me," Deon said, greedily munching. "You so smart, figure it out."

Giving up temporarily fidgeting with the remote control gadget and the Japanese instructions, Liz returned to the buffet table to continue her interrogation of Deon. She sat back down.

"So you have me to thank for you having money to travel around the world?" She asked like an airhead. "I'm curious to know why, I'd really like to know."

"OK," Deon said. "It's like this: Your birthday is June 17, right? Your mom, I guess September 29, and you lost your virginity the night before Christmas."

For once, Liz was dumbstruck. She was absent-minded as to how he even knew such information. Then with the force of a rushing avalanche, a torrent of unchained emotion threatened to overcome her sanity, which would make her react with monstrous excitement. She maintained her poise, albeit poorly, her throat knotted in anticipatory expectation of some exceptional news.

Her voice trembling slightly, Liz said, "You did it, didn't you?" They stared into each other's eyes. Deon averted her gaze, but he couldn't avoid her pressing him. Every time he looked up, she was there, motionless, but with eyes as wide as hypnotic saucers, a laser beam of aquatic, "tarheel" blue. It was almost scary, but he felt compelled to come clean. After all, it needed not have been a secret; but he wasn't too keen on telling everyone that he had won the lottery back home. For now that he was a multi-millionaire, people would be coming around begging. That was why he had to go home and get a new house for his family, his people. Liz had supplied him with the winning numbers some time ago, before the close of the previous year. Who would have thought that number would eventually hit? When he explained to Liz what had happened, she went into a fit of celebratory exuberance as if she too had won, or that she was entitled to some of the winnings.

Liz said, "The lucky charm must be me! I mean, my father once won the lottery a long time ago. He used my birthday too for his number, so the story goes. Omigod, I can't believe it. So how much is my cut?"

Deon scowled and said, "Your cut? The amount will be seen when you close your eyes."

It took a moment before "nothing" could register with Liz due to her excitement learning the unexpected, hammer strike of a news. Now horribly deflated, Liz snapped, "Oh, you do know that it's only appropriate to split some of your earnings with the person or people who contributed numbers or insights to a lottery win! Didn't you know that?"

"Hell nah," Deon said arrogantly. "B'cuz I ain't never won the lottery before. Nobody I ever knew did either, except for the daily, scared money takes."

Liz seriously thought, for whatever reason, that not only was she entitled to Deon's win, she really did think he was going to break her off a chunk of his fortune. She picked up the remote for the music box and picked up the joint Deon rolled up.

She said, "I kinda want a cigarette. I keep quitting then starting back again.."

Deon wasn't listening. He polished off all the toast, cold eggs, sausage on the breakfast platter, then wolfed down the pancakes drenched in as much maple syrup as he could squeeze out of the condiment packets. Liz watched and stared in awe; his cheeks inflated like a hamster as he chewed with excitement. She couldn't remember Eddie or even brother Halbert to be so greedy, as her eyes didn't allow belief that one person could have demolished all the contents like a pack of canines had shown up and licked the plates clean. "Damn," was all she could say after witnessing the sight. She gathered up the platters one by one and set them outside in the hallway.

When she came back, she picked up the joint. She said to a milk-guzzling Deon, "You wanna try this?"

Deon held out his hand and took the miniature white torpedo blimp. He shook his head with a laugh. He liked taking a toke or two of the pot when he used to do it with Taffie. Oftentimes, he liked to use it afterward as opposed to before. Otherwise, he wasn't a pothead. Still, he kept recalling how his pal Paz would chide him on how he should indulge every so often, so he could relax. "Don't be so uptight," was what he would say.

"All right," he said. He held out his hand, awaiting a lighter. Liz had ventured to the storage amenity corner and returned with an ashtray, and she supplied her own lighter. Deon took it and lit up the J.

His first two pulls were small and exploratory, intended to merely make the smoke burn evenly, and he didn't inhale. On the third, he drew in deeply, held it for a moment or two, then exhaled a swift white fog. His eyes opened wide before narrowing to weird, barbaric slits. One more hit of the spliff, which was actually a coolie—cocaine-laced weed—and his head was spinning. Reeling like his head had been detached and it spun on a merry-go-round while his body remained still. He exhaled again a white apparition, and the immediate area had more smoke than the hot fires of Hades.

Deon managed to place the joint in the clear ashtray, but his head didn't feel right. His sight was reeling in his eye sockets; multiple images of Liz appeared. Dizzily, he closed his eyes in hopes that she would stop moving or that the room would stop spinning. His sight went pitch-black. In an instant, he returned to the world of the living, but he was in a cold sweat.

Liz, who had been watching him, grew somewhat nervous when Deon's eyes went all white in his sockets; his head had fallen back as if his neck had turned to chewing gum and couldn't support it. She had never seen anyone react to pot that way, but she too had seemed to forget that she had boosted the potency of the recreation with her added ingredient of coke. She had always wanted to try it. Hastily, she was like, "Let me try."

Perhaps her tolerance was a bit higher or stronger than Deon's, but Liz didn't react the same way as he had. She did experience the brief, euphoric delirium always enjoyed when partaking of the drug. This, she thought, would be her last for a while. For when she returned to the United States and reunited with Carver, she was more than likely going to try and be a mother, or a married chick. She couldn't be like Mandy, who almost got herself killed trying to cheat guys and use them for money. Steve had nearly beaten her to death. Becky was now serving time for trying to smuggle contraband to her thug Mexican Chavez; in so doing she ruined the reputation of the law firm she worked at and got Lamar kicked out of school. It was a big mess back home, so she didn't want to wind up like her friends. She had learned what she felt was a reasonable start of knowledge about herbs and "medicines" she could use to embark on her health spa project; if not, she could take a refresher course at some point. She could see her future through the smoke she had blown into the air, like from a genie's lamp.

Only, from the smoke would not emerge one of Alladin's fairy-tale friends. Deon was now standing up and looking as if he was trying to maintain his balance. His chest was now slightly exposed; perspiration made his skin glow with an oily-like gloss. His forehead was covered by two or three yarn-like strands of his black hair, and standing there in his white robe, he bore a striking resemblance to Sugar Ray Robinson Primetime in a boxing ring.

Liz found it amusing, him standing there. She wondered if he would fall. Then she said, "Good shit, huh?"

Deon closed his eyes. Clasped his head, palms on either temple, then brought them around in wiping motion down the front of his face. He shook his head as if the fit he was reacting to had dwindled and waned. "I dunno, Elizabeth," he said. "This shit has got me feelin' . . . crazy . . . fucked . . . up . . my world. . . is spinnin'."

Just then, Liz's attention was wrenched away by some frenetic '80s tune that suddenly began transmitting through the Dolbys. "Omigosh! Is that *Debbie Gibson?*" She jumped up and turned the volume way higher than it needed to be, Deon felt.

"When this song came out"—Liz danced around joyously—"I was in high school. I couldn't decide if I was gonna join the volleyball team again or be a cheerleader."

Deon was suffering and dealing with a cramp that had formed in his abdominal area. His mouth wasn't dry, but there was a heated rushing of breath from his diaphragm to the back of his throat. He heard Liz singing, and the tone of her voice blended so evenly with the song being broadcast he could swear they were identical. Not that it wasn't pleasant, but Deon wasn't really enjoying it. In fact, the sound of Liz and her being in his presence was creeping under his skin and settling in a disagreeable way.

"*I remember how it used to beeeeeee . . . / how much I miss you . . .*" Liz was singing and dancing. She lit up the unsmoked portion of the three inches left of the joint. Some of her hair fell out of the back of her robe as she melodramatically half-sang and half lip-synched as if she were in a karaoke room.

Deon said, "Liz . . . stop . . . stop . . . turn it down . . . turn it off . . ."

Ignoring him with utmost disregard, she sang louder. Trying to bug Deon as would Eddie, or her older brother Halbert as kids. With expert mimicry of the song's artist, she bellowed on, like, "*Only in my dreams . . . / real . . . it may seeeeeeeeem, / only in my dreams!*"

Deon was fighting with himself. He couldn't take it. Like a madman, he almost had to force his hands over his ears, struggling to shut out Liz's harmonic outburst. "Stop it!" he half shouted, but the volume at which Liz had the sound blasting, she didn't acknowledge him. In fact, with every new verse of the song, Liz's performance intensified accordingly, as if each one was directed at an unseen person in her life from the past.

"And I realized, how much I miss you . . . / And I wanna start againnnn . . ." This one, she was thinking of Carver.

Deon screamed, "Liz, please! Shut that shit off!" He didn't know how much more he could take. Her singing had wrecked his nerves to smithereens, totaled like a Cross Bronx Expressway wall banger, eighteen-wheeler off a bridge.

"Couldn't see how much I missed you, / now I do . . ." This one was for Eddie. Here was when she began to succumb to the emotional baggage she had difficulty freeing herself of. *"If I only once could hold you . . . / only in my dreams . . . / la la la!*

Deon had had his fill. In an outburst of what was either rage or passion, he snatched the remote control device from her with so much demented force he broke one of her nails. She had been using the remote for an imaginary microphone. Her face weakened in fright and sadness as he wrenched it from her, and, in the same motion, yanked away the tie to her robe. As one side of the garment flew open, it bared one-half of her naked body, Deon disarmed the radio broadcast with the remote and threw it away to the sofa's cushion on the other side of the room. At the sight of Liz's nudeness, peach skin contrasting with the snowy white cotton robe, he couldn't restrain his own protuberance. His heart pumped with sudden exigency flowing at dangerously high levels. His eyes couldn't hide it, like his robe couldn't hide his swollen, inflated breeding muscle.

Liz trembled with fear or possibly the apprehension of vicissitude. The figure of Deon approached her like an apocalyptic, dark shadow despite the fact that it was early afternoon. The reason for this, Liz noticed with added throe was because rain clouds had materialized and veiled the once sunny landscape. A soft cry bolted from her lips, but no words could form. Deon lost his robe to the floor beneath his white socks, approaching her with a demonic gaze, nostrils wide in either intensity of fury or impaired breathing. Liz backed away slowly, feeling terrified, or yielding to doom, having nowhere to run save for a twenty-story jump from a window.

A jag of lightning slashed across the sky, as if to add more melodrama to the morbid moment. Liz winced out weak words, "Hey, what . . . Dee? What . . . are you going to . . . do?" As if she didn't know. Deon snatched a handful grip of her robe's right collar, issued a tremendous tug, and Liz stumbled toward him. With the same motion, he curled his knuckled fist inward, his strength sending her tumbling forward, at which time he tore his hand back in the opposite direction of her movement, peeling off her robe halfway.

"Deon . . . no! Please!" she screamed, freeing herself from the trapping of the robe's sleeves, which impaired her movement caught in the forceful yank Deon applied. Her struggling had advanced her in the direction of the bed, no doubt, as Deon consciously, or subconsciously, had been stalking her to move toward.

Liz fell back, and her bare bottom was caught by the side of the full-sized bed. She pleaded with Deon to get ahold of himself, as if it would actually resonate with him. He was in a trancelike state, like a zombie. Liz wanted to cry, but her tears wouldn't come. Only the increased pattering of her heart.

She said, "Don't do it, Deon . . . don't you dare . . ." Her hands gripped the sheets of the bed as her body shivered in horrified contrition, or angst.

Deon was past all reasoning. Liz's words uttered to him trailed off like an incoherent jumble of futile babbling and useless disparagement. For when she asked him why he was behaving this way, even he didn't know. He couldn't explain the sudden change that had absorbed him and made him feel so disconcerted, and so anxious. He pushed Liz's head back to the bed amazingly gentle, methodically and handily, as to almost seem as if he were a refined romantic. Liz was trying to cry, but instead, she used her elbows to crawl herself backward, like she was attempting to escape Deon as he crept slowly, following her on the bed toward the headboard post, where three fluffy pillows awaited her head.

Deon raised Liz's thighs and knees, his nails looked like pink peppermint candy atop caramel-coated fingers as they stroked long, slim lines at her narrow, slender waist. In a last act of defiance and animosity, Liz brought her leg up in the air and violently kicked her foot out, aiming the force of her heel at Deon's nose! Then something happened. Her attack stopped short of its target, as if prevented any further movement by an unseen force field or invisible barrier. Her foot made contact with Deon's face, but only lightly, as if she was tapping his moist, slick lips with her toes, rubbing her blistered soles across his teeth and his slightly coarse tongue.

Without realizing it, Liz attempted to launch another such strike upon Deon's face with her kick, as the first undertaking had seemed to mysteriously fail. The same results would be rendered. In her mind, Liz was kicking and stomping Deon's face bloody, and she would escape to the hallway, screaming, yelling, and attaining the assistance of the police or proper authorities—damn the risk, just save her skin! But reality was a quantum leap from her abstract delusion. She felt the soft but rough, heated skin of his face and the moisture from his mouth soothe her ailing pods, and she purred like a feline, but with outrage yet to be allayed.

Her head was cushioned into the soft pillow, which circled her like a cumulus cloud when she burrowed deeper, closing her eyes tightly, body tense from titillation. She inhaled a clenched-teeth gust of sultry air as Deon's heated tongue had shifted its consideration from her legs to the tips of her breasts. Biting them. Lavishing her nipples with a rapid rotation of ravaging. Liz tried to use her other cup's partner to batter Deon's face and render him helpless, but both breasts were overwhelmed to the extent the double team was ineffective. Liz was again forced into submission as Deon's hot, slimy kisses to her jugs left them bruised, slippery, and tickled. She whimpered. Crying. But it escaped into the silence of the room, almost like a laugh. Rain poured outside and pelted slightly against the windows like a multitude of miniature finger taps.

Liz cried out, "Dee . . . please, stop! We can't do it . . . not like this . . . not here, not now, not with you . . . Oh! Dear Gawd!"

Deon was now far gone and enveloped deep into a spellbound state from which he could not escape. The only cure he felt could quell his abrupt tension. His pain sought the relief that could solely be extracted from a peculiar attribute only Liz seemed to be able to provide him at the moment. His head retreated from her torso and dragged a wet, streaked print to her straw-colored love nest, his widened nostrils traipsed steadily within the urine-trickled golden grass, masked heavily with herbal-scented residue. Descending his chin beneath the knoll, abandoning her abdomen for a more unctuous destination.

Approaching the gates of her pristine, deep-pinkish quim, he bade to make his presence known. His mouth packed an emissary to prognosticate a future invasion of darkness. His tongue led the way along a piquant and brackish pattern along her vulva, causing her to emit a piercing cry of orgiastic rapture, which for her, she reasoned ineffably, was a release of fury and resistance.

Seeing an opportunity to trap and subdue her antagonist, Liz summoned the boa constrictor, serpent-like strength of her volleyball-trained legs, enhanced by aerobics and kickboxing classes, to wrap around Deon's head, locking him into the Candy Box and suffocating him, which would force her release and subsequent escape. With her right hand, she pushed his face against her and deeper between her thighs. Her other hand wiped slowly across her wobbling breast rack, as if to rid her nipples of the saliva residue Deon had left, but only served to stimulate them further, increasing her aroused juddering.

Deon, held captive by the muscular constrictors of Liz's thighs within her pudenda's sugar walls, considered his escape. He employed the usage of rapid contortion and wriggling patterns, which, to her, felt like hundreds of tiny feet marching its way out of its entrapment inside her female grotto. Exploding in a fervor of ecstatic chaos, her legs flew wildly apart, and Deon freed his head.

Liz flailed and thrashed with pandemonium, her body and mind still resisting, words of hostility only existing in her head. What escaped her vocal chords were only heated wails and loud murmurs, drenched in stress. Or impatience. A pre-intercourse emission from the depths of her woman's humidor formed crystal-like damp substance on her heated vulva as she felt the tip of Deon's guest of honor arrive at her heavenly gate, ensuring his entry to be free of friction or rigidness.

Deon's reprobate eyes glowed eerily phosphorescently in the graying dim of the room besieged by a gloomy afternoon storm. His heart pounded like a heavyweight boxer's inside his ribs. He could no longer wait. He pushed forward, and he felt himself sink into the heated fleshy cavern of Liz's body. Her petulant cries abruptly replaced again by her need to suck in a gust of air through gritted teeth, sagging in soft surrender to his rock solid invasion inside her womb that hadn't welcomed any activity for a span of time thought much too long previously.

Though she uttered silent, whiny words sounding like "No . . . no . . . please," her actions betrayed such as she softened from the tense state of her condition. Moments of fright dissipated into expectancy. She rollicked in a frenzy of wild abandon as Deon's waist pummeled tumid penetration to her, filling up her empty space. All she could do to resist him now was throw her arms around him, pull him closer, her hands creeping downside his back until they clasped his stone-hard buttocks. His weight crushed her like a citrus fruit, but only served to make her more juicy and ripe for his taste. Their lips finally met. For the first time.

Like two escapees liberated from the imprisonment of a house of hatred, the fugitives of circumstance locked lips. Liz's mouth opened immediately to unleash her own tongue to wrestle Deon's to a potent standstill in intensity. Both of her hands fastened to his cheeks and pulled him to her face with the power of passion. They were both caught in the rapturous moment, like two damned souls seeking to devour one another. Like a collection of interworking circuits of electricity, mystical sparks flickered into a fire—one that Deon could feel at the very depths of his soul. It was growing and spreading inside of him like a blaze, threatening to consume him in a fiery combustion. Before too long, this burning had arrived at his sack of mojo. He could hear voices of his ancestors, but they weren't speaking English, Spanish, or any language his Black ass could understand. Still, he pressed onward, as he couldn't turn back now even if he tried. Liz had now become his willing hostage, as exemplified in how she now clung to him for dear life. Her arms and legs fastened to him like a peachy white squid attempting to absorb him into her repository.

Liz writhed as Deon jammed tightly inside; together they twisted and squirmed in desirous embrace. She turned him over, to mount his cock pit. It was her turn to now black out; she left the moment and time and saw herself existing in space. Taffie had brought her there too. A sea of blackness enveloped her, like she was floating inside of a pool, but lit up by the stars of the galaxy. The universe was visible, and Deon brought her to the top of the world where she could see the stars shining so wondrously bright. She had reached a zone where no drug had ever taken her—or had it? The answer didn't come, but she was about to. Instantly, she could see not only the future, or eternity, she could also see her two beautiful bi-racial daughters, twins. The thought suddenly must have been a wake-up call, because the telltale signs of elated communion were imminent.

Deon's thrusts increased with intensity, and his gasps for air matched Liz's. Like a pinball machine, every ball he fired, and every contact made with her chambers put Liz on instant tilt and every bang. He heard the muddy slush of her acceptance to his every offer, her voice, which before had caused him severe grief and irritation, now whispered out an outlandish, almost alien harmony. It compelled him to stay as his voice thundered alongside the rain outside the window.

The unseen heat had touched his core, and Deon's mojo sack had no recourse but to cool things down by releasing his soul blood. Liz could feel it soak her inside. She gasped for air as if drowning. Deon released a sea of chaos within her that could have conceivably flooded cities like Atlantis. Simultaneously, Liz was hoisted to the Milky Way, gazing at the stars once again as her climax lifted her up. Weightless. Then at once she was free-falling toward the green earth, and well before she hit the ground, she passed out.

79

THE INCLEMENT WEATHER receded, and the day suddenly ebbed into the early evening. The night. The sun had beat a hasty retreat and delayed its return until the following morn, leaving darkness to creep its way back to the cityscape, and into the hotel suite. Liz woke up halfway underneath Deon, one leg pinned underneath the weight of his body; the other was curled around the log of his thigh like a forest vine wrapping itself around a black tree. He was still asleep; his coconut-scented hair was almost as bedraggled as Liz's, only now, as he rested his lightly snoring head on her right shoulder, his natural strands now resembled a collection of wet tarantulas, whereas Liz's looked like a long flowing cape of golden strands that extended to the small of her back. She gently eased out of the bed, sliding her body from underneath Deon's mass. She sat on the side of the bed, running her hand through her hair, massaging the side of her face and temples. At that point, she wasn't trying to fool herself into thinking that she was going to run away or "escape" from Deon. Surely, he would have an explanation for what he had done. Pretending that she was still aggrieved for his defilement would be useless. She stared at him still sleeping, his normal features now distorted due to the way his face was buried and pressed against the pillow, lips abnormally thicker and cheek appearing inflated. Sort of cartoonish, Liz thought. Somewhat cute. But there was nothing adorable about how he had pounced on her earlier.

Crawling out of the bed, wishing she had a cigarette, Liz walked with problematic, post-intercourse steps; soreness invaded her like it never had previously. There was no way she could deny it—no one had ever made her feel like the way Deon had. Not Eddie, not Carver, no Serge, no football jock, or Hollywood playboy, or LA socialite—no one. She made a move for the robe that Deon had vigorously removed her from, then picked up the one he had been wearing, as if she was trying to straighten up the place. She draped herself inside of the robe so she wouldn't be prancing around in the nude. The wide open curtains exposed the windows, and the buildings in view felt like spying eyes despite the appeal of a breathtaking sight's evening coruscation. While trying to clear away the table, she disposed of the empty bottles of consumed drinks, then saw the remnant of the burned-up roach to the spliff they had indulged in. It was the likely culprit that was a conduit for Deon's sudden erratic behavior that changed both of their lives that day. She dumped the ashtray contents in a wastebasket and noisily discarded the bottles as well. The clamor roused Deon from his slumber, causing him to open squinting eyes, but he was slow in movement. He raised himself up, like he was doing push-ups on the bed, turned, and stared about as if in a state of disorientation, or as if to quietly wonder where Liz was.

Liz heard him stirring and stretching himself, groaning as if he had been well rested and his lascivious desires satiated. He was welcomed back to the world of the wakened state by Liz firing a bundle of robe viciously into his face and torso. Angrily. Her face covered with a dark, unforgiving look of contempt. Their eyes met for a moment; then Liz quickly turned her back to him and went to the computer. Deon wiped the sleep out of his eyes and sat up in bed. He didn't put the robe on right away and didn't appear as if he was in a hurry to leave the comfortable soft *Sealy* mattress.

Inside the small, telephone-booth-sized compartment room, Liz sat upon the stool and checked her computer. To assuage her feelings of guilt, she planned to draft some type of rapprochement e-mail. She hadn't planned to sleep with anyone else, it 'sort of "just happened." She could try to say it was a "rape," she but didn't have the energy to fool herself. Much of her efforts were more concentrated on fooling others. Without realizing it, she began scrolling her pages listlessly while thinking of what she would say to Carver. Then, what she and Deon would talk about for the rest of the night, or however long they were to be together. Her mind was almost blank, stalling for time. Then she noticed something on her screen she had neglected to notice from previous Hotmail visits. She clicked on to the second page!

In between random ads she had yet to delete, scrolling back a month's time, she saw an unfamiliar e-mail address. She had once heard a geeky guy like Eric Cravens say that there were some types of e-mails people should not open or click on, because they contained a virus, or something of that nature. But Liz wasn't the type to leave any rock unturned. She had to find out who had sent it or see what it was. Even if it was just another ad.

She opened up the e-mail, and her chest was lit on fire. She gasped in hopes that a cool gust of air would extinguish her shock. It was from Taffie! But dated several months ago, the first of the year. How did she miss it? The question's answer was self-explanatory. Neglect to check her Hotmail account, busy schedules, partying, exchanging e-mails with Carver, obsessing—any reason could have been a factor, but the fact was she missed it before, and now she saw it. She didn't even remember giving Taffie her e-mail, but then again, it could have been possible, nonetheless. With no further delay, she dove tempestuously into the message, but was quickly disheartened.

> *My once dear friend,*
>
> *Please forgive if my English is not that good. My friend Takuto help me with it now to write mail to you.*
>
> *My reason to send you this letter is to say goodbye to you. We will never meet with us again. I cannot be a friend to someone as you. I really thought that we are friends, but I was wrong about you. I thought I can trust you. I thought I can believe you. But it was not case.*
>
> *But, what I told you is not lie before. I love you. You were a special person to me. I never forget you. But we cannot be together and we cannot be friends. When you find out this mail, I will move away to another place in Japan. Please, do not try to contact me anymore.*
>
> *This e-mail address is discard.*
>
> *TAFFIE Amelie JOLIE*
> *P.S> I was there on the night!*

Click for attachment

The letter itself was a heartbreaker. For Liz had no idea at all, whatsoever, about why Taffie had arrived at the opinion whereas she would think that she wasn't her friend. Or that they could no longer be friends. Had she come to her, Liz knew that they could have talked it over and worked things out. Granted, that was what she thought—before she studied the postscript. What did she mean by "I was there on the night"? She clicked the link below the postscript and got her answer.

Deon felt better, well rested, and refreshed, overall glad that he had recovered from that whacked-out trip he had with that weed earlier. Next, as he used his hands as a makeshift hand towel, he was wiping sweat and Liz slobber and scent off his chest and removing strands of her hair from his jib. He sat on the side of the bed and tried to figure out what he was going to say to Liz, because there was no way they could pretend that nothing had happened. Before he could make a move to put on his robe, he felt a stinging slap blow to the side of his head.

"Bastard!" Liz screamed like an agonized lynx or jaguar. Then she pounced on Deon, robe and all, like a bobcat. She leaped on the bed, and her weight caused him to fall back against the pillows. "How could you do that!?" she yelled as she tried to slap him with her hands in a rainfall pattern.

Deon, still seeing stars from the volleyball spike Liz issued to the side of his head and knocking loose his "Mickey Mouse" ball, covered his face while Liz vented. He tried to wait until she tired out, but Liz was in good shape. She worked out a lot and had decent stamina. Moreover, her strikes were unfocused but a little strong. Deon grew tired of taking a pounding, so he grabbed her wrists, then forcefully yanked her close to him to where her naked chest was upon his, their faces inches apart. Liz snarled at him with antipathy as she struggled to free her hands from his tight grip.

She said with a shivery, ice-cold tone, "Come take a look at this . . ."

Deon let her go, and Liz backed away. She adjusted her robe tight and stood at the computer closet, waiting for him to get appropriate, but Deon just let the robe lie. He walked over stark naked. Liz tried to act like she wasn't interested in staring at him, but she was too angry for frolics. She directed Deon's attention to the image on the computer screen. The result of the clicked-attachment link.

Deon stared at this photo. One of him and Liz hugging and cradling one another in a wide bed with satiny gray sheets. While he was reeling from the sudden shock of seeing this and trying to figure out if it was real or fake, Liz was ranting and asking similar questions like, "What is this? When was this taken? And where? Who took it? Why did *you* send this picture to her?"

Deon was like, "Me?! I didn't send this picture to anybody. This is my first time seeing it. I never even knew this shit even existed till now. Who is this from?"

"It's from Taffie, you fucker! You sent this to her, and she thinks we had an affair! That's why she left. I can't believe you would do something like this!" She tried to hit him but telegraphed it horribly, and Deon imperturbably blocked it and grabbed hold of her robe sleeve.

Deon said, "I'm not lying. I didn't send this e-mail or photo to Taffie. I didn't even know she had an e-mail account. Me an' her always contacted each other by phone. And hell, even if I did know her e-mail, why would I send her some fucked-up shit like that? Doesn't seem smart to me."

"Well, who did?" Liz angrily tore her arm away from his clench. "And where was this shit taken? When have I ever been so drunk or fucked up that I wouldn't remember sleeping with . . . you . . ."

Then it hit her. Probably at the same time Deon pointed out to her, answering her question about where the location was of the photo, she realized. Deon had said, "Look, that's the guestroom at Worm's cribbo. The only time I was ever there with you was the morning of the Christmas party. By the time I came out of the shower, though, you was gone. All y'all party guests had sat down for breakfast and broke out by the time I came down. That Worm told me his wife let me oversleep because I snored or some shit."

Liz remembered. Now knowing Deon's penchant for taking long showers, she recalled the night as well. Somewhat. It was an ecstasy night. She was drinking like a fountain fish. She crawled into bed with Deon, yes, but also Taffie—or so she had thought. But she never put together the pieces to the puzzle and get the picture that Taffie had been the one who had spied her and Deon in bed. But Deon's deductive reasoning enlightened her, even if slightly flawed.

Deon said, "I get it. Somebody probably set us up. Knowing Worm, he probably did it. When I got to the party, I was fucked up. One of my friends, Lester, he got married, and we partied that day before I got to Worm's Christmas thing. I never seen so much liquor before. But, I guess I was thirsty too, so... I was so wasted and tired I figured I'd take a nap, save some energy for when Taffie came later. Only, I guess I was so beat that nap turned into a full-fledged kayo. You probably got fucked up like you always do, and somebody, Worm maybe, put you in the bed with me and took the picture as a prank."

Liz shifted uneasily. She knew then that Deon was partially right. She said, "No . . . no . . . he didn't. Deon . . . it was me. I did it. I remember. You're right. I was messed up. I popped a side of X that night. I was in another world. Like you. Today. But you don't understand, me and Taffie . . . we had a special relationship. We talked about threesomes . . ."

"So you was trying to have a *menage a trois* with me?" Deon's face wrinkled in alarm.

Liz averted gaze. She said in a lowered voice, "Something like that." She ran her hand through her already-tousled do as if troubled. "All I remember is, yeah, she and I had talked about doing X together and getting into some really . . . outlandish . . . things while we got zoned out. It's just some fun. Gimme a break, dude . . . I . . . I was depressed. I was trying to get over a breakup, OK? It was a really fucked time for me. So . . . yeah, I got into the bed with you, but I thought Taffie was there too. We just ended up . . ."

"Passed out," Deon completed her sentence.

Liz broke out in tears, then ran out of the room. She paced around restlessly. Deon followed her out and decided to get dressed. Apparently, however, her tirade offensive had yet to run its complete course, and Liz was in a feisty mood.

"So what now?" she asked in a demanding voice, arms slightly akimbo.

Deon had plopped down on the sofa couch, as if preparing to slide his legs through a pair of black boxers. He stopped and replied, "What you mean?"

"Us," Liz stated. Her face looked dark from the dim light of the room. Deon lit the lamp beside the sofa to his left and gave the room a tangerine-ginger shade. Liz stood like an avenging angel with an extensive halo of marigold entrenching her angry face, making her look scary.

Deon felt a chill of augury, but he was determined not to back down. He had to confront the beast, whether that "beast" be himself, or her. He stood up and walked over to her. "What about *us*?" he said.

They stood before each other, about the same height, but were she to wear heels, she would have the slight edge. For the time being, however, his brown eyes stared into her sea of blue shining sinisterly in the rusty marmalade of light in the room. They were silent for a moment, facing like two fighters before the start of a match. Liz's face was so distressed with angry emotion she seemed to be fighting only tears.

"Why did you . . . take me . . . like that?" she asked with slow, deliberate elocution.

Deon didn't know what to make of her display of emotion. He could barely control his own. The beating of his heart increased, and the feelings he felt earlier were returning. Still naked, he came closer to her, until their bodies almost touched. Liz didn't retreat, though. She didn't back away.

Deon said, "Because . . . I needed to. I don't know why. I needed to do it, just like . . ." Some veiled, obscure force had sequestered his control of actions as he leaned into her, pressed his lips on her forehead. "Just like . . . I need you now."

Like invisible magic, his hands were suddenly inside of her robe, encircling her abundant mastitis, then spreading his palms wide in opposite directions, undraped the robe to expose her bare shoulders. Liz frowned an agonized face and put up resistance, for once now retreating from him.

"Deon . . . no!" Her rebellion against him was short-lived. It was as if his touch had numbed her. His face found its way to her neck, under her chin. His lips pecked light assault to her collarbone, reverberating tremors torpedoed to her central nervous system from wherever his kisses contacted. "We can't . . ."

Deon's spellbinding caresses wouldn't cease tranquilizing her. His arms slid down her back within the confines of the garment, and he stroked her soft skin. "Why we can't?"

Liz's poise shattered and crumbled her into tears. "Because . . . you don't love me . . ." As Deon held her close, she fell into him. If not in compliance, then to smear her wet, sorrowed face on his shoulder for an instant. "Two people like us . . . could never be together . . . could we?" She spoke as if she knew the answer yet didn't know.

Deon cupped her face in his hands like he was Humphrey Bogart and stared at her. For the first time ever, she suddenly became beautiful to him. He noticed her allure and attractiveness up close, and raw without the masquerade of makeup she polished her face with. But he knew it was just as shell. Underneath, he was aware that she was a ruddy, wild witch. Still, he was under the spell of a force he had yet to rein in inside of him. His racing heart alerted him that his beast within was returning for a repeat performance of the earlier tryst. His womb sweeper was quickening to a Medieval lance, outright and poking the opening underneath her robe's tie string.

Liz felt him and his member ease between her luscious thighs; she heard Deon whisper to her, "Yeah, we can." He kissed her face; she stood motionless as the feeling of her robe sliding off her body grazed her legs on its way to the floor again.

Liz said, "You don't love me!" in one last feat of opposition.

"I do love you . . . If not, I'll figure out how to," Deon said. Then before Liz could say anything, his lips trapped hers. She closed her eyes and welcomed him into her mouth. She answered back and met his tongue with her own in an equal display of amorous passion. Deon's answer must have been good enough for her; she threw her arms around him. Deon couldn't believe that he was kissing the mouth of a "slut" who had probably glazed across several hundreds of male penises, swallowed unnamable substances of all sorts, ingested all types of drugs, and no telling whatever the hell else. Yet at that moment, she was his lifeline to sanity and the only person who he felt could cure his insatiable need for love and affection. The way she held on to him, it was if she needed the same. *Their* needs were the same.

Liz finally uttered "Me too..." Then felt his hand form an iron-clamp grip, squeezing her soft, round behind and lifting her up off her feet like she was a baby. He walked with her to the bed again. Gently, he laid her down. She readied herself for him, allowing his access to her once again, with no roadblocks. Again, they became lost in the rapturous moment of coming together as one under the banner of love and passion. In her head, Liz was sending Carver a message that she wouldn't send on e-mail. "Sorry, Carver. I guess I played with your heart again." Her eyes closed as she floated into a dreamlike state, wondering what it was going to be like as a parent.

She never returned to California—at least not to live there. With Deon and the twins born of their improbable, uncommon but extraordinary union, she relocated to the Eastern United States, residing around the Emerald Coast of the Carolinas. She eventually kicked her substance abuse, which was another saga in itself, yet still followed through in her creation of a health spa and often made return visits to Japan and other parts of Asia. Who would have ever thought? she often wondered, that she would get involved with a *"whatever Deon was"*—those people she thought were the menaces to society that her parents once hated. Still did, but Mother Ida melted like butter upon seeing Leana and Deana; and since they were just as rich, who really needed their approval? She remained the vain sort of woman that would still give herself credit, for "transforming" Deon, for "taming him," and turning him around—changing him from being a drug dealer to a legit music studio owner who operated capoeria martial arts schools in the United States and Japan. Deon was planning on doing all of that anyway but allowed Liz to bask in her own "glorious" description of how the story went.

Regardless, there were times she wondered about what things would have been like had she stayed with Eddie. Or what would have happened had she returned to the States and reunited with Carver like she had planned. But both of those were forlorn memories ever after. Like Japan, like the colorful contour slopes of its countryside, the neon fireworks at night—the nightclubs, the lounges, the Candy Box . . . It was all like a dream. A dream she was seeing in a rearview mirror of her mind. In that same blurred vision, Liz thought she had saved Deon from jail, prison, or death; but it was actually *him* who had saved *her*. Not once with Brad, or many other times, he saved her from herself and made her believe in him. All the way up until . . .

THE END

EPILOGUE

Eddie Roman yawned exhaustedly as he walked the corridors of the Sakai City Hospital Maternity Ward, headed back to his now-wife Hiroko Okada-Roman's in-patient room. Now the proud father of a darling daughter, yet to be named, but he and wife seemed to be settling on Erica, or Erika, because it had elements of both a Japanese and a Western name. Mother-in-law Eriko didn't mind the title, the obvious reason being that the charming newborn's name would be similar to hers. She had stayed with Eddie all night while he was waiting for Hiroko to give birth, sometime during the wee hours, but remarkably maintained her youthful, pleasant features belying her forty-six years of age, while Eddie looked haggard. Swelled patches under his eyes denoted fatigue from stress, worrying; and pacing all night long made him look like an older man approaching his mid-thirties. After holding his daughter, spending time with her and the mother, his wife, all day long, he was paying Hiroko one final visit before Eriko carted him back to their home. Hiroko and the baby had to stay overnight for observation, and the next day, Eddie and Eriko would be back to pick her and the baby up.

Hiroko was up, in reasonably peppy spirits, and had been watching the news on the pay television in her room. She livened up upon seeing Eddie, who entered and showered her with kisses on her face, his now-bearded chin prickled her forehead. They commenced to talk about future plans. She would be on maternity leave, and Eddie would continue on with the CHET Program. His work performance had remained stellar, but his liaison with Hiroko had caused somewhat of a stir at the workplace and around that Hannan City area as well.

For the fact that PE Soccer Coach tried to expose Hiroko and Eddie's secret affair. She didn't fight the accusation; in fact, she embraced it and, with fortitude was prepared to face the possibility of losing her job in shame and disgrace, but without any regrets that she had fallen in love with the foreigner. Due to the fact that she was a good teacher, with also a good work performance and the ongoing need for eligible educators for the school system, Hiroko wasn't fired. Unexpectedly, she was instead transferred to Sakai City, her hometown. So in essence, things turned out for the better. With Eddie's longevity in the CHET Program, his seniority enabled him to eventually get a placement in Sakai City as well, teaching at another junior high school in the Mikuni-ga-Oka area. Soon after, they would marry. Now they had a daughter.

Just after Eddie had kissed her good-bye, preparing to go home and finally get some shut-eye, vowing to return the next day to pick her up and their new family member, Hiroko halted him. "Oh, I forgot to show you this from the other day!" she said as she grabbed a cluster of magazines, newspapers, and postcards. Eddie squinted seeing the pile of paper and hoped that she wouldn't have him reading something for long, or else he was due to collapse right then and there on the hospital ward floor. Yet he could understand how her being cooped up in a hospital bed all day long, a teacher with a mind like hers needed to be occupied.

"Did you know this girl?" Hiroko showed him a Japanese newspaper's photo of a Black female, ensconced within a sea of Chinese and Japanese characters. The girl did look familiar to him, because it was Taffie. But Eddie couldn't quite place her face, only having met her but just once or twice and seemingly eons ago.

"Can't say I do," Eddie said honestly, as her face sent off some alarms of familiarity, but he dismissed it thinking she was some singer or famous R&B vocalist. "Who is she? An actress? A singer?"

Hiroko said, "She's dead. She was strangled. In Tokyo. Hey, look at this: this is the guy who killed her." She grabbed another newspaper, then showed him a photo of the man he *did* remember, the one who he had known to be Serge. He would never forget the face, even though the night he met the man, Eddie was a little drunk. But the dude, to him, looked like a pale vampire with big feet. Intimidating then as he was in the newspaper, only this photo, looked like a mugshot image. A bandage covered the man's chin.

"Can you believe it?" Hiroko said in a mystified-sounding voice. "I used to know him!"

Eddie was like, "What!?" Clearly taken aback.

"I thought you would have known them, because they used to be French teachers at Bozack. Because your former girlfriend, Elizabeth, worked there, I thought some of them you maybe knew about. But when I was a teenager, as you know, I studied abroad in Canada. My roommate, she was Chinese, her name, Ming." She shuffled through a series of postcards from various places—Shanghai,

China; Hong Kong; Bangkok, Thailand; Indonesia; and, finally, Tokyo, Japan. This one she held out and stared at.

Hiroko said, "Ming sent postcards from everywhere she went and said she'd look me up if she ever came to Japan. But . . . on this card, when she came to Tokyo was the last card I ever got from her, and look what it says!"

Eddie ran his weary eyes over the message on the back of the postcard. Basically, he read where Hiroko's friend Ming had been depressed and in a state of utter melancholy because she and her boyfriend had suddenly broken up after a day in Japan. He disappeared and never came back. He deserted her. Cold.

Eddie shook his head in disbelief as he handed the postcard back to Hiroko. "That's crazy!" he exclaimed shortly. "So, who did he kill? That Black girl?"

"Not only her," Hiroko said as she opened a newspaper again that displayed his mugshot-type photo. Being Japanese, she, of course, could read and understand the article. "He was a murderer a long time before he came to Japan. It seems that he had killed his friend, a guy named Serge and had assumed his identity for many years. His real name was Gui Pierre. Living off Ming, he used her to travel to different places in Asia, looking for a quack surgeon who could perform an operation, like plastic surgery, to alter something about his facial appearance and remove his fingerprints. It says he found one such surgeon here in Japan. In Tokyo. He must have been working various jobs, at Bozack, at various nightclubs, it says, in order to raise the money needed for the operation. I guess he met this Frenchwoman, Taffie . . . and by chance, I guess he must have stalked her and . . . murdered her."

"Taffie?!" Eddie was swirling the name around in his head. Although it still didn't register with him, the ghastly news made him feel empty.

Just then, Hiroko's mother, Eriko, came, and the subject and mood changed. It was refreshed to small talk and chitchat involving Hiroko's mother asking how she felt and if she needed anything. When reassured that everything would be fine and she would be ready to return home the following day, Hiroko bid her husband and her mother a fond farewell for the time being. She was excited about being a mother.

At home that night, Eddie fell onto his futon mattress like he was a ton of bricks. He now resided with his in-laws, his wife's mother and grandmother. Hiroko's grandfather, unfortunately, had passed away the year before. Eddie was now the man of the house, but he and his wife bedded down in their own private room, which used to belong solely to Hiroko. Without bothering to stand up, he shucked his clothes and threw them in an unknown destination in the room, then switched off his floor lamp.

After a sexless five months, an erect perch emerged from his boxers, and he couldn't wait until Hiroko was home. He was in need of her and was tired of stroking his erections in her absence or her inability to give him pleasure other than some oral sex occasionally; but both of them felt guilty doing even that with Hiroko's protuberant belly. So Eddie grabbed hold of himself. No lotion on hand and too beat to go get up and look, a few dabs of spit would do the trick. He shut his eyes and let his eyes go blank.

In a deep, deep relaxed state, he brought his hands up and down in anticipation of her. She would disrobe, her breasts now expanded and more inflated, possibly because of having given childbirth and being filled with milk, Eddie guessed. But he didn't care. That, plus her slightly bubbled-up belly not yet returned to its normal repressed state after being expanded for nine months, didn't deter his wanton desire for her. He had gone for so long without her, and with his need for attention to the stiff organ he was stroking. She was speaking tired, incoherent Japanese to him, sounding like her grandmother, but he was disregarding her scolding. All he wanted was for her to come closer.

She knelt, and her thick thighs straddled him, and he impaled her dark, wet and sticky cavern; and as he did, her eyes went white in their sockets. She let out a husky gasp as her head tilted toward the heavens, like she was seeing a ghost on the ceiling. Sweat appeared on the older woman's forehead. Eddie was so consumed with the joy of feeling himself inside of her viscous, gelatinous fleshy passage, suckling her breasts, fingering her anal inlet, hearing her hoarse, hussy howling like a bitch in heat—he didn't realize that this wasn't his exhausted, delirious dream, and this wasn't Hiroko.

Too late, he realized, that Eriko was a contemptuous woman, and always had been, and didn't seem to have changed at all after so many years. Not only had she maintained her mantrap, youthful features to an extent, but just as she had ruined her marriage with her own husband, Hiroko's father, she now looked as if she would do the same to her daughter's.

Eddie climaxed and released himself full throttle inside her while she rammed her slimy tongue in his mouth. Her breath smelled like a putrid *Seirogan* medicine. Then with horror and shock, he looked up and stared into the face of his mother-in-law.

GLOSSARY

50cc. A small motor (scooter) bike slightly smaller than a Western moped, and in Japan measuring at fifty cubic centimeters regarding piston displacement.

100 yen store a store where various items and gifts are sold at low prices similar to "One Dollar" stores in the US.

893. A pseudonym for the Japanese mafia known as *Yakuza*, the numbers are a play on the Japanese translations if shown in Chinese *kanji* characters.

ALT (assistant language teacher). A person usually of foreign extraction who is hired to assist or teach her/his native language in a public school in Japan.

ATE (assistant teacher of English). The same as an ALT, only an ATE is a specific teacher of English in a Japanese public school, and may not always be of foreign descent, and English may or may not be their native language.

bento (box). A boxed lunch in Japan, often a portable-sized container or takeout package.

Black Cat (or kuroneko). A convenient courier service of Japan, similar to America's UPS, accessible from many locations including convenience stores.

blasian. A term coined by some to refer to a person of black / Native American, black / Latino, black / African, etc., and an Asian parentage.

bonenkai. A year-end party often thrown by businesses and places of social familiarity where associated guests and participants gather at a year's closing. Considered a significant social event.

bullet train (Shinkansen). A high-speed type of transport system that runs faster than traditional railways and commuter transportation. Japan's major system is called (the) Shinkansen.

business hotel. Most often a lower end, inexpensive hotel that has minimal amenities primarily used by businessmen, not intended for extended families or vacations.

C. Cocaine.

capsule hotel (or capsel). A pod hotel that offers small, coffin-like abodes, and stacked in rows like that of a morgue or crypt designed to accommodate backpackers, budget travelers, and transients.

coolie. Weed smoked in a joint laced with cocaine. (Also called a **woo.**)

chu-hai. An alcoholic beverage sold in Japan, which is a favorite of many because of its high level of alcoholic content but said to be unnoticeable within a soda or soft carbonated drink taste.

delivery health. A type of "escort service" that dispatches undercover hookers (or gigolos) to soliciting johns under the guise of another legitimate business or service.

(a) double. *See* **blasian.**

Dragon City. Nickname for the city of Nagoya, Japan's third major city, situated between Osaka to the west and Tokyo to the east.

eikaiwa. A Japanese word for an English conversation school. In most cases, these are businesses that do not offer any accreditation for students who learn and study at their schools, but generally offer English language lessons for people interested in learning for recreational study, travel, or career advancement.

enka. A type of Japanese folk music often characterized by haunting love ballads, the singing of cautionary tales of deviant lifestyles, and hinting of extramarital affairs.

freejack. A slang term for the foreign language teacher in Japan who negotiates her/his own contracts regarding jobs, like a free agent, or a backpacker colony teacher who makes a short-term living on part-time jobs to achieve a financial goal.

freeter. A Japanese slang word that denotes a slacker, mooch, freeloader, or free eater.

gaijane. A female foreigner of Japan, or foreign female living in Japan temporarily.

gaijin. Short for the actual term *gaikokujin*, which translates to "outsider" or "foreigner" in the Japanese language. Considered by some to be a contemptable and/or offensive term.

gaijin bar. A bar in Japan, most often in urban areas, where the theme of the establishment is made to resemble one that exists outside of the country, and its patrons are mostly foreigners as well. The most common of these in Japan resemble European pubs.

gaijin hunter. Usually (but not limited to) a Japanese person who stalks foreigners as their target language group or community. Sometimes a detested individual as these are said by some to have no interest in the foreigner outside of learning their language or attaining something from them without paying for it otherwise. (Also **gaijin killer,** but this term is used more by Japanese.)

gaijin pet. A foreigner to Japan who becomes a "fake friend" or trophy acquaintance used to display to their family, friends, or social circle, but not given much or any consideration to acknowledge them being on the same level as other Japanese people.

gokon. *See* **kompa.**

hapa. A term coined by some to describe a half-Asian and half-Caucasian/white person.

happa. A Japanese term for marijuana. (Also **kus-sa.**)

hiragana. The commonly used syllabic writing used in Japanese language used for the functional vocabulary words, similar to *katakana*; annunciates Japanese written language. *See also* **Katakana.**

inkan. A stamp or seal of varying shapes, sorts, and sizes, but most often a female lipstick-sized apparatus required for formal or official documents in Japan.

itchy-man. A term for a Japanese bill of currency equaling 10,000, which is literally its pronunciation in Japanese for the numeric amount.

izakaya. A Japanese bar, diner, or restaurant that serves alcohol, dinner, and snacks and comparable to dining caverns catering to afterwork socializing, similar to pub culture.

J-dude. A Japanese male, usually younger (possibly used with contempt by some).

J-girl (gal). A Japanese female, usually younger (possibly used with contempt by some).

JR (Japan Railway). Japan's most prominent railway, commercial transportation, and operates the Shinkansen. (*See also* **bullet train.**)

JT/JTE. A Japanese teacher (JT) or Japanese teacher of English (JTE) is an official Japanese teacher employed by the school system and the "partner" teacher to an assistant language teacher. (*See also* ALT or ATE.)

juku. A cram school or preparatory learning center.

Kansai (area). The western area of Japan's mainland (Honshu) island, with highlighted cities: Osaka, Kobe, Kyoto, Nara, Wakayama, and Okayama (plus Shiga and Mie prefectures). Other related term: **Kinki** (*kin-ki*) **Area.**

Kanto (area). The eastern area of Japan's mainland (Honshu) island, with highlighted cities: Tokyo, Yokohama, Chiba, and Saitama.

karaoke (bar). A bar or saloon where karaoke singing is the major feature.

katakana. The basic written sound/language of Japanese intended to pronounce nonstandard Japanese language or vocabulary of origin outside of Japan. (Similar to *hiragana. See also* **hiragana.**)

Kinki (area). *See* **kansai.**

KIX. Kansai International Airport.

kissaten. A tearoom, teahouse, café, or coffee shop, often quaint establishments operating privately and the preferred meeting places for some because of lesser bustle.

kompa (*also* **gokon**)**.** A blind-date arrangement where people are introduced to one another with the possibility of a matchmaking occurring in a party-type setting.

kuroneko. *See* **Black Cat.**

last train. References the final train operating on a particular commuter or subway line on a daily schedule. Usually (or in most Japanese major cities) around midnight.

Loop Line. In Tokyo and Osaka, a centralized route of the Japan Railway Line that circles the inner city and makes stops at large express-stop stations; one of the most crowded trains during rush hours. (*See also* **JR Line.**)

love hotel. Often an extravagant or gawdy anonymous reception, short-stay "fashion motel" designed to accommodate guests seeking intimate or sexual trysts; not so much for vacationing travelers or families with children.

mansion. Widely used in Japan, this a misleading term describing housing or a dwelling that is actually an apartment of one or two rooms or more, not a large house.

master cylinder. A very large can of beer, and in some cases in Japan can be as large as quart size (or 1000 ml); not to be confused with a keg.

mercy fuck. Noncommittal sexual agreement usually between two foreigners (or expats); term originally applied to lonely (foreign) people seeking affairs with those they would not otherwise consort with or date, but settle for them due to limited options. The dissimilarity here being the people involved aren't necessarily friends. (*See also* **wet handshake.**)

Minami. South Town (*see also* **Namba**)

Namba. One of Osaka's popular, colorful districts, bustling with commerce, also referred to as Minami by locals.

Nankai (line). A smaller, independent railway servicing the southern (southwest) area of Osaka and parts of Wakayama. Major terminal in Namba District of Osaka City.

Nengajo a Japanese practice of sending mass postcards to friends, family or familiars at the year's end

ninja. A slang term used as a verb to describe the action of riding a train (usually long distances) for free or minimal fare, deceptively and/or illegally.

nomikai. A drinking party or social function arranged usually by a company or business; designed to allow members to interact outside of the normal (work) environment. Usually considered a significant social affair and can be held anytime throughout the calendar year with no special day appointed; can include welcome/farewell parties.

okonomiyaki. Nicknamed at one time "Japanese pizza" it is in actuality more like a pancake that contains a variety of ingredients, but usually octopus (or bacon) and within a wheat-based flour batter. Roughly translated as "cook (it) as you like it," this dish is very popular in Osaka and Hiroshima.

OL an "office lady" or woman who works in an office.

onsen. A type of Japanese spa, indoor or outdoor public (or private) bath of varying types and descriptions. Often enjoyed on vacations. (*See also* **sento.**)

Osaka Airport. References Osaka's "Itami Airport"; a small hangar/runway strip that flies domestic primarily.

sento. A neighborhood, "public bath" designed much the same as an (see also "**Onsen**") but local, of lesser quality and/or grandiose and caters to the immediate community in which it is located; not attached to a resort or hotel like an "Onsen".

shinkansen. *See* **bullet train.**

shinenkai. Similar to a year-end party, the only difference being it is held at the start or beginning of the new year as opposed to the latter or year's close. (*See also* **bonenkai.**)

shot bar. A shoebox canteen, tavern, or pub, generally smaller than other commercial establishments, serving alcohol and snacks, sometimes even meals.

shochu. A clear, distilled drink high in alcoholic content and made from either barley, potatoes, or rice; a product of Japan, but enjoyed also in Korea. Not to be confused with *sake*, or Japanese rice wine.

shotengai. An indoor arcade or tunnel located in the downtown area of a Japanese town or city inaccessible by commercial traffic or vehicles; designed to be a shopping strip catering to foot or bicycle shoppers.

sizzle. Dope; illegal drugs or substance

snack bar. An exclusive bar, clubhouse, or pub catering to pricy-membership customers most often, who purchase bottles of alcohol to leave at the establishment and be consumed over a period of time. These places also include attractive women, called hostesses sometimes, who drink with the gentlemen and entertain with conversation, song, and/or both.

square. A slang term used by some people to refer to a regular, tobacco cigarette, or a socially awkward person. Also "L7"

takoyaki. A small, round meatball-shaped fried dumpling filled with pieces of octopus; a delicacy enjoyed throughout Japan, but especially popular in the Osaka (Kansai) area.

udon. Thick Japanese noodles not to be confused with *ramen* (*larmen*).

urban liner (the). A rapid express train servicing the route between Osaka and Nagoya cities, not quite as speedy as the **shinkansen** (*see also* **bullet train**), but speedier than the regular commuter trains of the same/similar route. Also referred to by some as **urb (the)**.

url. To vomit; throw up.

V. Viagra, or any male enhancement drug.

wet handshake. Noncommittal (usu. illicit) sexual affair between two common friends, associates, or coworkers; often blamed on drunkenness or loneliness (similar to **mercy fuck**).

white girl. Cocaine.

X. Ecstasy (or "exstasy") drug.

yakitori (spot). A restaurant or bar or diner found everywhere throughout Japan specializing in open grill chicken skewered on long wooden toothpick-like shafts. (*See also* **izakaya.**)

yellow fever. An affliction said to curse its victim with an addiction to people of Asian origin; to the extent they can have attraction for no other race, or difficulty in having such. Sometimes used with contempt.

yen. The currency of Japan, also called *en*.

Yolo You only live once

Zousanashi usually describes a heavy set, or full-figured woman with big legs: literally translated to "Elephant Legs"

FOOTNOTES AND ADDITIONAL TERMS

(*1) This tower is called "(the)Tsutenkaku" and 'Osaka Tower' is not its official name at the time of this recount/tale.

(*2) This game "hangman" was later unofficially banned in Japanese classrooms.

(*3) Izakaya is sometimes pluralized for this writing. It is a Japanese dining establishment specializing in quaint Japanese/Asian dishes, not to be confused with a family restaurant.

(*4) Bonenkai is a year-end party or celebration that is considered a big event.

(*5) Sensei is a Japanese word translatable to "teacher" or "instructor" and is usually a term denoting respect.

(*6) O-hana-mi, or hanami sometimes, but not always referred to as a cherry blossom viewing, and not necessarily a picnic.

(*7) Nomikai is a popular drinking and dine-out social event common especially among coworkers. These do not always follow a calendar schedule and do not necessarily befall on any particular date like Western holidays.

(*8) Eikaiwa is a term for (an)English conversation school, usually an independent academic entity, not connected with an official educational institution, designed to provide English lessons primarily to adults, but also children in many cases.

(*9) Mizu shobai—Literally translated as "water/liquid business" prostitution industry legitimized with weasel-worded statutes and laws.

(*10) Itchy-man – Translated from the Japanese word *ichiman*, meaning ten thousand (yen) as of money, equivalent to roughly 100 US dollars. It was coined by some non-Japanese speakers as an easy way to remember Japanese words by changing the Japanese to sound like English.

(*11) Sushi-go-round – The non-Japanese English speaker's coinage for *kaitenzushi*, or "conveyor-belt sushi," a restaurant where sushi is served on dishes distributed to customers by way of a perpetually rotating conveyor belt.

(*12) Pink-chirashi – Leaflets advertising quasi-legal prostitution formerly distributed randomly in mail receptacles of residential homes (until outlawed later), called such because of the pink color of the paper opposite an often-provocative photo of a nude or semi-clad woman.

(*13) 84 Spray – A small aerosol can of deodorant or antiperspirant available in tiny cans, able to be easily stored, which became a favorite of on-the-go people.

(*14) Honme/tatemae – An expression in Japanese society emphasizing the two-sided nature of human interaction; whereas how one speaks to others face-to-face might be different in reality.

(*15) Gaijin card – A wallet sized form of picture ID card (similar to an American 'green card') which foreigners in Japan are required to carry/have on their person; actual name is "gaikoku torokusho"./ also called "alien card".

(*16) Zabuton – A decorative cushion designed for sitting upon, especially in Japanese tatami-style rooms.

(*17) Azuchi-machi and Bingomachi (or Bingo Town) – Area of Osaka between Hommachi and Kitamachi.

(*18) Chuo-Odori – Chuo Boulevard.

(*19) Omikuji – A type of Japanese fortune telling usually purchased at the beginning of the calendar year, which predicts the future of that following year.

(*20) 100 yen store – Similar to a dollar store in countries like the United States. Sometimes food items and beverages can also be bought here.

(*21) Seafront Avenue, or Kaigan-Dori – Translated by some in English as Seafront Avenue.